THE REDWIND

To Kathryn,

aloha,

E Mele Kalikimaka,

Ian Mitchell—

OTHER BOOKS BY IAN MACMILLAN

Light and Power, (stories) University of Missouri Press, 1980 (Winner of the 1979 Associated Writing Programs Award for Short Fiction)

Blakely's Ark, (novel) Berkeley/Putnam, 1981

Proud Monster, (novel) North Point Press, 1986, The Bodley Head (London), 1987

Orbit of Darkness, Harcourt, Brace, Jovanovich, 1991, Ediciones B. (Barcelona), 1993

Exiles from Time (stories) Anoai Press, 1998

THE REDWIND

IAN MACMILLAN

MUTUAL PUBLISHING

Library of Congress Catalog Card
Number: 98-65468

First Printing, October 1998
1 2 3 4 5 6 7 8 9

Casebound
ISBN 1-56647-205-9

Softcover
ISBN 1-56647-203-2

Design by Jane Hopkins

Cover illustration © James Fitt,
represented by Expressions in Art

Mutual Publishing
1215 Center Street, Suite 210
Honolulu, Hawaii 96816
Telephone (808) 732-1709
Fax (808) 734-4094
e-mail: mutual@lava.net
Url: http://www.pete.com/mutual

Printed in Australia

ACKNOWLEDGMENTS

For Susan, Julia, Laura, and for parents: Donald and Elizabeth Trout MacMillan, George V. and Dorothy Robertson Bates, Richard and Lola vomSaal.

I would also like to thank Carl and Sandy Pao of Kailua, Hawaii, for information about Kailua's past, including the story of how to build a roof-sheeting outrigger canoe, and the late Dr. Dempsey Huitt, for information about medicine.

ACKNOWLEDGEMENTS

THE REDWIND

Prologue · 1994

He was dull green with a blunt unicorn's horn, and when you saw him go inside the crevice, wriggling on his side, you dove down and hooked your fingers, pulled down and looked inside, water dancing in the top of the mask and tickling your forehead, and you waited, lungs already robbed of oxygen so that your trunk began to contract in little involuntary convulsions, waited until shapes emerged out of the blackness, eyes jerking across them to accelerate definition, and locking on an eye materializing, and then the horn, the kala's body way back and jammed there with its dorsal spines splayed, behind him and to the right a brown eel watching, and you moved the spear toward the kala's eye, concentrating while your lungs squeezed, and ignored that and waited, aiming, and then thrust, pulling the hinge trigger, and then felt the surge of the fish and the vibration as you eased him out, and once free of the crevice he wriggled on the spear as you backed away, your lungs burning, and you planted your feet and burst for the silver plane of the surface.

Standing on a path halfway up the small cone-shaped island, they watched a half moon emerge from behind a single cloud hovering over the Koʻolaus, so that a lane of silver opened up on the water between them and Lanikai. The little island was a mile off Oahu, and the line of mountains was broad and sharp against a blue-black sky, backlit by the surreal, ashy glow of Honolulu. To their left, between them and the line on the horizon dividing the ocean from the sky, waves broke against the smaller of the two Mokulua Islands.

"So your friends goin' be there when you go nex' week?" Anika asked.

"Nah," he said, "It's just you and me and the airport scene."

His feet were sore from the climbing. He had left his zoris on Lanikai beach. The moon oozed from the edge of the cloud, half dark and half a phosphorescent silver, the slightly tipped, cut half looking like a bright shark's fin rising from the cloud. He reeled a little, feeling dizzy from the marijuana, and she turned and looked at him.

"When Keoni dem comin'?"

"Soon," he said. "He had to get home from work."

He wished Keoni and Junior would show up. Earlier in the summer after he had met Anika, he wanted to be alone with her all the time, but now she was taking the thing too seriously—to the point that she had introduced him to her parents, and wanted to know all about his family. It was no longer me Ben and you Anika, let's have plenny fun.

The smoke from the campfire down on the eighty yard beach facing Lanikai drifted up past them. Some haole kids were camping on the island too. He squinted at the patch of sand where they had left their stuff—fins, spear, cooler, wave-ski. Earlier he had gone in the water toward Lanikai to the reef and caught a unicorn fish. He had surfaced gasping with laughter, feeling an exhilaration he hadn't felt in a long time, because it had been years since he had fished. When he brought it to Anika, speared through the head so that the flesh would not be ruined, the strong odor wafted off it. "Ho, Ben dat stink!" Anika said, and he said, "Yeah, they're famous for that." Now it was in a plastic bag buried in the sand near their towels, and he could not get the strong fishy smell off his hands.

"No trades," he said. "You can drop a feather straight down. My grandfather calls it horse latitudes weather."

"I thought you said you were gonna see him today."

"I know, but he wasn't home." He felt bad about it anyway, about promising to visit and then finding an excuse not to. "He's out in the old shed I told you about. In the woods up the coast."

She put her arm around his waist, and the warmth of her flesh against his caused a strange flash of something in his trunk, like fibrillation, a subtle marijuana zap that left him feeling airy and without substance.

She giggled. "Dat good dope."

"Keoni grew it," he said. He turned to her. "So, speaking of birds—"

"I wasn't."

"I know, I was just curious about how you got into birds just the way you were curious about how I could get into business law."

"My dad taught me all about dat. We hiked a lot when I was little, so I was always interested. 'Ass how it started."

They looked at the half moon now sitting to the right of the cloud. He shook himself, almost as if waking up. "Anyway, I'll take the wave-ski in and call Keoni. I got one other thing I gotta do."

"Da taro inna car."

"They're just plants. I gotta deliver them."

"To who?"

"Whom," he said. "I'll be back. Gotta pick up more beer too."

"Why you talk li'dat? Like one teacha. Chee, you da mos' haolefied local guy I evah met."

"What do you speak at school? King's English, right?"

"So? This isn't school."

"You get good grades. You're a scholar, going to be an ornithologist. In the end you'll speak the king's English."

She scowled at him, and he snorted softly. It was stupid to say that. But he was going to plant the taro. he image of it sent a rush of giddy exhilaration through him.

"You doing something dumb I know. Dat Keoni, he a bad whatchucall—influence. Nice guy but."

"It's only a bet, and hey, I've known the guy since I was little."

He turned slowly, scanning the horizon—water, then Lanikai and the strip of houselights, then Kailua beach with the mountains far beyond, a fan of faint, salmon colored light over them.

He looked at her face, colored an ashy dark gray in the moonlight. She had large, beautiful eyes, and broad shoulders, from paddling, volleyball, surfing.

"So, your grandfaddah haole," she said. "Buggah's black."

"The sun. His name was Dennis and he used the Hawaiian spelling—Kenika. The Hawaiian and Portagee is from my mother's and grandmother's side."

"Wasn't he supposta be waiting for you?"

"He just forgot. He's up messing in the shed. Building something is all." He visualized the old man, wondering why he would go up there when his grandchildren would be visiting. He had been a little surprised to see how frail he had become. "We made all kinds of things up there. My sister and I helped him with canoes and stuff."

"What about your dad?"

He felt his face flush, and shook his head. "Well," he said, and turned slowly again, scanning the lights, then the mountain he always thought looked like an alligator's forehead and snout in the water, the rock formation jutting off the Marine Corps Air Station to the northwest of them.

She looked again at the moon. "Chee," she whispered, "'ass unreal."

He brought up in his mind the image of his father, dressed in filthy, grime-blackened jeans and a dirty sweatshirt, sometimes with a half rotted flannel shirt over it, and wearing a red bandanna whose red you could barely see, wandering barefoot along Kailua Road, or downtown Honolulu, or climbing into the dumpsters behind supermarkets. Years ago when he was twelve or thirteen he and his friends would ride past him on their bikes, and he would pretend he didn't know who the man was. No big deal, jus' one nodda bum. Just anodda ol' druggie.

The last time he had tried to talk to him, four years ago when he was on his way to college, he had seen him walking on Fort Street in downtown Honolulu. His father walked slowly, looking down at the sidewalk before him, seeming to contemplate some cryptic riddle, his left hand to his chin. As he approached, Benjamin took a couple of deep breaths because he was shocked at how dirty his father was, how dark, how slowly he moved. The man was only thirty-eight years old but looked sixty, his hair tangled in a reddish pony tail, a huge mat of it hopelessly snagged near the bottom.

Then as he got to within three steps, before his father looked up, he saw the red eyes, the rotted teeth, and the long dirty fingernails. "Dad," he had said, and then looked around, worrying that someone he knew might see him. But it was just downtown traffic. The man stopped and looked at him, seeming not to recognize his son. "Hey Dad."

"Eh howzit," he said. Then he cocked his head. "You smoke?" he asked, mimicking the act, his thumb and forefinger holding the imaginary joint before his lips.

"I just wanted to tell you," Benjamin had said. But there was no recognition. His father had looked into the middle distance before him and thought. Then shook his head slowly as if reacting to something in his mouth that had begun to taste bad. "No," he whispered. "No. No." He turned and walked away, back the way he had come.

So Anika wanted to dig. She wanted to dig it all out of him.

"Okay," he said, "You know the one who— Well, he's always barefoot, wears jeans and a sweatshirt, sometimes a flannel—"

"You mean a homeless guy?"

"We both saw him yesterday? Right there—Kailua?"

"Yeah, I know who you mean. I mean there are plenty of—"

"He's my father."

"Not."

"He is. The family's dirty secret that isn't a secret. I mean most people know."

"Not." She stepped away from him. "I know you dis way two months. I like you an' you nevah tell me dat?"

"I was afraid."

"Why? Of what?"

"You. Your parents. I mean I like your parents. I wish—"

"Why he like dat?"

"A long time ago he got into drugs, and Hawaii's stupidest profession—bank robbery. Can you believe that? A bank robber in Hawaii? He blew his brains out on paint, correction fluid, antifreeze, you name it."

"But why?"

"I don't know. I mean, it was a regular family and all. He had two older sisters, grew up normal and all." He laughed, shaking his head. "Once there was a standoff with the police at my old house. He robs a bank and eventually what does he do? What do all local bank robbers do? He comes home. Then the cops are all around with their bullhorns." He barely remembered that—the blue lights and yellow tape with writing on it stretched across the street.

"Why you nevah tell me?"

He scanned the lights again. Somewhere over there his father was probably sleeping, or stumbling along contemplating the mysteries of the universe. "I don't know. I just thought, you know, you and me and all that." He stopped. He didn't want to put words to it. He was twenty-two, she was twenty. It was out of the question, stupid. Why the hell would he do this to himself again?

"I guess I'm a little shy about all this stuff."

The look on her face was a mixture of expectation and anger, and he touched her cheek and shook his head slowly. "C'mon, let's go. The pakalolo's wearing off." And because of that, the thought of the taro in the car caused a twinge of shaky dread.

"I no go unless you tell me," she said.

He looked at her, then at the ground and thought, okay, put words to it.

"Well, like we're sort of—involved, right? I was just wondering if we should like, stay involved? I mean later on? Like whether or not you'll be around Christmas vacation and all that kind of let's keep in touch stuff?"

She heaved a huge, artificial sigh, and then giggled. "You lolo. Let's go."

As they made their way down the path, which was a flat gray in the moonlight, the brush on either side black, he hobbled on his sore feet while Anika explained that her parents were more understanding than Ben might expect. "An' of course everybody knows about your sister. I like meet her sometime."

He snorted—Pua the model. "Hey, she's just like you and me." He could hear the excitement in her voice because he had mentioned being "involved," and now he was unsure of himself for having said it. he got hooked into it somehow, on the beach at night on the other side a quarter mile east of Sandy Beach under the moon. What was the way of putting it? She gave herself to him in a simple ritual of such unabashed devotion that it scared him half to death. And in a way she was being presumptuous to assume that she could so easily appropriate his freedom like that. But his attachment to her was strong—he thought about her all the time, and he was confused about the idea that a girl who came from a background so like his should have this effect on him. Sometimes he even thought he hated it. When the word love entered his mind he would snort with embarrassment, and feel a strange shame, and the more objective and analytical side of his thinking ridiculed him. Moron. Like, what the hell you doing?

"An' your grandfaddah, he's kinda famous yeah?"

"Well," he said, "he's famous for canoes and some arty stuff, but mostly for canoes." As they approached the little beach, he laughed. "I mean Jesus, he was born in someplace like New Jersey. New Jersey or New York or something. That's why my name is McKay."

So what else could he tell her, since she was so interested in digging. That the heart of the family was torn out a half a million years ago? That most of the old folks were dead? He didn't understand it himself. He understood only that his own escape came in the form of being taken away from the windward side, away from where everything bad happened, and at thirteen he had been elated to be rid of it.

He scanned the water between the little island and Oahu. Nothing. "Look, I gotta go. Keoni'll be here soon."

"It's something stupid," she said. "Why you do it?" She pulled the blanket away and shook it, then ballooned it down on the sand.

"Just impaired judgment," he said, "and a problematic self concept." He visualized the twelve little plants with their rings of tiny roots, all in a paper bag.

"Me too," she said. "What it comes down to is that I don't like my clothes. I gotta see one shrink about dat."

"Yes, I understand. In my case, I'm really a lazy savage, shiftless and dumb."

She laughed, then sat down on the blanket. "What about dat kala? I can still smell um on you." She looked at the spot where it was buried. When he had brought it out, she had stared with a kind of scholarly interest at the strange unicorn's horn on its forehead and at the dull green color of its hide. "Gotta clean um," she had said, and he said, "Uh uh. Kala you cook guts in. My grandfather taught me that." Now, looking at the spot where it was buried, he shook his head. Where the hell did he go?

"Keoni dem bring food?" she asked.

"Yeah, hot dogs, hamburger, poke, tents, all that."

"'Kay."

He got his belt pack and tied it to the thick, nylon handle next to the seat depression on the ski, and picked up the ski and kayak paddle. "So," he said, "hold the fort."

He went to the right end of the beach near the other campers because the rip came straight from Lanikai between the islands, opposite the break. The water was warm on his legs and calm, and he sat down on the ski and put his feet in the nylon stirrups.

Two-hundred feet out, where the rip waves weakened, he stopped paddling and floated along, rocking with the gentle bumps made by the waves. All around him the ocean was black, except for the pathway of light coming from the moon ahead to his right. He looked behind him at the black shape of the island and tried to see Anika, but could not. It was stupid to leave her there. Willful, asinine behavior.

He squinted in the moonlight and opened his pack, rubbed the water off his hands on his bathing suit and felt around for matches and the half joint he had left there. What the hell. He was going back to the mainland in a week and felt that he could cut loose a little. His mother would be mortified. In fact she would be mortified to know what he'd been doing for the past two months—especially his hanging out with his old friends in Waimanalo. Earlier in the day, before he picked Anika up, he had sat on the beach with them and regressed into the easy, pointless joking around that his mother would have disapproved of: "Eh Ben," Keoni had said, "go back ovah da t'ree priorities of life fo' us idiots, 'kay?"

"It's surf, pussy, and dope. Agriculture is fourth—growing number three and planting taro."

"You no do um," Keoni said.

"You wait."

"Eh, what about beah?" Keoni said, holding his Bud can up.

"Beer may be generically classified along with dope."

"Not," Junior said. "Den whackin' off would go wit' pussy."

"No, beer is a form of dope, whereas—"

"Chee," Keoni said. "Fuckah blows me away wit' dat 'whereas.'"

"—whereas whacking off is a mere imitation."

"Howevah," Keoni said, and laughed. "See, I can do dakine too. Howevah, in my list of priorities, surf come firs', cause I do dat mostly mornings, den beah, den pussy cause dat laters."

"Clever," Benjamin said. "Linear thinking. Eh, Sakata, you Japanee, how you put pussy first?"

"Paht Hawaiian," he said. "From da hips down, brah."

"You fuckah," Keoni said to Benjamin. "You haole from da neck up. How dat happen?"

"Brainwashing," he said. "My brain has been washed of all its ignorant savagery."

"Shit!" Junior Sakata said. "You heard dat? Eh Keoni, you ignorant savage, what you tink?"

"I tink da idiot's pussy whipped. Anika, she got you, brah."

"No way."

"Ho, she got you good."

"Nobody gets me. All I gotta do is plant some taro and get outta town."

"Nah, you'll chicken out."

"No. No I won't"

He held the first puff in his lungs until he felt the desire to let it out tickle his chest, and exhaled. By the subtle movement of the houselights, he knew he was drifting along the beach to the right, and studied the lights for the arrangement that indicated the right-of-way between two gigantic stucco houses recently built in the contemporary Taco-Bell architectural style, immense monstrosities of the sort he had seen in Los Angeles. His car was parked there at the end of the lane between them, on the street.

He drew again on the joint until he felt the stream of smoke burn his lips, and smelling the remnants of the kala on his hands, threw the joint in the water, still holding the smoke in his lungs.

A sluggish electrical charge moved like a sigh, or a yawn, through his flesh, and the lights of the houses grew prismatic halos. He giggled and began paddling again. Another hundred yards, and the dome of stars seemed to shift to the right, as if he were in a gigantic, slowly turning sphere, and the lights were not lights but dashes, bright hyphens along the shore, and his body felt out of balance. On the beach his father waited for him, he knew now, and between them was a treacherous obstacle course where he had to maneuver the ski past sucking abyssal whirlpools, sharks, vengeful aquatic dead who would rise up wearing feather capes and helmets. He felt hated, by whom or what he could not be sure. Behind him Anika hated him for not taking her seriously, for the cool superficiality he had spent the past few years cultivating.

He stopped paddling and rocked with the little bumps. In a week he'd be in L.A., and that was a relief. He loved the life there, the excitement that he imagined he had looked for ever since his mind opened up to a world larger than where he grew up. He supposed it was typical of anyone who grew up in Hawaii. The only thing that compromised what felt like total freedom was that for two years he had been involved with a girl, even secretly thought of getting married. Then he began to sense that she liked to be with him most of all because of the color of his skin and the cut of his features. It was almost too easy to read—expressions, little things she said. Walking with her into an apartment where a party would be going on, he could almost hear the voice in her bearing: here I am, and isn't he beautiful? Isn't he just so cool? He wanted to stop and look at her and say, listen, I am not as different from you as you imagine. L.A. and a blonde girlfriend might have been a novelty for him, but when he found out what a novelty he was for her, he didn't like the feeling. He broke up with her.

Then almost immediately he allowed himself to get involved with Anika. It seemed strange to him because he had known her most of his earlier life, from grade school and all the innocent stuff like May Day shows for the parents out in the blistering heat on the playing field, to Kailua Intermediate School, where she had grown up, impressively any boy would have to admit. Even though his family had moved, his school baseball team went back to play in Kailua a couple of times a year. One afternoon he had jumped down out of the bus and seen her riding out of the parking lot on her bike, and boys sitting on the concrete tire bumpers whistled at her and yelled, "Hey, get chance?" and she passed by them and said with haughty composure, "Eh! Kiss my ass," and they yelled, "Anika, I like try!" Pedaling away she looked back and yelled, "Try come ass-ho! I kick you inna alas!" The boys looked at each other with appreciative awe, and then sang at the tops of their voices, "Swee-eet okole! I like get some swee-eet okole!" He bumped into her at the beach, and stared at her, thinking, Jesus, that's Anika. That's Anika Nahoopii, from the old days.

He felt more or less settled again, and looked back—the little campfire was still going, and black figures moved in its light. She'd be all right. He went on with his paddling, knowing he was moving but seeing no movement because the water was black and the lights stood there the same distance away as he moved. The out-of-balance sensation returned, and this coupled with the optical illusion of non-motion made the water tip in a blatant violation of natural law, and he gasped as the lower half of his body went in. He held onto the ski, and struggled back up, for a moment almost hysterical at the idea of the thick tentacle which barely missed him as he propelled his legs out, and he ended up shaking, holding the paddle against his chest. "I shouldn't do this," he whispered. "I shouldn't."

When he got to the dim strip of sand he found himself a hundred yards off the right-of-way, and walked back shivering, dragging the ski behind him. He left it in the bushes at the end of the right-of-way, pulled out his zoris, and digging his keys out of his bathing suit pocket, made his way out to the street between the two houses, from which he could hear televisions on the same channel in a crude stereo effect.

He didn't clean the sand off his feet or worry about salt. Always buy cars with vinyl seats. He giggled, then felt around near the floor on the passenger side and found the bag. He gently pinched a little taro shoot—it wasn't hot or slimy. The heat didn't get them.

He drove through Kailua, and remembered as he passed the police station that he had left his bag tied to the ski. No money. But he decided not to go back. He'd get the beer later. Now he was technically without an identity, and if there was a surprise DUI roadblock he would be toast. Anika would worry, would think he had drowned. He got through town and went up the Pali Highway toward Castle Junction. He was so unsure of his grasp on things that forgetting his wallet felt like a mistake that had aggravated itself like a rapid infection, so that he thought he was forgetting his own name, or his imagined future and real past, as if these too were as easy to mislay as a wallet.

He turned right and passed one golf course, behind which was another new one. A few years ago it replaced a complicated jungle just under the Pali Lookout that had mango and avocado trees, bananas, stands of bamboo, lilikoi vines, mountain apple trees, starfruit. As a child he had gone there with his grandfather, and come out so laden with food that his knees would nearly buckle. There had been a lot of protest about the building of that course, but it got built anyway. Both golf courses ended on the west side against a state park, and tucked behind the new golf course was a huge house, nearly finished but as yet unoccupied, with a little driving range and putting green on its grounds. It was a corporate retreat for Japanese businessmen masquerading as a single-family house, and there had been controversy about the building of that, too, because people claimed that it had been built on sacred land. The land was at the base of the almost vertical face of the Koʻolau Mountains, sharply eroded so that looking up your eyes fell into deep V's down which water ran when it rained, a gigantic curtain topped with clouds. But now the mountains were a flat black silhouette, and cloudless at the top, with a surreal blue-black sky behind.

He had done this twice before, with sprouted coconuts, so he knew the way in. It was willful and asinine, but he felt for peculiar, unanalyzed reasons that he needed to do this, a stupid prank masquerading as political rebellion. Besides, it impressed his friends when they read the paper the next day, or better, saw it on TV. Keoni even recorded one TV story for him, although it was very brief. The problem was that the last time he was up here was only a few weeks ago, and he had to be extra careful.

He parked on a cul-de-sac near the state park entry, and carrying the taro and a little garden axe went across a vacant lot between two houses into the brush. Behind him a car came in and turned around, gangster rap rattling the house windows, and left, the deep booming of the speakers resonating in his ears.

The hard part was the woods. Walking, he felt that it was only a personal, deeply-remembered sonar that gave him his bearings, because he had come here dozens of times with his grandfather when he was little. There, an old rock wall, built hundreds of years ago maybe, and beyond that, the remains of a banana patch, mostly rotted, papery stumps and thin, frail plants.

A dim, ashy light on the other side showed through, and he knew he was going in the right direction. He stopped, mesmerized by the silence, as if nature had stopped to listen to him as he moved. Then the clicking of a gecko. He clicked back, imitating the gecko by popping his tongue away from the roof of his mouth repeatedly. Then he became dizzy again so that the earth rose under him and then fell away, and he stumbled to right himself, felt his zori slip on something soft, and smelled rotten avocado. He was under one of the few avocado trees left here.

He went on, his heart beginning to beat too fast, and then a fear similar to the fear he had felt on the water expanded in his flesh — something out there did not like him, whether entrepreneurs or Yakuza vacationers here to practice their putting or the spirits of the dead, he didn't know, and he moved over the flat, soft forest bed trying to ignore what he knew to be a paranoia induced by the pakalolo and a reason he secretly didn't like smoking it, because friends would sometimes metamorphose and reveal themselves to be vicious, ridiculing monsters who had been barely able to conceal their condescending pity for him, barely able to control their derisive laughter until he was out of earshot.

He shook it off when the dim outline of the huge building showed itself beyond the bushes, undulating with the rhythm of his walking. In the driveway sat a stretch limousine. When he was little and one went through Kailua, people came out of their houses to look. Now you saw any number of them every day, various lengths, gold fittings, the works.

No one seemed to be around, although the limo made him uneasy. He made his way out of the brush, climbed over the little fence and walked along the driving range. A minor bit of construction compared to everything else—the developers saw a chance to make bundles off those golfers willing to pay to stay in the house. The little signs here and there were in Japanese.

Out in the moonlight, he thought he could see the green of the grass, although when he concentrated he realized it was a flat gray, a little brighter where the putting green and the flag were.

He felt the soft smoothness of the green under his feet and stopped. He turned slowly, scanning the black wall of mountains, then to the east the peaks of Olomana, and to the left of the peaks the subtle glow of Kailua. He was sure of it, had been the first and second times—there had been an avocado grove here. Standing there, he shook his head, imagining the dark, ragged shape of his father, locked away probably forever, the synapses, or the tubes and resistors and chips, all the delicate wiring of his brain shorted out and burned into stumps. And then his grandfather, that willful old fart, running off just to aggravate them with his eccentricities. He and his sister had not maintained enough contact with him, that was the problem. As a boy Benjamin and his sister had spent a lot of time with the old man up in the shed and he knew, even at eight or nine, that his grandfather was trying to teach them everything he knew about wood, tools, canoe building, carving. He was even aware at the time that the old man's only son, brain already half shorted out, should have been the one to learn all this, and the grandchildren were the next-generation surrogates. Now he had forgotten most of it, and the old man was alone, he imagined going nuts like his father, the wiring of his brain shorting out.

There was no answer to it. There was no remedy for anything. He snorted, and lowered himself to his knees.

The first satisfying whack of the axe produced a perfect, two-pound divot in the well-fertilized soil. He took a taro plant out of the bag and placed it in the hole so that the little root, fringed base was just one inch below the surface of the grass that seemed nearly as smooth as the surface of a pool table. Then he broke the divot up and packed the loamy soil around the shoot. You must measure out the distance properly, he thought. Someone told him that, Kenika, old fart, but he felt guilty thinking that, and then suddenly afraid, because something felt wrong, and he had no clue about what it might be. But then it was not his business. Right now planting taro was. The length of your forearm. Then the next divot. They should be in a straight line. Speak to them as you plant, compliment them on their procreative strength. "Yeah," he said, putting the second one in, "you're bursting with growth, aren't you, you little shit? You feel hot in my hand, you'll explode when I cover you. We'll just see if those fuckers can find their balls once you get going."

He heard a noise, and stood up, his back stiff. Rat, bufo, whatever. He stretched, the axe still in his hand.

When he turned something blasted all the air from his lungs and he sat down, heard yelling, but from where he didn't know. The axe was gone.

"You son of a bitch! What da fahk you doeen? You son—"

He didn't understand—the voice was disembodied as were other sounds, and he tried to stand up but felt a shaky lack of tension in his knees. He giggled as he stood. Someone had thrown a rock, that was it, and he reached to his chest, felt something wet and looked at his fingers. Black. Now the voice was louder.

"Who tol' you to bring dat, you goddam jerk!"

Then a higher voice: "He was gonna—"

Bring what? he wondered, and then was knocked off his feet from the side, coughed so hard from the ground's impact that he thought he had ripped his throat. He tried to sit up, and the side of a white, phosphorescent sneaker came at his face and he went back in a sickening, silver flash.

"T'row dat away!" someone yelled.

"It went off," the higher voice said. "I din' mean it. He was gonna hit Herb wit' da axe."

He reached for his face with his left hand, the one not pinned under his body, and tried to feel his nose, but both his fingers and nose were numb. Someone nudged him with a foot.

"Get off him!" the voice bellowed. "Oh Jesus, oh Jesus!"

A black silhouette of a head hovered over him. "Brah!"

He tried to speak but could not.

"Goddam jerk—you shot him! Goddammit!" Then the head appeared again. "Brah!"

"I—" He was confused. Pain seemed to search his body with long feelers for a location to put down roots. Then one did, high in his chest on the left side, and then he felt blood bubble in his nose and run down his cheeks.

"Why you kick 'im?"

"I thought he'd get away." A different voice.

"Goddammit!"

"Well, he didn't get away dis time, did he braddah Fred? Hah? No mo' fix greens fo' us, ah?"

"Get outta my face!"

The pain now had a center, as if someone had thrust an iron into the hollow of his shoulder.

"Brah, don't move."

He tried to speak again, but his nose was plugged up. "My friends are on—" The sky tipped again, the sphere rotated, the stars became hyphens.

"Oh God," the man said. "You keeds, why you do dis?"

"I—" He was confused again, as if he were waking up in the morning, a sigh in his flesh. A dizzy yawn.

"Oh Jesus." Then the head vanished.

"You son of a bitch!" he yelled. There were voices off toward the building.

"They're calling nine-one-one," the man said. "You stay heah. Relax."

"My father wanders—" No. He was scared. Anika was alone. It was stupid of him to leave her there. The thoughtlessness of it, someone so— If Keoni didn't show up then—

He tried to move, but had no strength. His head went up, flopped back, and he felt the pull of the earth stretch his face, his whole body. Gravity. Only place you can get away from it is in the water.

"My friends," he whispered. "They are on— They need to be notified, so they know— They're on an island somewhere. It's—" He couldn't remember the name, could no longer fix the location, and now had no idea where he was, why he was here instead of somewhere else, and a horrible cold sensation overcame him, seemed to choke the breath from him.

A hand patted his chest, and he heard a voice, but he could not understand the words, which came across tinny and hollow and flat. It was as if the man had suddenly decided to speak in another language. He saw the hulking form of his father, dirty and slow, moving across the green, his hand to his chin and his eyes fixed on the ground, and then other shadows floated above him, his grandfather whispering to him, other people in the background, and then there were the translucent shapes of ghostly red fish sweeping by. He swallowed blood, and then could breathe through his nose, and smelled something.

Earth.

Grandaddy Kenika sits on the submerged reef at low tide, water lapping around his stomach, and when you burst to the surface and breathe, you say, "I no see um." He is black against the bright sky. The Mokes are green with the shimmering movement of windlashed grasses.

"He's there. Go down with your chest sliding on the reef and just turn into the cave—that way the first thing you see is the ceiling."

"Cannot. Mask fill up wit' dakine, 'ass why. Wattah."

"Suck air in your nose and it'll stick."

You try it. Ho, suck da eyeballs out. "'Kay den."

"Go in spear first. He won't move. I'll watch you from here." He places his mask on the water so he can see down through the glass.

Cold. To the bones cold, like everything inside is straight out of the refrigerator. Take three big breaths.

You crawl down the face of the reef and the top of the cave comes to you, and then you crawl like a snake upside down and fold your body into the cave and move the spear into the blackness thinking, remember what he said, hold your arm steady and a little tense and pull the trigger with a little push forward so that the spear will have the right thrust.

Breath running out. On the black ceiling of the cave nothing, and you are ready to turn out when you see it, a red ghost, and when the eyes adjust it is as if you can see through it, a strange, faint light deep red like translucent blood in the shape of a fish, and then it intensifies into the black-red, the spines on its top splayed, jammed into a depression in the ceiling, its huge eye looking back at you and its mouth open as if it is thinking. You turn the spear slowly, moving the point toward its head. You are out of breath and the ticklish desire to breathe causes little hiccups in your chest.

Red-black, he looks, not moving, and you begin to choke in your throat. You settle your body as he said, waving the flippers to keep it in one place, and move your arm. Then in one motion you thrust and pull the trigger and feel the spear point drive into the rock, and then it is jiggling in a fine vibration followed by being pulled to one side.

Your breath is gone. You thrash out of the cave gripping the spear and explode to the surface and the mask slides down over your face so the strap is around your neck. Bursting into the blinding light you scream, "I got um!"

You raise the spear and there he is, still splayed and thinking, then wiggling on the spear. Menpachi.

"Hey, that's a big one," Kenika says. "Here, I'll put him in the bag."

You cough, splutter, snot running down your upper lip.

"I got 'im! One big fahkeen menpachi! Oops."

But Kenika laughs. "Yup. Ten, eleven inches. You got him right through the gill."

Kenika slides his thumb and forefinger under its gills and then runs the menpachi down the spear to the rear end and off, and pulls the inner tube toward him. Hanging inside is the bag, into which he slides the menpachi.

"Grandaddy, I sorry I curse," you say.

"You were just worked up."

The shivers run the length of your body, vibrate your jaw.

"Come on up here," Kenika says. "Your lips are blue."

You climb up on the reef into where the water is only a foot deep, look in the seaweed for vana, and then sit down next to him. He drapes his stringy arm over your shoulder and around and grabs your left upper arm with his dark, scarred hand, and the warmth seeps into you.

"Oh ,he big," you say.

"Aweoweo does the same thing," he says. "That's the one that has the sort of mottled red and silver look. Next we find aholehole, the silver ones."

"Where dey?"

"You look for a place where there's a current where you can look in a hole and see them sideways, but it's usually where there's a current."

"Dey heah?"

"Over that way," and he points toward Kaneohe. "A hundred yards or so, where there's a rip current. The water goes back and forth, and you see them in little schools all standing still fighting the current. Then you pick one. Tomorrow. You're too cold for any more."

"Not."

"We've been here two hours. Your mom's gonna get mad."

"Not."

One · 1947

Dennis McKay's only escape was the water. In the moment of entry, the coldness of it shocked him into an exhilarated flurry of energy in his legs, propelling him past the bright bubbles, and he left behind everything that tortured him on land, whether it was stuff from only days ago like Junior Kaaiai punching him in the face, or centipedes stinging him in his bed, or the more horrible stuff he could not shake from before he was brought here; the memory of the fire and the sound of the terrified cows struggling in their stanchions as they burned to death; or his mother's stiff form, head down on the kitchen table, her eyes staring dully at nothing. The long rides with The Captain on the train, and then the droning plane ride across the Pacific during which he sat dazed at a porthole watching the translucent whirr of a propeller, and then the strangeness of the new place. None of those new things could obliterate the memory, which seemed to overlay his brain like a bright tattoo. But he had discovered that the water seemed to dull and then to somehow neutralize consciousness, so that he became reduced to an organism with a pair of eyes propelling itself weightlessly through the dense medium in serene, thoughtless motion.

He took the same route each time, gliding over the rubble-strewn sand to the first dark green lump of dead coral covered with fine plants waving in a surreal unison with the gentle sways of the water. At the coral head he would bear left, feeling the coldness of the water seep into his flesh, and he would hum into the snorkel, sustaining the soft rattle of the little residue of water caught in the bottom of the black rubber U under the mouthpiece. Sometimes the ounce of water swaying against the glass in the bottom of the mask, just covering his nostrils, would become pink from the residues of blood. Then the pressure of the partial vacuum he created to keep the mask mashed to his face would make his nose throb up to his eyesockets. But the welcome, advancing chill would finally cancel even the memory of Junior swinging at him.

The morning sun slanting into the water animated everything with a brightness and density of color that seemed possible only in a dream, and sounds of clicking and soft, grinding squeaks came from all directions. The yellow butterflyfish and black and yellow Moorish Idols were as intense as neon lights. He would look at his free hand, the one not holding the spear, and it would glow with a tan so rich it bordered on bright orange, huge because of the magnification of the mask, which made a soda bottle look quart-sized rather than six ounces.

The spear had been given to him by The Captain a week after they had arrived. Until he got the spear and fins and mask he hated it here and lived each day in a hopeless misery at the idea that he was two thousand-five hundred miles away from the continent, with no way to escape. But then he found the water. The spear handle was a two-inch thick section of dowel with a hole bored through it end to end, with one leaf of a heavy door hinge screwed into its side, the other leaf loose and bent over one end so that the thin, six-foot spear could go through the dowel and one of the hinge's screw holes. The loose leaf of the hinge was bent to form a crude trigger, and the spear was propelled by strips of inner tube so that it worked like a slingshot, cocked against the sides of the screw hole until you pulled the trigger.

Forty yards out there was a shelf with a cave underneath, which funneled water back and forth with the gentle waves, leaving the broken shells and pebbles on the bottom dancing over each other, creating a soft-hissing sound. Deep in the funnel, in a dark space with a single vertical shaft of ashy light cutting down through it, he had seen the green side of a large fish, and another time the strange, surging undulation of an octopus. If this little cave so close to shore held all those fish, he had reasoned, then the hundreds of yards of reef which stood a foot out of the water all along the beach at low tide, all hollow underneath, must have an unimaginable wealth of them. So far he had speared only one fish, a strange black one with dull white speckles, shaped like a box with a mouth on one end and a tail on the other.

Bringing it up, shaking with excitement, he had found that it was no larger than a pack of cigarettes. Disgusted with himself and moaning with shame, he slid it away from the hinged barb to the back end of the spear and released it. Still gulping but swimming sideways and then upside down, the dying fish dissolved into the blue like a ghost.

He stopped, pulled his legs under him, and planted the black fins on the sand. Then he stood up into the cold, gravity-laden air. Balancing against the gentle surges of the waves, he slid the mask up on his forehead and looked back at the little hundred-yard beach where Momi Santiago sat under a fringed white umbrella. This was the fifth time in three weeks that they had come over the mountain to Waikiki so that The Captain could look for a cottage. Soldiers back from the war had a lot of them, he said, and the prices owners charged were higher than before the war.

Momi seemed to be looking at him, but did not wave. He did not entirely understand what was going on between The Captain and Momi, although he knew enough to know they slept together sometimes. But as guests at the Santiago house on the windward side of the island in Maunawili, they could not stay more than a week or so, The Captain had said, because he did not want them to overstay their welcome.

His little room at the Santiago house was in the back, one floor lower than the rest of the house, a converted toolshed nestled against a stone foundation held together by oozing, cracked cement, and after they had been there two days he woke up in the middle of a humid, sweaty night being stung on the side. He had turned the light on and looked around in the moist sheets thinking it was a wasp, and then stumbled back in terror as a brown centipede that had to be six inches long moved out of a fold in the sheet, and when he looked more closely he could see the dark pincers, like ice tongs, on the sides of its head, and its legs were a pale blue. His shadow covered the centipede, and its feelers unrolled slowly in a perfect opening spiral. He moved to the side so that the light hit the centipede, and the feelers rolled back down to its head. Then it moved, and like a string of dark liquid crawled back under the sheet. On his side the welt had already begun to harden, and he went out to get The Captain. The worst part of it was that when they looked for it, The Captain with a flit gun ready, they couldn't find it, and after The Captain reassured him and left, he sat on a wooden chair the rest of the night with the light on. And that was how he had slept since then, and in his half dreams he always settled on the image of the hideous, sort of prehistorically-formidable creature, perfect for this place because it seemed to him more exotically venomous than any insect he could imagine.

Behind Momi, bright in the morning sunlight, the steep, rocky flanks of Diamond Head rose up, darker green in the erosion-cut gulleys and parched and light brown on the outcroppings. He turned and saw, out on the exposed reef, Junior Kaaiai and Angela Santiago stepping gingerly over the seaweed and spiny urchins that crowded the tiny holes in the reef. He was not sure how far out it was proper for him to go, but figured that since they were on the reef and the same age, he should be able to go at least a few yards beyond them in the water, which interrupted the reef in a single, wide blue swath. He was sure Momi Santiago was convinced that he could not swim.

He had learned to swim in an indoor YMCA pool with water so heavily-chlorinated that it felt like a fine oil, the air above it in the loud, cramped hall dense with a stinking chemical vapor. That was in Paterson, New Jersey, when he was twelve, five years ago now, when his mother had left him there every day in the summer.

He did not want to irritate anyone, or cause them to worry about him. He still did not know why it was that The Captain, a friend of his mother's, had declared himself guardian, but was grateful enough that he tried to do everything right.

He decided to swim out and around the exposed reef, where he could remain in the water safely out of Junior's range. A cousin of Angela's, Junior always behaved well in the presence of Momi or The Captain or Momi's old mother, a shriveled lady in black who spent her days sitting in a rocking chair over at the Maunawili house muttering unintelligibly to the wall. But when they were alone at places like Kailua Beach, Junior and Angela and the young friends, Junior would punch him in the face and say, "Eh, haole boy—you fuckah—you rat. You tell an' I kick your ass." And Angela would stop Junior before he could carry on with the beating: "Stop dat Juniah! I tell!" She explained it to him later. "Local boys no like haole boys, 'ass all it is. Dey like beef wittum whenevahs. No worry, he stop bumbye." It all seemed absurd, because one of the other boys was Chinese, another Japanese.

As he churned in the shallow water on the beach side of the exposed reef, he imagined that it would all pass, that Junior would let off if for no other reason than bruised knuckles.

Junior was way out on the reef, Angela closer in, standing on the reef and apparently singing while the small waves sent fans of white spray over her legs. He was always a little nervous in her presence. She had a strange directness, where she would walk up and talk to him with her face a foot from his, the huge brown eyes boring straight into his head. He stopped in the water, listening to the rattling in the snorkel. She was tall and in all ways she was big. There was something about her proportions—long legs and a kind of lithe roundness, so that in the bathing suit, her body was different from pictures of sort of normal beauties in magazines—Lana Turner, Betty Grable, Rita Hayworth. There was none of that angular definition he saw in those pictures. Instead she seemed smoothed off, rounded with a covering of thick, very brown skin, and hair that was almost black but for the strange dark-copper color that became lighter in the pony tail.

When they were together she did most of the talking, told him about Pearl Harbor and after, about how scared everyone was that there might be an invasion, about trenches dug in schoolyards, about barbed wire on the beaches and gas masks and scrap drives and the Junior Red Cross which she belonged to throughout the war. It fascinated him because in New Jersey he had spent the war reading about the events, following them day by day all the way through the Russian invasion of Germany and the Allied invasion from the west. Her stories fascinated him also because of the way she talked, the beautiful lilt of pidgin and the peculiar word selections, and watching her as she talked, he would become mesmerized by her voice and her face, with the full lips and broad nose, the sensuous pudginess around her eyes.

"An' den, ho, we tink, if dey fine one smaw submarine right dere Bellows Fiel', den dey get dakine huge ones too, right? So da neighbors, dey check rifles and stuffs, make shuah dey have ammunitions and all li'dat. Us kids, we climb da ridge behine da house an' sit an' watch da ocean fo' ships and all dakine. Ho, was scary."

The Captain had explained to him in Maunawili that these people, and he gestured as if to indicate the entire neighborhood, these people were Hawaiians, Polynesians like Momi, or like old Elizabeth, or Angela. They were a dying race who would disappear through genetic assimilation. They were people of another time, stuck in the twentieth-century and like children who needed tending. They had been led out of their savage past by America, a country which had taken on the task of keeping them safe and secure. And didn't Pearl Harbor teach everyone that? Didn't the modernization of this beautiful place preserve for them some semblance of civilization, and a reasonable future? These people, he said, gesturing again, were a race of magnificent creatures out of the past.

He could not explain to The Captain the effect she had on him, was ashamed to admit it, even thought the reason The Captain was out here was to be with Momi, or at least so he implied.

When The Captain had announced where it was they were going, he said that most of what he owned was in storage there, and some of his best friends lived there. On the map it was a tiny string of islands making a dotted arc in the center of the Pacific; the remotest populated place on the globe, The Captain had said. And even at the airport he understood how alien a place it was. Japanese people wandered around, smiling cordially and chatting, Hawaiian girls walked around in leaf skirts, people wore flowers around their necks, and because he was so tired it had all felt like some bizarre dream.

He floated away from the shallow water into the hazy, bluish-white area where there was no reef. Fresh water from Diamond Head had run down into the ocean, The Captain had told him, and prevented the reef from forming, creating a fifty-yard wide, shallow aquatic canyon, sandy-bottomed and sometimes murky. The reef rose from each side, and at its deepest the sandy part was twenty feet. When he dove down to look into hollows and deeper caves in the sides of the vertical reef wall, he had seen shafts of surreal light in the distance, with the shapes of large fish moving through them like figures from a dream.

Angela was singing as loud as she could, her voice drowned out by the waves and the wind. He rose up and hooked his fingers on the reef, looking around to make sure his knees wouldn't hit anything sharp. She was facing away, and he looked up under the skirt of her blue bathing suit at her buttocks.

"...Dann-dy," she yelled. Then he heard, "Do or die..." It was a song from a movie they had seen at the Princess Theater downtown. She turned partway and yelled, "Bon on da fot' of July!" then saw him.

"You catch anyting?"

"No."

She got down on her knees, right there above him, and then down on her elbows, stretched out on her stomach, her face only two feet from his. He backed up a little. "Hah," she said, "get hana butta all o' you face."

"What's that?" He reached up to touch his face.

"Snot."

He fell back into the water and shook his head in it, and then rose back up and opened his eyes. "Isn't Hana a town?"

"Yah, but snot too," she said. "Try come. Can walk all ovah."

"'Sokay. I'm gonna fish."

"Da Captain gonna marry my auntie?"

"I don't know."

"You get brown eyes," she said.

"I'm gonna fish. I—"

"Get us one 'uhu," she said. "Da big green one wit' da beak. Parrot fish."

He had seen them, but they were always beyond what he considered his range. He hung there on the reef, looking to her left, her right, toward Diamond Head. Her forwardness scared him, and he avoided her eyes. When a little wave washed over the reef, tipping her so that she had to brace herself against it, she drew a mouthful of water from the wave and shot it into his face. Then she laughed. He shook his face in the water once more, and then came up blinking the drips from his eyes. "We be cousins den," she said. "Juniah no mo' beat you up. Cannot." She looked directly into his face again, and he began to shiver from the chill, his chin wiggling. "How's your nose?"

"No problem."

"Juniah—he one hothead."

"'Sokay."

"It's not personal, like I to' you."

"'Sokay."

"Dat all you say? 'Sokay?'"

"Well, I—"

"Eh, get one 'uhu. Nobody punch you den."

He pushed off the reef and hung there holding himself up by churning the fins. Off to the side now, he looked at her lying on the reef, the water washing over his thighs and forearms. She was studying something in a little hole in the reef. Because she was not looking at him, he stared at her brown skin and the way the bathing suit seemed too small for her, depressing her flesh at every seam. The bathing suit skirt had washed up onto her lower back, which was arched from the way she was propped on her elbows, and the profile of her thighs and buttocks was almost black against the sky. When she looked at him he said, "Well, I'm goin' in," and put the mask on.

Moving along the reef he felt his limbs growing weak, and shivered. If he climbed out here there was always the chance that Junior would work his way in from the outer reef, so he decided to swim all the way back to the beach and the safety of Momi's presence.

He thought that it was his re-entry into the world of gravity that caused it, but once he had dried himself off and sat down on a towel, a safe-enough distance from Momi that he would not have to talk to her, because he just didn't know how, he found that all he had forgotten in the water came back, and as had happened before it came back with a pinpoint lucidity that he hated: nine in the morning and he had overslept.

He had planned on going to the school to sign his quitting papers, because he didn't want to do the last year. But he was going to have to argue with his mother about that, once she got up. Outside, the loud morning traffic of Paterson had already died out. He walked down the hall to the kitchen and there she was, drunk again, her head down on the table and the bottle next to it. There was a two-day-old *Paterson Morning Call* on the floor. "Ma," he said. He approached, and then touched her shoulder. There was a strange stiffness, as if her entire body had been flexed rigid against his touch. "Ma." He turned his head and stooped over her, to make eye contact. Hers were half open, and drying liquid pooled under her slack mouth, a small insect mired in it. "Ma." He knew and he didn't know. He touched her hand, and it was cold, the flesh stiff. He thought that if he waited she would come around. He looked at her hair, parted in the middle and then flowing down over her face, and he moved it out of the way and looked at her cheek, then at the pool of drying liquid. He touched her cheek, felt the same stiffness. "Ma."

He did not know then, and did not know now, sitting on the beach with the sun beating down on his back, why he stood there so long, knowing she was dead but then not really knowing, and after that, he did not know why he didn't cry, in fact felt no more than a peculiar airiness, the strange floating sensation of a blank dream, where he moved from here to there answering questions from neighbors and then police, his voice sounding to him tinny and flat. He didn't know why he waited until the right time, four o'clock in the afternoon, and then went as he always did to the stinking YMCA pool. He didn't know why he went home that evening either, to the empty apartment, and then spent the evening answering the door, to one neighbor or another offering casseroles and cans of food, or men who inquired if it was really true, that his mother had died, and then asked him how he was doing, stricken expressions on their faces, asked him what he was going to do now that his mother was gone. He would close the door thinking, what to do? What I always do—wait, and then go to the pool. Why would anything be different?

And after a week it was The Captain, whose real name was George Angstrom, someone he remembered from years ago when he was little, and then a few times when he was nine or ten, a longer stay when he was thirteen. He was a well-dressed man who had a smell, like soured talcum powder. When The Captain told him that it was time to leave, that the rent had not been paid and there was no longer any use in staying here, he looked at the man and said, "Are you my father?" and the man said, "No, I am not," and so he said, "Then who is? Do you know who he is?" No, The Captain didn't know. And he thought, Then who am I in the mirror? Why are my eyes not blue like hers? Why is my face not her face? "I thought you might know because—" and The

Captain got a pained expression and said, "That is not the issue right now. The issue right now is that there is no point in staying here any longer, and it's time you came along. I promised her I'd take care of you if—" and as he went on the understanding slowly emerged: so this man is a guardian, so this man will take care of me now, at least until I'm old enough to— "We're going today," The Captain said. "You'll need to pack up your things." And so he packed up his things, into a green duffel bag left in the apartment by a soldier his mother knew, and the name crudely stenciled on the canvas was "Richard Keach" and he thought, no, no, my name is Dennis McKay, my name is Dennis McKay, my name is Dennis McKay. And that was the first time he cried: packing the duffel bag, his hands trembling badly, and repeating his name to himself. He cried because he would miss the YMCA pool, because his only refuge from anything was that stinking water.

He was warm enough now, sitting on the beach watching Angela Santiago and Junior Kaaiai walking on the reef, that he decided to go back in the water. Momi sat now with the umbrella down, her face to the sun. For an older lady she was pretty, he thought, with a dark, aristocratic face and dark hair like Angela's. He supposed that if The Captain married Momi, there would be a normal life, he a kind of adopted son. Then he would get a job, come home every day to a cottage in Waikiki or maybe to the musty house in Maunawili. Angela, Momi's niece, would come over from her house just down the road in Kailua and they'd listen to the radio or go swimming, and Junior would have no more right to punch him. If he was exiled here, then that seemed to him an acceptable life, at least until he got up enough money to leave. But to where? Paterson? He shuddered at the thought that there was nothing there, and nothing anywhere else. The army maybe.

He made his way to the water and got the equipment on, and eased himself in, trying to disregard the coldness which shocked his flesh, and with the weightlessness he could almost see memory receding, moving backward so that it became tiny, as if seen through the wrong end of a telescope.

If his only escape here was the water, it made sense to him because it had been his only escape back in New Jersey, that snot and piss-polluted swimming pool, and for a while before his mother died a muddy pond in upstate New York, with dark green moss and weeds and frogs around the edges and a bottom with muck as smooth as pudding. Water, its silence and density, which made buoyancy possible, seemed a strange neutralizer of all he hated. It shut out hearing, clouded his vision when he opened his eyes into it. And the deep chill it produced eroded memory to the point that floating along face down in the pond and opening his eyes to a hazy, flat yellow, sometimes made darker by the slow ballooning of clouds of silt from the motion of his feet, he would think, I do not really exist, or if I exist, I am a lower form of life.

In Paterson he had lived with his mother in a three-room apartment over a confectionary store, across the street from a bowling alley. From the time he was seven or eight he understood what was happening each night when she would come home with a different man. Long after he was put to bed he would hear them, the clinking of glasses and the low, secret laughter, then the sounds of bedsprings squealing as if they were playing some bouncing game on it, and then soft speech, more clinking of glasses, and the smell of cigarette smoke materializing in the air he breathed.

Sometimes these men remained for days or weeks, and he became used to expecting to see them when he got home from school, listened to Yankee and Dodger games on the radio with them. Once he went to sit on a man's lap, and a hand covered his face and shoved him away. "Get atta heah, kid. I ain't no friggin baby sitter." Once he got out of bed to go to the bathroom and heard the bouncing game in the closed room down the hall from his, and stopped to look in the keyhole, and in the dim yellow light from the single bulb hanging there, he saw the bed and the man's flesh moving in rhythmic surges, and then saw a section of his mother's bare thigh, and then a hand on her side so that each fingertip depressed the flesh, making an arcing line of dents. He had heard about all of this at the Y, and from the Italian and Negro boys on the street, and tiptoeing to the bathroom, he tried to hold onto the dim belief that maybe Uncle Steve was not hurting her because if he was she would surely scream.

But the men would leave and in the afternoon his mother would sit at the kitchen table and drink whiskey and smoke and listen to music or the news on the radio. Then it was Germany invading Poland and the threat of war, and once it started, there was a string of soldiers who came to stay. During the summer she would drop him off at the YMCA, where he spent the day swimming, his eyes raw from chlorine and his skin puckered white. Once, in that pool, boys were playing a game at the edge and he dove off the board under them and, trying to rise to the surface, he was repeatedly pounded in the head by thrashing feet and knees, and trying a second time to claw his way through the legs and feet, got hit on the nose, again on the head, until he felt his lungs begin to surge in powerful convulsions, trying to draw in the air they wanted. He clawed at the legs and feet, and could not get through, and the water stung the inside of his nose, bored into the center of his head, and then he became nauseated and dizzy so that he didn't know which direction was up, and for a moment, or far longer, he couldn't tell, a strange sensation of blank serenity overcame him so that he felt the strange, weightless pleasure of— And he didn't know what it was, even as it was happening, only that he felt good, felt like laughing. And then this feeling was interrupted by a powerful jerk of his arm, and then noise, the sharp din of the echo of voices against the walls, and then the smell of his own vomit, and a hand stinging his back with repeated whacks that hurt so much that he thought he would die.

He never told his mother, because he was afraid she wouldn't let him go back. The memory of that feeling haunted him every time he went to the pool, a sensation he got only the tiniest hint of when he held his breath under water, something like a soft, sweeping dream.

When he was twelve he delivered *The Paterson Morning Call* to sixty houses in the Italian section of the town, leaving the apartment around dawn every morning and wheeling out on his bike into the darkness to the Maratini brothers' soda shop and then into the neighborhoods, his tires hissing over the macadam. Even that early in the morning, strips of light sliced at the edges of blackout curtains over kitchen windows as he rode past and sailed the folded papers onto porches, and he knew by that time what the differences were between these families and his, if he could call his a family. Sometimes when he got up at four-thirty to get ready to go out, the light would still be on in the other room, and cigarette smoke would hang in the hall, and the low voices would still be going, or the bed would creak with the man's lunges, and he knew it was a reverse of normalcy, that he would be getting home from school when his mother would get up and start the day with a donut and a little glass of whiskey.

"We landed in Messina," he would say, holding the paper out to her, "the Eighth Army."

"Oh, that's good," she would say.

"And the Red Army cut the Kiev railway."

And then a year later the Russians were in Warsaw. "That's in Poland, and that guy McGuire from New Jersey, you know, Ridgewood, was killed. He got thirty-eight Jap planes before—"

"McGuire," she said. "Yes."

But she would be in a numb, remote fog, and it amazed him that she could be so oblivious to what was going on.

Eventually he understood that their situation was unique, that no other kid he knew lived it. Around Christmas he would do his weekly collections and his customers would give him little envelopes with oval holes cut in the paper, out of which Washington peered at him in his stern dignity, or sometimes even Lincoln. One family, the Libonatis, invited him into their house every year, and he would stand shivering at the door, hunched up in his coat, his hands almost numb in his gloves, and Mr. Libonati would study him and say, "Come on in here, son," and then he would yell in the direction of the kitchen, "Annie! Bring the boy a glass of wine."

And each year the little girl wearing the white Christmas dress would bring out a small glass of red wine which Mr. Libonati would encourage him to drink to warm him up, grinning his jovial Italian smile. Way down the hall of the huge house boys played pool in one of the back rooms, boys he didn't know because they went to the Catholic school. Each year the girl would be taller, and then she had breasts to go with the black hair and dark eyes. And he would close his eyes and drink the wine while the girl and the parents watched, laughing and encouraging him. Then Mr. Libonati, who was a contractor, would give him five dollars and send him on his way. That, he thought, is a family. He dreamed of Annie Libonati, of the beautiful dark eyes and the swollen chest with the little gold cross sitting there on the white lace.

When he was sixteen one man came to the apartment every night, an older man who had been in Europe in the war and who was interested in settling down. He did not sleep with her in the room as the other men had. By the time Dennis McKay was sixteen he even knew what she charged, twenty dollars, and knew exactly what it was all about. The boys on the street talked of it all the time, said that on the rooftops of the neighboring buildings they had girls all they wanted, daytime or night, and he would see the same girls on the street, their faces made up so that they looked like sharpened Rita Hayworths or Mae Wests, and they threw tough language around like boys, gestured at them with middle fingers raised, making the boys grab their crotches and shake, which made the girls laugh and walk off, talking amongst themselves, and the boys would tell stories about what they had done to this one or that one. And the Negro boys would try to top them with stories about that they did to their girls, who were tougher even than the toughest white girls. He was very close to getting in on all this when the man who came every night apparently made some kind of a proposal to his mother, because she told him that they were moving to upstate New York, they were getting out of the filth and the noise of Paterson, and already he hated the man because he was losing the YMCA, and losing his chance to do all the things to the girls that his friends talked about every day. She told him to never never never say anything about all the other men, that this was her chance and she was not going to have it ruined.

≈   ≈   ≈

Lon Carlson's dairy farm was huge, five hundred acres he said, and he had seventy cows, black and white Holsteins, and he had a pond, which served as a replacement for the YMCA pool but for the frogs and the mud on the bottom. Dennis helped Lon Carlson every morning with the milking, helped him take in the hay, throwing bales of it up to Tom Skiles, who worked for Mr. Carlson. The breeze would blow the golden chaff down into his face and it would stick to his sweaty skin, but he quickly came to understand this arrangement because it was no longer all those different men but now only one, and he went to sleep every night more or less praying, to what or whom he wasn't sure but he supposed to God, whoever or whatever that was. He had never been in a church to find out, but understood that He was a vengeful being whose face his mother had more or less held her middle finger up to each time she accepted a twenty, or two tens. But now, far off in the other part of the house he would sometimes hear, especially on calm nights, the subtle squeaking of bedsprings, and he would wait as it went on, tense with a strange satisfaction that after all this time it was over, there was actually something you could call a family in this house.

He volunteered to paint the barn. It was located behind a knoll fifty yards from the house, and Lon Carlson kept scratching his head and speculating on the size of the job, looking at him as if assessing the capability of someone as skinny as he was to do all this. Lon Carlson kept shrugging uncertainly, even as he loaded the paint onto the bed of his International flatbed parked in front of the hardware store, as he paid up for the brushes and scrapers, as he drove back into the long dirt driveway, looking at the barn. "I don't know about this," he said.

"I can do it."

"I can get Tommy to help."

"No. I can do it."

"Well—"

"I can do it."

The man did not understand. Dennis wanted to do it by himself and not have any of it contaminated by anyone's help, not even Lon Carlson's.

He settled into living on the farm by painting the barn and wandering over the fields and through huge stretches of woodland, and by floating in the dirty pond. Each day was another day in which a twenty or two tens did not change hands, another day in which he did not think, whore, another night in which he did not have to worry about what depraved plans this man or that man had for his mother's body.

He had to wash red paint out of his hair with turpentine, and all his clothes looked as if spattered with dried blood. Once when he was high up on a thirty-six foot extension ladder a cow started rubbing her horns on the first two rungs, and he yelled, holding onto the eave, until Lon Carlson came running out of the barn to chase the cow away. "I don't know about this," he said, scratching his head and watching the cow walk off, her bag swinging. "I don't know."

"'Sokay!" he yelled down to him. "I'm all right."

"I don't know," Lon Carlson said.

When he had finished half of it he began hearing the strange inflections in their voices, especially on windless nights. He held onto the hope that it meant nothing, and kept on painting each day until his right arm became so fatigued that he could barely lift it, and his hand grew water blisters. Once when he went for relief in the pond Lon Carlson told him that there was a swimming hole in a brook just there, and he pointed, about a mile over the hill. Boys and girls his age swam there, especially on Sundays.

He went one Sunday and swam in the hole, clear water in a deep part of a brook that ran under a rusted steel bridge, and they began showing up, big blonde boys who said hello, how ya doin'? and went on with their own swimming, and then girls came, until there were nine kids in all, sunning themselves on the grass and diving in from the muddy bank or from the girders of the bridge.

The boys did not yell and curse in the girls' presence, but they did make subtle references to them. "Hey," one called from under the bridge, "what's the three basic parts of a stove?" and the three girls giggled and whispered amongst themselves. No one answered, and then another boy yelled, "Hey, Chuck, do a crow's nest!" and they giggled again, hiding behind their pale, drawn-up legs.

When Dennis had the chance he asked one of the boys about the stove, and the boy said, "Lifter, leg and poker," and then laughed and dove into the water. It took him a full five minutes to figure the joke out, because he visualized at first only the steel device with the heavy wire coiled around the handle that was in Lon Carlson's kitchen, used to lift the hot, round plates off the surface so you could see the fire, and the ornate, chromed legs of the stove, and the poker itself. He never found out what a crow's nest was.

And he painted on the weekdays, shirtless now because he was ruining all his good clothes, and became more and more tanned, then brown, and at the swimming hole the boys began to notice this, and made subtle jokes he thought were at his expense: "Hey, Chuck, what's the sound of a knife thrown into a barn door?" and Chuck yelled from the rusty, dripping bridge girder, "Wop! Ginnieginnieginnieginnie!" And at home he looked in the mirror at his face, at his eyes as brown as molasses and his hair, far too curly, and at his skin and the strange thickness of his features, and a wave of terror washed over him, and he thought, mulatto? Or Puerto Rican? Is that what she did? Did twenty dollars change hands seventeen years ago?

On especially calm nights he heard their voices, the strange tension, and during the day he saw the looks on their faces, his mother's showing a calm, fatalistic resignation, Lon Carlson's showing a peculiar, sustained question, the expression of a breath held. One day Lon held money out, for painting the barn, and Dennis said, "That's all right. I don't want any money."

"C'mon, take it," Lon Carlson said. "It's a real good job, would cost me a lot if I had it done."

"I don't want any money."

"C'mon, take it."

"'Sokay."

"C'mon."

"Nope. Uh-uh."

And at night, the tense conversation migrated to the kitchen, and he could not avoid it: for god's sake, I have a child. Oh yeah, well I ain't talkin' about that. I ain't fond of so well-used a piece of property. So take us to the bus then, we'll get out. So when was it you became a whore, huh? How much did you charge? Was it all white men, or was there niggers too? Did you spread for Chinks too? I'll bet you did. I'll bet you spread for anything.

He walked down the stairs, making enough noise that he was sure they would hear him. He did not know what he would do or say to Lon Carlson. He walked into the kitchen and stood there staring at him. He stood and stared for a full thirty seconds, watching as his mother played with a drink glass on the oily, plastic table cloth and Lon Carlson sat and looked at him, eyebrows raised.

"Well, can I help you?" Lon finally asked.

But he stood there staring, and then turned and went back up the stairs.

They moved their argument back to their room.

If he just held on, he thought, it would blow over. Lon Carlson was doing the milking later and later, so the cows would be let out into the darkness to go up to the pasture, and each night he would wait for Lon in the milkhouse so that he could help with the milking. It bothered him because he liked the cows, liked their calm, placid simplicity and their huge, watery eyes, and the hot blasts of their breath, which smelled of hay and grain and a rich, sweet fermentation. When they were not milked they became jumpy and alarmed. The more Lon and his mother argued the later the milking got. He would turn the lights on in the manger and wait, looking around for something useful to do.

He would go and stare into one or another cow's eyes and say, "You wait now, he'll be here soon."

On one night of bad arguing he decided he'd put a new coat of whitewash on the manger and drive ceiling. He got a broom and began at one end, working in the light of the line of bulbs that ran down the middle drive past the two lines of the cows' bony rear ends. He swept cobwebs, swinging the broom over his head, removed chaff and dust with a kind of imbecilic focus, making sure to get every single dot of dirt, every web, every little golden needle of chaff. Then he went back out of the barn and to the little knoll that separated it from the house, and listened. The voices were raised to a shout, his louder: you goddam whore! How many've been in you? Goddam cheap whore!

And he turned and went back over the knoll to the barn and swept and swept, then hit a socket with the denser part of the broom and heard a subtle crackling static up beyond the hole that the ribbed, metal-wire casing came through, and smelled ozone. He wasn't sure if that was important or not. He left the barn and went over the knoll toward the house. Get out! Goddam sure I'll take you to the bus, whore! Then she screamed.

He continued walking, across the dirt driveway past the red Farmall tractor and to the kitchen door. He walked in and there they sat, Lon Carlson with his eyebrows up in that can I help you? expression, and his mother, redfaced and wiping her eyes with a hankie.

"Did he hit you?"

"Denny, go to bed."

"Did he hit you?"

"This ain't none of your business, boy," Lon Carlson said.

"Yes it is. It is my business."

"Denny."

"Did he hit you? Because if he did I'll kill him."

"Don't talk like that," she said. "This is adults' business. Don't you say that."

He stared at them. Lon Carlson looked down at the table, shaking his head. His mother gestured with subtle flicks of her fingers—get out of here.

All right, so he went upstairs to his room and sat on the edge of the bed and waited. For a verdict, he supposed, delivered by Lon Carlson. Now he heard them clearly: a man stomps all over that goddam continent and comes back wanting to set something up, a man gets shot at, sees all kinds of horrible shit and he comes back and wants to set something good up, and what happens? Honey, I can't do anything about the past, that's all dead and gone. No it ain't! The kinda filth you wallowed in, that don't ever die, never! Is it because you think about them? Is that it? You think about them when we're— I think about you! About how dirtied you are! I think about all them men with you in broad daylight lookin' at you tryin' this an' that an' laughin' and movin' you around with their hands. About all the junk that's been in you and why? For a few bucks, that's why. Sometimes it was two, or three, right? You do this while I do that while you watch. Here, lemme take a picture of that. For a few lousy bucks you spread for a thousand men, all kinds, all colors. I think about the filth, the filth! Then I think we should go. You're goddam right you should go. You're goddam tootin' right about that. To think I stuck it in there where a thousand others have— How about ten thousand, Lon? Fifty. You're not the hotshot you think you are, buster.

He sat on the bed, waited. He could hear Lon Carlson walking somewhere in the house, not the kitchen. The bedroom wall across from him held an orange glow in the center of which he saw his own hunched form. The orange glow intensified and then died back, some strange sunset thing. But sunset was an hour ago. He turned to the window.

The immense billows of smoke bloomed above the barn roof, and all the windows were a bright, dancing orange. He ran for the kitchen and yelled for Lon, who had already seen it and was running over the knoll. He followed, saying, "Oh God, oh God, oh God."

Lon ran to the door and grabbed the handle to open it, and then pulled his hand away as it drifted open, revealing a wall of fire. Inside the roar and the sharp crackling he heard them, hooves sliding and hammering on cement, groans and then loud mooing almost like shouts, and the sound of the cows lunging against the thick stanchions and then jerking back. Then the smell came, the odor of burning hair and the hot, molasses smell of burning grain and then the salty, rich smell of cooking flesh. As the windows turned into thick blowtorches of roaring flame, they backed away, and turning, he saw the shafts of headlights bouncing above the road out in front of the house.

No one could do anything. A police car came later, and he sat in the kitchen with his mother, who cried into her hankie. "We have to go now," she said. "Why did you do that?"

"It was an accident. I was coming to—"

"We have to go. Maybe the policeman can take us out. Go and get your things together. My God, I can't believe you did that."

His hands shook so badly he could hardly pack. He kept repeating, it was an accident, it was an accident, but he knew no one would believe him now, not even his mother.

On the bus ride, during which he watched the hills and pastures sweep away behind them, he waited to ask her, all the way until they crossed the state line into New Jersey. "So why did you tell him? You told me not to say anything, so why did you tell him?"

She looked at him, annoyed that he would ask. "He kept needling me," she said. "He kept asking over and over, so I told him." She took a swig from a flask she carried in her purse. "Shit," she said, wincing, "this stuff is poison."

When he turned back to the window and watched the trees sweep out behind them, he pictured the farm, the woods, the clean swimming hole and the boys, and the girls with their long, pale legs, and thought, then you should have lied.

≈   ≈   ≈

The cottage The Captain found was on Royal Hawaiian Avenue, right in the middle of Waikiki. It was clean, no place for centipedes, had three bedrooms, one separated from the other two by the center of the house so that if The Captain and Momi wanted to do it in their room, there was sufficient distance that he would not hear them, especially on nights when the tradewinds blew. If he wanted to fish, then it was a mile or so to the beach with the exposed reef, past the Moana Hotel and Kapiolani Park up at the beginning of the rich neighborhoods on the lower foothills of Diamond Head. In a few weeks all the kids would be going back to school, and he would not.

On that first day they settled in, The Captain flopped down on the rattan couch in the living room and said, "So, my boy, what do you think?"

"When are Momi and Angela coming over?"

"Oh, weekends maybe. You wait. I'll get the rest of the furniture out, and we'll have a great place. Did you notice the family next door? From Kansas of all places."

"Yeah, I saw them."

"You see their daughter? What an absolute doll. You should meet her."

And he thought, what about Angela?

During the weekdays he fished and walked up and down Kalakaua Avenue through the center of Waikiki. The Captain had friends at the Yacht Club, and usually went there to sit around and socialize, or go out on people's boats, leaving him to do as he pleased. He wanted to get a job, but understood from talking to a restaurant owner that everybody wanted jobs. The GIs had taken most of them, and unemployment was high. Secretly he didn't mind that, at least for the present, because his interest in simply seeing things seemed inexhaustable: he went to the reefs off Diamond Head, where he spent so much time with his face down in the water that he lost two layers of skin from his back. If he did not fish he hung out at the beaches fronting the Waikiki hotels with the tourists sunning themselves, sunburned girls slick with oil that smelled of coconut, dark beachboys taking long wooden boards and outrigger canoes out to the small waves that rolled in all day just in front of the widening lines of white surf under the horizon.

He understood what the attraction to this place was—the trees along the beach created patches of damp shade smelling of plumeria, with soft Hawaiian music drifting in the breeze. The tourists lay out in the sun on their towels, mai tais or mixed drinks or beer in the sand next to them, the men eyeing the sleek Hawaiian and mixed-race girls walking by, the women looking at the dark, muscular local beachboys, who instructed them in the art of surfing, so that those same women would lie on their stomachs on the boards in the shallow water while the beachboys looked down at their rear ends as they struggled awkwardly to learn the sport, giggling with demure embarrassment.

One day he sat on a towel at the beach at the Royal Hawaiian Hotel, and just six feet away from him a fat man wearing a gold watch sat with a petite, dark part-Oriental girl, a sleek little bombshell who sat before him with her knees up and legs spread, playing with a little umbrella from a drink. The man reached out and pinched her side, at which she shook with a coy, defensive giggle, and then after he whispered something to her, they both got up and went into the hotel. After that he sat staring at the two depressions her buttocks had left in the sand and imagined what they did, saw the rich man removing the girl's bathing suit, and in broad daylight, maybe even in view of the white breakers out the window, the man doing whatever he pleased with her, his watch glinting in the sunlight.

The first legitimate fish he caught was what The Captain called a menpachi, a smaller red fish with large black eyes that looked like bottomless wells, or like some strange doorway into space. It looked big enough in the cave, and he held his breath, carefully aiming the spear, and pulled the doorhinge trigger, and the fish froze on the point, shot through the gills, its spines up. When he brought it up into the air, he was disappointed at its size, about ten inches, but walked back home with it still dangling on the spear like a little red flag, realizing that if he was going to catch more, then he needed a bag. Although The Captain said he was not a fan of cleaning fish, he did that one, showing him how to slit the belly and remove the guts, and how to scrape the scales off. They cooked it in a frying pan with butter and salt and pepper, and ate it. Within days of that catch he caught a wrasse, and a couple of convict fish, with their dull black stripes up and down on yellow bodies.

The family from Kansas in the cottage next door were the Hendersons, the daughter Carol. The Captain had called her a doll, and she was that, with hair the color of wheat, a round, attractive face and a pale, freckled body that had a luscious softness that fascinated him, the same softness he saw every day on the beach. If he was at the cottage when she came home from school, she would peek through the tall panax hedge and say, "So, how's the tan?" or "Wow, you made progress today." She began inviting him over to listen to records and talk, but only on weekday nights, because The Captain reserved weekends for trips over to Kailua to visit Momi, or for Momi, Angela and sometimes some of her friends to come over to the cottage for the day. The strange courtship between Momi and The Captain seemed to him ridiculously slow, because they did not see each other during the week, Momi's time taken up with a job in Kailua, and The Captain's with his Yacht Club friends.

One weekend Momi and Angela came over for a long day at the beach, during which Dennis fished and Angela sat on a towel next to Momi and The Captain. He fished with a kind of furious impatience, wanting badly to catch something so as to impress them, but got nothing, although he stayed in the water so long that he ended up feeling barely conscious, and finally saw them waving him in. The Captain invited them to stay the night. He would take them all out to dinner, and then they could see a movie and turn in without having to worry about driving over the mountain to Kailua. Momi would sleep in the small guest room, Angela on the couch.

The Captain insisted on a movie called "Sinbad the Sailor" with Douglas Fairbanks Jr., because he claimed to have met the actor's father, who, he said, could jump over a table from a standing position. "The most athletic actor ever," he said, "and I want to see if his son is cut from the same block."

"It's fine with me," Momi said. "I like adventures."

Dennis watched her as she spoke, wondering about her having no kids at her age. She struck him as somehow strangely tragic despite her regal bearing.

They got back to the cottage at around ten o'clock, and were just inside the door when someone knocked. The Captain answered. It was Carol Henderson, looking for Dennis, but once she saw the people in the house, she said, "Oh, I'm sorry, you have guests."

"That's all right, sweetie," The Captain said. "Like to come in?"

"No thanks, no. I'll come by another time."

After she was gone Angela bumped Dennis on the side and said, "Dat your girlfrien'?"

"No, just a neighbor."

"She pretty. Bumbye no mo' neighbah. Girlfrien'."

The Captain was going on and on to Momi about how the son couldn't come anywhere near the father, and that the ginger chicken was too sweet. Dennis and Angela were left sitting on the couch, and after a short period in which he felt awkward in her presence, as if there was no place to go and he had to figure out what to say to her, he felt woozy, as if his brain had become waterlogged. The movie had seemed to him flat and tinny, because he was so tired.

"You like play cahds?" Angela asked.

"Nah, I gotta go to bed."

She looked disappointed.

"We're going for a walk," The Captain announced, and then held his elbow out to Momi, who laughed and looked at the ceiling, then took his arm.

"Da fisherman say he go bed," Angela said. "Den I go too. I go dream about Antony Quinn. Oh, he so cute."

"Okay, I'll get the sheets," The Captain said, and went to the hall closet.

Dennis slept as if drugged. Before dropping off, only half covered by a sheet because it was hot and still, horse latitudes weather The Captain called it, he envisioned fish sweeping past him with powerful but graceful flashes of their tails, some so bright that they reflected sunlight into his eyes.

In the few minutes before awakening he was aware of a presence in the room, but could not move. He was lying on his back, his nose and throat irritated, and dreaming of those girls on the beach, the ticklish sensation of desire moving through him like some sluggish electricity. Then he felt a breeze on his cheek, and was aware that it smelled of human breath. When he opened his eyes, another pair were there staring at his, huge and brown. Angela.

"Hah, you snore," she said.

He reached around as if drunk, and found the sweaty sheet and pulled it over his chest. "Wha— I mean, what happened?"

"I jus' wakin' you up, lolo," she said.

"But—" He opened his eyes wide. What was she doing in his room? Then he realized that he had been sleeping on his back in his underpants with a rock-hard erection and only the sheet to cover him. He blinked at her. Her hair was curly, draped over her shoulder.

"Breakfas'," she said. "Den we go beach."

"But what are you—" He tried to focus. She was wearing The Captain's pajamas which smelled of that strange talcum powder, and she was on her knees at the edge of the bed with her elbows on the mattress, her chin on her forearms. She continued to stare at him.

"Get potagee sausage an' egg," she said. "No rice." Then she stood up and sat down on the edge of the bed. In that single motion of getting up and sitting down he saw that she was wearing nothing under the pajamas, that the heavy, liquid bounce of her breasts was clearly visible, sliding inside the fabric, that her whole body had moved with a soft liquidity inside the loose, thin fabric of the pajamas. He remained rigid under the sheet. He felt his heart slamming in his chest, and worried that the pulse would be visible in his face which, he imagined, was surging into a thumping bloat with each beat.

"Whatsa matta?"

"Nothing, it's just that I'm not— Not awake yet."

"Try come, da egg get cold."

She got up and walked out, and again he saw it, the soft bounce of her buttocks, clearly visible sliding inside the loose, insignificant fabric of the pajamas, and then the unmistakable shape of a woman's body, as if the pajamas were some translucent vapor loosely clinging to her skin.

He put his hands up to his face and whispered, "Oh Jesus." He stared at the tan waterstains on the ceiling. When you peeled away everything that got in the way, money, bragging, foul language, hatreds, or the elegant distance of a Hollywood actress, there she was with her woman's body, and being unaware of what seemed to him a majestic sexuality, and it frightened him. He thought of the boys in Paterson and their word, fuck, and even that word paled in comparison to what he imagined. There were no words for this.

It was high tide, too murky for a couple of hours for him to fish, so he was stuck with them on the beach, sitting on a towel and staring out at the surf, and at the black shapes of barges heading toward Honolulu Harbor. The Captain was casting with a little fishing rod in the roiling water, uselessly it seemed, on the other end of the beach. Angela stood up from her towel and held a small pair of scissors out to Momi, who looked up, shielding her eyes from the glare. "What do you want me to do with those?" she asked.

"I like you cut my skirt off."

"Why for heaven's sake?"

"Esther Williams, 'Ass why. Da odda lady too, Colleen Gray. 'Memba 'Nightmare Alley?' She get one two-piece."

Momi shrugged and took the scissors. "If your mother finds out I did this, she'll—"

"C'mon auntie, nobody know."

He watched as the scissors went schwick-schwick-schwick and the edge of the skirt dropped in little jerks down past Angela's knees. Then it was off. She looked down, turned, and he looked away, then back. He found himself staring straight at the middle of her body, the graceful shape of hips and the slight, muscular bulge of the stomach centered by a flat plane of fabric over the subtle cone around her navel. And below, the bulge which made him look away again, because a couple of dark hairs peeked out from the edge. He saw Momi looking at him, then squinting slightly, and he felt his face become hot. Then Angela walked down and into the water, squealed once because it was cold, and ducked under and came up. "Eh, Denny, try come!"

In the water they stood working their legs and arms against the push and pull of the waves. "How come you no mo' skoo?" she asked.

"I quit. I didn't want to finish."

"I go nex' week. Da lashear, senior."

"That's good."

She stared at him, working her arms. "You comin' ovah still?"

"I guess so."

"'Ass good." Again she stared at him, so he ducked under and came up shaking his hair. "I like see you," she said. "I don't tink we gonna come dat much an' I like see you."

He didn't understand what she was saying exactly, and shrugged, looked toward where The Captain was casting and reeling his line back. "Well, I can come over weekdays sometimes too, I guess. I guess I can do anything I want right now, you know, like hitchhike over the mountain or around that place—"

"Waimanalo side," she said. "Makapuu Point."

When they went back up on the sand Momi was gathering towels together, and he dried off, sneaking peeks at Angela doing the same, and was again aware of Momi watching him out of the corner of her eye. As for going over the mountain, he wondered if he would be allowed, then wondered also if not being allowed would be a relief.

There was a party at Carol Henderson's cottage on Sunday night, and she came over to invite him. Her parents had gone to a double feature, and would not be back until late, and the kids had the house to themselves. Before he went, The Captain said, "Hey bucky, behave in the presence of that young lady. My God, what a doll."

There were four other boys there, and five of Carol's girlfriends, kids mostly of military people. Ricky Staton was from California, Joey Branch from Illinois, and so on. The girls were demure and well-mannered, like Carol, and the boys did as The Captain had ordered him to do, behaved well, except for the subtle references to sex that reminded him of that swimming hole in upstate New York. They listened to Glenn Miller records and drank soda, ate cookies and candy, tried dancing. He felt awkward in their presence because they were all friends and he didn't know them. When they started talking sports the boys became more personable. He easily fell into conversations in which the names of baseball players were dropped: Williams, DiMaggio, York, Ott, Kiner.

During a lull in the conversation the girls went into Carol's bedroom. When they were gone Joey Branch suddenly stood up, his hand on the top of his head, a thunderstruck expression on his face. "What?" another boy asked. Then Joey Branch ran out the front door making a strange sound, and out by the gate, fell down on the lawn, and there, rolling around, he continued making the strange sounds, as if he had either won some million-dollar lottery or maybe knew he was dying.

Dennis followed the other boys out as they went to Joey Branch, who was now making wheezing sounds, and gesturing at the sky, his eyes wide with awe. Then Joey sat up, his face a mask of stunned wonder. He looked up at everyone with an expression of monumental pain, of complete devastation. "There are twelve tits in that house," he whispered. "Did you realize that? There are twelve tits in that house." The other boys groaned and laughed, and Joey Branch struggled to get up, staggering and out of balance. "Oh God," he said. "There are twelve tits in that house. Twelve. Some are—" and then he was straight, his hands on his friends' shoulders. He coughed, wiped his face with his hand. The girls had now appeared on the porch, looking on with concern and whispering to each other.

"It's all right," one of the boys called. "He'll be all right in a minute."

Then, in a conspiratorial whisper, so that the girls would not hear, Joey went on, "Twelve. Some are bigger than others. Oh my God!" and he staggered again, his eyes glazed. As if he were about to weep with joy, he whispered, "It's bilateral symmetry, do you understand? Bilateral symmetry." He got his bearings, cleared his throat and said, "I'm all right now. I can make it now, gents. It's just—"

He staggered a little. "It's just that I never knew the essence of it in biology. It was only a fact. But now I see into the true soul of science, the heart of reality." He stopped, shook his friends off, and held both hands up to the sky. "Twelve!" he bellowed. "Twelve! Thank you, God! Thank you!"

"What's the matter?" Carol asked.

"Nothing," Joey Branch said. "I'm sorry," and as the boys snickered, Carol turned to her friends and said, "Another stupid joke."

Back inside the house they continued talking baseball, Joey Branch from time to time bursting out in an imitation of weeping. "My God," he would croon softly. "Six times two is twelve. I have seen the light."

A half an hour later everyone left, Carol following them out to the street. She stopped Dennis before he made his way around the hedge.

"What was the joke?" she asked.

"Oh, I don't know," he said. "Just, you know— A joke."

"C'mon, tell me—sort of dirty, I'll bet."

He snorted. "Nah."

She looked at the hedge separating the two cottages and said, "So how do you know those local folks?"

"Oh, family friend of The Captain's," he said.

"That girl—"

"Angela Santiago."

"You're good friends with her?"

"Nah, I just know her a little."

"I was wondering," she said. "You know, if she was sort of your girl or something."

"No."

She looked once more at the hedge. "My parents'll be home any minute. Anyway, I thought she was, and then thought, well, maybe not."

"Why?"

"Oh, you know," and she laughed, a kind of secret, knowing laugh. "You know."

He laughed too. "Hey, I don't, really. I just got here about a month and a half ago."

"Well, I shouldn't go on like this, you being a family friend and all. It isn't really— Proper, you know." She moved closer and looked around. "Those girls, they do— Well, they mate with their brothers, even when they're, you know, really young."

He laughed again. "I don't— I mean how—"

"It's traditional," she said. "They do that with their fathers and uncles and brothers. I mean I have nothing against them but that's the story."

"She doesn't have any brothers."

"Well, you know what I mean. It's a general thing. I just thought about diseases and all that stuff."

"That's hard to believe."

"It was for me too," she said. "But that's the story here." She peeked out the gate. "Oops, here come the folks."

"See you later," he said.

"Okay, hope you had fun." She touched his arm, a soft, cool touch.

"I did," he said. "Thanks."

In the cottage he sat on the couch and considered what she told him. He didn't really believe it. The image of Carol's face faded away and was replaced by the image of Angela walking out of the room in the pajamas, which were now neatly folded on the end table. He picked them up and smelled the fabric, but all he smelled was that strange sour talcum smell of The Captain.

By Monday afternoon he had decided to try hitching over the mountain to Kailua. He didn't know his way, but The Captain had a map, which he asked to borrow. "What for?" he asked.

"I was thinking of hitching to Kailua to see Momi and Angela."

"Why? We see them all the time. Besides, the kids are all in school, like you should be."

"I know, but—"

"I understand there's a storm moving in anyway," he said. "We're supposed to get a good deal of rain."

"Well, I don't mind the rain."

The Captain stared at him with what looked like perplexed sympathy. "So Carol doesn't catch your fancy, eh?"

"I don't know what you're talking about."

He laughed with a kind of paternal mystification. "Oh my," he said. "A gorgeous doll like that."

"I don't know what—"

"Yes, you do," The Captain said. "Look, let me give you a little tip. Don't get all worked up over the brown girl. She's not for you. Besides, she's no more than a large child."

"I'm not worked up," he said, flushing. His face prickled. "I just wanted to see how the fishing was over there."

"I think you can do better. Their whole way of life is different from ours. They're like—" He waved his hands around. "I can understand your attraction. There's something about these people, and about Japanese and Chinese and even Negro women, but that's just for fun." He looked up at the wall. "I know, I know," he said. "It's a powerful attraction, like they exude something, and you want it so badly that— I like Japanese women a lot," and he screwed his face up, almost as if in pain, and said in a kind of growl, "Oooo." Then he shook his head. "They do that to me, but you see it's only for fun." He stopped, looked around at the hall, and said, "Here," and went into his room. He came back out holding something. "Take some of these."

They were rubbers. He had seen them in Paterson. Boys carried them in their wallets so that you could see the circle through the leather, bragged about using them on their girlfriends on the rooftops.

"You're seventeen and free as a bird," The Captain said. He put the rubbers, wrapped in foil, on the pile of pajamas that Angela had worn. Dennis stood there hot with embarrassment. This, he knew, was one of those man-to-man talks he had heard about, but not "Boys Town" or Andy Hardy. He didn't want to touch them.

"Boy," The Captain said, "you can't be satisfied making love to your hand."

He flushed again and looked away. How did he know?

"Unless you tried the other way already in Paterson?"

"No."

The Captain laughed, almost as if he had just heard a great joke. "Oh my," he said, "you and I should go on an inaugural crusade to Hotel Street."

"What's that?"

"Downtown Honolulu, the whorehouses."

"No."

"Because once you have one, you'll want plenty, believe me. This fascination for her will evaporate. In fact I can set you up with a Hawaiian girl far more—well, you know what I mean. When I was in the Merchant Marine, I had my fill. Jesus, I was twenty, twenty-two. Talk about a hard-on? We used to say to each other, 'Hey, my God, I got a soft-on.'" Then he laughed, nodding, encouraging him to appreciate the joke.

"I don't know what that has to do with my wanting to go fishing though."

"That is pure horseshit, Dennis. Why would you go all the way over there when what you really want is next door? You don't have to be all goody-goody with her—she's a girl your age who might just be as interested as you are. Give the girl a chance. I mean, what a doll."

"But—"

"But nothing. Take those and keep them. They have two uses, one is if you're a soldier and you want to keep your rifle muzzle clean. They put them over the end of the barrel. But the war's over, boy, and the other use is," and he clapped his hands, "to put it over the muzzle of your gun so as to keep it clean. Get it?" And he laughed again.

"'Kay."

He picked them up, feeling the hard circle of rolled latex with his thumb, and stood there holding them. He hated the idea of them and didn't know why.

"So that's how life works," The Captain said. "Do you know what all boys your age do? What I did? Manufacture sperm." He laughed again. "That's the way it goes. You'll have a good time and later on pick one of the nice ones, and white too. Besides, Angela is the niece of one of my best friends."

"What about that, about you and Momi?"

"What do you mean?"

He knew he should not have asked the question. It was too personal, not his business. "I mean, are you going to sort of, you know, get married?"

The Captain laughed again, stared at him with that strange, perplexed look. "What ideas you come up with. No, we're just friends."

He felt a peculiar emptiness that he did not understand. It was not a bad feeling, just a strange sensation of an isolation, from what, he was not even sure. Of course it was stupid of him to assume anything about The Captain and Momi. It was just the way life worked. An airy feeling of mature flippancy overcame him, and he said, "You mean like you and my mother."

The Captain stared at him, thinking. "Dennis, she was a lovely woman, as you know. She endured an awful lot of heartache. We were very good friends."

"For twenty dollars, you mean."

"I don't think you should have said that."

"I knew by the time I was seven. You know, on the plane I sat and tried to remember how many times you stayed with us. Maybe four or five times? Every few years, and you'd stay a week or so. I remember you as one of the ones I liked. Yes, Captain Angstrom. But they all left, you too."

The Captain sighed, looked down.

"I thought that you might know about who my father is, or was. Doesn't matter, but— She never told me. I mean was she ever married? Do you know?"

"I don't, really," he whispered. "I swear on a stack of Bibles I don't." He waved his hands around before him. "These things happen. It does not diminish you, or her."

"That's okay, I don't bear grudges. I just wondered."

In his room he sat on the edge of the bed and stared at the four little packages on the night table. So that was it. The Captain's advice was easy to appreciate. The rubbers would keep you clean and avoid kids so that without worry you could go out and look for girls to fuck. "Valuable advice," he whispered. And then that series of vivid pictures rested in his perception in a strange, multiple super-imposition, like map overlays; Lon Carlson, Richard Keach, The Captain, younger but still smelling of sour talcum powder, the long line of them that went back to when he was born or maybe even before that, men who smelled of whiskey and cigarettes, who may or may not have had much in common except for the willingness to spend twenty dollars, or at least that much during the war; probably less in the thirties when bills changed hands in front of his face and he didn't know numbers, looking up at them from the perspective of two feet tall, huge jovial men who got what they paid for in the room down the hall. One of those men was a Mr. McKay. Uncle Bobby McKay or Uncle Phil McKay, who whispered to his mother, Hey, I got twenty dollars to spend.

The next morning he put on fairly-good clothes, got out his spear and fins and mask, and walked out into a shower. He slid his toes into the go-aheads and, wondering if his feet would be able to take it, walked out of Waikiki to the east, imagining that if he kept on walking, he would find that point Angela had mentioned and then, if he walked beyond that, Kailua. He chose this route because he did not know how to get down through the city to the Pali Road. Going over the mountain might make more sense, but he wanted to remain near the water.

He was only a few hundred yards past the little Diamond Head beach where he usually fished, walking up past a lighthouse, when he realized that the rain would be too much. In the distance to the east he could see the black clouds, and the ocean, down to his right, was swept by wind and rain and was visible only a quarter of a mile out. He was drenched, which was not that bad because he wasn't cold, but he turned and went back.

On the radio at the cottage a newsman described torrential rains, especially on the windward side, and flooding all along the coast. The Captain was holed up at the Yacht Club, and so Dennis sat and listened to the roar of the rain on the roof, watched it cascade in windblown sheets off the eaves, with only a few tourists running past the opening in the hedge, hunched under umbrellas.

He waited. He did not want a job and he did not want to go to the movies and he did not want to go over and see Carol when she came home from school. He would wait until it stopped raining and then go again. He would hitchhike around the end of the island because he did not want to take one of those rubbers over to Carol's house and find out if she was interested in doing it because they were such good friends.

The Captain came home flushed with rage about a stamp collection he had kept in storage. He had it all wrapped up in plastic sheeting, came running through the hedge and then into the cottage dripping, shaking the water out of his gray hair. "This is one reason I could hate this place," he said, holding out the package. "This is one thing I always thought I could learn to hate about this place." After he dried off he slowly opened the package on the kitchen table, moaning with sadness—"Oh boy, oh my, oh my"—and when he took out one large blue volume and opened it, Dennis could not at first see what he was talking about. "Shouldn't even open this in weather this bad," The Captain said, "because of tropical stain. But then it would appear to make little difference now. Oh my."

On a page half-filled with mounted stamps, American and old, there were tiny holes, only a little more than a sixteenth of an inch, perfectly round as if punched out with some precision instrument. "Look," he said. The holes ran straight through the album and through many of the stamps. "Look here, Columbian Exposition, five-dollar black, mint, very valuable, I assure you." It had three perfect perforations, one right through Columbus' profile. "Never try to keep stuff like this here. Anything metal, anything paper, valuable books, nothing," The Captain said. "They don't last. Only glass and marble. Oh my, oh my." He shook his head. "Thousands of dollars. Termites, termites." He looked at Dennis with a kind of fatalistic acceptance. "The holes, of course, run straight through the volumes from front to back. You know, a million-dollar Stradivarius would end up the same way, full of holes."

"Termites."

"Yes. Let me tell you something. In New England or Europe, things last. Civilizations endure because their artwork and furniture and so on last. Here? No," and he shook his head gravely. "No, and this is what I could easily learn to hate about this place. Do you realize what the impermanence of things here means? A kind of death." He looked out the door. "It doesn't even rain a normal, American rain. Look at it. It'll go on like this for hours, and rain more than a foot. It's one of those maddening tropical rains. I hate it."

"Yeah, it's different all right."

"Different!" The Captain said. "Damn straight it's different." He placed his hand on the page gently, as if comforting someone wounded. "This is why I could never see myself living here forever. The most beautiful things you would ever acquire in a lifetime rot, get eaten by termites or ants, mice, or get stained because of the climate, or just melt! It's awful."

After that, as they ate dinner, Chinese food left in the icebox from yesterday, he seemed inconsolable, looked around as if he were ready to pack up and leave right away.

"I don't want to go if you're thinking of that," Dennis said.

"Oh, I'm not, at least not now," The Captain said, digging into some greasy noodle mixture with his chopsticks. "It just frosts me, that's all. The impermanence of things here. It's a kind of—of nothingness, that's what it is. It's a death. I suppose that's why people never wrote anything down here." Then he came out with a derisive snort. "Hell, their alphabet has only twelve letters—you'd think they might have tried. But what would be the point after all, if it would just melt? That's why people live for the moment here."

"I was thinking of going to Kailua tomorrow."

The Captain stopped eating, put the chopsticks down, and cleared his throat. "Everything's being washed away right now. Roads are out. It's bad."

"But then it'll clear up."

"True," The Captain said, studying him. "If you must, just let me know."

"I'm letting you know, I guess."

"Don't ever decide to collect anything fine," The Captain said. "At least here. Never buy good furniture, don't keep nice books. If you think your clothes will last, forget it. And your belt buckles will rust away." He stared for a second, a look of a kind of skeptical sympathy on his face. "I don't understand this business with Angela," he said. "What I see is you allowing yourself to be taken in by something here, and that is not what I think your mother would like. Oh, I see you down the line, boy, still here and vanishing into the nothingness. I see men around who are like that. They came out here and got sucked in, and now they're toothless drunks." He shook his head sadly. "Maybe I shouldn't have brought you out here."

"I—" But there was nothing to say.

"I know the attraction," The Captain said. "They know too. What, did she do something that would—"

"No," he said. "She didn't do anything."

"C'mon, you can tell me. She let you put your hand somewhere, is that it? What'd she show you?" He laughed then, heartily. "Hey boy, I've seen her in a bathing suit too."

"She didn't do anything."

"She did," he said. "I'm a little surprised, although I know I shouldn't be. I mean they start early here, after all. Half of them are sluts by the time they're fourteen. Where'd it happen, here?" He came out with an amazed laugh. "There are so many of them you could lay, and you pick her, and that creates a very sticky situation, if you'll pardon the pun."

Dennis felt suddenly tired of the argument, and looked away. "I don't wanna lay anybody," he said.

"Don't look away from me," The Captain said. "Understand something. We are Americans, and this is not America."

Yes, it was someplace else—a place where fat men with gold watches went to do what they wanted with beautiful, dark girls, for a few bucks probably.

"Then why are we here?"

"Hasn't the war taught you anything? Without us this would have been no more than a Jap outpost. We saved them. We give them our culture and technology. What we get in return is, well, a place to go and have fun, don't you see? Do you know how much sex there is here? I'll get you a beautiful, really experienced woman, a real darkie if you'd like, who'll hug your face with her thighs, none of this bashful doctor playing with that—"

"I told you, there wasn't any—"

The Captain laughed, picked up his chopsticks and worked at the noodles. "You'll see," he said. "You just don't have enough experience yet. When you get over this thing about that girl, then you'll see."

≈   ≈   ≈

The go-aheads hurt the flesh between his big and second toes so much that he took them off and walked barefoot on the damp, pebble-littered roadside, the fins, spear and go-aheads in his left hand. He held his right hand in a fist, the thumb straight, in anticipation of the next car. The rain had washed everything clean, and large pools of it sat in the lower areas. He stayed on the road along the coast, looking out over the ocean as he walked, and turned to stick his thumb out when he heard a car coming up behind him. He remained patient, enjoying the quiet, inching his way. He saw himself inching slowly on the globe of the planet, and when he looked out over the bright horizon, he thought he could see the gentle, sweeping curvature of the earth.

An old pickup truck with a square cab slowed down, then pulled off to the side. He went and looked in the window. "Eh, jump in," the man said. "Put da stuffs inna back."

The old man was Japanese. Feeling a little unsure about this because he didn't know what he was supposed to say to a Japanese person, Dennis put his gear in the bed of the truck and stepped up on the running board, which was perforated by rust.

"Wheah you go?"

"Kailua."

"I go Waimanalo," the man said.

Dennis got in and he pulled back onto the road. Then he reached down between his legs, where there was a mayonnaise jar, and picked something out of it. The truck made a lot of noise. The man rubbed the object between his thumb and forefinger and then popped it into his mouth. Dennis took furtive glaces at him, studying the Oriental profile, black hair peppered with gray. The man picked the jar up and held it out to him, the jar jouncing because of the rough road. Dennis picked out a pale, rubbery disk and looked at it.

"Tako," the man shouted. "Rub da salt in an' eat um."

He did so, and the rich, fishy taste along with the salt stung his jaw. His teeth worked against the rubbery meat, and then the flavor flowered out into his mouth.

"'Ass good, yah, dat tako," the man yelled.

"What is it?"

"He'e. 'Ass octopus." He offered another. This one had a little sucker disk on the edge. Dennis wondered if he should eat that, too. The man looked at him and nodded encouragingly, and he put it in his mouth, felt the sucker disk with his tongue so that it popped off, and then chewed. "How do you make this?" he yelled.

"Clean da guts an' beak out an' lomi dem wit' sea salt," the man yelled. "Even hammah dem onna flat rock. Make um aw squeaky-like, no mo' slime." He ate another. "Braid da legs an' hang um in one screen box a week. Den t'row um onna hibachi an' cook um up good all dakine black black black until all da legs wen' snake outta da braid. Den dice um up li'dat," and he pointed to the jar and went on, the veins on his neck bulging. "Some get dakine green stuffs on um. No worry. Jus' rub um in wit' da salt."

He held the jar up and Dennis looked at it, trying to focus against the bouncing of the truck. Some of the disks had moss on them, and he shuddered at the thought of eating those.

The man laughed, his face wrinkling around his eyes. "Yah, 'ass good, da mossy ones mo' bettah." Finally he put his hand on his throat and imitated the expression of gagging, and then put his finger to his lips.

Dennis nodded, and the man concentrated on his driving, every few minutes or so holding the jar out.

The road went past expensive-looking houses and then inland, and after twenty minutes back to the shoreline past farms where cattle baked in the sun and people rode horses. Past that, the road went over a hill and became winding and bumpy, along steep, rocky bluffs above the ocean, which was now deep and blue-black, and closer in a vibrant blue where the waves crashed against the rocks. He got the impression that the dark water with its larger swells was the same as it might be in the frightening, blank vastness of ocean he had seen from the porthole window of the plane.

They passed the deeper water to an area of what looked like tidepool marshes and black, jagged lava on the shoreline, and then went up another hill past a mountain, where the road and shoreline angled to the north. He didn't want to make the man talk any more but yelled, "Is that the point on the east side they call—"

"Makapuu," the man shouted.

When they broke over the highest elevation in the road the man slowed the truck down because the road narrowed, seemed nailed like a bookshelf to the side of the mountain. There were two larger islands offshore, about a mile out, and he remembered them from the maps. Angela had told him they were used for target practice during the war. Beyond them he saw a strange, windswept coastline that disappeared into a salty mist. In the middle distance there was what looked like the double humps of a little offshore island, and right under the road, a bright, sandy beach that was interrupted by rocks, and then ahead, a thin arc of bright tan, a beach that swept away for a couple of miles.

The only other times they had come to the windward side of the island they had come over the green, cloud-topped mountains past the Pali Lookout, and then down the narrow, winding road into Kailua, past the gouged, trashy remains of an army tent-city. But from this vantage point it looked bright and prehistoric, as remote in a way as the Amazon, and the separation from Honolulu seemed extreme as he studied the wall of the mountain to their left, bare gray with alluvial fans of thousands of rocks halfway down, covered with light-green lichens. And the beach was empty as far as he could see. They went into a populated area, cottages, chickens in front yards and horses out behind, all in a strip of land that began at the base of the line of mountains that became greenish-black rather than gray, hanging under the clouds like dark drapery, with the white needles of waterfalls in some of the vertical depressions.

"Cannot feesh today," the man shouted. "All murky, 'ass why. Runoff."

"I was just going to look around a little."

They approached another cluster of buildings, a town. "Dis Waimanalo," the man said. "Kailua nodda two, tchree miles up da road. I take you but."

"That's okay," he said. "Thanks a lot."

When he stopped the truck in front of a little store, the old man turned in the seat and said, "I Shige Sakata."

"Dennis McKay."

The man laughed and said, "Eh, you Kenika. 'Ass your name."

"Kenika," he said. "Thanks."

The man grabbed the back of his hand and turned it over, and shook about a dozen of the octopus disks into it. "Put um in your pocket," he said. "No fo'get da feens an' li'dat."

With the disks in his shirt pocket, the fishy smell wafted up under his nose as he walked. He was not sure how he would recognize Kailua, but figured he should work his way along the shoreline which was now beyond some smaller mountains on his right, while the dark curtain of the bigger mountains loomed on his left.

The road wound up into some bluffs on the flank of a lone mountain with three peaks, and after half an hour he broke over a hill and saw the large, flat area with marshes and, he supposed, flood ponds that ran for miles through the low elevation, which was dark green. In the late morning sun it glittered, speckled by thousands of palm trees, tiny against the wet patchwork. He had no idea where the house was from this perspective, because his only other orientation to the place had been from the road that came down the Pali.

In the near distance there was a cowpasture that had a dirt road through it, and it aimed toward a cluster of buildings about three miles away over some bluffs. He switched the gear to his free hand and kept going, and then discovered that it was all fenced off, that he would have to walk until he reached the road that ran through the town, still miles away.

Shige Sakata was right. The shoreline water was murky and in places a brownish color, fringed by sandy beaches and dunes that ran a hundred yards inland to pale, low hills of coral. The sand was nearly white and as fine as flour, not like the light greenish-brown sand off Diamond Head. The breakwater was a mile out, which meant that the town was on a shallow bay. If he wanted to fish, he would have to go out there, but the prospect gave him a strange, expectant satisfaction. Who would go out that far? And he thought, I would. The breeze blowing off the ocean into his face was salty and fresh, and it came from the open ocean he imagined thousands of miles north, the Aleutian Islands maybe.

But he could not fish. He imagined that school would be out by now, and turned and trudged off the dunes back toward the road that led to the Santiago house, a cottage perched on a hillside near the beach at the base of a cluster of smaller mountains at the east end of the bay. Walking, he began to feel foolish about not having let anyone know he was coming. If no one was home then he would walk back to Waikiki and get ready to make the same trip tomorrow.

A very large, dark man was outside the house cutting tree branches. It was probably Angela's father. He had only met her mother, up at the Maunawili house. To the right, a few houses away, he could see someone on a bicycle talking to some little kids who were playing in the street. Angela, and his heart began to thump. She wore blue jeans rolled almost to the knees, and a white shirt. He stopped, standing there with the gear in his hand, and looked at the man. Finally he looked up, his eyebrows raised. "Eh," he said, and went back to cutting branches. Dennis stood there until the man looked at him again.

"I just came over to—" What? Say hello? He looked down, trying to think of something to say.

The man straightened up again.

"Uh, I'm a friend of Momi and Angela's."

The man turned and yelled in Angela's direction, a strange, high pitched "Hu-ee!" and she looked in their direction, then came down on the bicycle. "She watchin' da Nahoopii kids," the man said.

"Eh, Denny."

"I just came over to—"

"'Ass my dad," she said. "Daddy, dis Dennis from da oddasai. Da people I to' you about."

The man put his hand out and Dennis shook it, and it was so huge and soft that he felt no bones.

"How much rain you get?"

"All day and all night," he said.

"My dad was up aw night. Works wattah depahtment," Angela said.

"Odda side Kailua Road all flooded out," the man said. "Dat stuff in your han' pahtayou or does it come loose?" he asked. He nodded at the gear.

"Dennis, he means you can put da stuffs down. Come. I show you my records."

It was the last thing he would have imagined doing, but he sat on the floor in her room, his feet sore, and listened to records while Angela ordered the Nahoopii kids around— "No feet onna bed! Look, your feet all pilau. Kaipo, keep outta my stuffs!" The mute awe with which the four little kids looked around at the room meant that they were allowed in there only infrequently.

"Auntie Angela," one said, "I like heah Toots Paka."

"'Kay, 'kay," she said, turning the sleeve pages of an album. "'Kay, firs', Hilo Hattie an' 'Manuela Boy.'"

"Auntie Angela," a little girl said, "braid my hair, braid my hair," and she did so, bouncing to the song.

"I like play bug-face," a little boy said.

"Bug-face is wit' gas masks," she said. "We kep' ours."

He sat and watched her as she concentrated on braiding the girl's hair, mouthing the words of the song, from time to time looking over at him with a sort of unself-conscious smile that made him think that she was barely aware of his presence. It didn't matter—maybe The Captain was right. She was no more than a large child, and seemed so engaged in taking care of the little kids that in a way she seemed one of them. They were now all staring with open-mouthed wonder at the record player, their lips moving with the words. But he couldn't change the fascination he had for her, for something that didn't have a word. It was as if there was nothing that separated her from whatever space she occupied. Different from someone like Carol, who was cool if the space was warm, or refined if the space was coarse, or distant if the space was familiar. He realized his own feet were dirty, and tucked them under him to prevent her from seeing them. The room was clean and simple, with magazine-pages taped to the walls; Lauren Bacall,

Tyrone Power, Shirley Temple, newspaper clippings about the Junior Red Cross taped to a square of cardboard leaning against the wall, and school books on a little desk; the record player and a tan woven mat he thought they called lauhala on the floor.

With another song, "Ukulele Lady," she stood up and swayed with the music, her hands out, making the kids laugh and mimic the movements, squirming on the floor. He watched, staring at the middle of her body as her hips moved with the music, and saw what he thought of as the woman rather than the child. The Captain had told him that missionaries considered the dance savage, and he understood why. The expresson on her face was innocent and absorbed in the music, and her body exuded sex in so unabashed a manner that he felt uncomfortable being there.

The door opened, and Angela's mother peeked in. "Dennis, what are you doing here?"

"I hitched."

Angela turned the record player off.

"Momi says Mr. Angstrom hasn't come back from sailing yet, and was supposed to. Does that sound right?"

"No," he said. "I mean he's always precise about time."

"She called the Yacht Club. They're all worried. She just left a little while ago."

He stood up. "I don't know. He's always precise about time. It doesn't sound like him to be late for anything." He felt a stab of fear for a moment, and looked at Angela. "I better get back. I mean it might be nothing, but I'd better go."

"How you get back? It's quatah to foah."

"The way I came?"

"Mommy," she said. Angela's mother shook her head, looking at the floor. "Of course we can—"

"No," he said. "I can do it. Can I leave my stuff here?"

He sustained an anxious haste for three miles, walking through the town and up the road toward the Pali. Once he was through the town he began to run slowly for a few hundred yards at a time, then walk, waiting for cars to come. Most of the traffic came down the mountain toward Kailua. By the time he was walking uphill, he had exhausted the nervousness out of himself, and settled into a patient gait. Finally a truck pulled over.

≈　　≈　　≈

He was led to believe that The Captain's disappearance was "not unusual," that it happened all the time, that, as the days passed, he could still be found. Carol Henderson's parents were optimistic, sometimes even jovial as they invited him over for dinner so that he would not have to eat alone. Momi and Angela came over the second day after the disappearance, to return his fishing gear and cheer him up, and drop off some food. They, too, thought that what with the weather's being fair, The Captain and his two sailing mates could still be found, perhaps having drifted down to the southwest with a broken mast or something. He remained in a kind of fog during their visit because he had spent most of the morning in the water using The Captain's mask and no spear, until his brain seemed so sodden that normal reality took on the tinny, bright superficiality of a dream.

"Dey look wit' planes," Angela told him. "Happens alla time. No worry yet."

But as the time passed, sunrise and sunset, the time taken up with snorkeling or sitting and staring dully at the wall or looking at the blank, blue page in the atlas, the center of which was Hawaii, he began to believe that it was true: The Captain was gone, and it was not unusual according to the paper, according to Mr. Henderson, according to anyone he talked to about it. The atlas showed the awful, blank blue of the Pacific, with its pitiful little outposts of land, and he let his eye move slowly to the southwest to The Gilberts, or to Howland or Baker Islands, and understood that it would be not unusual for The Captain to drift until he starved to death or died of thirst, because the little outposts of land, Howland, Baker, Palmyra, were so tiny in the blank vastness of the Pacific that he wondered how anyone in his right mind would choose to live in the center of it, in the remotest place on the planet.

The fifth day, late at night after he had accepted an invitation to eat at the Hendersons', Carol kissed him before he went around the hedge. Then she put her arms around him, her head against his chest, and whispered, "Stay here with us. You can do what you want now. Stay."

He put his fingers up to his lips to touch the strange shadow of that contact from her, and said, "I don't think I can do that. I mean—" Then he became nervous. What was she doing? Why all of a sudden was she doing this?

"Let me talk to my parents."

"I think I'm supposta go, I mean back to the U.S. or—"

"Are you still seeing that family, that local family?"

"Yeah, I mean I went over there a week ago, just to—"

"That girl?"

"Well—"

She pushed herself away, and folded her arms.

"I mean it's not anything that—"

"Oh, I understand," she said, and he could hear a strange, lilting pain in her voice. "I get it." She laughed. "What'd she do? Something I can't compete with, I'll bet." The expression on her face had turned hard. "Yeah, I saw the way she threw her tits around. Did she let you do it?"

"It's not—"

"I can do that too, you know. I can do all of it."

"I wasn't—"

"It's interesting," she said. "Almost like choosing to be with Negroes rather than us. They're way ahead of us, I know. I've heard plenty about those girls. But you know, I can do anything she can."

He opened his mouth to speak, but nothing came out.

She shook her head and went back into her cottage.

He continued on to the front door of the cottage, feeling muddled and ashamed. He was supposed to respond somehow, but he hadn't any idea of how to do that and now Carol was mad. He supposed that his reaction was not unusual, considering the circumstances. He could not get out of his mind the atlas's picture of the Pacific, of the curved string of tiny dots indicating where he was at that moment, in the middle of absolutely nowhere. And he envisioned himself now as standing somewhere in the middle of the continent where there was land everywhere you looked, and the ocean was no more than some vague and exotic concept to those he would know there, something a thousand miles away.

"I get lost."

"No, it's just up the gulley only a hundred yards. The leaves are oval and shiny. You can fill a bucket in five minutes."

"I no like go alone. You come too. I get plenny whistles anyway."

"This is an oeoe. It makes a neat sound."

"'Kay."

He sits with a hand on each knee. The tattered tank shirt he wears has a logo on the back, "Amalgamated Chicken Fighters Local 69," around a faded circle in the center of which are two fighting cocks.

You do not know what the word "amalgamated" means.

"I like get one fighting chicken," you say.

"Get the kamani nuts first, then we can talk chickens."

"I no like go alone."

"Okay."

You follow him out, down the steps and onto the soft, moist floor of the woods, the blackish water under the bed of leaves squirting up around your feet. Then it's across the narrow little stream that comes down the gulley, and up under the tall trees, toward the dark base of the mountains. He stops and looks around. "See this?" *He places his hand on a tree.* "See how it's all green on this side, and gray on the other side? All these trees?"

"Yeah."

"That's how you never get lost. The green side is mosses and lichens and stuff like that. That side is always on the north."

"Fo' real?"

"Yup. So if you're on this side of the island, you walk north, and you'll never get lost."

You follow him. The black boulders ooze water, leaves drip, the smell of rotten fruit wafts down in the wind. Guava, bananas, mangoes. You are out of sight of the shed now, and Kenika is the only other human in this deep and secret place, the hush like a voice in the trees. The spirits watch, the boulders have eyes, in the distance up the gulley the red-eyed pigs wait. It is only the two of you but a million eyes watch.

"Someday I'll take you to a place someone showed me once, way way up the gulley, a burial cave."

"No way. I not goin'."

"It's your ancestors."

"Yours too, but—"

"No, not mine. I'm not from here. But you are."

"What ancestors you get?"

"My mother."

The tree is up on the right side of the gulley, and the round nuts have fallen down and into the stream. Kenika looks around, picks three up. "We take the husk off, and you have the nut. We drill three holes, one big and two small, clean the meat out and put the nut on a string, and when you whirl it over your head it sounds like someone screaming." *He cocks his head, looks around.* "Hey, I hear someone screaming right now."

"Not." *You look around, listen. The greener sides of the trees are on the north. Kenika looks, then laughs.*

"You wen' try freak me out," *you say.* "I not scared."

"C'mon, let's get a couple pocketfuls of these. We'll make a bunch. We used to sell them in Waikiki."

"Oeoe," *you say.* "I make one fo' when my daddy get outta jail."

"'Kay. And we'll make one out of a coconut. You gotta hear that. Your great-granduncle Benny and I made dozens of them."

"Unca Benny da boat man?"

"That's Uncle Benny."
"I like make one big honkah oeoe. Coconut."
"Little one first."
"'Kay."

≈   ≈   ≈

The next day, before he was able to get out and wander around in Waikiki, Momi showed up at the door of the cottage. He saw her through the window and wondered again how he would be able to talk to her. When he opened the door he could tell from the puffiness of her eyes that she had been crying.

"Dennis," she said. "We have to go over something here."

He backed away so she could come in. "Any news?" he asked.

She shook her head, a pale, fatalistic expression on her face. "I'm afraid not," she said. She sat down at the table they had eaten at just weeks ago. "There's a simple reality here—the rent on this place is due soon, and you're still a minor. Technically you have no family."

He sat down across from her and realized that the table was cluttered with garbage, plates with dried Chinese food stuck to them, dirty milk glasses, stained chopsticks. "Well, my mother had a family I guess, but—"

"I am aware of some things. I mean, Mr. Angstrom told me about your situation. I am also aware that he left a will, if we can assume he is really gone." She went on to point out that the bank had the official copy of his will, that they would act as executor in the event that The Captain were to be declared deceased, and she knew that there were no provisions in his will for anyone but a sister in Ohio. "Besides," she said, "he wasn't rich. He had a few things, a little money, and that's all. No property." She looked toward the hallway leading to The Captain's room. "We do have to do something about his stuff."

"There's hardly anything here," he said. "Most stuff is in storage, he told me. And I don't need, I mean I don't expect—"

"He also told me about you."

"What'd he say?" He took two plates to the kitchen alcove and put them in the dirty sink.

"He had a letter he told me about. It was from your mother to him, written in 1930. He had planned to give it to you when you turned eighteen, and I guess you're close enough that I'll tell you what I remember."

"Okay." He sat down again. Before him was a week-old newspaper with a circular depression from the plate.

She got a pained look, then a look of distraction, as if she wished she were not put in the position of having to tell him all this.

"I know what she was," he said.

"Who?"

"My mother. She was a prostitute."

"No," she said. "I mean yes, that I know, but the letter describes your mother as having found you in an alley in a city. Newark, I believe. That your biological mother died shortly after you were born. He told me that your mother didn't know her full name, only that she was very young and a— A girl of the streets."

"What color was she?"

Momi looked at him with surprise and a perplexed wonder. "Why, Caucasian, I presume. Why would you ask?"

"I was just wondering." He slid the paper off the table and folded it, and held it on his lap.

"She knew of this girl, that she was pregnant and so on, and by chance was nearby when she gave birth, apparently tried to help her, but she was in such a weakened condition that she died. A man had planned to, well, put you in a garbage can and as I understand it, suffocate you, and your adoptive mother, I suppose she would be, begged the man to let her have you. She managed to make her custodianship of you official by some means, I don't know." She shook her head, stared at the table. "So strange a story, it made me wonder about this Newark, how something like that—"

"It's not that unusual."

"What are you going to do?"

"I don't know." When he said that the familiar, airy flippancy swept over him, a sensation of lightness and lack of substance, and he thought, so, she was not my mother, my mother was a girl of the streets in Newark, and has no name. I was meant for a garbage can. "So I have no name, technically I mean."

"Legally you do."

"You mean illegally I do. McKay is my mother's name, but I don't know anything about her really, if she was even ever married to a guy named McKay. I asked her when I was little and she said she didn't want to discuss it."

"What's at issue here is what you plan to do."

"Go back, I guess. Paterson or— Or Newark."

"Before you do that you need time to get up the money and so on." She rubbed her chin, thought a moment. "Angela thinks you should work for a while for my brother Benjamin."

"What does he do?" He got up again and stuffed the newspaper in a waste basket.

"He builds boats, supposedly, and carves things that they sell in Waikiki. He's an—artisan I guess you'd say. Ours is, or was, a family of canoe builders, although he hasn't been involved in making one since long before the war."

Again she rubbed her chin, and shook her head as if she were considering just how bad an idea this was.

"He isn't hiring," he said, wanting to laugh, because he was still captured in that sensation of airy casualness. In fact every emotion he had ever felt seemed somehow wrong, at least for the occasion. He shrugged and sat back down.

"He requires some explanation," she said. As she talked, he confirmed to himself what he had read in her expression, bad idea. Benjamin Santiago was a difficult and eccentric man, in fact eccentric enough that Momi and Angela's parents rejected the idea when Angela brought it up, but Angela was one of the few who could be considered a sort of favorite of her uncle, and the idea that she could talk to him about getting Dennis a job more or less opened the door. "We don't see much of him," she said, "and he may just laugh the idea off."

"Does he work here or in Kailua?"

She laughed then, almost hopelessly, he thought. "No, he works in a huge, dilapidated shed out beyond Kaneohe, up the windward coast. I mean, how on earth would you even get there?"

"Is the fishing good out that way?"

She told him to pack up his things, and she would pick him up in two days. It might be a good idea to clean up a bit, so as not to irritate the landlord. He could stay in his room in the house in Maunawili. He wanted to tell her, no, he could take care of himself, but she pointed out that the house was big, the room remained empty, and he thought, I know why—centipedes. She herself could use a little help with the vegetation, Benjamin's job normally, but even though Benny's room was right there in the house, Benny was never there. He kept a room sometimes in Waikiki, or else slept out in the shed. In any case the vegetation was overtaking the place, again something Dennis knew about. There were rotted palm fronds thrown over a bank above a stream, a huge mango tree in the backyard that left a perpetual sweet mire of orange, fly-drawing slime, and there were thick, vigorous grasses and odd bushes all over the place. The idea that he could be of some help with that old place reduced the embarrassment somewhat, but he said to himself, so I am a temporary guest. It struck him that he had been a guest, a visitor, all his life. Everything was temporary.

He watched her leave, walking past the garbage cans sitting next to the hedge, and a strange shock of retrospective dread washed over him. A garbage can.

On the day Momi was to pick him up he waited in the cottage living room which looked stark and bare after he had cleaned it. He thought he should say something to the Hendersons next door, but they were not home. Besides, it was a relief not to have to face Carol, and he couldn't figure out how it was that he had reacted to her like a mute dummy. His things were packed in the duffel bag stencilled "Richard Keach," and seeing it sitting there on the scratched linoleum floor next to two boxes of sheets and other junk brought back a morbid cyclone of recollection, because it was happening again. At least this time the uprooting had nothing to do with anything bad he himself had done. It seemed odd to him that a girl of the streets in Newark had accepted a twenty from a man and he was the result, and now, seventeen years later, his chances of finding out who this man was, and his name was not McKay, had dimmed out of existence. So he was nobody in particular, and any evidence of whoever he was or whatever he was now had receded like an object dropped into the ocean. Then, when he went to comb his hair for the fifteenth time, he stared at his face in the mirror, at his eyes, and they seemed to him as flat as clay, as vacuous, empty and devoid of identity as two holes in the ground.

≈   ≈   ≈

He was awakened by the rapid tickling of something on his bare leg, and bolted upright in the bed and then jumped out, sweating because of the moist, windless heat. When he turned the lamp on the light blinded him, and focusing, he saw cockroaches running around on the floor, one of them two-inches long, shiny like a brown date, and sensed that somewhere in the sheets a centipede sat, waiting for him to come back. He was in his dank room in the old house, and stood there thinking, why am I here? and then the reality of it formed in his mind: Momi had picked him up late in the day, had deposited him here in this room with its dresser and wooden chair. By the door were the two cardboard boxes with sheets and some of The Captain's junk that Momi thought he could use, the brown tube with the fishing rod taken down and put inside, shaving stuff, and on the dresser was the deflated duffel bag. The Captain was probably dead. They had eaten something called laulau for supper, a ball of greenish-black spinach with pork and fish and a wad of fat inside that had seemed to him so repulsive that eating it was only possible if he simply ignored what was going into his mouth. The other food that went with it was poi, a purplish-gray slime that he refused. Then the old lady, Momi's mother, sat there smiling at him and speaking, but because she mixed languages, English and Hawaiian, Momi said, he barely understood what she said, most of which had to do with things that happened fifty years ago, and people long dead. He figured she was just senile and that was it.

He had no idea what time it was, but outside it was black and wet, as if the air itself were a slab of jelly, and when he ran his hands over his chest and sides, he saw that he had been sweating in his sleep. He went to pull the sheets around to find the centipede, but it was not there, had probably retreated and was snaked around a spring, waiting until he got back in. He sat on the chair, and as he had done when he and The Captain had visited, tried to doze off.

He heard roosters crowing a little later, and began to see the faint change in the square of the single window. He was so groggy and tired that he longed for sleep, but was afraid of the bed, so he put his clothes on, wormed his feet into the rubber slippers, and stepped out the door to the backyard.

By the time Momi appeared on the little porch next to his room, which led into the kitchen, he had raked up all the rotted mango skins and pits from under the trees, and pushed the piles, along with oozing, blackened palm fronds, down the bank.

"My God," she said. "When did you get up?"

"Around dawn, I guess."

"You should go to the beach. It's Saturday, all the kids'll be there. Angela likes Lanikai, around the point from their house."

He knew the place, the long, open stretch of beach with a few houses and cottages at either end.

"What about the— That work thing? Your brother."

"He says he doesn't want anybody up there, but we'll see. Just needs a little time." Then she pointed at a shed at the edge of the bank. "It's miles to the beach. There's an old bicycle in there. Pump the tires up, maybe you can get it to work. But come on in and eat first."

It was a girl's bike, and he rode it with a hopeless mortification that he might be seen by anyone, holding the spear and mask and fins in his right hand, which remained gripped on the handle until it had rigidified into a numb claw. And as he rode, burping back the taste of Portuguese sausage and looking around at the mountains and the ocean in the distance visible over the tops of the palm trees in Kailua, he understood the absurd remoteness of where he was, and vowed to save every cent he made to buy a ticket out of this place. Even though it was October it was as hot and sticky as some outpost in the Indian Ocean. He hated it. For all the bizarre profusion of life around him, he thought that there was as The Captain had said a kind of death here, a horrible impermanence, a rot that sucked the breath out of you.

Only the water soothed him. Different from the little beach off Diamond Head, Lanikai had no reef inshore, but he could see it way out, two-thirds of the way toward the two little islands that sat a mile or so offshore. Since no one was at the beach yet, because it was still too early, he went in and churned his way out toward the reef, the cold leaking into his flesh and gradually numbing his mind. Pale fish darted over the sand at the bottom, seven or eight feet down, and the sparsely-placed coralheads had only small fish moving around their hollow bases. Then, ahead, the bigger reef materialized in the soft blue, and he knew by the size of it that it was as good as or maybe better than the one off Diamond Head.

After he explored the reef for a while he heard voices mixed in the wind. He looked around and saw dark boys on surfboards paddling out toward the islands. The boards were long and made of a dark wood. Then he recognized Junior Kaaiai, who had stopped and was looking in his direction.

"I like do what Tarzan Smit' did," one of the boys yelled to the other. "Alla way to Maui, whooeee!"

Junior paddled in his direction, then stopped the board where the reef began. "'A fahk you doeen?" he called. "Come heah learn fo' surf? What? Your boad sink, ass-ho?"

"Nothin', just fishin'." He raised the spear out of the water, proof that he was here on more or less legitimate business.

"Notting my ass, haole shit!" he yelled. "Dis my beach, dis my wattah. Dis all my feesh! I gut you like one fahkeen peeg! I catch you onna shore, I gut you!" Then he turned and paddled toward the two islands, catching up with his friends, once looking back, the fury on his face so bewildering that Dennis turned, muttering into the snorkel, and headed back to the shore.

Looking down at the white sand sweeping under him, he thought that maybe Junior was right, this qualified more as a trespass than his appropriation of the water off Diamond Head, and it reminded him of the way boys claimed blocks in Paterson and would fight with ferocious devotion to validate their claims. All it meant was that he could not fish here, regardless of how rich in life that long stretch of reef was, regardless of what he had seen, parrotfish, schools of blue and brown cattlefish as the book called them, one large silver fish that shot away so fast he did not even get to see its shape.

Angela was sitting on a towel on the beach, near the bicycle. When he stood up in the shallow water he remembered to lean over and clean the hana butter off his face, and smooth his hair back.

"Eh, Denny!" she called. "Try come!"

He went to her. "Your cousin Junior just told me he's gonna gut me," he said.

"Dat mullet," she said.

"How long would he stay out there?"

She pointed. "See da island onna right? 'Ass wheah dey ride. All morning, up to one or two. I got out wit' dem too, but— Boys get pilau mout', make me sick."

"Pilau? What do they say?"

"'Ass talk dirty, an' I no tell you— Den I get pilau mout' also."

His heart started beating harder—the same involuntary sensation had crept over him again, the entire fleshy magnitude of her had done something to his mind.

"What?"

"Nothin'," he said. "Sorry." He looked down at the fine sand. He imagined that the sun, stark and powerful even at this time in the morning, had relocated his perception into the present, and he had for the moment forgotten all about The Captain, about his mother and all the rest. "Hey, who's Tarzan Smith?"

"He took one surfboard to Maui. Lashear."

She flopped back onto the towel and closed her eyes, and he took the opportunity to look at her, at the black, curly hair fanned out on the towel, the shoulders, breasts, ribcage, hips— The radiation of heat and the slight tinge of sweat and flowers coming off her like some vapor bored into his flesh and created a strange, ticklish sigh of pure desire, like a breath held almost too long, and the sensation made him afraid.

"You come ovah tonight—we do one cookout."

"Okay, what are you cooking?"

"Fish, chicken, dakine."

$$\approx \qquad \approx \qquad \approx$$

They had beer at the cookout, and Angela's father offered him one in a brown bottle, Primo. He had had beer before in Paterson, on a rooftop with some of his tough friends, so when he took the first sip he did not grimace as he had in Paterson.

"T'ree weeks from Monday you staht," Angela's father said. "Momi say he pay fifty cents an hour."

"Fifty?"

"Yah, j'like one sugah workah, good money," he said, then went off to his fire, built in a lava-rock fireplace with a metal grate. Carrying his beer, Dennis went to the other side of the yard where Angela was talking with Momi. Junior was there, along with one of his surf friends. It seemed best to avoid him, even eye contact, but whenever he sneaked a look in Junior's direction, he would be looking back with an expression of jovial aggression on his face. So he found himself thinking, fifty cents? Hey, Junior, fuck you and the horse you rode in on. I'm making fifty cents an hour.

And Junior's face said, I'll get you alone, haole fucker, and I'll kill you.

"Denny, come."

Angela had gone to a tree in a more or less remote corner of her yard, away from the others. She had a plate on her lap. Approaching her, he felt his heart kick up again, and his walk felt jerky and uncoordinated. He sat down next to her.

"Try," she said, holding her fingers out.

It was that stuff, poi. "I don't really care much for—"

"No, no," she said. "Dis soaked in lomi juice. Try."

It coated the ends of two of her fingers, a long, swinging drip hanging on because of its gooiness. He reached for her fork, and held it up.

"Babooze," she said. "Jus' lick um off."

He opened his mouth, and she stuck her fingers in. When he wrapped his lips around the soft fingertips, feeling the fingernails with his tongue, the rich, tangy taste of onions and fish stung his jaws, and as if he could not resist it, he sucked on the fingers until his mouth made a popping sound.

"Good, yah, dat poi?"

"Yeah," he said, and nodded.

"Try, jus' roll um on your fingers."

He watched her roll the poi and swish it around in the pinkish juice, then put it in her mouth until she made the same popping sound. "Eh, lemme have some adat beer," she said, peering around the tree. "Anybody watching?" He shook his head, no, and she took a swig, swallowed, and then came out with a loud, drainpipe belch. "Oops."

For a moment he was embarrassed, until she laughed and tried to manufacture another belch. "'Me show you somethin' neat," she said. She got up and walked toward the backyard, and he followed, looking around to see where Junior was. He didn't see him, and felt a tingling rush of fear going out of sight of the adults.

Angela walked into the bushes behind the backyard and he followed her, up a path that went above the house. Finally she stopped and turned. "Look," she said. From where they stood they could see the long, white strip of Kailua beach curving to the north to the Marine base, and the thousands of palm trees inland. "Da pavilion onna beach was one USO club, an' back about a mile dat way—one German spy lived in a two-story house. Dey caught him. Mr. Koon or sometin' li'dat." She paused, then cleared her throat. "Momi say you saving fo' go away."

"Well, the thing is—" But he didn't know what to say. He shrugged and looked at her, and the serious expression on her face frightened him. Her eyes met his for a second, and then she looked down, and he looked back at the trail, trying to think of a way to get out of this. But there was nothing to say.

"I like you stay," she said.

"But the thing is, I—"

Then she was right in front of him, and he held still, looking down at the trail. She put her arms around him and then he felt her lips mashing his, front teeth meeting, and he could feel the breathless, shaky agitation in her body, as if her heart were beating much too fast. She backed away then, with a look of horror on her face, and he opened his mouth to speak, but could say nothing.

"'Kayden," she said, and was gone back down the trail, running. He stood there for a full minute, the taste of her lips on his mouth and the shadow of sensation on his sides and back from the contact of her hands and arms. He whispered, "Oh God, what did I—" and then gestured at the water. When he finally made his way down the path his knees were so weak that he felt as if he had suddenly become sick.

During the rest of the cookout Angela stayed with her mother and Momi, and he wandered around the edge of the yard, from time to time looking in her direction. A couple of times she was looking in his direction when he did that, and both times her head jerked back to what she was doing. And he remained flushed with shame because he had done it again, had lapsed into the dumb, gawking paralysis that seemed to him now like an incurable disease.

It seemed pointless to wait out the days to go to work when he should be getting on a boat or plane. Angela wanted nothing to do with him, he was sure, and with that, the conviction that he would leave as soon as he could was fixed in his mind. He didn't belong here, and when he walked along the beach past little groups of the dark, local people he felt that his banishment in this foreign country was merely interesting, and of course temporary, and in a few months he would be gone. He didn't care any more about Junior's threat, and spent the days fishing off Lanikai. Tuesday he caught two large brown fish with sharp barbs on their tails, and one of them left a cut on the tip of his thumb. He decided to stop at Angela's house and, avoiding her if possible, give the fish to her father.

He found Mr. Santiago in the front yard bundling up hedge clippings. "I caught these," he said, holding them up on the stringer. "You want 'em?"

"Eh, palani," he said. "Good stuff."

Dennis worked the piece of wire, which was tied to the end of the stringer, out through the gills.

"Watch da tail."

"Yeah, figured that out," he said, holding his thumb up.

Thursday he stayed in the water until his brain had become numb. All through the reef were hollows and caves, and he fought the currents and waves trying to get his body inside, aiming the spear, banging his knees and elbows against the reef. As he had practiced with his friends in that dirty YMCA pool in Paterson, to see who could stay under longer, he breathed deeply ten or twelve times, saturating his lungs with oxygen until he was dizzy. Then he would be able to stay down so long that it seemed like it was too long. That dizziness dulled the pain and gave the water a mesmerizing effect, and each time he saw a big fish slide into one of those holes he would lunge after it mindlessly and hit something, and ignore the pain. He caught one more palani and made his way toward shore, miserable because of what he did not catch, a huge, fast-swimming silver fish that he had surprised gleaming in the back of one of those caves, its side bluish-green and iridescent.

On his way in he saw them on the shore sitting by their long wooden surfboards. He decided to ignore Junior as he had ignored the bruises and scratches on his body, and aimed for his towel, which was more toward the Kailua end of the beach.

The group of kids moved along the beach toward his towel as he approached. Some were girls, but Angela was not among then, although he knew that had she been, she probably would not have minded Junior's abuse anyway.

Rising out of the water felt like a strange dream. He took off the fins and mask with an exaggerated care and then dipped the fish again and again in the water as one would a teabag, to clean off all the sand. Then his back was stung with what felt like birdshot, and he turned, the stinging raising the hair on his head. Junior had thrown a handful of sand. "Hey, haole fuckah, I got you now."

"Junior, cut it out," one of the girls said. The other kids stood at some distance. "Hey, he caught one fish."

He looked at the girl, held the fish up a little, and walked out of the water. Junior lunged at him and pushed him on the shoulder so that his head snapped, and he fell down in the gritty pebbles in the shorewash. When he tried to stand up again Junior punched him on the crown of the head, and he sat back down. His neck hurt.

"You fuckah, I wrap dat spea aroun' your neck." Junior rubbed his fist, looked at it.

Dennis took a deep breath and then felt as if he would begin to cry, and swallowed the feeling. Then his skin began to bristle, and he stood up again, still tightly holding his gear. Junior looked ready to swing again.

"You touch the spear and I'll kill you." With that a feeling of tremendous exhilaration raced through his flesh. Junior could run him over with a truck, gut him, do anything, but he would pay if he bent his spear.

"You stay away from my cousin, you fuckin' rat. You stay away from dis beach."

"I'll go where I want, and if you touch the spear I'll kill you."

"Ho!" Junior said, turning to his friends. "Da assho like beef wit' me!"

"I don't wanna beef with anybody."

"Well you gonna, you little piece turtle shit."

The boys laughed.

"Fuck you," Dennis said. Now his head hurt, and all the bruises on his body began to throb.

"Take his fish," one of the boys said.

"Nah, I no wan' his goddam stoopit fish. I want da goddam haole rat outta heah."

"I'll go where I want."

Junior snorted. "I not in da mood fo' kill you now. I like tink it ovah, maybe tomorrow, maybe not."

Dennis walked back to the water and dipped the fish again. "Whatever," he said, and trudged on down the beach to give the palani to Mr. Santiago or Momi, but even that seemed stupid now. Making sure that no one watched, he rested the bike in the weeds and buried the fish in the sand.

≈　　≈　　≈

The longer he stayed at the house in Maunawili, the more he sensed that he was an imposition. It didn't matter how much he cleaned up. He could have painted the house and it would not have mattered. The still, windless heat was first uncomfortable, then maddening. He would be tickled awake by a cockroach or, he was sure, centipedes, and find himself bathed in sweat, and would stand staring out the window at the damp vegetation with the sharp outline of Olomana behind it against the slightly-lighter night sky and feel no movement of air, and sleep would be impossible.

At times the subtle but tangible shadow of sensation on his lips, from her lips, and even what he thought of as a slight toothache from the collision of their teeth, stayed with him like a tattoo of regret that he had not done what he was supposed to do, did not say something sophisticated as Robert Taylor or Errol Flynn would have said. He had stood there like a dummy, and now she hated him.

Where fear of insects was concerned he tried to convince himself that he was being a baby, that there was really no threat. But then one night he was bitten on the foot by a centipede that had to be six inches long. When he scrambled out of the bed to find the light switch he was aware of it wrapped around his big toe, prickly and tight, and he kicked it off onto the floor, grabbed a little rectangular mirror from the dresser and slammed the edge of it so hard onto the centipede's head that he cut the palm of his hand with the corner. Then he focused on the centipede. The nearly-decapitated brown head sat there, its black ice-tong mandibles opening and closing, and when he finished decapitating it, working the mirror edge through the sinewy flesh, it snapped its mandibles again and again while a foot away the headless body writhed, brown segments catching the light, its blue-white belly glistening, and then the body righted itself and slowly walked away and burrowed under his sock.

He was trembling badly, and briefly studied the little oozing hole in his hand, then the hot welt on the top of his foot with the two little holes from the bite. He wanted to go to the bathroom to do something about both, but was afraid to leave the centipede's head, and wanted to keep an eye on the body, which now hid under the sock. The idea that the body would walk off like that was nothing short of a nightmare, such an aberration of nature that he wanted to figure out how to get a ticket out of this place before even going to work. He opened the window screen and then pushed the head, mandibles still opening and closing, up onto his go-ahead and flipped it out. Then he did the same with the body, long and brown, which held onto the slipper until he flipped it into the darkness. He went and washed off the cut, and put a white burn cream on the bite. But he could not sleep after that and sat and waited for the chickens to crow. He could not escape the image of the headless body coming back in the window or snaking its way through any of those damp holes in the lava rock wall, or the head itself making its way back, walking on its pincers, bent on vengeance. The longer he sat there the worse the bite itched, until he could barely stand it.

When he worked in the yard sometimes Momi would stand briefly at the kitchen window, and he would see that her stare seemed flat, and he would think, I know, I know, I'll get out of your way as soon as I can. But he was stuck until he could make enough money to go. Mountains he had thought of as beautiful seemed as flat and distant as her stare, and he hated them too. He supposed it had been that way always, that his "mother" and The Captain and those clients who came to the apartment in Paterson to get in bed with her, all of them saw him as an imposition, and he longed for a place where he could live without being anyone's responsibility.

Only the peculiar properties of water managed to neutralize the pressure, and he thought of it as somehow mysterious in its capacity to do this. There was no gravity and hardly any sound, only the strange squeaking and ticking that came from everywhere, and he moved through the dense medium in a perfect solitude, and it leached his memory of everything to the point that he wondered if being a lower form of life might be preferable. He spent so much time in the water that he began to welcome the numbing chill which made its way through his flesh all the way to the center of his being.

He had become familiar enough with the reef that he headed directly to those dark caves where he had seen the biggest fish. He became used to holding the spear next to his face, cocked and ready to thrust as he would simultaneously pull the trigger, giving it maximum velocity. He would shoot at the biggest fish, usually from too far away, and miss. That he missed all the time was not bad, because he didn't know what he would do with a fish anyway. Bury it in the sand probably, and this brought back the image of Angela, and he would grunt or snort into the snorkel, and gradually the image would melt away and his location in time would melt away with it.

The best of the caves faced the ocean and had a strong current that pushed him toward the inside unless he held onto the reef with one hand and kept his flippers up near the surface, to hold himself steady. On one trip he approached it, and thought he saw something, a sickle-shaped part of a large tail. He surfaced, amazed at the size of it. Then he breathed deeply fifteen times, until he felt that slight dizziness. He slid over the reef, approaching the lip of the cave, and tensed his arm, his finger on the cocked trigger. When he pulled himself over so that he was upside down, he was blinded by the blue-silver side of a huge fish, its eye locked on his, its mouth half open as if in a kind of irritated surprise. It had a high, curved forehead, and an iridescent blue stripe from gill to tail. He thrust the spear as hard as he could straight at the head.

He was pushed by current into the cave so that his knee went into a hole, and the silver fish thrashed in tight circles, banging into his head and shoulder. The fish surged powerfully, tearing at his grip on the spear. He grabbed the rear end of the spear and bent it around, pointing at the arc of the gill, and drove it in with all his might, and the spear end thrust out the fish's mouth. He bent it back toward where it had entered the gill, and felt a charge of gleeful exhilaration. It was his.

Something struck his right knee, and he looked down at the hole where it was stuck and there emerged the broad, bulbous head of a brown eel whose jaws were locked on the flesh above his kneecap. He shouted into the snorkel, and the current slammed him into the back of the cave, the fish still thrashing so that the point end of the spear had now bent to a right angle and was scraping his chest. The eel's body had emerged partway from the hole, surging back and forth, and water began to fill the mask. Then the current hit again, and he was turned over, blasted against the back of the cave, the fish's belly against his cheek, and felt a piercing rip in his side. With his free hand he punched at the eel's head but his fist slid off to one side, and he grabbed at the thick head but the skin was rubbery and slick, and the eel's body came all the way out in an upward surge and snaked around his leg. Involuntary spasms erupted in his chest and he held them back, and then his perception reduced itself and he was inside a bright dream. He could just see over the water dancing in the mask, and staring in a mesmerized trance, tried to push at the eel's head. Buried down in the brown, rubbery skin, the eye looked back as if either blind or unconcerned, flat and black. More spasms jerked in his chest, and minute bubbles rose before his eyes, luminous little planets each in its orbit in the blue-white infinity.

The eel's head came at him and struck his mask, mashing his nose against the glass, and then the body slithered along his neck in three slick, powerful undulations, but his leg was free. He tried to look down but the water in the mask blocked it. The fish continued to jerk, its mouth opening and closing, and he saw the teeth, again felt the searing pain in his side as if someone had closed a pair of pliers on his flesh. The bent rear end of the spear danced before his eyes, and he felt a tugging at his side. His throat filled with acid and he fought it back, swallowing, and tried to push away from the fish. It thrashed, and he was upside down again, his back bouncing against the roof of the cave, and then with the water dancing in the side of the mask he saw that the spear had been driven into his side so that its tubular shape was visible under his skin in a hard ridge, and as the current pushed him he saw the point appearing and disappearing, peeking its way out of his flesh five inches away from where it had entered.

He felt a serene dizziness, and relaxed, and realized that he was not afraid, that the ticking hush of the ocean was comfortable. He thought he tasted chlorine, felt feet and knees banging his head and shoulders, and wondered about his mother's reaction to his death. The current relaxed, and he felt himself sliding back upright, the water in the mask turning slowly to level, and he tried to push away from the cave wall, but couldn't. He closed his eyes, both arms around the fish, and his chest heaved inward in crushing spasms, and vomit filled his throat and mouth. He opened his eyes and saw in the bright water pink smoke ballooning before his face, and then felt a long sweep of current hurling him away from the cave wall.

Cold wind stung his face and vomit erupted from his mouth and hissed on the water. The sun blinded him, the two islands' black cones loomed above him, and he coughed, breathed, coughed until he was sure he was breathing, then saw the mask and snorkel sinking away from him, and lunged after them. Then he blew the remains of the vomit from the snorkel, put the mask on and looked down. His knee was lacerated in a series of slits, each billowing little clouds of blood into the water. He still had his arm around the fish, and looked down at his side, his vision jerky and his body numb. The spear had gone through under his skin and the point was out along with the hinged barb. He touched the hard ridge of flesh encasing the five-inch section of spear, and felt no pain there. It was numb, as was his knee. The water dancing in the bottom of his mask had turned pink.

He floated into a pleasant delirium. Motion was a good idea, he thought vaguely, but he did not have the will for motion. With his arms around the fish, which was quiet now except for fine, high-pitched vibrations along its body, he floated and breathed, aware that the bottom and the taller columns of reef were sweeping slowly under him, and dimly he understood that he had achieved motion without really trying to, and raised his face from the water. In the distance, cottages. The white strip of beach, the green, jagged range of mountains way beyond, so dark and beautiful, a huge half circle of vertical chasms, and above, a sky so deep blue that it looked like space.

That beach was Lanikai, those mountains were the Ko'olaus, inside those cottages were people, and around the corner of that little mountain right there at the end of the beach where his towel was led to the Santiago house. He was only a half a mile from there, and his mind worked sluggishly on an idea. All he had to do was move his feet, if he could, and then he would be alive. And when this thought struck him he went rigid with panic, and scissored his legs, aiming for the shore.

The swim took what felt like hours while he was locked in that same peculiar delirium, and when he reached the shorebreak and tried to struggle to his knees, the cuts shot blood down his lower leg. Gravity meant pain, so raw that he could barely breathe. A woman screamed, others spoke with voices that were harsh and flat, voices from a dream. When he had made his way ten feet up the beach he fell, still holding the fish against his chest, and felt the sun warm his back. Just as the pain had exploded throughout his body as soon as he hit gravity, it vanished when he placed his cheek on the hot sand.

After that he lay there with his eyes closed, opening them from time to time to study the fine sand, feet, then someone's knee bent toward him in a kneeling position. He was turned up a little, and saw a hand holding a pair of heavy wirecutters, and his eye followed them down to the spear point emerging from his side. "No," he said. The voice that spoke back said something in English that he did not understand, but it was Mr. Santiago's voice. When Mr. Santiago clipped the spearhead off he felt the twanging shock of it in his trunk. Then there was a drawing in his flesh, a sensation of ticklish sliding, a pulling toward the front of his stomach, and the fish was pulled from his grasp. Without it his balance seemed to change, and he felt a sweeping heaviness pull his head back down.

He imagined that he might just sleep in the sun all afternoon, but felt himself being lifted so that all the pain which had dozed with him now woke up and scalded his flesh. He was being told that he had to go to a doctor. "A good one, one guy who sews up cane cuttahs 'ass why."

Despite whatever the eel had done to his leg, he was able to walk on it. He stumbled, held up by Mr. Santiago, one towel tied around his leg, another around his waist, now fully awake and embarrassed for causing all this, and hoping that Angela was not around, and sitting in the car he worried about salt and blood soiling the seat fabric, and became so cold that he shivered almost uncontrollably. He tried to speak but his speech was jerky and breathless. "Wha' happen to the fish?"

"Put um inna sink in back—tail sticks up, ho!"

"Wha' kind is it?"

"Ulua. Ho, da big! Speah like one pretzel."

That shivering stayed with him throughout the visit to Dr. Ebesu, who leaned on his thigh while treating it to counteract the shivering. He washed the cuts out with a brown soap and squirted water in them, then sewed them up. He muttered that the spear had slipped aside anything serious so he did not have peritonitis to worry about. As for infections, if Dennis had the resistance to hold that back, good, because the penicillin series was—hahaha, one big pain inna ass. As he spoke and sewed, Dennis wanted to tell him that he shivered because he was cold and no more, but he did not, because he found himself watching the sewing, the way the doctor hooked the thread through with a semicircular needle and then quickly looped it so that it tied with each stitch.

When it was over he said, "How much will this cost?" and Dr. Ebesu said, "I give George da bill."

He left and went back to the car, and now the fatigue overtook him and he fell asleep. He was half asleep when Mr. Santiago helped him to his room, only blearily understood what he said, that Momi would be home soon and he'd be okay here, jus' res' an' take um easy, we come check on you laytahs, we cut up da fish an keep da tail, ho, big lahdis', and he held his hands up. We make dakine fillets and steaks. I get one frien' in town—he freeze um.

"We freeze little pieces too. No worry."

"I got blood on your car seat."

"No mattahs, go to sleep."

And he did, realizing dimly that for once, the idea of centipedes didn't matter to him at all.

From ten feet down the boat is a black shape like a long shovel head and the surface of the water is silver. Pua can dive deeper. Why?

Grandaddy Kenika's feet hang next to the shovel head. You surface, spluttering.

"See anything?"

"How can she ho'd her breat' li'dat?"

Pua comes up spluttering, hair draped over her mask. "I see one!" she shouts. "One big spotty one!"

"You guys cold yet?"

"No ways!" Pua shouts. She goes back down, her ass last.

"How can she?"

Kenika shakes his head and shrugs. You could tell him now but you will not. Anyway his eyes have drifted to the spot on the water where Pua went down. Then he holds his mask on the water so he can see her through the glass.

Anyway, you rode your bikes around him. Junior and Keoni and you. "We go aroun'," you said. "He jus' one o' druggie, 'ass all. He bite you."

"Not," Junior said.

He hulked, walking with a stick, his face dark and his clothes filthy, and his hair matted and reddish all the way down his back. Dad.

"J' one o' druggie," you said. You pumped the pedals. Get away. Get away fas' so dey won't evah know. Hope he fo'get wheah da house is. Hope he fo'get.

The undulating shape of Pua's bathing suit writhes under the surface and then she breaks up, spits the mouthpiece out. "I get one fish!" she screams. "Grandaddy, look!"

She brings it out and holds it up, the spear bending. Ho, a big fish.

"Wow," Kenika says. "That's a spotted hinalea. I think they call it 'opule.'"

Pua motors to the rubber boat. "Can cook um, 'kay?"

How she do dat? How she ketch dat fish? So little?

"This weighs almost a pound," Kenika says, sliding it off. It flaps at him, spraying his face with water. "Good eating, too."

"Can go da Moke and make one fiah?" Pua asks. "Can?"
"Sure," he says.
How she do dat? Ho'd her breat' li'dat, ketch dat fish?
But anyway, you went around him. You tell Kenika an' he go look
for him. You nevah tell.
Pua climbs into the boat and you follow, skin dragging in a fart-
like sound on the rubber. "I got dat palani odda day," you say.
"Nani nani poo poo," Pua says. "My fish bigga."
"Shaddap," you say. "I ketch plenny fish. You get lucky, 'ass all."
Kenika has skin like a brown turtle. You would say, "Grandaddy,
I see my dad odda day," but cannot. No wan' him fine out wheah da
house is. Nevah. Den he come walking. Mento druggie.

≈   ≈   ≈

It was the blood on the car seat, it was being fed and doing nothing for it, it was the doctor's bill, the fact of being a burden that tortured him, and he saw himself as having a kind of race, to heal up fast enough to be able to work whenever it was that Benjamin Santiago would let him work. He dreaded the idea of seeing anyone any more than he had to, and Momi was nice about it, but he sensed in her bearing that same attitude of flatness that made him think, okay, okay, just hang on, I'll be out of here as soon as I can, but he realized that first he would have to pay the doctor's bill, first he would have to make up for any work not done in the yard, which sprouted vegetation and collected palm fronds and grew grass at a rate that seemed to him unnatural. But he had to wait until the swelling went down on his knee, until the itchy, red patch around the two holes in his side became less tender.

Luckily Angela had to watch the Nahoopii kids weekday nights, so there was little probability of his having to see her. She did visit the first weekend day after the accident, and brought cookies, and it seemed to him that she acted so normal and cordial more out of duty than anything else. They were in the kitchen and Momi was there. The fish was forty-two pounds, she said. Her father cut it up into steaks, fillets, and saved the tail for him which, she said, he could nail to his carport wall whether it was in Hawaii or New Jersey or wherevers. She told him to come to the beach, the sun would be good for his knee.

He did go to the beach, but not Lanikai. When the stiffness started to go away he tried taking the bike out, and instead of going to Lanikai went to the far end of Kailua Beach, and walked in the dunes dully studying the junk in the high-tide line. And when it was time for him to have the stitches removed, he went himself on the bike, and Dr. Ebesu was impressed at his progress, and explained that because the eel had bitten straight in and he was not able to pull his leg from its mouth, the damage was lessened. Eels are not normally aggressive, he said, but apparently the knee coming at it caused a defensive reaction. He had seen it before. Eels behaved like pit bulls when they're cornered. The greatest damage was done when the teeth sliced, which in this case they did only a little bit. Again Dennis asked about the bill, and he said, "I sent dat to George."

≈ ≈ ≈

He got a ride in a truck driven by a neighbor of Momi's, who was going out to the north shore to buy piglets. He was a Japanese man who smiled a lot but said very little, except to say that he would drop him off at the base of the road Benjamin's workplace was on, and he was to ask another man up the valley how to get to the place itself. He rode on the back of the truck to steady the bike, which bounced around when the truck went over potholes. His lunch was two baloney and cheese sandwiches, and he would either ride the bike home or hitch on a truck to get back. If he had to ride the bike, then he would work his knee more than he wanted to. Even the jouncing of the truck hurt his side and made it itch. The prospect seemed to him a little on the absurd side, and he wondered how it was that people got jobs they could walk to and then home in a matter of minutes, even an hour. After they passed waving gray-green fields of sugar cane, the shoreline around Kaneohe Bay became damp and jungly, the air smelling of mulch and rotted fruit. Then out by the cone-shaped island they called "Chinaman's Hat" the landscape opened up so that the bright mountains loomed over the road, so verdant that his eyes were driven nearly shut, and he saw it all through blazing slits of vision. As the truck bumped along, rumbling at one point across a steel landing strip for planes, he held onto a fatalistic patience, thinking, go ahead, make it fifty miles, a hundred.

As the man instructed, he rode the bike up a dirt road toward a dark valley in the distance, his lunchbag clutched over the grip by his left hand. There were houses along the road, all with corrugated roofs and chickens and dogs in the yards, patches of banana trees and huge mango trees and perfectly laid-out grids of papaya trees. At one house there was an enormous, muddy pig who watched him as he passed. Some of the dogs ran out and paced him, tails wagging. The house where he was to ask about Mr. Santiago was supposed to have a sign in front that read Marumoto.

He was short and thin and had gray hair. "So you come help Benny," he said. "Come, I show you. Leave da bike heah." Behind the man's house were screen structures full of orchids.

He leaned the bike against the man's garage and carrying the lunchbag followed him into the faint remnants of a road behind the house, no more than two depressions in the grass that went into dense woodland, at one point blocked by a four-wire fence. "Dis training area fo' da ahmy," Mr. Marumoto said. "Benny no care. He jus' insai fifty yahds or so."

Then the man fiddled with the fence and opened the top two wires.

"So this is supposed to be— Whatever, off-limits."

"Yah, but Benny, he no care."

"But what if I'm caught in there?"

"I dunno. Whatevahs. Jail maybe."

Dennis stepped over the wire, and the man hooked the strands up again and left.

When he entered the woods it was so dark that he could barely see. The dense canopy of treetops blocked out all the light, and he felt as if he had walked into some damp, oozing prehistory. Even sound itself seemed absorbed by the denseness of it. The forest floor was sodden and muddy, and he went down an incline to where a narrow stream bubbled by, the two tracks of the faint road crossing it, and when he stepped over, his foot sank into the muck. He hopped and then pulled his foot out, leaving his slipper in the mud. He saw the broken strap sticking out. Great, now he was barefoot.

He pulled out the broken slipper and walked the rest of the way carrying it, his left foot squishing in the leaf mulch so that black water squirted up between his toes. In the distance he could see the building, up on thick stilts, the rusted, corrugated roof coated with moss and leaves, smoke wafting up from somewhere in back. At the base of the stilts there was a pile of huge, black logs half submerged in muck. He took a deep breath, feeling foolish because it had to be obvious to Mr. Santiago that his having come this far, even for fifty cents an hour, meant that he was either crazy or desperate, and he hoped the man would not think of him as imposing himself.

He walked in a cloud of black mosquitoes, and waved them away from his face. Then he came to a slime-covered flight of wooden stairs, and looking up, saw that the shed was screened all the way around. In the dim light inside the shed he could see a figure sitting on a chair. Beyond the shed, down in another gulley, there was an outhouse sitting under large, light-green banana leaves, and vines clotting trees which were fringed on the ground by dots of yellow fruit.

His eyes had now adjusted to the dimness, and he walked up the stairs, pushed the screen door open, and stepped into the shed. There, sitting on a wooden chair, was an immense man with thighs bigger around than the average person's chest, a massive belly hanging over a leather belt, shoulders and upper arms stretching a sweaty, white tee shirt to the point of disintegration. He turned slowly and looked, his dark, bloated face splotched a bluish-purple around the eyes, one step short of some bizarre birthmark, and his hair was black, short and curly, glistening at the temples with sweat. His feet, huge and splayed in the toes, were also a dark, bluish-purple, coming down from scaly, tubular ankles.

"Uh, I'm Dennis McKay."

The man looked at him as if not understanding.

"I'm here about the job."

He turned back to his table. On it were pieces of wood, each about a foot and a half long, one locked in a rusty vise. He picked up a wood rasp and began sweeping it along the side of the wood, with the grain. Spread out on the table were other tools, chisels, sanding blocks, wooden mallets.

Dennis stood and watched. He stood for around three or four minutes, until the man put the rasp down and looked at him, and his expression went through a moment of recognition, then a kind of search of his memory. Oh yes, the guy at the door.

Then he said something unintelligible. It sounded like "Heyaha kay lah?"

"I don't understand."

He said it again and pointed, apparently at the lunchbag. Dennis held it out, and the man said, "Mai, mai."

The chair creaked, and the man stood up and stepped toward him. He was not actually immense in height, maybe a little over six feet—his immensity was horizontal. He held his hand out, and Dennis handed him the bag. He opened it and looked inside, and stood there studying the contents for what seemed like thirty seconds. He sniffed it, then thought. Then he turned and walked across the shed to the back and dropped the bag into a fifty-five gallon drum, and sparks and smoke appeared at the rim, the smoke lazily sweeping down and out through the screen at the back of the shed. He turned and went back to his chair.

"Okay," Dennis said.

The man went back to filing the wood.

He stood there for another five minutes, and when the man rose up from his work and turned to look at him, his expression seemed to say, oh, you're still here. I forgot.

"If you want me to leave, I'll leave."

The man cocked his head, then looked down at the floor, apparently not understanding. Dennis scratched his head in embarrassment, wishing they'd told him about this. He now smelled the burning bread, and, he guessed, singed baloney and mustard. Mr. Santiago waved him over, this time to the drum, and he walked to his left around the table, and heard a voice from the other end of the shed. It said, "Why?" in a soft, high-pitched tone, like singing.

"What was that?" he asked.

Mr. Santiago waved him toward the drum. Dennis went the rest of the way, along a huge log that was partly covered by a canvas tarpaulin, the black ends sticking out hewn narrower. He was frightened now, either by the voice beyond the drum, or by the man himself, who, he imagined, might now throw his employee into the drum after his lunch.

The man held up a gray coconut. Then he stooped over, a slow process because of his size, and rose up again, holding a sickle-shaped piece of coconut shell, the dry, light-brown fiber on the inside crawling with little insects. Then he threw the piece of shell into the drum. So, it was firewood. Then he reached behind him and held a machete in his hand, and Dennis backed away a step. In the firelight he got a better look at Benjamin Santiago's face—the bluish-black discoloration around his eyes and on his cheeks might be from his obesity, but he did not appear to be ugly in the old sense of the word. His eyes were a dark copper color and a sheen of skin oil glistened on his forehead and broad nose, and his lips were nearly the color of liver. He saw the resemblance to the man's brother, Angela's father, right down to the huge hands. He held the machete out, and Dennis took it.

Then Mr. Santiago rattled off something in what seemed to be Hawaiian and pointed down the ravine, where the tops of palm trees were just visible above the bank. He stooped over again and held up another sickle-shaped piece of husk and threw it into the drum, and then picked two halves of the hard inner shell off the bench, halves apparently cut by a saw.

"I got it. This is like firewood. And you want the inside shells."

But the man had already turned and gone back to his table.

Before going out Dennis found a piece of twine on the floor and repaired his slipper while Benjamin Santiago watched, appearing both fascinated and perplexed by the repair job. He tied the twine to the V and passed it down through the hole, then wound it around the broken-off plug so that it would not pop out of the hole, and put the slipper on. The twine would kill the flesh between his big and second toe, he knew, but he did not want to let on. He stood up and walked out, feeling the rubber plug through the bottom.

If he made it through the day, then he would go to Angela's father and ask him about this even though their house was out of the way. He would find out if what he was doing made any sense, or if he should give up and quit.

The ravine was deep and had steep, vine-covered sides, and he was halfway down when he realized he had no bag to carry the husks up in. "Fuck it," he whispered. "Use the shirt." And why was he carrying the machete down? Dumb. But then, he would do the work down there so his "boss" wouldn't see him make mistakes like ruining the inside shells.

Because of the idiocy of what he was doing and the cloud of mosquitoes, and the flies that kept landing on the scabs on his side, he worked in a fury of jovial despair—this would most likely be his only day of work for the strange monster in the shed, so he might just as well do what he was told. The gray, parched coconuts had apparently been rolling into the ravine for centuries, because under those he picked up to hack apart, always making sure not to damage the shell inside, he saw older ones and under them rotted remnants of more. He was in a coconut mine and deep down underneath in air pockets and oozing grottoes thousands of centipedes lurked, confused because they were trying to sleep. He imagined that at night, under the moon, the surface of the mine would glisten with thousands of them.

He took load after load up, and walked bathed in sweat and covered with filth into the shed and dumped them out of his shirt in the corner. His knee itched, and irritation radiated out from the scabs on his side. Mr. Santiago would look up each time and watch, his copper eyes swiveling like periscopes inside their dark, fleshy lids. Each time he brought up a load he stepped in that one place and heard the voice across the room sing "Why?" and stepped on it as he walked out, as if for verification. It was something about the floorboard that made that sound. It was a singing floor.

Later he leveled off the fury of his energy and settled into pacing himself, now more aware of what was around him, birds singing, one in fact whistling a complicated series of notes right above him, the bizarre, almost Martian vegetation, the funky, sweet smell in the air. Finally he heard a hooting sound from the shed, "Hu-ee!" and looked up the bank. "Mai mai mai!" Mr. Santiago yelled.

He took his three-quarter load up the bank and into the shed— why?—and turned and stood there, the mosquito welts burning on his sides and back. Mr. Santiago had a steaming metal pot on the table, and paper plates. He opened the pot and spooned out rice, and then picked out something wrapped in leaves, which steamed as he dropped it on the table. He opened it. Fish, what kind Dennis couldn't tell. He spooned fish onto the rice on each plate, and motioned him to come over.

Then he said something that sounded like "Maki-maki o-ee-why?" It was a question.

"Uh—"

"Pia," he said, and went to a large galvanized bucket. From it he drew two brown bottles of beer.

"Hey, I get it. Pia—beer. I get it."

He handed Dennis the beer, and then the plate of rice and fish. He had no forks, and began picking at the fish with his fingers.

≈   ≈   ≈

"Dat lolo!" Angela's mother said, and slapped her forehead.

"Does he speak English?"

"Of course he does," she said. "It's some stupid thing with this culture stuff. He gets these manias, you know, and I think this language thing is a mania. Working way out there is a mania too. He doesn't really remember the language, not much anyway. It's just something he's got on his mind." She shook her head. "Actually we would be spanked for speaking it in school when we were little."

"A couple of times while we ate he said stuff, but I don't remember, except one, where he pointed at the plate and then the drum where he threw my lunch and said something like 'A holy haole cow cow.'"

"That's 'a'ole haole kaukau—no haole food. 'A'ole means no and kaukau food. When my mother got mad at us kids she'd say 'no!' about five times, and then she'd say 'a'ole,' and that's when we'd know to stop."

"So you think I should go back?"

"Of course. He'll stop that. Don't give in. And make sure he pays you."

"'Kay. Well, I should be getting on. Been a long ride."

"Angela should be at Momi's soon," she said. He nodded, and then she said, "What about tomorrow?"

"Bike, I guess. Gotta get used to it."

"It's more than twenty miles," she said. "How long does it take? And your knee—"

"Couple hours. No problem."

"This is ridiculous."

He was so tired by the time he got to the dirt road in Maunawili, in near darkness, that he no longer had the energy to feel awkward in Angela's presence. Embarrassment got left behind somewhere in that ravine. But he had a large pile of coconut husks in the shed, and understood that tomorrow they were going to saw the nuts and clean them up. Mr. Santiago showed him a wind chime, the half nutshell hanging like a dome with little pink and red baseball bat-like things that made a glassy, tinkling sound as they bumped into each other, strung down from the edge of the half nut on pieces of fishing line. The nut was polished a deep brown, and he had to admit that it was beautiful the way the grain rippled and little white threads ran through it, the way the hard wood of it shined up.

But as he approached the house, bumping along on the dirt road, he began to feel the slight irritation on his lips, the shadow of the contact of their teeth, and decided that if Momi's car came down the road he would hide in the woods until it passed. But it did not, because it was already in the driveway, and he pulled the bike around to the back of the house near the door to his room. He was fatigued to the point of being asleep on his feet, but wanted water, and headed for the kitchen entrance. No one was around, or they were in the living room at the front. When he opened the kitchen door and walked in, he saw it in the dim light on the table curled in a horrible sweeping arc, and he stumbled back out gasping, shaking so badly that he thought he might faint. It had to be three feet long, and upside down so that its pale-greenish belly was up, its blue legs thick and menacing, its head somewhere at the other end, mandibles he imagined five inches long. He stumbled back to the landing, dizzy from the vision of it. The starker the color, he imagined, the more venomous the bite. But that big? No, it couldn't be. He was sweating, and knew that in the looming shadows all around, back there where he had thrown the wet, oozing palm fronds and the mango slime, thousands of them were waking up, the biggest ones the horrible blue and green of this one.

"Denny?"

"Get— What—"

"'Sammatah? Denny?"

It was Angela. She stood in the kitchen doorway across the room. It occurred to him then that he had to have been mistaken, that what he had seen was something else, but he was still in the process of getting his breath.

"How you get so dirty?" He sensed a kind of conversational formality in her voice, and looked down at himself.

"Uh, work."

"Come," she said.

"What's that on the table?"

"'Ass one jade flowah lei," she said. "We jus' made it, fo' aunty Clarice Malama's birt'day."

He went into the kitchen and looked at it, moving closer carefully. Then she turned on the light, and the colors almost jumped off the table. The greens and blues were almost brilliant, and he could see how the flowers' shapes, like curved, elongated teardrops, might be mistaken for a centipede's legs because of the repetitious precision of their arrangement, points all curved out in a line, so that the arced shape of it resembled a single being curved to look seductive and lethal.

"Pretty, yah?" She pulled at it, straightened it out, and he became more aware of her. She wore a gray sweater and blue jeans.

"It looked to me like a centipede."

She stared at it, her mouth open. "'Ass awful," she said.

"They come in my room at night."

"Really?"

He stood and looked down, trying to think of something to say. Then to his relief Momi came into the kitchen and asked about work, and he went through the story again. When he was finished she sighed and said, "That man—I know he's my brother, but this is idiotic, some mumbo jumbo stuff that's on his mind."

"It's okay."

She shook her head. "That man," she said.

"I should wash off," he said, looking down at himself. "Not the bathtub, though. Maybe the hose."

"I do it," Angela said. "Put your bathing suit on."

He did so, again almost asleep on his feet, and left his dirty clothes outside his room door. Then he went out into the yard in the dark, to a patch of grass, and Angela turned on the hose. He cupped his hand over the sores on his side. When the water hit him he gasped, and then let it numb him, his eyes closed. When it stopped he stood there with his arms around himself shivering, and saw her coming with a towel. "Take dis," she said, and he did, his teeth chattering, and wrapped it around his shoulders and went into his room to dry off.

"Denny?"

She was on the other side of the door. "Yeah?"

"Momi say we eat in a half hour an' you can res' till den. I wake you up."

"'Kay. You goin' home?"

"No. Make leis, 'ass why. Momi an' me, we sell um to one lady who has a shop Kaimuki."

Waiting for the tickling of centipedes' legs, he drifted into a stuffy half-consciousness in which his own heartbeat sounded like the whacks of the machete, and garbled voices in other languages ordered him here and there, birds scolded him, the air danced with the gray sickles of husks, dirt, potholes, macadam swept under his handlebars, and sandwiches burned in a hot drum. Then he was cold, his flesh like meat from an icebox, and didn't have the energy to reach for the covers.

"Denny?"

The whisper of her voice seemed to come from hundreds of yards away, and he tried to open his eyes. When he did he saw her face in the doorway, and remembered waking up over in Waikiki that day with her sitting on the bed.

"We eat in ten minutes," she said. He pulled the sheet up, but it was tangled at his feet. "Don't be like dem wit' my uncle," she whispered. "Don't you do dat."

"Okay."

"No, I mean it," she said, her voice low so Momi would not hear. Her head went outside, came back. "Benny always sad," she went on, "but he not lolo."

"Okay."

"He sad because his wife wen' die. He sad about Darnay. Darnay his boy."

"Okay, but what happened to him?"

"Everybody know," she whispered. "He one mahu."

"Oh," he said. There was a silence, and he focused on her face in the doorway. "What's a mahu?"

"A boy who like boys."

His mind worked on the information sluggishly. A queer. He looked at the ceiling, then at her face in the doorway. "What happened to his wife?"

"She die of diabetes."

"Does Benny have any other kids?"

"No. 'Ass why so sad. You no talk stink about him." He could hear the combination of anger and warning in her voice, and the distance. Almost as if he were the enemy now.

"I won't," he said.

"So what you tink now, eh? You hate him too, right?"

"No, I like him."

"Why? You tell me why you like him. You jus' one more haole an' you tell me you like him? No lie to me."

"One more— Look, I don't know what I am," he said. "He fed me, he talked to me, even if it wasn't in English. He hired me. I don't know what I am and he hired me anyway."

He shouldn't have said that. It made no sense. The fact that he had said it made him colder, and he began to shiver. It was as if whatever caused heat in the body had turned itself off, and he felt hollow and wasted.

"What's wrong?" she asked. "What you mean you don't know what you are?" She came into the room, two steps. "Denny?"

The bed dipped with her weight, and she was right there above him. "Ah, you sick?"

"It's okay, I'm just tired, a little cold." He shook his head and rolled it a little sideways, embarrassed at her closeness, and then wary, even a little angry at the imposition of her presence. Then it was as if he could hear her thinking, and he began to smell thinking in her breath and in the sweet smell of the heavy sweater.

"You so cold," she said, and then crushed herself down on his chest, and he could feel her breasts against it. "I no want you to leave," she whispered.

"I won't."

"Ever."

"No, no."

"You mean it?"

"Yeah, I do."

"Momi an' my mom, dey say you will."

"No."

"You freezing," she said. "Come, put your hands under."

He wormed his hands up under the sweater, and the backs of them slid up to her flesh. "Ho, da cold," she whispered, and giggled. "Denny? You not lying?"

"No."

The hair slid up off his face, and he felt her lips slide on his cheek. Then she kissed him, almost experimentally it seemed, once and quickly, and he ran his tongue over his lips, holding his breath. The contact of her body suddenly felt familiar, or natural, and whatever chill he had felt was now gone, replaced by something else. His legs had been so tired, his buttocks so sore from riding the bike that the lower half of his body had forgotten itself, but now it was awake, and then he realized too awake, and he was almost horrified at what was happening, sliding inside the shorts so that she must surely feel it against her side.

She sat up and said, "I go help Momi inna kitchen."

"Yeah, been ten minutes, I bet," he said.

She took one step toward the door, and then stopped. He grabbed his shirt and punched his fists into the sleeves and tucked the tail in. She turned, about to say something, and then apparently changed her mind and left.

While they ate dinner, the four of them sitting around an old round table with huge eagles' feet clutching wooden balls, he listened to the conversation—did Auntie Clarice have all the tables she needed, would Uncle Benny show up, probably not, who had Pele's hair for the leis—he found himself looking at Angela when she was not looking at him, trying to figure out exactly what had just happened. When she stopped talking and looked at him, she appeared to be thinking the same thing, exactly what had happened and who was it, exactly, sitting there looking furtively at her when he got the chance?

And Tutu Elizabeth spoke up from time to time, sometimes in English and sometimes in Hawaiian, and Angela and Momi nodded, or said yes, or offered her more sweet potato. Once she stopped eating and said, "She was so beautiful, so beautiful," and Momi said, almost vaguely, "Yes, Mother, she was." Then to him she said, "Kaiulani, a princess who died a long time ago. She knew her."

After dinner while they worked on leis in the kitchen, he watched for a while, from time to time studying the venomous jade flower lei, and then went to lie down again.

This time when the sound made its way into his consciousness he bolted from the bed, turned the light on, and pulled the sheets back. But it was Angela, peeking in the door. She stepped in and stood before him, now looking shy and almost distant. Then the expression of a peculiar anguish crossed her face. "Denny, I wasn't kidding."

"Me either."

"Make me feel like one idiot."

"Me too."

"I gotta go."

"Yeah, I gotta leave really early. No ride this time."

Then she sighed quickly and said, "Well," turned to go and then stopped, and he could hear her thinking again, he could feel it in the air, something tangible like powerful radio waves or electricity.

She stepped to him and put her arms around his neck, pulled his body to hers, all the way to the thighs, knees colliding so that he winced with the contact on the healing cuts, and she was shaking, breathing against his neck. He put his arms around her, closed his eyes and smelled her hair. She whispered, "Oh I scared, I scared—Denny, I not kidding, I not kidding," and he nodded against her face. "Ho dis crazy," she whispered, "I get all funny an den' scared. Denny, I love you," and she pulled harder, almost as if she were trying to crush him. "I do, no lie, an' I scared," and when he buried his face down in the hollow of her shoulder and nodded again she whispered, "Oh, chee you not kidding, Denny, you not kidding either—oh I know you not kidding," and he shook his head no into her shoulder. "Oh you not, Denny."

He straightened up a little and said, "No, I'm—" and she looked straight into his face with a look of awed wonder, almost surprise, and it was as if he could not get his breath to speak, so he nodded, yes, yes, I'm not kidding. Then she was gone, and he could hear her telling Momi she was ready to go home, and there was a shaky excitement in her voice, as if she could not hide her state of mind. Finally he heard the car leaving, pebbles plinking the insides of the fenders.

He stood there by the door, staring at his hands, then around the room, then at the bed. He was not kidding either. He had little idea what it really meant, and then wondered how it was that he could have so easily changed his mind from wanting to get out of this place to the way he felt now.

≈   ≈   ≈

In the morning he was surprised at the strength in his legs, that the miles swept under him, macadam, dirt, potholes, and although his body felt wracked with pain and stiffness, some other energy drove it, so that by dawn he was more than halfway there, skimming along the muddy shoreline of Kaneohe Bay, maneuvering the bike around the odd dips and pits in the broken macadam. The sun rising out of the ocean illuminated the mountaintops in a copper glow, and the salty air felt almost like some strange inhalant that increased his strength.

And the hard coconut shells—he sawed and then filed, working each one with the same energy. He understood where it came from. He had only a vague idea of what it might mean eventually, and muddled visions flooded his mind, the dark, beautiful face, the totality of her, and he saw them alone someplace and thought of sex on rooftops and car backseats, and shook his head. He looked over at Benny, who worked in silence, concentrating on his sticks, which he was shaping into little canoes. He had gathered pieces of the burlap-like fabric from the large pods housing the coconut flowers, and cut them into little sails, and he used carefully-selected sticks to connect the hulls to his little outriggers. Watching Benny, he recalled The Captain's speeches about these people, but whatever warning The Captain had meant to convey now meant nothing. Why should race make Benny or Angela creatures of the past? And anyway, where race was concerned Dennis himself had none he could really define.

Because Benny had a deadline to meet, he worked on his models even as he ate his fish and rice and bananas, and the day was passed mostly with the sounds of tools and not voices. During lunch on Wednesday Benny left his tools idle. He would eat, belch, stop and then look at Dennis, studying him with his strange, copper eyes, his face glistening with a sheen of oil and half-dried sweat. Then he said, "Apopo," and pointed at the sun, then swept his arm over his head to the west. Tomorrow. Benny cupped his hands around his eyes and produced a sound with his tongue—blp-blp-blp—and stuck his huge, dusty feet out, moving them in an imitation of a swimmer's kick. The water? They were going to the water. "Mai poina," Benny said, and pointed to his temple.

"I won't. I mean, what is it? 'A'ole loa."

No, he would not forget. How it was possible to have a job where you would go into the water? He would not forget that. When he got the chance later, he pulled the cuff of his pants up and studied his knee. There were still deep scabs, like little plugs, in the stitch holes, but the cuts themselves had healed over to the point that new, pink scar tissue was emerging from under the flakes of dead skin. He decided he could do it.

Riding home, with the same energy he had had for two days now, he realized that his hands were in trouble—the tools, the repetitions of filing and sanding, had raised water blisters, and the skin around them was red and tender. But the water would be good for them, he figured. He recalled the same problem from painting Lon Carlson's barn, and then laughed, watching the macadam sweep under him, because Lon Carlson's barn now seemed a million miles away. The images of his mother and The Captain presented themselves, and he slowed the bike down. They were dead. Everything that was a part of them was now dead, and he felt a strange sensation of being between two lives, and he looked at the mountains and ocean, and then visualized the string of dots on the map of the Pacific.

Angela was busy with the Nahoopii kids and homework, so he ate alone, before Momi and Tutu Elizabeth, and then slept. He was awakened at four by the subtle sounds of movement on the floor. He sat in the chair the rest of the early morning with the light on and watched the cockroaches race across the floor, the geckos walk on the ceiling, and then before dawn ate cereal and left, the spear, mask and snorkel, and the fins clutched along with the handgrip by his right hand.

Benny had his gear ready, little goggles and no snorkel, a mesh bag, and gloves. He looked at Dennis's gear and nodded, then took the spear and studied it, playing with the doorhinge trigger and stretching the strips of rubber, making him feel a little stab of fear when he looked at the fire drum, but no smoke came from it. Benny leaned the spear against the screen. Then he fiddled with a second bag. Something was wrong with it. "Eh, Kenika, lavay mai hay schkroodrivah." He held his hand out.

He grabbed the screwdriver off the clamp on the wall and gave it to Benny. Kenika, that name the old Japanese man called him. Benny worked the clamp on the top of the bag, and then put the screwdriver down. "Ho!" he said, and carried his gear to the slippery front steps.

Benny led the way down the path to the little stream. He stepped through it, sinking in almost to his ankles, and turned and said, "'S your middle name?"

"Huh?" He stared at Benny, trying to understand, but his mind was blank. Then he realized it was English, and it took him five seconds to process the words. "Middle name?"

"Yah, what dey call you?"

"Reuben, leas'ways so my mother told me."

"What 'leasways'?"

He jumped across the stream. "At least."

"I look da name up, den," Benny said. "Cannot do notting about your las' name, but da firs' two, can change um."

"Why are you speaking English?"

Benny pointed at the little stream.

Following Benny toward Mr. Marumoto's house, he figured it out. You could speak English on one side of the stream, but on the other side you could not. Kenika. Kenika McKay. He turned the sound of it over in his mind.

Benny's car was a 1938 Pontiac that had the little Indian's head on the hood, with the feathers stretched back into a silver stream that melted into the hood seam. The front seat was covered by a salt-stained tarpaulin. Whenever he hit the brakes to avoid a pothole, beer bottles rolled out clinking from under the seat, and the waving feelers of a cockroach stuck out of a knob hole in the dashboard. As he drove he explained what they were doing: 'ina, or pencil urchins, are hard to find, and when you found one, you would break off only the five biggest pencils, so that the urchin could grow them back. When it came time to fish they would fish, so no speah today, 'ass why. It would be easier, he said, to find the 'ina on "da oddasai" around Makua or Waianae, but it was too far to go, and he knew where they could find them outside of Laie Bay. "But jus' five," he said, holding up the huge hand. "I heah about da ulua," he said. "But da knee look pretty good, yah? Can do um?"

"Yeah."

At the beach Benny showed him a plant called naupaka, the pulpy leaves of which you used to coat the glass inside the mask with a thin layer of clear sap, by crushing the leaf and rubbing it on. "Mask nevah fog," he said.

The magnification of things underwater took on a new meaning. Gripping his mesh bag, he churned alongside Benny, who was startlingly huge, a dreamlike leviathan working along at a gradual, stately pace, his scissoring legs and slowly fanning arms an impossibly rich brown. Every thirty seconds or so he would lift his head out to draw another breath of air. Dennis would motor out ahead of Benny, then circle back around behind him, then pull up alongside to watch as he moved, the huge thighs flexing with each kick, but Benny moved at such a slow pace that he was made to feel like some overexcited, spastic remora shadowing his host. When they went through huge breakers he had to dive under and fight the powerful roiling water, white and silver with racing bubbles, but Benny, like a log, rose up and settled down over them, his stately progress unchecked.

When they reached a broken reef he assumed they would stop there, but Benny turned right, making him backpedal to give him room, and went another hundred yards, out to where the bottom swept away and they were in twenty feet of water. At one point Benny stopped and surfaced. "Get one mano," he said, pulling the goggles away and shaking water out of them. He pointed down to his left, the oceanside direction, and Dennis put his face down in the water.

The shark cruised along the bottom, changing its direction in jerks, one eye on them. The flat, wide head resembled the blade end of some huge medieval fighting implement. Its pectoral fins were swept back, and it appeared to be eight feet long. Then it moved far enough away that it vanished into the blue. He pulled his face from the water.

"No worry," Benny said. "Not big enough fo' me anyway." Then he laughed. "Nah nah nah—hammaheads get smallah mout'. He no bodda us." From that point Dennis motored alongside Benny with his eyes darting around in search of the shark, but he didn't see it again.

Finally they came to shoal-like outcroppings that didn't break the surface of the water but had the bubbles of current around their crowns. The pencil urchins were in depressions in these outcroppings, the fingers, or little baseball bats bristling a bright red. Benny rose up and went down head first, churning his flippers to keep himself in one place as he carefully twisted the little bats off an urchin. Dennis kept looking for the shark, and finally reasoned that if Benny wasn't concerned about it, then he wouldn't be.

After about two hours he understood that Benny had, like a whale, the protective layer of fat that might allow him to stay in the ocean all his life, but Dennis did not. He was frozen to the point of numbness, even in his fingers, which could no longer feel the sandpaper surface of the urchin bats as he picked them, and then it began to affect his brain, so that as he searched the outcroppings and picked the five bats from each urchin, he felt as if he had made his way into a bright, absurd dream, and he was as mindless and bug-eyed as any of the simple organisms that lived out here. He was giggling and moaning with what he thought they called hypothermia, his jaw vibrating on the mouthpiece, his trunk leached of all warmth. It went on like this much longer, until his mind was emptied by the bright pastels, the darting fish, the absurdly-complicated richness of the surface of the outcropping flashing with light from the sun on the dancing water, and reality became timeless. Finally something immense and dark floated before him and an appendage waved before his eyes, and he hung gawking at the huge brown thing for a period of time before he found himself thinking, yes, yes, I understand. And what was that period of time before recognition? It seemed to him that his brain had labored for minutes before the rudimentary shadow of something resembling consciousness became evident, and it found itself thinking, wait, that's Benny, and I exist, that's what I forgot.

By the time they reached the shore he imagined that his heart, the center of his being, would be cold to the touch if he could get his hand in there. Then he convinced himself that some other kind of warmth kept it beating. That she was not kidding presented itself to the front of his mind, and he stared with a dumbstruck awe at the huge waves crashing outside the bay.

"Angela," he said.

"Hah?"

Benny. "Oh, nothin', I was just—"

"Ho, you look dead," he said, and then laughed, a high-pitched "Hee-hee-hee-hee," which seemed totally out of place considering his size. "Come, get in da cah," he said, pushing him on the shoulder.

Benny told him that there would be no work on Friday because that was his Waikiki day when he would deliver the products to the stores. He parked the car at Mr. Marumoto's and got out carrying his gear, walked toward the path and then stopped. "We pau today," he said. "When you go, can squirt off wit' Hiroshi's hose." Then he stared at the trees. "Gotta be twelve-tirty—I owe you twelve twenty-five."

Dennis stared at him, thinking. Six, then seven and seven, and then today— Benny must've had some kind of an adding machine in his brain. "Yeah, that sounds right."

"You come eat, den go home. Col' food but. No mo' fiah 's why. I gotta stay tonight, pack up an' all li'dat."

"'Kay."

"Bumbye I teach you how make all kine stuffs, toys an' whistles and all li'dat. Den we make canoes bumbye. You know da shed inna yahd Maunawili? Get tools an' stuffs. You can practice."

"'Kay."

He rode to the Santiago house in Lanikai, the gear in his hand on the grip. When he was within a mile of it, pedaling along North Kalaheo Avenue past the dunes and the big houses, he began to shake and his heart started thumping in his chest. His legs felt weak, but not from the fatigue. He did not know what to say to her, or how to even stand in her presence. It seemed ridiculous to him that he should be so afraid of her.

Her parents were home, and he heard music coming from Angela's room, Toots Paka he thought the name was. "Dennis," Mrs. Santiago said, "since we're eating more of your ulua, you stay."

"Okay."

She had a dish with inch-thick steaks on it, the pink meat reflecting the kitchen light in a blue-green iridescence. "Angela's in her room."

He went down the hall and stopped, stared at the door, and then knocked. He could hear her singing with the record. When she opened the door she stopped, then backed up. "Denny," she said.

"Hi," he said, and then looked around at the posters, the walls, the floor, anywhere but at her, and he hated his embarrassment, hated the shakiness in his legs and the slamming heart that he could feel in his neck, and the sweaty hands and the inability to figure out what to say.

"Can come in."

"Oh, yeah." He stepped in and closed the door. The record stopped, and they stood listening to the hiss-click, hiss-click of it turning. She went and picked the little arm off the record, producing a loud, grating squeak.

"We got pencil urchins today," he said, and then shrugged, scratched his head.

"I did dat wit' Benny," she said. "Can ho'd his breat' two minutes. My cousin Darnay, he can blow one shell a whole minute."

"Really?"

"Yeah."

She stood there, and the look on her face seemed a combination of terror and nausea, he imagined like his expression. She looked away, then swept her hands down her sweater as if there had been crumbs on it, and then seemed almost to be in pain trying to think of what to say next.

"Mommy get one chime in da kitchen."

"Really?"

"Yeah."

"Da win' only need blow tiny bit an den 'tinkle tinkle' li'dat. So pretty." Then she frowned and shook her head.

"Yeah."

"Chee, I gotta go camp not' shore dis weeken'."

"Really?"

"Church camp. I got watch kids, cook."

He thought he should do something, maybe walk to the window and look outside, and tried that, and as he did, she circled away, watching him. He looked, saw the Santiagos' car, the road with sand blown in little dunes over it, in the distance a brown chicken.

"How's your side?"

"It's okay," he said.

"'Me see."

He pulled his shirt up, and she stepped closer to look.

"Scabs got all green from the water today, but they're okay I think."
She came closer, stooping down. "Wait, you get sand on um." He
felt her touch, very light, next to the scabs. "Dat no good," she said.

"It's really okay," he said. "I mean I don't think sand can hurt
anything because it's just sort of, sand, you know? It's kind of clean
because it's—" He ran out of breath, and then rattled on, "I guess it
would just sit there and then get kind of what? encrusted by the scab
and maybe kind of pop off later? I mean it would be worse it if was like
dirt or something because that would mean germs, but sand is sort of
clean because it's just, just sand after all and—"

His arms were around her and her head mashed his cheek, and
the sweet, curly hair was draped over his nose, and her flesh was so
hot that it startled him, and she was against him all the way to his
knees. He could feel her heart racing and her breath hot on his neck,
and he felt a powerful, breathless shudder, like electricity, suffuse his
body, and put his hands under the sweater and slid them up her
back, and that she was wearing nothing under it sent another shock
through him, making him slide his hands around, his thumbs first,
so that they slid across stubble in her armpits and felt the hard,
rounded sides of her breasts pressed against his chest. Looking down,
she let her upper body move away from his, and almost experimentally,
waited for him to touch her, and when he did he felt the hot, soft
liquidity of them, could feel the blipping of her heart through them.
What was happening below she must now have felt, and he thought of
backing away and started to, but she put her hands on his buttocks
and pulled him against her so hard that it hurt.

"I wish we were someplace else," she whispered. "I not scared of
dat. I like you put your hands everywhere. All day, all night, 'ass what
goes on in my head."

"I—"

"Shh. No say anything. I already know."

He let his hands slide down her sides, feeling dizzy, and then
heard the high pitched "Hu-ee!" from the kitchen.

Something in both of their expressions must have showed, because
Angela's mother looked first at her, then at him, and got a perplexed
expression followed by a strange smile. And as they ate, he chewed
the ulua, then caught himself staring at his hand, remembering with
fright and amazement the feeling of the heavy, soft liquidity of her
flesh, and what she said to him, and the vision of it caused the erection
to throb so that he became uncomfortable sitting there. Angela did
not hide it well either. She moved too much in her chair, stopped and

stared at him open-mouthed, as if finally having calmed down from some strange surprise. Then she went back to eating, studying her food as if she were involved in some cryptic science experiment.

He tried to get his mind off it. "How much do I owe you for the doctor?" he asked Angela's father.

"Eh, you awready pay. Whassat on your plate?"

"Lu— Ulua."

"'Ass right. Plus da palani. Pay me 'mos' twice 'ass why. I dryin' da tail fo' you."

"Thanks."

"Put um onna tree or cahpawt pos'."

Then they continued eating, and he looked at his hand and then at Angela, accidentally at her breasts, then back at his hand. Then the discomfort attacked him again. When they were nearly finished, he found himself looking at her bowed head as she ate, the almost black, curly hair sweeping down over her shoulders, and her hands, one holding the fork and the other a piece of bread, and the sudden, frightening reality of human physiology dawned on him like a shocked awakening. He was made up the way he was, and she was made up the way she was, with all those parts that the boys in Paterson talked about and that he had dreamed about with a kind of aggressive lust because they were all there for the boys to get like trophies, body parts to grab and get into like enemies captured on a battlefield, on rooftops or in the backseats of abandoned cars, but this reality had nothing to do with getting anybody. It went beyond that into the realm of a terrifying, reverential magnetism, and if anything, he was frightened by her, because he was sure that when they were alone, it would happen, like two locomotives on the same track heading toward each other, he at fifty miles an hour and she at a hundred. He choked on a piece of fish.

"You okay?" George Santiago asked.

"Yeah, yeah," he wheezed. He swept his hand across his forehead and then on his pantleg.

"Bone?"

"No no, it's okay."

"Angela," Mrs. Santiago said, "you ride out to the north shore with the Nahoopiis Friday, okay?"

"'Kay."

Then Mrs. Santiago looked at Dennis and said, "Church camp."

Her expression had taken on that perplexed smile again. Did her mother know something? Was the weekend camping a kind of defense against something? He suddenly suspected that Angela had said something to her about him, or about her— What would it be? About her liking him, maybe. And then the whole question of church invaded his mind. What Angela wanted to do was unacceptable. That old image of the angry, vengeful God presented itself, and he felt somehow guilty of thinking of her in the wrong way, or maybe they were both guilty, and the funny smile on Mrs. Santiago's face showed that she knew they were both guilty.

When it came time for him to leave so that Angela could do her homework, he found himself confused about the idea that anyone could know. She went outside with him, and looked around while he got ready to jump on the bike.

"I don't wanna go church camp," she said.

"I know. I—"

She looked at the house, then up the hill behind it, then around at the houselights in the neighborhood. "I don't wanna go skoo, I don't wanna do any of dat." She stepped to him and put both hands on the handlebar, then moved her face close to his. Then she ran her nose up his cheek, and giggled. "Hey, get stubble."

He looked at the house windows for heads looking out.

"Yeah, but your parents—"

"I no care."

≈   ≈   ≈

Over the weekend he skipped fishing and tried carving wood in the shed. Out of a four-by-four piece of redwood, which was soft and easy to chisel, he made an image he found in a moldy book that sat on a shelf, a kind of squared-off gargoyle-like monster which, in the picture, was identified as a god figure. It had a flared mouth like an eight on its side, and teeth, and a stout body with muscles hacked in the simplified surface, and bowed legs. He tried refining the muscles, rounding them more in the style of Greek statuary. He worked with sweaty energy, his concentration on the carving so intense that the muscles in his arms and back became sore. At one point, looking up through the dusty window, he saw Momi come out of the house looking in the direction of the shed, maybe wondering who had left the door open. He walked out into the sunlight, the hair on his arms clotted with redwood shavings, and said, "Benny said it was okay. He said I could practice carving here."

"Oh, that's okay," she said. "Nobody uses that stuff anyway."

She cleared her throat. "So how are things with Benny?"

"Fine. Everything's really okay."

"Is he still playing his language game?"

"Yeah, a little bit, but I'm doin' okay, you know, 'apopo'—tomorrow, 'lawe mai'—bring, like that."

"I was just curious about your saving up to go. If everything is working out."

He didn't know what to tell her, that he wouldn't go, didn't want to, that he thought of everything outside of this island as dead. He shrugged and said, "Well, I don't know if—" Then he concentrated on picking redwood shavings off his arms.

"I just wondered more or less because my sister-in-law wonders," she said, and then he felt the blood run into his face, and knew that his expression could not hide it. "I was wondering because with your experiences in Paterson—"

"It wasn't—"

"With your experience in Paterson—"

"There wasn't any experience in Paterson."

She laughed. "Oh, come on," she said. "After all, you're what? A sort of student of George Angstrom? You don't need to—"

"I hardly knew him."

"Understand something—once this was a big family and now it's not. It came down to my brothers and me, and then Angela and Darnay." She snorted, and then gestured with a wave of her hand at the house. "Of course my parents had all sorts of hopes for us, and I suppose we disappointed them. But do you see how important Angela is to us?"

"Yes."

"Well, she has come up with some strange ideas about you, and that concerns us. We only wondered what you planned to do before you leave."

He looked away. The sunlight on Olomana made it look greener than was natural. He felt a defensive willfulness come over him, and shrugged. "I don't think it's strange," he said.

"Excuse me?"

"I don't think it's strange. I don't want to leave, I mean I'll go from here if you want, but I'm not goin' to Paterson or any place like that. I'm not. I want to stay here and I don't think it's strange. Where An— I mean with An—" He felt his face flush again, and dropped his shoulders and laughed hopelessly. He folded his arms on his chest. "I'll go if you want."

"I wasn't saying that," she said.

"But nobody's making me go back. I'm not gonna do that. I don't care what anybody says, I'm not goin' back. I work with Benny. We make things. That's it."

She nodded. "Trinkets," she said. "My, but that's a noble enterprise."

His scalp prickled. "No, it's more than that. He said we'll make canoes."

"That would be a surprise," she said. "Listen, that's all dead and gone. I don't know what he told you, but you have to understand that he's a hopeless dreamer, and this 'job' will come to nothing."

He stood there with his arms folded, trying to think of something to say. Finally he said, "We make things. That's all I know."

≈   ≈   ≈

Jumping over the little stream, he felt a twinge of excitement and then doubt about the redwood image, which he carried in a grocery bag. He could see Benny at the table and could just hear the faint tapping of a mallet on a chisel. Another little canoe. He stopped halfway, and looked around at the trees and at the clusters of ginger plants along the stream that vanished up between mossy boulders. Did Benny know about Angela? If he did, what would he think? He felt the redwood statue through the paper, and a sensation of an odd self-contempt washed over him. In more ways than one he had imposed himself, and all of them including Benny were tolerating him and doing their best to conceal their dislike.

Benny would think the statue was amateurish, and along with what Momi may have told him, decide that after all this job arrangement was not a good idea. He went up the steps and through the screen door. "Eh," Benny said. "Pehea 'oe?"

"'Oia mau no." Something like "okay."

"Keoki, Momi Anela? Pehea lakou?"

"Uh, maika'i no lakou?" Yeah, that's it. "They're fine."

Benny nodded. When Dennis drew the redwood image out of the bag to show him, he squinted, and then struggled up out of his chair. He reached out, and Dennis placed it in his hand. He stared at it for thirty seconds, slowly turning it over in his hands, a look of wonder on his face. Maybe he did like it. "Maika'i," he whispered.

Benny looked off to the side, as if listening for something, and looked once more at the image. Then he took two steps to the fire drum and threw the image in. Within fifteen seconds the rich smell of burning redwood spread throughout the shed.

"Okay, I guess I see what you mean."

Benny shook his head and looked into the drum. He watched, waited, then took the galvanized water bucket and carefully poured water in, creating a furious hissing and then billows of steam, which sent the birds sitting on the branches just outside flapping off into the ravine. Black water ran out of the bottom of the drum, and through the cracks in the floor. He looked in, poured more water, until the fire was out.

He pointed toward the door and went out, and Dennis followed, adjusting his walk to step on the board. This time the voice said "Wha-a—?" more or less halfway between why? and what?.

Benny waited for him on the English-speaking side of the stream. When he jumped across, Benny said, "You gi' me dat akua an' I felt one icy chill. I tink da spirits all huhu now."

"Spirits?"

"I gotta show you sometin'. Dis impahtent. Long walk but." He looked into the ravine, the floor of which rose into the darkness of a gorge with nearly vertical, greenish-black walls. "I been tinkin', an' I wen' figgah sometin' out."

"Okay."

"You Catlick? Protestant, what?"

He looked into the ravine, then shook his head. "I'm nothin', I guess."

"I knew dat. Come," Benny said, and walked up through the brush on what appeared to be an old path. Dennis followed, looking at the huge legs and buttocks, the broad back. They walked for about ten minutes, rising up at a gentle, and then steeper incline, and the walls of the mountain jutting out on either side of them made it darker. All around them was a still hush except for birds. As beautiful as it was, the landscape was an exaggeration of that dripping, prehistoric aura of the area around the shop, and he became more and more uneasy. Finally Benny stopped, panting and bathed in sweat, and sat down on a flat, black rock. From where they were the ocean was visible through the treetops, and the immense wall of mountain loomed almost straight over their heads.

"Momi to' me about you, all about how you were found, an' dat you don't have any real name."

"That's right, I don't."

"Momi to' me you like Angela."

He looked down, embarrassed, and Benny laughed—hee-hee-hee— "Chee, I mention her name an' you turn purple."

"Well—"

"J' like boys who do too much li'dis," and he pumped his fist up and down in an imitation of masturbation. "Dey get big earlobes, you know dat?"

"Well," and he looked around, scratched his head, then surreptitiously pinched one of his earlobes.

"Got you!" Benny said, pointing. Then he went into his hee-hee-hee laugh again. "Only one joke, but work every time, ah? Look, dis serious. I tink an' tink, and den unnastan'. I know why you get no name."

"Why?"

"Because it's heah."

"I don't understand."

"Come, we go on. I get my breat' back." He stood up. "I watch you work like all pupule wit' hacking an' den wit' sandin'. You no need work dat hahd. I tink you melt, too much li'dat. Come."

And they walked on, up the trail, which veered a little to the right, approaching a cliff of some sort, and again a flash of fear raced through him. Benny would throw him off. Benny would punish him for liking Angela, for making the image. But he shook the fear off, because the trail then veered back toward the ravine, deeper into the mountain-shrouded darkness. Again Benny stopped, and because there was no rock to sit on, he sat on the ground with a slow, wheezing groan.

"You okay?"

"I'm awright," he said. "Jus' res' a little. Mos' deah."

"What's there?"

"Eh, I show you," he said. "Listen, from heah on we no say notting, 'kay?"

"'Kay."

"Den back at dis spot, we talk story."

After another few minutes of walking they were in near darkness, although behind them the ocean was a rich blue, the trees below them bright in the sunlight. Benny went thirty feet up a little path that left the narrowing ravine floor, and crooked his finger for Dennis to follow. Beyond some dense brush there was a strange malformation in the rocks, so that at the bottom of a nearly-vertical wall that rose straight into the clouds, a two-foot high opening just above ground level appeared, like a slightly-open mouth, but eight or ten feet long. Benny pointed to it, then cupped his fingers around his eyes. Look. Then he grabbed Dennis's shoulder and shook his head, no. He meant don't crawl in.

Turning away from Benny, he crouched down and approached the opening. Then he got on his knees and looked inside, smelled a rich soily odor, and it took a few seconds for his eyes to adjust to the blackness. Staring back at him were pale gray skulls, some embedded in black silt up to their eyesockets. To the right and behind, the cave had a higher ceiling, as high as a room, and there he saw rotted wooden pillars lying half sunk in the silt, and their shape was unmistakable—they were images like the one he had carved over the weekend. There were other objects, rotted cloth, boards, long bones jutting out of the silt, and right near his face, a huge white molar.

When Dennis backed away from the cave Benny returned to the narrow ravine floor, and they walked back toward where they had last spoken, but before they got there Benny walked off the path into another patch of dense brush, and then up a steep incline toward the cliff. But the cliff was another twenty yards away. When they broke over the incline they came to an open space, and the remnants of a large square made out of black rocks, with a parched, level floor tufted with weeds and grass, and littered with shattered pieces of stone. It was man-made, about forty by fifty feet. All around the edges the rocks formed a kind of foundation, now just visible because of the brush and grass. It had been carefully arranged, so that the surface of one rock matched the surface of the one against it.

Benny motioned him away, pointed back down the path. He went down, assuming that he was supposed to go where they last spoke, and waited.

Finally Benny came down the path, panting and wheezing, and sat down. "'Kay," he said. "Da burial cave—dat da ol' ol' ol' Kupuna. Da statues was hid inside way way way back early paht of las' century after one queen, Ka'ahumanu, who was Kamehameha's wife, wen' break ol' kapu system. Dat taboo in haole talk. So den, da secon' Kamehameha awdah da destruction of alla o' gods, an' da akua statues were hid. Da heiau, dat da sacred place. Dat where da spirits stay. Dey proteck da ol' gods. I wen' tell um you didn't know about da akua an' all I ask dem not be mad atchu."

"Okay."

"Now you gotta go make nice wit' dem an' so fot'. You gotta introduce yourself to dem and make nice wit' dem."

"How do I do that?"

"Tell um your name. It Kenika Le'upena. I look dat middle one up."

"Le'upena."

"Den say whatevah you figga good fo' say to dem. You'll know."

"Okay."

"Kenika. Dis mos' impahtent ting of all," he whispered. "I know what's happening. You da person from nowhere. You get no name, 'ass why. An' I know what's gonna happen too. Angela. Every time I mention her name." He studied Dennis. "See? Every time. Go, make nice wit' dem."

Walking back up the path, he found himself at first feeling foolish going along with Benny and his bizarre superstitions, and then he felt nervous and afraid. Benny saw right through him. They all did. And making that image—he had offended what Benny called the spirits, and he wondered about the vengeful image of God that he had conceived way back there when his mother took twenty-dollar bills from men. This was something else entirely.

He approached the square, and stopped. All of them might have disliked him on sight, probably did, Benny, Mr. Santiago, Momi, even Angela. But with these people it seemed that all you had to do was give them an excuse to like you, and they did, despite your imposition on them. Especially Benny.

He drew a deep breath and let it out, and then stepped into the square. He took three steps toward the center, crunching on the parched stones, and suddenly felt a horrible panic that the ground would drop out and he would be falling. He made his way to the center and stopped, and looked up the sheer face of the mountain, then at the ocean. He took another breath because it seemed that he didn't have enough air.

He whispered, "Hi." The sound of his own voice embarrassed him, and he gestured at the air in front of him. "I'm Kenika Lo—" He had forgotten his middle name. "I forgot," he whispered. Then he cleared his throat and tried to go on: "I am a visitor here." He looked up the mountain again, and felt so awkward that his knees began to shake. "I'm from another place but I learned to never offend my— Host, I guess you'd call it, so you don't have to worry about me." It occurred to him that if these were the spirits, then like the living, they might like him if he gave them the right excuse to like him. But they had no reason to like him, he knew, because he was only a visitor. "There's Angela," he whispered. "I have a problem with—"

There was movement, no, something else. He looked down at the rocks. At his feet, then a few feet away, dark splotches appeared. A little rain. Then it stopped, and he looked up at the mountain face vanishing into the clouds, and then felt a strange, airy lightness in his flesh. "You have a beautiful place," he whispered, and stepped back to the entrance. "Bye."

He ran back over the rise and down to the path, feeling more winded than he thought he should. Walking down to where Benny waited, he decided that whatever the reality was, he would go along with it simply because there was nothing else to do.

Benny was sitting on a patch of grass in the sunlight, looking like some scaly, tattered Buddha. "You feel anyting up deah?"

"No, but I— Like you say, I made nice with them."

"I like tell you all about dis," he said, waving his hand around at the trees.

And so Benny talked, and Dennis sat there mesmerized by the lilt of his way of speaking. He was always a problem for his family, one shkroo-up, because he drank and got into fights in Waikiki when he was young, because even though he married a nice girl and had a son he couldn't make anything work—he was da whatyoucall, black goat of da family. Sheep, you mean. Yeah, sheep, whatevahs. So his wife divorced him and then died and he went on fighting and getting into trouble, and he found out about his son being one mahu and he was all shame and drank and fought more. Da was what? When Darnay was fo'teen, jus' when da wah staht.

So then there was the war and the island was crawling wit' da haoles, all walking around like dey owned the place an' den it wasn't the place he knew any more, because of the martial law and all da Japanese were suddenly enemies, even Mr. Marumoto, who wouldn't hurt a flea. And he had to stand on line downtown six hours fo' get one slip of peppa fo' get one lousy fricken case beah, until they figured out how to get it other ways, and Benny drank and fought more, and was arrested in Waikiki and spent a few nights in jail. And he went to his trial and the—whassat word? Da atmospheah of it was like he was a foreigner who committed a crime in their country. And they sentenced him, to what? To give blood. How can you make a man do dat? He heard one soldier call him a "gook" and even though he had no idea of what a gook was, he knew it was bad just by the sound of it.

"But dey took my blood," he said in a low, angered whisper. "Dey made me give dem my blood. I saw it inna tube." And all the time this was happening he had stayed away from the family, shame, 'ass why, and found out later that the military, the same people who called him a gook and then took his blood, just decided to fence off parts of the windward side for their own use, fo' practice, fo' who da fahk knows? Fo' t'rowin' goddam grenades at trees? Fo' shootin' birds, fo' what? An' da family, they couldn't do anything about it and didn't want to, and when Benny found out about it he didn't really care either, because he wanted nothing more than to go to the beach in Waikiki and chase wahine an' talk story wit' his braddahs and drink. And so he did that, but was all the time thinking, dey took my blood, dey took my blood. It was like what dey call one revelation. He got up one morning in a dingy little cottage and saw beer bottles and shit all o' da place, an' his buddies sleeping it off, an' da sun like slanting in da window. An' da dust like all swirling inna sunlight. And he remembered the land on the windward side, how he and his father had built canoes in the shed, long time back, and remembered his mother, who sat day in and day out muttering under her breath, talkin' story to nobody, because she was trying to hold on to something nobody wanted to hold on to, and he understood maybe for the first time everything she had told him when he was little, about what this place was before the haoles came, about how there were wooden images more than a hundred years old in a cave near that property, that she was staying alive to make sure no one would ever forget that they were there, that there was a whole way of life that she was trying to keep in her mind even though her mind was fading, even though whatever was left of what she was trying to remember was scattered and all out of focus like trying to see underwater without goggles. He remembered what she had told him when he was ten or twelve, that once upon a time this was a place with kings, later a queen, and this place was stolen from the royal family by men who put money above everything else, and at the end of the century there was one last chance and one last princess that she herself knew, but she died, and everything died with her. Kaiulani. He had forgotten most of what she had told him, but remembered one funny thing that would make her face light up when she told it: America decided to take Hawaii because if they didn't, somebody else would, and her favorite was some stupid pilau secretary of state who said that Hawaii was a ripe pear ready to pluck. Stupid, cause no pear evah grew in Hawaii.

So he came back to the windward side. He went up to the land and saw that it was fenced off. He hadn't been there in years, and remembered helping his father build some of the bigger canoes there, because the logs had all been hauled up there years before that, but he also remembered that when he was twenty-two or four or whatevahs he was so bored dat he felt like punching his own faddah out. But this time it was different. When he saw the fence he asked Mr. Marumoto if he could borrow his wirecutters, and he cut the fence and went inside. Then something else happened—it was the spirits. He walked down through the rotten leaves to the little stream and jumped across, and exactly when he did that he heard voices, felt some different kind of wind passing over him, knew that he was not alone and there was a reason for his being here. He did not understand the voices because they were all like whispering all around him and he stood there all scared wit' chicken skin, so his hair sort of stood up on his head like he was electrocuted or something and he thought he should say something to the voices so he said the only thing he could think of. He whispered it, dey took my blood. Dey took my blood. And he stood there thinking that the whispering voices would instruct him, and that was when it all fell together. He looked at the big old shed that he had hated, and felt like shit because the roof was full of holes. He knew why his father did his work here. Because the voices were here. Then the voice inside his head more or less said it, but he thought that it was the whispering ones that had whispered in his ear without his even knowing it. He ended up knowing what to do at the same time he didn't have any idea of what to do—you know how dat is? when you know and you don't know alla same time? He himself knew nothing, didn't know his own language, had no idea what he was supposed to do, stood there staring at the shed scratching his head tryin' fo' figgah, now what? So he stood there a long time, the whispering having gone away so that there was nothing but a sweet wind, the smell of rotting mangoes and vegetation, and the voices of all the birds, who he thought had now carried the whispers in a kind of translation.

"What you do is figga out somethin' to do right here. Make canoes, den. Whatevahs. Because da fahkeen haoles took his blood. Not you Kenika, you haole but. Leas' paht, anyway. You different, an' now you get one new name."

"I didn't know about any of this. I mean I read papers and stuff, but this—"

"You one kid, how you know?" Benny said. Then he leaned forward and grabbed Dennis's forearm. "It's Angela," he said. "Oh, I love her, she so pretty, an' da only one I can tink of inna family dat—" He let go and leaned back. "Oh, I don't know, maybe dis all booshit," and he looked over his shoulder and said, "Eh, sorry, I not talkin' about you guys." He turned back and said, "You look at Angela an' what do you see?"

"I—"

Benny did his hee-hee-hee laugh again. "I know what you see. But I see dakine sweet, old-time girl, like from two hundred years ago, 'ass what I see." And he went on, "Is dat impahtent? I dunno, cause I know a'mos' nottin'." He knew only that the whispering or the birds were telling him that all this was right, that Kenika was right even though he was from nowhere and was nobody, didn't even have any real name until now, Kenika Le'upena, and maybe that wasn't even a real name, but so what? It was still right.

"I know," he said. "Out Laie? I bet you woulda died raddah den tell me you was cold. I coulda stayed until sunset an' you wouldna said notting, you woulda ended up floateen face down, dead but still lookin' fo' urchins." He looked around, thinking. "Dat stuff wit' da ulua, dat strange. It mean someting. Da speah go tchrew da fish an' den you, ah? Dat strange."

In the distance they could hear a roaring sound, the sound of treetops being thrashed, and in a few seconds a wind roared up the mountain, blowing leaves around them.

"See?" Benny said. "Dat a sign." He looked around, waited. "See? It all quiet now." He stared at Dennis long enough for him to become self-conscious, then said, "I look at you an' what do I see? I don't know, I tell myself. What dis? Is he paht popolo? Dakine Mexican? What?"

"I don't know. What's popolo?"

"Dat Negro."

He thought at first that Benny's speculation might be an insult, but saw that it was not.

"So 'ass why I know why you heah," he said. "You an' Angela, you make babies. Dat make me happy cause da family, all bus' up now. She da on'y one lef' can make babies. I tink dat make da spirits happy too. I mean 'ass how it feels."

"I don't think your brother or Momi would like it."

"Da hell wit' dem," Benny said. "You know when I wen' jump across da shtream an' felt all kine funny? One odda thing I tot was how we wen' church when I was little, an' standin' deah I rememba also Kane an' Lono an' Ku an' Pele an' alladem, an' dat odda guy nailed up onna cross all li'dat? I tink', who's he? No mo' notting fo' do wit' me. Halfway around da worl', who's he? Heah he no count, I mean right heah on dis mountain. Momi dem, dey no care about alladis. Fac' when da ahmy took dis little patch it was fo' whatdeycall 'Pacific Combat Training Centah,' Momi dem all proud. Not me."

Benny rolled to one side and heaved himself up, then brushed the twigs and dirt from the seat of his pants. "We gonna build one canoe now. Wa'a."

"Really?"

"You stay heah dis week, sleep heah, so I can teach you how fo' do dis. We work fifteen hours a day, an' take time off fo' make winchime. Da big log inna shed? Dat one outrigga canoe. Koa. Den nex' week we do same, work onna wa'a until it done. Take months, seven eight nine, maybe a yeah."

"You mean I stay tonight?"

"No, go home, tell dem about dis, bring extra clothes and stuffs, toot powdah, whatevahs."

Dennis realized that it meant he would not see Angela, and looked down the path in the direction of the shed.

"I know, I know," Benny said. "Eh, she wait."

He rode home along a shoreline that was periodically lashed by showers that he could see coming, white columns racing across the water and drenching him briefly, then racing up the foothills to the mountains. The thought of building a boat made him pump the pedals as if he were racing—he had seen them in Waikiki, narrow, sleek things at least thirty feet long, the koa wood gleaming with a dark richness. But he hated the idea of not seeing Angela. Sure, she would spend the weeks watching the Nahoopii kids, probably, but he still didn't like it.

He was almost dry by the time he reached Kailua, and he found her watching the kids on the Nahoopiis' front lawn. Two of them were running around in green gas masks, the straps holding plumeria and hibiscus flowers, the cans dangling underneath, and the other two kids were hiding from them.

"Denny, you look wet."

"Almost dry," he said, shaking his head. "Look, Benny wants me to stay out there during the next couple weeks to start building a canoe."

"Really?"

"Yeah, so— I mean I won't be around."

She looked at the kids, then back. "You be back Friday night week afta nex'?"

"I think so."

"We can go movies den. Or Sad'day."

So he went out on Tuesday with a bag of extra clothes and his Dr. Lyons toot powdah. Benny was standing by the log in the shed when he went up the stairs and said, "Pehea 'oe."

"Yeah, I'm awright," Benny said. "We gotta cheat an' talk haole dis week." He looked at the log and then scratched his head. "I donno if I can do dis," he said. "I ustedto help my dad but I hated it, and now I fo'get, an' stay all confused. Dis awdah came from a racing group called 'Hui o Pa'ani,' one rich haole who wants to staht one club. Pa'ani mean spoht."

"Sport?"

Benny went through his hee-hee-hee and said, "'Ass it, spour-t! 'Ass it. Now, da wa'a. How we do dis?"

He had old charts laid out on the table along with various chisels and axes and saws lined up. Sitting on the workbench was a two foot model of an outrigger canoe. "Dis I made when I was one kid," he said, "an' I use it fo' teach you what we do. Reason you stay heah is dat I want you to see canoes all day, tink canoes all day, dream canoes all night. No pretty wahines' chichis an' okoles to look at, no whatchucall— dakine distractions."

"'Kay."

"Alla words dat go wit' ho'owa'a are Hawaiian. Ho'o means to make, or like make happen. Ho'o—make. Wa'a—canoe. Dis shed is one halau wa'a—canoe house. Heah one you like do: Ho'oipoipo."

"What's that?"

Benny did his hee-hee and said, "Make love." Then the smile vanished. "I wanna do dis right. It's like a reputation, dakine. I worried about dat."

"'Kay."

"You gotta put it all in your memory."

"'Kay."

Then he went into a background description that struck Dennis as a trip backward into some fantastic antiquity. That ugly black log sitting over there was alive, and inside was a canoe like a baby inside its mother. It was for them to bring it out, and it must be approached with reverence. A canoe is not a rowboat, it is a sacred work of aht. The log came from the Big Island forty years ago, rough hewn into the suggestion of a canoe, from a kaekae or canoe tree. Tchree kines koa, he said, koa la'au maia—dat yellow an' light, koa 'awapuhi or ginger koa—dat middle density and red brown an' what we call female koa, and den koa'i'o 'ohi'a—dat dark an high density. We use ginger koa fo' canoe. Olden times when dey wen' get a kaekae it was one huge ting, ovahseen by da kahuna kalai wa'a, da mastah buildah. Firs' dey would eat an' stuff an' da kahuna would dream. If he get good dream, den he say, 'kayden, we go. Den dey followed da 'elepaio bird way into da fores' to fine da tree, an' da bird would sit one one, den anodda. 'Elepaio is da goddess Lea, one pretty little bird wit' a tail dat sticks up, an' it scol' you when you get near um.

'Kay, when da bird lit on one special tree da kahuna would say like, "Ho, dat da tree I wen' dream of,' an' den dey would give offering, pig an' banana an' all li'dat at da base of da tree once dey fine um. Den da kahuna kalai wa'a would sleep one mo' time, an' if his dreams was good den dey would cut da tree down, but hahd work. Dey make one cut one side den stuff um wit' hapu'u stalk, to keep from cracking 'ass why. Hapu'u? You see Momi's orchids hanging onna lanai? Dat black fibah dey grow on, dat hapu'u, from da tree fern. Den dey lay hapu'u onna ground wheah da tree goeen fall. So dey cut da tree down, an' wait fo' da 'elepaio bird come check um out again. Da bird come, an' if he run all along da trunk wit'out stopping, den perfeck log. If he stop in one place, den lot rotten wheah he stop. If he fly in circles above it or onna side, den you gotta roll um ovah an' bring undahside up and hollow it out along deah.

'Kay den. Log perfeck, right? Right. So den da kahuna put on one loinclot' an' get up on um wit' da axe and do one chant dat say mo' less, "I hit wit' da axe an' hollow da canoe!" Den he walks all along da log an' say, "Hit wit' da axe an' hollow um out. Give us one canoe!" Den with' a couple mo' prayers da kapu lifted an' dey put one 'ie'ie wreat' on um. Dat one vine. I show you dat, like I show you da Lea bird. 'Kayden, on da odda end all dis, when we finished, we gotta get one kahuna fo' da lolo ka wa'a, dat one nodda prayah. But jump way ahead. We gotta make um firs'.

"Did they do this stuff with this log?"

"Some of it. My fadda wen' get da log, alla ones down below too, long time ago. But funny, Kenika, I tell you alladis an' I feel funny cause I not tink of um for long long time, like fo'get mos' of it too. So I gotta go talk story wit' odda buildahs. My faddah, he knew one buildah an' his name was li'dis, see if I remembah—Kawaikaumaiikama-kaokaopua Kalokuokamaile."

"Jesus."

"One mout'ful, yah? Ho, my brain not dead yet."

"So what happens next?"

Benny sighed. "Kenika, dis gonna be hahd. You know in odda countries, France an' alladat? When dey build one cateedral? Dis what we doin'. What we gotta do is as difficult, an' what? Cannot get da word. Precise, 'ass it. As precise as building one cateedral. Odda makers, dey wanna make one shit canoe, dat dere business. We make cateedrals." He picked up the model and stared at it, thinking. "Problem is dat we good wa'a makers. My Granfadda Santiago was one sailah on one whaleboat, way back middle las' century. Dey rowdy guys come get drunk and get laid alla time, trash stuffs up, but dis Emilio Santiago, one big, tough guy he was, have one revelation or whatevah. He fall in love wit' my gramadda, stay insteada go wit' dem aftah whales. He was one cowboy in America before becoming one dakine, but anyway, he stay, an' my gramadda's fadda wen' teach him how fo' make wa'a. Funny how dis guy come from way fah away an' 'ass how we Santiagos, 'ass how it is we make canoe. An' now we gotta do um. Lotta stuffs I fo'get, so I gotta go talk to some odda makers. You gotta put alladis in your head an no fo'get."

"Mai poina."

"You get brain like one gas tank. I tell you little bit little bit each day, we cut little bit each day. Five, six, eight mont's, I donno, we finish, give da wa'a brains, an' 'ass it."

"Brains?"

"Da las' ceremony called lolo 'ana ka wa'a i ka halau, means putting brains inna canoe."

"I know that word lolo."

"No, when you say low-low, it crazy, but when you say it little faster like lolo, it brain."

"'Kay."

"You might tink dis nuts, but I tell you, nobody stupid enough to go in one canoe dat no mo' blessed. Bad stuffs happen, it crack, da guy die, whatevahs, but nobody go in a wa'a dat not blessed. People can change religion, eh, no sweat. But da ocean have all kines mystery. It can be frien'ly an' den, ho, it can be angry. It huge an' deep. You try sell one canoe to a man an' say, eh, I get dakine Jesus fo' bless dis instead, 'kay? an' you know what he do? He pat his pocket an' say, chee, I broke, cannot buy um. Da religion of da canoe fixed insai an' cannot evah change. 'Ass why it stay same alladis time, cause da religion paht cannot be separate from da canoe. It inna wood, 'ass why. Nobody nuts enough to change um."

Benny picked up a short-handled adze, and stepped to one end of the log. "Come," he said. "I show you." He turned the adze and began chipping lightly into the black wood. Underneath, it was a bright reddish-brown, grain so rich and deep that it appeared to have been cut down within the past week. "'Ass pretty, yah?"

"Sure is."

"Kenika, listen. You gonna learn alladis, all. No mo' fifty cents. No mo' dat shit. Time we finish, you pahtnah, fifty-fifty. No mattah how much kala, fifty-fifty."

"'Kay."

"But you gotta learn all of it. Time we done, you know more den me. You get fresh brain, mine all foggy an' fulla all kine shit. I tink it hahd fo' learn what you awreddy fo'got, but you, you learn firs' time 'ass why. Tryin' fo' do dis, my brain get all kapakahi but your brain all fresh, can file stuffs away easy."

"'Kay, I won't forget."

"Put a han' on um, onna axe cut."

He did so. The wood was cool, as hard as stone.

"Dis canoe name Lapa Uila, and dat mean lightning flash. 'Ass da name we give um."

"Lapa Uila."

"You gotta feel da life in it," Benny said. "Den inside da head, make nice wit' it."

"'Kay."

"Feel um buzz like?" he whispered. "Is alive 'ass why."

"What do you guys want to name her?"

"I like name it aftah one turtle," Pua says, and you laugh.

"Dumb."

"Not," she says.

Kenika has cut the piece of wood and you can almost see the canoe inside, two feet long. He puts down a block plane made of wood with the little steel tongue that runs diagonal through it and peeks out the bottom. Outside the shed the wind increases, seems to groan. Kenika stands up and walks to the rusty drum in which a slow fire burns. He places sickle-shaped chunks of brown coconut husk down in the drum, and sparks shoot out, sweep quickly in different directions before disappearing.

"'Kay," he says. "Turtle is 'honu' so now Ben makes a word to go with it."

"Big an' shtrong," you say. "Like one supahero."

Kenika thinks. His skin is darker than a turtle's. He says "'E'epa."

"What dat?" Pua asks.

"It means extraordinary, or like something with great powers."

"I like dat," she says.

"So it will be called the Honu 'E'epa."

"Ho, dat nice," you say.

You pass your hand along the side of the rough-cut canoe. Hull is "ka'ele." Even though it is rough cut it gleams when you look at an angle from the side.

"Grandaddy, I nevah get to make one wisso," Pua says.

"'Kay, we make a whistle instead of a canoe," he says, and laughs.

"No!" Pua shouts. "I like make one canoe."

"Did my daddy make one?" you ask.

"No."

"He one druggie."

Kenika looks at you, then nods slowly. "Well—" But he doesn't continue. He goes to the drum and pulls out the black lunchbox, makes it dance steaming in air between his hands as he carries it to the bench. "Hot hot hot," he says, and drops it on the table. When he opens it steam billows in one puff above the lunchbox. Inside is a dish of fried rice and a dish of chicken with Chinese noodles. "And a can of sardines," he says. "Little kids like you need fish."

"Uh-huh," Pua says. Her eyes are big. She will go for the chicken first and you won't get any. Her eyes are too big. Kenika twists the little key and rolls the tin up like a cigarette. The scars on his knee shine pink. There are the dull-silver sides of sardines. He stopped that time in Nanakuli because the water was black but there were no clouds. He said I know what that is, get your stuff, I want to show you guys something. Halalu. You and Pua followed him into the water, into a school of a million halalu, each one bright silver, all of them in bright sweeping lines like lightning sweeping away as you swam through them, and it almost hurt your eyes watching them and then you felt as if you were in a silver dream, laughing into the snorkel while they swept away from you like oozing walls of fish, the silver walls bending and then sweeping into points, and then you were in the middle of the school and you turned around, and by the millions they circled, like being inside a silver drum and watching it spin. At the store they lie wrapped in plastic in a styrofoam tray, big black eyes staring, only little fish. But in Nanakuli they were a silver dream.

Out beyond the screen the wind sweeps through the woods, drowning out the song of a thrush. Way up that valley are the ghosts,

the wild pigs, way up that valley the pigs get red eyes and chase you,
the ghosts know where you are because they can smell your breath a
mile away.

Kenika dumps the sardines, juice and all, on the rice, and holds
out little white plastic forks. Later, on the way home, we will stop at the
store in Heeia and stand before fat jars of crack seed, the jars with
masking tape around the lips so the big lids won't chip them. Pua will
stand and look and look and look—wet li hing mui, no, pickle mango,
no, sweet whole seed, yah, I take dat, cuttlefish, yuck. And when she
sees the red coconut balls she will gasp, as if she has seen them for the
first time in her life. Every time. It takes her all day to pick out what she
wants, and all day to eat it.

The extraordinary powerful turtle. That is one cool name for a canoe.

≈   ≈   ≈

Friday afternoon after nearly two weeks in the shed he got a
ride home with Benny, who stuck the bike in the back seat angled
from the floor corner up to the opposite window so that the muddy
tire slid up and down against the glass when they went over bumps,
and over the steel runway plates at Kualoa. Rain lashed the
windshield, swept across the road and into the mountains, and the
ocean was frothy and gray. He kept nodding off, the fatigue so great
that he felt washed of all energy, his hands sore, his arms twitching
with little spasms in the muscles. His mind was so hopelessly muddled
with canoe terminology that he wondered if it would ever be possible
for him to commit it all to memory. But he would sleep in a regular
bed rather than the cot, and his flesh swooned at the thought of it.
He had no idea about whether or not he was supposed to go to a
movie with Angela, or if he would even be able to stay awake through
one. He wanted only to sleep. The problem with sleeping at the shed
was the woods. All night there were sounds, rustlings, and he found
himself awake way before dawn staring into the damp blackness for
shapes, listening to Benny's snoring from the little room he slept in.
His own cot was placed at the back corner, behind the fire drum, and
was so creaky, the canvas and wood so old, that he slept imagining
he might fall through it any time.

Benny asked him something. When he turned, Benny said, "You
can come out Sunday? Gotta get more dakine fo' win'chimes 'ass why.
We make some, den go back to wa'a."

"Sure."

"Dey wan' um Wednesday 'ass why. I pick you up an' take you
back."

"'Kay."

Benny dropped him off at the Maunawili house. He sat there and looked at it for a few moments before Dennis got out of the car. "Ah, hell wit' it," he muttered. "Go Waikiki."

The house was empty. Momi and Tutu Elizabeth were gone off somewhere, and in his room he looked around, shuddering, because it seemed damp and moldy with the rain beating down outside. He got a towel from the dresser and then went through his usual ritual of squirting himself off in the back yard, gritting his teeth because of the bone-chilling coldness. He ran back into the house, pulled the wet bathing suit off, dried, put on a pair of underpants and got into bed, too tired to worry about centipedes or food, and waited for the warmth to seep back into his flesh.

He dozed off in the multiplied imagery of his work, of the sawing and planing, the curled ribbons of koa on the floor, the woman's voice that came from the far end of the shed whenever he stepped around the roughhewn suggestion of a canoe to pick up a tool or break off another chunk of wood—"Wha-at?" so softly that he could not convince himself that it was only wood squeaking, and then he thought the voice was saying "wa'a," because it had a soft V sound at the beginning and then a sort of haunting ahh. In drier weather the word was why, now it was wha-ah.

Later on, in an ashy semidarkness, he was dimly aware of the rain pounding on the roof, and in his half sleep he felt something like breath on his face and recalled that morning at the cottage, even thought he felt the edge of the bed dip, and in that ticklish yawning of half-consiousness, there was a whisper over the roar of the rain, from close, "Benny call you Kenika, den I call you Kenika too." He felt the radiated warmth against his shoulder and face. He opened his eyes and looked at her, at what appeared to be an expression of pain.

"What?"

"I hated it, you gone all week li'dat."

"Oh, I didn't know you were—" His heart was thumping, jolted awake like that, and he stretched his legs out, tensed his arms and aching back, and went into a long, shuddering yawn. "Where you guys been?"

"Dey out," she whispered. "Church, won't be back till ten." Something was wrong. She radiated a strange agitation, and he worked on waking up, blinking at her in the dim light. "Kenika," she whispered.

"Yeah, that's what Benny—"

There was a ghostly shape of quick movement and the mattress moving, and he squinted up at her, and her hair settled against his neck and shoulder. She held his hand by the wrist and then placed it on her side, and he could feel through the hot flesh the rapid heartbeat and the same shaky agitation, and then all along his chest and stomach, and then his thighs, he felt skin on skin, hot and dense, and somewhere down there felt the slight scratchiness of hair. "Kenika, take um off."

He did, only half understanding, and didn't think to become embarrassed by the painful, thumping erection which rested against her somewhere. She wormed her way closer, pushing up at his arms, and he did what her hands told him to do, rose up to make room for her, and then she had her hands on his back and pulled him down. When his stomach melted onto hers the heat raced into his flesh so that he gasped with disbelief at the sensation, and then her thighs slid up around his hips and she whispered, "Do um." He didn't know how, but someone else or something else did, and he felt the sensation of opening, of soft, hot flesh spreading, and then something stopping him. Her hands went over his back and down to his buttocks, and with a strength that surprised him she pulled up, and in one rush he felt a hot, almost scalding liquid immersion that made him gasp again, as she did, and then her arms were locked around him with such strength that he couldn't breathe. A rich smell rose around them, of something like woods after a rain, or the ocean, something raw, dark and fresh. They were both bathed in sweat, sliding against each other, and then it seemed that they were writhing like sea creatures, like eels, until he felt the powerful-ticklish explosion, like a slow electricity radiating throughout his flesh, that in a few seconds left him empty of strength.

She was whispering against his neck but the roaring of the rain made her voice sound like a dream in another language, and when he felt the first hints of embarrassment creep over him he thought he should rise up on his elbows and pull himself out and away, but when he tried to do that she gripped him with her arms and legs. "No," she whispered, and then relaxed a little, writhing slowly under him.

He opened his eyes and tried to focus, and saw, close up, her forehead glistening with sweat, and looking down, saw her shoulders, gray in the bleak twilight, and then her side under his side. He slid his hand down her side, making her shudder as if avoiding being tickled, and she giggled. "Dat was so nice," she whispered. "I all weak."

And he thought, nice? He couldn't think of any word for it. Then he felt her tense a little, as if waking up, or as if something were occurring to her. "I gotta go bat'room," she said, and slid out from under him, and when she left, her heels thumping on the floor, the sheet slid off him and followed. Suddenly he was cold, and realized also that he was naked, wet, and that the bed was wet, and he sat up quickly and said, "Oh God, what did—" He saw the white shape of his underpants on the floor and quickly pulled them on, then got back on the bed and sat with his arms around his knees.

He stared at the hall and at the slice of light that came from the partly-open bathroom door. He whispered, "We did it," and then laughed softly, and then was paralyzed with fright. They were not supposed to do that, but they did, and he stared again at the slice of light, at the quick flash of a shadow that dulled it every few seconds. He felt a sudden, sweeping surge of pride, and with that an awed, almost breathless understanding of, and he thought, what? Anatomy. So this was why they were made up the way they were made up. The beautiful logic of it was beyond any words. He could not believe the luscious softness of her, the heat, the feeling of such total contact, as if it were some strange kind of melting together.

Enough time had passed that he felt himself begin to swell again, and he didn't know what to do about that. He was glad it was dark, and wished he had something to cover himself with.

She came back out of the bathroom wearing the sheet like a gown, up over her breasts and the other end dragging on the floor, and he held his breath, trying to think of what he should say. Then she was in the doorway, and turned on the light. It blinded him so that he squinted, trying to see her. She was grinning, holding the sheet against her chest, and he sat there hiding behind his knees, unable to think of anything to say. "Oh, you cold," she said, and came and sat down on the bed. "Close your eyes." He did, then blinked them open and closed them again. His heart began that ticklish pounding, and in his mind he held on to the fading vision of her breasts, moving a little as she unwound the sheet so that he could put half over his shoulders. "You looked," she said.

"Sorry."

"I no care."

"I'm a little scared about—"

"I no care about dat too. Catlick girls at skoo? Dey talk about dis method. I figga, hey, you no have to be Catlick to use um, right?"

"But—"

"You still got your eyes closed."

"I know. Look, I think we should get married."

"Me too. Denny, I mean Kenika, open your eyes."

He did. She had the sheet over her shoulders and sat next to him. She still had the grin on her face. She looked around, then said, "Chee, da spot—I gotta wash dat." Then she whispered, "Dere was blood an' stuff. Stopped but."

"I wash my sheets," he said. "I mean, I put them in the washer, ringer and all. 'Sokay."

She turned to him again, stared straight into his eyes. "You mean it, about getting married?"

"Yeah."

She looked at him, then seemed to carefully study his face, her mouth open with a kind of speculative awe. "We can do dis all we want. Hey, you know what time it is? Look my watch. It only seven."

"Really? God, I woulda thought it was eight at least."

"I'm gonna turn da light off again." She moved to get up. "Close your eyes."

He did so, and the bed rose. "Open your eyes," she said, and he opened them. She was standing right in front of him without the sheet, and he gaped at her, the breasts and stomach, slightly lighter where her bathing suit had covered it, then the triangular patch of pubic hair. He could see the beating of her heart in her ribs. "I like see you, too," she whispered.

≈   ≈   ≈

They went to the Kailua Theater Saturday night. It felt to him like some confused dream, because people acted normally, spoke as they had spoken the day before, as if nothing had happened. But of course for everyone else nothing had happened. It was a double feature, "Tarzan and the Leopard Woman" and "Da Bandit of Sherwood Fores'." Her girlfriends were there, and boys from the town, some of them blonde and tall, some of them stocky local boys, Japanese and Hawaiian. He looked around for Junior but did not see him. He had the impression that the people were all looking at him and Angela, and even heard one of her friends, a jovial girl who was astonishingly fat, say, "Oh, he cute," and Angela giggling and whispering to her. Did she tell them? On the way in, another girl pointed at the poster for the Tarzan movie, at the picture of a little boy with curly hair, and said, "Cute yah, dat Johnny Sheffield?" While the movies went on he sat with his arm around Angela's shoulders, trying to act nonchalant and normal, which she seemed to find easy. He watched as Johnny Weissmuller swung on vines, watched Jane run through the forest in her little leather suit, and cute Johnny Sheffield with his curly hair.

But he couldn't concentrate on the pictures. Waves of fright washed over him at the thought of what they had done, about the possibility that nature might have taken its course and she would be pregnant, or as they said, knocked up.

After the second time, when she got back into the bed, he asked if they should worry about that, and she whispered, "Too late now." Besides, she wanted him to touch her, wanted to touch him—chee, dat smoo' like polished wood—and mortified by the feel of her warm hand on him, he tensed and she came out with a little shriek of surprise. "How you do dat? Make it jump li'dat?" And then he touched her, and fell into the stupefied awe because of the hot, resilient softness of her flesh, because of how she moved when he did, when she pushed his hand down between her legs and writhed against him with a breathless urgency, and then they were like eels again, more forceful this time, so that he was afraid that the power of her arms or his arms would cause them to crush the life out of each other, would shatter ribs, crush pelvic bones.

The girls in the theater whispered about how cute Johnny Sheffield was, and the boys made suggestive catcalls about Jane. But sweat beaded his forehead, and the panic washed over him again. They had done it, and were cooked now. They were in trouble.

How Angela could be so convinced that the Catlicks were right seemed crazy to him, and how she could assume that Momi and Elizabeth would be out until ten seemed even riskier. But on they went while the rain pounded outside, and the thought, six times? How could they have done it that many times? How could the human body in a state of such debilitating fatigue keep coming back like that? And how many times could they do that and have it just as much of an explosion of electrical release as before? And when it did seem close to ten, she said, "I don't wanna stop. You like one hot octopus."

"We have to."

"What about tomorrow, or Sunday?"

"Oh, I forgot, Sunday Benny wants me to pick urchins."

"Really? I did dat too. 'S he comin' heah?"

"Yeah. You wanna come too?"

"Yeah, I get fins, mask, dakine."

They were ready when Momi and Tutu Elizabeth came home, playing cards, and his hands shook ridiculously as he tried to hold them steady. Angela looked up at Momi and said, "I beating da octopus. He one junk player," and giggled.

They were waiting on her parents' lawn when Benny drove up in his Pontiac. Angela ran to him and kissed him on the cheek, and then backed away and stood next to Dennis. With his strange light-brown eyes Benny looked at her, then at him, and nodded knowingly.

Did it show? Was it like enlarged earlobes? On the way out toward Laie Benny mentioned that since Angela was here he would sit on da beach an' read da peppa. No worry about da shahks, you no see um dat much. The sky had been gray above Kailua, but it was a brilliant blue above Laie Bay, and they left Benny on the beach and went into the water.

He swam, carrying the mesh bag, looking to his side at her with her hair trailing behind her and waving over her back, the sunlight giving it a strange copper glow. She was huge and bright, the brown skin so dense in color that he was held in a sustained wonder, and the water sweeping down her chest and over her back animated her flesh so that it shook in a dreamlike slow motion, clearly visible through the insignificant fabric of her two-piece bathing suit. She stopped, blew the snorkel out, and put her mask up on her forehead, and her face was wet and eager, teeth bright in the sun, and she pushed his mask up and pulled him to her so that they were against each other all the way to the knees, and she kissed him on the mouth and laughed. "I wish 're was a little island out heah," she said.

For a couple of seconds before they were pushed by a wave, they were face to face, and he looked straight into the dark brown eyes without even a hint of embarrassment, realizing that it was the first time in his life that he had been able to do that, and the face staring back was focused on him without any reservation. He might as well have been looking into a mirror. It occurred to him that he thought he knew who he was, or if he didn't at least the question of who he was had become trivial.

At the shoal they dove and picked the little red urchin bats, and he surfaced for air and watched her scissoring her legs and pulling herself down on the sections of reef where the urchins were. Hovering on the surface, he watched as her legs worked in the rhythmic push to keep her down as she picked the bats, and he focused on her buttocks and the thin section of bathing suit between them going front to back, the water moving the fabric. He vaguely remembered all those words the boys in Paterson used to identify what was there, and understood the triviality of those words. He found himself receding into a kind of dream, that here they were, and there was no time. It had either stopped or at least no longer went backwards. It was stopped where they were with him looking down at the dark, woman's body, the refracted sunlight dancing over her skin, and time no longer had any meaning. She had wished for an island, and in a way they had found it.

≈   ≈   ≈

During their work, whether on the canoe or filling orders for trinkets, he became aware that Benny drank too much. He would be drinking beer in the morning, and by afternoon he would be making mistakes with tools. With the canoe you could not make mistakes, and Benny seemed to understand that—he wanted the apprentice to measure out and shape the pepeiao or "ear cleats" where the seats would be located, and watched as Dennis worked on them. Dennis kept silent about the drinking, tried to cover for the errors, always wondering what it was that made Benny so apparently pulled into himself and sad.

Despite that they went on with it, and the hull took shape. They went up the mountain in search of big 'ohi'a trees to find strong U-shaped roots for the wae, or spreaders, which fit under the ear cleats and gave strength to the hull.

Dennis spent the days preceding the Christmas luau fishing, pulling in aholehole, parrotfish and something new, he'e, or octopus. He saw it sitting at the base of a rock, looking up at him with strangely-expressive eyes, and he speared it. The octopus undulated up the spear, its skin shifting in color and its slippery, suckered arms winding around it, and he swam in with it on the spear because he didn't know how to get it off or what to do with it when he did. George Santiago considered he'e a prize. The fish built up in the ice-box, and he fished almost compulsively because he didn't know what else to give the family for Christmas. Angela said, no worry, jus' fish. He didn't have much money anyway. And Angela—he had no idea what to get her either, and was aggravated by a vague embarrassment because he was not sure how he was supposed to fit into the scheme of things, and because he feared what Benny's drinking implied.

What if he decided to quit? The thought of any other type of job was detestable, and he worried that somehow circumstances would conspire to end what they were doing.

There were around thirty people at the luau at first. George and a cousin, Richard Stevens, who was as Hawaiian as you could get despite his name, dug a pit and roasted a small pig wrapped in chicken wire in it for a day and a half before Christmas. There was Irene's sister Aunty Clarice Malama, Momi and Elizabeth, families of more distant relatives from the other side of the island, even as far as Waianae all the way up the leeward coast. Junior and his family showed up, but he remained away from Dennis, sometimes looking in his direction but then looking away. Angela told Dennis that the family was "goeen move Big Island." Benny was there, already a little drunk, and kept to the side of things for no obvious reason, even though Angela went over to him to talk, Junior too. Dennis was impressed by the gathering— the people did seem all of one family, huge men who shook his hand with their large, soft hands, huge women in muumuus who sat around in the shade fanning themselves and talking story while the aroma of pork escaped from the ground, and they all talked with the familiarity of a family even though, as he understood, they hadn't seen one another in a year.

"Dey love da fish," George said to him. "Come, I show you sometin'."

Standing at the deep sink behind the house, he showed Dennis how to properly clean a fish. "You see da ass-ho deah?" he said. "You go in wit' da point an' run um down wit' da fish's nose in drain hole, 'kay? Dat steady um, an' alla guts come right out. You shot alladem right in da gill, an' 'ass da way fo' do um."

"I see." He picked up an aweoweo.

"Put da knife right tchroo da gill and cut da troat paht," he said.

"I see."

"Den you pull um out. Look, Angela's mom tol' me all about you guys."

"Oh, I—" He stopped, frightened, and looked at the large black eye of the aweoweo. He didn't know what to say. The sound of chatter came around the side of the house, the smell of fresh fish guts wafted up out of the deep sink. "I—"

"Angela say you wanna get married."

"Uh, yeah."

"Early fo' dat, yah? But bumbye maybe. Angela's mom tink about um." He stopped. "Da scales," he said. "We get dis tool heah," and he held it up, a circle of steel teeth with a handle. "Aweoweo no need cause it get skin mo' den scale, but we scrape fish wit' dis. Later, we do anodda he'e. I show you how we lomi da slime off an' hammah um onna concrete to soften um up. Get six or eight? We put um in dakine. Washin' machine."

"Really?"

"Angela's mom only worry because haoles—dey go away."

"I'm not—" He was going to say "a haole" but instead said, "Not going anywhere. I'm staying here. Nothing back there means anything to me any more."

"'Ass good. Her mom worries about getting hapai."

"Oh." He lifted the fish, turned it over, and picked up the scraping tool, then stopped. "Uh, what's hapai?"

George patted his stomach. Then he heard someone calling him from the front yard, and left. Dennis put the fish back into the deep sink and turned, and found himself face to face with Junior Kaaiai. He quickly went over his options: call out, run, or stand his ground. He decided to stand his ground.

"Eh," Junior said.

Dennis nodded.

"So you work fo' Benny now," Junior said. "Make canoes?"

"Yeah."

Junior looked down into the deep sink at the fish, then scowled distractedly at it. He looked again at Dennis. "One big canoe?"

"Yeah, forty feet about. Called the Lapa Uila."

"I like do dat some time. But we going Big Island."

"You could do it there, I guess."

"Yeah," Junior said, looking again at the fish. "You want one beah?"

"Sure."

Junior went around the corner of the house, and Dennis stood there staring at the space he had occupied. Then he raised his hands and smelled the strong fishy odor coming off them. Junior came back and handed him the brown bottle. He took a sip.

Junior looked at the fish in the sink, then leaned back and looked around the corner of the house. "You like eat?" he said.

"Sure."

"Come, I hungry too."

"'Kay."

They walked around the corner, and Dennis saw Angela looking at them, and she appeared both curious and wary. She joined them as they went toward the table where the food was set out. "Get some food," Junior said to her, and she watched him as he went and picked up a paper plate, then turned and looked at Dennis, who shrugged and said, "You hungry yet?"

When the luau was in full swing and up to around forty guests, he seemed to spend most of his time shaking hands and explaining who he was and what he did, each time apologizing for the fishy smell on his hands. No one gave him any reason to feel like an alien, yet he did whenever Angela was off talking with someone else.

At one point there was the sound of breaking glass in the yard, and those nearby went silent. Benny had thrown a beer bottle against one of the big rocks at the base of the hill. George looked at Momi, who looked at the sky and shook her head, Angela looked at her mother, and nobody seemed able to figure out what to do. Dennis nodded to George—wait—and went over to Benny and sat down next to him in the grass.

Benny stared blearily at him for a moment, then smiled dully. "Kenika," he said.

"What's the matter?"

"Darnay, dat goddam boy, he no mo' come da luau."

"Oh."

"I see 'im I bus' his face. Goddam boy."

"No, you wouldn't. Look, I don't know Darnay, but he's your boy. He's just not thinking about the family right now."

"Goddam boy."

He put his hand on Benny's huge shoulder. "You don't really mean that. Remember when you told me about you and your father? How you didn't want to go up to the shed? It's just one of those things. Look, let's get some food. You'll feel better. I caught fish, aweoweo, 'uhu, all that."

"How many?"

"Ice-box full," he said. "C'mon, let's go."

He was a little surprised, but Benny slowly got up. "That's the way," Dennis said, pulling him by the wrist. "Hey, you'll feel better."

He helped Benny pile up a plate, poi, kalua pig, sweet potato, potato and macaroni salad. Then he led Benny back to a spot under a tree, aware that nobody nearby was talking. They all appeared to be watching them. When he sat Benny down with his plate, Benny looked up and said, "Eh, lawe mai—"

"Pia."

When he went to get the beer they were still staring. Momi said, "How did you do that?"

"Look, I work with him all the time. But I think I'd better eat with him if that's all right."

"Any of us and he'd throw another bottle."

Angela stepped over to him and put her arms around him from the side. "Kenika, you so nice," she said. "Can I eat witchu too?"

"Sure," he said. He saw Junior looking on, holding his plate. "You wanna sit with us?" he said.

They got plates of food and sat under the tree with Benny, the same tree they had sat under that day she held the poi out to him on her fingers, and a century ago it seemed. And Benny ate quietly, drank his beer, and looked blearily at them. "I love you keeds," he said. "An' you Juniah, you buggah, you goeen away." Junior nodded. Benny ate more, drank another sip of beer. "Angela," he said, elbowing Dennis on the side, "dis buggah one wa'a man now. Should see da guy work, ho."

≈　　≈　　≈

Benny had estimated that it would take around five months to build the cateedral, which it did not. It took closer to eight months, but he said, no worry, racing season is summah, 'ass why. When Dennis worked in the shed through the rainy season fashioning the component parts for the canoe under Benny's instruction, he could not get the image of Angela out of his mind, and when on weekends he was at her house or at the beach when the sun was out, he would find himself thinking of the Lapa Uila, unable to get out of his mind the images of the parts, and the exacting work of making them. During the weekdays Angela did as she had always done, watched the Nahoopii kids and did homework, but on weekends, there would be awakened in both of them the hot magnet of their attraction, now a logistics problem they addressed in sudden, whispered speculations: on the beach one day, Angela sat up and turned to him, and looked directly into his eyes and said, "'Kay, cannot go my room, your room, cannot go woods." Then she nodded toward the two islands sitting off Lanikai. "We go out deah."

He was a little embarrassed talking about it this way, but got up on his elbows and looked. The Mokuluas. They could get their masks and fins and stuff and swim out. Once there, well— And he felt himself starting to swell a little, and turned over on his stomach. He could do nothing about it, except jump in the water. But she was right. Nobody would bother them out there. "Let's go now," he said.

"Gotta get da stuffs."

"They're right here," he said, pointing.

"No, mines," she said, and then there was a jerky urgency. Now that the idea had formed itself they were both standing up, she looking at the islands, then down the beach to where her house was. "I'll go get um."

"No, I'll do it," he said, and turned and ran. In his haste he hadn't looked ahead, and almost knocked an old haole woman down. Just in time he was able to sidestep her with a brief yell of surprise, and ended up sitting in the sand. She laughed at the slapstick idiocy of it, and he said, "Sorry, sorry, sorry," and sprinted on.

They started the long swim out in a sprint, churning over the coralheads and rilled sand. After a while she surfaced and pulled the snorkel away and said, "Eh, we be too tired, les' slow down," which they did, and when he had settled into an even pace, looking over at her, again magnified and dense in color, he began to see himself as a canoe knifing through the water, and settled into envisioning what he was working on at the moment, a kupe'ulu or single-piece manu. The wishbone shaped section ended in the high projection that rose to a point off the prow, the top gently curved in the back, and flattened vertically into an elliptical oval in front. This V that cut the wind would be mounted on the ni'ao, or rim of the hull, the flat oval in front helping to deflect water. The aft manu or la'au hope was the same but smaller. Benny had explained to him that the two-piece manu, two sections of the wishbone joined at the point, was easier to make, and Dennis had told him that he wanted to make the kupe'ulu instead, as if the harder the project was, the better it would turn out. When Benny told him that manu meant "bird," he undersood the logic of their naming of things—the manu rose in a beautiful sweep up from the hull as if pulling the canoe up and ahead with its wings, its head the forwardmost part, perched on a neck which seemed to strain powerfully in the act of pulling.

The ocean did strange things to his head, he knew, and the fact of his thinking of the canoe while he and Angela swam to the island made him look once again at her, at the richly-colored, magnified reality of her flesh. Benny had told him once, when they had worked on planing and measuring the hull thickness and Dennis had paused and gazed out through the screen at the ocean peeking through the leaves, that the canoe was a woman, and now you are thinking of the other woman, but 'ass okay long as you keep da two women in dere places. As they approached the bigger of the Mokuluas, the image of the canoe vanished.

They stood shivering on the little beach, looking back at Lanikai and to the right, Kailua. It took five minutes for the sun to do its work, and once the warmth had worked its way into the flesh, she looked at him and smiled.

"Well," he said. And he thought, what now? Where do we go? How can we do this in broad daylight? It struck him as odd, that they should be standing here for this purpose, and he would be locked into a peculiar shame, as he imagined she was, trying to figure out how to broach the subject.

"Get no towel," she said.

He looked around, then back at her, and then she made a sort of jerky, bashful movement in his direction and slid her arm around his waist. Her arm was hot from the sun, and that contact of flesh on flesh made the shame evaporate, and they were against each other. He pulled away and looked around, then whispered, "'S look over here," and they picked up their gear and walked up the beach toward the brushy base of the mountain. When they got to it, a gray bird waddled up out of a shallow hole in the sand under a bush, gurgled at them and raised its wings, and then went back into its depression in the sand. "Sea bird nest," she whispered.

"'Kay, 's go this way," he said.

They walked toward the west end of the little beach. The sand was hot, the island parched in the powerful sunlight that beat down on his back, drying him so that he felt the tightness of salt on his skin. Walking along, hearing the water slosh up on the rocks, and hearing it crash against the ocean side of the island, he felt a strange, hot dizziness, as if the brightness and heat were draining him of consciousness, and the only part of him that was wide awake was his desire. When he looked to his side at her, the expression on her face seemed to reflect his own state of mind, as if they were now beings from a thousand years ago discovering this place for the first time. The visual reality of her physical presence brought up in him a subtle, sustained amazement, and sometimes on the path in front of him, she was so close and seen with such lucidity that he thought something had happened to his eyes, that they had become refined enough to read a paragraph on the head of a pin. Ahead of him, every pore on her back, every tiny detail, the movement of her bathing suit on her buttocks, seemed to present themselves to him as microscopic, and when he looked at her face, with her looking back at him with a shameless eagerness, he thought he could see even the shimmering light on each hair of her eyebrows, or eyelashes, the precise geography of each bright tooth.

When they found a place, a shaded, sandy depression under the face of a huge rock, they both looked around, wondering who or what could see them, and verified that once they were down, no one would.

He remembered vaguely, as if from a far greater distance in time than a year or two ago, that the one thing forbidden and cut in stone was the sight of nakedness, and now, with that same visual lucidity he had experienced out in the blazing sun, he watched her as she sat on her knees in the sand before him and took off her bathing suit top. He sat leaning against a smooth rock, and reached out and lightly touched one breast, staring at the dark nipple with the few little hairs around it, and then let his eyes travel over her stomach, watched as she pulled the suit bottom off and the breasts shook with a heavy, liquid animation. "Eh, yours too," she whispered, and when he took them off he watched her looking down with wonder, then up at his face. "Dis way?" she said, and then came forward, walking on her knees, until their upper bodies met, and then she looked above his eyes, moving herself downward, feeling her way with her body, her breath warm on his forehead, until he felt that slick, liquefied encirclement and then the sensation of being engulfed by the soft, electrifying heat. Just as he slid his arms around her, he closed his eyes.

That depression in the sand became their place. He made a float out of an innertube and a piece of plywood so that they could bring along towels, drinking water, picnic stuff, and keep their things nearly dry. The explanation was that they were fishing and picnicking on the island, and he felt sure that her mother and father saw right through it, that he sported huge, dangling earlobes and Angela, walking around in the house before and then after, must have shown what she was up to, radiated some aura shamelessly demonstrating that she was full of sperm, and he had been as The Captain had told him, manufacturing it at a hysterical rate.

≈   ≈   ≈

The Flash of Lightning was given its brains on Mr. Marumoto's lawn the Sunday after Angela graduated from high school. A couple of Benny's friends came up to help carry the hull to the lawn. Benny had contacted a kahuna named Kelemeneke Makaila, a rail-thin man with skin the color of coffee beans, white hair and teeth missing, who walked around and around it before the ceremony. The hull gleamed the deep red-brown of varnished koa, and in the sun it seemed elevated somehow to what Benny had said canoes were, works of art. It was forty feet long, the sleek hull just nineteen inches wide, and weighed four hundred pounds, verified by a scale Benny brought to the shed and hung on a chain from a beam. They had the 'iako and ama loosely lashed in place. Kenika stood and watched as everyone else studied the canoe, Angela and her parents, Momi, who would look at the canoe, then at Benny or Kenika, then back at the canoe as if to confirm the truth that the canoe and the makers were really connected. Angela would look at Kenika and giggle, and he kept wondering why it was that she would look at him and giggle, for no apparent reason. There was the buyer, a haole man wearing yacht club clothes, his friends, three haole sailor-types who were younger, in their twenties maybe, Mr. Marumoto and his wife, and Benny, who explained certain refinements in its construction: the outrigger booms or 'iako is hau, da bes' wood fo 'iako, it has one little keel, a half inch maybe, running six feet under from da bow an' stern, good fo' wave riding, it get one one-piece manu, Kenika's work, da bes' manu evah.

When he had finished it Benny had placed it on the hull, and then had Kenika hold a flashlight on the other side, and he tried to detect light coming through where it joined, but could not. Kenika held his breath throughout the test, fearing the worst. He had shaved and sanded, placed it on the hull a thousand times, but was not sure. After that Benny tried blowing air through the joint, but could not. Then he tried the color test. He painted a mixture of berry juices on the hull and then pressed the manu on, then lifted it off and turned it over, and the berry juice had contacted all of the surface where the join would be—there were no spaces in there, no chance for a weakness in the joining. He patted Kenika on the shoulder and said, "Ho, da nice. Dis betta den I could evah do um. Ho, da beautiful."

The haole buyer seemed a little impatient with the ritual, and Kenika thought, watch yourself—only an idiot would get in a canoe with no brains. He did not like the buyer, who kept looking around at the woods, then at Mr. Marumoto's house where, outside, tables were set up with food, the expression on his face showing a sour disapproval, as if the mud, the smell of the neighbors' pigs and chickens, the damp, funky atmosphere were all just a little too coarse for his tastes. It was a tragedy that such a beautiful canoe should be wasted on a jerk like him.

The ceremony called the lolo 'ana ka wa'a i ka halau lasted ten minutes. Kahuna Kelemeneke Makaila had them stand in a circle around the canoe, and then got inside the circle and walked along the canoe, touching it and speaking rapidly in Hawaiian, words that the wind stole from Kenika's hearing. Then the kahuna drew out a bag of pink rocksalt, and turned away from the canoe. "I put um aroun' da canoe an' den close da circle. Olden times we would use one pig to get eensai and sniff um, but modern times. We do um dis way fo' sake of efficiency." He walked around the canoe sprinkling the salt in the grass, speaking rapidly in Hawaiian. When he had almost completed the circle he drew out a book of matches and held them up. "Now I close da circle," he said. He lit a match and dropped it where he had sprinkled the last of his handfuls of salt, a foot from where he had begun the circle. "Maika'i ka lolo ana," he said. Kenika thought that meant, "excellent it brains has," but was not sure.

"Dis good spell," the kahuna said. "You go fas' in dis canoe. Dis canoe displace less wattah, ride highah. Strong canoe dis, an' safe too. Come," and he gestured for them to approach. "Take little salt, sprinkle um onna ama, in hull."

"Will the salt harm the wood?" the buyer asked.

"What, you race dis inna bat'tub?" the kahuna asked. "Salt make um mo' durable. Salt a blessing." He shook some into the buyer's hand.

The buyer turned to one of his friends and smiled jovially. "I don't believe this," he whispered.

"Eh," Benny said. "No take chance, yah?"

"Whatever you say," the buyer said.

Kenika went to Angela and said, "C'mon over. Let's put some salt on it." They went and stood before the kahuna, who sprinkled salt into each of their hands. Kenika looked at his bony hands and the leathery skin on his arms, until he looked up at them. He looked from Kenika to Angela and back to Kenika, and smiled.

They threw their salt on the manu and into the hull, and then he helped Benny undo the lashing.

"Should we get the trailer?" one of the sailors asked. It was parked on the road behind a large pickup truck.

"We're supposed to eat," the buyer said.

"Come," Benny said. "Cannot bless one canoe an' not eat."

Another of the sailors was talking to Angela, and Kenika could see the look on his face, a kind of awed lechery, so he went over to her. "Hey," he said.

"You helped build it?" the sailor asked, but he had not taken his eyes off Angela. Kenika nodded. "Good work. Boss might come back sometime, dicker with Benny for another." Then he walked off toward the table, where he caught up with another of the guys, to whom he said something, both of them looking back at Angela.

"Kenika, 'ass one beautiful canoe," Angela said.

"That's what I want to do," he said.

"Cannot believe you did dat," she said. "Jus' cannot."

"It was Benny."

"Still."

"He taught me."

Throughout the little feast Kenika studied the buyer, and then looked at the canoe, then looked back at the buyer. The one thing that bothered him was that all this work, this cathedral, was for that man over there, sneering at the tako poke or the poi, looking at his watch and then at Benny, and growing more and more impatient at the idea of having to humor him and these old people any longer.

When they left, the Lapa Uila bouncing on the trailer and disappearing down the hill in a swirl of dust, he felt a sudden, almost shocked sadness that the canoe was gone, as if something had died.

Mrs. Marumoto was showing Angela something in the kitchen, and the others were in the garage talking. He wandered off toward the spot where the Lapa Uila had been blessed, and looked down at the small pink crystals of salt lying in the parched grass. Benny appeared at his side. "Eh, no feel bad," he said. "Dis business. We make more."

"I hate it," he said. "I don't understand it, but I really don't like this."

"I no like see um go too," Benny said. "Heah, take dis."

It was a two-inch thick wad of bills folded in half and held tight by a red rubber band. He squinted. They were twenty-dollar bills. "Wait a minute," he said.

"No, I said fifty-fifty. Dat man pay two tousen' fo' Lapa Uila. Dis half."

"Two thousand?"

"Canoe one complete log, 'ass why. C'mon, take it."

"But—"

Benny reached down and pulled Kenika's pants pocket open and stuffed the wad of bills inside. "Put um inna bank. Bumbye you buy one house, cah, li'dat. Whatevahs."

Benny patted him on the shoulder and went back to the food table. He followed, his hand on the outside of his pocket, holding the dense wad of bills against his thigh. For the next hour he kept his hand there most of the time, and stumbled around as if in a dream, staring at the square bulge in his pocket and then at the space where the Lapa Uila had been blessed. Finally Angela came out of the kitchen and caught up with him. "You okay?" she asked. "What, too much Primo?"

He told her about the money and she did not believe him until he showed it to her.

≈   ≈   ≈

The Malolo, or Flying Fish, was a log at the base of the shed, lying on top of others which were so buried in dead leaves, mud and rotted palm fronds that Kenika could not tell how many were under there. The Flying Fish would be purchased by the same buyer who drove off dragging the Lapa Uila, but Benny told him that they would go slowly on this one, that there would be plenty of time for Kenika to do some of the things he might want to do, four five mont's at leas'. They went back to making wind chimes, oeoe whistles, miniature outrigger canoes.

Without a canoe to work on Kenika became secretly impatient with what he thought of as a static situation. He took the thousand dollars to the bank in Kailua and placed it along with his little savings book before the pretty Japanese woman who had months ago entered ten dollars one week or twenty dollars the next, and said, "It's a thousand dollars," and she picked it up and began to count, the bills a little limp and greasy from his having counted them thirty or forty times. She didn't ask him where he got it. Finally she said, "How's Mr. Santiago?" and he said, fine, fine, and understood then that he didn't need to tell her where the money came from. People already knew.

On the days that Benny dropped him off early, he rode the bike around Kailua, his mind stewing over what he knew he had to do. But before doing it, before going to Angela's parents to ask them if they could get married, that old question he had seen asked a hundred times in the movies, he wanted everything else to be settled. He asked Benny about it one Friday as Benny negotiated the car around the potholes in Kaneohe. "Eh, I show you," he said. "I tink you ready fo' dis now."

He drove the Pontiac to the east side of Kailua where, above the cowpastures Kenika had seen from the other side of the valley that first day he hitched around the end of the island, roads were being put in and houses were being built. The little development was above the marshland that stretched from the base of the little cluster of mountains above Lanikai to the foothills of Olomana mountain at Maunawili. Many of the houses were already occupied, and Benny drove the car up one street to a point where they could look down over most of the development. "Guy know to' me dese houses cos' eight tousen'. Pay on time, fifty bucks a mont', get one house."

They looked down at the new rooftops. People had their cars parked in driveways, some of the lawns had already grown some grass. It all looked stark and parched because there were no trees, and the road that led to it ran along a mangrove-clotted swamp which, a quarter of a mile away, became a lake. "Would they let me buy a house you think?" he asked.

"Why not?" Benny said. "I help you too if—"

"I only have eleven hundred some—"

"No, you buy um on time."

He picked Sunday. He didn't know if Angela should be present or not, and it happened that she was up at the house in Maunawili with Momi on that day. He waited until they got into working on leis, and then told them he had to go do something, and left on the bike.

Because it was hot and bright outside he could not prevent the sweat from soaking his shirt. He found Angela's parents in their living room sitting a few feet away from a fan. He knocked on the screen door and stepped in. "Hi," he said.

"Eh, howzit," George Santiago said.

Kenika stood there, the sweat beading on his forehead, his hands clasped behind his back. When he tried to form the words but could not, both parents looked at him, then at each other. "Well," he said, "the reason I'm here is—" And the sweat ran down his face. He glanced out the window. A black car went by. "The reason is that—" He shook his head.

"Wait, wait," George Santiago said, and heaved himself out of the chair. He turned the fan and aimed it at Kenika. Angela's mother laughed, then quickly stopped herself.

The air that swept across his face and upper body made him suddenly shiver, and he swept his hand across his forehead. George sat down. "'Kay, now what was it?" he asked.

"George, stop it!" she said. "Denny, I mean Kenika, when do you two want to do this?"

"Soon? As soon as possible. Look, I was looking at those houses above the marsh, you know, the new ones. I wanna buy one of those so we'll— And I have eleven hundred dollars in the bank, more too when we do another canoe. Look, what I think I'm saying is that—" Then he was breathless and had to pause. He looked out the window. "I mean I'll take care of her," he said.

"Where do you think we should do this?" she asked. "I mean with all the guests and food and—"

"Maunawili," George said. "Eh, I call Howie Shigemura."

"Who's Howie—" Kenika said, but they didn't hear him.

"—needs time to get all this ready," she said. "I mean you have to have at least a three-week period of time so—"

"Dat too long. Two weeks. Eh, I twis' his ahm. He get da pig an—"

Now George and Irene had begun to sweat.

"Well what about invitations?" she asked. "You can't just—"

Kenika stood there before the fan, his hands clasped behind his back, but they now seemed oblivious to his presence.

Nobody needed him for anything. The way he understood it, he went off to the shed to innocently make wind chimes and tiny outrigger canoes with Benny while back in Kailua there was a sustained explosion of preparation, as if what he had instigated by asking that simple question had generated an event that could only be bettered by the marriage of the Queen of England. Benny would stop filing a canoe hull and lean back, and look at him with those strange, bovine eyes and go over the subject again and again: "We get da bes' music evah," or, "Cannot believe dis happening. Ho, da nice." Then he went back to his filing, and stopped again after a few minutes. "Kenika," he said, "dat da sweetes' girl. You be good to her, ah?"

"I will, I tol' you."

And then Benny went into a fit of that strange laughter, "Hee-hee-hee-hee!"

After three days of this, Benny said, "Come, I teach you how fo' drive. I take you to town, get one license, and we look fo' nice ring too, ah?"

"Drive? What for?"

"You be one married man! What, you go groshery staw and wanna buy stuffs an' you walk? You tink Angela like do dat too? No, you gotta have one cah. Chee, what a dummy!"

"I'm saving to buy one of those little houses, I tol' you."

"Nah nah nah. I like buy one new cah, one Chevrolet, get what dey call dakine vacuum shif', go vvvvrup, vooo, li'dat. You take mine. Come work on time, go home on time."

"I can't do that."

"'Kay den, I t'row um away. Buggah no like have my cah, den I t'row um off one cliff." He stopped, squinted at the ceiling. "Pali, I tink," he said. "Or Makapuu lighthouse road. Ho, what a dummy."

"Jesus, Benny, I can't take your car. I mean, maybe I could buy it."

"'Kay, cos' you one dollah."

"Benny, for chrissakes, I can't—"

"Ho, one assho, pass up one good deal. Eh, maybe I make one mistake aboutchoo. What, you fail mat in skoo?"

Kenika sighed in exasperation and looked out through the screen at the waving banana leaves. "Benny," he said, "what is this? What are you doing?"

Benny went back to filing the hull of the miniature canoe. He turned to say something, then went back to the filing. Now his expression had changed, and he looked sullen and distant.

"Benny?"

He put his file down. "So I like gi' you my fockeen cah," he said. "So what!"

"Okay."

"I mean," and he stopped and looked out through the screen. "Look, I like gi' you da cah, 'ass all. Call it a wedding gif' den, 'kay?"

"But—"

"Shaddap!" he said. "No gi' me 'but' dis and 'but' dat. You take da cah, 'kay? I teach you how fo' drive so you can go da goddam mahket, 'kay?"

"'Kay, but—"

Benny heaved himself out of his chair. "Ho! I kill you, you say 'but' one mo' time."

"'Kay."

"Ho, dri' me crazy dis guy," he said to the screen.

"Sorry, but— No no, I mean I'm sorry."

Benny went to the water vat and drew out two bottles of beer. "Come, we take one break, den learn how fo' drive."

"'Kay."

By the next day Benny was sending him on stupid errands so he could practice. "H'mm, I like you go Kaaawa buy crack seed. Get me wet li hing mui an' cuttlefish," or, "Dis poi all hahd, no good. Go back Waiahole, memba da place I to' you? Get one dish poi, tchree fingah. Soupy kine."

By the end of the week it was Kenika who drove back to Kailua. "But I don't have a license," he told Benny, who waved his hand before his face as if waving away flies.

"Nah nah nah, nobody care," he said. "Eh, watch da pothole."

"Where?" Benny bounced up and down. "Sorry."

"Ho, check da shocks."

≈   ≈   ≈

He thought it might have been that he had had two beers partway into the party, but he floated throughout the early part of the day in a strange, half-conscious daze, as if he were in some elaborate dream. In his pocket he had the ring, a gold band with fine carving of vines and flowers on it, and inset with black enamel spelling the word kuʻuipo, which meant "sweetheart," Benny told him. He got it at a jewelry shop in downtown Honolulu, and it cost twenty-five dollars. The cars parked in front of the Maunawili house went right out of sight in both directions, tipped down into the runoff ditches on either side of the road, and both the front and back porches had an absurd profusion of slippers, shoes and high heels piled up by those who went into the house. One Waianae cousin came in a suit with a vest and gold watch chain, and Kenika found him sitting in the grass taking off his shoes before going into the house, and told the man that he really didn't have to do that, but he said, nah nah, 'sokay. His hand was shaken by the meaty hands of dozens of uncles and cousins and friends, and he was mauled with mammoth hugs by huge women wearing startlingly bright muumuus, who planted kisses on his cheeks and put leis over his head until they rose all the way to his nose. Angela introduced him to most of the relatives, and more than once he heard one auntie or another say, "Oh, he cute!"

A three-man guitar and ukulele band showed up just after noon, and played Hawaiian songs as the people chattered. George and his friends drew the chickenwire-wrapped pig out of the pit in the backyard at two, but Kenika thought it surely had to be superfluous because there was so much food everywhere, heaps of little crabs, shrimp, various kinds of fish and octopus chunks, Japanese and Chinese and Filipino delicacies, little squares of coconut cake, beer, juice for the kids. But with the pig came the sweet potato, poi, lomi salmon, fried chicken, and more obscure vegetables and meats and desserts from the aunties and uncles and calabash cousins of different backgrounds and mixes of races. There were even haoles there. He met them all, shook every hand, allowed himself to be mauled by every woman.

In the middle of the party was the ceremony, for which Angela and Kenika went inside the house and changed, he in his room, trembling and whispering, "Oh boy, here we go," and she somewhere at the front of the house, with Momi's and Irene's help. He swept his eyes around every corner of the room and over the rocks, the habit of checking for centipedes, and then took off his leis and set them on the bed. He could hear the chattering in the house as he pulled on white pants and put on a white shirt with puffy sleeves, as if he were one of those swashbuckling pirates in the movies. Benny came into the room with a red sash and a maile lei, and told him to stand still as he wrapped the sash around his waist and tied it at his hip. "You got da ring?" he whispered. Kenika pulled it out of the pocket of the pants lying on the bed, and slipped it into the pocket of the white ones. Then Benny draped the maile lei over his shoulders so that it hung down in front, and stood back and looked at him. "'Kay, you aw set," he said, and left.

As he had noticed before, the usually reserved Momi and Irene switched to pidgin in the excitement: "Suck your tummy in! I to' you no eat so much!" "'Ass too tight!" "Ho, da pretty!" Kenika then went outside to wait with the other people facing the back door of the house.

When she came out, followed by the two Nahoopii girls in white dresses, she was wearing a white holoku which clung tightly to her midriff and had a little foot-long train dragging on the ground, and puffs at the shoulders. She wore an elaborate haku lei on her head.

He was instantly dumbstruck with awe at her beauty, the dark skin made even darker by the blindingly white dress.

A Protestant minister said the sentences leading up to Angela's saying, "I do," and his repeating it, and then he slid the ring on her finger. Then Kelemeneke Makaila stood before them, placed a withered hand on Angela's head first, and spoke a kind of chant, a series of Hawaiian phrases, then placed his hand on Kenika's bowed head and repeated them. Throughout all of this flashbulbs crackled, and when it was over the band picked up again with a wedding song.

The band went on playing Hawaiian music, some of the songs a little off-color he understood, at least if the reactions of some of the guests were an indication. "Ho, pilau dat song!" followed by giggling. During one, an immense auntie from Nanakuli whispered to Angela, who nodded as they listened to the words, and then Angela sat up straight, her hand to her mouth. "Auntie!" she said, and the woman leaned back and erupted with laughter.

Benny pulled Kenika off to the side and said, "Momi an' da parents gi' one gif', one week at da Moana Hotel. You drive to it but I tink you go aroun' Makapuu side. Do da Pali when you mo' experience, 'kay?"

"'Kay."

"Goddam Darnay, he no come but. Eh, 'ass okay I guess."

"Yeah, no point in being mad at him."

"Eh, you keeds have fun, ah?"

"Yeah, we will."

"No tink about wa'a fo' now. Bumbye we do um, but not now. You take two, tchree weeks off. You have fun," and he nudged Kenika with his elbow. "Plenny good fun, yah?"

"'Kay."

They went to the table for more food. Angela, still in the holoku, stood looking down at the four Nahoopii kids, and again he stopped and stared at her. "I can't," she said. "I married now, like I to' you."

"Den you come play wit' us tomorrow 'kay?"

"Cannot. Going Moana Hotel, 'ass why. Now I get too o' fo' play witchoo guys."

"Not."

She knelt down before them, and said something to the oldest, a girl. Then, "'Kay?"

"'Kay but." Then the little girl giggled. "I know what you be doin'," and then she sang, "Nani nani poo-poo."

"No talk dirty," Angela said. "I spank you."

"Cannot. You married now 'ass why. Nevah spank us anyways."

"Uh-oh. 'Ass true, I cannot spank you. Ho, maybe I get unmarried fo' ten mintues an' do it." The four kids ran away from her.

Then all four of them: "Nani nani poo-poo. Hana kokolele, you cannah catch me!"

She moved toward them and stopped, looked at Benny. "Eh, unca Benny, unmarry me fo' ten minutes so I can give dirty lickens to da keeds," and they all shrieked and ran around the corner of the house.

It went on like this into the late afternoon. Kenika wandered around, and stopped to talk to one guest after another, "Yeah, it's forty feet long, and we tried putting that little half-inch keel in the hull," or, "Eh, I heah about da ulua you speah, den yourself," "Yeah, that was strange, especially that twang when George clipped the spear." At one point, after telling the story of the ulua to a distant Santiago cousin, they ended up comparing scars. Knee, side, the cousin's hand, bitten by an eel. Angela came over, and then pulled the hem of her dress up. "Fell off my bike," she said, pointing to a scar. Then she held out her thumb. "Tack. Try put um in upsai-down 'ass why," at which the female onlookers laughed. "Talk fish story alla time, you!" she said to Kenika.

As he understood it, the last event was the opening of wedding gifts, and he calculated that it might take an hour and a half, and then they would be off. People began crowding into the house, and the footwear now made two dunes that flanked the path leading to the landing and door. He had not expected this, but the relatives had brought boxes, bags, envelopes, and they were all piled on and around the table he and Angela had played cards on that rainy night. Angela sat on the couch between Momi and her mother and began opening presents while Irene carefully recorded each object and gift-giver's name in a little notebook. He stood there leaning against the wall watching as she opened box after box—toaster, iron, salad bowl, and envelope after envelope— "Auntie Clarice dat too much! You so sweet!" and "Benny! I to' you no mo' gif's!" and "Ho, Liberty House fo' table setting!" and with each gift she jumped up from the couch, went to the giver, and threw her arms around his or her neck.

≈   ≈   ≈

When he had first come to Hawaii with The Captain he had regarded the Moana as the most beautiful building in Waikiki. It was white and resembled an elegant European hotel, with a wide flight of stairs going up to a hall with a gleaming wooden floor, and across from that was another flight of stairs down that went right out to a circular bar under a huge banyan tree, and then the beach. To the right and left of the shallow hall were the rooms.

He understood quickly that without the barrier of logistics they were free to do as they pleased whenever they wanted to. At first, when they looked around at their third-floor room, which had a little lanai facing the ocean, Angela had a strange, perplexed expression on her face. "Auntie Beatrice from Waianae?" she said. "She tell me, 'Eh, go head, put juice onna sheet.' Ho, da aunties talk dirty!" She looked out the window. "Look, sun awready wen' down an' dey still get canoes out."

He went out onto the little lanai and stood next to her. The freedom made him nervous, and he supposed by the expression on her face that it made her nervous too. Yes, there were canoes out there just inside the phosphorus-white dotted line of breakers, which expanded and then merged into a single white line, then broke again in a surreal changing of its shape. But then she slid her arm around his waist, and they backed their way into the room.

In less than an hour he understood the beautiful logic of allowing them to be alone while the rest of the world went on about its business outside. Even though the desire had an urgency about it, the urgency was offset by the knowledge that there was no rush. The hot, liquefied merging of flesh drew sweat from both of them. It was because of the exhaustion of the long day that they fell asleep, and in the morning, he woke up with a sudden, shocked confusion, because he didn't know where he was. Then he looked at her, lying on her side with her fists down between her knees and her breasts squeezed together between her arms, her hair draped over her shoulder, three or four hairs vanishing into the corner of her mouth. He watched her sleep, and then reached up and pulled the hairs from the corner of her mouth. She opened her eyes and saw him, and apparently unconcerned about the brightness in the room, the sun slanting across the lanai, she pulled him on top of her.

They were dressed and ready to go get something to eat by eleven, and she brushed her hair, then looked around at the bed. She walked to it and pulled the sheet back, and put her hand to her mouth. "Kenika, I like get away now, before da maids come." Then she said, "Take showah an' I still aw gooey. Ho, go bat'room one mo' time."

During the days they walked the beach, from the little one off Diamond Head they had gone to with Momi and The Captain, all the way to the downtown side where the Ala Wai Canal met the ocean. During these walks she asked him about "Pattasan," and he explained it all, from when he was little all the way to Lon Carlson's barn. He explained what he wondered about when he looked in the mirror, something he thought might bother her, but it did not.

He studied every canoe they came across on the beach, the short and heavy fishing canoes, the tourist canoes the beachboys took visitors out in, and the finer ones sometimes sitting in the sand in front of the Outrigger Canoe Club. Twice they went out on one and paddled, along with pale tourists and a beachboy who did the steering in the small, breaking waves.

At night they went along Kalakaua Avenue past the luau torches and the lei stands to different bars to listen to the little bands, and she taught him to slow dance. She wore heels, so she was as tall as he was, and he liked that because they were face to face or ear to ear.

The men always looked at her, followed her with their eyes whenever she went to the ladies' room, and sometimes even when she was sitting at a table with him, the ring on her finger clearly visible. They looked with a kind of aggressive sizing-up, and he always felt a little uncomfortable when they leered or whispered to each other. One night a couple of crewcut soldier-types did this, and one leaned over to him while Angela was in the ladies' room and said, "Hey, Mac, how 'bout givin' us a chance with the jungle bunny."

"Huh?" For a few seconds he worked on processing the sentence.

"Hey, plenty meat to go around, eh, Mac?"

He swung from a sitting position and there was a wet, slapping sound as the man's head jerked back, and then they were both up on their feet. He caught one in the nose, and it caused a sickening, silver flash, and then got the man on the side of the head, hard. Then it was over. Someone very strong was holding him from behind.

"Come on outside, fucker," the man said, trying to wrench himself free of the grip of his friend.

Kenika turned to look to see who held him. The bouncer, a huge local man with an expression of bland, almost casual warning on his face.

"Kenika! What happened?"

It was Angela.

"I'll get you," the man said. "I'll wait for you outside, you goddam bastard."

"Fuck you, haole son of a bitch," he said.

"Kenika, stop it!" she said. Then he was confused. What had he said?

"You guys, you leave now," the bouncer said. Then he squinted at Angela. "Eh, dat you Angie? Angie Santiago?"

She gasped. "Unca Henry!"

The two men left, one holding his head, saying, "I'll wait for you buddy. I'll tear your balls off and stuff 'em up your ass."

Uncle Henry let him go. Angela stared at Kenika, and he looked down. "Sorry," he said.

Then she explained to Uncle Henry that she was just married, "To him, Kenika McKay. 'Ass my name now."

"Lemme see your nose," Uncle Henry said. "Little blood, look okay. So! Married."

"Just three days ago," Angela said. "Oh, I shoulda sent you one invitation!"

"Eh, I no see George eight, nine yeahs now. You wen' grow up. So how all da folks?"

He did not want to explain to her, later, what had caused the fight, because now it seemed to him stupid, violent behavior that served no purpose. But in the hotel room, sitting in the stuffed armchair with a wet washcloth draped over his nose, he did, and she giggled. "'Ass what I am," she said. "Yoah jungle bunny." And the next morning she said, "Ho, I should get you in a fight every day. Dey gonna hafta buy one new bed too much li'dat."

≈   ≈   ≈

The Malolo, or Flying Fish, was to be thirty-nine feet long and weigh four hundred pounds. The prototype design was the Malia, built in 1930 and thought of by those in canoe racing as the ideal design for a racing canoe, and Benny regarded it as an artist might regard the ceiling of the Sistine Chapel. He found out from a friend when it would be on the beach at the Outrigger, and took Kenika over to show it to him. As far as Kenika was concerned, there was no question—already nearly twenty years old, it looked to him somehow almost futuristic in its sleekness, because the manu was not as large and it had a fairly narrow beam.

It took them a full day to winch the rough-cut hull of the Malolo up the side of the shed and put it in its proper position on the soft hau cradles for the sculpting. The shed was built in such a way that a forty-foot log could be placed in its hau cradles and worked on, all outside of the roof support beams, which were inset eight feet from the screen. The log sat on a section of floor on a foot-high level bench, the floor supported underneath by the massive posts that supported the shed, but set out at the floor's edge. You had only to roll up the sections of screen to bring the log in. They got some help from Mr. Marumoto during the phase of sliding the log on smooth short, slide-logs angling from the upper slope of terrain to the floor of the shed, so that the angle of rise was not sharp. Benny poured water on the logs to make the sliding part easier, and he and Kenika pushed the log up a few inches at a time, while Mr. Marumoto held the log in place by tying it off around the heavy roof-support beams. The trick was to work slowly, inch by inch.

The Malolo would have an ama kaka, the outrigger booms curved up more for rough water, the fore-end of the outrigger float, or lupe, sharper and higher for cutting through the water. The client wanted an open-ocean racing canoe.

By the time they were exploring the wooded uplands, searching for U-shaped 'ohi'a roots for the wae, he and Angela had settled in at her house and day by day watched the building of their new one, a little two-bedroom, one-bath house overlooking the rooftops of others in the development, below which was the marsh and in the distance cowpastures, and the lush, triple peaks of Olomana. There were almost no trees, and hardly any grass anywhere on their block, because the hillside had been scraped and then filled in a loose, stairstep pattern, each yard around seven-thousand square feet. He did not like where they were at first because it seemed raw and scarred everywhere he looked, with posts sticking out of the ground, broken cinderblocks lying around, bright nails and pieces of tarpaper on the dusty, parched ground. But then it seemed that in no time at all, green appeared in the form of hardy grasses and weeds. And in the neighbors' yards, faster-growing plants rose up and obscured the dirt: papaya trees, tomato vines, skinny, almost leafless mango trees that seemed to leaf out in a matter of weeks.

The house was bought with the help of George Santiago, well known to the bank people in Kailua. Kenika hated the idea that he should be helped this way because he thought that it was supposed to be solely his responsibility. George told him, "It is your whatchucall. I only standin' between you an' dem." He had eleven hundred dollars, and they had another five hundred from the gifts. That made the down payment, far more than the minimum required, and they would make their monthly payments to George, who would take them to the bank. The problem was, as Angela's mother put it, "They're not inclined to write a mortgage for someone eighteen years old." And the look on her face seemed to say, someone who barely shaves yet.

They were staying at the Santiago house in Lanikai until their house had walls and running water. The parents got them a double bed, and at night they did what they could to avoid making noise, but the expressions on the parents' faces in the morning seemed to Kenika crossed with a thinly-veiled amazement that those kids could stay up that late and do all that work, and then get up fresh and ready for breakfast the next morning. Kenika was mortified. The four of them would sit at the kitchen table eating fried eggs and aholehole or aweoweo that Kenika had caught, and he would try to remember if this screech of the springs or that house-shaking thump might have been heard by the parents at two in the morning. The problem was that the strange intensity of the nights at the Moana Hotel did not abate at all, and if anything, it was heightened because they knew they should try to make as little noise as possible, so he would put his hands on her, both of them trying not to even whisper, and then he would be on top of her, trying to do it with a kind of calm restraint, but that only made her more vigorous, crushing him with her arms, or, if she were on top, he would try to hold her in check as she thrashed, her hair swinging around above his face, and just past the final moment, she sometimes fell on him as if shot, so that her forehead crashed down on his nose or cheek.

"Ah, was leaning over to pick up a tool, hit my head on the workbench," he said one morning when George inquired about a bruise just in front of his temple.

George smiled, and Angela looked down at her breakfast and chewed thoughtfully, apparently assessing the believability of the lie, then might as well have waved a flag, because she inadvertently reached up and fingered the less-visible bruise on her forehead. Throughout all of these conversations, her mother tended to continue gazing at her daughter with a secret, amused smile.

At the Moana and then at her house, they went through a strange, undiscussed evolution in terms of sex. First it was the hands and how they affected her, and then added to them was the mouth and the tongue. He had heard the filthy stories in Paterson, had assumed earlier that sex between normal, good people was reserved and elegant. But he and Angela failed that every time, and when she, or they, discovered his tongue and all the interesting effects it could have when used in certain places, she went around during the days sometimes seeming to stop, to consider whether or not what they were doing was normal. In the mornings after the discovery was made she would find a way to get his head down there and then present herself to him bathed in blinding sunlight coming in the window, and he would go ahead, now knowing where the tongue went and what it did best, all the time amazed at this moist, sunbathed anatomy lesson. When they did this at her house the first time, he immediately got up and went outside to see how high up that window was, and sighed with relief. It would take a ladder to see in.

Then she told him one day, after one of her knowing giggles, "I asked my mom about dat. Know what she said?"

"Really? I mean you asked straight out? Oh, Jesus."

"Yeah, an' she say, 'Well honey, you do what makes you feel good,' an' so I ask her did you an' Daddy evah do dat an' she say, 'Well, yes we did.' An' I clap my han' on my mout' an' say, 'Mommy! Not!'"

He was flushed with mortification. What was it about women that made it so easy for them to talk about stuff like that? And he could easily imagine Angela framing the question: is dat okay when da woman wants da man put his face, I mean li'dat, down dere? I mean do dat chickachickachicka stuff wit' his tongue? And he could see the combination of amusement and maybe a little well-maintained shock on her mother's face as she said, well honey— After that he walked into the kitchen in the mornings feeling as if he sported huge, crusty earlobes that dangled on his shoulders.

≈   ≈   ≈

Because the work at the shed was sporadic, Benny announcing that there would be no work for two days one week, three days another, they had time on their hands, and Kenika hatched an idea based on something he had seen happening at the Filipino Camp on the east side of Kailua Town. He had to walk to Kailua to get a tube repair kit and had gone into a little dirt side road, more or less exploring, and saw the camp, a little cluster of cottages, close set to one another and crisscrossed by dirt paths, with patches of weeds and vegetables between them. Chickens pecked at the parched dirt, and he could hear the grunting of a pig back in there somewhere, and dark, wiry old men sat on their haunches in the shade, smoking and spitting into the dirt. The women and children went on about their business, and he saw a teenaged girl walking across the road from one house to another, and she looked once in his direction. She was petite, dark and pretty, with large breasts between which glinted a gold cross, huge doe eyes and black hair.

He was struck by her exotic beauty, but not for the usual reasons. It was more the atmosphere of the place, as if it were some strange, jungle village and he was looking in at the goings-on of a clan. Then he saw a tall, lanky and very dark man a little older than he was carry an aluminum box from one house across the dusty road to another, and when he did, two men rose from the shade and went and looked inside. One reached down and came up with a large menpachi, then another. He placed the fish into a piece of newspaper produced by a woman at the cottage door, and then looked into the box again. He took out two brown palani, and turned and gave those to the woman. When the tall man closed the box the old Filipino man pulled out a wad of bills and gave the man what looked like three dollars.

He told Angela about this. "Dat Filipino Camp, like da one jus' insai Lanikai. Sugah workers and li'dat. Dey buy plenny fish. Hey, you know what?"

"That's what I was thinking."

"Bet I catch much as you."

"Uh-uh," he said.

She held up her fist, one pinky extended into a hook. "Bet."

He had never seen this before, but assumed that he was supposed to close the bet by hooking his little finger in hers, which he did.

They went to the reef two-thirds of the way out to the Mokuluas, in sight of that spot under the rocks they used to go to. They used their innertube float, and put mesh bags inside to hold the fish. He started by going to familiar caves, turning upside down and looking at the black ceilings, and the menpachi and aweoweo would materialize, the ghostly, almost transparent red shapes, dorsal spines up. By the time he had stuffed three of them in the mesh bag, Angela had come up with an octopus. It writhed on her spear, the tentacles snaking around it, and he looked at the brownish-gray head which dangled on the spear, fighting gravity.

"Benny show me how fo' kill he'e," she yelled over the wind, and then spluttered in the water, blowing snot from her nose. "Watch." She got her elbows up over the innertube and then held the spear, the octopus right in front of her face.

"Hey, can it bite? The one I got that time had a black beak, sort of."

"Watch!"

She cupped the slippery head with one hand, and then drew it to her mouth. Then she worked her teeth around the protruding eye and bit it, grinding her teeth behind the eye. She did this with the other eye, and the octopus was limp, its skin still flashing different spots. He stared at the shifting color changes, all variations of gray, black and dull pink, and they raced like a slow electricity under its slimy skin.

"Where'd you find it?"

"Eh, I tell you, I lose da bet."

"Suppose we go over there to our old beach and—"

And she said, "'Kay, deal."

They wasted an hour, and then, straightening herself up, she explained. "Squid eye, it called. Benny to' me I had squid eye. Once you see um, you got um. You stick speah in um and den shake it aroun', and he come outta da hole an' right up da speah. Try come, I show you." Then she shook herself. "Kenika, you get san' on dakine— You know?"

"No."

She shook again. "Fee' like it. I wonder—"

"Maybe you should ask your mother."

She giggled. "'Mom, Daddy evah get san' on you know, dakine?' 'Well, honey, of course.' 'Dat okay?' 'Well, honey, if a little sand feels good, then—'"

She found one but did not spear it. She called him over and blew the snorkel out of her mouth. "It's right undah me," she said. "You go get um."

He looked down through the glass, but saw only a bland, rubble-littered bottom, but off to the left there was a dull circle in the sand, and it appeared to darken as he looked. He dove down, and inside the circle he could see the two eyes up in the lumps of their sockets looking back at him, strangely-expressive eyes somewhere between those of a cat and a human, the skin around the eyes shifting in color, then puckering up so that it appeared to have short, dark thorns. He speared it between the eyes, but could not get it out of the hole, and out of breath, he exploded to the surface.

"Jus' shake da speah," she shouted. "He come out."

When he drove down to the camp, he had the fish and octopus in a small cooler like the large one he had seen the tall man carrying. He waited until he verified that the tall man was not there, drew a deep breath, and carried the cooler into the camp. Within twenty minutes all the fish were gone, and he had twelve dollars in his pocket. Three menpachi, two dollars. One octopus, skin still flashing color changes, dollar fifty. Six aholehole, two dollars. He wondered at first how much money he should charge, but the old men instructed him as to the pricing. With the little kids watching, and the wizened smiles of the men, who handled the fish with their dark, battered hands, he had the strange feeling that he was charging too much, so he asked George about it. "Fresh fish is fresh fish to dem," he said. "'An dose men'll nevah cheat you."

The off-day fishing expeditions went on throughout the rest of the summer, and he would find himself stopping on the surface to watch Angela, magnified and richly-dense in color. During these pauses he experienced an intense sensation that no dream he could ever have hatched in the shadows of those grimy buildings in Paterson could come anywhere near this.

He calculated that the tall man did his selling on Monday, Wednesday and Friday, so he went to the camp Tuesday, Thursday and Saturday. He knew that the supply had now outstripped the demand, so was not bothered when he drove home with fish left over. They took it to the Nahoopiis, put some in the Santiago icebox, took some to Momi and Tutu Elizabeth, and gave fish to neighbors that the Santiagos knew less well, but well enough for them not to be surprised. Then one day as he carried the cooler to the road leading into the camp, he saw the tall man selling his fish, on a Tuesday. Wednesday the tall man was not there, and within a week they had reversed their schedules.

One day weeks later as he went in on Wednesday the tall man was back, this time he guessed, ready to do another reversal of the schedule, but he was coming out, carrying the empty cooler. Kenika stood there as he approached, tall and very dark, and wondered if he would be punched. But the man simply said, "Eh," and kept going, but then stopped. "Wheah you get da mos' aholehole?" he asked.

"Left side of the Mokes, but in holes where there's current."

"In front or by da side?"

"Side, not in the rip. I don't know, but I think it's incoming current."

The man looked at his cooler and said, "Yeah, same place I go too." Then he nodded and said, "Hey," and went on. This time Kenika distributed three-fourths of the fish to the neighbors.

He did as much as he could helping to paint the rooms of the new house, and worked on painting the outside, set up gardens and planted trees, and by the time they had moved in, the hull of the Malolo had taken its shape. Each day as he got back, Angela, Momi and Irene would be sitting, paint-splotched and beaded with sweat, in the barren front room, drinking juice and eating whatever pupus either of them had brought along for the day's decorating work. He would go immediately to the yard, garden tools in hand, and continue what he had left the previous day, a garden set off by patio bricks sunk edgewise in the dirt, or a panax hedge made from cuttings from the one bordering the ocean side of the Santiago house. Day by day the greenery defeated the raw, wounded look of the yard.

If you were to look at the profile of a canoe from absolute ground level, Benny told him, then you would see the following: from the center of the profile would begin a razor-thin angle toward the fore end, and the angle would open up to a quarter of an inch at five feet, more at ten, and then it would sweep all the way to the point where the manu rose up. From the center of the canoe again, if you looked aft, you would see the canoe's bottom contact the earth for one-fourth of the total length of the canoe, after which the same razor-thin angle would open, but this time sweeping up to the aft in a total of one-fourth, rather than one-half of the canoe. What would that be with the Malolo? From the center to fore end nineteen feet six inches, Kenika said, and added, why didn't you tell me about this with the Lapa Uila? Cause not time yet, Benny said. 'Kayden, try meashah. 'Ass right, Benny said. Nineteen feet six inches, and with one piece chalk make a mark. Then, Kenika, you get down onna haunches and look. And as Benny leaned on the hull, pushing it to make the quarter of the canoe contact the level plank it sat on, Kenika looked and said, I see the light dying out at more like seventeen feet. Ho, seventeen, Benny said. 'Kayden, get da sanding blocks an' planes an' let's make um nineteen-six. 'Kay, but how come I didn't know this last time? Cause I tell you, san' heah, plane dis an' dat. Too dakine— complicated fo' explain firs' time. Now you ready fo' dis paht. Like alla lashings, called 'aha. Bumbye I show you dat too. An' den how fo' cure 'iako? Ho, dirty job. Go ocean, fill up dese cans wit' wattah, come back and put um insai horse trough down undah shed. Fill um up. We get hau fo' 'iako but mus' cure in salt wattah. Well, why don't we cure them in the ocean then? No, my dad no like do dat. 'Iako mus' be heah fo' cure, make um feel good. 'Sides, he try ocean and lose beautiful ones. No mo' ocean cure. So, go. Fill um up. But—

He made five trips to the ocean and filled the trough, into which they immersed the 'iako logs. We didn't do this last time. 'Ass because awreddy cured, 'ass why. Was o' ones, but good, ah?

But wouldn't it make sense to— Nah nah, we do um dis way.

And then hollowing out and finishing the inside, checking and rechecking the exact inward-turning of the hull for the subtle, calabash cross-sectional shape. He measured, he was sure, a thousand times, feared that there was a flaw anyway, always in the back of his mind, pregnant, hapai, with child, how many other words? Angela believed that it happened in her room, and he put his hand on her stomach, again and again, staring at it, then up at the eager grin on her face. "It make me so happy," she said, and he said, "Me too, but—" And she got a look of suspicious doubt on her face, and he said, "No no no, it's just that I'm a little scared."

"Me too," she said.

He followed her around, watching her, until she said, "Eh, I not made of glass you know."

As for sex, she had asked her mother. Yes, up to a certain point. As for fishing, yes, but up to a certain point. In any case the work with the Malolo had cut down the fishing to once a week.

And in the yard, replacing panax cuttings that had died before rooting, he understood that at least half of the child's blood would be known, that however obscure his was, Angela's was not, and he imagined that over the long road of procreation, someday the fact of the obscurity of his blood would be diluted out.

≈   ≈   ≈

Component parts: wae, of 'ohi'a, so hard a wood that he felt as if he were trying to shape a metal. From the vise upside down to the hull, back to the vise upside down and back to the hull, he would address it with the different planes Benny had hanging on the wall: jack plane, horn plane, smooth plane, all of them wooden with steel tongues that ran diagonally through the middle, the wood rounded off and shiny with the skin oil of its users, and it sent thin sheets that curled into pale, transparent corkscrews out the opening. And then it was the pepeiao, or ear cleats, extensions of the hull interior into which the notched wae fit. These supported the seats and with the wae gave the hull its stability. Each set was different from the next, from the tighter U's fore and aft to the heavier, larger ones toward the middle.

One day he stopped and said to Benny, "She's too big."

"Lemme see it," he said, staring at the wae.

"Angela, I mean."

"Eh, gimme dat li'l smoo' plane." He was working on the pale kai, the V-shaped splash guard that would be mounted behind the manu. Kenika handed the plane to him.

"I take her to town, to Kapiolani Hospital, and they show us cutaway pictures of the baby upside down inside? A picture says 'five months,' and Angela's about that, but she's much bigger. Now she's seven months and Jesus—"

"Cutaway one haole wahine. Hawaiians biggah, 'ass why. Angela a big girl."

Kenika smiled. "I won't argue that," he said, and then looked down again. "If she's a big girl, then wouldn't her stomach be smaller, considering that a small woman with a baby would—" He shook his head and went back to shaping the wae. It didn't feel right. When she was three months she asked him, "Why you tink I get no braddahs and sistahs an' li'dat? Mommy tell me she lose two babies, one before me an' one aftah." Every morning he would awaken and look at her, lying on her side with her hands down between her knees and her stomach toward him. At times the stomach would move, slowly undulate and change shape, and he would stare, breath held. He tried to give some optimistic explanation: maybe because it was him she was having the baby with, the chance that something could go wrong would be reduced by half. And how about Benny? Why did he have only one child?

"One irresponsible fuck-up, 'ass why," he said.

"I'm scared about it all the time."

Benny looked at him, his face shining with oil and sweat.

"Look, come down wit' me unda shed. We pull out one goodlooking wiliwili log fo' ama. Den you go up da mountain."

"What for?"

"Go heiau." Benny looked at him, apparently waiting for an expression of skepticism, but Kenika looked down at the bright coils of shavings on the floor. "Why take chance?" Benny said.

"'Kay, but—"

Benny heaved himself up and went to the lunchbox. He pulled out a banana. "Look, do dis, 'kay? No ask questions. Onna way up pull off two ti leaves, nice bright ones, an' make one cross onna groun' an'—no no, not dat cross. Den put banana deah, pull leaves up and tie um in a knot. Go put dat onna rock up deah."

"What do I say?"

"Eh, dat up to you."

Walking up the trail, which was overgrown because of the spring rains, he hefted the banana and wavered between feeling foolish and feeling afraid. As the sharp mountain-outcroppings rose above him and then loomed almost straight overhead, he got that feeling of walking into a place he did not belong and whose inhabitants might find his presence irritating. The sensation that this was foolish went away, leaving only a strange fear. He tried to ignore that and thought, no take chance. When he thought he was within a hundred yards of that optically-confusing area of blank space over the knoll, below which was the heiau, he found ti plants and snapped off two healthy leaves, and as Benny had instructed, tied the banana up in them.

The dirt knoll was muddy, and when he went over it and stood facing the black, rectangular worshipping place, he stopped. Unsure of whether or not it was a good idea to go in wearing his muddy slippers, he kicked them off and stepped out onto the rocks. They were hot, and he tiptoed farther into the center, and found one stone that was lying on top of the smaller stones and sun-dried dirt, and placed the wrapped banana on it. Then he rose up and looked around, at the gray and in places mossy mountainface vanishing into the clouds on his left, and then at the mountains sweeping away down to the dark blue ocean to his right. Then he whispered, "Well, I—" He thought, please make this work. Please let nothing happen to Angela. Please give us a healthy baby. But he became nervous at the idea of trying to form the words, and whispered, "Please." Then he shuddered, feeling as if something were behind him, or maybe watching him from somewhere. He pointed down at the wrapped banana and whispered, "That's for you," and then slowly backed his way out of the square.

As he had done the first time he ran a little just after going over the muddy knoll. When he had slowed his pace to a walk, he whispered, "Okay," and went on.

"What happens if I didn't say anything?" he asked Benny.

"D'jou lea' da banana like I to' you?"

"Yeah."

"'Kay," he said, nodding.

Twenty M and M's are lined up on the bench next to the Honu 'E'epa. You look at Pua's eyes and see them stay there even when she waves a mosquito away. "Firs' is junk an' a po," you say.

"One two tchree," you say, and Pua's flat hand wins.

"Peppa covah rock," she says. "Na-aah."

"'Kay, Pua goes first," Kenika says. He points.

"Pale kai," she says.

"Why?" he says.

"Pale mean to defleck."

"Not."

"No, she's right," Kenika says. "How about kai?"

"Wattah."

"Right."

Her eyes widen. Her hand hovers over the M and M's, and she whispers, "Green," and then, "No, yellow." She takes a yellow one.

"Your turn, Ben." He points.

"Mo'o board."

"'Kay, but it's not easy."

"Mo'o mean lizard. Mo'o also mean dragon an' supah wattah ghos'. Also mean one little shtrip lan', an' story, an' den also dakine, line." You hear something in the distance, a hissing. "Grandaddy, what dat?"

"Rain," he says. "Very good, though. You got every meaning. Take one."

You hear it coming, hissing down the mountain, and you look. Pua looks too, waits. The hissing is louder, like something flying through the leaves, and then you see it, the ashy gray materializing and then blotting out the trees, and then it roars on the roof followed by a wet, cold wind that blows through the shed, rolling one M and M off the bench and onto the floor. Kenika picks it up and puts it back, and then water is dropping in silver sheets off the roof. And then it stops, and the trees appear again dripping, then bright with sunlight.

Brown. You tuck the M and M next to your teeth. Does brown taste different from green or red?

Kenika points.

"Ka'ele," Pua says. "Ho, fo'got dat."

"And what does it mean?"

"Mean empty, an hull. Mean hollow."

"'Kay, you get two."

Pua studies the line of M and M's.

"Ho, take all aftahnoon."

"Shut up," she says. Her hand hovers. Green, then red.

Kenika points, his finger touching the bottom of the model.

"Kuamo'o, mean backbone an' pat', or dakine. Lane."

"Uh-oh, you guys are too smart. I'm gonna run outta candy."

"Not, I saw da bag," Pua says.

"What bag?"

"Lie! I saw da bag."

≈   ≈   ≈

The Malolo was to be given its brains in April. Benny told him not to come to work any more, until the baby was born. He needed to be home to take Angela to the hospital, no worry, I finish da mo'o, and Kenika said, I already rough cut the boards for them, they're under the bench. The mo'o was the gunnel board that ran along the top of the thin, graceful hull. I get kokua from da Kama boys, Benny said, no worry, dey help me take um out. And with that, Kenika stayed home, in the mornings staring wide-eyed, almost with a sustained shock, at the size of Angela's belly.

The obstetrician, Dr. Kanemori, estimated the birth at the second week of April, and on the Sunday morning Kenika knew to be the day of the lolo ka wa'a up at Mr. Marumoto's house, Angela woke up, felt around, and then jumped out of the bed and went down the short hall to the bathroom, her heels thumping on the floor, leaving a dotted line of clear drops, and he got out of the bed and knelt down to touch one of them. It was like a fine oil, slippery on the tips of his fingers. From the instructions they got at the hospital, he knew this to be what they called the Bag of Waters.

Irene and Momi went over all the possibilities and determined that no one in either of their families had ever brought identical twins into the world. Clarice Mahealani McKay was the first, delivered around the same time that Kenika paced the parking lot at Kapiolani Hospital, his knees weak and his body slick with sweat, and then came Elizabeth Kaiulani McKay, delivered three minutes later. Frightened to the point of becoming sick to his stomach, which had not seen food in twelve hours, he waited in the hall outside the delivery room, his tumid, electrified brain radiating pleas, promises, and offers of trade, his life for hers, or for theirs, with or to whatever spirits might have decided to occupy the cool, alcohol-scented air of that hall. A nurse offered him a little sandwich and then went on down the hall, and he bit into it, but the bread and baloney and mustard lying on his tongue felt like a mouthful of clay, and he spat it out into his hand and put the sandwich in a scrap basket.

Mahealani meant "the full moon," and Kaiulani meant "the high point of heaven," possibilities discussed months before the birth. On Angela's list they were numbers one and two, and for a boy, if there was one, George, or Keoki, middle name Lanakila, which meant "victorious."

When he was finally allowed into the room, he walked in on legs that felt weak, ticklish and rubbery, floating toward her airy and faint.

She was propped up against pillows, a baby cradled in each arm, a broad, triumphant grin on her face. There was a chair by the bed and he sat down, feeling out of balance, and looked at the two dark, angry little faces. "Look," he whispered, as if to show them to Angela. "Oh, look at them, I—" He tried to say more but his throat had tightened in on itself, leaving him breathless and dizzy, and her voice came to him as if from a great distance, tinny and flat. Kenika, when did you eat? Are you all right?

He was not sure if time passed or did not pass, but Irene was speaking to him, telling him he'd feel better if he ate something, and when she offered him another of the little snack sandwiches that was the same as the first, he stuffed it into his mouth, chewed three times and swallowed, and said, "Do they have any more of those?" at which Irene and Angela looked at each other and laughed.

At home there were always cars parked along the street, and inside, the babies went from auntie to auntie, the air roiled with the aromas of the dishes they brought, and the chatter went from nine in the morning on into the evening. It was apparent that Clarice and Elizabeth were to orient themselves to the new world with the help of an army of women, who advised Angela as she nursed or changed their diapers, and who delighted in having half-digested breast milk burped up onto their muumuus.

When she nursed in the evenings he would watch as they chomped away, always beginning with Angela shuddering with pleasure as gooseflesh erupted on her arms. "Ho, dat tickle," she whispered. And the babies sucked away, their brows furrowed, their fine black eyebrows drawn together in a kind of angry concentration. And when, for no reason he could figure, one or other would open huge, dark eyes and stare at him, he would stare back, sometimes would touch the soft skin and feel a strange satisfaction that yes, this was Polynesian skin, more like Angela's than his, and that these were children who would know who they were and where they came from. These were children sprouted from land they belonged to as surely as 'ohi'a trees rooted in the upland forests.

≈   ≈   ≈

Between the Malolo and the Puaho Akua, or Divine Arrow, there was a two-year period of trinket-making, and two fishing or 'opelu canoes, their orders coming with names, the Leilani and the Moana. They were to be stout, between eighteen and twenty-feet long, and heavy. "Eh, no ask me about da names," Benny said. "Some guy in da touris' business to' me dat's da names. Get no whatchucall— No, you know, dakine."

"No real creativity."

"'Ass it. Names a big ting. My names strange, I know, but I like um dat way. Dis racing canoe, Puaho Akua, no need make um till way aftah neckshear, but I made da name. Buyer no wan' um till he expand his space, 'ass why. But make name anyway. Da log right undah us, make um feel good."

"Good idea. I like the name too."

"I cannot even walk up to a log I like cut until I have a name."

"So where do we get short logs?"

Benny turned in his chair, leaned over and reached into the beer tub while Kenika listened to the chair squealing in its loose, abused sockets. He came up with two Primos, opened them and handed one to Kenika. "We go Big Island. Strip of fores' dat run not', sout', from Milolili up to Honokahau, but up, tousan' feet. I buy um from guys I know who cut um. Cured ones."

"Hey, that's gonna be fun."

"Hey, not you. You stay wit' Angela an' da keikis. Take a week off."

"Seems like only last week they said their first word."

"What was it, mama, daddy?"

"It was 'not.'"

"Can you tell um apaht?"

"Yeah, Clarice weighs about an ounce more than Elizabeth."

Benny smiled at him. "I watch your face when you talk story about dem. Ho dey so pretty."

And they were. A little more than two feet tall, with huge heads and cascading black hair, kinky like Angela's whenever it was humid, they ran naked around the house and in the yard, their bodies plump and strong. Slowly weaning them off breastmilk had meant no more than sitting them before bowls of poi, into which each would immerse a fist, and then oozing the purplish gray goo onto their laps or the floor, the fists went to the mouths and there were the loud popping sounds of it being sucked off with the same zeal with which they had nursed. It ended up in their noses, all over their faces, in their hair, and Kenika got the impression that the entire house was sticky.

Angela had recovered from the birth easily, and they returned to the same sweaty vigor of the days before she got pregnant. Again they had to remain as silent as possible, especially on calm nights. Sometimes shortly after they were finished and cleaned up, he would hear the thump thump thump of them coming through the darkness to crawl up into bed with their parents. Angela would put them back to bed after they fell asleep, or if she fell asleep first, Kenika and Angela would wake up in the morning with them rolled up into little balls, one between their heads, the other down by their feet, or both of them, rumps up, between their waists.

The one-year baby luau was held at their new house, and cars lined the street all the way around the corner. George showed Kenika how you did one of these: in the carport you put chairs around a beer tub, for the men, while the women talked story inside. Next to the beer tub was a little table with dishes of tako poke and ahi poke and potato chips. We talk story out heah, bumbye somebody get a little drunk, drop beahcan? 'Ass why we heah and not in house, 'kay?

Then the twins were talking more, so that the routines of the late afternoon after he got home were based on a kind of absurd joking: "Da, get one co'," and the other, "Me too, Da, get one co'," and they stood side by side, their mouths wide open so that he could look into their pink throats.

"You swallowed a gecko."

"Not."

"Angela! She swallowed a gecko!" and Angela produced a loud, theatrical gasp.

"Well, I see a gecko down there, in yours, too. I told you not to sleep with your mouth open."

"Not, I no sayo gecko."

"Me too, you no hea chirp chirp da trope."

"Wait, I think I do."

"Not."

He began noticing a change in Angela, that on such social occasions as food shopping or buying little shoes and panties for the girls at the Liberty House store, she used proper English in addressing the salesgirls. He suspected that Momi and Irene had probably conversed in pidgin and with maturity abandoned much of it in favor of social propriety, except at those times when there was some excitement. At the same time the kids were developing their language, partly from Angela's proper example at banks and stores and at Momi's, and partly from the other little kids on the block, with whom they played in the front yard in the blazing sun: "Dat mines."

"I like mo' taffy."

"Eh, dat manini piece."

"Dis my dolly my faddah gi' me."

"So, den dis my sistah, cannot have."

"Dis dolly mo' pretty den dat."

"Not."

"I no mo' pleh witchoo."

"'Kay den."

"Eh, watch dat, get sand on her okole."

"'Kaywait, I show you guys how fo' make one perm.'"

The fishing-canoe logs came to the halau wa'a on a flatbed truck, rough hewn and muddy and scarred from being dragged by chains out of the forest by their maku'u, the large knob left on to accommodate logchains. Benny borrowed a tractor from a neighbor of the Marumotos and dragged them to the shed, plowing through the mud and rotten leaves. By the time they were near filling the order for the Leilani and the Moana, names which Benny could not utter without a sneer of disgust, the girls had elongated, so that ribcages and muscles were more defined, legs were longer, skin darker from the sun. As they grew they more and more took on the full-lipped, broad-nosed and dark-eyed character of their race, although the frequent visits by aunties contradicted that because they were continually impressed by what they called the hapa in them, or half haole. He didn't mind this. No one could look at them without seeing Angela. And he could not look at them without seeing what he thought of as beautiful, even magnificent prototypes.

Their twinness fascinated him. He would find them staring at each other, he supposed not yet understanding that they might as well have been looking in mirrors. Each took the behavioral prompt from the other. When they took them to the doctor to get their shots, the jovial nurse swabbed Elizabeth's arm, and while he watched, tensed up with vicarious pain, poked the needle in and plunged, then swabbed again while Elizabeth stared gape-mouthed at her. Then the nurse did the same with Clarice, while the sharp, cold pain of the needle searched its way up into the channels of Elizabeth's brain, at which her face slowly contorted and her lower lip moved out. And then Clarice, whom the nurse had just innoculated, looked gape-mouthed at Elizabeth, and produced a reaction that was perfectly identical, and the wail that came from Elizabeth's mouth was followed by one from Clarice's, but delayed by precisely the amount of time it took to convince anyone that this was like a repetition of a film clip.

≈   ≈   ≈

If Benny had always had a problem with drinking too much, he now drank way too much. Kenika reasoned that it was either something to do with Darnay, or something to do with filling an order made by a man who thought those two names for canoes were proper, or creative. When they finally made their way past the two fishing canoes and winched the Divine Arrow up into the hau cradles, he expected the drinking to stop, but it did not. Benny sat and watched, downing beer after beer, and smoking cigarettes, something Kenika had never seen him do before.

"'Ass it, no be afraid of da adze. Swing so you take only quatah, eight' of an inch."

He did so. It was not his place to say anything about the drinking. It was not his place to complain. Now when Kenika stepped on the singing board, it clearly said, "why?"

He worked on, dripping with sweat while Benny sat and watched.

"No worry, plenny time," he said, but there was not plenny time. Here they were shaping the hull of a canoe that was due for delivery in five months, not to mention that Angela was due for delivery in six. It would be the fastest building job they had ever done, but it was no longer they, it was he. Worse, there was a late standing order for more model canoes with their little fiber sails.

"What about the baby canoes? Shouldn't—"

"Fuck dem. Junk models made out of junk koa. I no mo' do dat. Eh, like one Lucky Shtrike?"

"Sure. I didn't know you liked cigarettes."

"Doctah say cannot—blood presha. Momi an' George too. Did long time ago, but cannot."

He had smoked cigarettes a little in Paterson, and lit one up. He took a small puff and drew it into his lungs, and then coughed. His mouth filled with the taste of the smoke. He didn't like it. "Jesus, tastes like shit."

"I donno," Benny said. "I nevah try eat dat yet. Tell me what shit tase like," and then he laughed—hee-hee-hee—

"But the baby canoes—"

"No. Dat man can get his little shit canoes from some odda assho, not me. 'Sides, dey bring dat stuff in from da Philippines now. Wooden hula girls wit' stupid cellophane grass skirts, an' dese wooden hands wit' da middle finga stuck out. I saw dat Hotel Shtreet. It ugly shit."

Kenika bristled with anger, fear and doubt, and that was exaggerated by the taste in his mouth. He threw the Lucky Strike into the fire. It was as if Benny had spoken blasphemy when he referred to his baby canoes, but here was the Puaho Akua, and they had very little time to do it right.

At home he decided he would not talk stink about Benny, but his fear that something could go wrong, that the canoe would not be perfect, tortured him like an unbearable skin condition. He had come to think of the Hawaiian canoe with its leanness and grace, its strength and durability, its absolute beauty, as an invention equal or superior in its genius to that of the internal combustion engine or the V-2 Rocket. He could never see one, whether in Lanikai when they took the girls to the beach on weekends, or in Waikiki, or even the crude little models Benny made, without seeing every canoe he had seen and the perfect one he had dreamed of, the way he imagined an artist would pause before any work of art, not because of the piece but because of art itself.

Benny left early one Thursday, saying that he didn't feel good, that he had to "take li'l time off—quit early today." When he didn't show up in the morning Friday, Kenika sat at the bench and waited. When he imagined it to be ten o'clock, he decided to fill the baby canoe order himself. He could not work on the Puaho Akua without Benny's instruction. He placed a cast-off piece of koa in the vise, and began filing and planing, assuming that he could do five or six of them by the end of the day. But as he planed, he found himself stuck to the principles of shaping that went with a full-sized canoe. He balanced it, measured and did the mathematics for something like a one-to-thirty ratio, peered under its sleek hull searching for the razor-thin angle of rise from the center to the fore. Benny's baby canoes were hollowed-out bananas more or less, and he could not make himself do it that way.

By the end of the day he had one canoe three-quarters done. He knew it would not work, that he would never be able to fill the order, but as he studied the model, the surface of the hull already gleaming dully from the oil of his hands, he reasoned that in a small way he had almost finished another canoe, and was already sweeping his eyes around the littered floor searching for likely pieces for the wae, manu, splash guards, 'iako and ama.

Benny did not show up Monday, so Kenika worked on the baby canoe, finishing the tiny component parts and gluing them in place by the end of the day. Before he left the shed he ran his hand along the rough hull of the Puaho Akua, and then felt a little rush of urgency because time was passing and they had less than four months. By Thursday he had done three more baby canoes, working along with a slowly-growing irritation at the idea that Benny's "li'l time off" was apparently more like a week. He took the finished model home with him. The girls studied it, their mouths open, while Angela stood with her hands on her growing stomach and watched.

"I like one," Clarice whispered.

And then Elizabeth. "I like one too."

"'Kay, I'll make you each one, but really fat, like rowboats, 'kay?"

"No, I like one li'dis. I like one skinny, pretty one jus' li'dis," Clarice said, and then Elizabeth, "Me too, I like one jes' li'dis."

"Eh, what about me?" Angela said.

"'Kay, I'll make you one, too."

"Yah, make one fo' Mommy," Clarice said.

"Yah, Da, do dat. Make one fo' Mommy, den we aw get canoe."

When the girls were in bed he told Angela about not seeing Benny for nearly a week. "Would he be at home?"

"No, I tink Waikiki. Momi hasn't said anyting about his being up home."

He went Friday and started another model. All during the weekend, teaching the girls to swim, working in the yard, and going to the supermarket, the fear worked at him, and he couldn't shake it off. Angela moved the grocery cart along the aisles while the girls gawked and whispered before boxes of cereal, cans of peaches, rolls of toilet paper. At the meat and fish counter they pulled themselves up to peer over at what was inside and beheld oozing slabs of beef and liver, and Clarice whispered, "Ho, da stink," and Elizabeth said, "Stink, yah, dat meat?"

Kenika looked at Angela and said, "What if he never comes back?"

When the girls climbed up on the cart Angela whispered in a voice of sweet, motherly warning, "Oh, no climb on da caht, girls, you faw an' crack your face."

Maybe she hadn't heard his question, but in any case the problem was his, not hers.

Monday it rained, and as he squished through the rotten leaves to the shed he could see that Benny was not there, and he felt a flush of anger. Inside, he dried himself off with an old towel, and looked at the Puaho Akua. So then, it was his to finish. He would turn it over and shape the outside hull. He was afraid of doing it, but not as afraid as he would be if it were the inside hull, which took a sixth sense he thought Benny had and he did not.

It probably weighed eight hundred pounds, but its positioning in the hau cradles was such that he could rock it up with the heavy cant hook and brace it with an 'o'o, or crowbar, then slide it into position. When he had the point driven into the wood and the arced pincer in place, he rolled it up until it was balanced, and then let the cant hook fall off onto the floor. Next was to tip and let it slide, which worked, but when the log fell into place with a thud that shook the entire shed and made birds fly off in a panic, something shot at his face and struck him on the right side of the forehead, so hard that he almost sat down. When he got his bearings, his hand on his head, he felt the blood oozing onto his palm. He looked around on the floor, still dazed, trying to understand what had happened, and saw it, a chisel. He stumbled into the little screened room where the cot was and squinted at his forehead in the mirror. It was the handle that hit him, not the blade, and he breathed carefully, staring at the oozing welt, his mind concocting the other variables of what could have happened: the sharp blade could have taken his eye, could have cut his throat, the handle could have knocked out his teeth.

"I can't do this," he whispered. "I can't."

It was not because he didn't have the skill. It was something else. Why did whatever or whoever caused the accident permit him to be struck by the handle? Because it was a warning, not a punishment. He did not think himself superstitious, but Benny's advice whispered inside his head: eh, no take chance.

The path through the dripping woods was muddy, and a little trickle of water ran down it, so that pebbles and roots were cleaned off in the little channel. The bleeding on his forehead had almost stopped, so that when he reached up to touch the welt, he came away with rainwater tinged pink. He carried a banana, trying to go over in his mind all the things he should say, or think. When he reached the place where the ti plants were, he pulled two good-looking leaves off and wrapped the banana up in them. Because of the chilly discomfort caused by the rain, lighter when he approached the vertical ridges which vanished into the clouds only a couple hundred feet up, he did not feel the same uncertainty and fear that he did back before the girls were born. He walked over the muddy knoll and right out onto the wet rocks. He placed the banana on what he thought was the same rock on which he had placed a banana the last time.

"'Kay," he whispered, and then cleared his throat and in a normal speaking voice said, "I shoulda come up before about the girls. Thank you. I was taken up with them and forgot. There's another on the way, and—" He remembered the single word, please, from the last visit. He looked around, and for the first time, his presence here did not feel odd. "I want to thank you for warning me without doing anything worse when I know you could have." He looked down at the wrapped banana, then off toward the ocean, but there was nothing but fog. "But I have a problem. I need to be allowed to finish a canoe. I promise that I'll do the best I can because I love—" And he thought, canoes. Then he reasoned that he should be succinct. "I know I'm not doing this right, but if you give me permission, then I'll go ahead. Next, I want you to help Benny and take care of him because it is not my place to do this without him. He's one of yours while I'm not, that is, I'm just a visitor. If you have a choice," and he gathered it all together in his mind, "then first take care of him, Angela, the girls and the next one who is on the way, because they're yours. If that's like piling up too much, then I'm sorry. Thank you."

He left. It was the best he could do, and if he caught a chisel in the eye, then so be it.

When he went back over the knoll he did not run as he had in the past. He left hoping that he had said the right things, and determined that he would continue with the canoe. Benny was a believer in signs, and on the way back to the shed he looked for one, but there was nothing but rain, and down near the shed, fifty feet from him on the trail, a wild pig with a huge head, long legs and a tall, narrow body, and it snorted, and then sniffed in his direction, its black disk of a nose twitching and moving around, its blue-black skin visible under the coarse black hair. He stopped, and it turned and crashed into the brush, followed by piglets, he couldn't tell how many, who squealed in panic and ran after their mother, their little hooves clattering on the rocks.

After he dried off he approached the upside-down Puaho Akua whose hull was black and shiny with moisture. He picked up the heavy adze, and then lightly chopped off a quarter-inch piece, and touched the rich, red-brown wood inside. "'Kay," he whispered, thinking, make nice with her. "I want you to be patient with me, 'kay? You hang on, you're going to be a beauty."

There were two measures, one with gradations of eighths, quarters, halves of inches, the other using the human eye. He stooped down so many times to run his eye along the hull, to try to measure with his eye the curve that would permit the subtle, calabash-shape of the hull, that his lower back flashed with a dull ache. The Puaho Akua would be forty feet long, twenty inches wide at the hull rim. He measured three hundred times. Every curl of wood that fell in its reddish corkscrew onto the squeaking floor of the shed brought it a half a millimeter closer to the shape. Sometimes he would run his hand along the hull and feel an almost triumphant satisfaction, and other times he would run his hand along the hull and shudder with fear and something approaching self-hatred. He was screwing it up, as surely as the sun rose. He would work the planes until his arms were weak and trembling like jelly, and relax, limp with fatigue, and whisper, "Benny, goddammit!"

But the time came when he had to stop. He hovered over the aft section, the ko'i 'auwaha or scooping adze in one hand, but could not strike the wood. How do you know what the exact, curving angle is as it sweeps fore and aft in its narrowing, upward curve? This was not for him to decide. Component parts he could do. He could make a hexagonal 'iako whose planes were all exactly the same width. He could fashion wae that when he put them inside and then raised them in the quarter-circle arc into place, they fit so snugly into the hull that they seemed almost to suck themselves into place. But some things were for Benny to do, and his "li'l time off" had come to an end.

When he got home he found Momi there, sitting at the table with Angela and the kids, who had colds and sniffled with such swinish gusto that he wondered if they might injure themselves. The kids went through their ritual of greeting, jumping up to hurl themselves into his arms so that they could study the little scab on his forehead, imitating Angela who checked it each day. He had told her that it was simply a mistake with a tool. "Daddy, da owee bettah, yah?" Clarice said, and Elizabeth, "Yah, da booboo aw 'kay now."

Then they went back to their drawing, and as he and Angela had observed, Clarice drew with her right hand, Elizabeth with her left, elbow to elbow, their long pencils resembling two waving cockroach feelers. There was ten minutes of the usual chatter, and then the girls went to play in their room. Angela giggled and said, "Why?"

"Put them in a canoe," Kenika said, "and they're always balanced."

Momi snorted. "You, you always find the right explanation, even if it is by the canoe."

"I gotta ask you something," he said. He explained what had been going on. He explained that he did not want to talk stink about Benny, but his time was up and he needed him back.

"I think he believes that you're better at this than he is," Momi said. "He wounds easily."

"He's the master and I'm only the student. He knows that."

"But Lapa Uila," Angela said, "an' Malolo. I nevah see canoes like dat."

"Has anyone seen him?" he asked.

"He hasn't been home," Momi said. "He's probably in Waikiki. This is nothing new. I mean he's done this before, disappeared for months."

"All right," he said, "then I'll go the next step with this." He went on to explain the incident with the chisel, at which both of them cringed, and then lifted their eyes to the healing welt on his head. He told them about the first time he had gone with Benny to the heiau, and the second, and then this last time. They broke in only once, to tell him that yes, they knew of that place, Momi had gone up there when she was a girl, Angela had gone too, with Benny and Darnay, and it did no more than raise chicken skin, at which she left, scared of it. He spoke almost in a monotone because he was embarrassed to admit to what his instincts told him should be a secret. When he was finished he took a deep breath and shrugged. "So, the chisel thing? I think I was fooling around where I shouldn't and got a slap on the wrist, head, whatever. I thought I was going up there just to kind of think, but I really went up there to ask for help. So that makes me what, a supersititious fool? But it still doesn't feel right and I need him back."

Momi nodded, thinking. Angela got a stranger look, as if she were using her eyes to feel something in the back of her mind. Then she said in her formal way, "Kenika, we all feel what, fear, and like a reverence for what we don't know."

Momi nodded again. "That's right," she said. "I don't think it matters who you credit your good fortune with, but I think it's wise to credit something. Do you realize what you've done? Look where we're sitting. Look in the other room. To tell the truth, you amaze me."

He looked down, shook his head.

She laughed. "Look at him blush," she said to Angela. "I think that's what makes people like him. Anyway it's what makes me like him."

"Me too," Angela said, and then she stared at him again, with a look of thoughtful assessment, and it made him uncomfortable.

"'Kay," he said. "How can I find him?"

"We've been through this before," Momi said, "when our father died. There's Waikiki and his friends there, and there's downtown Honolulu and his, well, associates there."

"What about Darnay?"

Momi sighed, looked out the window. "Yes, he would be in contact with Darnay most likely, but that's something else. Darnay lives in the Hotel Street district. Lately he's been—" She stopped, looked at Angela, who nodded. "He's been dancing a sort of, well, dirty hula at one of those places, on a stage, I mean."

"Do you have his address?"

"Unfortunately, yes."

Late at night he found himself wide awake for some reason, and turned and felt for Angela, but she was not there. There was no faint glow of light from the space under the bathroom door either. He got up. He found her standing in the dark at the living room window that faced the mountains, and she was looking out at the faint black silhouette of Olomana. She heard him approach and turned.

"What?" he whispered.

She put her arms around him, so that her belly pushed against his, and said, "I always thought you were—what's 'at word?"

"Objective, rational."

"Yeah, rational. I'm glad you're not."

"'Kay, good."

"'Cause I'm not either. Even Momi, I know her. Could you ask— I mean would you go up again? I mean," and she drew away a little and looked down.

"I already covered that," he said. "I made sure about that."

≈   ≈   ≈

According to Momi, Darnay lived in a second-floor apartment on Maunakea Street, half a block off Hotel Street, the center of the old red light district. The narrow, busy strip ran down a hill toward a canal or shallow river of some sort, and had the look of a kind of trashy energy. Peep shows, strip joints, bars and strange Oriental herb stores lined either side, and in the storefront shade, dark, wiry men sat on their haunches spitting and smoking cigarettes. Tiny old Chinese and Japanese and Filipino women walked on the sidewalks carrying groceries. What he imagined to be prostitutes, out for some reason in daylight, walked on high heels in one door or out another. At one corner, waiting for cars to pass by, he found himself standing next to a tall, heavily-made up woman who looked at him with an expression of venomous hatred, and he did not understand what made her do that until she walked across the street with the athletic lope of a very muscular man. He whispered, "Oh boy," and wondered about this Darnay.

He found the apartment building, the ground floor a Chinese restaurant, and went up the narrow, creaking stairway to the second floor, a long hallway with doors on either side. He smelled the aroma of fresh cooking, and heard voices behind doors. He knocked on the door to No. 6, and after a few seconds it opened a crack.

"Yes?" a woman said.

"I'm looking for Darnay Santiago. I'm related to him."

"How is that?" Kenika realized that the voice belonged to a man.

"I'm married to his cousin."

The door opened a little more. The man inside was wearing a shiny robe, and was balding and appeared to be of mixed race. "Well," he said. "I think he went to the Liberty House store, up around the corner. He and a couple of friends."

Kenika did not know how he would recognize him but assumed he would be more or less Benny's magnitude. He was wrong. Off by the men's clothes he saw him, and he was immense both horizontally and vertically. He appeared to be horsing around with two much smaller men, part-Oriental it appeared, and there was no mistaking their movement. His two friends were muscular, one with a tattoo, and walked with a languid femininity, but there was nothing soft in their appearance. They looked menacing, and when one turned and saw Kenika, his expression seemed lethal. Darnay was walking quickly down one aisle with the powerful grace of some large animal, and his chest, thighs, feet, were huge, the thighs almost monstrous inside frail and shiny chino pants.

Kenika paused, now eyed by both smaller men. This was a bad idea. Their faces radiated violent challenge, and when one moved down the aisle toward Darnay, he seemed to deliberately exaggerate the languid swishiness of his walk. He whispered to Darnay, who turned, and Kenika saw the resemblance to Benny. Darnay walked in his direction, his face aimed in on Kenika's, and he said, "Eh assho, give stink face to us, ah?"

"No, I came to see you. Are you Darnay?"

"Eh, I Darnay?" he asked his friends. "Dat who da fock I am? Eh, gotta check my goddam wallet."

"Eh, you hungry?" the tattooed one asked. "Haoles tase j'like chicken. I like one breas'."

Darnay turned back to Kenika, stepped closer, and he loomed above him, the jovial, lethal sneer on his face so pure and unrestrained in its hatred that Kenika could not speak. Finally he swallowed and said, "I work with Benny. I'm married to your cousin Angela." When he said that an amazing change came over Darnay. The menacing expression softened and melted and within three seconds was replaced by a look of such warm geniality, even brotherly affection, that Kenika became embarrassed. Darnay turned and whispered to his friends, whose expressions also simply turned themselves off, and then went on looking at the clothes.

Kenika briefly explained his problem, and Darnay turned to his friends and said, "Hui!" in a high-pitched voice. "I go asai wit' my cousin, ah?" Then he turned back and said, "Come, I show you. Gotta take da bus but."

"No, I have a car."

Outside on the sidewalk, Darnay explained that Benny hung out in Waikiki, and he named friends, cottages where he might be found. As Kenika listened, he was struck by the husky but soft manner of speaking, in a lilting, almost syrupy voice that sounded as if it belonged more to a portly Hawaiian grandmother, or to Tutu Elizabeth. As they walked toward the car, Darnay stopped and said, "Kenika, sorry fo' dat inna staw."

"That's okay, really."

"Angela, she so sweet. An' twins! Ho, I bet dey beautiful. I heah about dat from Benny but fo'get."

As they approached the car, Darnay said, "Benny to' me he give dat to you fo' wedding present."

"I didn't want him to, but—"

Darnay laughed. "I talk to him, he talk about you. Talk talk talk. You know, I supposta be jealous of you."

"Well—"

Darnay elbowed him on the arm. "Not, though. I glad somebody does what I supposta do. Dat keep 'im offa my back."

Following Darnay's instructions, he drove the car up King Street, aware that it was listing to one side because of the weight imbalance of Darnay's presence on the right side. They went to Kalakaua Avenue and into Waikiki, right past the block The Captain's cottage was on, and then into the clusters of cottages on the little streets off Kalakaua. Darnay looked, they stopped once and he struggled out of the car to ask a woman about Benny, and when he got back in and the car dipped, he said, "'Kay, Kalakaua den."

They saw him from two hundred yards away, sitting on a bus stop bench, his hands on his knees, apparently addressing the people who walked by. The bench was near the Waikiki Theater and there were a lot of pedestrians there, and Kenika looked for a parking space as they moved slowly in Benny's direction. "I'm sorry," Kenika said. "I shoulda checked here before causing you the—"

"Nah nah nah," Darnay said. "I happy to meet you an' hea about da keikis. But you talk to 'im firs', 'kay? He mad at me."

He found a space, and they got out and walked past the well-dressed tourists, and he became aware of the threadbare rattiness of his shirt, the grime and stains on his shorts. Some of the people stopped before Benny, then went on, laughing and whispering. Darnay stopped fifty feet from the bench, and Kenika went on alone. When he got there, Benny looked up, bleary-eyed and drunk, and said, "Eh, when you get back in town?"

"Benny, I never left."

"Eh, I come hea fo' play tie games wit' wahine, an' no mo' notting."

"Benny, it's time to come back. The Puaho Akua—"

"I no mo' do dat. You do um."

"I can't, I need help."

"Nah, you no need help."

"Dennis?"

He turned. A woman standing next to a tall man in an Air Force uniform had addressed him.

"Eh, when you get back in town?" Benny asked the man.

"Excuse me," Kenika said, "but—"

"Carol?" she said.

It was Carol Henderson, and he stared, then nodded. "Of course," he said. "Hey, sorry, I just—"

"This is Jim Nichols," she said, indicating the man. He extended his hand and Kenika shook it. Carol told the man about the cottage days while Kenika looked back at Benny, who appeared to have fallen asleep. Then he became embarrassed, looked down at his own clothes, then at Benny, who looked awful. There was a drying urine stain on his pants, he was dark and sweaty-looking and his face was puffed out with drunkenness, the dark, blue-black patches high on his cheekbones made darker. Then he saw Darnay approaching, and felt a little relief because Darnay could tend to

Benny while he made his way through the embarrassment of trying to explain all this.

While Jim Nichols looked with a horrified amazement at Darnay, Kenika told Carol about being married, "Angela?" and he said yes, and described the twins, his buying the house, his work with—and he pointed—the best canoe maker in the world. Then he shook his head and looked at Benny, now gazing up at Darnay.

Benny asked Darnay when he got back in town, and Darnay sat next to him and spoke in that soft voice, "Daddy, you come wit' Kenika an' me now, 'kay?"

Twice Carol said, "How nice," while Kenika explained his work, and Jim Nichols grew fidgety and impatient.

Then Kenika saw something in her expression, that she looked at him and at Benny with a thinly-veiled sympathy, while Jim Nichols looked at him with thinly-veiled disgust.

When they finally went on down the sidewalk, he considered those expressions and decided that it was his own embarrassment that had caused them to interpret them that way.

"I not coming witchoo," Benny said.

Darnay looked at Kenika and shook his head sadly.

"Benny," Kenika said. "I only want you to come out and show me, 'kay? Not today, maybe day after tomorrow. Also I'm filling the baby canoe order, or some of it anyway. Is that okay?"

"Why da fahk you ask me?" Benny snapped. "You do um. Make baby canoe, make big canoe, I no mo' give a shit. I too o' fo' dat anymore."

"No, you're not." This began to scare him. The single reason things worked sat right there, drunk and surly. He sat down beside Benny on the bench. "I can't do this without you. Don't you understand? I know nothing without you."

Darnay nodded encouragingly. Keep going.

"I don't know who to take stuff to. I don't know how to do the angle going up to the manu. I'm afraid of hollowing the—"

"You look at da plan onna table!" Benny shouted, and passersby stopped and watched. "You look at da fahkeen hull, you feel um wit' your eyes! How many times I to' you?"

"But I need you to tell me again."

"Don't you use dat goddam word 'but' wit' me!" He looked at Darnay with an expression of weariness and pain. "I tell him an' he say 'but dis,' an' 'but dat,' an' it dri' me nuts."

Kenika got an idea. "Darnay, would you and Benny come over Saturday and have something to eat with us?"

Darnay nodded again. "We'd love to," he said. "Daddy, we go Kenika's house Sad'day, 'kay?"

Benny considered this. "Come see Angela anna keikis?"

"Yeah."

"Who else be deah?"

"Anyone you'd like," Kenika said. "George and Irene, Momi, the Sakatas."

Benny looked up at Darnay. "You goddam boy, fo' once I get you come odda side, ah? Ho, I like slap yo' head."

Darnay had extracted the information about where Benny was staying, in one of the little cottages off Kuhio Avenue, and when they got him there he simply toppled onto the bed with a foundation shaking crash and fell asleep.

Outside, Darnay said, "'Kay, now it's ho'oponopono."

It had something to do with ho'o, to make, and goodness or something, pono. "What's that exactly?" Kenika asked.

"Now it make nice wit' da family, fix stuffs up, an' I been so bad about dis. Ho, I feel bad about dis, but good, make nice wit' da family now. Glad you look me up."

They arranged logistics. Darnay would come with Benny in Benny's Chevy. What about Angela? Well, if I told her that I passed up on this chance because it would put her out, she would slap my head. "By the way," he said. "What is a 'tie game'?"

"That's thigh game," Darnay said.

≈   ≈   ≈

About half an hour before the guests would be driving up, Kenika stood at the back living room window watching the girls running around in the backyard. Their colds had almost run their course but the running caused them to cough in a way that bothered him, although Angela said it was all right.

Beyond the yard and the other rooftops he could see Holsteins grazing in the pasture under Olomana, and remembered with a warm flash of old shame the fire that had killed all of Lon Carlson's cows. He shook that off and thought about Benny. He had explained Benny's situation to Angela, and she said, "Lemme invite da Kams. Dey been arguing a lot, so we can double up onna ponopono, 'kay?" And he said, "Good, we'll do that." So, this was all an elaborate ploy to what? Shepherd old Benny back into the pastures of reason? He didn't know if it would work. The notion that Benny would simply quit and never go to the shed again was his greatest fear because he could not see himself alone there, making trinkets, or worse, canoes, without the benefit of his advice, or maybe without the approval of whatever or whoever it was who populated that place. As for them, Benny was his go-between, and without him he felt alien and vulnerable. Besides that, the huge, oily form of the man, black patches on his face, scaly ankles, the entire massive, sweaty, belching monster, had become so much a part of him that he seemed almost like a father.

He had thought it would be a small gathering, but Angela, who loved these parties, said, "No wase dis on six people!" Eighteen, maybe, and Kenika had to go do some fishing. She wanted regular fish, but also 'uhu so they could eat big chunks li'dis, an' lobstah if you can, an' no fo'get da glove. He had learned that you don't grab a lobster without gloves, the spines on their shells easily perforated your hand. An' octopus, she said. Then, 'kay, what else? We shop, potato an' macaroni fo' salad, fruits, limu, all dat. Ho, we gotta get goeen! Beer, he said, and she snorted. I don't hafta write dat down.

So he fished, sneaking up on holes looking for the green sides of 'uhu, struggling upside down in the darkness searching cave roofs for menpachi and aweoweo, looking for the feelers of lobsters sticking out from under rocks.

He did see an octopus, and dove down to get it. The octopus intrigued him because once seen in its hole, it was dead, and he felt a secret sympathy for the animal because despite its one weakness, that once seen it was dead, it had many tricks of camouflage, and its defense methods outside the hole, vanishing into clouds of its ink, changing color so that it went limp and resembled sand, pumping itself up with ridges and points to resemble a chunk of coral, and so on. He got down close and aimed the spear, then paused, looking at its eye which looked at him, the pupil so deep a black that he felt as if he were looking into some vast space, like a night sky. Then it closed its eye, its eyelids like those of a human, and waited. He started to pull the trigger and stopped. The octopus's tubular gill vent surged, sending out little bits of sand. He surfaced, got more breath and dove down again. The octopus looked at him, its skin changing color and becoming darker, then puckered with points. The strange shifting of color caught his eye, and when he got ready to pull the trigger again he found that he could not.

He went into shore without it, muttering, "Stupid, stupid stupid," into the snorkel, moaning with shame that he could allow himself to be taken by an eye simply because it looked so human. It seemed that the fatal weakness of the octopus had revealed another kind of weakness in him.

George, Irene, Momi and Tutu Elizabeth, and Benny and Darnay, all arrived at the same time, while Larry Kam was helping Kenika set chairs up in the carport. When Kenika nodded to Benny he saw a little twinkle of amiable penitence in his eye. After the appropriate amount of socializing, the men would sit out there in the cool semidarkness in the smell of mosquito coils and drink beer and tell their stories while the women would sit inside and tell theirs. There was a ten-minute span of chatter in the driveway, Angela and Darnay particularly, and then they all went inside to see the children. But they were in the backyard with Becky and Stacy Boy Kam, and Kenika went to the window to call them. "Oh no," he said.

"What?" Angela said, then looked out. "No let um do dat."

"What?" Irene asked. She looked out too, and then all of them moved toward the window.

"This is your fault, George," Kenika said. "This is a snot-shooting contest."

"Wait," Irene said. "Let them go ahead. Let's watch."

As the children had observed in Lanikai, George was an expert in placing his knuckle against one nostril and then blowing snot from the other. Kenika and Angela were there the first time they saw this, and the girls stared with a kind of speechless admiration at the display, and when he walked off, went to study and point down and whisper about what was in the grass.

Becky Kam was seven, Stacy Boy Kam six, the girls just over three. But because they were both recovering from their colds, they had far more ammunition than did Stacy Boy. Becky remained above it all. Clarice stood there staring off into some mysterious middle distance, focusing in on the subtle sensations of the movements of the ammunition inside her sinuses and nasal cavities, and then said, "'Kaywait. Watch." She placed her knuckle against one nostril, drew her whole body up, arching it backwards, and then lunged forward just as she blew with all her might, and the greenish string that shot out of her nose made Stacy Boy jump back in disgust.

"I can do dat too," he said. "But I no wanna now."

"Cannot."

"Can."

"You guys stoopit," Becky said.

"I got one!" Elizabeth shouted, and just as she put her knuckle to her nose she saw all the adults in the window, and whispered to her sister, who pulled the skirt of her pretty little dress up over her round belly and used it to wipe her nose.

The kids came in, and went around offering demure hellos to the adults, ending with Darnay, towering far above them so that they seemed to be looking almost straight up, their mouths open, at which Darnay whispered to Angela in that voice Kenika had now become used to: "Oh, Angela dey so-o sweet!"

Within twenty minutes the remaining ten guests arrived, school friends of Angela's, Auntie Clarice Malama and her husband Kimo,

Waimanalo friends of George, including a man named Frank Sakata. Kenika asked him if he might be related to a Sakata named Shige, and he laughed and said, "My faddah."

There was half an hour of chatter inside and around the house, during which people went to the table to fill paper plates. Kenika showed people papaya trees, the garden plants, the joists and carrier beams in the crawl space under the house. When more of the beer was brought out Angela clapped her hands and said, "'Kay, you guys go cahpo't sit an' tell fish story, compare scars." She turned to the women, who sat on the couch and on chairs. "Talk talk talk, brag brag brag, dis big," and she held up her hands. "Dis big, dat big." Then she turned back to the men and said, "Go on, we stay tell story inside, dis big, dat big," and she held up her hands. Then she said, as an afterthought, "Not about fish but," at which all the women laughed, and Momi said, "Angela, for heaven's sake."

So the men sat in the carport and drank beer kept cool in a washtub on the floor and in the dim light of the single forty-watt bulb told fish stories, getting up only to refill their plates, "Ho, dis lobstah ono," and "How she do dis poke?" Every ten minutes or so the girls, sometimes along with Stacy Boy and Becky, would come out and stand and watch, then run back in. Kenika furtively kept his eye on Benny, wondering when, or even if he should ask about Monday. As it grew darker the beer loosened the tongues of the more reserved of the men: "So I tchrow da net in dat frot' an' ho! can hahdly hol' um," and "Frank Frank Frank! Tell about dat hammahead. Ho, dis a good one!" They all knew the story of Kenika's ulua, so he needed only to provide parts of it when they asked, turning to point at the clipped spear leaning right there, against the wall. Gonna file a point on it, put it back to work. He felt a strange stagefright at having everyone listen so intently, but the beer eventually loosened his tongue too.

The only silent one was Benny, usually a jolly storyteller, but he sat and drank his beer, from time to time going inside to talk with Darnay and Angela.

Finally the beer loosened Benny up, and to Kenika's relief he began talking: "I tell you about buthead o'dea? I tell him, dis what you do, an' he say, 'but wait,' an' 'but I tink dat so an' so'. I know dat word, but chee, now I gotta look um up inna dictionary fo' two hunnahd ways he use it." That he went on like this at the expense of his host made Kenika feel good, more optimistic about the work, and then Benny went on with the pencil urchin picking story, and after that, "Da bes' one dis." He looked at the doorway to the house. No kids.

"Dis from right aftah Kenika get married. Next day—"

"But—"

"See dat?" Benny said. "'Ass what I gotta put up wit'. But anyway—Oops, dere's dat 'but.' Get me sayin' it too. Anyway nex' day we work, an' he hack an' chop an' sand an' saw, den tchrow himself off cliff an' come runnin' up wit' coconut husk fo' fiah an' I tink, ho, 'ass why he so skinny. Always li'dat, fac' one day I look at my weight onna scale an' see I lose ten pounds, from *watchin*' da guy."

"Nah nah nah, not you Benny!" Kimo Malama said.

"But now he married," Benny went on. "An' Kenika chop chop, sweat, snot drip off his nose, so I say, 'eh Kenika, how many times you do dakine las' night?' an' he give side-eye to me, den say, 'once.'" All the men laughed and looked at Kenika, who said, "Go on, Benny, I gotta hear this."

Benny stood up, took a long swallow of beer, and put the bottle down. "So I say, 'Eh, no worry, bumbye you get da hang of it.' Nex' day, chop chop, sand, hack dis an' dat, tchrow himself offa cliff fo' get coconut husk, drip sweat, an' he skinniah. I say, 'Kenika, how many times you do dakine las' night?' an' he tink, den say, 'Eleven,' an' I clap him onna shouldah an' say, 'ass my boy, you getting da hang of it.' So nex' day at work, he slam chisel an' hack an' saw an' tchrow himself offa cliff fo' get coconut husk, all dirty an' cut up, mo' skinny and drip drip sweat an' I say, 'Kenika, how many times you do dakine las' night?' an' he say, 'Twenty-seven,' an' my jaw wen' drop onna table. 'Not,' I say, an' he say, 'Yup, I counted.' Eh, look like one skeleton nex' day. He hurl himself offa cliff, hack, chop, sweep, no meat on his bones. I say, 'Kenika, how many times you do um las' night?' an' he say, 'Ninety-eight,' an' I say, 'Not! Cannot do um ninety-eight times. What, you one machine?' He goes back work, chop chop, sand, alladat. Aftah while no can stand um any mo' so I say, 'Kenika, tell me how you do um dat many times?' an' Kenika tink, den say, 'Like everybody else, just li'dis,'" and Benny drew back and thrust his belly forward and said, "One!" drew back and thrust forward again, "Two!" and again, "Tchree! Foah! Five!" The roar of laughter lasted ten seconds while the men pointed and hooted at Kenika, who put his hands on his face and shook his head. Angela poked her head out the doorway and said, "What was dat?"

"A joke," George said.

"Pilau, I bet. Kenika, you hana hou dat fo' me laytah, 'kay?"

"'Kay."

When the girls came out for about the tenth time, Frank Sakata asked Kenika how he could tell them apart. "Easy," he said, looking at one of them, but in the dark he could not. "You're Clarice, right?"

"Maybe," she said. Then the two of them ran back in the house.

"Uh-oh, I know what's coming," Kenika said. "Benny, by your head there on the shelf, that little empty paint can? And that skinny brush?" Benny struggled around in his chair and held them out to Kenika, who took them, and then dipped the brush into his beer and set it gently in the can. "'Kay, watch what kind of games I gotta invent every day."

The girls came back out. "Where's Becky and Stacy Boy?" Kenika asked.

"Play cahds eensai," one of them said. "Junk."

"Are you Clarice?" he asked.

"Well," and she touched her chin with her index finger, and squealing with laughter, they ran back in, and came back out in about thirty seconds.

"Look, can I paint a C on your forehead?" he asked Clarice.

She came out with a little gasp. "What color?"

He looked into the can. "Green."

"'Kay."

Elizabeth stepped up behind Clarice, then tried to look around. "Nope, stand in line, 'kay?" She did so, and then Kenika said to Frank Sakata, "Provide a little distraction," which neither of them understood.

"'Kay, close your eyes." Clarice did so, and he painted a large C on her forehead with the beer-sodden paintbrush. Then he leaned down and whispered, "Look, yours is real. I'm gonna put a fake one on Lisbet, 'kay?"

"Why?" she whispered.

"I only need one to tell you apart, but we don't wanna make her feel bad."

She reached up to touch the C, and he said, "No no, it takes fifteen minutes to dry, so don't touch, 'kay?"

"'Kay."

"And pretend to Lisbet that hers is real so she won't feel bad, 'kay?" She thought this over, then nodded gravely.

He turned her around and then pulled Elizabeth forward, preventing her from seeing Clarice's forehead. Clarice stood off by the beer bucket looking at the ceiling, so her paint wouldn't run. "Daddy, mines is da E, 'kay?" Elizabeth said.

He painted the E on Elizabeth's forehead, and then whispered to her exactly the same instructions as he had to Clarice. When they finally looked at each other in the dim light, Clarice stole a glance at Kenika and said, "Well, dat look really nice."

Elizabeth, taking the prompt from Kenika, said, "I like dat one betta den mines."

Then they walked slowly into the house, looking up as if balancing something delicate on their heads. "Remember, don't touch," Kenika called after them.

George figured it out first. "Dirty guy!" he said, and the other men laughed, "Ho, dey gonna be mad atchoo!" Benny laughed and said, "Ho, you mean buggah, you."

About five minutes later they were both back out, standing before him with their hands on their hips. "Daddy! Boo-lie you!" they yelled.

The party broke up gradually, with family staying, sitting in the living room and talking. The talk was more about the babies and the one on the way, and about relatives. All of the people, Kenika noticed, abandoned the pidgin. Then Kimo Malama talked about the POW deadlock in the Korean thing, and about bombing in North Korea and General Mark Clark. After a while Kenika wandered out into the backyard, remembering his fascination with the European War and understanding now his almost total insularity from the activity of the outer world. Almost anything could happen and it would pass him by. Angela, the kids, Benny, canoes and the ocean, that was what was important in his life. As if Benny had somehow tuned into these speculations, he joined Kenika in the yard.

"You know," Kenika said, "I fished yesterday and found an octopus and couldn't shoot it."

"Really?"

"Yeah, explain that one. I just looked at it, and it just looked at me, and we went into a stalemate."

Despite the darkness he could see Benny staring at him. He cleared his throat and said, "Look, I was wondering—"

"Yah, I come."

"You sure?"

"Yah. Dis stuff jus' one phase. No worry."

"You want another beer?"

"Yah."

"Wait, I'll get a couple."

≈   ≈   ≈

The Puaho Akua received the lolo ka wa'a ceremony on Mr. Marumoto's lawn on an overcast day in October, a cool wind blowing up the mountain and rustling the leaves of the trees. Kenika was saddened by the wizened, frail look of Kelemeneke Makaila, as if this might be the last time he would have the strength to give brains to a canoe. Standing next to Kenika, Angela cradled Keoki Lanakila McKay in her arms, bouncing him to keep him distracted, and Clarice and Elizabeth stood side by side, all decked out in pretty little pink dresses, their hands folded before them as Kelemeneke Makaila circled the beautiful canoe.

Kenika looked at the baby, at his dark eyes and fine, copper-brown hair, red lips and tongue searching the fabric covering Angela's chest for a nipple. As was true of the Malolo, there was a kind of race to finish the Puaho Akua so that there would be time to take care of Angela, and although the birth was an easy one, the month and a half period prior to it was not. There was some bleeding and there were premature contractions, and after the boy was born the obstetrician explained to them that he did not advise having another child because of the danger of miscarriage. There were various contraceptive methods that he could discuss with them. One night about a week after the birth Angela cried about that, cradled in his arms as they lay in bed, because she had wanted at least four. He explained that as far as he was concerned the luck that they had experienced with the children was such that he was as happy and satisfied as he could ever have imagined himself to be. She accepted that, and the next day he saw her holding the tiny boy at the window while the girls played in the back yard, seeming to survey the logic of what he had said, and the contemplative, almost wide-eyed expression on her face told him that yes, they had three children and it wasn't a good idea to become blind to their good fortune.

The buyer was a Hawaiian-Chinese man named Clarence Lum, who was wealthy and good-mannered, and went through the ceremony manifesting a reverence for the tradition that made Kenika like him. Four of his friends attended, paddlers apparently, because Benny wanted those who would use the canoe to be present at the blessing. The Puaho Akua was beautiful, the rich, red-brown grain of its koa so deep that it caught the weak sunlight in a flashing iridescence, and the hull was, it seemed to Kenika, more refined in its shape than any of the others.

He had had to track Benny down only once before the canoe was finished, a one-week binge in Waikiki, but at the back of his mind felt the needling inevitability, that some day he would retire, and Kenika continued to fear that inevitability. He did learn more about the selling aspect of the business, even to the point of taking a box of his canoe models to a gift shop in Waikiki. Benny had looked at them and said, "Dese good, you take um," and gave Kenika the address. At the shop the owner, a haole man named Maxwell, studied them and said, "This is not tourist junk, you know. These are scale models. How much do you want for them?" and Kenika said, "Five dollars each," at which the man snorted and said, "You're a dismally incompetent businessman. I'll give you eight apiece for them and even that is taking advantage of you, so take a little advice—if you want to hack a coconut up to make it look like a monkey, then you're competing with plenty of others, but when you do stuff like this, stand up for it." And Kenika said, "'Kay," and walked out of the shop with ninety-six dollars in his pocket.

After the ceremony was over they went to the table set up in Mr. Marumoto's carport. Kenika set up two chairs for the girls, who went around the table and spooned fried rice, poi, fruit, and fish onto their plates, and Angela went to the back of the carport and sat down to nurse the baby, at which the girls got down off their chairs and dragged them into place so they could watch. They loved to do this, and Kenika would watch from a distance appreciating the picture, of the two girls staring in that rapt attention, their mouths open and moving slightly to the rhythm of Keoki's sucking, their lips sometimes popping while they watched, and Angela's bowed head would be above and he could just hear her whispering to them.

He turned back to the table, and Benny stepped over to him and whispered, "He gi' me a check, so I take um bank, gi' you da two tousen' nex' week, 'kay?"

"'Kay. Good time for it. We're adding a couple rooms to the house." He visualized the mess it was right now—joists, plywood, plumbing for the second bathroom, room for the stuff they were accumulating from garage sales and stores. Angela liked to buy art books, and they were all over the place, required that they buy bookcases for which there was no room. So it was time to make room. The girls would sit all day and watch while the carpenters hammered and sawed, and at night they would set up their dolls and toys in the bare rooms. "Anyway, that man can have our canoe any time," Kenika said. "I could make lots of canoes for a guy like that."

"He want a fishin' canoe too. No rush. Maybe two yeahs. Logs hahd to get now, so I ask him, 'What about one checkabo'd canoe, be cheapah too.' He says okay, so we make um wit' pieces. I no like use what's lef' at da shed, excep' fo' special stuff."

A canoe that doesn't come from a log? Kenika considered the idea. There could be more of them, but then what about the whole idea of the canoe? "'Zat seem right to you?" he asked.

"Kenika, bumbye no mo' logs. We gotta figgah how fo' make wa'a wit' pieces. Eh, maybe soon dey make um wit' plastic."

Clarence Lum stepped over to them and nodded to Kenika. "You're the apprentice, eh?" Kenika nodded. "I want to call the fishing canoe simply 'Aukai.'" He laughed. "Benny thinks I should have a name now."

"Sea traveller," Kenika said. "Good. But putting it together this way might take longer."

Clarence Lum looked at the Puaho Akua. "No rush," he said. "That is an absolute beauty. You folks are good."

Later Kenika filled his plate and stood at the table eating and watching Angela and the kids. Of course it was true, someday there would be no more logs. The koa forests were being cut for everything, wall paneling, tables, parquet floors, and the way things were expanding now, with new houses going up all around his neighborhood and everywhere else on the island, then that meant a lot of tables and parquet floors.

The idea of no more logs felt more like a technical problem than a threat, and he had this absurd vision of himself and Benny taking pieces and making a huge log, and then hollowing it out. He chuckled at the idiocy of it and went on eating.

With the money from the Puaho Akua they would be safe from any skimping for a while, even considering the cost of the addition. And with the birth of Keoki, he felt that another threat was averted. That month-and-a-half period before the birth frightened him as he knew it did Angela. In the hospital during the four hours the birth lasted, he had sat so tense and breathless that when it was over and the obstetrician congratulated him, he stood there, the sweat on his forehead suddenly cooled by the draft of air the obstetrician brought with him through the door, his body so sore that he felt as if he had spent those hours holding a log on his shoulders. In his mind he gave thanks to that indistinct entity he felt had followed him, or watched him, throughout the past few years.

What that entity was he could not say, and in a way he did not want it defined too precisely. Benny called it Ku 'ohi'a Laka, the god of canoe builders, or Lea ka Wahine, the female god of canoe builders, who showed herself as the 'elepaio bird. Kenika accepted that. But if a broom hitting a light fixture on a manger ceiling could cause a spark that would do what that one spark did, then life itself, and its management, was something you had to take care with. He thought of it as similar to making a canoe. It required a lot of measurement. When you cut, you held your breath against the possibility that you might cut too deeply and do something you could not undo. He began to understand why he respected his superstitions, even though he wasn't sure how they functioned.

Halfway through the week the somewhat penitent Benny had come back to work, he leaned up in his chair, wiped sweat from his forehead with a rag, and said, "I know why you no shoot he'e."

"It's the eyes?"

"No, you no shoot um because he yoah 'aumakua."

Kenika thought a second. God. "What is that exactly?"

"He yoah own personal god."

"Why him and not—"

"Heah da funny paht. He change shape an' color. You change shape and color."

"Jesus," he said. He liked the logic of that. "Do you have one?"

"Honu. Hawkbill turtle, I tink."

"Why?"

"I donno, but I nevah like see um get shot, lay upsai down onna beach wit' eyes runnin', like dey cry."

"So you never shoot them?"

"No, I no mine somebody else shoot um, but I nevah."

"'Kay, I'll never shoot a hawkbill turtle, or an octopus either."

What the octopus did for him he didn't know. Benny told him only "proteck" but how the octopus might do that was another question, and he left it all in that region of peculiar, misty indistinction in his brain where all the other superstitions dwelled.

Others made more sense to him. One day while he was sitting at the dining room table he wrote his name and Angela's name and the names of the children in the margin of the newspaper, and saw the children's names as if for the first time. It was Keoki's that struck him first. The initial three K's of Keoki Lanakila McKay seemed to gather themselves up and welcome, and then blend with the alien K in his last name. It was either coincidence, he thought, or something else. Then he looked at the girls' names: Elizabeth Kaiulani McKay, so the one K welcomed the alien K. It took a little more time with Clarice Mahealani McKay, and he decided that the Hawaiian M welcomed the alien M. And it worked with the parents, Angela's middle name being Maile, and the alien K's in Kenika welcomed by and meshing with the K of his birth. He also realized the almost childish foolishness of this observation, and mentioned it to no one. But Benny's old admonition stayed with him, no take chance.

≈   ≈   ≈

Keoki ate with the same animal gusto that the girls had. He had the benefit of competing feeders, each standing before his little highchair with spoon and jar. "My turn," and Elizabeth would spoon peaches or apple sauce or poi into his mouth, and he would either squish it out between his gums, or spit it at his feeder and squeal with joy, or swallow it, making the loud popping sounds with his lips, his brow furrowed with the same concentration he had shown when nursing. Then Clarice would take her turn. After that Angela would change the diapers and they would watch, fascinated by his pudgy baby-boy anatomy, and wrinkle up their faces at the yellowish contents of the diapers: "Ho, da stink," and, "Mommy, why da poop yellow?" or "Dat wheah shi-shi come from, dat little button ting?"

By the time the 'Aukai, or Sea Traveller, was finished, he was waddling on his fat, sturdy brown legs in the backyard, chasing his more fleet-footed sisters as they went from tree to tree in a yard that was now half shaded by the growth. The shady spots bore the brightly colored fruit that had dropped before they could pick it, mangoes, tangerines, lemons, papaya. The yard was alive with mynahs, rice birds, mejiros, doves. From the middle of the backyard Kenika could look all the way up the hill to his left and see houses, all the way across the cowpasture, more houses. The neighborhood had become three or four neighborhoods, and in the nights they could hear people arguing, especially when it was calm, from up to two hundred yards away.

Closer in, just down off the corner of their yard, it was Larry and Denise Kam, whose arguments were particularly violent and whose relationship was a cruel mystery to Angela, who could not stand listening to them. "Take fish to them," she said once. "Take fruit. Make them feel part of things here."

He tried that, feeling a little foolish, one day when it was oddly quiet. Because the Kams' yard was fenced he went down around the block to the street below theirs and approached the house, wondering if after all Denise Kam was dead, and knocked.

Larry answered, and Kenika could see Denise in the kitchen. "I got some fish for you, aholehole, one small 'uhu," he said, and handed Larry the bag.

"Eh, tanks," he said. "How you guys?"

"Okay, and you?"

"Eh, awright," he said. "Eh, tanks."

But at night it continued, with Angela lying with her head on Kenika's chest, the arm around him tense. Larry Kam yelled and she yelled back, and he used the word "fahk" and "fahkeen" in such a way that the four letters came out in a loud, harsh burst much louder than the yelling around it, so that, dozing off at one in the morning, Kenika still heard the word coming across the cool air like a series of random gunshots.

One evening when they were going at it Angela walked to the corner of the yard to try to mediate, and just before she was about to call to them Denise Kam came through a louvred bedroom window and ended up flat on her back in the grass a few feet below the sill, broken louvre pieces lying all around her. She got up, looked herself over, probably amazed that she was not cut, and yelled, "I calla cops, goddam you!"

Angela asked if she was all right, and she ended up climbing over the low chain-link fence, using a car fender as a step, and then Angela's hands as she jumped into the yard. No, Larry wouldn't hurt the kids. No, she didn't want the cops called. She wanted that stoopit son of a bitch to stop gambling away all his salary on some stoopit fahkeen chickens in Waimanalo, that's what she wanted.

Kenika went over the fence to go talk to Larry, and found him sitting before a beer in the kitchen. "I like cut her head off," he said.

"Well—"

"But cannot, ah?"

"Maybe you should lay off the chickens for a while."

He snorted, drank some beer.

"Need any help cutting new louvres?"

"Nah, I can do um."

Then Denise and Angela were at the door, and then in the kitchen. Denise stood there with her arms folded and glared at Larry, who snorted and looked away, then back. "You hurt?" he asked. She shook her head.

"Somebody might get hurt," Angela said. As soon as she spoke they heard the thumping of feet, and Becky and Stacy Boy came running out.

"Auntie Angela," Becky said. Their expressions showed such normalcy that Kenika was amazed.

"Hi, sweetie," Angela said. Then she looked at Larry and Denise. "So den, everything okay, 'kay?"

"Yeah," Larry said vaguely.

"I'll stop by later," Denise whispered to Angela, which she did, and Kenika, staying out of their way by working in the carport, heard them talking on into the evening.

During long stretches of trinket making, he went alone to the shed, made models of canoes, wind chimes, oeoe whistles, little bowls. Benny's absence was not due to drinking this time. He was given to feeling fatigue and his color was off, as if he were paler than before, so that the dark, bluish patches high on his cheeks were more gray than blue. And he did not seem as strong as he had been. Beer made him fall asleep and he did not have a good appetite. When he suggested that Benny see a doctor, Benny said, "Nah nah nah, I be awright. 'F I see anybody, it Makaila, or one kahuna la'au lapa'au."

"What's that?"

"La'au mean herb—he one herbal doctah. Anyways, it only flu, whatevahs."

"How is Makaila?"

"Not bad," he said. "Memba, he in his eighties."

But Kenika worried about Benny, even though he seemed to drink less beer. It bobbed in the tub at the shed, softly clinking in the water.

During one absence Kenika assumed was like the others, he did his work day by day until he got word of Benny's activities from Momi, who was at the house one day when he got home. "Isn't this cute," she said. "He's down in front of Iolani Palace with a big sign that says, 'No

Statehood!'" She went on to explain that all this statehood stuff was just the kind of thing that would get Benny riled up, and sure enough he was now making a total fool of himself. "I mean he should just wake up—it's nineteen fifty-five, not nineteen hundred. It would be one thing if he wasn't drunk, but—" She had been shopping in downtown Honolulu and had gone up King Street and seen him, and parked the car at the post office and had gone over to talk to him. "He told me to mind my own business."

She had watched for a while as passersby stopped and talked with him, and saw that he was being ridiculed, and then thrown her hands up and left. Kenika had seen the articles about statehood, all of them in favor of it, and had only vague ideas of how he was supposed to think of it. There were articles condemning the idea of the Puerto Rico-type commonwealth status for Hawaii, articles about the Reds and how statehood would put them in their place, about Governor King's plans. Benny, he was sure, hated the idea partly because of his experiences during the war and partly, he guessed, because of the lingering death of all the old traditions that were a part of his family. But what were you supposed to do about a place that had become so Americanized that ninety percent of its people saw themselves as Americans? That same ninety percent felt that it was unjust that Hawaii was not a state. What Benny probably wanted was a complete restoration of a monarchy, with a king and queen.

"I don't know," Kenika said. "If I understand how he thinks, I think he just never liked the idea of this place being diluted by another culture." Secretly he felt a surge of sympathy for Benny. If he knew the mysteries of canoes so well that Kenika would accept everything he said, then what of the mysteries of politics?

"He's a total throwback," Momi said. "That stuff is dead and gone. This is the twentieth century."

"I know."

"I wondered if you might talk to him. I mean it's embarrassing, the whole thing."

"I'll go over tomorrow," he said. "If he's there I'll talk to him."

"You're the only one who can," she said.

It was one of those days when the sky overhead was a deeper blue than he imagined you would see anywhere else, and the sun was almost startlingly bright. He parked at the post office and right away saw him sitting on the sidewalk by the front gate, the sign next to him leaning on the wrought iron fence reading, "No Statehood!" He squinted at it—the sign appeared to be half a piece of sheetrock, four feet by four feet.

Behind Benny, Iolani Palace baked in the midday heat, people in aloha shirts and business suits moving in the recesses of its multiple arched lanais. It was small by European standards, he supposed, but it was still a royal palace, built for a Hawaiian king and queen, and now it was haoles and Japanese walking along in the shade of the lanais and pulling their cars into parking spaces along the flanks and then going down the stairs into the basement section of the palace to their offices. In a way Benny was right. If a queen could be held prisoner in her own palace and her government overthrown, then somewhere down the line someone would have to remind people of that, even if it was Benny. And an illegal overthrow was so blatant a violation that, for some reason, it had become obscured and confused by modern times, to the point that it had now become a mystery to people that it could be thought of as a violation.

He walked across the street and over to Benny, who now seemed to sleep sitting there, huge and dark, not toppling over because of the bulk of his stomach. "Benny?"

He opened his eyes. "Kenika, come sit."

"You should get out of the sun."

"Dey no let me insai da fence," he said. "Da cops I mean. 'Sokay, I Hawaiian. Sun no bodda me. You what? Mongrel. Sun no bodda you too."

Kenika laughed, looking around. He felt a wave of embarrassment creep over him, because the spectacle Benny presented was grotesque and comical. Every detail of his dark, crusty obesity was magnified in the sunlight, all the way down to his huge feet with their jagged, overgrown toenails.

"Dis guy Rayburn?" Benny said. "Speakah da House? He wen' block da statehood vote." He looked at the traffic, thought a moment. "A guy comes by, ask me if I one 'Red,' an' I say maybe an' maybe not, an' he get all huhu."

"Looks like you're about the only guy who doesn't like it."

"What about you? You like it?"

Kenika looked at the palace, then at the lines of parked cars on either side. "No, I guess not, but it might be time to come back to work."

"Nah, you do um."

A line of tourists walked past, half of them looking at the sign and then whispering to one another. Benny waved to them and said, "Eh, howzit? Wheah you folks from?" No one answered him.

As the tourists made their way up the long driveway toward the entryway to the palace, Kenika watched them, wondering where they had come from. They were all spectacularly pale. When they disappeared into the palace, he said, "Well, whaddaya say, you wanna have something to eat?"

"Nah," Benny said. "Not hungry."

"You gonna stay here all day?"

Benny looked at him with bleary irritation. "What, you tink I nuts?"

"No. I just thought we had stuff to do out at the shed."

Three men walked past, then stopped. One was Oriental and the other two haole, one of the haoles wearing aviator's sunglasses. "I like the sign," the one in the aviator's glasses said, coming back toward them. "I mean, the letters are—well shit, they're perfect."

Kenika felt his face flush. The expression of ridicule on the man's face was obvious. The other two, who had moved down the sidewalk, stopped to wait for him. He stepped up closer to Benny. "Hey, my shadow fell on you!" he said enthusiastically. "Does that mean you'll have me killed?" He turned to the others. "Isn't that what they did in old Hawaii? If a person's shadow fell on the king he'd be executed?"

The other two men appeared bored, the Oriental glancing once at the sky.

"Just an expression of an opinion," Kenika said.

"No shit," the man in the aviator's glasses said. The man stepped back to look at the sign, and Benny squinted when the sun hit his face again.

"You no like my sign, den go on," he said. "I no bodda you."

"Oh but you do," the man said. "I think I spent all that G.I. time in the Pacific for a reason, and this ain't it." He stared down at Benny, and Kenika moved closer to them.

"Why don't you just move on," he said.

"Why don't I?" the man said.

"Why you not move allaway back America?" Benny asked.

"Because I live here, mister, that's why. And I don't like your sign."

"Fuck you den," Benny said.

The man's face brightened up, and then he appeared to have become loose and jovial. "Well," he said. "Did you hear what the king just said to me?" He turned to his friends. "You hear what he said?" he called. "Me, who fought for his country? I'm disappointed."

"Not yoah country," Benny said.

"Really!" he said, drawing the word out. "Whose is it? Yours?" The man had moved closer to Benny again, and Kenika stepped partway between them.

"Lay off, okay?" he said.

"You say somethin'?" the man said to him. Then he looked down at Benny. "Hey, you fuckin' slob, you work? You got a job? Or is this your job?"

"He has a job," Kenika said. "So let's just cut it out, okay?"

"You gonna make me?"

Kenika's scalp prickled. So the man would not quit. He stared at the aviator's sunglasses and waited.

"Are you?" the man said. Kenika said nothing, so the man took off his glasses. The skin around his eyes was bluish-white while the rest of his face was sunburned, now almost florid. He folded the glasses shut and put them in a case that looked like a chocolate bar, and slid the case into his back pocket. Kenika felt a surge of tension race through his flesh, and got ready for whatever the man was about to do.

"I guess I am," he said.

The man looked at him. "Well, before I go I want to fold that sign up," he said.

"No, you can leave the sign alone."

"Chip!" one of the friends called. Chip waved them off, staring at Kenika.

"Well," he said with breathy resignation. "I have been warned not to touch the sign!" He shook his head in mock amazement. "So any fuckin' slob can just go ahead and take a day off from being what? A garbage man, perhaps. And sit in front of the legislature with a sign like that."

"Yup," Kenika said.

"Dat a royal palace," Benny said. "It one legislature because you guys stole it."

The man gasped with prissy indignation. A group of five tourists came out the gate, and the man looked at them. "Howdy folks! Beautiful day innit?" They laughed and went on.

"Kenika," Benny said, moving to get up, "gi' me a han', I wanna break dis assho's head."

Kenika put his hand on Benny's shoulder. "That's okay," he said. "He doesn't really mean any harm."

"What, you gonna protect the bum?" the man said.

"Yeah, I'm going to protect his right of freedom of speech."

Kenika began to suspect that the man was all air, and felt less tense than before. The man stood there considering Benny and the sign. "Hey," he said, "at least he spelled the words right."

"He sure did," Kenika said. "Amazing innit?"

Benny laughed—"Hee-hee-hee-hee."

"Any time anywhere," the man said. "I'll take you on."

"'Kay, meet me at Kaena Point tomorrow at dawn," Kenika said.

"Where's that?"

"Hmm, I think we have a problem."

The man now appeared aware that he was being ridiculed, and apparently didn't like the sensation. He snorted, somewhat deflated, and walked off toward his friends.

"Bawk-bawk-bawk," Benny called, imitating a chicken.

"Hey," Kenika said. "Shh!"

"'Kay, we go work now," Benny said.

≈   ≈   ≈

The expansion of Kailua that seemed at first nice, because it brought more neighbors to them, now spread toward Maunawili, and the city was boring a tunnel through two mountains at the pass over to Honolulu. It was said that the tunnel would not harm the beauty of the Pali Lookout, where you stood at the edge of a five-hundred foot drop, sometimes leaning into a fifty-mile an hour wind, with a panorama of the entire verdant bowl that formed Kailua and Kaneohe, and the ocean beyond. Benny felt that it was about the same as taking a drill and running it through the chest of a man, just as he felt that all this talk about statehood was America getting ready to finish the job and drive the point of its flag into the heart of a prone, weakened Hawaii, just like that picture of the flag raising at Iwo Jima.

Although the bid for statehood failed this time, Kenika didn't know what to think, about statehood or the tunnel, except that he suspected the result would be more people, and his own town seemed the perfect example: it seemed always under construction, at least the areas near his house. Huge tracts of land lay wounded and parching in the sun and then blown by the lashing winds that came off the ocean. The areas were cut with deep crevices from the powerful, driving rains that came between November and March, so that the stream outflow into Kailua would make the ocean water brown. And the marsh, that was changing too, because one of the city's projects was to fill part of it in and expand the buildable areas around the lake, and later he saw that it was by backfilling with clay, huge chunks of sidewalk, black slabs of macadam, odd rocks and other debris.

But their original little outpost of houses was being engulfed by the expansion, as if the town were coming out to absorb it like an amoeba. Even though they always went shopping with Angela, the girls still seemed to think of Kailua town as a place as remote as Honolulu, and would always gasp with delight when they learned they were going there. It meant the shopping and a trip to the Harada store to buy cracked seed. Angela started resisting their pleas for seed because they had developed a tendency to gasp at the wrong times. One incident occurred while they were playing marbles with fish eyes after dinner, something they always did. They never had any problem with fish bones, but one evening Clarice decided to eat one of the hard, white fish eyes, and just as she put it in her mouth Elizabeth told her that the eye was looking down her throat, at which she gasped, and then choked on the eye. Angela had to slap her back until she coughed it up, and said, "See? I to' you, how can I let you buy seed when you do dat?"

They promised not to gasp. They had been eating seed since they were tiny, traded it with Becky Kam at the back fence. Kenika couldn't stand it because it was too sweet and/or too salty, with a strange, heavy licorice taste. This mystified Angela, and he told her that he grew up on haole candy and supposed he could never change the way his tongue reacted to such things. Angela finally let them know one day that the suspension was off, they were going to the Harada store to buy seed, and they both began their gasps of delight, but managed to gag them off into a kind of grotesque hiccup before they were finished.

At the store they would stand before the double line of heavy jars, taped around the top to keep the glass lids from chipping them, each with a hot, sweaty quarter in her fist. It would take ten or fifteen minutes for them to choose, while Angela talked story with the proprietor and Kenika stood there reading the dizzying list of offerings: Li Hing Mui, Sweet Whole Seed, Rock Salt Plum, Dry Lemon Peel, Sweet Sour Plum, Wet Li Hing Mui, Dried Strip Mango, Pickled Mango, Shredded Mango, and on and on. He would look at the jars and see some of the stuff sitting there looking like rotting fruit, in a smoky liquid that darkened toward the bottom. All he could handle was dried cuttlefish, dried tako, which was octopus, and dried aku, or tuna.

The girls decided that they should see "The Wizard of Oz" down at the Kailua Theater, because every kid on the block went around all day singing "Over The Rainbow." They had never seen a movie before, so Angela arranged for Keoki to stay at the Lanikai house so they could go see the movie. It turned out to be a nightmare. Apparently the girls had some trouble convincing themselves that it was only a story, and there was so much gasping that Angela made them spit the seed out into a popcorn bag and collected all the rest. When the house spun up in a tornado, when monkey-like ogres flew off a castle parapet and finally when the witch melted, her shoes rolling up like party favors, they burrowed in terror under their seats or behind their parents' backs.

Finally they took the twins downtown to the school, shepherded them to their assigned room, and watched them as they walked in, each with a pink dress, new go-aheads with little daisies wobbling on the straps, and identical lunchboxes, braided hair swinging behind them. Kenika and Angela observed with guarded pride that they took to the expanding world beyond their own yard with a fearless interest in exploration, which secretly scared Kenika into allowing his imagination to concoct all sorts of disaster. When they came home late from one of their forays up the little hill across the road or down to the construction sites on the extension of the block below them, Angela would always sigh with relief and exasperation, her nightmarish fears gone, and say, "Where have you been?" or if she had been particularly worried, "Wheah you was!" Sometimes Kenika would go out and look for them, and find them walking past Becky Kam's house dragging cast-off lumber and carrying sweaty, metal-smelling fistfuls of nails. They finally took them to the Liberty House store and bought them little watches.

There was a golf course hole just over the hill to the north of their house, one of the holes for the course at Lanikai, and one day the girls came back with balls, and then proceeded to dig little holes all over the yard, into which they sank little flags made of construction paper and twigs, and using metal curtain rods which turned at a ninety degree angle at the ends. They spent hours playing "garf." Angela asked them where they got the balls, and Elizabeth said, "Inna weeds, an' den some come bouncin' up da lawn an' we got dem too."

The golf course? "Dat too fah!" Angela said. "No go dat fah any more!"

Another time they came sprinting around the corner of the street in breathless terror and yelled to Kenika that "Da reds is comin'!" Kenika went out to the driveway to meet the reds, and the first one who walked up to him, dressed in a black suit, his face burned to resemble the shell of a cooked lobster, asked him if he was aware that the return of Jesus was imminent.

≈   ≈   ≈

For a long period of time Kenika went to the shed figuring there would be a fifty-fifty chance that Benny would show up, and got used to going on with the manufacturing of tourist junk by himself. When Benny did show up he would work along on the canoe models and wind chimes as he always had, or if he was tired, he would go into the little back room and sleep. At least when he came to the shed and slept, Kenika knew where he was, and went on with his work without thought of any more than simply making enough stuff to take over to Maxwell or to the other vendors he was gradually getting to know. But at the back of his mind was a gnawing worry that the manufacturing of canoes, something he felt he was almost skilled enough to do by himself, was for some reason going the way of blacksmithing and the manufacture of buggies. He would wait for Benny to show up, thinking that he would squish through the rotted leaves to tell him that it was time to build another canoe, but it didn't happen.

Despite the declining orders for trinkets and the lack of any for canoes, he had to keep up with things. So he was a manufacturer of tourist trinkets, and it was a decent job. When Benny was not at the shed he sometimes got bored with making trinkets, and sat sometimes for hours trying to figure out what else he might do with wood. He went down to the log stash next to the foundation of the shed and pulled away rotted palm fronds and dead leaves, and found one rough hull a little less than forty-feet long inside the hauling knobs, and two very large but short logs, and a split log that looked useless. All of the logs were partly submerged in black silt which had built up against them over the years, and he doubted that any of it would be much good. Under the shed he found large, two-inch thick crosscut pieces of koa, tables Benny had told him, and studied the gray surfaces, trying to detect the quality of the grain. He took one small crosscut section out, about thirty inches in diameter, and carried it up into the shed, sanded it a little and found a beautiful, swirling grain that held the faint suggestions of surf, or clouds.

On his way home he considered the idea of making a picture in the wood using chisels, a relief picture he thought it was called, and decided to look into the art books they had accumulated over the years.

When he got home he saw a hole-perforated sheet of corrugated metal roofing in the backyard. "What's that?"

Angela looked up from a lei she was working Spanish Moss into and said, "Girls brought that home. I could hear them coming a mile, dragging that thing all twanging and bonging. Then they asked me for a coffee can and two spoons."

"What for?"

"I don't know, but they went off."

They came back as usual just late enough that Angela was up from the table and standing at the door. "How many times I to' you, five o'clock!" The girls each raised their arms and scowled at their little watches.

"It five-fifteen," Clarice said.

"Five-sixteen," Elizabeth said.

"Not."

"Your watch junk!"

"What's that black stuff all over your clothes?"

Kenika looked out the door. Their coffee can was full of tar. It was on their hands, knees, shorts.

"We making one canoe," Clarice said. "Dis fo' fill up da holes. Road tar junk but."

"Light po' tar mo' betta, j'like bubbugum."

"We scrape um offa road and light po'. Daddy, can we have a hammah an' nails and wood and stuffs lahdat?"

"We foun' two-by-foah fo' wae an' broken basebaw bat fo' manu, den we make ama wit' big tchreebranch."

"Yeah, an' we squeeze dat roofing fo' make hull, make one ono canoe."

"I like make paddow too."

"Me too, I need one paddow."

"Borrow Mommy's cookie pans and nail um to sticks."

"We make seat fo' Keoki."

"Inna front."

"Yeah."

"Daddy?"

The creativity of the idea, and the breathless zeal with which they described it, amazed him. They were not quite nine years old, but their plan had merit, so he helped them build it, deciding not to change any of the ideas they came up with. It was, after all, theirs. The project took two days over one weekend, interspersed with trips to the beach to teach Keoki to swim. They bent the corrugated sheeting, and he used pliers to turn the sharp edges over so they would not be cut. The project had one keen observer, Keoki, sitting in his sand box with a soup ladle and a toy dumptruck, asking questions throughout: "Can I ride dat by myse'fs?" "You make me one paddow too? But round?" "Why you put black dots on um, hah?" "Hey, can make room fo' Mommy too, yah?" "Can make shi-shi in deah?"

"Clarice," Elizabeth whispered after a string of questions that lasted a full minute, "how you like we put his seat onna ama, yah? Ho, talk talk talk da boy."

When it was finished Kenika had one bad flash of irrational fear: who would bless it? He had to laugh at himself, carrying that requirement to this canoe, but he was still scared. The girls had named it Wa'a 'Aka, the mixture of "laugh" and "canoe" so it meant, to them at least, the Laughing Canoe. He found the stamp "Boise Cascade" on one of the two-by-fours, and reasoned that of course the metal was not mined from this island, so the materials were alien, even the ama, shaved into a slight banana shape out of a light four-by-four piece of redwood. Nevertheless, the night it was finished he went outside with a tiny handful of the coarse sea salt Angela used in cooking, and sprinkled it on the galvanized hull so that it produced a metallic tinkling, and whispered, "Okay. Maika'i ka lolo ana."

≈   ≈   ≈

One morning when he walked across the lawn at the Marumotos' toward the path, Mrs. Marumoto came out of her house and waved him over.

"How you doin'?" he asked.

"Fine, okay," she said. "Benny call Kenji, send message."

"Which means Benny can't come today?"

Mrs. Marumoto, who knew about Benny's waywardness, laughed and shook her head, then said, "Come come."

Mr. Marumoto told him that Benny had an order from a Mr. Stevenson, the buyer of the Lapa Uila, who wanted another single log canoe. "Yeah, I remember him, but I didn't like him much," Kenika said.

"Seh peh six tousan' fo' new canoe," Mr. Marumoto said. "Beeg money. Buyah no' mo' fine single-log canoe. Peh beeg money."

"There's one good one left. Listen, is Benny coming up?"

"Cannot. Benny sick, 'ass why."

"Where is he?"

"Wit' Darnay? Memba him?"

"Darnay takes good care of him. Is it his same apartment downtown?"

"No, Seaside Avenue, Waikiki. Benny deah. Sick but."

"Did he say how sick?"

"On'y dat he cannot come. He tell, get Kama boys he'p winch log. Kama boys live up da shtreet heah, little way." He pointed up the dirt road. "But Benny, he like see you bumbye. Soon."

"Did he sound like he'd been, you know, boozing at all?"

Mr. Marumoto shook his head, and took on a strange, perplexed look. He reached out and grabbed Kenika's upper arm. "Come eensai," he said. "Drink juice."

Kenika did not like the look on Mrs. Marumoto's face either. She poured him a glass of guava juice, from which he took a sip. He had never been all the way in their house before. Through the doorway to the living room he saw a wall of framed photographs of what he assumed were their many children and grandchildren, and beyond that, a little shelf with a Buddha and incense sticks in a sand dish, and he could smell the faint traces of incense in the kitchen. "You have a really nice place here," he said. "I see all those pictures. That's what I'd like to have when I'm older."

"Kenika, you will," Mrs. Marumoto said. "Oh dat Angela, she so lovely, an' your keikis, oh my!"

"Thanks."

"Kenika," Mr. Marumoto said, "Benny me fren's long long long time. I know him from smaw kid time. He tell dat he sick, not hung ovah, but sick, no lie. He like see you."

Kenika felt a little swoon of fear, and then a sensation of regret that he had been so stupid to assume that Benny's pale look was no more than drying out. "Did he say how?"

"Weak, get headache, hahd fo' get air. No like eat. Sick pretty bad I tink."

"I no like dis," Mrs. Marumoto said. "We get um heah, we fix um, but he no go doctah, li'dat."

"Use dakine kahuna," Mr. Marumoto said. "Chant, make tea outta leafs, stuffs li'dat. Good, but why not go doctah too?"

"I'll go see him," Kenika said. "Do you have the address?"

He did. He pulled it off a little pad and handed it to Kenika, then smiled. "Kenika," he said, "I memba you come chucka chucka chucka up da hill on dat bike. I tink, 'ho, dis da boy from Mahs?' But Benny, he come all whatchucall, positive when you come. Beeg change, fo' once he all excited about stuff."

"Well, he means a lot to me."

He found himself grinding his teeth as he drove, his arms tense and his hands gripping the steering wheel too hard. He went around Makapuu Point because of all the construction on the Pali Highway. He knew Seaside Avenue because it was just a block from the cottage The Captain had rented what seemed like a hundred years ago.

The apartment was in a two-story stucco building with plumeria and ti plants surrounding the small parking lot, and he recognized Benny's Chevrolet parked in one of the stalls. Darnay's apartment was on the ground floor, and his knock produced a thin, younger man of mixed race, who let him inside the darkened living room and then went into one of the bedrooms. Benny and Darnay were sitting on a sagging couch watching a television set, apparently a cowboy movie, Benny with a bottle of beer between his huge thighs. He did not look as pale as at the shed.

"Kenika, come sit."

"How're you guys?"

"Fine," Darnay said.

For five minutes they talked about family, stopping when Ken Maynard rode his white horse through the sagebrush with unshaven bad guys in hot pursuit, their guns blazing, producing puffs of smoke that the galloping horses left behind.

Finally Kenika said, "So, we're gonna build a canoe."

"Look," Benny said, "I may seem like I'm awright, but I not."

"Hey, you're havin' a beer."

"On'y to make stomach fee' good, 'ass all."

"Kenika," Darnay said, "he can't really eat, and gets dizzy spells and headaches. He cannot."

"Have you seen a doctor?"

"No, but I getting bettah. Be okay bumbye."

"Okay, you want me to start it?"

"No, dis one fo' you."

"What does that mean?"

"Time fo' you make one. I get bettah, I come he'p, but you do um. Kama boys uppa road, dey come he'p you winch um, an' any odda heavy stuff."

"What name does it have?"

"You name um."

"No, that's your job."

"No no. Yoah turn. Tink up one good name, not da usual Hoku dis an' Hoku dat or wahine names. Make up a good one."

Kenika looked at Darnay, who nodded his head once, then looked at his father. The expression said, do it and don't ask questions.

"'Kay."

"Box eensai sleepin' room, have alla stuffs, phone numbahs of guys who can come if you get problem. You know alla guys we sell touris' shit to. Take time off canoe, make win' chime, alladat. Call um up, ask how many dey want, 'kay?"

"'Kay."

"Den when I bettah, I come up."

"When do they want it?"

"Mahch."

"I was wondering. How old is that log?"

Benny stared at the ceiling, then said, "Come up I tink nineteen eight. Fifty yeahs."

Kenika shook his head and shrugged. "What if it isn't any good?"

When he left, Darnay walked out into the parking lot with him. "What's the matter with him?" Kenika asked.

"You ever heard of uremia?"

"No."

"Kidney trouble. He has high blood pressure too, and I'm worried about him. He won't go to the doctor, so I went and asked, and they suggested that I change his eating, not let him drink beer. I've been about half successful, but James cooks for him, the right kind of food."

"James?"

"My roommate."

"What about Momi, Irene and George?"

"He doesn't want to bother them with this. I asked him to stay with me, and I'm glad I did. We've said more to each other in the last few weeks than in all our lives, I think."

"Good, that's gonna help him too. Thanks."

≈   ≈   ≈

During the week following his visit to Benny, the weather became foul, with lashing rain and wind, and he went to the shed only two days. There he sat, unable to think of what to do, and the prospect of making models didn't help, although he knew he had to because his income was mostly from stuff like that. The old Pontiac was on its last legs, there were always little bills from the pediatrician, and now he was beginning to regret that extra prepayment on the house. The canoe meant big money, but he hated the idea of having to make a canoe alone because it was not his to do alone. He was not ready for that. Benny would get better, and then they would make the canoe, and Benny would name it.

His doubt must have showed at home, because he found Angela looking at him from time to time, with an expression that seemed to suggest that she suspected he was sick and had decided not to tell her. He had explained Benny's illness to her, along with the business of his having to make a canoe by himself, but did not mention anything about his fear of it.

One windy night after they put the children to bed she sat with him at the table while he showed her a picture of a relief carving. He described what he was thinking of, making a picture and trying to sell it. "All the real standard tourist things come from the Philippines now, shell stuff and all that."

"I like making things like that," she said. "You know, I've been thinking."

He felt heat rising into his face. He had heard this before, that two of her friends went to college, but most of them were working, had been for years, downtown at Liberty House and in the new supermarket. And when he thought of her working he pictured her stuck as a checkout lady with a demanding, unreasonable boss.

"Kenika," she said, and giggled. "Even inna dark I see you turn purple."

"I'm not turning purple. I just—"

"Momi an' me talked." She giggled again. "She said you'd turn purple." She put her hand on his arm. "I'm talking about opening a flower shop, that's all. Momi an' me."

"Really?"

"Make leis, flower, kukui nut, seed, all that. Kailua's so big now, so many kids graduate from school, so many weddings. Momi said she take care of permits and all, and there's a store for rent right in town." She went on to point out that Keoki would be going to school, they could use the money, at which he flushed again, and she liked nothing more than making things like that. They would sit and make stuff all day, talk story.

Finally she said, "Can I?"

And he said, "Sure, I mean," and she cut him off by clapping her hands and producing a huge, artificial sigh of relief.

"Why did you ask?"

"Man da boss, right?"

"I never felt that way."

"Really?"

"In there," and he nodded his head toward their room, "am I always on top?"

She laughed, but too loud, then put her finger to her lips. They waited, listening for the kids, and then she said, "Top, side, upside down. You pilau buggah, you."

"Sorry, but I can get enough of the jungle bunny."

"Oooo, heah come da skinny ginnie, heah come da octopus."

"You juicy savage."

"Oooo, I like sit on you tonight, but wheah?"

"Uh, listen, my jaw is still healing from—" She slapped him on the arm, again too loud, and they waited, listening.

"Aren't we getting a little old for all this?" he asked.

She thought, then said, "No."

$$\approx \qquad \approx \qquad \approx$$

If she had the energy to think of starting that shop, then he would throw off all the doubts and build the canoe. At the shed, which shuddered in the wind that pasted leaves and red and yellow flower petals to the screen, he held the plans down with pieces of wood and then grabbed the cant hook, a shovel and a flat-blade chisel and went down the stairs to the log. He began digging at the silt under it, muttering as he went, "So, you're not Hoku this or Hoku that, eh? No Shooting Star or Morning Star or what, Hokuwelowelo, Comet, huh?" And then the wahine names, "No Malia or Leilani or Maile, is that it?" What the hell, he'd figure something out. When he had removed most of the dirt from the underside facing him, he decided to rock it and check whether or not it was rotten. It bore the crude shape of a canoe, hulking with the cut V where the inside of the hull would be. He drove the point of the cant hook into the side, and then kicked the hinged point of the swinging ice-tong grip into the wood a foot and a half over the log, and pulled. There was a sucking sound, and he could see the length of it move. Good. Then he reversed the cant hook and pushed to see if he could roll it up a little.

When he pushed up he heard the sucking sound over the wind, and at the same time felt something prickly moving on his foot, and let go of the hook and looked down. Like a six-inch string of some dark fluid, it went over the rest of his foot, tickling the skin, and went into a little gulley, and again like a string of dark liquid oozed down over stones, twigs, and then vanished into a crevice under a rock. It was grayish, and had those light blue legs, as he had noticed centipedes that hid in very wet places sometimes had. He stood there staring at the crevice for a minute, the wind from time to time nudging him. He thought he should lift the rock and kill it, and then thought, no.

He went into the shed. He looked at his foot and saw no little holes there, and knew he had not been bitten, but still his foot itched, and he kicked his go-ahead off and rubbed where the centipede had walked on him. Then it dawned on him what was wrong. He had stomped down there like a fool and moved a log that had not been moved in fifty years. It had lain there sleeping, waiting for the day some worthy person would come along to move it, and then find the canoe inside. Whether or not he was worthy was one thing, but the arrogant assumption that he was had caused him to step over the line. He had driven the point of the cant hook into it without thinking, leaving a hole that seemed redder than koa should be, like a wound. He needed permission, or at least he needed to tell them that he wanted to do this, and he thought, whether they liked it or not? No, he could not think that way either.

The path up through the woods was drying out, although the wind was stronger the farther up he went. He carried an orange from his lunchbox, and stopped at the ti plant to wrap it. The sharp, vertical mountains were shrouded in swirling clouds, and off to his right and down toward the ocean, which was barely visible because of the salt mist blowing off it, clouds of ferrous dust swirled toward the mountains like reverse breaking waves.

He walked out onto the flat rectangle of black rocks. He leaned down and placed the wrapped orange on the same rock he had earlier placed bananas, stood up, buffeted by the wind, and whispered, "Hi." Then he thought about Angela and the kids, and said, "Thanks." In the near distance the trees shook violently, and he looked up at the mountains. "I have two things, one, Benny is sick and if there's," and he thought, if there's anything you can do to help, I hope you will. "Down there," he said, "I was being sort of arrogant. I didn't mean it. I'm here to ask permission to make a canoe." Then he thought, all right, done, and turned to leave. But something was not right, he felt, and stopped. It wasn't anything in the setting, or in the way he presented himself. It was the name. He turned back and said, "I have no name." Then he added, "For the canoe." He could not leave without giving the canoe a name, and he became confused. Hoku this and Hoku that. He had to give it one, and he stood, staring at the mountains disappearing into the clouds, and at the waving trees. "Makani," he whispered. Wind. He laughed. But what kind of wind? Divine? Royal? Fast? "Makani," he said. Then he whispered, "'Ula." This was even worse, wind that is red. But he hung onto a strange, almost gleeful sensation that it now had a name, no matter how strange it was. "'Kay, it is called Makani 'Ula," he said, again feeling as if he were exuding some kind of willfully-stubborn and inadvisable confidence in the sound of the name. He backed out of the heiau, and went down the path.

At the shed he sat, still feeling the itchiness of the skin on his foot. Wind-red. Makani 'Ula, actually more properly translated as The Red Wind. He moaned at the illogical strangeness of the name, but knew that he could not change it now. He could not assume that deviating from the process he had learned was legal. He had to look those words up, because he knew of the pitfalls of the language, that there might be something in the haphazard selection of those words that would ridicule the canoe. You could find a beautiful, lilting Hawaiian word and name your child with it, he knew, and discover ten years later that the other meaning of the word was something like "rotted cabbage head."

He went back down the stairs to the log. He picked up the flat chisel and placed its blade on the wood. With the shovel shaft he tapped, until a quarter-inch thick curl of the black wood turned up and fell off. It was gray inside. He placed the blade on the gray wood and tapped again, and the gray curl rose and fell off, and underneath, what he saw made him draw his breath in, because not only was the wood fresh, bright and beautifully-grained, it was ginger koa that bore a fiery hue that anyone would call red, as if it had lain there in the mud all those years waiting for someone to call it red, and he knew then that he would not change the name. "'Kay," he whispered, "you are The Red Wind."

As he drove home he found again that he gripped the wheel too tightly, because he feared the words. He was almost afraid to look them up.

One of Angela's afternoon things with the kids was weeding the gardens in the backyard, and while they were doing that, Keoki down on his haunches picking tiny shoots while the girls showed him what this plant was and that plant was, he went to the dictionary to look the words up. 'Ula bothered him the most, and skipping over the extended explanations and definitions that didn't apply, he read the following: "Red, scarlet; brown, as skin of Hawaiians; to appear red." And the second meaning, "Sacred; sacredness; regal," the fourth, "Blood of great value, as royal blood," the seventh, "A ringing in the ears, as due to rising in altitude, believed by some to be a sign that one is being talked of," the eighth, "Ghost, spirit, footprint (of) spirits." He felt a surge of a kind of breathless amazement shoot through his flesh. If anything the word was perfect. Then he looked up Makani: "Wind, breeze; gas in the stomach." He worried about gas, but then reasoned that "wind" as gas was figurative, and that, for example, the author Margaret Mitchell did not mean "Gone With The Wind" to be interpreted as "vanished in a fart."

He sat back in the chair and stared out the window at Angela and the kids in the back yard. So it was The Red Wind, and the oddness of the name, which had all along held its own logic, and which he himself had been unaware of when it made its way into his head, seemed much more like a gift than an invention.

Through Mrs. Marumoto he got the Kama boys to come and help him put the log in the shed. Mrs. Marumoto went up to their house to pot orchids with Mrs. Kama, which they sold to nurseries in Honolulu. On the day they were to show up, Kenika found them waiting just on the other side of the little stream. They were both around six feet tall, and their upper bodies were massive, their legs thick, hands and feet huge, and their skin was almost black from the sun, their hair singed to a dark copper.

The log weighed around three thousand pounds, and the method of getting it into the shed was to slide it up the two wet, oozing logs, while inside the shed Kenika pulled on a rope sent under and back over the log. When the log was pushed up a foot of so, he would pull, then wrap the rope around a beam so as to keep the log from sliding back.

"Uh, do you guys know how to—"

"Uh-huh," the older Kama boy said. His name was Kopa, short for 'Iakopa, or Jacob. Kopa also meant soap. The younger, about eighteen, was Alika, or Alex.

He didn't need the cant hook. The Kama boys went to one end of the log, got under the hauling knob, and both lifted at once, and in that sound of sucking mud it came up, the two bodies under it vibrating powerfully, their feet sinking into the mud. They pivoted it around and dropped it down, then went to the other end and repeated this. "Lightah," Alika said.

"Closah da shed too," Kopa said.

When the log was in position to slide up into the shed Kenika found a space under it and ran the rope through, and then took it around one of the heavy beams set inside the bench.

Within half an hour the log sat, V cut up, in the cradles, and the Kama boys were covered with mud and rotted leaves. He told them to have a seat, and reached for his wallet. Ten dollars each, he thought, because it was hard work.

Kopa Kama shook his head. "Was one favah, 'ass why," he said.

"But look at your clothes. C'mon, take it."

"Uh-uh. Favah."

He stared at them. Then he turned and pulled three beers out of the wash tub. "You want one?" he asked. Kopa nodded, and Alika looked at Kopa, who nodded, at which Alika nodded to Kenika.

Through a silence that lasted three or four mintues they drank. At one point Alika burped and said, "Excuse me."

"'Kay," Kenika said. "What if I asked you back for something that isn't a favor?"

"'Ass okay," Kopa said.

He stood up and pointed to a two-man saw hanging on a hook on the wall. "That's a rip saw," he said. "We have to saw the log lengthwise over this V here," and he touched the log at the point under which the ni'ao, or hull rim now waited. "It'll take one or two days, because rip cutting is slow. Can you do that? I mean do you have the time?"

"Yeah."

"Uh-huh."

"The cut has to be precise, so the whole thing will be measured out before we start. Take a whole slab right off the top, almost level, but just a little curved down at the center. We sort of imitate the line of a finished canoe so we can find it inside."

Kopa nodded.

He got out three more beers and they sat in silence for a few more minutes. "Where do you guys go to school?" he asked.

"We go University. Manoa."

"Really. What do you study?"

"Plant biology," Kopa said. "Him too," and he indicated his brother. "The scientific side of agriculture. If, say, you know all the most damaging pests in, say, the sugar industry, then study the most profitable and nonpolluting ways of getting rid of them, then you're doing something. Long way to go but."

"Hey, that's great," Kenika said. Kopa had slid into formal English without any transition, and had ended with pidgin where he started.

"We gotta go," Kopa said. "Surf's gonna be up."

≈   ≈   ≈

If a human being can fall in love with a piece of wood, then Kenika found that he was in a love affair the intensity of which he could not put into words. Every careful chop of the adze, which produced a deep, resonant sound from the entire length of The Red Wind, brought away a chip of wood whose richness of grain astounded him, and he felt guilty, in fact horrible at times, that Benny was not there to see it.

It was the log that a person like Benny might have dreamed of all his life, now in the hands of a confused novice convinced that it would be wasted on his own haste or incompetence. The wood was sacred. The Red Wind was in the hands of an alien, one not born worthy of it, and more than anything else he feared that he didn't have the skill to do it justice. He had to have the nerve, or the arrogance, he wasn't sure, to cross beyond that. He went to Darnay's house to talk to Benny about it as frequently as he could, and tried to put his doubt into words.

First was the name itself. "Eh, what you call um?" Benny asked, just after Kenika and the Kama boys had finished the removal of the top slab, for which the Kama boys made thirty dollars each, pay Kenika thought was miserly and they apparently thought, looking down at the bills in their sawdust-plastered hands, extravagant to the point of ridiculousness. And he cleared his throat at Benny's question, said, "Makani 'Ula," and waited.

Benny considered the name for five seconds, staring at the blank television screen, and then smiled, nodded, and said, "'Ass beautiful." He kept nodding. "Beautiful."

Then he showed Benny a chip of the red wood, and he studied it, nodded again. Kenika went on to explain that he had pulled the name out of the air up at the heiau, the word red totally arbitrary, even though he had seen how red it was from the cant hook hole, and cut into the log to find what Benny held in his hand.

"Dey gave um to you," Benny whispered. He shook his head in contemplative amazement.

"That's what I thought."

In their talk he hinted around the possibility that Benny might come up and advise him, and noticed now, after all the haste and excitement about relating to him the name and the beginning of the work, that Benny did not look good, that the characteristic oily, dark face, the sharpness in his strange eyes, the healthy burliness of his body, had all changed. His ankles and feet looked swollen to the point of bursting and the skin was bluish and scabbed.

So he finally asked, "How are you doing? Healthwise, I mean."

"Eh, I getting bettah. Bumbye I chase wahine o'hea," he said, indicating the direction of the beach. "No worry, I come shed bumbye."

But he did not. There came that time when Kenika rose up from the hull and whispered, "I can't do this," and sat on the chair. He was supposed to use Benny's steel calipers to measure hull thickness, but he was afraid of that, because he was not sure he could close one end and look at the other and see the exact gap he wanted. The calipers themselves might lie to him. As for the thickness of the bottom of the hull, again he feared the curve, feared that he would not be able to achieve the perfect shape as the thickness of the hull increased in the bottom curve, and swept inward as you went fore and aft. Benny had a method of measurement that seemed backward, but was at the same time foolproof—he had two long sticks that you held in one hand, one stick up to a little brass plate on a ceiling beam, the other, gripped with the first, down to the bench. You extended the two sticks that were made into one by your grip so that you touched the plate and the bench, and then made a mark on the stick. Then you put the bottom stick into the hull of the canoe and the top stick against the brass plate and looked at your mark, then added another mark where the bottom stick had slid in your grip upward: four and a half inches. That was how thick the bottom of the hull was, at least in those places where the hull contacted the bench. Out fore and aft, you had to brace the hull at an angle so that the bottom contacted the bench. Four and a half inches. Too much.

His answer to the problem was to work tentatively, to measure ten times more than might be necessary, and he knew that if he was too tentative, the hull would weigh five hundred pounds rather than four hundred. Some of the measurements required that he walk around the canoe on the singing board, and now it said, "why?" each time, so that he would mutter, "I don't know why." At times, bent over and planing for hours, he would develop cramps in his back and shoulder blades. He would take a break and pick up the thin adze called ko'i kupa 'ai ke'e, swivel-headed for narrow spaces, and gouge in the raised, narrowed ends of the inside of the hull so that he could stand up straighter. He would lie down inside the hull, and plane or chip with the ko'i kalai or carving adze in a prone position, and more than once, fatigued to the point of giggling helplessly, he put his head down and fell asleep, and in the curved belly of the Makani 'Ula, dreamed of it cutting through the water like a barracuda, the shafts of paddles thumping its beautiful red sides like a heartbeat.

Benny reassured him. "No be afraid of it. Jus' feel wit' da eyes, a'ways feel wit' da eyes." And week by week Benny seemed thinner, more wan and almost listless, as if Kenika's descriptions of the Makani 'Ula meant less and less to him, and the possibility that he would be coming back got more and more remote, like something dropped in the ocean and fading down out of sight. And Kenika would say, "God, I wish you could see it. I wish—" and Benny would put his hand on Kenika's shoulder and say, "Eh, I will bumbye. No worry."

He took days off because he was ahead of schedule for a March deadline, and helped Momi and Angela at their flower shop, a little storefront on Kuulei Road two blocks toward the ocean from the town's four corners. There was a shade tree out front, so it tended to be cool inside, and gradually took on the fragrance of all the flowers Momi and Angela had collected from aunties and neighbors, from growers in Waimanalo and Kaneohe. The Santiago family had so many connections that the shop became the concern of around thirty or forty close relatives and friends, and Kenika imagined that without some control, imposed by Momi, the place could easily have been chest-deep in orchids, bird of paradise, ti leaves, Pele's hair, ginger, and all those other flowers prized by the women and unknown to Kenika because of their Hawaiian names. So he would walk in at three-thirty or four and find Angela and the kids, Momi, Irene and the wizened Tutu Elizabeth, sometimes Clarice Malama and others, all sitting at a huge table spread out with flowers and various kinds of seeds: Job's tears, kukui nuts, and others whose names went in one ear and out the other because of their verbal complexity. Canoe terminology was the best he could manage, at least for now.

His contacts at the shops in Waikiki turned out to be good targets for their seed work, mostly leis and other decorations made out of seeds. Mr. Maxwell studied one of their creations, a lei made out of tiny, brown haole koa seeds that Angela had boiled and dried, strung on thin fishing line and then a number of these strung lines braided and tied in such an elaborate manner that he looked at the knotting with a jeweler's eyepiece and said, "Three dollars, and I'll take all of these you can make. This is amazing. How'd they figure this out?"

Kenika told him that he watched them make them sometimes, but he had no idea how they did it. Then at the shop he told them about Mr. Maxwell's offer, at which their eyes widened, and Clarice and Elizabeth stared at each other, and when he asked about how they figured out the knotting, they looked at each other and shrugged. "Mommy taught me," Angela said.

And Momi said, "Tutu Elizabeth, I guess."

"We know how fo' make um too," Clarice said.

"Yeah," Elizabeth said. "We get tchree dolla too?"

"I guess," he said.

"Den me too," Keoki said, "'cause I make um too. 'An I go skoo."

Yes, Keoki went skoo. After school the girls would walk with him the short distance to the shop, and they would stay there until it closed at five. And on weekends they would either go to the beach and fish or paddle the Wa'a 'Aka, or they would go into the woods on the mountain side of what was left of the original Pali Road and look for Job's tears, bananas, avocado, mountain apple, haole koa seeds, thimbleberries. He would watch them in the shop, and his appreciation for all that they had made for themselves would be offset by the cloying fear of what seemed inevitable, that he would inherit from Benny the responsibility of the business, and he didn't feel either prepared for it or qualified for it. With the responsibility came the problem of protecting the reputation, which went back more than a hundred years. It was as if he was the lucky imposter who had all of this dumped in his lap.

But he made his way through most of the component parts. By then it was rainy season and Christmas vacation, and during one of Kenika's visits to Waikiki, Benny claimed that he was going through a phase of better health, to the point that he walked on Waikiki Beach and visited friends who lived in the cottages off Kuhio Avenue.

Kenika took Angela and the kids to visit him on New Year's Eve so they could watch the neighborhood fireworks, and blow off a few of their own. Inside Darnay's apartment James had set up a table of exotic foods, sashimi, various kinds of poke with seaweed, asparagus which he had dyed blue and devilled eggs he had dyed pink. There were blue peach slices, there was purple macaroni salad, orange daikon radish, bright red cauliflower chunks, and champagne. The three children went around the table filling their plates, and the expressions on their faces seemed to show that they felt they were in some bizarre but pleasant dream, the roar building outside and this incredible layout of brightly-colored food before them. The girls would look, gasp with delight, and whisper, "Ho, da pretty!" James stood by the hall watching with a kind of giggling triumph because everyone, adults included, seemed to stare a long time at what they were putting on their plates, as if some process of recognition were necessary for the selection of each food. Nothing was eaten without some slow, careful experimentation, eyes searching blank middle distances while the tongue interpreted, considered, and then accepted. Of course, macaroni salad.

Benny sat in his easy chair, and when Angela asked him if he was coming out to watch the fireworks he waved his hand at her and said, "Nah nah nah." In driveway after driveway there was the setting off of thousands of firecrackers, many of which were strung in dense lines on the pavement and then up, suspended from long bamboo poles along the street, so that they could detonate up rapidly in an ear-splitting roar that would become a brief but violent explosion at the top. In a jovial competition of noise, each family tried to outdo the next, so that the roar was universal. Kenika's five bundles of firecrackers in the apartment parking lot didn't add much, although he got the chance to school Keoki on the use of matches and firecracker lighting. By the time midnight was upon them the visibility was around a hundred feet because the air was so thick with smoke.

When the noise died down around one in the morning they were able to talk without shouting. The girls fell asleep on the couch, and

Keoki crawled up on Kenika's lap and did the same, drooling on his shoulder. He and Angela sat on chairs facing Benny and Darnay. "So, nineteen fifty-nine," Benny said, holding up his beer. Then he took a sip. "Ho, go fas' da time yah?" Angela said. Then Benny went on, "So now we gotta go troo alla statehood junk again, an' dis senatah and dat represen'ative all sayin' Hawaii be one state. We wen' troo alladis awready." He took another sip and said, "Junk! 'Ass what it is."

"Daddy," Darnay whispered. "No wake da keeds."

Benny looked at them, then smiled. "Ho, so sweet," he said. "Eh, how da Makani 'Ula?"

Kenika described to Benny where he was with the canoe, and Benny said, "Two mont's den. I caw Makaila."

"Is he still—"

"Yah. He come up."

Kenika inwardly cringed at the idea. The man was too old for a trip that far. "What if he can't?" he said. "Would someone else do it?"

Benny thought a second. "Everybody do um different. Dis ceremony from way way way back. Dis how we a'ways did um."

"Yeah, I remember you telling me that."

"Makaila get dat ceremony from his faddah," Benny said. "But main ting is bless da canoe." Benny looked at Darnay, then back at Kenika and Angela. "'S late," he said. "Gotta go bed."

So they gathered themselves up. Kenika took Keoki on his shoulder, and Angela woke the girls up, and they said a groggy goodbye and left. "Wait," Kenika said, and turned. "I was gonna ask him about the buyer, I mean what I'm supposed to do." He handed Keoki to Angela.

He was about to knock on the door again but instead looked in the window to wave at them because of the sporadic noise, with Angela standing just behind him. Darnay was holding both hands out to Benny, and then pulled him up to his feet. Then Darnay supported Benny and they walked slowly toward the hall, Benny shuffling wearily, his huge body looking deflated and frail, shoulders hunched, legs apparently too weak to support him. Kenika watched the two men go down the hall, step by tortured step, Benny so debilitated that he could not get to the bathroom on his own.

Kenika turned and looked at Angela, who stood with her free hand to her mouth. "Oh my God," she whispered. The girls stood groggily watching the remaining flashes of firecrackers, and had not seen Benny. Then Kenika realized something else—that he had not seen Benny anywhere else but in that easy chair for the past four or five months.

They drove out of Waikiki, past dunes of red paper in every gutter from the firecrackers, and past sudden tail-end ratatats of firecrackers going off in driveways, which shook the kids awake only momentarily. Out of the smoke and the noise and on the Nuuanu approach to the tunnel, he told Angela what Benny had told him, that he had walked around Waikiki.

"He no wan' anybody to know," she said. "Oh, he looks bad."

"Darnay told me it was uremia," and he went on to explain what that was. "—but then he still drinks beer."

"I'll talk to my dad," she said. "He just looks really bad sick."

So it became clear that Benny would not see any part of the construction of the canoe, and whether or not he would ever come back seemed now to have been reduced to a vague hope for some miracle. For the present, Kenika was on his own, and the simple truth of Benny's condition was irrefutable. This caused in him an odd feeling of a kind of gloomy but determined industry. It was up to him, and because he had to do it, he did it now with less doubt than when he had expected Benny to squish his way across the muddy stretch of ground and come up the stairs. And he stuck to the conviction that his only way through this was to make every part perfect, if he had to measure every part ten thousand times, if he had to plane and sand until his arm fell off. He had to bring every square inch of her to the point of being as smooth as ice.

Within a week he found himself at the point of varnishing the hull, which was to be done before most of the component parts were installed. He prepared the hull exactly as Benny had, stirred the varnish until his arm wilted with fatigue, and then dipped the brush in. He held his breath and touched the brush to the wood, and drew it along a section of the thin fore-hull, and it was as if the color had been in the varnish and not the wood. The color was rich and deep, the variation in the grain creating that optical illusion of one's being able to see into the wood because of what appeared to be an iridescent three dimensionality. The varnish was its layer of protective skin, the wood inside now locked in this varied and fiery color.

Benny told him to get the Kama boys for the weighing. "Befo' you finish try fo' get um as close as you can to foah hunnerd wit' pahts inna hull. Den, like I to' you, you ovah by ten poun' o' whatevahs, no worry, if mo', den shave little from insai fore an' aft but not middle, 'kay?"

"'Kay."

"Foah hunnerd t'ree poun' good." Benny took a sip of beer and looked at the blank television screen.

"The buyer didn't come up to see it."

"No problem."

"Did you always work this way? I mean no down payment, everything done by whatchucall—verbal agreement?"

"I do um way my faddah did. Do everyt'ing way he do um, from ripsaw to lolo ceremony."

"What if they don't want it?"

"Dey wan' um."

"And Makaila, he's still—"

"He come, no worry."

Kenika mistrusted the scale. He cringed and held his breath when the Kama boys lifted the hull and set it gently on the long, rounded tray. The boys whispered when they saw it, he thought because of its beauty, and then he thought, maybe because something was obviously wrong with it, some blatant violation of proper shape, so stupid that the boys thought it best to humor the sadly-incompetent builder and let him dream on.

Benny set up the meeting with Stevenson, not the elder but his son, who was part of a paddling group interested in long-distance racing. The blessing would take place March fifteenth on Mr. Marumoto's lawn. Kenika would meet with Stevenson in Waikiki a few days before the blessing to set the details up and discuss money.

"I to' dem six tousen', an' what dey say? 'Eh, whatevahs.' I mean like dey tchrow money aroun', like dey light ceegah wit' dollahs."

"Any chance you can come up?"

"Eh, I try."

≈　　≈　　≈

It was done two weeks before the deadline, and in the shed he was locked in a teeth-grinding tension, circling and circling, looking at every part, studying the seam where the mo'o boards joined over the hull rim, running his eye from fore to aft searching for flaws. He tried passing time by making miniature canoes but it didn't work. He went home early, and almost as if he were going from some sort of a pressurized container out into the free air, he would step into the flower shop, be greeted by the kids and Angela, and feel the tension drain from him. His exhaustion was more mental than physical, and he would stop from time to time and shake his head with self-critical amazement that he could be so vulnerable to doubt. He would take Keoki to the school field and kick a soccer ball around, and try to teach him how to throw, using a glove and baseball they had given him for Christmas. The boy was well-coordinated and fast on his feet, and as he watched him run after the baseball or kick the soccer ball, his copper-brown hair bouncing on his head, he was able to forget everything that had to do with the canoe.

George stopped by the house one evening to tell them that Benny was in the hospital, Queens, that he had had fainting spells, vomiting and diarrhea, and that, according to Dr. Chun who was now treating him, his kidneys were failing. "Cannot go see Benny now, but he say tomorrow can."

"What do they do for it?" Kenika asked.

"He to' me but it was all dakine technical, but he had a tube in his ahm fo' dehydration. Now da mos' serious problem is infection. Deal wit' dat firs'."

"Kenika, we go see him," Angela said.

They did go the next evening after dropping the kids off at Momi's. But the visit lasted only five minutes, because Benny was asleep, covered up to his chin with a sheet, his face flaccid and oddly-colored. Dr. Chun was not there to talk to, so they left and went back over the Pali. "He's gonna need money," Kenika said. "The three thousand'll help."

"Momi said that hospital stays are expensive. But hey, it wouldn't be that much."

"The canoe'll take care of it," he said.

He was to meet Stevenson at four o'clock the next day at a bar in the basement of the Reef Hotel, which was on the beach in Waikiki. Kenika had seen the rusting steel skeleton of its construction a few years earlier when they had taken the kids along that stretch of beach. He wore better clothes, and went over in his mind just how it was that he should present himself, if the man would want to know anything technical about the canoe, or simply arrange to meet at Mr. Marumoto's and then take the Makani 'Ula off on a trailer. Stevenson called out "McKay?" as soon as he walked into the cool, suntan lotion-scented air of the place.

He was about twenty-five, with a blonde brush cut, and resembled the actor Tab Hunter, whom they'd seen in a movie called "Battle Cry," and another called "Island of Desire." Unlike the silent type Hunter played in the movies, he was vigorously jovial, moved a lot in his chair, and yelled out to the waitress for three beers, the third for a friend of his named Mike from his fledgling paddling team. Kenika was immediately reassured by the man's good-natured enthusiasm.

He took a sip of his beer and said, "So you like the long-distance races, right?"

"Damn straight," Stevenson said. "Got some strong boys, too. My dad said Benny's would be the canoe of canoes."

Kenika swallowed and said, "That's right, Benny Santiago's canoes are works of art. This one is a single log. As your father specified, it has a little keel, just a half an inch that runs from the manu to—"

"Hey, whatever. So when do we come get it?"

"Anxious," Mike said to Kenika. "Guy runs on two-twenty current all the time."

"It's a Malia design as specified," Kenika said. "But thirty-seven and a half feet, which means that the hull base is a little thicker, so it's a strong canoe. The only difference is that we gave it a traditional manu, with a flat up and down oval plane, for deflecting water."

Stevenson's expression changed. "I heard Benny was sick."

"Yeah, he is."

"Was he able to do that baby before he got that way? I mean you're the helper, right?"

"That's right. He was on this one from the beginning. I do the dealing for him now."

Stevenson watched a badly-sunburned girl in a bathing suit walk by, then shook his head in an exaggerated appreciation. "Jesus," he said, "I love Hawaii. Imagine, touch her where she's burnt and she says 'ouch,' touch her where she isn't and she says 'more.'"

"So I'll just go over what we do," Kenika said. "I wrote the directions for Mr. Marumoto's place on—"

"'Sokay, my dad already told me."

"'Kay, we'll do a little ceremony, and have some food—"

"Wait wait wait," Stevenson said, "let's just cut the ooga-booga shit, put that fucker on a trailer and move."

"Wait," Mike said, looking at Stevenson and shaking his head. "Tell us about this ceremony." Stevenson snorted and looked at the ceiling, and Mike said, "C'mon, just listen, willya?" Then he turned back to Kenika.

"Okay," Kenika said, "from the beginning, but briefly, 'kay? Benny and I named it Makani 'Ula, which means The Red Wind, but you can name it what you—"

"Damn straight," Stevenson said. "I'm gonna call that baby the Yankee Clipper," and he nodded brightly to his friend. "Shall we say," he went on, imitating someone sophisticated, "in honor of the impending statehood vote in Congress." Then he snorted again. "Besides, what the fuck kind of name is Makani whatsis?"

"We give all our canoes names, so that we can build them knowing what we are building," Kenika said slowly, realizing that the heat had risen into his face. He shook it off, drank some beer. "Okay, okay," he said, "lemme finish. We have a kahuna named Kelemeneke Makaila come up to do the blessing—"

"Ah, a medicine man!" Steven said with sudden excitement, but Kenika knew he was being ridiculed. "Hey, how 'bout that, Mike? A fucking witch doctor! Hey, does he have a bone through his nose?"

"Let him finish," Mike said.

"The ceremony is called lolo 'ana ka wa'a i ka halau—"

"Ching chong chee hoi doi," Stevenson said, screwing his face up, at which Mike looked at the ceiling.

"—and its purpose is to more or less," and he paused, thought a moment, and said, "I guess to impart a kind of knowledge to the canoe." Then he added, "No, he does not have a bone in his nose."

"Isn't 'lolo' crazy? The crazy ceremony?"

"It is a matter of pronunciation," Kenika said evenly. "'Lolo' pronounced 'low-low' means feebleminded, whereas a faster pronunciation, like 'lull-o' almost, means brain. When it's written they use a little line over the vowels, called a macron."

"Ah so," Stevenson said.

"Which means to draw out—so 'low low' has macrons. But I'm not an expert in language," Kenika went on, "because it is a very complicated language. I am merely trying to describe this ceremony to you."

"Yes," Stevenson said, again adopting that false propriety. "Very well. I see. Absolutely."

Kenika stared at the table, trying to hold onto his composure. "By the way," he said to Mike. "When are they gonna vote on this statehood shit?"

Mike laughed. "Tomorrow, I guess. What the papers said anyway."

"A real fucking patriot," Stevenson said. "Hey, you one of those commies? Christ, are we dealing with an American here?"

"Okay, I'll just finish this," Kenika said, aware that Stevenson was now staring at him with an expression of jovial hostility. "The lolo ka wa'a ceremony, that's a shorter way to put it, lasts only a few minutes, then we just throw a little sea salt on the canoe and it's done."

"Sea salt?" Stevenson said, and then he laughed.

"Exactly," Kenika said. "Precisely."

Stevenson zeroed his eyes in on Kenika, and he took a long sip of his beer. "Hey, how do you like that mumbo jumbo?" he said, looking at Mike. His eyes shifted back to Kenika, and he thought a few seconds. "Hey, buckaroo," he said, "you sit on the back porch and eat bananas with 'em, too?"

"Huh?"

"Watermelons?"

He had processed the statement but didn't really understand it, as if his ability to interpret language had failed him. He sat, not breathing, and stared at Stevenson.

"Listen," Mike said. "Don't—"

Then he felt language returning to him, but slowly, as if he knew no more than the rudiments. "'Djou say?"

"Aw, for chrissakes," Stevenson said. "Let's get another beer. We'll come and get the fuckin' boat. Jesus!"

"I don't like you," Kenika said. "You're a jerk."

Stevenson looked at him and smiled. "Fuck you," he said amiably. "I don't like you either." But then his face took on a very flat, almost shocked look. "I don't like you much at all." He stared at the table, thinking, his face screwed up in an expression of speculative disgust. "What, are you some kind of a goddam commie in cahoots with a gook witch doctor?"

"I have an idea," Mike said.

"Really?" Stevenson said, not taking his eyes off Kenika.

"Let's start this over."

Kenika drew a deep breath and then let it out. He now felt much cooler, and much more under control. "No," he said, "that is too good a canoe to be wasted on you, Mr. Stevenson. You can't have it." He took another sip of his beer, then held the bottle before his eyes, and Stevenson drew back a little. "No, I'm not gonna throw it. I mean I want to, but I won't. I'm just suggesting that you go back and tell your father that he should teach you some manners, and that if you want a canoe, go get some lumpy glued-together piece of shit from somebody else."

"We made a deal, asshole," Stevenson said.

"No. No, we didn't. I thought it would be you coming up to see if the canoe was worthy of your six thousand dollars. Now it turns out that you're not worthy of the canoe. You can't have it. Even at ten thousand."

"The fuck I can't. I'll be there."

"Listen," Mike said.

"Well, it's my fucking boat, man," Stevenson said.

Kenika leaned forward and put his elbows on the table, one cooled by a little pool of condensation from his bottle. "It's a canoe, not a 'boat'," he said softly. "If you come up anywhere near that place, if you even lay eyes on my canoe, I'll kill you. I'm not kidding either. I'll take the same flat-bladed chisel I used to shape part of that canoe and I'll bury it in your face." He leaned back. "Just so you're clear on this, 'kay?"

Stevenson snorted. "Tough guy," he said. "I oughtta take you outside right now and clean your fucking clock."

"Up to you," Kenika said. "But I'd love that. Please do." He got up from the table. "So, I'll be on my way, unless you want to follow me out. Thanks for the—" He stopped, then shook his head and pulled out his wallet. He carefully removed three dollars and placed it on the table. "That's for the beer," he said. "Take your business elsewhere."

It was not until he was in the car that he realized the enormity of what he had done. Six thousand dollars down the drain, and it wasn't necessary. It was stupid, willfully idiotic behavior, and he became hot with shame. He began to sweat, and held the wheel tightly and whispered, "Stupid, stupid, stupid." And when he drove out into the traffic on Kalakaua Avenue, he was shaking so badly that he could barely drive, and it was not from any fear or threat, it was because he had made a mess of a family business more than a hundred years old.

When he got home there was a note on the table: "All went to see Benny, love, A." He had to go see Benny too, to own up to what he had done, but he would have to do that alone. Then he got an idea. He would get Benny to call Mr. Stevenson, the father, and patch things up. There was still plenty of time. The two older men could talk without insulting each other, and all this could be forgotten.

When Angela and the kids came home, she reported to him that Benny was doing well, that Dr. Chun had begun to control the infection and Benny was in good spirits. Did everything go okay with Stevenson? Yeah, he told her. We're working on that. So it was set. He would explain it all tomorrow.

He went out to the shed the next day to check the canoe over for the hundredth time, and planned to leave early and go see Benny and explain the whole thing. But at the shed he did not check the canoe. Instead he sat and stared at the trees moving in the wind and at the birds, stuck in a mindless suspension of will. Then he left.

People were tooting horns on the bumpy shoreline highway to Kailua, and he knew what it was. As they had predicted, Hawaii was now to be a state. He didn't know what to think of it, as he didn't know what to think of anything political. At the flower shop Momi, Angela and the kids worked on seed leis as usual, but cars on the street blared their horns, and shop windows already had the afternoon paper taped up facing out. The headline read simply "Yes!" the word framed in a rectangle of stars.

"Daddy!" Keoki yelled, "I like one fifty-stah flag!"

"Sure, I'll get one."

"Ho, da noise!" Angela said. "We got ukubillion oadahs fo' leis."

And then Clarice, looking up with an angry scowl, said, "I no like be one state. Dat mean we no mo' Hawaii?"

"Nah nah nah, we still Hawaii," Elizabeth said.

The newspaper said that Congress voted them in at ten in the morning, and Kenika figured that was at about the time he was sitting in the shed watching a mejiro usher two babies out of a nest it had built in a branch just off the mountainside corner of the shed. He shrugged, still not knowing what to think of it.

After dinner the kids settled in to watch television, and he spoke to Angela in the kitchen, briefly explaining what had happened the day before at the Reef. She dropped her shoulders and shook her head, then put her arms around him. "You hothead," she said, looking sadly at him. "Nevah change."

"I'm gonna ask Benny to call Stevenson."

"Even way back when you punch da jungle bunny man." Then she looked more serious. "But you cannot always do that," she said. "You cannot follow your canoes the rest of their lives."

"'Kay. Anyway, I'll go."

There was a three-hour visiting period from six until nine, and he got there at eight, having to maneuver the car past people walking around tooting little horns and waving little flags, and past cars whose horns blared as they approached at one pitch, blared at a lower pitch after they passed by. In the parking lot he could hear the horns from a great distance, downtown and Waikiki. As he walked down the hall toward Benny's room, he saw George and Irene coming out, looking back in and waving. He kept going, then stopped at the door. "How is he?"

"Really relaxed now," Irene said. "Tired too, I think."

"Chun say no stay too long," George said.

"'Kay."

Kenika did not think he looked relaxed. There was now a greater appearance of deflation, as if Benny had lost a great deal of weight. That was supposed to be good, but with Benny it looked all too wrong.

"Kenika," he whispered. "Come sit."

He pulled a chair up to the bed, sat and cleared his throat. "The canoe deal fell through," he said. "It was my fault."

Benny turned his head on the pillow. "How come?"

He went into an explanation, trying to reconstruct the meeting with Stevenson as he remembered it, statement by statement, and finished by saying, "He insulted us."

"Bananas," Benny said, and smiled.

"I know it's business, and now I know it was a mistake, because you need the money for bills, for," and he waved his hand around the room. "For all this. I wondered if you think it would be a good idea to call his father and explain. Call me a hothead, a mullet, whatever, and then we can set it up again."

Benny looked at him, and Kenika wondered for a moment if Benny had sort of lost consciousness because of the blank look of his stare. Then he said, "Kenika, you good boy." He raised his hand and patted him on the forearm.

"Would you call?" he asked.

"No," Benny said. "Fo' once we tell um fuck off."

"But what about the money?"

"Not wort' it," he said.

He closed his eyes, and then seemed to sleep, and Kenika studied the face, the grayish pallor and the dry look of the skin, so unlike the oily brown he was used to. He thought he should go, and moved to get up.

"Eh, no go, Kenika. Sit."

"'Kay."

"No worry about da Makani 'Ula. Wait fo' good person to buy um."

"But—"

Benny shook his head and smiled. "Nevah change," he said.

Dr. Chun came into the room. That probably meant that the visiting hours were over, so Kenika got up and moved his chair aside so that Chun could talk to Benny. Benny whispered to him, and then Dr. Chun turned to Kenika and said, "You can stay longer, as long as you like."

"'Kay."

He put his chair back and sat down. "Listen," Benny said. "Toot toot, aw day. Ho."

"Yeah."

"I tink back when you firs' come up. I sit inna shed an' I tink how fo' get ridda dis boy? Ah, no speak English, 'ass how. Tchrow his lunch inna tub and smell um burn, 'ass how. Den I watchoo fix slippah wit' twine an' I tink, ho, dis boy no whine, no mo' notting. Den, off da cliff fo' coconut husk. Den nex' you try fo' learn Hawaiian an' I tink, ho, he pupule o' what? Dat was funny. Den I tink, 'kayden, I practice Hawaiian too den."

"You almost convinced me."

"Nah. Nottin' I can do. Burn lunch, make you go off da cliff fifty times, whatevahs, cannot get ridda you. No mo' place fo' go, 'ass why, ah?"

"Sort of."

"You good boy 'ass why. I tink, what da boy doeen heah? He do dis, do dat, nevah say notting." Benny rattled on, going over other things he remembered, until he seemed to tire out to the point that he might fade off to sleep mid-sentence. Kenika was tired too, in fact exhausted, more from the tension of what he had done than anything else.

Benny remained silent for a minute, but awake, staring off into some middle distance. "You know, I wanna see Makani 'Ula bumbye."

"You will."

"You know da fat log, shawt but big big big? I got one idea how fo' cut um. Cannot tink how exackly. Take one half canoe, manu to middle, odda half manu to middle, see?"

"Yeah."

"Cut da log almos' like two halfs all nestled togeddah, den you get two halfs an' you attach um inna middle."

"Yeah."

"Now, how fo' cut um?"

"Because the fore and aft are thin, you look in the log and see fore and aft next to each other, with the middles cupped around each other on the other end of the log, you know, cupped like roof tiles. You see the angle increase to the middle, right?"

"'Kay, now cut um."

"I start at the fore-aft end and cut until— But—"

"Got you," Benny said. "'Ass one fo' you to figgah."

He went silent again, looking out the window, and then said, "I go sleep now. Kenika, can you do me one favah?"

"Sure."

"Ho' my han'."

"'Kay," he said, feeling a little twinge of embarrassment.

He did, felt the heat of Benny's low-grade fever in the soft flesh, sitting there with his forearm on the edge of the bed. Benny closed his eyes, and he waited for him to sleep. In his own fatigue he felt his own head drooping, felt his arm going to sleep until it was numb, but did not want to remove his hand from Benny's until he was sure he was asleep. He concentrated on holding Benny's hand.

With his own eyes closed and the feeling of the tingling numbness in his hand, his head filled with bright, oddly-arranged flashes of imagery, swimming with Benny at Laie and picking 'ina bats, the time he sat with him way up on the mountain and Benny went on for so long about what made him go there, the dark, looming form of him standing in the shed like some black monster. He had only known the man eleven and some years but it felt like a lifetime. He thought he continued considering this, but went into a transition in which his mind rendered sound, the hissing of canoes over water, the thumping of paddleshafts against wood, the calls of seabirds skimming only inches over the water, and the sounds of chisels, files, sandpaper against wood, sawing, muttered speculations about measurement, the endless tap tap tapping of making things, and the verbal squeak of the floorboard which said why, or wa'a.

Someone shook him, and he felt drool on his chin, and wiped it off with his shirt. His hand was asleep, and he looked up and saw a Japanese nurse, who was pulling it away from Benny's. She moved toward the door and signalled his attention, and said, "He's gone," and when Kenika turned to look he saw that they had already covered him with a sheet.

He walked out into the hall, and then stopped. He had to go home, that was it. His mind was numb, as if he could not decide if he should make his leg move forward for the next step. When the nurse's shadow appeared on the floor next to where he stood, he turned. "Was there a cause?" he asked.

"Mr. Santiago most likely died of congestive heart failure. You felt no movement?"

"No."

"Then he went quietly. I'm to call his brother, a Mr. —"

"That's George Santiago."

"Yes," she said. "I'm sorry. He was so fun. Talk story all day."

In the car he sat and listened to the honking of horns in the distance, and then the sporadic bursts of firecrackers. He stared at the other cars in the lot, and then whispered, "Benny Benny Benny." He felt a strange emptiness, as if he had been painlessly gutted while he sat there next to the bed, and his heart, if it was still there, seemed to float somewhere above where it should have been, but empty, like a helium balloon. When he finally thought he was really thinking, he realized that he wanted to go home, and when that thought struck, it felt like a desperation to get home, as if he had forgotten for the moment that there was one to go to.

≈   ≈   ≈

Benny Santiago's body was cremated according to his own instructions to his brother George. He wanted it simple and quick— the sooner he got to the ocean the better. He had instructed that his ashes be spread on the ocean off Kualoa, and that George, Kenika and Darnay would be the ones to do that. He requested that his ashes be taken out beyond the breakwater in a six-man canoe, and that if possible other canoes paddled by his friends might accompany his ashes. After that, all of the friends would go to the Santiago house in Lanikai and eat, drink, and talk story.

George and Irene amended Benny's list of requests by adding to it a brief memorial ceremony to be delivered by Jerry Moniz, a Methodist minister who would go with the friends and family to Kualoa. George called Benny's friends, secured the ashes which would be taken out in a koa box, and made all the other necessary arrangements. The ceremony would take place Saturday afternoon.

Kenika could not lift himself from that numbed stupor that overcame him at the hospital, and at home, listening to Angela on the phone talking to Momi, or Irene, he sat and gazed out the window at the profile of Olomana, unable to make his mind function beyond simply resurrecting images from years ago. From time to time the saddened children would come over and talk to him: "Daddy, unca Benny wen' die, yah?"

"Yeah Keoki, he did."

"No fee' bad, he wen' heaven ah?"

"Yeah, if anybody should go, it would be Benny."

And Clarice and Elizabeth: "Daddy, no fee' bad, he go home you know?"

"Yeah Dad, ocean, 'ass his place."

"Yeah, that's his place."

They would look straight at his face with deep, unabashed concern. "I so sorry fo' Benny, an' you too."

And Angela. He would lie down in bed and stare at the ceiling, and when she was finished checking on the kids and turning off all the lights, she would come in and get in the bed and put her arm over his chest. "So sad. I know you feel bad, but it happens."

"Yeah, I know."

"But I know what he meant to you."

"Yeah, he meant a lot."

The water off Kualoa was shallow, and the men familiar with canoes studied it wondering about depth, because it was just after low tide. Kenika stood by the line of four canoes in the sand, one of them the Puaho Akua, brought by Mr. Lum so that one of Benny's own canoes could take the ashes out. One of the other canoes was white, and as Kenika stood looking at the water, he would glance at it as the men worked on the outrigger lashings, and wonder why they had painted it. He walked over to the men working on the lashing and introduced himself. The men knew who he was—"Eh, Benny talk about you plenny!"

"So you guys from Waikiki?"

"Yah, 'ass us."

"Well, Benny talks about you plenty too."

They laughed, and Kenika put his hand on the canoe. "Why is it white?"

"'Ass fiberglass," the man said. Kenika had heard of it, and spent the next few minutes studying the hull, running his hand along the mo'o and tapping the hull with his knuckle, which produced a strange hollow sound. As Benny had predicted it was in effect a plastic canoe.

Reverend Moniz delivered the prayers for Benny to the bowed heads of the family and friends, all of whom held elaborate leis of different colors and sizes. There were about forty people standing in the sand facing the ocean, half of whom were family and the other half his friends, all dark, many of them heavy-set local men in their fifties. All but a few had come in their bathing suits.

With the leis piled inside the canoes, they paddled out slowly, Darnay holding the koa box on his lap while George steered and Kenika, Clarice and Elizabeth sat in the three middle seats and Angela sat in the kamani'ula, or bow seat, Keoki between her feet. As Kenika paddled he watched the sharp, bony shoulder blades of his daughters working, and ahead of them Angela's broad back. The water was calm and clear, hardly breaking at the outer reef, and when they saw the bottom tip and recede into a darker blue, the four canoes turned, and Kenika turned in his seat. "You do um," Darnay whispered to Kenika, and George nodded.

Kenika took the box and opened it. Inside the ashes looked like dark-gray sand, and he tipped it, and the ashes fell on the water, hissed and then vanished down like a cloud of slowly-billowing smoke, a little bit of it from the box lifted by the breeze across his face so that he could feel it on his lips with his tongue. Then all the paddlers threw the leis in graceful, spinning arcs onto the water, and they paddled back in.

At the Santiago house in Lanikai people came and went throughout the day bringing food, and the atmosphere was what Benny would have wanted. It resembled a luau, and one looking in from the street and hearing the laughter would not have known why all those people were gathered. Kenika went through the day in a stupor similar to the one that had afflicted him since Benny died, but the company of all those people made it comfortable, even enjoyable if that was possible. Talking story was the center of it, and by the time the day was over his voice was hoarse. When they finally got home he slept as if drugged.

Had he not dreamt of canoes, he was sure he would have forgotten, but early in the morning he woke up from the echo of the familiar sound, of shafts thumping wood in an even comfortable heartbeat, and the hissing sound of the hull sliding through water, and then sat bolt upright.

"What?" Angela said.

"The lolo ceremony. What day is it?"

"Sunday."

He flopped back down, his heart beating. "Jesus, I would have forgotten it. This afternoon at Mr. Marumoto's."

"But you said the deal fell through."

"I know, but Mr. Makaila. I should call him and cancel."

"I think you do it anyway."

"But who would— I mean, who would come?"

"We come. I get Darnay too, cause he staying in my o' room. Mommy an' Daddy, I don't tink so. Dey exhausted. Momi maybe, but Tutu Elizabeth sick, so maybe not. Look, Benny would want you to."

"I gotta go early and set it up. The Kama boys—"

"I caw Momi."

He drove out at noon. Momi, Angela, Darnay and the kids would come at three and Mr. Makaila would come at four. When he got to the Marumoto's house he found that yes, they had heard that Benny died. Irene had called earlier in the day. They were sorry they could not come to the service because they had just come back from Molokai where they had visited family, and yes, the Kama boys were coming. Kenika explained to them that there would be fewer people at the ceremony because the deal had fallen through.

Kenika and the Kama boys carried the hull on their shoulders, squishing through the rotted leaves and then over the little stream, and placed it on Mr. Marumoto's lawn. Before he went back to get the outrigger parts Kenika turned and looked at the Makani 'Ula, which in the sun, took on an even brighter sheen, the koa so rich in color that he was momentarily amazed by it. Just aft of the center on the right side there was a knot that in the shed was only a knot, but in the sun resembled a whale's eye, peering out of the wood's three-dimensional iridescence. And when Momi, Darnay, Angela and the kids got there, it was already loosely lashed, and they all circled it, staring. Angela stood with her hand to her mouth, and he could tell that her eyes were wet and didn't understand why, so he stepped over to her. "You okay?" he whispered.

She looked at him, almost as if shocked. "Benny nevah see it? He nevah?"

"No."

"Oh my," she whispered, turning back to it. "Oh my." Momi had that look on her face too, standing at the other end. Then she looked up and caught Kenika's eye, and shook her head slowly in a kind of contemplative wonder. But he did not feel overcome with pride. If anything it was something like the opposite. When he backed up one more time and looked at the hull, the powerful sun making it radiate color, he was almost overcome with devastation because no, Benny had never seen it.

Makaila's black 1938 Buick coasted to a stop at the edge of the lawn at four, and Mr. Marumoto went out to say hello. Kenika felt an embarrassed regret that, counting the Marumotos, there were only eleven people there, standing around the canoe. Clarice and Elizabeth whispered to each other, watching the car, and Keoki stood holding Angela's hand. Then two women got out of the car wearing bathing suit tops and kapa-pattern sarongs tied at the waist, and together strode across the lawn toward them. Clarice and Elizabeth stared, and their mouths dropped open. The women were not twins but appeared to be sisters. They were tall and dark and almost astonishingly beautiful, at least five-ten, with black curly hair swinging all the way down to their waists, the confident stride showing a lean, physical grace that approached a kind of feminine magnificence. The twins' amazed expressions were easy to read: would they ever, ever be fortunate enough to grow up to be women like that?

They were Lehua and Pualani Makaila, Kelemeneke Makaila's great-granddaughters, and would help him in the ceremony. He could not walk on his own. They had heard about Benny's death and expressed their great-grandfather's condolences. Clarice and Elizabeth edged in closer as they talked, staring up at them, and Kenika saw that when Clarice got closer she sniffed the air wafting off those beautiful bodies. He understood—the sisters radiated their beauty like a vapor. The fourth generation down from the wiry little man seemed to have been the end of a process of genetic refinement into something approximating mystical perfection. When Lehua saw the girls she crouched down and introduced herself, and then both of them stood there gaping at her, face to face, unable to speak. "Are you girls twins?"

"Uh-huh," Elizabeth finally said.

"What's your name?"

For five seconds neither twin spoke. Then, as if the sight of Lehua had scrambled their sense of themselves, they reversed, Clarice saying, "She's Elizabeth McKay," and Elizabeth said, "My sister is named Clarice."

"Isn't this a beautiful canoe?"

"Yah," Clarice said. "My dad make um."

They returned to the car to bring their great-grandfather out, and just as those women turned everyone's eyes, so did Makaila, but for another reason. He was so frail and thin that, standing between the two sisters, he could have been a child devastated by some emaciating illness. He shuffled, step by careful step, the girls each holding an arm, and when he got closer Kenika understood that like Benny, he would not see the canoe either, because he was blind, or close enough to it that his eyes searched what was before him by looking around it. He smiled, showing a couple of large, bright teeth, and Lehua whispered to him that the canoe was right here.

Thirteen people formed the circle, and Lehua drew the old man inside it and then placed his hand on the manu. She whispered to him, her hand on his shoulder, and backed away. Kenika looked once to his left, at the ocean, and in a flash of that feeling of blank emptiness realized that only twenty-four hours ago they had spread Benny Santiago's ashes on that water. He moved to his right, grabbed Angela's hand, and held it against his thigh.

Then, supporting himself with his hand on the smooth hull, Kelemeneke Makaila slowly shuffled the length of the canoe, whispering and then stopping, eyes closed, sometimes whispering a little louder so that his faint voice was just discernible over the sound of the soft breeze rustling the trees, and in a ceremony that lasted about five minutes, gave brains to The Red Wind.

Two

You whisper, we are The Red Wind.

Two hundred yards out, and you cannot see him. He would be standing on the finish line wearing the faded shirt and shorts, but there are thousands of them on the beach.

The Makani 'Ula, red wind.

Paddleshafts bump against the hull of the Makani 'Ula, Keoni's broad back up front, Richard, Kimo Parker, youl and behind, big Skippa Moniz holding down the stern of The Red Wind. Last, skinny Junior Sakata to steer. Only eleven, but he is back there to steer.

It is a dream: fourteen lanes, the flags a quarter of a mile away over the silver water. You run your hand on the outside of the hull, over the red koa, and just feel the little ripple in the wood, where it has an eye that will follow you as you walk past it, watching. Makani 'Ula means The Red Wind, Kenika said. What kine name dat? Junior asked, and Kenika said, red like you guys' skin, like a Hawaiian's skin. 'Ula means sacred too. The red sacred wind, like canoes blowing across the ocean, like a thousand years ago.

And he said, listen up, guys. Remember to keep the pace and pull, and fight your fatigue. You are not on The Red Wind, you are The Red Wind. Remember that.

'Kay, Skippa Moniz said, I da Red Win'.

But I Japanee, Junior said. I no mo' Hawaiian.

Eh, Keoni said, You like us, brah, you black skinny buggah. Dat not chopstick you get, dat one paddow, brah. Babooze, we to' you dis lashear.

Just remember, today you are The Red Wind, Kenika said.

'Kay den, I da Red Win', Keoni said. We da Red Win'.

'Kay but, Junior Sakata said.

I to' you, Keoni said. We all da Red Win'.

Keoni roils the water with his paddle, and the manu dances left, straightening in the lane. Junior steadies it behind. They are talking, rapping encouragement down the line, but their voices are a dream language. You set.

'Kay den, Junior shouts, you watch dakine Red Win'. 'Ass us.

The first flag is up, then the second, then the go flag waves, and you pull The Red Wind under you, thrusting it forward with your heels and buttocks, and lunge forward, the little spray of water lashing across your face, you dig in a lunging reach and pull, sending The Red Wind further out in front of you. There is a moment when the paddles are off synch and The Red Wind drags left and the ama rises out of the water, streaming long drips into the wind, and Junior Sakata pulls it straight and the ama slaps down. And he said, look at the water, at your paddle—imagine that you reach out as far as you can and are hauling the ocean past you, holding the paddle face always straight away from the canoe. And Kenika said, listen to Kimo, hut-hut-hut, and always be with him as The Red Wind shoots out from under your heels and buttocks, and the paddleshafts thump the hull as one, and you pull, your chest beginning to burn from the gasping for air, and ahead all the paddles enter and leave as one, and hut-hut-hut-ho! they swivel over heads and you are pulling The Red Wind out from under you on the right side. And you pull, the rhythm settling in, and there is no memory, only the thumping of the knees and heels on wood and the water surging off the paddle face, and now your chest and thighs are burning, your gasps of breath salted by the water, your arms and shoulders scream with fatigue, but you peek once to the side, and see the manus of the other canoes, see the flying hair and paddles, but the manus are all just out from you and not Keoni, and you are a third of a canoe out ahead, and you dig, thrusting The Red Wind out from under your heels and buttocks, listening to Kimo, hut-hut-hut, and you peek again, and see the manus surge and drag, surge and drag, one appearing in front of another and then

*behind, all the manus surging and dragging, now a strange rhythmic
pulse, and they are all off you and not Keoni, and you pull The Red
Wind under you and it sweeps away and you lunge out and catch up
with it, your chest near bursting, pull so it leaves you, hut-hut-hut-ho!
and now you hear them yelling on the beach and peek to see Kenika
but you can't, because there are thousands of them, and along the line
of manus they are surging and dragging, surging and dragging, the
boys' hair flying and spray shooting from their paddles, and you thrust
The Red Wind out from under you.*

*As you cross, Keoni stands up in the front with his paddle over his
head, a black silhouette against the silver water and the sky, and you
wilt, your forehead on your knees, The Red Wind still knifing through
the water, and the screaming from the beach fills your lungs with air,
and you stifle the urge to vomit. The urge vanishes, and you run your
hand along the smooth hull of The Red Wind, over its eye. Makani 'Ula.
The best canoe in the world.*

≈   ≈   ≈

As if in step with the blank emptiness Kenika felt whenever he
envisioned the shed, he accepted as normal the fact that for months
he got no calls, no orders for anything, and went about the business
of making baby canoes and wind chimes to take over to Mr. Maxwell
and the other vendors in Waikiki, some of whom looked at what he
brought with lessening enthusiasm. Oeoe whistles they wanted nothing
to do with—they couldn't sell them, they said, and the stuff coming in
from the Philippines was so cheap that Kenika was at too much of a
disadvantage. Angela's and Momi's handiwork seemed far more
attractive to them because of its artistry and use of natural materials.
Mr. Maxwell still accepted the scale-model canoes, in fact he could
use as many as Kenika could make. So he went to the shed and he
made them, but with a sensation of dullness, sometimes horrific
boredom. He didn't bother to light a fire in the drum, and when he was
hungry ate fruit and cold malasadas and drank beer. From time to
time Mr. Marumoto would come squishing through the woods and
have a beer with him and talk story, and Kenika always welcomed the
diversion.

Mr. Marumoto would come up the stairs, step inside and walk on
the singing board—why?—and then smile and sit down in Benny's
chair. Against the screen on the mountain side sat The Red Wind,
covered by tarps, its rigging lying inside the hull. "I ask aroun'," he
would say. "Bumbye somebody caw an' make offah. Dat too good a
canoe fo' jus' sit li'dat."

"Nobody's got six thousand dollars, I guess."

"Eh, no worry, Kenika, bumbye you get caw. Now you come, eat lunch wit' us."

The shed seemed to exude the strange shadows, or the aura, of Benny's presence. Everything from the deep shine on the handle of each tool, from his skin oil, to the nine and a half cases of Primo stacked next to the beer tub that Kenika refilled every few days, so that the bottles bobbed there in amongst squirming mosquito larvae, to the odor in the little sleeping room, the cot, still with the reed beach mat and old army blanket Benny had used, the squeaky chair which Kenika did not sit on because it was Benny's chair—all of it was Benny. It occurred to him as he sat there on his chair staring at the empty one a few feet away that the difficult, wilful and eccentric man had been the closest to a father he would ever know in his life, and now he was dead. And as if to seal the finality of Benny's death, Kenika learned from Mr. Marumoto that Kelemeneke Makaila followed him within one month of his blessing of The Red Wind.

And then it was Tutu Elizabeth. She got sick just around the time Benny died and never got well. She was taken to the hospital and, after Momi consulted with her doctor, it was clear that she would not come out. She died just two months after Benny, and was buried next to her husband, dead twenty-five years, in a small cemetery in Nuuanu. The family stood around the square hole in the ground before the already-weathered stone and watched as the casket was lowered into it with thick straps. Then they went to Maunawili to sit and talk, this time with very old men and women Kenika had never seen before, obscure friends from half a century ago.

When school was out, he discovered that given the choice, he would rather stay home with Angela and the kids, even though not going to the shed made him feel guilty. He worked on the skills of baseball and basketball and soccer with Keoki, and spent a lot of time fishing. If not that, then he sat in the cool, moist air of the lei shop, while outside, they could always hear the grinding of earth-moving equipment and the pounding of hammers, the high-pitched roar of huge trucks sending rivers of concrete down their chutes into the forms for all the buildings going up in the town. The center of the town seemed to have moved somewhat up Kailua Road to the east, where the new shopping center had been built across the road from the Liberty House store. Kenika noticed that now, driving up that road toward home, he passed houses all the way to get to the street that had once been one of only six, the little outpost of houses on the bluffs above the lake and marsh, separated from the town by more than a mile. Now the marsh was gone, filled in and blocked out for new houses, a lake in the middle.

He began filling orders for a new client, Angela, who needed drilled, cleaned, smoothed and buffed kukui nuts for the leis she couldn't make enough of. He collected them in the woods, drilled them end to end with a hand drill, breaking so many drill bits that he wondered if he might end up buying out the entire island of Oahu of that particular sixteenth of an inch size. He put the drilled nuts under the shed for the ants to clean out. Another time Angela showed him Job's tears, little grayish silver seeds, very hard and slightly tear-drop shaped, and asked him if he had seen any of these in the woods.

"Sure, in the tall grass down the hill where the stream runs through."

Angela turned to the twins and said, "Go wit' Daddy to da shed an' get ukubillion dese, 'kay?"

The kids could not contain their excitement. They had been there a few times before, with Angela who was after flowers of some sort, and they liked nothing better than sitting inside and making believe that it was a castle, or a secret hideaway, or the beginning of a school they would build as a more than agreeable alternative to the one they went to.

"An' no walk off inna woods!" Angela yelled after them.

If his "business" was floundering, as if Benny's death meant to all his clients that it no longer existed, then Kenika could offer whatever he had that was useful to Angela, whose business was booming so much that she was already contemplating buying another house just like their own, "fo' kids someday," she said. Down one side of the house and across the back hedge she had planted 'ilima bushes, which had a thin orange flower that, stacked hundreds upon hundreds on a thin thread, made a lei that looked like a bright orange rope, and she got four dollars apiece for them. A wind chime got a dollar-fifty, one of her Job's tear leis got two. An oeoe whistle got zero, the simplest orchid and plumeria lei got a dollar.

Then, in a monkish rejection of the making of any trinkets, he began drawing on the table cross-section he had taken to the shed so long ago, thinking of making a relief picture in the koa. Benny had cut the cross-section at an angle so that it was oval-shaped, making the swirling of the grain more evident. His relief picture showed the fore manu and prow of a stout, traditional fishing or 'opelu canoe, with a rounded, almost bulbous ihu wa'a or bow and a wide manu high up in the wood, and the grain more or less determined its size and angle. He carved background first, and then from there visualized the canoe sweeping in foreshortened diminishment into the wood, the fists and bowed heads of the paddlers smaller and smaller as the canoe narrowed into the distance. He used the smallest chisels he could find, V-shaped routers and small blades to dig the pictures into the wood. Under the ihu waʻa he found variations in the grain that suggested water, and again let the grain determine the shape of it.

What it would come to he didn't know, and didn't care. In effect he was idling his time, almost as if he half expected to hear the squishing in the mud and look and see Benny hulking through the mulch to the shed. His work took on the intense, almost demented focus of an obsession with the visually minute, so that he might work for six hours carving a fist the size of a pea. Then he would forget the relief for weeks and make baby canoes. Vaguely he reasoned that he was doing it because he loved koa and he loved canoes.

One windy day in November someone did squish through the rotted leaves, a man wearing a suit, and Kenika stared at him as he approached, wondering if he was some official out to inform him that he was on government property, or some official here to inform him that he had never paid taxes. The man stopped and looked toward him, then said, "Yoo hoo!"

Kenika went to the screen door and waved him in.

The man was an official. His name was Milton Robertson and he was the headmaster of a private school called the Central Pacific Academy, on the other side of the island just outside Honolulu. Kenika offered him his own chair and sat on Benny's. The man looked down at his shoes, which were muddy and wet. "Wait," Kenika said, and got a rag. He stooped over and quickly wiped the mud from the man's shoes. "Sorry," he said. "Prob'ly better to meet somewhere else."

"I got your name from Clarence Lum," he said. "He said I should just come up, see what you have here. This is quite a place."

"We made a canoe for Mr. Lum."

"Let me explain why I'm here," the man said.

The Academy wished to commission the building of a canoe, he said, but not a racing canoe. Rather they wanted a traditional fishing canoe which was called ʻopelu, and that they were interested in its being built as much as was reasonable according to the old methods, such as lashing of certain boards together rather than using screws and glue and nails.

"ʻOpelu canoes run around eighteen or twenty feet," Kenika said, "and they're deeper, wider and heavier than racing canoes. If you have a twenty-foot ʻopelu it might weigh three-hundred-fifty pounds or more because the hull bottom will be four or five inches thick."

"We don't really know what we want," Robertson said. "That would be up to you. I just learned the word 'opelu' today."

"I can make it," he said. The wind lashed against the screen, and they sat and waited for it to die down.

Then the man got an uncomfortable look. "The school has budgeted two thousand dollars for the canoe."

It was far from enough. The log alone was worth that much. Kenika thought, then asked, "What are you going to use it for?"

"The school wants it for the kids to use, and for them to learn about canoes."

"Does your school have a religious, uh, orientation?"

"It's a small Episcopal school."

"What would happen if, say, I made this canoe, and the people who were going to use it came up here for a traditional blessing in which a kahuna put a sort of spell on it?"

"That would be fine. I think part of the reason for having the canoe would be educating them about various rituals of the past."

"This is a ritual of the present."

The man looked at him, and he detected a little squint of skepticism. "Well, that would be fine."

"I won't make a canoe that isn't given brains," he said, and then laughed. "Sorry, let me put it this way. I won't make a canoe whose users are not present when it is given a kind of intelligence."

"Well, we can—"

"If I understand you correctly, all these kids are going to use the canoe. That means I won't make the canoe unless they are all here when it is given its brains."

"That's three hundred kids."

"It has to be that way."

The man thought, looked around the shed. "But what about kids who will use it five years from now?"

"They'll be all right."

Robertson studied him. "All right?"

"I mean they'll be safe."

"So what do you do? Take some boards like those over there," and he pointed at a pile of planks, ripsaw leavings, leaning against the bench, "and sort of laminate them into a hull?"

Kenika looked at the boards, then at Robertson. "No, this will be a single log."

"My understanding is that single logs are rare."

"If this is a sort of demonstration canoe— Wait, do you think you'd ever sell it?"

"No, not any more than we would sell the administration building."

"Okay, then it'll be a single log. And I'll do it for two thousand. I have a rough-cut one right down below, came here about, oh, eight years ago."

"How much would you require in down payment?"

"Nothing. When it's done, you can look at it and then pay me. I mean, that's the way we always did it."

The man studied him some more, almost as if he suspected him of being a little off his head. Kenika got up, went to the tub and got out two Primos, and opened them. "Here," he said. Robertson took the bottle, and Kenika took a long swallow of his, too much because he was suddenly excited about the idea of making the canoe, and belched. "Oops," he said, and sat down again in Benny's chair.

"I was given to understand that a single log canoe would cost twice that much," Robertson said.

"It would, even more maybe."

"Why would you do it for two thousand then?"

Kenika looked at the screen, watched the trees wave in the wind. "Because I think schools should have canoes."

"We could do a fund raiser or something, you know, to add to the payment."

"I'll tell you what," Kenika said. "Use the fund raiser to get yourself a good trailer, with cradles, and maybe build a good place to store it." Then he stopped. "It," he said. "Look, it has to have a name."

"Well, we'll—"

Kenika laughed again. "I didn't tell you, but I won't touch the log until it has a name."

Robertson took a sip of his beer. "Hmm," he said. "Why would that be?"

It had taken all this time for the recognition to hit, and now his heart was thumping. He had waited what felt like too long a time for this, and now it was happening, and he realized that he would make the canoe for nothing, because someone wanted a canoe. He got up and went around Robertson to the mountainside wall of the shed, and began pulling the tarp off The Red Wind, and in the breeze it ballooned up, Kenika holding onto it. Robertson stood up and walked a few steps toward the canoe, stepping on the singing board, but the why? was obscured by the rustling of the tarp.

"My God," Robertson said.

"This is the Makani ʻUla, which means The Red Wind. The man who taught me to make canoes made it possible for me to make this one. We named our canoes first. He's dead now. His name was Benjamin Santiago. I'll make the ʻopelu for two thousand if you allow me to name it."

"Well of course," Robertson said.

"We'll call it the Peniʻamina."

"Which is?"

"It's the name Benjamin written in Hawaiian. Would that be all right?"

"That would be fine," he said.

"One other thing. If it's all right with you, don't mention that the shed is here, okay? I mean, we do the blessing out on Mr. Marumoto's lawn and people more or less assume I brought it there from somewhere else. I'd like to keep the location of this place a little secret because of all the tools."

"Sure thing," Robertson said. Then he laughed. "Mr. Marumoto's got a grandson in the school."

"Really?" Then he began putting things together. "So was it Mr. Marumoto who called Clarence Lum?"

"Clarence Lum is on our board of directors. I think it's a great idea by the way."

"A conspiracy," Kenika said. "That calls for another beer."

"Oh, not for me," Robertson said. "I should go."

After Robertson left he stood there for a few minutes feeling a rush of exultation. When he went to cover The Red Wind, though, he suddenly felt an odd sensation that something was wrong, and thought that it might be that The Red Wind had been sitting there in that spot for eight months, and the fact of its not having a buyer left things unsettled. In fact it was bad business, his making a canoe for two thousand dollars when this one was not sold. He was just finishing his fourth beer when he saw Mr. Marumoto making his way over the stream. When Mr. Marumoto came into the shed and sat down on Benny's chair, Kenika got him a beer and said, "As Angela would say, kolohe buggah, you."

"Eh, dat not mischief. I on'y get togeddah wit' Clarence 'ass all," and he laughed, very close to the impish tee-hee-hee Benny always came out with. "Besides, alla odda guys da boa'd gotta vote too, ah? Dis not one gif'. Dis one job."

"'Kay."

"Get ti'ad fo' watch you sulk."

"You sound like Angela."

"So, I caw Kama boys?"

"'Kay."

Later, feeling a little drunk, he made his way up the mountain, his gift a cone sushi from his lunch box. On the way he reasoned that Clarence Lum and Mr. Marumoto could just as easily have advanced their conspiracy in order to help some other canoe builder. But they were doing it for him, and as far as he was concerned, if they had to coerce board members of a school to accept the idea of buying a canoe for their kids to use, then they were involved in a good conspiracy. Benny, he imagined, would have told him "'ass business, word of mout'. No worry."

He walked out into the parched rectangle and placed the sushi, wrapped in ti leaves, in the center, and then stood up straight. "It is named Peni'amina, after Benny," he whispered, "and it's for kids, a lot of them yours. If Benny is there with you, ask him what he thinks. I think it's good to name a canoe after him, because it guarantees that it will be a good one." He stopped, looked around. He felt a kind of swoon of relief, because he could now build a canoe, and the sense of wholeness that created caused him to nod at the rocks, whispering, "Yeah, yeah, yeah. That's it." Then he backed out of the middle of the rectangle and whispered, "Thanks for—" and then thought, making this happen. Just before he left, though, that same sensation of something being wrong hit him, and he walked down the mountain still unsure of why he felt that way.

≈   ≈   ≈

Alone in the shed, chopping with the adze, measuring, eyeing the hull, he talked to the canoe, as if hearing his own voice gave him company: "There you go, Benny, there you go. Hell, we'll make the hull base five inches thick, 'kay? Any canoe with your name ought to be thick at the base, right? Right." When rain lashed the screens he talked louder so that he could hear his own voice. When he ate lunch he held up the beer bottle to the hill and toasted: "Here's to you, Benny You relax now, you be patient, 'kay?" And ever since he had made that recognition that it was wrong that The Red Wind still sat in its cradles, the problem continued to gnaw at him.

Part of the tarp blew back against the hull one day so that he could see the red koa, and the swirl of grain that resembled an eye watched him. He looked at it, thought, a buyer is what I need.

≈   ≈   ≈

At home late in the afternoon, after the shop was closed, he sometimes walked in and found Angela sitting alone at the table. She would be flipping through books or fiddling with seed leis. But one day she was simply sitting there waiting. He walked in, and she looked up, then looked furtively around and said, "Well, Keoki's at soccer practice and the girls are at the school at a scout meeting an', chee, cannot pick um up until seven."

"But it's only five-thirty. What now?" With that a powerful rush of a rubber-legged urgency coursed through him.

"I know. Ho, boring."

"Listen, I have a sort of technical question, of a strange personal matter involving your, uh, person. What color underpants are you wearing today?"

She gasped, put her hand to her mouth and said, "Oh! S'kebei you, I no tell."

"I was just wondering. Is there any connection between the color of the fabric and the heat of the skin under them?"

"Cannot tell. Dirty ginnie, you."

She got up from her chair, walked around the table looking at him with artificial disgust, and then walked around him to the front door and closed it. "No want any neighbors heah you talk pilau. Shame on you! Well, now I gotta go make da bed. Hope nobody boddah me in dakine."

He followed her into their room, and when she bent over to pull the sheet, he said, "Red! Can I have them?"

"No."

"I just want to look at them. Red implies heat, so—"

"Ho, pig, you wanna do some nasty ting, eh?"

"Well, it's not really the underpants themselves. It's the connection between their temperature and skin. I just wanna—"

"Cannot. I no show you dat."

At which the wrestling match began. This became something they did only during the day. When they made love at night it was more "normal" he guessed the word would be. But in this silly wrestling she was so strong that at times he thought she had wrenched ligaments, forced him to pull muscles as he tried to get some article of clothing off while she giggled, trying to keep the noise down because next door was only thirty feet away. Once she kicked too close to his head and caught him just under the eye with her heel, and he collapsed on his back, feigning being unconscious, and she did everything to wake him up, pulled his shorts off, put the condom on, crawled over him, whispering, "Pua Kenika, out co', an' oh so skinny an' aw dead to da worl', 'cept fo'," and she gasped, "ho! What dis down heah!"

Afterwards they lay staring at each other as if each judged the other as abnormally foolish. "Chee, you strange, Kenika. Like one pig. Ho, I gotta ask my mom 'bout dat."

"Jesus, look at the clock! It's only six!"

"Ho, boring."

"Uh oh, I think something's happening!"

"Shh! What, now tell me. No be shy, tell da troot."

"It's this impulse to— Well—"

And he rolled up on his elbow and looked at her.

"You can tell me," she said. "I your terapis'. Fac', show me an' I'll tell you if you okay, 'kay? Oh your pua eye!"

"Well, I had this dream that if I put my hand down here—"

"Go ahead, no be shy. I tell you laters if it okay, 'kay?"

"Then if I just push around like this and look, what do I see? I mean, what is that?"

"An' den?"

"What if I just took this thing here and—"

"Lemme tink. Now dat feel good, da han' li'dat. Suppose—"

"That's what I was thinking. Look, lemme just—"

She gasped again. "Ho, what you doeen?"

"Well, I'm not sure but—"

"Who said you could stick dat in dere? Ooo, but wait, dat feel good."

"Well, you said to."

"Lemme tink, should I tell dis man dis dakine inappropriate fo' him fo' do dat, or, ho, dat even bettah—"

And later, sitting around the table: "Daddy, why your eye all puffy li'dat?"

"Well, I ran into a foot, kind of."

"Foot?" Keoki said. "What, you play soccer today?"

"Sort of."

Angela cleared her throat. "Girls, sit up, no slouch while you eat, 'kay?" She thought a moment. "'An when you make signs for the store window, let me see them first, 'kay?"

Clarice and Elizabeth giggled, then went on eating.

"You know ant'urium?" Angela asked.

"Yeah," Kenika said. It was a strange, waxy flower with a sort of heart-shaped, red base, out of which stuck a long, whitish thing that looked like a thin finger.

"Dey made a sign an' put it in the window, 'Boy flower, ninety-eight cents.'"

The girls giggled again.

"Shut up," Keoki said.

"Ho, put me out of business."

≈   ≈   ≈

Component parts, 'ohi'a root, hau, mo'o boards, but this time he had to lash them rather than use screws and glue, and this meant traveling to different parts of the island to talk to old friends of Benny's who knew traditional methods of canoe building. Kenika decided that the Peni'amina would be ninety-five percent traditional, but for such things as sennit cord, which he tried making one afternoon at the shed. You had to pull thin, tough strings of fiber, one by one, out of a coconut husk, each around five or six inches long, and then you braided little sections, which then would be braided section into section in overlapping lines. He realized that in order to create the lashing for a single canoe he would have to hire ten or twelve people to work for about six months or a year just to create the sennit cord. Benny had told him a long time ago that women made sennit cord, and it was so valuable that it was like money, a ten-foot section worth about as much as a pig. He went to the hardware store and bought rope somewhat thinner than they used for ama lashings, and dyed it brown with a mixture of wood stains. All the time he worked, the koa eye watched him, and he wondered if being alone all day like this was doing something to his head.

Kelemeneke Makaila's nephew had taken on his uncle's duties, and would do the blessing. Kenika asked him if he used the same ceremony that his uncle had, and he said yes, he did, with some modifications, but it was still essentially the traditional blessing.

Kenika would go home and report the progress to Angela and the kids, and if the kids were not at home: "Can I help you?"

"Oh, I'm sorry, I walked into the wrong house."

"Well, I J. B. McKay, a terapis'."

"Sorry to disturb you. What does J. B. stand for?"

"Oh dat jus' a name. Eh, why da long face?"

"Oh, it's a personal problem."

"I an expert on personal problems. What's wrong? You can tell me."

"Oh, it's just that, well, nothing about women gets me at all excited. I'll never have kids. Well, I'll be going."

"Wait, why don't you tell me more about dis problem?"

"No, it won't work. It's psychological. I look at a woman with no clothes on, at everything, and nothing happens."

"Tsk, dat serious. Come wit' me, see if I can help. You look at aw da body pahts an' notting happen? We fine out now."

"'Kay."

"Dis very techincal. Stick out da tongue."

"Ahhh."

"Can you move it?"

"Ahhgkch! No."

"Get all dakine stuffs down heah?"

"Ouch."

"Uh oh, I tink so. Put da han' unda heah an' feel. What you feel?"

"A breast, but wait. I thought— It's soft. I thought that it would be sort of hard?"

"Why?"

"The only other one I felt was on a big plaster statue in school. The one with no arms, Venus de whoosis."

"You get one serious problem. When I tell you do something, you do it, 'kay? On'y way dis can work."

"'Kay, but like I told you, it won't work."

"My office is in this room."

≈   ≈   ≈

The Peni'amina was given its brains in late September by Kalani Chun, Kelemeneke Makaila's nephew. Chun was in his seventies, Kenika guessed, but healthy, and he resembled his uncle in being thin and very dark.

Those participating in the blessing came in five buses and a number of cars, and although he thought they might have considered it an inconvenience, the two-hundred-fifty or more kids, from five up to thirteen, seemed to think that there was no better aspect to acquiring a canoe for their school than coming up here for the blessing and for the immense quantity of food heaped up in Mr. Marumoto's garage, various plates brought by parents. The parents and various chaperones took the whole thing with good humor and, to Kenika's surprise, an obvious respect for the ritual. No one appeared to sneer or whisper to a neighbor when Kalani Chun shouted that this canoe would be a safe one because of dis ritual, that dis canoe would proteck its passengers, and that dis canoe would ride highah inna wattah an' bring in mo' fish den one nevah blessed, that the soul of this canoe was in the wood and then rose up over it in one dakine invisible canopy dat enfolded da paddlers like one dome fo' proteck.

Kenika stood there looking at the Peni'amina as Kalani Chun spoke. It was stout and high, wide, with manu fore and aft in lighter koa, with two 'iako of hard hau and a wiliwili ama. The hull was thick, strong and dark, like Benny, and had long, sweeping lines of redder grain that went iridescent in the powerful sunlight. There was no question in his mind about it. It was a strong, and now with the chant, a smart canoe. And when he looked at the huge circle of kids, their colorful clothes almost dizzying in the light, their hair black, brown, blonde, he thought that there must be no better future in the world for a canoe than this. He imagined that some element of Benny's spirit resided in the dark grain, aware that for as long as this canoe lived, it would be a kids' canoe, feeling them crawling over the mo'o boards to find their seats, their little feet flat on the wood at the bottom of the hull.

Kalani Chun closed the salt circle, lit a match and dropped it into the gap, and called out, "Maika'i ka lolo ana—dis spell complete!"

Angela and the twins helped pass out the salt, only a tiny pinch for each child, taken from wooden bowls they held out as the long line approached the Peni'amina. Clarice and Elizabeth were a little nervous and awed by all this, never having seen any of these kids before, so they gawked, mouths open, when older boys came up to reach into the bowls, and seemed to study each child going by, as if each one were some strange, exotic creature from some far-off country.

Later while everyone ate, Kenika explained to a small group of teachers and parents all he could about traditional lashing, about component parts, about shape. Mr. Robertson then drew him aside and said, "Everyone is very pleased." He drew out a check. "It's for twenty-five hundred. We allocated a little more, given the cost to you."

"Thanks." He looked at the canoe. "Listen, I get the impression that people are a little baffled about a lot of this. What if I made a model, say two feet long, and marked parts, maybe put some stuff down on paper?"

"Well, that's—"

"No, there's extra money here in this check. I'll just go ahead and make the model."

≈   ≈   ≈

He didn't know if it was the effect of beer, or the weather, which was too hot for late fall, but manufacturing the model of the Peni'amina was taking far longer than it should, because he became too involved with doing it right, drawing diagrams, looking up all the Hawaiian words so that the parts were correctly named, the seats, the riggings. The singing board simply groaned at him when he walked across it, as if the entire shed were bored, or in pain, and he felt somehow alienated even when he was there. At night he would sometimes awaken from dreams he didn't understand and didn't like, and it was as if he knew something but didn't know he knew it. In some he was a boy tied up tightly in ropes and being carefully stalked by something that resembled a carrion bird, in others he ran glue-legged from vicious dogs on long chains, a dream from his childhood. In other dreams he was denied breath, or light, and had to endure those denials without understanding why, but did so with a patience that just managed to outweigh his fear.

Christmas and the sustained explosion of the fireworks on New Year's Eve, and the multitude of family activities distracted him from it, but whenever he returned to the shed, that same sensation would return to him. He thought that he might never have really been the right person to be doing this, to be muttering encouragement to a two-foot model of a canoe that he did not have the energy to complete, which he escaped from by making wind chimes, or applying a little pen knife to the relief picture which he also did not have the energy to finish.

And when the model was finally done there seemed nothing left, no reason to go out there again. He called Robertson and took the model over the mountain to the school, and asked him how the Peni'amina was doing. Robertson told him that by then every student in the school had paddled it, some more than once. He was impressed by the model and by the written explanations that went with it, and promised Kenika that should they ever want another canoe, they'd call him first.

And so two days later he found himself back at the shed, without energy and without any idea of what to do next. The thought of another wind chime disgusted him. The thought of scale models wasn't as bad, but he didn't have the energy to do them. He hated the relief picture, because it looked amateurish and crude, and he draped it with a piece of tarp and sat down and drank beer. By the time he had finished his fourth beer it was two-thirty and he had done absolutely nothing. He contemplated going up the hill to ask, but at the same time felt that even they were irritated with him for some stupidity obvious to them but a mystery to him.

But the shed was one world, home the other. The twins were growing up. They were tall, with beautiful eyes over which hovered black eyebrows. They were dark little versions of Angela but for a leanness she did not have and may never have had, and he assumed that it was the Kenika in them that caused it. One day, giggling with amazement, Angela told him that when they took their showers and she was in there, she saw that each had a little round patch of pubic hair the size of a fifty cent piece, right up there in front, and it was also obvious that she had to go to Liberty House and get them training bras. Later in the spring he was sitting in the living room while at the dining room table fifteen feet away Angela watched them do their homework and then said, "Sit up straight. Why you go aroun' wit' da shouldahs hunched alla time?"

They both shrugged.

She squinted at them, and then said, "Stand up."

They groaned and did so.

"See dat? You get hunchback too much li'dat." She studied them for a few seconds and then put her hands on her own breasts. "What dese?"

"Chichis," Elizabeth said.

Clarice snickered. "Chichi balls."

"Stick yoah chests out."

"Why?"

"Does Daddy have to be heah?"

"Ne'mine him. You get chichis, so stick dem out. No try fo' hide 'em. Does Annette on TV hide dem?"

"Ho, she can't," Clarice said.

"So?"

The twins looked at each other, then at Angela, who shook her upper body so that her breasts shook.

"Mommy!"

"So? Dey chichis. I to' you, you girls, so take a deep breat' an' stick dem out."

The twins then took deep breaths and stuck their chests out, their backs arched.

"Dat too fah. You get cramp da back."

"'Kay, den li'dis?"

"'Ass bettah. Now when you go skoo, put da shouldahs up an' no worry. What you tink, boys aw say 'oh look da twins. Get chichis!'"

"Well, dey will!"

"So?"

"So I not gonna go stick um inner faces."

"I not askin' you stick chichis anywheah, jus' no try fo' hide um. You girls. You get chichis an' nice roun' okoles."

"I no want roun' okole."

"Either me."

"Well you gonna get um, so no try hide dat either, 'kay?"

"'Kay."

"Den bumbye you get boyfrien' an', 'kay, talk about dat laters 'kay?"

"Hah," Clarice said, "I see you stick chichi in Daddy's face."

"No talk stink! Wheah when you see dat?" Then Angela began to think, and her face dropped into an expression of suspicious wonder. "Hah? Wheah when?" Now her eyes were wide, because she must have been imagining one of those ridiculous afternoon games. "Wheah when?"

"We watch TV an' you all ovah him. Ho, poke his eye."

"No talk stink," Angela said, now obviously relieved.

After that conversation the girls walked around the house with their chests stuck out, to the point that Keoki, one afternoon after baseball practice, looked at them and then at Kenika, his face twisted with wonder and disgust, and said, "Why dey go roun' ho'ding breat' alla time?"

Keoki was eight, and so ferociously energetic in any sport he played that Kenika always worried that he'd get badly hurt. He would approach a ground ball or a player about to kick a soccer ball, with no fear, his dark, eager face radiating challenge, and when he did get hit he would shake off the impulse to drop to the ground sobbing as other boys sometimes did, and play on. His soccer and baseball coaches both watched him, shaking their heads with amazement, and once his soccer coach elbowed Kenika and said, "Ho, get lakas, da boy!" And Kenika stood there thinking, balls, the boy's got balls. As a consequence of his obsession with sports, in fact any sport, he wasn't much of a student academically, unlike the twins, who were always nearly perfect in their grades. Their room was full of books, papers, seed-stringing projects, while his room was a mess of sports equipment: shin guards for soccer, dirty uniforms, baseballs, sneakers stained with the red dirt of the playing field.

But Kenika had to go back to the shed, to do what felt like some penance he did not understand. He forced himself to make canoe models and wind chimes, and the beer he drank would leave him open to running chisel heads over his hand and cutting himself, or screwing up his work by applying too much pressure in the vise and cracking coconut shells.

One day late in spring as they sat at the table eating dinner, he was aware that the girls and Angela were looking at him, then at each other, as if they were getting ready to ask him something.

Finally Angela said, "The girls are joining a canoe club."

"Hey that's great," he said. "Which one, Lanikai?"

"No, a new one called Olomana," she said. "It's small. They can't enter most of the races. But they're allowing girls to paddle with boys because they don't have enough boys, in the twelve and under bracket."

It was proper speech, which meant that she was not finished.

"Olomana has two canoes, one thirty-three feet long and way over four-hundred pounds, the other forty-five."

The girls went on eating.

"Lemme think about that," he said. When Clarice drew breath to speak, Angela put her finger to her lips.

So, they wanted The Red Wind. Later, wandering around in the backyard picking up fronds from under the palm tree and folding them up for the garbage, he knew that he could not let them take it, and felt a hot swoon of shame and embarrassment, because it was a reasonable request. It was business, and he had to sell it. When they went to bed he was surprised to find that Angela said no more about it, and because of that he found that he could not sleep.

He escaped from the house just as the kids got on their bicycles and headed off for school. And when he got to the shed he squished through the mulch, jumped over the stream, and stopped. Benny had been a believer in odd sensations, da co' chill, the impressions that things in nature looked at him, and Kenika stood there staring at the dark, looming shed and felt that every rock regarded him patiently, watched his every move, and he felt a growing, subtle fright worming its way throughout his body. He shook it off and went up the steps into the shed and stepped on the board, and again it groaned as if sick.

Sitting at the table staring at a piece of junk koa, planning to shape it, he sighed and gave up, and with his elbows on the table, rested his face in his hands and whispered, "Oh shit. Oh shit." He opened his eyes again and looked out through the screen. Nothing. Silence. He ran his eyes around the interior of the shed, and saw the tarp pulled back again from the bow of the canoe, and got up to cover it. When he approached, the feeling came back again, but this time it radiated from under the tarp, and he wondered for a moment if something had gotten in there, rats or something. He stepped closer, and the feeling of radiation intensified, and he thought he heard something like whispering, and he was sure that something or someone was there.

When he understood it, all the hair on his head and arms stood up, and he felt choked off and breathless and unsteady on his feet, as if the floor would collapse under him. If he had ever had any doubts about a piece of wood being alive, they vanished, because it was clear that the voice had been pleading to him for years, and he was too stupid to listen. "I'm sorry," he whispered. He pulled back the tarp. "I was stupid, stupid." The strange field of something like electricity hovered around the wood, and he placed his hand on the manu, and shook his head in wonder. Every canoe they had ever built went from the blessing to the water, except this one. Every canoe felt the water sweep under it as it knifed along, the paddleshafts thumping its ka'ele. Every canoe felt flesh pressed against its seats and hull base. The Red Wind had sat in the cradles for—what was it, two plus years, and had never felt water, and it had been miserable for those years, lying in its cradles wondering why it was not allowed to feel water sliding under its hull. It was in exile from its element because of Kenika's foolishness or selfishness or whatever, and he had sat right over there like a gleeful dummy chattering away to the Peni'amina while The Red Wind had lain there waiting to feel water and flesh, and he realized that once it had been done he had stopped talking to it, had left it there as if it were some inanimate object, and it was forced to sit there waiting patiently, ignored and agonized by thirst.

He was dimly aware that it might be his own paranoia that caused all this, but ran back out to the Marumotos' to borrow their phone, to call Angela. He was made a little breathless by the run, and when she answered he said, "Look, tell the girls to tell their coach that they can have The Red Wind. Don't let them get any other canoe, 'kay?"

"'Kay. Kenika, what's the matter?"

"Nothing. Just tell them not to forget to tell their coach, 'kay? I'll get her there as soon as I can but the Kama boys are— Well, you know what I mean."

"Kenika, dey won't practice till nex' week."

"'Kay, but don't let them get—"

"What happened?"

"Nothin'. Just occurred to me is all."

He couldn't tell her. He couldn't tell anybody.

When he went back to the shed he pulled the tarp off. "It's time for you now," he said. "Wait, lemme get a rag, clean all that stuff off. Yeah, now you go to the water. How about you and a bunch of kids, eh? Forty-five feet is too long and you're thirty-seven and a half." Rubbing the dust off the hull, he whispered, "Okay, now you'll breathe."

And breathe she did. He could feel her glow when he pulled the trailer up to the right-of-way and could smell the water and felt the glow behind him when he went to meet the coach, whose name was Junior Ho, and some of the paddlers, whom he asked to help carry her from the trailer to Lanikai beach. They approached her and their faces all changed expression when they saw her shape and color. In fact as he watched, he had the impression that her heart was thumping as they all stood around gawking at the strange, red fire of the hull, when they ran their hands along it and felt no lumpiness or imprecision on the surface, when they studied the carefully-carved wae and the manu. He had to answer "Yes I did," to the question did you build it, ten or twelve times.

And from the moment he helped the men of the Olomana Canoe Club lash her to the moment when they carried her to the water and he felt the sudden buoyancy as the bow was lifted, he could feel the vibration of joy in the wood. He had asked the coach if it was okay for now that the Makani ʻUla be used by the younger crews and by the novice and junior women crews and the coach agreed, saying, "Eh, perfeck fo' dem. Da big one da men's." Junior Ho didn't know that Kenika was treating the Makani ʻUla as a kind of virgin of the water, that he couldn't help but cringe whenever he saw someone put a hand on her hull or saw a child turn and strike part of his or her paddle against it. He knew it was foolish to be so protective, as if the canoe were a piece of fine china, and tried to override those fears as he watched them practice on the days he left the shed early. At night she took up temporary residence on a beachside lawn behind the house of Jerry Cambra, one of the senior paddlers, and kept company under a giant tarp with the Hokuʻaeʻa, or Wandering Star on one side and the short, stocky Akelina, or Adeline on the other.

The boys' twelves, including Clarice and Elizabeth, practiced right after school, repeating their quarter-mile sprints over and over. Junior Ho asked him to help with coaching the kids, and he quickly said he would, again because he wanted to keep watch over The Red Wind. Junior then said, "Eh, you like paddow mens?" Like the other men of the club, Junior had large shoulders and a muscular upper body.

"Sure," he said, "but if I get another canoe order, I won't be able to."

"Cannot now anyways, cause you'd be a team of one," Junior said. "We get boy's twelves, women's novice, men's junior an' men's senior an' 'ass it. You be one benchwahmah. But somebody get sick, 'kay?"

That was all right. He built canoes. He did not have to paddle them any more than to help the kids and refine the lashing to avoid drag. The fore of the ama had to be toed in somewhere between three-quarters of an inch and an inch and a half, and for The Red Wind, it turned out to be an inch.

Through the late spring he watched the kids sprint, their hair flying, their shrill voices calling out the switches and the pace. As for the real races, he did not expect much. The boys were skinny except for one, who was maybe too fat, and the twins were taller than any of the boys. The twins sat in the three and four seats, the fore of the powerhouse, and he reasoned that this made sense because one was left-handed and the other right-handed. The heavy boy, Clayton Shigemura, sat in the fifth seat in front of the steersman. That they could do well in a regatta was something that sat at the back of his mind. That they paddled a smart canoe who would protect them was at the front.

He had thought that turning over the canoe to them would automatically make going to the shed less alien, but it did not seem to have that effect. Each time he went he had that feeling of the boulders and the mountains regarding him with a kind of brooding doubt, as if penance for his error could not be wiped away so easily. The sensation of the presence of something in the air was not frightening, but it was not comfortable. It was just there, as if the next thing he should do would be to blurt out, "What do you want then?" But he kept his mouth shut.

≈   ≈   ≈

The King Kamehameha Regatta was held on the first Sunday in June only a mile away on Kailua Beach, and leading up to it, Kenika was aware that an entirely new group of friends had made its way into their world: Angela discovered that Junior Ho's wife had gone to high school with her. "She one snob, but no mo'. She so nice." After practice Kenika drank beer with Junior and Jerry Cambra and some of the other men. Angela and the women plotted potluck parties for the regatta days.

All of this was aimed at that first Sunday. On Friday, Junior Ho got all the kids together and told them, "Eat plenny rice an' poi nex' two days, get plenny sleep."

For Kenika, whatever encouragement he could give them came in the form of something he felt embarrassed to express, so he held back until just before the race. There were probably fifteen-hundred people lining the carefully blocked-out course, which had buoys and flags marking the lanes, and a large tent at the finish line inside of which were race officials, huge, dark women in sarongs, men sitting at tables with rosters and field glasses so that they could see which manu crossed first, second, third. There were eleven clubs there, each with its own tent and food table, some with people playing guitars and ukuleles and singing. Kenika walked the beach first and studied each canoe, found the Lapa Uila, and looked around, found no one nearby, and leaned down, whispering, "Hey, how you doin'? How they treating you?" He looked around for Mr. Stevenson, its owner, but did not see him. Then he went down the line of canoes, stared at the lashing, shape, parts of each and went back, hearing a garbled male voice on a bullhorn.

In their club tent all the paddlers were sitting around, and all the paddles were blades down in a line, suspended by two post-supported parallel clotheslines looped over the handles. Up on the grass on two reed mats sat George, Irene and Momi. The schedule was simple: the youngest would go first, and that meant that the twelves would be in the first race. Junior gathered them together and gave them a little pep talk, and when the time came and Kenika thought it might be possible to talk to the kids without any other adults around, he went around and whispered to each of them to come down and meet at the canoe. He found himself fearing ridicule even from the kids, but could not let them go without trying to put into words what he felt they should know, whether or not they believed it.

When they were all there he looked at them. The twins stood holding their paddles and he noticed that, yes, their shoulders were already bigger, their skin very dark from the sun, the ends of their long hair singed dark copper. Just as he was about to speak an adult did wander over, Angela, and although he might have thought better of this, he found that he felt no embarrassment at all. In fact, her presence made sense. "Listen," he said, "do you know why this is called the Makani 'Ula?"

"Uh huh," they said.

"It means The Red Wind, but 'ula means red like your skin. 'Like the skin of a Hawaiian' the dictionary says. We named her this because it's like a thousand years ago when your ancestors came here, 'kay?"

"'Kay."

"I mean like sweeping over the water, like a wind made of people. Try to imagine that, people paddling thousands of miles in a kind of red wind. That's why the wood is this color. That's why we gave her this name. Here, put your hands on the hull, 'kay?"

They did so. To his surprise, Angela did too, and looked at him, waiting for him to continue. "The Red Wind is alive," he said. "If you concentrate, you can feel her making little movements. You can feel her mind tingle in your hands. The man who blessed her and gave her her brains is dead now, but she has them and she'll always have them."

He looked around at them. Not one showed anything but a concentration on holding the canoe. Clarice and Elizabeth stared up at him, their large, almond eyes caught in an expression of something approaching a mystified awe. One boy turned and saw men carrying a canoe to the water for his crew's short warm-up, and he got an anxious look on his face.

"You won't be paddling The Red Wind. What I'm saying is that you *are* The Red Wind. Her flesh is your flesh. You want to do well and she wants to do well. She wants to feel your heels and okoles on her body. She wants you to pull the ocean past her as hard as you can because she knows who you are. If you remember that you are The Red Wind then she'll glide through the water like a knife, 'kay?"

"We are The Red Wind," Clarice said, and the other kids said, "Uh-huh," and "Yeah, 'ass what we are."

"Don't be afraid to talk to her. Don't be afraid to bang your shafts against her, even though a good stroke doesn't do that. And do what she wants. She doesn't want any other canoe to get out ahead of her, 'kay?"

"Yeah."

"'Kay, we no let um do dat."

"We da Red Win'."

"That's right. She is you. She was born for you. She sat inside a log fifty years waiting to feel your flesh on her, and now finally she feels you, 'kay? Do you feel like a heartbeat? Does it feel like something breathing?"

"Uh-huh."

"Ho, I feel um. I do."

"Yeah, me too."

"But suppose you do let other canoes out ahead?"

"We no do dat."

"Uh-uh."

"But if you do, she won't be mad, 'kay? Just remember what she wants. What happens is something else maybe. But don't worry about it after the race."

"'Kay."

"Let's get her in the water."

As they paddled out toward the start line down the beach, Angela watched, then slid her arm around his waist. Then she whispered to him, "Aftah dat I bet dey win."

"They don't have to."

He waited on the finish line, standing in the sand down from the officials' tent and under their line of vision of the finish, which stretched in a dotted line of flags hundreds of yards out into the water. Angela had gone to the start, and would follow them as they raced. From where he stood, the sun beating down on him, the canoes looked like a cluster of black dashes against the water, maneuvering slowly around each other, the men who would hold the sterns steady bobbing in the water. Then all eleven of them were lined up, and a quarter of a mile away they looked tiny, the Makani 'Ula number six out of eleven, the figures perched on her seats appearing to him smaller than those in the other canoes. He wished he had binoculars.

A large inboard-motor sport fishing boat plowed its way through the water out to the finish line, its engine roaring. Then he looked at the line of canoes, the tiny arms all raised up, waiting to plunge their paddles into the water. Then with the flags, the race started. He saw the sixth canoe swerve, and the ama rise up and slap down. "It's okay," he whispered. The canoes crawled out, and he could see the tiny arms going up and down, up and down, little splashes of water shooting away, and then he heard people cheering down the beach, but faintly because of the sound of the breeze and the little waves near his feet. Although the canoes were moving, he could not perceive them coming closer. After about thirty seconds they were just a little closer, large enough that he could make out manus, and the glittering splashes of water off the paddles were clearer.

Because of the sharp angle of his vantage point, he could not tell if anyone led, but the yelling from down the beach told him that someone must have led. The manus rose up and floated down, the arms went up and down. At about a third of the way they all seemed to stop, but he knew it was an illusion. The bows were larger, all lined up, and because they were coming obliquely toward him, he could no longer see movement, as if it were some strange dream. Four, five, six. They were still there in the middle, their arms going up and down, the water now clearer fanning away from the bow, the manu clearer. They still did not seem to move. He looked down the beach and saw figures fast-walking or jogging along, one of them Angela. Half way.

Now the yelling was clearer. The manus were clear too, as were paddleshafts and sprays of water, and the canoes were moving again, enlarging as they approached, and four, five, six, it was still there in the middle, apparently not ahead, but not back either, and he began to see hair flying, and the faint sounds of thumping came across the water, then voices, and he could see the line of manus now, surging ahead, dragging back with each pull of the paddles. Two thirds.

Now he could see three of the canoes behind and the rest about even, and five, six, they were still in it, and coming now toward broadside in his vision, closing toward the line of flags, and the kids were not giving up, they flung themselves into it, spray from the paddles going up and hovering, then dropping behind the canoe, and the thumping of wood on wood was clear, the figures black silhouettes, and the manus surged ahead, dropped back, surged ahead, the uneven line approaching the even line, and the yelling was right down the beach from him.

The wide angle of the two lines closed, and five, six, their arms and fists went up and down. The lines were like scissors slowly closing because of the foreshortened view from the distance into the shore, and he could not tell who was ahead. The canoes farther out seemed to inch toward the line while close in they raced at it, closing the distance with a speed that the canoes farther out did not seem able to match. Then he finally could fix in his vision the manu of The Red Wind creating another irregularity in the line, which caused a deafening shouting behind him. It was two feet out from the line, and as it seemed to inch at it, the kids' hair flying and spray shooting, the one closest to the beach raced at the flag, and he stooped down, his hands on his knees, and just made out the manu of The Red Wind break the line before the canoe closest to the beach shot across it, and with that, all the skin on his body erupted in gooseflesh. He saw Elizabeth holding her paddle over her head, Clarice slumped over on her knees. The other members of the club ran down the beach waving, holding up their fists, followed by others carrying leis, but he stood there rooted to the spot. Practice, rice and poi, or, and he thought, that other—it didn't matter. He stood up and turned, and saw Momi and Irene coming down the beach with leis draped over their arms.

By the end of the day The Red Wind had also placed third in the women's novice half-mile, fifth in women's junior. When its day was over it went back to sit with the Wandering Star and the Adeline. Around dusk, while they ate on Jerry Cambra's lawn, Keoki playing in the water with other little boys and Angela talking with Jerry's wife, Kenika wandered across the back yard to check on the kids in the water, and saw the twins sitting on their seats on The Red Wind, facing each other and talking, slowly rubbing the hull and looking at it. Then they both placed their hands on the hull and he could tell that they were feeling it, and didn't want to bother them. He imagined that The Red Wind, after the long day of knifing through the water, liked nothing better than feeling the flesh of the two beautiful children on her.

On Monday he went back to the shed, and just as he jumped over the stream, he felt a welcome coolness in the breeze, and imagined a whisper of invitation coming from the wet air around him. He walked without any sensation of strangeness or alienation up the mossy steps into the shed and it was as if the gentle breeze more or less sucked him into it, and standing there, having no idea what to do next, he saw the prospect of an infinity of choices as a gift. The Red Wind was back on Jerry Cambra's lawn, snoozing with her friends, and even the vague presence he had felt all these years, that undefined set of shapes that seemed to reside everywhere and to watch the outsider they had still yet to finally judge, now regarded him with affirmative nods. He grabbed an old mesh onion bag from the pile Benny had kept in the corner, and went out and climbed down into the ravine as he had done that first day, and collected dry coconuts for some trinket making. This time, he thought, he would find small ones out of which he would make bracelets, into which he would etch little pictures, canoes, palm trees, birds in flight.

≈   ≈   ≈

On the wall in the little alcove they called a study, he had mounted three maps, one of the world in a Mercator projection, so that the south and north poles took on a bulk many times in excess of their actual sizes, and Hawaii remained a little string of dots in the middle of the Pacific. He had stared at just such a map years ago and perceived the awful remoteness of where he stood, but now, next to that map, he had a larger one picturing the island chain, so that Oahu was as big as a dinner plate, and then next to that one, he had a full-sized map of Oahu showing topography and reef placement, including ocean depths and currents. In the study he had a small desk, and books on shelves made of koa scrap, from an encyclopedia to books on navigation and boating, and books on flora and fauna, arts and crafts, which Angela liked to collect.

When he was in there he would go to the map of the island chain and understand that there, on that island the size of a dinner plate, in fact only on the northern side of the eastern tip, everything happened, at least for him, and on the bigger Oahu map he could reach out and touch the reefs he fished. The outer world took on for him the remoteness of outer space, and although he was interested in manned satellites circling the earth, was interested in the threat of nuclear war with Russia, was interested in watching sports on TV, especially with Keoki, that world seemed almost artificial to him. It was as if the maps were actually in scale, so that Oahu was more or less the same size as China, its mountains, surrounding water, clusters of population constituting a kind of "mainland," which reduced the rest of the world into a weird place where weird things happened and he was a distant, casual observer. He knew full well the insularity of their lives, had heard one acquaintance or another proclaim that it was time to get off this rock, heard the twins talk about what a big world was out there, and whenever he heard this, there would be a small, inexplicable rush of heat throughout him, as if any compromise of this insularity was hateful. The world he understood was about six-hundred square miles, only a few of those his. He was part of the center of a family that he and Angela had increased by three, while time had decreased it by two.

In September after the regatta season was over and the girls had won two races, had come in second in two and third in another and had their little medals mounted on the wall in their room, Darnay's friend James was murdered in Waikiki by two men trying to mug him. They saw film on TV, of police lifting a heavy, lumpy bag onto a stretcher on wheels, which they deposited into the back of a large station wagon. Shortly after that Darnay gave up doing dirty hula on Hotel Street and got another job, working at Angela's flower shop, and rented a little apartment in downtown Kailua. Rather than thinking of this as an imposition, Kenika felt a twinge of satisfaction that now every member of what he considered to be his family was situated within walking distance of his house.

He would drive home and stop at the shop, and might walk in to find Angela, Irene, Momi and Darnay sitting around the table, flowers lying in a bright profusion of color before them. And when they talked, there was very little difference in the sound of their voices, Darnay's soft voice resembling that of a Hawaiian grandmother, his enthusiasm for the beauty of the leis as bright and feminine as Irene's or Momi's. And although Kenika had wondered what the presence of the immense mahu might do for business, if anything it increased it. Unlike that distant, vague thing called Paterson, where queers were vilified universally, where the idea of homosexuality was one most men and women despised, here Darnay was accepted as an equal, was in fact popular among the patrons of the shop. When haole parents came to pick up leis or lapel arrangements for one ball or another, they sometimes looked somewhat wary in the presence of the gentle monster, but local people chatted with him in the same tone they might use with an auto mechanic or bank teller. Even when Darnay let his hair grow so that he could draw it together in a pony tail in back, that bizarre development in his personal appearance seemed to go unnoticed.

There was a kind of sleepy stability in the neighborhood, except for routine problems: dogs barking at night, arguments, the old neighbor who was an alcoholic and would stumble past the house, get to within fifty feet of his own just four houses up the block, and then wilt into the roadside grass and fall asleep in the blazing sun. Kenika would walk up and half carry him into the carport where there was a filthy old couch. The man's wife would not let him into the house when he was in this condition. And there was Becky Kam, three years older than the girls. She had caused a shift in the nature of the violent arguments they heard drifting through the fence, because she was getting into trouble with boys, which would have been none of Angela's concern but for her contact with the twins. The girls would sit behind an 'ilima bush in the corner and talk with her and pass candy or cracked seed through the fence. One day Kenika and Angela were killing little black ants who had set up a nest in the bedroom screen frame, and their conversation was audible, punctuated by the twins' familiar gasps of surprise. Angela had assumed that their conversations were only about girly things, clothes, rock and roll, boys, but it went farther than that:

"You know, I gi' one dakine blowjob to one soldiah."

Gasp. "Not. Really?"

"Yah, an' I let um shoot dat stuff in my mout'."

"Not. What it tase like?"

"His dakine dis long."

"Really?"

"An' den we wen' inna backseat. Ho, was so fun. 'Kaywait, I tell you da ho' ting."

Angela stared wide-eyed at Kenika, then called out the window. "Girls!"

"What?"

"I— We goin' Liberty House! You like go?"

At night it was Denise Kam screaming at Becky. "Why you do dat! You slut! Why you let um touch you dere? Ho, I bet it was moah, ah? You let um do dakine didn' you?" And Larry, "You do dat one mo' time I lock you inna house a mont'!" But when they ran into them in the supermarket, Becky would run over to Angela and say, "Auntie!" and kiss her on the cheek.

In early spring he got an order for a racing canoe, from the Central Pacific Academy. Clarence Lum and Mr. Robertson came to the house, and this time were prepared: it was to be called Hokulele O Kamali'i, or the Shooting Star of Children. The school had had a naming contest, and this name won. He liked the oddness of the name, and its length. This time they would pay handsomely, because they had the money budgeted and the Academy was planning to expand to become a K through twelve school, and Clarence Lum believed that canoe racing was going to expand to the point where all schools would have teams, and he wanted his school to get a good canoe now.

"No full logs though," Kenika told them. "You guys want another beer?"

"Sure," Clarence Lum said. Kenika got up from the table and went to the refrigerator and got three out, and opened them. "But I've got a fat log about twenty-two, twenty-three feet long. Benny and I talked once about how to cut it," and he went on to explain that this canoe was in there, but folded over on itself, and had to be cut out and joined in the middle. "I was thinking that I would inset four strong ribs in the hulls which would cross that joint, and the joining'll be a kind of sawtooth thing."

"So it's a single log, technically," Robertson said.

"Yeah. It'll take longer though."

That was no problem. The school wouldn't need it for more than a year, but was still prepared to offer a substantial down payment. No, Kenika told them, I'll make it and you come out and see if you want it.

It would be forty feet long. It would have a thinner beam, maybe seventeen inches, thus making it possible for him to stay at four hundred pounds and have the hull thicker so that the stabilizing beams running through the joint would be strong. All component parts would be traditional, including 'ohi'a for the spreaders and hau for the 'iako and so on. Newer canoes tended to have small, short manus, making them look like trivial decoration. 1963 or not, he would put on manus that were tall and regal, with the traditional flat, vertical oval rising up. This canoe would appear to have been made fifty years ago, but it would still be light, and would slice the water like a knife. And Kelemeneke Makaila's nephew Kalani Chun would bless it and give it its brains. Were they prepared to haul all those kids up to Mr. Marumoto's again? They were.

It didn't matter to him that other builders had invented all sorts of labor-saving techniques, the use of power tools, chainsaws and so on. He did not want to save his labor. As far as he was concerned a canoe should be built the way it had always been built except that adzes and shaping materials were of steel rather than stone. The canoe needed to feel the shaper's hands, and feel the tools that helped it emerge from the log, working tap by tap rather than by the brutal, rapid tearing of a power tool.

For days he stood outside the shed in the cloud of black mosquitoes and studied the log, whose narrower end would be the fore and aft. He drew pictures of it, trying to figure the best way to separate the two hull halves, and concluded that he would shape the hull halves partway right where the log sat, and when he removed enough of the wood, working lying on the log and reaching down into a crevice and then working some sort of a tool in a trench at the base of the curve of one of the hull halves, until he could reach no further, he would drive a six-foot 'o'o with a wedge point in just the right spot and try to split the halves away. Or two or three 'o'o's.

The wood resisted him. Because of the mosquitoes, he wore a long-sleeved shirt and pants, and, constantly shaking his head and trying to blow air obliquely across his face, he dug the trenches the length of the log, following his plan to separate the trenches in a thin V, thus distinguishing the thin fore and aft points. He worked in the rain, remaining drenched all day. Where the two hull pieces spooned around each other, the trench for that distinction running obliquely along the log, he hacked with the adze, deepening the trench, but the awkwardness of what he was doing caused him to sting his hands when the tools caroomed off the wet, slippery wood. He sometimes became cramped, his muscles screaming when the fatigue of digging with the hand tools made them limp.

By the time a month had passed, he realized that the plan might not work. The awkwardness of trying to reach into a curving gap and scrape made the work so slow that he wondered if a power tool might be the way to go. And there was something else. The wood itself was surly, and did not give him any help. It was as if he were making it into something it didn't want to be, and he couldn't figure out why. He talked to it, in fact argued with it. "Goddammit, c'mon, give me just a little curl of wood, huh?" But it wouldn't. It sat there, stubborn and resistant, and at one point, probably irritated because of the rain, he kicked the log in a fury of impatience and nearly broke his toe.

When he left the shed he felt an immediate release of pressure. He limped home defeated, as he had walked into the house defeated before. He was beginning to hate this project.

Angela was at the table. "Jesus, I gotta shower," he said. Later, back in the living room he said, "Where's everybody?"

"Everybody?" she said, and then lowered her eyebrows in confusion.

"The kids?"

"What kids? I—" She shrugged. "Something's not right."

"What's the matter?" he asked, stepping toward her. Was something up with the kids? A wave of hot shock ran through him.

"Do I have kids?" she asked. He laughed. Of course. It was formal English.

"Yes, Angela, you do."

"Is that my name?"

"Yes."

"What are you?"

"I'm Kenika. I—"

"What is a Kenika?" She squinted at him. "You don't have any of—" And she put her hands on her chest. "These things here. Why?"

"Males don't."

"Are you a male?"

"Yes."

"Don't come any closer," she said quickly. "What else does— What did you say you were? A Kenika? A male? I thought male was something that guy stuck in the box out there."

"No, a male is a way of distinguishing sexes, although your definition suggests strange similarities, that is, 'box' and so on. I have various things that you don't, and the reverse. You have things I don't."

"Why? What is a 'sexes?'"

"It's hard to explain. If you take some of those clothes off, I can show you."

"I can't do that. Can I?"

"Well, if you want to know, you'll have to."

"All of them. Even—" and she looked down at her lap.

"Yes, that particularly, because the most interesting distinctions are there. But I'll help you. Don't worry, this is all in the interests of showing you the difference."

"But why is there a difference?"

"All I can do is show you. I know it's, well, embarrassing for you to do this, but you'll see."

"Well," and she looked down at herself, shook her head in mystified confusion. "Okay." She suddenly squinted at him, looking below his waist. "Excuse me, but do you have a banana in your pocket?" They both started laughing, but she gripped her mouth and held it back. "Well, where should we go?"

"There's a nice room in here with a bed in it."

"We have to be in a bed to do this— Comparison?"

"Yes, you'll see why."

≈   ≈   ≈

A log with so despicable a mulishness should not be shaped for children. The whole thing was turning out to be a mistake. Pretty as the wood was, it resisted, seemed to laugh at him, and he bruised his knuckles, fought the hand tools until he wilted with fatigue, lying on the log. At one point, drawing a small adze back toward him to get another niggling little scrap of waste, he ran a thick splinter into his forearm. When he pulled his arm out he saw that the splinter had entered the skin, moved under it about an inch, and then exited, and before he pulled it out he stared at it, feeling a twitch in his side. Just as the spear had done. He climbed up the stairs to get the little first aid box and doused the two holes with mercurochrome, and waited for the sting to pass. Something was fundamentally wrong, and he would not continue until he figured it out.

Sitting by the log, he drank one beer, then another. He stared at the log, whispered, "What's wrong with you?" By the time he was on his fourth beer, the pain of the holes in his arm began to dissipate, and he studied the log, waiting for an idea to form itself. He sat there, listening, thinking that there must be whispers in the air, stared at the wood until he became dizzy staring. Then the idea did form, and when he figured it out, he was amazed at the simplicity of it, and at his own ignorance. "Blood doesn't run both ways in a single vein, does it," he said to the log. "I'll call Kalani Chun. He'll help you." He got up, patted the log, and said, "You'll be okay now."

When he got home he verified that today the kids would be home earlier—Angela was busy in the back yard, throwing fertilizer around the bases of the 'ilima bushes—and called Kalani Chun. A woman answered and he asked for Mr. Chun, and she yelled, "Hui! Uncle!"

"I have a complicated problem," he told Chun. "It has to do with a log." He went on to explain that he was building a canoe, and tried to make clear the technical description of how he was cutting the log. "The wood resists me," he told him, "and I think it has to do with grain, that when it's done, the direction of the grain will be opposite back from front. Do you see what I'm talking about?"

"What you tink wood is?" Chun asked.

He paused, wondered what Chun was getting at. "Flesh," he said. "A kind of flesh."

"Whatchoo mean by dat?"

He cleared his throat, then felt embarrassed. "Well, I think it's alive. It's living flesh."

"'Kay," Chun said. "Den we on da same page."

"Is this a real problem?"

"Dis canoe fight itself. You join um li'dat, den back en' like go back an' front odda way. Come ho'opilikia whole life da canoe. How you figga dat out?"

"I sat and looked at it."

"You akamai boy figga dat."

"Is there any way to fix that?"

"Yah. I come up, talk to um an' bless um shtraight. Mus' let um know it awright fo' two sides join dis way. Look, dis not common. Fac' I nevah heard dis befo'. Make good sense but."

"Should anybody else be there except me?"

"No. Eh, have one beah wit' Marumoto laters, 'kay?"

"'Kay."

Chun would come up the next day, he said. When he hung up, Kenika stood there wondering as he had always wondered if his peculiar superstitions were so extreme that even kahunas found them strange. That Chun had never heard of this before made him suspicious, and he feared that the man might be simply indulging his manias. But he trusted Chun, and would do as he instructed. And he did not want to continue making a canoe that would spend its life fighting itself. Regardless of his belief in reason, he believed that the one thing about which he could never be cavalier or scientific was the canoe.

Chun parked his car at the Marumotos' and walked with Kenika down to the shed. It was raining, but he didn't want an umbrella, and he jumped easily over the little stream, approached the raw-looking, oddly-hacked log and said, "Ho, da big!"

"You want to cover yourself with a tarp or something?"

"Nah nah nah. 'Kay, which paht da fore-end?"

"This part here," Kenika said, touching the protrusion around which he had gouged the trenches. "This down here is the aft, I think."

"Once I do dis, cannot tink. Gotta be dat way, 'kay?"

"'Kay."

"Fo'get, den da canoe be slow, ride low inna wattah."

"I won't."

When Kalani Chun leaned over and studied what would become the aft section of the canoe, Kenika backed off a little. Chun held his hands over that section of the wood and spoke to it softly in Hawaiian, moving his hands and nodding his head. After two minutes of this, he turned and gestured for Kenika to approach, which he did. Chun grabbed Kenika's wrist and moved his hand to the wood, so that his palm fell on the wet aft section, and then Chun muttered more words, and ended by saying, "'Kay, 'ass it. She ready now."

"I wouldn't ask you what you said, but then I was wondering what you were saying more or less when you put my hand there."

"I ask um fo' let you be da one reverse da grain."

"But only the aft part, right?"

"'Ass it. Aft paht da paht give you troubles."

Kenika thought about that. "Yeah, the aft part put that splinter through my skin here," and he pointed to the dirty, rain sodden bandage on his arm.

"Anyways, we go Marumoto's."

"Lemme go in the shed and grab three beers."

"Eh, get six. Nine maybe."

"Before that though," Kenika said, drawing out his wallet. He took two twenties and a ten out and handed them to Kalani Chun, who smiled, revealing the huge, white teeth, and put the money in his pocket.

They sat in the Marumotos' kitchen and drank the beer, and ate pupus. Mrs. Marumoto looked at Kenika and Kalani Chun, went into the hall, and came out to the kitchen with two huge towels. "Put dese on," she said. "Kenika! You shivering. Come, put um on."

They did so, and in the next hour Kenika understood Kalani Chun's perspective on things that could be thought of as mysterious. "Da boy come wit' mana'o dat grains fight eachodda. I nevah heard about dis, but den wait." Chun went on to explain that we learn things until the day we die, and how many canoes might dere be wit' dis same problem? "Da boy feels da soul of da wood so he knows," and he looked at Kenika, nodding. "Akamai da boy," he said.

As for the wood accepting him after that, he was sure it did, although the work continued to be hard. He got to the point of separating the halves in April, and needed help. The Kama boys, Mr. Marumoto said, were off at college. He'd have to find someone else.

At the flower shop he found himself looking at Darnay. With a body that huge, maybe he would be enough. Angela worked on a bunch of lapel arrangements they called boutonnieres, and Darnay on some kind of floral arrangement of birds of paradise and strange, drooping plants called hanging heliconia, a string of closely-attached red and yellow triangular pods in a kind of sawtooth pattern which always reminded him of a string of huge pieces of candy corn.

"I think they sleep because they're growing," Darnay said to Angela.

"But chee, soon as dey get home?"

"Uh, Darnay?" Kenika said.

"Yes?" he said, not looking up from the arrangement.

"How'd you like to work one day with me up at the shed? I gotta winch a canoe up."

"Eh, Darnay mines," Angela said.

"It's all right, sweetheart," Darnay said. "Jus' one day?"

"Yeah."

"Monday den. I no been deah 'mos twenny yeahs."

Then Angela went on speculating on why the girls slept all the time. Kenika had only seen this a couple of times, but on Saturdays they wouldn't get up until eleven, and on weekday nights they would finish their homework and go to bed.

"I wonder if dey sick," Angela said. "Afta dey got period, dey sleep. Darnay, you weah boro-boros Monday. Muddy 'ass why."

"'Kay, get paint-splotched ones."

At home, sure enough, the girls were asleep, right after coming back from paddling practice. They had dusted off The Red Wind a month ago and were paddling women's novice now, because both had grown three or four inches in the past year. They were now about five-seven, eight maybe. Angela and Kenika went to their bedroom door and peeked in, and both were out cold, clad in tee shirts and underpants. "I know what it is," he whispered. "Look at them."

She did. Clarice was lying on her back with her fingers entwined behind her head. She was not a child. She had full, perfect breasts, and her legs, one resting straight over the other, one heel hooked over the other ankle, were the legs of a woman, long and dark and well shaped. She jerked in her sleep and muttered something unintelligible, and Elizabeth countered that with a loud fart. Angela snickered. "Animals," she whispered. Elizabeth was lying on her stomach with one leg drawn up, and those were not the buttocks of a child, that long, muscular back not the back of a child either. Angela squinted. "How many times I to' dem," she whispered, "no weah flowahs an' go bed." Each pillow had a loose rainbow plumeria on it, squashed and brown edged, and she tiptoed in and took them, pulling them away from their luxuriant, copper-brown hair. "Stain da pillowcases 'ass why," she said.

Sitting at the table with Angela, he said, "They're growing their bodies. You know how much they eat." The girls would come home and each eat an orange, a banana, five or six pieces of bread, drain a half a quart of milk, and a half hour later would say, "Mommy, when we eat?"

She had a look of wonder, even a kind of awe on her face. "I notice but den I don't," she said. "But 'ass what it is. Dey eat like pigs. Cereal bowl inna morning? Dey fill um up tchree times, eat, burp, go skoo. I should give 'em laundry tubs."

They usually went to the beach Saturdays while Keoki went to baseball practice or soccer practice or basketball practice, and now he was learning the skills of football with his friends. The twins would take their bikes and Angela and Kenika and sometimes the grandparents would join them later. One Saturday Angela sat on a towel and watched as the girls ran down and dove into the water while three boys who were walking along the beach watched, then seemed to lose their balance, acting as if they had been made dizzy by just seeing them. Angela nodded knowingly. "Ho, dey stacked," she said. "An' okole? I should nevah have bought two piece-suits."

As the morning went on they noticed that every male on the beach was distracted by them, even from a hundred yards, and when they horsed around throwing sand at each other, their bodies jiggled with a lucious animation, and Kenika wondered if they even knew the effect they had. "Are they interested in boys yet?" he asked.

"See a boy coming, dey run like rabbits an' hide," she said. "My God, they are so beautiful." It was a pronouncement made in proper-sounding English, and he had to agree. Not only were they beautiful, they exuded so powerful a sexuality that he was amazed that he had not seen it coming. And that potent aura was made even more potent because of their seeming lack of any hint of self-awareness.

"They remind me of you," he said.

≈   ≈   ≈

As for Darnay, Kenika found on Monday that he had underestimated his strength because he didn't suppose a man of his, what was the word? orientation, would be particularly strong. Kenika had removed most of the outside waste and started two six-foot 'o'o's and had pounded them into the thicker end of the log about a foot, and they took turns hammering them for an hour. In Darnay's huge fists the sledge hammer appeared to be light, made of some other material, and when he drew back and hit the ends of the bars, he rarely missed. It was on one of his powerful shots that Kenika saw the crack widen, and then saw the two crowbars lying loose in the crevice.

Then they pulled the halves apart, turning one half with the cant hook. Darnay helped him roll out one half so that it tottered, and then slammed down into the mud. "'Kay," Kenika said. "That's it. Now I do more cutting."

"No, we put um inna shed, right?"

"These halves weigh seven or eight hundred pounds."

"So?"

"Too heavy."

"Booshit. Get dat rope an' slide um undah dis one."

"But—"

Darnay laughed. "Memba dat? 'But dis,' an' 'but dat'?"

Kenika slid the rope under where he figured the fulcrum on the log would be and checked the positioning of the two slide logs, and then climbed into the shed, rolled the screen back, and played the rope around the thick beam. He moved to go back down. "Nah, jus' pull um when I lif'."

Darnay picked up one end of the log, so easily that Kenika slipped as he pulled the rope to wind it around the beam. Then Darnay hefted the log end up to his shoulder, and Kenika thought he had to be bearing five hundred pounds, and took two steps and set it down on the slide logs. The log slid, hanging on the rope, and Darnay steadied it. Within another twenty minutes the fore of the canoe was in the cradle. The same thing happened with the aft end. Kenika stared amazed as Darnay put one end on his shoulder and walked it to the slide logs.

When they were finished Kenika said, "I think you need more exercise. Those logs only weighed a half a ton each."

"Nah, less den dat."

"C'mon up, have a beer."

"Cannot. All muddy 'ass why."

"Nah, that's okay."

Darnay sat down in Benny's chair and said, "Yeah, 'ass it. Dis fit perfeck." He looked around. "Eh, fiah drum get pukas."

"Yeah." The perforated drum was on its last legs. "Gotta get a new one."

Kenika drew out fifty dollars and held it out to him.

"No, I not take money from you."

"No, c'mon, that's what it would cost me to hire people to do this. Take it."

"No, I not take um."

"C'mon, you gotta pay rent."

"'Kay, gi' me twenny den."

"Thirty?"

"No, jus' twenny."

He gave Darnay a twenty and got two beers.

They drank beer in silence for a while, Darnay looking around at the tools, and out through the screen at the up slope of the mountain. Finally he said, "I no take money 'cause you guys save me at one really bad time."

"Hey, that was sad, what happened to James."

"Was sad, yah. Was awful fo' me. T'ought I would die. You guys might not know dis," and he shifted in the chair, making it squeak with that familiar sound. "You guys might not know, but when dese tings happen to us folks," and Kenika knew he meant mahus, "it is jus' as bad. Read the paper, and what does it say? That a man was murdered in Waikiki. TV? You see a body bounced around in a bag. Ask anybody, eh, jus' one mahu, who cares? But you gotta unnastan', we feel tings jus' like you folks. You think mahus' hearts don't beat when they look at each odda jus' like when you look at Angela? You tink we don't love eachodda? You tink we don't worry about eachodda? You tink we don't kiss eachodda on da lips? Eh, I saw dat expression. But no worry, you what dey caw no'mal, an' cannot help dat. No no, no need fo' be sorry."

He went on to explain that when he was fourteen or fifteen he already knew, and Benny knew too, and one day, right here from this shed, Benny took him up the hill to the heiau, you know where that is? Kenika said yes, he was familiar with the place. Benny wanted Darnay to go to the heiau and he wanted whatever was in that place to straighten Darnay out, to tell him not to be a mahu. But when Darnay walked alone out onto those stones, and it was a really hot day and he was sweating from the long walk up the hill, he stood there dripping, and waiting for something to happen. He thought, eh, I one mahu, what you guys tink? and waited more for something to happen. And then something did. It was just a little breeze coming down the mountain, 'ass all, but when he turned to leave, he realized that he was just told that it was all right for him to be what he was, that nothing was going to change it, whether or not Benny wanted grandsons or a normal son or whatever it was he wanted. If you wanted to call whatever was up there spirits, then that's what they were, and they whispered to him not to worry about being what he was, and when he got back to the place where Benny had waited for him he told Benny that they had said it was all right for him to be what he was, and Benny just looked up the hill and thought for a while, and then nodded and said, c'mon, les' go back down. He never brought the subject up again.

"I memba dat. Tinkin', eh, I one mahu, whatchoo guys tink of dat? An' right at dat time, I feel dis breeze, and all of a sudden everyting okay."

"That's strange. You know, I went up there to name a canoe once."

"Makani 'Ula," Darnay said. "Benny to' me 'bout dat. He loved dat name."

"Benny trusted the spirits," Kenika said.

Darnay laughed. "'Ass good, cause it kep' 'im offa my back aftah dat." He looked across at the hulls. "So when you ripcut da top?"

"You know about that?"

"Yeah. My dad to' me all about dat."

"Well, you don—"

"Nah nah, I help you."

≈   ≈   ≈

Forty feet. As he worked, he had the impression that this canoe was not merely two and a half feet longer than The Red Wind, but ten feet longer. It might have been that he had the two halves separated as he hollowed out the hull, but walking along it all the way to the aft end, and stepping on the board which said "wa'a" now because it was heading for summer, he felt that it was somehow too large a project.

He would stop and run his eyes along the rough cut hull and wonder if something was wrong in his measurement. But then the building of any canoe was a large project, and each time, he knew, he was taking on something that he secretly felt he was not qualified for. But when he went down to Lanikai in the late afternoons to watch the twins at their practice for their half-mile races, he would run his eyes along the graceful hull of The Red Wind and think, well, there she is, and wonder how it was that he had been able to do that, and he was convinced that never in his life would he be lucky enough to repeat all the circumstances that made The Red Wind possible.

Into the slightly-thicker hull he embedded five ribs, each about eight feet long, three from the outside and two down from the inside, inset an inch and three quarters. The mo'o boards stabilized the joining, and then the wae went over the joint, topped by a strong seat on the ear cleats. He also embedded deep bow-tie insets over the joint, so that when the joint was complete, it might as well have been a single log.

The Hokulele O Kamali'i, which he had begun to think of as the Children's Shooting Star, was to be given its brains on Mr. Marumoto's lawn in November, but the blessing was delayed a month by the assassination of the President of the United States. On the world map Dallas, Texas was simply a little circle, whose size indicated the estimated population of that city. In the days following the assassination they spent a lot of time in front of the TV, and the more that was revealed about what happened, the more Kenika wondered about the modern world and its weirdness. And the vice president who would now be president was a man with huge ears and an exaggerated Texas drawl, who was pictured taking the oath of office on a plane while Kennedy's wife stood next to him in a blood-spattered suit. The clips of the event itself were repeated so often that after a while the movements of the people involved were fixed in his memory in a pinpoint lucidity.

He realized also that he knew little about the politics of the outer world. In fact the kids knew far more than he did. "What happens if this Johnson gets shot then?" he asked, and Clarice said, "Speaker of the House is next. And then if he can't, the president pro tempore of the Senate." Elizabeth stared at him. "It's all in the constitution," she said. "As Mrs. Wong says in class, Jefferson was a genius."

He hadn't known how the consititution was written. He hadn't known anything really about why Kennedy might have been shot: Castro, or the Mafia, or disaffected government people, or the KGB, or whatever. The twins discussed the various ramifications of the event with a grasp of current events that amazed him. What he did know came from all the reading he had done in Paterson. From reading encyclopedias in grade school he could explain exactly how World War I started, from the assassination of the Archduke Franz Ferdinand by a student named Princip, to the expansionist desires of the different European empires and so on. He knew the names of all the big World War II generals, ours and theirs. He could explain exactly how it was that a tribe in the Gobi Desert could conquer much of the known world in the 12th century. But he did not know what the ramifications were that so and so was a democrat and that other guy a republican.

He had the uneasy feeling that their isolation was no longer the insularity of the old days. And the wiser and more knowledgeable the kids became, the more that outer world seemed to cross the ocean and take up residence in the place he once felt was immune to it. Beautiful, healthy and strong as they were, his children seemed to him to be quite comfortable as residents of a planet rather than an island, and the implications of that troubled him.

At eleven Keoki was tall for his age, his skin almost black from the sun, his body muscular and marked with permanent, pinkish abrasions on his knees and ribcage from the fiberglass surfboard they got him for Christmas, on his elbows from sliding into bases. His face was square and well-formed and ferocious, and at school he liked nothing better than taking on any bully he and his friends ran across, better if the bully was a haole. He would come home with bruises on his face, but with a triumphant smile, and when Angela asked him what happened he would say, "Notting. I wen' beef wit' one haole boy. Ho, he look like shit."

"I to' you no talk li'dat," Angela would say, and he would mutter, "Sah-ree."

"Oh, you so kolohe, you! I no like you fight."

He had his allegiances and his jovially, cultivated hatreds, picked up from his friends, Kenika imagined. Haoles, no. Japanese without dark skin, no. And so on. Once when they sat on the little beach on the larger Mokulua island, resting after fishing, Keoki asked him, "Hey Dad, why you no talk like us?"

Kenika explained that he talked the way he did because of where he came from, and told him that it always sounded ridiculous to him when someone not from here tried talking that way. "You know, some big blonde guy saying, 'Eh, you like go feesh? Get dakine pole?' It just doesn't sound right."

Keoki laughed at that, and said, "Yeah, tryin', but no good, ah?"

Kenika did his best to adapt to anything that interested him. He also tried to interest Keoki in things the boy did not naturally find

interesting, like hiking in the woods under the Pali Lookout looking
for avocadoes and bananas, or going out in The Red Wind with the
twins. Paddling seemed to frustrate him—he thought that the best
thing to do with a canoe was to go out and ride the big breaks, and
those times they went fishing out by the Mokuluas, Keoki took his
board with him, and ended up leaving his gear on the little island
beach and paddling out to the small, rip-current waves that came in
opposite of the ocean break. Kenika usually followed him out there,
scouting the reefs while he surfed. In the woods Keoki liked mostly
climbing up the avocado trees and shaking them down, and when the
two of them went, he tried to push Kenika to walk closer to the lookout
and try climbing the sharper ridges under it.

And the twins, now taller even than when he and Angela were
convinced they had stopped growing, were finally aware of boys, but
this awareness caused them to be so shy in their presence that they
would try to hide behind each other. When from time to time one or
another friend who was a boy would come over to study with them,
they would be amazingly gracious and soft-spoken when they let him
in and showed him where to sit and where to put his pile of books,
and they would giggle and whisper to each other whenever they were
out of his sight, as if arguing over how to behave in the presence of
this strange creature. Their room resembled what he assumed a college
dormitory would look like: posters on the walls, homework all over the
place, their little shrines where they kept their medals from all the
canoe races they had won, their record player and records, no longer
Lena Machado and Hilo Hattie. No longer Bill Kaiwa, whom they once
considered the cutest singer ever. Now it was Elvis and the Everly
Brothers and Johnny Mathis.

While they were incredibly shy in the presence of boys, they
were incredibly coarse with each other, or when one or another of
them babysat particularly difficult kids. For a while Clarice watched
Frank Sakata's boy, and the sounds that came from the room or
the yard were absurd: "Fock you!" the boy would yell, and Clarice
would put her fists on her hips and say, "You pilau little shit, I give
you dirty lickens," and he would snap, "Assho! I wanna go home!" It
was as if the behavior that was so proper and restricted in the
presence of any visitor had to be balanced off by behavior which
was extreme in the opposite. One evening Angela and Kenika were
sitting on the couch having a beer and easily overheard their
conversation, and it was more absurd even than Clarice's arguments
with Frank's boy;

"Ho, da stink! Whatchoo eat?"

"Wait, dis bettah."

Angela looked at him and said, "Uh oh, it's another futting contes'."

"Dat manini, listen to dis one," and even that sound made it to the living room

"Should't feed them beans when they're in this mood," he said.

Then there was hoarse laughter. "I amos' shet my panties. Wot, you got one bigga assho den me?"

"You get da bigges' assho evah."

"Shut up, you twat."

"Fuck you."

"Shithead."

"Mullet ass."

"What dat? Mullets get no asses."

"Get assho but."

"'Kaywait, I got one big one coming. Stan' back. I blow da fricken windows out."

Then there was more giggling.

Angela had warned them any number of times that they could be heard easily. In fact she believed that they could be heard half a block away, and the girls would stare at each other open-mouthed, then giggle with prim mortification. But they simply forgot that there was an outer world when they were holed up in their room.

One day Kenika was weeding one of their little vegetable gardens next to the house, pulling nut grass and clover from around cherry tomato plants and straightening all the bricks. Angela was getting ready to go to the shop to work with Darnay on boutonnieres, and the twins were in their room. Keoki was off playing basketball at the park. Kenika heard Angela talking to someone at the front door, but forgot about it when the twins started up.

"You get bigga chichis den me." It was Elizabeth, he thought, because sometimes her voice sounded a tiny bit deeper than Clarice's.

"Not. We twins 'ass why."

"No, look. Eh, watch um rotate." And then there was giggling, followed by a horrified gasp, again Elizabeth's.

"Dis one bigga den da odda!"

"Not."

"No, I try lif', and dis one heaviah."

"Not, you right-handed, so it feel lightah cause dat ahm shtrongah."

"Ho! Nobody evah marry me!"

This, he heard easily, and from the lower end of the garden. "Hey!" he called. "I can hear you way down here!"

"'Kay!"

"No marry you cause you so ugly, 'ass why," one of them went on in a lower voice.

"Den you ugly too, assho!"

"'Kayden, we bot' ugly. So fricken what?"

There was a ten-second silence, and Kenika went back to straightening the bricks.

"I like try dakine tampons."

"No, you like fuck yourself wit' dakine tampons."

"Not, in Seventeen—"

"Oooooeee! Lisbet like fuck herself wit' tampons."

"Fuck you den."

"Shitface hag."

Then another silence, and Kenika remembered that Angela had talked to someone in the house, and then shook his head. Maybe not.

"Ho, industrial strengt' twat itch!" one of them yelled, and he looked around, because that, he was sure, could be heard a block away.

"Hey!" he said. "Keep it down."

Silence. He went back to work, but within thirty seconds they started up again.

"Get itch fo' boys, ah?"

"You get hots fo' Steven Lee."

"Not! Eh you slut, I see you look at da bulges in da pants. Ho, what a fricken slut!"

He groaned, rose from his work and went around to the front of the house, just to check and make sure no one was there. He walked in the door and found Clinton Murakami sitting on the couch, looking up at him with an expression combining nausea and awe.

"Hey, how you doin', Clinton?" Next to Clinton on the little table was an empty glass, ice cubes still in it. Angela had given him soda before going.

"Fine, Mr. McKay. We're gonna work on our project for English."

"Ho, fahkeen panties all up my ass, man!" one of them yelled.

Kenika cleared his throat. "I'll go tell them you're here."

"Eat me, fuckface!"

He knocked on the door. "Clinton's here."

"Oh chee! Study!"

Within thirty seconds they were in the hall, peeking around at Clinton Murakami, each trying to hide behind the other. "Clinton! You jus' get heah?"

"Uh, yeah yeah, I mean, just a few— Yeah, like just—"

"'Kaywait, we get our books."

"Yeah, 'ass what we do."

After that as they sat with Clinton at the table and discussed with a studious earnestness the themes of "The Devil and Daniel Webster," their voices were so soft, their demeanor so refined and he thought almost elegant, he could barely believe what he had heard a few minutes earlier.

When they missed a couple of practices at Lanikai he asked them why, and they told him that the Beatles were staying at a mansion on Kailua Beach and they, like their friends, spent the afternoons hanging out on the beach waiting to get a glimpse of them. George, Ringo, Paul and John. At that time he was also aware that one song played over and over in their room, in fact he counted ten times in one afternoon. Angela seemed not to notice it, could somehow tune out the sound, but Kenika would hear it start again and his brain would be captured as if in a net, gulping for breath. He also recognized fundamental contradictions in the song, so he went and knocked on their door.

"Entah!" one of them said.

He went in, stood almost as if at attention, and cleared his throat. He could see the impish smiles on their faces. "'Kay," he said. "Let me analyze that song."

They shifted on their beds. "'Kay," Elizabeth said.

"In order to do this I have to sort of sing, 'kay?"

"Oh, do it, Daddy!" Clarice said.

"'Kay. It goes sort of like this: 'Lizzun, do you wanna know a segrut?' he says. No, I'm only pronouncing it the way they do. Then he says, 'Do you promise not to tsell?' Notice that he doesn't say 'tell.' He puts an 's' in it."

"Ho'd it, lemme get my notebook."

"Then you have, 'oh ohhh ohhh closuh, let me whispah in yo eah, say the words you wanna heee-uh.' The girl, presumably, has edged in closer, her expression secretive and full of all sorts of anticipation, because after all a Beatle will now whisper in her ear. But what happens? Clarice?"

"You tsell me."

"When she is now close, her ear near this Beatle's mouth, what does he do? He screams, 'Whahm in love with you!' thus shattering her eardrum."

They both bounced on their beds and clapped, laughing.

"I just thought you'd appreciate this closer look at that song."

"Thank you, Daddy," Elizabeth said.

"Yeah, Daddy, we do appreciate that."

"How 'bout Bill Kaiwa? I like him. You think you could play some Bill Kaiwa?"

"We'll consider that."

When he was back in the living room, the same song started up again. Angela, oblivious to the sound, leafed carefully through a library book on shell jewelry, from time to time making notes on a pad next to her. Apparently she had the kind of brain that could control what went into it while he did not. And soon he did not have to be actually hearing the music. That song and other Beatles' songs began to taunt him all day, in the yard, in the shed, because he found himself involuntarily whistling them to himself, and he would mentally vow not to do it, stop what he was doing and select an old song to plant in his head, "Pua Lililehua," or "Lei Mokihana," to take up residence and lock The Beatles out. But only a few minutes would pass before the various tunes squirmed like aggressive, parasitic worms back into his ears.

Angela's various projects still engaged the twins' attention. When she came up with an idea, such as making polished opihi-shell pendants, the twins would spend the entire day with her at Makapuu or the north shore looking through the sand for them. Opihi shells were round and slightly conical and had interesting gray-silver patterns on the inside. Angela and the twins would string them on twenty-pound test sugi line chains that would be strung with what she called puka shells, which were actually the worn base whorls of cone shells the ocean had worked down into tiny buttons with a single hole in the middle.

Kenika and sometimes Keoki went out in the water looking for menpachi, palani, lobster, Kenika stopping to look closely at an occasional octopus. When they had had enough of fishing, they would go up on the beach and wait for Angela and the twins to finish up looking for shells, but they would remain apparently mesmerized by what they were doing, to the point that Kenika and Keoki would become fidgety waiting, frequently looking at each other and sighing with growing exasperation. Keoki would step close to one of the twins and say something, and get a vague "'Kay," for an answer. Kenika would finally say, "Time to go guys," and whoever was closest would say, "'Kay," and look at him with a distant, wistful distraction, but then would go on looking for shells.

"Hey Lisbet?" Keoki said one day.

"Yeah?"

"The Beatles just went by in a limousine. Dey waved."

"'Kay."

Kenika laughed and walked over to Angela. "I just heard on the radio in the car that the Chinese bombed Pearl Harbor."

Angela looked vaguely in the direction of Pearl Harbor. "'Kay," she said.

"Time to go."

Nothing. "Wanna go back in the water?" Kenika said to Keoki.

"'Kay."

There were mysteries of the weather and seasons that made it such that these shells would be on the beach in abundance, and Angela seemed to know when that would happen. The ones left around by opihi pickers, because the meat was prized, usually were damaged at the edge because you had to use screwdrivers to pry them off the rocks where the water sloshed up. The outside of the opihi shell was dark and finely rilled in a sunray pattern from the center out, and she experimented with filing the rills off so that the inside pattern would appear on the outside. Kenika remained fascinated with her interest in trying anything to advance the artisanship of natural decoration, and he would go to the shed sometimes wishing he were back in Kailua with her and the twins, moving on to some new scheme to make something out of whatever they could find. Snakehead cowries, brightly-colored pieces of octopus-crushed cone shells, tiny pink and white shells arranged into patterns, driftwood, anything could become raw material for something Mr. Maxwell would stare at, scratching his chin, speculating on how much he should charge. Kenika was left staring at his relief carving, a project he understood now might never be finished. Or if not that, he sighed and turned to coconut shells he had cut for wind chimes.

And Keoki? Sports. If he wasn't surfing out by the Mokuluas with somewhat older and more experienced friends, permission for which involved long negotiations with his parents, at the same surfing spot Junior Kaaiai had gone to with his friends that day that seemed a hundred years ago, he was playing baseball or basketball, and at home, he wanted Kenika to sit with him and watch TV, cowboy movies or professional wrestling from the Civic Auditorium. The wrestlers were Rippah Collins, Johnny Barend, Lord Tallyho Blears, Curtis the Bull Iaukea, facing off against visitors from the mainland, Argentina Rocca, Verne Gagne, Gorgeous George and the rest.

Keoki liked to spearfish with Kenika, but only occasionally, because for him the ocean meant surf, its mysteries all having to do with waves and their properties. For some, Kenika knew, the ocean meant canoes, or fishing with poles. For him the ocean was a three-dimensional medium, and he could not fish with a pole—it was too frustrating to see the line and sinker disappear into a place he could just as well go with his mask and spear. Even when he paddled a canoe his eyes always automatically searched for likely coralheads under which choice fish surely hid. He saw it as the reverse of land, with its own topography and its own natural residents, he being the alien allowed to fly weightlessly in slow motion in this medium, and he imagined that if fish were technologically advanced, then in an alternate world a shark would rise out of the ocean wearing his own breathing equipment, and would float throughout the world of humans, perhaps diving down into someone's backyard to grab a human in its triangular, serrated teeth, and exultant, he would return to the ocean and shed his breathing equipment, and then display his terrified, drowning prize to his friends.

The twins made the state races for the third time in five years, but came in second to a crew from the Big Island. To their hoard of medals and little poi bowls with the medallions on the side they would add a silver, but Kenika understood that day at Keehi Lagoon that they were probably finished with canoe racing, or at least finished taking it as seriously as they had. There were four or five thousand people at the regatta, and in the twins' race, there was that irregular line of fourteen canoes knifing over the water, the manu of The Red Wind ahead except for one canoe, which was so far out ahead that, even after the turn at the flags, it was clear that no canoe would catch it. The Big Island girls won by thirty yards. The manu of The Red Wind crossed ten feet ahead of the third.

While the other races went on, Kenika, Angela and the twins wandered along the hard, pebbly sand and looked at other canoes, and came across the group from the Big Island. Angela, her eyes on the high tide line, kept going, looking for shells or likely pieces of driftwood. The twins stopped and looked into the Big Island crowd. The six women were under the poled-up tarp congratulating each other and talking excitedly about the race, and Kenika could see the twins studying them, their faces held in a speculative wonder. The Big Island girls were tall, strong, and so broad-shouldered and muscular that they seemed as strong and well-proportioned as men. Anyone seeing the twins would understand right away that they had to be athletes, because of the cut of their bodies, the long, powerful back muscles, the shoulders. But that day they were, he imagined, looking at themselves in the future assuming the training they would need in order to beat those girls—something about the shape of a woman was seemingly absent from them, as if in their training to become ace paddlers they had traded in what most identified them: softness. One of the girls, on recognizing the twins, walked over and said, "Hey, you guys give us one race."

"Nah nah nah," Clarice said. "You killed us."

The other girls approached, and they introduced themselves around. Clearly these were girls, giggling, gesturing about the race, but Kenika could tell that the twins were secretly vowing to themselves that they would pull up short of achieving this Amazon status. He could also tell from the girls' careful looks at the twins, that they were impressed by their beauty, by the appearance of softness they had managed to preserve in spite of all their training. It was a look of powerful envy, which for the moment seemed to neutralize the exultation they had felt only moments before. And Kenika understood what they were seeing, something approaching extraordinary womanhood, as if the twins had achieved exactly what they had dreamed of achieving that day they saw the Makaila sisters just before their great-grandfather Kelemeneke blessed The Red Wind.

In the far distance the heat boils off the road, and you pedal as fast as you can going down the hill past the golf course toward Waimanalo, and boy, would Mommy be pissed if she knew. If Pua evah tell— Keoni has a Pacman game. The profile happy face with the quarter-circle mouth opening and closing chomp chomp chomp as it runs through the little lanes. Keoni is fifty feet ahead and Junior Sakata is behind because his bike has little wheels. Hey wait you guys! he keeps yelling, and Keoni laughs and pedals, hunched way down to cut the wind. And boiling above the road you see him walking, know who he is before you even think you know.

You slow down and Junior comes up, says, What? Dat man, you say. He one druggie. He bite you. Not, Junior says. Keoni waits because he saw him too. Tall and dirty, with a clump of reddish hair allaway down his back.

One o' druggie, you say. We go 'roun. And thinking just in case Keoni or Junior asks, No, I no know da o' druggie, nevah saw him evah. But dey no ask.

Pedaling again, you look back. He walks, hulking, and you think, I hate you! I hate you! Don't you evah come home li'dat. And remember way back, you on his lap and Tutu Angela and Kenika and Mommy and TV and the yard with the 'ilima bushes wit' orange flowers like Christmas tree lights and the beach and water, 'kay, you sit onna boa'd an' Daddy show you how fo' paddow.

Pacman, the happy face in profile, chomp chomp chomp. If mom evah fine out, ho!

Look back again, and he is still there in the boiling heat by the little ranch on the side of the hill with the cows and the rodeo circle and Olomana behind it. He is walking. He will walk and walk and walk, and someday aim for the house. No mattahs. You pass Frankie's Drive-

*In and then Shima's market and then the feed store. Look back. No
way. He still walks up there by the ranch. Fuck him. Fuck him fuck him
fuck him. Chomp chomp chomp goes da happy face.*

≈   ≈   ≈

Of the remaining logs at the shed there were two shorter ones
which had rotted through the core, as far as he could tell, and one
which was damaged on one side so that a complete hull could not be
shaped from it, but the hull walls could be added after the fact. The
fore or aft, depending on how he cut it, would need completion from
other wood. From this log would be cut the Moanapahi, or the Ocean-
knife. The order was so long in coming that Kenika didn't believe what
the man was telling him when he called. They wanted a canoe. It was
as if he had forgotten how to make one. How many times had he driven
through town on his way to work and stopped at the flower shop, and
gone no farther? What had stopped him there was the speculation of
just what it was he would do out there—more wind chimes that nobody
wanted? The relief carving which would never be finished? Baby canoes?
There were the remaining logs by the shed, but he would not use them
until someone needed a canoe.

It turned out that someone did. It was commissioned by a small
private college whose location was in a series of refurbished buildings
in Pearl City. It was called Stimson College and was a satellite campus
of one of the same name in San Diego, actually an experiment in
alternative education, a two-year school whose students would finish
in San Diego. The representative who called him, Jonathan Scheck,
said that they hadn't really thought of naming a canoe that had not
yet been built, so he told Mr. Scheck that he would consider names
and suggest one. The college would pay ten thousand dollars for a
Malia design, hull-weight four hundred pounds. Kenika had a year to
build it, and he pointed out that because there were very few complete
logs, this one would have hull walls of matched wood but from different
sources, and that either the fore or aft would probably have to be
added to.

No problem, the man said. He had been advised about the difficulty
of finding koa logs, and about how expensive canoes were.

Kenika explained in a more or less dry, almost challenging tone
that he required that the canoe be blessed by a kahuna in the presence
of those who would use it, and that this was not an idle habit of his, or
some quaint sidelight to the manufacture of the canoe. Rather it was
crucial to the canoe's lifetime identity, crucial to the safety of those
who would use it, and if Mr. Scheck or his associates found this odd,
or old-fashioned, then they had a problem.

The man said that he was sure everyone would be delighted to participate in a blessing. He assumed, although he was not sure, that a kahuna was some sort of a priest.

Correct, Kenika said.

That would be fine, Mr. Scheck said.

He held the phone to his ear and couldn't think of what to say. He had thrown the blessing requirement in the man's face and had heard not the slightest hint of skepticism or veiled ridicule.

As to the matter of a contract and down payment, Mr. Scheck said he would arrange that and then a meeting where the details could be worked out. Kenika told him that a contract was not necessary, nor was a down payment. When the canoe was done they would come and look at it, and if it met with their approval, then it would be theirs.

There was a long silence, until Kenika asked him if he was still there. Mr. Scheck said yes, but didn't Mr. McKay think that for the protection of those involved, a contract should be drawn up? If you don't like the canoe, then you don't pay, Kenika told him. That was how he and his original teacher did business. That was how business had been done in this family for more than a hundred years. Mr. Scheck then said that he and two deans had seen two of Kenika's canoes, at the Central Pacific Academy, and if this one could be anywhere near those in craftsmanship, then they would buy it. As had happened before, the surge of adrenalin this caused gave him energy he always seemed to lack when there was no canoe to build. At the shed, he walked the length of the damaged log carrying a small adze, sweeping his hand on the blackened, oozing wood which was spotted here and there with lichens and moss, and whispered, "You'll be beautiful, if you let me put on wood from those you've been sleeping with here most of this century. If you think that being damaged you're somehow less than your friend The Red Wind, you're wrong. I'll make you so strong that you'll forget what happened to you when you fell, when you were dragged over rocks. I'll match the wood so that even you will forget what you lost."

He raised the adze and chipped into the black wood, which went gray a half inch in, and then with the next chop, became the warm, rich grain of koa. "See?" he said. "Most of you is in there, and if your grain looks like this, you'll be great."

It felt like a return to simpler times, his being able to stand there and size up a log. They could use the money, because soon the twins would be going to college, and they would also be burdened by this business of buying another house, which he and Angela had already more or less picked out one Sunday afternoon during the real estate open house hours of two to five. The twins thought they should buy a really big house on the beach, and Angela and Kenika considered that, but always ended up looking at their backyard at all the 'ilima bushes they had planted, the palm trees, the orange tree, the gardens, the little green empire they had made on the small lot. Besides, Angela told them, at the beach your clothes get salty, your windowscreens get salty, and after a couple months of wind off the ocean, you'll start to wish you were back here.

The house was two blocks from their own and nearly the same design, currently being rented by the Chang family. The asking price was twenty-three thousand dollars, a figure that made Kenika reel when he thought of it. He tried to reason out the mathematics, and concluded that if he bought one house at eight thousand when he made nearly three thousand in one year, then they could by one for twenty-three if he made ten in a year. Because of the success of the flower shop they had the money, but the idea of a house costing over twenty thousand dollars seemed preposterous to him. "But it's an excellent investment," the real estate man had told them. "You watch, prices will keep going up up up." Kenika didn't believe him. Angela did.

Secretly he imagined that acquiring houses was a good idea, as a hedge against something. The something was hard for him to gauge—it came in the form of the loss of familiar things and the introduction of foreign ones. The Kailua Theater was boarded up and would be torn down, something the kids considered one of history's significant crimes against humanity, because they had gone to that theater all through their childhoods. Kenika hated the idea too. The Filipino Camp was gone, bulldozed off for the construction of a shopping center of some sort. Cowpastures were gone and houses had sprouted in their places. It seemed to him that for years now he had driven past one stretch of open space or another only to see more bulldozers and graders churning away, followed by white, long-necked egrets pecking for insects and skinks where the giant blades had just scraped, and he could not look at the scraped ground without thinking of it as wounded. And after heavy rains the water in Kailua Bay would be brown, the silt and trash from the developments making its way down Ka'elepulu Stream and into the water at the beach. The lake itself, the small remainder of the huge marsh he had first seen, was now ringed with houses three quarters of the way around. And when he took trinkets over to Mr. Maxwell, his own and Angela's, he noticed that the building the shop occupied, which had at first seemed like a large one, was now dwarfed by buildings three times its height. Waikiki was still Waikiki, but it was taller, and there were fewer trees. There was something cloyingly urban about it, and when he walked toward Maxwell's shop, the air he breathed did not smell of plumeria as it once had, but car exhaust.

Making a canoe with the old tools was less like hard labor and more like a comforting way to pass the time. From all that he had learned about what others were doing in building canoes, or in building anything for that matter, he understood that he could now logically be called eccentric and hopelessly out of phase with the present. Benny had stored a number of saltwater-cured hau pieces for 'iakos under the shed, but now he needed more, and went out the windward coast to find perfectly-curved pieces in the more arid areas, because dryland hau was harder than wetland hau. The cure was just as old-fashioned as everything else. He carried saltwater up to the shed and dumped it into the cattle trough under the floor, and then put the hau pieces in the water and held them down with rocks.

The log had not been roughed out because of the damage, so he began by hacking with the heavy adze, standing on the log, planning to get enough off to use the cant hook to turn it. It was difficult work and it was hot for spring, but he went home every day satisfied that he was making reasonable progress.

And there were still those surprise days when he walked in to discover that all the kids were out and would not be back until such and such a time. Angela would have it all worked out before he got home.

He walked in and found her sitting at the table with her eyes closed. "Who's there?" she demanded.

"Uh-oh," and he cleared his throat. "Uh, well, I'm the plumber. I'm here to do repairs." Eyes still closed, she aimed her head in his direction.

"What repairs?"

"Clogged drainpipe, dripping faucet. Generally, pipes have to be opened up. I use a snake."

"A snake? That sounds a little, ah, strange. What kind of a snake?"

"Excuse me, but are you blind?"

"Yes, since birth. And I also have no feeling below the neck." Then she snickered. "Ho, I don't know wheah dat came from."

"Really, no feeling below the neck."

"So go ahead an' get out your snake an' do your repairs. I'm going to be in my room doing yogi exercises—" and she laughed, "an'—"

"Ma'am, I think it's yoga."

"Yes, yoga. You no bodda me in dere, please. I have no feeling or sight, but I have very good hearing."

"Hmm," he said. "If I need anything can I come in and sort of tap you?"

She gasped with indignation. "No! I do my yogi naked!"

"Very well. Could I use your shower?"

"For what? You have to be clean to do plumbing?"

"I prefer it that way, yes. I'm a professional."

"Young man, you know that this would not be necessary if those kids didn't stay up so late, don't you?"

"Kids? What kids?"

"So do your plumbing in the bat'room an' kitchen only. Stick your snake inna pipe an' den go."

And then, in a remarkable imitation of a blind person, she felt her way to the bedroom. It was so good that for a moment he imagined that he stood there burdened by a toolbox.

Sure enough at eleven that evening when he was just trying to doze off, he was assaulted by "Hey Jude" six times in a row, and ended up staring into the blackness trying to figure out what they meant when they sang, "The movement you need is on your shoulders."

≈   ≈   ≈

In April, after he had reduced the log to proportions he felt were manageable for winching, he got a call from Jonathan Scheck. Would Mr. McKay be willing to accept two apprentices for the remaining duration of the building of the canoe? The boys were American Studies majors whose practicum for the summer and fall semester was called Pacific Cultural Studies. They were juniors, soon to be seniors, and would be coming out from San Diego in May, and would spend the summer and fall in a small dormitory on the campus.

"Do they know anything about canoe building?"

"No, but this is part of the practicum."

Kenika didn't understand exactly what that meant. "Do they do work and then take a test or something?"

Mr. Scheck laughed. "No no, a practicum is field study. These students arrange these projects with their advisors. When it's all done they do a report, back in San Diego."

"Where I work is not exactly convenient, nor is it comfortable."

"No, these boys spent last summer on an Indian reservation. They're tough, and I think they're capable."

"What do I do? I mean, do I do what I always do? Just keep on making the canoe while they watch?" The idea seemed bad to him, embarrassing, because he talked to his canoes, he acted in ways any outside observer would consider ridiculous.

"Mr. McKay, this is only a request. If it isn't, well, right in your mind, then we don't need to consider it."

"What would they do if they didn't come up here? I mean, you said they were coming anyway, right?"

"They would have to work out something that would meet with the approval of the advisors. They might try to apprentice with another builder, or something like that."

"Oh. Chainsaws, stuff like that. How old are they?"

"They're both twenty-one."

Kenika thought about it more. Haoles from the mainland. The image of Richard Stevenson rose in his imagination, and he made their faces his face. But then he was building their canoe, not his own. Benny had always told anyone who commissioned a canoe to come up an' talk story, take one look da wa'a.

"Mr. McKay?"

"Yeah. Listen, I make canoes by hand. There's no electricity here and even if there was I wouldn't use it. They'd have to walk all the way up into the woods looking for 'ohi'a root for parts of the canoe, they'd have to sand until their arms fell off, the bathroom is an outhouse, they'd—"

"That is precisely what we and they hoped for. That is, some traditional process. Actually, there's an interest in outrigger canoe racing in California, so this more or less makes sense. But I leave it up to you."

"What are their names?"

"Seth Davis, from San Diego, and Keith Williamson, who is from Iowa I think."

He ended up agreeing with the idea, and he told Angela about the conversation, and tried to describe his own reservations. "—but I don't know. What would Benny think? I mean these people are not— You know what I mean?"

"Hey, he didn't kick you out, did he? For once you'd have somebody up there with you."

"Yeah but—"

"You're a mainlander, or were."

"I know, but—"

"So it's you an' Set' an' Keit'."

Set and Keet. He started thinking of them that way, more or less dreading the day when he would meet them. When he could trim no more off the log, he sat in the shed and in effect waited for them. If they wanted to learn about making canoes, then they could help him winch the rough-cut canoe into the shed. He made baby canoes and drank beer. Lunch didn't taste good, and constantly there was that vague tension at the idea that anyone should be allowed past that stream. By May he hated them, was convinced that they would sneer at the mud, at the dilapidated condition of the shed, that they would see the wood and think of it as just that: wood. He would have to mediate, be like a kind of diplomat between those ignorant, insensitive people and his living wood, and whenever they were not around he would have to apologize for their crassness and ignorance, would have to reassure the canoe that at least he, Kenika, knew it was alive. When they got back to their goddam dormitory they would describe their experiences, frequently gazing up at the ceiling as if in appeal to reason. He got one more call from Mr. Scheck, to get directions as to how they might find the shed. He did not withdraw his offer. His last chance was gone.

≈   ≈   ≈

On the day they were to arrive, he sat in Benny's chair with his arms folded, and waited. In the cooler was lunch for three people, Angela's idea, which he thought was unnecessary. She packed three laulaus, a little plastic container of lomi salmon, another of poi, and he chuckled, because that might discourage them, sweet potato and macaroni salad and fruit, and instructed him that he was to start a fire and heat this stuff up. He was wearing better clothes than usual, not the ratty boro-boros he usually did. Angela had even noticed: "What, you goeen church?" With the better clothes on he felt stupid, and ground his teeth in disgust at his having allowed himself to be put into this position. When he thought of cleaning up a little, collecting some of the little stubby, brown Primo bottles sitting here and there and maybe sweeping the floor, he immediately shook his head and whispered, "No, no, there's a limit to this."

He saw them enter the woods. Well, they looked big at least, kind of well-proportioned. They made their way over the stream, and approached the shed. Kenika got up and went to the door. "C'mon up," he said.

They introduced themselves. Seth Davis was brown-haired and handsome. Keith Williamson was brown-haired and handsome, but for a pink scar on his forehead. They were both fairly tall and looked strong enough. Kenika told them to sit down, Seth in the chair and Keith on the bench. He went to the tub and got out three Primos and opened them.

"Uh, are we allowed to do this?" Seth asked, pointing at the beer.

"Yes, you are," Kenika said. "We talk story first."

As Benny had once done, he went back into that region of mysterious antiquity in which the process of getting a log was so complicated that a normal, modern person would consider the average ancient canoe builders to be demented fanatics. He added things he had learned about the process, other bits of information Benny would add after that first day. But to Kenika's amazement, Set and Keet understood it all, listened with a respectful attention that showed not the slightest hint of skepticism. After a while he got out three more beers. He continued, and at one point Keet raised his hand. Kenika didn't understand.

"Oh, sorry," Keet said. "I mean, I had a question, or I mean not really a question but a sort of comment."

"Yeah yeah, go ahead."

"This bird—"

"'Elepaio, or 'Ella-pieyo. At the beginning you have what they call a glottal stop."

"Did they watch it maybe knowing that because it's the bird's normal feeding place that the bird would look for bad spots in the log for bugs? Like, it's the guardian spirit but it's also scientifically a valid judge of the better parts of the log."

"The valid judge came first, and the people blended the spiritual part in," Kenika said. "Probably."

It took two hours for him to go over it all, ending with the lolo ka wa'a ceremony. "Brains to canoe it means, more or less. The kahuna puts an intelligence into the canoe, and then it's ready to paddle."

He got three more beers.

"Uh, you want us to pay for these?"

"No."

"Brains," Set said. "That's neat."

"More than neat," Kenika said. "It's as important as the wood itself."

Set nodded thoughtfully.

He liked them. It was almost as if they were children, like the twelves who paddled The Red Wind. Their brains were indiscriminate sponges that soaked up what he said without question or judgment. The fact that they were haoles straight from the mainland, that other world he would just as soon imagine did not exist, made telling them about canoes seemed all the more strange. On the one hand it seemed to him special, secret information not to be given out to people like them, and on the other the telling convinced him that he wanted to give the information out for fear that it would be lost, and if he spread it carefully, to as many people as possible, it might somehow be preserved. But he worried about preservation of information being correct, that everything be relayed without missing any details. What would Benny say? Eh, no worry, dey good boys. No worry 'bout who dey are. And wit' dis infahmashen, no take chance, ah? Memba, I geev um to you cause you good boy, 'ass why. Watch um when you talk story. If dey keep on tinkeen, den 'ass good.

They stared at him as he added other details, their expressions thoughtful to the point of being almost dopey. One or the other would stare at the middle distance, seeming to imagine such things as trips in these canoes covering thousands of miles, men committing to memory the pattern of the dome of stars for guiding their journeys, even the idea of canoes with a special intelligence locked inside the beautifully-grained wood, thinking as they knifed through the vast ocean by day, maybe dreaming as they went by night.

"So after a while you can come over to Lanikai and I'll show you the Makani 'Ula. We'll take her out." He thought a moment. "I pay two dollars an hour for this work."

"Uh, we can't accept any money," Set said.

"No, then just don't tell anybody. I pay two dollars an hour for this work."

He liked them even more when they went to work. They were strong, so the winching took only an hour. As Angela had instructed, he heated the lunch, and explained what the food was. They ate like pigs, the laulau, poi, lomi, without the slightest hint of hesitation. "You ever eaten that stuff before?" Kenika asked.

"Nope."

"Uh uh."

"You liked it?"

"Yup."

"Yeah, that was good stuff."

He opened three more beers. "By the way, how did you get up here?"

"Bus."

"Yeah, then walked up the road, no problem."

It was fascinating to watch them work, bathed in sweat, curls of koa stuck to their salty skin, their faces held in a strange, rapt attention. At one point Set took a heavy plane and began working on the hull side, according to Kenika's instructions, and before he started he said, "Okay Moanapahi baby, this is gonna tickle just a little. Don't get mad."

Kenika laughed. Set stood up and said, "Well, you said you talked to them, right?"

"Yup."

On Saturday morning he went up to the shed to do a few things to the hull, to check the bottom angles without Set and Keet present, to make sure that he wasn't missing anything in the shaping, and when he got there, he found them sitting on the mossy stairs. "What are you doing here?" he asked.

Keet looked at Set. "Uh, you didn't say if we should come or not, so we thought we should come."

"No, you're supposta have weekends off, right?"

"I don't know," Keet said.

"Nobody said," Set said. "Doesn't matter. I'd just as soon do this than—"

At about ten o'clock, by the time all three of them were bathed in sweat and covered with grit, Kenika heard something in the woods. He stood up and squinted in the direction of Mr. Marumoto's house. Angela and the twins were making their way over the stream. Angela stopped, drawn by something to her left, some kind of seed probably, and the girls, wearing their somewhat too small two-piece bathing suits, stomped up the stairs and walked into the shed. Kenika's two filthy apprentices stood up, and for a moment seemed not to know where they were. The girls, who had been about to speak, stared at them, and then backed up a little. Set dropped a shaping adze into the canoe hull and winced. Then he looked at Kenika, as if the shock of his own clumsiness was dawning on him very slowly.

Keet stood there with his mouth open, and the scar on his forehead paled.

Kenika cleared his throat. "These are my daughters," he said. "Clarice, there in front, and Elizabeth behind her." Then he pointed at the boys. "Seth, and over there, Keith."

There was another silence while they looked around each other, not exactly at each other, and there were abashed nods, shrugs, some breath drawn in preparation of speech, but nothing came out of anyone's mouth. Then Kenika had a flash of a strange, fundamental understanding that vanished only seconds after he thought it: he was struck by the image of the four of them standing there staring at each other, and the air was funky and damp and smelled of the sweetness of ginger and mangoes, and then rotting vegetation, and the girls stood eighty-five percent naked, their dusky skin rich in color, and there was no coyness or reserved elegance in their bearing. They seemed too stunned for that. What passed across that space of sweet air between them was elemental and prehistoric.

He shook the vision off and spoke. "So what are you guys doing here?"

"Beach," Clarice said. "Uh, those— You know."

"Job's tears," Elizabeth said.

"Yeah, that it. But those heah. Beach is—"

"We—"

"Yeah."

"Eh! Try come!" Angela yelled.

The girls backed out the door and walked down the steps so gingerly that they appeared to be invalids.

Kenika turned to the boys and explained what was up. Angela and the girls came here frequently to collect materials they used in making seed leis, jewelry, and so on, for Angela's shop in Kailua.

"Oh," Set said, nodding. "Jewelry, yeah, neat."

"Yeah," Keet said. "That's, I mean, hey," and then he gestured around at the air, shaking his head as if this information had been some amazing revelation.

They were useless after that. He told Set that there was still plenty of wood in the base of the hull so they could keep on with the shaping adzes, and in thirty seconds he found Set in the hull swinging the adze so feebly that he removed no wood. Keet suddenly seemed unable to figure out how to use the tools they had used all morning. Their brains had been so shorted out that the simplest suggestion baffled them, and they tried their best, hacking while their eyes wandered off in the direction of the ravine, from which they could hear the swish swish of people walking there, and every once in a while, a voice.

Finally Kenika said, "Hey, listen, it's almost twelve. What about some lunch? I'll go down and see if they want to go down to Kahaluu and get some burgers or something, 'kay?"

Seth pulled out his wallet, and fingered nervously at the bills. "Yeah, here, let us buy lunch this time. I'll— What? Ten dollars?"

"Split it," Keith said. "That's—"

After a moment Kenika said, "Five each?"

It was not only the boys who had seemed to have experienced some combination of sunstroke and severe blows to the head, the girls did too. After Angela and the girls came up the ravine and he introduced the boys to Angela, he suggested that they all go to Kahaluu for lunch, and the girls looked at each other, then sneaked looks at the boys, and then nodded and garbled out their agreement: "'Ass what we do, yeah, go lunch," and "Yeah, me too."

"'Kay," Angela said. "We go in one cah, 'kay?"

Everybody agreed, and they marched out of the woods, the boys in front. Seth went to jump over the stream, and in an expert leap, he left the ground and then came down right in the middle of it, the horrified smile on his face showing that he could not believe how badly he had misjudged the jump. Keith stepped across like a debilitated old man. Out on Mr. Marumoto's lawn, the boys stopped and looked down at themselves. They were dirty. "'Ass okay," Angela said. "Sit on towels."

The girls stopped. Six people in their mother's car? Who would sit where? They held a conference off to the side, an urgent, whispered argument. 'Kay, girls in the front. But Angela ruined that. "Come sit," she said to Seth, patting the seat next to her, just as Kenika and Keith piled into the back. This left Clarice sitting in the window seat next to

Seth, while Elizabeth sat between Kenika and Keith. Kenika could feel the rigidity of Elizabeth's body next to his, and see the same in Clarice, and then Elizabeth escaped her embarrassment by putting her arm around Kenika's neck and leaning against him.

The saimin rescued them from their hopeless social ineptitude. They sat at a sticky picnic table outside the little hamburger/saimin shop, where flies buzzed above a plastic garbage can. Neither of the boys had ever used chopsticks, and the twins, in a strange lapse in their embarrassment, showed them how, Clarice Seth, and Elizabeth Keith. "Kaywait, I show you—hol' um li'dis, one from da base da tum an' onna middle fingah, da odda like one pencil," and then Clarice grabbed Seth's limp hand and formed the fingers in their proper positions while he watched, his mouth hung open.

What had dawned on Kenika a short time ago was obvious now— there they were, the two girls manipulating the chopsticks into the hands of the awkward, stunned boys, who would look at their luxuriant, dark hair, then at a brown shoulder, or at their hands, then at the tops of their ample chests. And when they were finally ready to try the chopsticks, it was the girls who looked, or gawked, each one at the boy she had just instructed, and then at each other, their beautiful faces held in a strange wonder. Angela noticed it too. She stopped eating and stared at them. It was as if Kenika could read her mind: uh-oh.

Kenika remembered it: the first time he had seen Angela at the beach under Diamond Head. He could not take his eyes off her and he could not make his mind and therefore his speech function properly. When she got up off a towel to walk down to the water his eyes locked on her, brown back, hair, buttocks, all in the fluid totality of movement, and never in his life had he seen a girl who could cause him to feel almost stunned, the ticklish currents of pure sensual fever racing through him like an unbearable, flashing electricity. He had learned from Angela too, that she had felt the same way looking at him, but secretly he didn't really believe her. There was nothing he ever saw in the mirror to lead him to believe that.

≈   ≈   ≈

From that day on it was clear to him that all four were hooked. He did not understand exactly how it worked, because all through high school the girls had gone out to movies and proms with different boys, none of whom caused in them that strange, dumbstruck wonder. It was some cryptic-instant chemistry that only they knew, and he kept visualizing that first strange time they all saw one another. Set and Keet did their jobs with a kind of furious diligence, sometimes asking him questions he thought they simply manufactured so that they could ask the father of those two girls a question: "Gee, how many canoes have you made?"

"Well, as I said—"

"Oh, right, right, and do, uh, Clarice and Elizabeth paddle—"

They would sand, then stop and cock their heads in the direction of Mr. Marumoto's house, then look at each other, amazingly with the same sustained dumbfoundedness that the twins showed when they looked at each other. The dirtier the job, the more they seemed to like it. One of the worst was the hau—they removed the sticks from the putrid, brackish water in the trough and stripped the bark from them, sitting amiably in a cloud of stench that would gag a maggot. At home in the evening the twins talked in their room, and he could hear their hushed voices from the living room but there was none of the usual coarseness, not as bad as when they were fifteen or so, but still their way of talking. There was a sound of a peculiar seriousness in the tone, yet he could not really hear any words. Then the boys began coming over Friday and Saturday nights to take the twins to the movies, and Angela loaned them her car.

One night Angela sat at the table flipping through another jewelry book, and he got up and went to sit with her. "What do you think?" he asked.

"No question," she said. "They look at those boys the way I looked at you, and this isn't like Becky and her boyfriends. They're really serious."

"I think I saw it happen. It happened in about five seconds."

"I know that—it's like what happens in the rain. I memba when you slept dat firs' night? It happen because it was raining so hahd. I memba lookin' in, an' was so mane'o, ho, it was comin' down an' I'm tinkin', I do dis now, I no can stop it."

"Something about this place, I think."

"But they're nice boys, so nice."

"Like I wasn't."

"I know what you looked at. Nasty greasah, you."

"You think they don't?"

"Of course they do. But you couldn't really hide it. At the beach I'd look away, then look back, an' your eyes would be right there between my legs. Ho, it only one body paht, but you—"

"But— Well, it's true, I mean the closer I got to it the better I felt. It was jungle bunny vapor. I could see it coming off you like smoke."

She snickered.

"Look someplace else, look back, the big eyes would be right there again, or down the top of my suit."

"But—"

"Eh, 'ass wheah I wanted you to look." She giggled. "Sometimes I'd move around so you could."

"Really? Hey, no wonder I saw so much."

"An' how many different ways did you have to sit not to show dat banana in your pants?"

"I know. It was torture."

"Remember the morning at the cottage? When I went in your room I had this sudden kind of dream that it was jus' you an' me an' nobody else."

"You think—"

"They're not babies any more."

No, they were not. Nor was this strange courtship anything like that of Becky Kam and her boyfriend, who were now married. That courtship had been paced by violent arguments and by Becky's pregnancy when she was seventeen, and her husband was a local boy who looked to Kenika about as lethal as anyone could, with scarred knuckles, a body rippling with muscles, and a face that radiated challenge.

Then Angela told him that both boys came from families that were more or less broken up. Seth lived with his grandparents because his parents had divorced and had more or less cut off contact from their children. Keith's family consisted of his mother only, because his father had been killed in Korea. His mother was an eccentric woman who barely subsisted on a small income and lived alone in a two-room apartment in San Diego. Kenika understood also that Angela's understanding of what motivated people to do what they did was very sharp. "They're like you," she said. "They come from strange families and are anxious to make their own, and as normal as possible." She looked at Kenika and thought, then said, "I know why you are the way you are, and I think that's the way they'll be."

He sat in the little study and stared at the wall. She was right. He was motivated by an unconscious desire for normalcy because he hadn't really had any. The boys, if her story was true, might have seen normalcy as a paradise of its own, and hence found the idea of a happy, swinging bachelorhood less important. But what bothered him was something he had almost forgotten, or was so buried in his memory that he had to deliberately bring it back up. Angela had mentioned nothing about the boys being haoles, as if that aspect of their identities meant nothing to her. The Polynesian he and Angela had made might now be further diluted by the Caucasian, but these were good boys and he had no right to disapprove, even though they came from that other world. The Polynesian in the Santiago family had already been diluted by the original Santiago, and his own blood, but then, Kenika had no idea what his own blood was. His children knew theirs, at least in part, and their children would know so much more that the indeterminate nature of their grandfather's blood might mean nothing to them. If his own mother was a half-black prostitute who had accepted ten dollars from, say, a Puerto Rican, then it might mean a great deal to him, but even the twins might think of it as not worth worrying about. Angela had told them about the mystery of Kenika's background, and they apparently thought it was sad and at the same time kind of exotic and interesting, like something you would read in a novel. But why was Angela so apparently unconcerned about blood? Or why was it that she seemed so generous with her own blood? Wouldn't she have preferred Hawaiian sons-in-law? He didn't ask.

The simple fact of his own extraordinary luck made it all seem trivial. Most people saw themselves as coming down from a complicated branch of a genealogical tree, and fixed their identities by it. He fixed his by what would come after him. He might have been conceived in a stinking bed in Newark, by a man doing as much as he could because of the money it was costing, to a woman who wanted to get this filthy business over as soon as possible so there would be time to open her legs to another man with ten dollars. And then, to this woman, a baby was no more than an impediment to her income, and when he was born he was to go from the womb to a garbage can, and that would have been the sum total of his life. That image always caused in him a stab of retrospective dread, because it was the intervention of another prostitute that prevented what was most likely supposed to be the sum total of his life, to live a few hours and then be suffocated, and all of this was finally his and his alone to wonder about. Nobody else thought of it as significant at all.

≈   ≈   ≈

One Saturday morning the twins were out picking 'ilima flowers and Keoki, skin almost black from the sun, his hair singed copper, was repairing his surfboard on the bench by the toolshed, mixing little bits of epoxy to fill in the dings. He began poking fun at the girls. "Oooo, da twins get haole boyfrien'."

They turned and looked at him their hands on their hips.

"So?" Clarice said.

"Den you get haole kids."

"So? Paht haole."

"Ha. Paht spic too. Dad paht spic, 'ass why."

"Is not."

"Ho, get dahk curly hair, brown eyes an' dakine cho cho lips, skin like us almos'."

"Not, dat from da sun, an' he no get cho cho lips. What dat? Spic?"

"Dat Mexican o' whatevahs. Hey, maybe popolo too."

"Not. Dat mean you alladat too, babooze."

"So? But you get haole kids."

"Ho, dummy, fix yoah boa'd an' shaddap."

"Nani nani poo-poo."

The twins began to find excuses to come up to the shed, sometimes convincing Angela to drive them out right after school, for Job's tears or various berries or flowers that would be used in craft projects. Whenever there was the sound of their approach, either Set or Keet would both stand up straight and start messing with their hair or straightening out their clothes. The twins would come up the stairs and then stand there in the shed, side by side, and ask how the canoe was going, and Set and Keet would launch into complicated explanations of what this was, or what that was, and even though the twins knew what they were being shown, they acted as if it were the first time in their lives they had ever seen or heard of such a thing.

And the boys did get to see The Red Wind, but not under the circumstances he had imagined. The twins still did their paddling, in the women's freshman division, but not with the fury of their youth. One day when they came out to the shed with Angela they proposed that all of them go to Lanikai and paddle, since there was no practice today and a canoe would be available. Kenika wanted to be there when the boys saw The Red Wind, so he agreed to bring them to Kailua and they would meet there at the end of the day. Angela had to go back and help Darnay close the shop and do the receipts for the day, and the twins stayed at the shed and waited impatiently while Kenika finished up what he was doing.

Then it was the seating controversy. Who would be the unlucky one to sit up front with Kenika? Set. Oh well, Clarice talked to the side of his head from the backseat.

When they pulled the tarp off The Red Wind the boys did a double-take—clearly their obsession with the girls was compromised for the time it took them to circle it, whispering, and looking from time to time up at Kenika, who stood there trying to control his wallowing in a kind of proprietary smugness. Rather than point anything out, he watched them touch parts and whisper, repeating Hawaiian names, wae, mo'o, kapua'i, kuaiako.

Then they carried her to the water and the twins ran back to Jerry Cambra's house to borrow paddles. In fact they went at a dead sprint. When they came back with four, Kenika smiled. "Kay Daddy, we be back soon, 'kay?" Elizabeth said, and then Clarice, "Yeah, we show um how fo' paddow, 'kay?"

Set said, "Uh—," and Kenika nodded to him. Go ahead.

The boys bought the twins' graduation leis from Angela, who tried to refuse the money. They were 'ilima leis, and Angela said that Set and Keet stood there like mules, their money on the table. No, we'd just as soon pay for these. Yeah, me too. Angela tried to get them to change their minds, but they would not. After the graduation, which took place on the football field at the high school in the blazing sun, they stood in their white gowns, startlingly dark and he thought startlingly beautiful, sweat running out of the hair at their temples and leis piled up almost to their noses, while boys in blue gowns wandered around with leis piled up to their noses, some made out of cans of beer woven in plastic mesh, or leis made of flowers and five and ten-dollar bills folded to look like little fans. Set and Keet stayed with the twins, sweating in their good clothes and shaking hands with the multitude of the twins' dark friends, throughout the graduation, and then all throughout the party in the family backyard, where fifty or so of the graduates socialized, barefoot but still in their good clothes, their polished shoes with dress socks stuffed in lined up around the stoop and all across the front of the house. The kupuna sat inside the house and talked story, Kenika and Angela, Momi, Irene and George, Darnay, Auntie Clarice Malama, and so on.

Kenika would have thought that the next phase was fixed: the girls would go to the University of Hawaii, and he assumed that the courtship would continue at a normal, even pace. But it did not. As the day of the blessing of the Moanapahi approached, he got the impression that he should also make arrangements with Kalani Chun for another blessing. One evening as he sat drinking a beer and chatting with Angela, Set and Keet knocked on the front door. The twins remained holed up in their room. Kenika told the boys to come on in, and so they did, and stood side by side, at attention. Set cleared his throat.

"What's up?" Kenika asked.

Angela groaned and looked at the ceiling. "No be mean, you," she said.

"I'm not being mean," he said. "I was just wondering to what I owe the pleasure of this surprise visit." He looked at Angela. "I mean surprise to me but not to you, right?"

"You so mean."

He could hear, faintly, a sort of scraping at the girls' bedroom door.

"Well, uh," Keith said, "I will speak for both of us about this."

"Yeah," Seth said, "Keith will, uh—"

"Neither of us is particularly well off, but we will be getting our degrees and will also get good jobs."

"That's good," Kenika said.

"Stop dat!" Angela said.

"And so," Seth said.

"We want to ask permission of you," Keith said.

"Come on out!" Kenika called.

The girls came into the room, looked around as if they were baffled by what they saw. "What's happening?" Clarice asked. "What are you guys doing here?"

"These guys need a beer," Kenika said. "Could you go grab a couple for them and cut the game?" Then he turned to the boys. "Sit down." They did so, Seth in an arm chair and Keith over at the dining room table. Elizabeth joined Keith and Clarice went and stood by Seth, and handed them their Primos. "Kids, get a beer for yourselves and one for Angela, 'kay? Might as well do this now."

When they all had their beers Kenika said, "Okay, it's set. When do you guys want to do this?" Seth and Keith looked somewhat confused about it all, as if all their elaborate preparations for asking him this crucial question were for naught, and being denied the opportunity to make this speech, they had both become speechless. "Uh," Seth said, "I'm not going back to California without—"

"That's right," Angela said. "We gotta get things set up."

"But it has to be after a month or so," Kenika said.

"December," Clarice said.

Kenika shrugged. "Sure, why not?"

Both girls squinted at him. "Daddy," Elizabeth said, "why you make dis so easy?"

"Because these are good boys and I know nature when I see it," he said. "Did you think of waiting?"

"No."

"Me either, uh uh."

"Did you?" Angela asked him.

"What about college?"

"Daddy, we still do dat. We get married, Set an' Keet go back San Diego until May, we stay."

"But what about—" They were going to spend time apart? It didn't seem right.

"It's okay," Seth said. "We'll finish up and then come back."

"You don't wanna wait?"

"Kenika!" Angela said, "Stop dat!"

As they chattered on about preparations he watched them, then looked at Angela, then looked back at the two couples. Set and Keet had become in his mind a strange set of twins, in their own way. It was about as innocent as anything could get. The girls had gone through high school without real boyfriends because they were just too shy in the presence of boys, and now this happened with the inevitability of certain kinds of weather, or tides. To try to do anything about it would be pointless. He could clearly see what they wanted, and they wanted it now. In fact, when he imagined them together he saw himself and Angela in all the unabashed forms of their sex, and although he was aware that he could have cringed at the idea of what his daughters would be doing with Set and Keet, in the same way he had sometimes cringed at the idea of what he and Angela did, it was after all natural.

≈   ≈   ≈

Kalani Chun circled the Moanapahi sprinkling salt, and came around to where he had started. He lit a paper match and then dropped it in the gap, the quickly-dying flame leaving a little puff of gray smoke. Malia design or not, it had a slightly taller, somewhat spatulate manu which seemed to proclaim above its sleek grace the majesty of older times. And it happened that at precisely the moment Kalani Chun finished giving the Moanapahi its brains, a breeze rolled up the hill and past the thirty or so people at the blessing, ruffling hair and clothes. Kenika felt it, and then nodded to himself, looking at the rich, deep grain of the hull. He looked up the hill in the direction of that rectangle of parched stone and imagined that in a minute, the same wind would cross over it too, completing the blessing and whispering to the timeless forms occupying that space that it was done properly.

The wedding took place in the backyard of their house. For Kenika it was a strange, dual repetition of his own, with the boys wearing black pants, white shirts and sashes, and maile leis studded with pikake buds, the girls white holokus and elaborate haku leis on their heads, and as was true with Angela the white of the holokus accentuated the darkness of their skin and the curly, luxuriant black of their hair. They were tall and beautiful standing next to their soon-to-be husbands, staring wide-eyed first at the Methodist minister, their faces beaded with sweat in the blazing sunshine, and then at Kalani Chun. There were more than fifty people there, and cars lined the street on either side and went around the corners at the end of the block. In the shade of the mango tree sat the elders: Momi, hair now almost white, George and Irene, Darnay, Aunty Clarice Malama and others, including the Marumotos, who insisted on driving in for the wedding. Kenika vaguely remembered that at his own wedding, elders sat in the shade, and now those elders were long gone. It seemed to him a century ago and then at the same time it seemed like two months ago. He divided his time between talking story with the men sitting in the carport drinking beer and eating tako poke and chips, and talking with the other guests, the more distant relatives from the Santiago family who were seen only at weddings and funerals.

Angela had arranged that the kids stay for two weeks at the Moana Hotel, the timing perfect because they were between semesters. They would come home for Christmas day and go back. Kenika had considered this suggestion and asked the girls if they wouldn't rather go on some longer honeymoon trip to the U.S. or something, and they looked at the ceiling. "This is the U.S., Daddy," Clarice said, "and no no no, we like go Moana Hotel." Then he understood. The Moana was a half-hour drive, that was why. They had something else on their minds.

After the gift-opening circus in the living room, during which Kenika wondered if the house would sink into the soft clay from all the bodies in it, Clarice cornered him and Angela in the kitchen and said, "Should we go now?" She had an anxious, jumpy expression, and Angela looked at her watch.

"Five," she said.

"'Kay, I'll get the keys."

They were going to change, grab their little suitcases and drive over the Pali in Angela's station wagon.

When Clarice went off with the keys to the lavishly-spread food table where Elizabeth and the boys waited, Kenika whispered to Angela, "Listen, have they— You know—"

"No," she said.

"Did you sort of, you know, talk to them?"

"Dey come an' ask, 'Mommy, what we do?' an' I tell dem bot' turn off da lights, take off da clothes, an' get inna bed. Da res' take care of itself." She snickered. "Dey bot' wen' gasp," and she imitated the familiar indrawn breath, "an' say 'Mommy!' an' I tell um no worry about da sheets." She laughed, peeking out the window at the crowd in the backyard. "Was so funny. Hey, dey wen' movies. What? Get no imaginations?"

"I suppose they're a little scared."

"Dey terrified," she said. Then she changed her expression. "I just wish the boys didn't have to go back, though."

"Me too."

"I remember the Moana. I hope it turns out for them like it did for us." They looked out the window. The girls were going from guest to guest announcing their departure so that the people could see them off.

≈   ≈   ≈

With Keoki surfing and playing basketball at the park at night, the house seemed suddenly, profoundly empty, and Kenika would wander from time to time to the girls' bedroom door and open it and look in. Everything was still there, along with the mountains of gifts each had piled on her bed, but the girls were not. He knew things were happening as they were supposed to happen, but he could not help but feel a hard tug of pain in his chest. He understood that after eighteen and a half years the twins were no longer "his" or Angela's. They belonged to themselves. They belonged to Seth and Keith, so to speak, and he wondered about life working that way, that families were not destined to remain together as he imagined they should, like tribes. But that was speculation on an imaginary world. They lived in a new world, one that was radically different from the one he had come out here and found when he was seventeen. Even though he had known it from the day the girls were born, he knew now more than ever the power of common blood.

Angela felt the same. How could it be that her babies grew up and were now on the other side of the island, and if they were there, where would they be next? They called every day, told Angela or Kenika what restaurants they ate at, where they went to dance, and so on, but still they were twenty miles away. Three days after they went to the Moana he found Angela in the study staring at the map of the island chain, then at the map of the world. She looked at him, her face screwed up in a look of suspicious wonder. "What?" he said.

"Look at us," she said, and pointed at the minute, curved line of dots in the middle of the Pacific. "Those boys are from over here," and she put her finger on southern California.

"I know what you mean."

"Do you?"

"I want the island chain to be like it is," he said, "and then I want nothing but blue all over the rest of the map."

"That's what I was thinking," she said. "I bet they go away. I just bet they do."

They came back from the Moana for Christmas, and spent the day in the aroma of turkey opening presents and talking about what they had done in Waikiki. In the backyard Keoki showed Seth and Keith his surfboard and fishing equipment, and Seth, fascinated by the three-pronged spear, tried shooting it into one of the palm trees, and they couldn't get it out. Kenika had to use a short crowbar and hammer to get the prongs out of the tough wood.

It seemed to Kenika somehow appropriate that the twins were married, ready to go back to the hotel, and he had something tangible to do at the shed starting the day after Christmas, because an order for a traditional fishing or 'opelu canoe had come to him through Clarence Lum, who had recommended to the directors of the Central

Pacific Academy's satellite campus on the Big Island that they acquire one just like the Peni'amina. Kenika explained that the canoe would not be made of a complete single log, because the ones he had left were damaged. As for the name, Clarence Lum told him that he had explained to the Academy people Kenika's, well, system, that the canoe must have a name and would be blessed in a traditional ceremony by a kahuna. They didn't know what to do about names, and told Lum that they would leave that to the builder.

The Hihimanu. The word meant "stingray," and according to the dictionary, its second meaning was "lavish, magnificent, elegant," appropriate because the stingray itself was a beautiful, dark and almost surreal animal, and the second meaning of the word in effect informed Kenika as to how it would be built: traditionally, as far as the materials would allow. He would use rope to tie the manu, which would be tall and spatulate, the hull stout and four or five inches thick in the base. He would lash the mo'o boards with rope, the pale kai, the seats. It would be closer to an original than the Peni'amina. Standing there in the shed, he closed his eyes and visualized the Hihimanu, saw the straight, upward projection of the manu, saw contrasting grained wood, maybe the lightest in color he could find, for the kaupo'i, or bow cover. Benny had once told him that this part had always been painted black with combinations of berry juices, but he decided that he would ignore that one feature, because in his mind's eye, the contrast of the ginger hull and the pale, gleaming kaupo'i seemed right. Rather than use koa for the seats, he would use kukui wood. Perhaps he would put wooden tags on the parts with their proper Hawaiian names: seat - noho 'ana wa'a, or noho for short; splash guard - pale kai, or pa'ele, or kua; gunnel board - mo'o, and so on.

When he went down the steps with the adze in one hand and the cant hook in the other, to test the wood, he realized something. Twenty-two feet of the damaged log would be cut away and shaped into a fishing canoe. The log had lain there for what? sixty-some years, and would now be made into a canoe that would go to the Big Island, the place of its origin. He would tell this to the log, and would feel the subtle, almost indistinguishable current in the air, of its reaction to this news. With that, he was convinced that the log would not resist him.

The newlyweds came back on the first of January, pulled into the shady space under the shower tree in front just as Kenika was sweeping up red paper from what seemed like a billion firecrackers the night before, all up and down the street. From all around came the residual popping of leftovers kids had found in the streets, and the baboom sounds of kids experimenting with making bombs that launched coffeecans into the air and tore up mailboxes. He stopped, studied the girls as he had on Christmas, wondering if he would see anything different about them now that they were married, but they seemed the same, came running over to hug him, then ran inside to find Angela. The boys loitered around the car, looking at the dunes of red paper in the street.

"Hey, you guys got time to help me winch a log?" Kenika asked.

"Sure."

"Yup."

"No rush, and it's only a fishing canoe. Twenty feet."

"Any time."

"Sure."

After they winched the log, an easy job because it was hollow and lacked full weight, Kenika delayed beginning work on the Hihimanu. The family, minus Keoki who was usually off surfing or playing basketball, sat around and talked for two weeks, either at the beach or in the living room. After a couple days it was Keoki and the new husbands off playing basketball, and Keoki was apparently impressed by their skill. "Eh, buggahs can drain um," he said. They were staying at the house, one couple in the girls' room, one in Keoki's, while Keoki slept in the little alcove in the study. In the middle of the night, sometimes, there were sounds, and Kenika couldn't tell what those sounds were, although he knew. Nothing could keep him and Angela apart when they stayed in Lanikai so many years ago, so why should anything keep them apart now? Kenika liked the idea, wished that, somehow, they would all stay nearby, but he knew that was a fantasy.

Angela wanted them to share their other house, providing that the Changs would not find moving too much of an inconvenience. The girls had other ideas. They would go with Seth and Keith to California. Apartments were cheap. Then you'll come back? Angela asked. Of course, they would all come back. But they wanted to see some of that other world. Kenika could see it in their expressions—there had to be so much to see over there that they could spend their lives exploring it, but of course they would always come back home. Kenika could also see in Angela's expression the creeping suspicion that the call of that other world meant something she had, in her innocence, not anticipated—these were children of the next generation. The difference from her own childhood, television, cheap air tickets, a university campus crawling with mainlanders with stories about this place and that, even husbands from back there, was so extreme that there was no way she or Kenika could hold them.

One night when she crawled into bed she put her arm over his chest and her head in the hollow of his shoulder. "They're going away," she whispered.

"I know. They'll come back though."

"I wish—"

She didn't continue.

"What?"

Nothing. He felt her breathing on his neck. "Uh-oh," he said. "What's that I feel?"

"That's the hot wahine savage jungle bunny wants to see what the ginnie's got."

"Shh. Keoki."

"He surfed today. You couldn't wake him up with a shotgun."

"But I'm a working man. A celibate canoe maker. Nothing could get me going now."

"Not even dakine?"

"Which dakine."

"Da*kine* dakine. I don't know. I haven't figured it out yet."

"H'mm. Well, what if—"

She gasped. "What is this?"

"One of my tools. It's a boring tool."

She laughed, and he said, "Shh, the girls."

That made her laugh louder. "They're as bad as us," she said. "God, las' night? I hear giggle, then a funny squeal, then thump thump thump for however long, then squeal, then a giggle. What's that, do you think?"

"H'm, I think they're building something."

"Must be. So where does this tool go?" Then she made a strange sound, "Gk-tscht."

"What happened?"

"Uh oh, I jus' wen' click into slow motion," she whispered. "Oh no." He could feel her moving very slowly. "Now everything move way too fas' fo' me. We cannot be in synch. I hate dat. When it happen inna kitchen? Take five minutes fo' poa one glass juice. I drop a banana an' it take so long to faw allaway down. It so frushtrating."

"Well, what if I clicked too?"

"Can you do that? You go slow too li'dat? Take long long long time you know."

"Gcht-tchkik!"

≈   ≈   ≈

In all there were nine people present at the blessing of the Hihimanu, and that included the Marumotos, and for October, the weather was perfect, cool and breezy, unlike the usual dead-wind time in early fall that they were used to. But only nine people? True, the intended users of the canoe lived on the Big Island, but Kenika stood there as Kalani Chun circled the canoe, and wondered if there was any reasonable possibility that this ritual he loved would survive time. More important than his love of the ritual was the function of it, that those who would step into a canoe not properly blessed risked death, if not a bad fishing day, and he began to wonder about how many people there were left who understood that, or took it seriously.

Angela stood there with a distracted look on her face, because her only contact with the twins now was by phone and by letters, and proof of their need to communicate with each other was a phone bill that was in excess of a hundred dollars a month. They did not come home for the summer because Seth and Keith got jobs at a state park in the Black Hills of South Dakota, which, after Angela talked to them on the phone one day, Kenika found her squinting at on the map hanging on the study wall. He could see the look of doubt, even dislike, on her face, that yes, there was that huge world out there and the twins were in it, talking excitedly day by day about everything they had seen; huge mountains, bears, moose, Indians, open plains and hills as far as you could see. Every description seemed more and more an insult to that perfect, ideal little homeland they seemed less and less interested in. But why? she asked him. And he could only shrug and say, I guess it's their age—they just want to see things. They'll come back. And Angela said, when? When will they come back? I ask them and they talk their way out of it, because next is what? Canada? Europe?

The telephone was a nice invention, but it was also a trick, because you thought you were really seeing them when you talked, and the fact was that you did not see them. And she was not fond of the idea of that world, in which a bizarre war in Southeast Asia, the assassination of Robert Kennedy only months ago, and then Martin Luther King, all of those horrible things could happen, and now could somehow invade their place like some kind of virus whose function was to destroy the last vestiges of that perfect insularity the girls had grown up in, that Angela had grown up in. And what is this draft business? she wondered. To fight way over there, for what? Would they try to take Seth and Keith? And what about Keoki? If someday they tried to take Keoki she would sit on the front porch with a machete waiting for them to come, because they could not have him. Benny may have been right— becoming a part of the rest of the world would cost the identity of their own.

Her pain was his, too. He remembered that time so long ago when he and Angela had gone out into Laie Bay looking for the little pink bats for wind chimes—he probably did not know it then, when he watched her dive down, the brown skin so rich in color and the black hair waving in the water, that it was in its own way a perfect world, but one which was doomed to extinction.

As Kalani Chun neared the end of his circle, a longer and more painstaking process now because of his age, Kenika moved over and put his arm around her waist, and she held his hand against her side.

With the dropping of the match the Hihimanu was given its brains, and it was a good spell. The canoe sat there, stout and lashed in traditional fashion so that you could see the winding of the stained rope around and through the precisely-cut openings joining the mo'o boards to the hull, and the two halves of the manus on either end. Had he had an extra lifetime to use up, he was sure, he would have spent part of it making sennit. The joining of the extra pieces for the hull and the aft portion, because of the damage to the log, was visible but not intrusive to the eye, because he had made a kind of decoration of it, insetting bow tie-shaped pieces of koa along the joint so that the insets looked almost like a line of stars. He worried so much about the canoe's strength that he may have overdone the joining, but reasoned that overdoing was better than underdoing. But as he looked at it he again wondered, how long would these works of art, these products of ancient genius, mean anything at all?

≈   ≈   ≈

Without a canoe to work on, he went back to the relief picture. By the time he was nearly done with that, he had at the back of his mind the idea that the girls had now been gone a year, and both he and Angela had settled into more or less accepting the idea that they were citizens of that other world. In their own, they were more and more perplexed by Keoki's behavior. Where his tendency toward a good-natured waywardness seemed almost all right when he was twelve, it became more and more worrying now that he was heading for seventeen. He was six feet tall and weighed a hundred seventy pounds, and was like one long, complicated muscle. Neither Angela nor Kenika cared particularly for his friends, who would usually be seen working on old cars in front of their houses in one part of Kailua or another, beercans lying in the gutter, rusty motorblocks and large patches of black oil on their front lawns. They were both aware that he came home from his sports with beer on his breath, and Angela would sometimes confront him with that: "Wheah you was! I get beah stink. Wheah you get dat!"

And he would shrug and say, "Sah-ree," and wait until he would be allowed to go to his room.

It worried Kenika enough that he brought the subject up while they sat on the little beach on the bigger Mokulua island on one of those days that Keoki wanted to do some routine surfing and fish a little. He told Keoki about his mother and about what alcohol had done to her. "Beer doesn't bother me that much," he told him, "but then too much of anything can be a problem. One day I got up to go to school and she was slumped over on the kitchen table, dead."

"Fo' real?" Keoki said. "You jus' go out an' fine 'er?"

"Yeah, and there wasn't any other explanation except booze."

"Chee, I no like go t'roo dat. What? You wen' phone police?"

"I went to a neighbor who called."

"Chee," Keoki said. "'Ass bad."

One of Kenika's new activities was the business of checking up on him, even to the point of going downtown to play basketball with him and his friends at night in the park. He had played in Paterson, but he discovered that these boys modeled their games on the heroics of Wilt Chamberlain and Jerry West, Walt Frazier and Earl Monroe. You had to jump and shoot while you were suspended in the air. Kenika did the best he could, and the boys were respectfully tolerant of him. Keoki, who was good at it, could jump so high that he could flip the ball downward through the basket. A dunk, or stuff-shot they called it. When he was there he was aware sometimes that they whispered to each other, and he knew what it was: don't do such and such tonight, because Kenika's here. What that such and such was he did not know, but from the little comments he heard he understood that during their rests between games they sat and smoked pakalolo, what in Paterson kids had called reefers. And the basketball court was located right behind the police station.

During the vacation periods of big north shore surf, Keoki would be gone sometimes two or three days in a row, staying at friends' houses out there, after careful diplomacy with his parents. Bobby Kaeo, a boy from a family they knew, invited him out there, which seemed safe enough. Kenika and Angela would sometimes drive out to see just what they meant by "big surf," and check on him. The times they did that they were both a little shocked at what they saw: at Chun's Reef or Banzai Pipeline or Ehukai or especially at Waimea Bay, the waves would be so huge that they appeared to be breaking in slow motion, and on the light-blue face of the waves there would be the tiny, dark figures cutting in the powerful curl, usually going forward off the board as the mountain of water curled over and broke right on top of them, spitting the light, fiberglass surfboard twenty or thirty feet in the air. You could feel the break of the waves in the sand you stood on, while on the beach other surfers and girls with bathing suits so small that they might just as well not have been wearing anything socialized. When Keoki came out, sometimes bleeding from the knee or elbow, having collided with his board before having fifty tons of white frothing surf bury him, he would be grinning broadly, and those girls would run down to say hello to him.

"H'm, I think I understand why he likes this more than football," Kenika said to Angela on one of their visits.

"Ho, but dose girls so pretty!" she said. "Dey haoles mostly. Oh look, hippies."

"Those girls are from California, I think," Kenika said. "At least that's what Keoki told me." And yes, there were the hippies—boys with long hair, so odd a picture that when Kenika first saw them at the beach with their backs to him, he thought he was looking at topless girls.

"I know why dey run afta him," she said. "He beautiful 'ass why."

Which he was. Kenika had never in his life seen a specimen of young manhood so ferocious and almost charismatically electric. It was as if he glowed. In a strange hapa mixture, he was part-Hawaiian and part whatever Kenika was, and apparently whatever he was, the Puerto Rican or Mexican that had gotten mixed in had produced what appeared to be an almost godlike human being, broad-shouldered and powerful, with a face that was first Polynesian because of its resemblance to Angela's face, but made leaner by the alien blood, almost as if he were some magnificent prototype of the distant future when all races blended into one.

What evidence Kenika could see of the world Keoki moved in secretly bothered him. Everything from the music they listened to to the bumper stickers on their cars signalled a set of ideas that seemed peculiar: Turn on, Tune in, Drop out - Make Love Not War - Girls Say Yes To Boys Who Say No - Ban the Bomb - Up With Chaos - and one he thought ridiculous, Fuck Tomorrow, Get High Today. As far as he was concerned nobody needed bombs, and war, at least the one they were fighting now wasn't a good idea, but getting high today and shaking your fist in enthusiasm for chaos and dropping out didn't make a lot of sense either, and he hoped that Keoki wouldn't take that stuff seriously. If what took him out to the North Shore was surf and girls, fine.

So they permitted him the freedom of what seemed like a vigorous youth, although Kenika continued shadowing him sometimes when he went to play basketball at the park, some of the time running through hundreds of flying termites, from the swarms coming out of hedges and poles, so that each floodlight would have a dense, yellow halo of them. From time to time he got the impression that Keoki did not appreciate his presence, and rather than push it, he began to back off, assuming that as Keoki grew up, the danger that he would do something stupid would decrease. At school he made his way without causing more trouble than being sent to the principal for fighting, and once he was caught in an English class with beer on his breath. He did not play on the high school basketball team or any other team, because surf became his main sport.

≈   ≈   ≈

By the time it was a year and a half that the twins had not come home, he began to wonder if they'd lost them altogether. They did call, but without the frequency of the early days of their marriages. They did not yet want children and according to Angela would wait, were on birt' control pills, and planned to have a good time first. What that meant was traveling, as far east now as New York, as far south as Mexico, as far north as Canada. They were involved in various activities in the protest movement, and Seth and Keith had draft exemptions because they were both graduate assistants at UCLA, continuing their cultural studies.

Seth proved to be an enterprising businessman. He and a couple of his friends made a good deal of money marketing what were called "X-Rated Conversation Hearts," a box of which came to Angela in the summer, along with photographs of the four of them and an apologetic letter explaining that they would not be able to visit until Christmas because they were spending the summer in Europe, using Eurail passes to travel around, all the way, Clarice wrote, to North Africa.

When she read that, Angela jumped up from the table and grinned at Kenika, because they would come, even if it was six months off. As for the conversation hearts, she wrote, there was a kind of fad of group games involving these candies, hence the success of the product. In the photographs the twins looked the same, but a little lighter of complexion because they did not have the same intensity of sun where they were. Set and Keet both had long hair, and long sideburns, and mustaches, and wore loud, tie-dyed shirts, while the twins wore little mini-skirt things with sloppy-looking blouses. Angela screwed her face up at the pictures, and said, "Ho, wheah dey get dose rags?"

The gift came in a heart-shaped box, and had a little warning label written out by Clarice: for use in the privacy of your own home.

Angela opened the box, and looked at the mound of hearts, then squinted at one: "Eat Me," it said. "Hey, try look," she said to Kenika. The next one she picked up read "Suck Cock," the next, "Fuck Slow," and so on. Within five minutes Kenika was amazed at how many combinations of four letter words there were.

"What kind games dey play?" Angela asked.

"Let's see, you take ten each, face down, and then roll the dice, 'kay?"

Angela laid out ten candies face down, and Kenika did the same, trying not to see any of the words. He went into the closet and got out the Monopoly game and took the dice back to the table. "'Kay, let's say I roll the dice, then you roll the dice. The highest number means the winner gets to— What? Do what the heart says, drawn by the other player?"

"'Kay," Angela said. She rolled a seven. Kenika rolled a nine. "'Kay," Angela said, "You do what dis one says," and she turned over a heart. "Eat cock." She thought a moment, then said, "But I don't have one of those."

"H'm," Kenika said. "Try again."

They rolled a second time, and Angela won. Kenika turned over one of her hearts. "Suck tit," it said.

"'Kay, you have two of those, so—"

Keoki walked in. "'S'op?" he said, and went to the refrigerator and took out the half-gallon container of milk. Angela quickly put the candies back in the box. "Junk game," she whispered, and ate one of them. "But I like play laters, 'kay?"

"Do what later?" Keoki said. "Hey, can I have one of those?"

"I saving dem till later," Angela said.

"Ho, stingy," Keoki said.

The box of conversation hearts went into the cupboard. When Angela put it there, Kenika could see the look of perplexed doubt on her face. How was it that her daughter could send that as a gift?

"Look," Kenika said after Keoki was gone to his room. "It's just the spirit of the times. Remember that you didn't really keep it that much of a secret."

She giggled. "Now I know how surprised my mom must have been."

At the shed Kenika finished the relief picture, polishing it with kukui nut oil, a technique Benny had taught him. He crushed five nuts and put the meat in a rag, and then pounded it with a chisel handle until the oil had soaked the rag. Then he polished the koa, the tiny fists and faces of his paddlers as they worked, forcing the fore manu outward over the water. As a picture it seemed fairly good, although he knew that because he had been looking at it for so many years he had no idea if it was any good at all. It was just too familiar to him. But as a picture partly determined by the swirling grain, he liked it, because the grain had told him how the little waves should break off the hull, how the canoe itself would be placed inside the oval shape of the plank.

He took the finished piece over to Waikiki to show Mr. Maxwell, whose shop was now so dwarfed by the huge hotel buildings that it seemed to be some pitiful outpost from the past, enduring in its smallness now for no logical reason. He had to park on Ala Wai Boulevard because everything closer was taken. Maxwell was there, but his showcases and trinkets were not. Kenika stood there holding the thirty-pound relief picture under his arm and looked around at the empty walls, different layers of paint now visible where the wall cases had been mounted, wires sticking out of junction boxes in the ceiling. "What happened?" he asked. Mr. Maxwell stood looking at him, then shrugged.

"We're being torn down," he said. "What's that?"

"I think it's called a relief."

"Let's have a look."

Kenika took the oily rag off the relief picture and set it on the floor against the wall. Maxwell stared at it, leaning forward to study the little fists going smaller and smaller in the foreshortening of the canoe.

"I can't sell this," he said. "But I know some people who have a shop in Ala Moana Center who could."

"'Kay."

"But I don't want somebody cutting a piece of glass and screwing in legs and making a fucking coffee table out of it."

Kenika laughed. "Well—"

"Because that's what they'll do. We'll put like a two-thousand dollar tag on it. That'll cancel out the coffee table people."

Two thousand. Kenika scratched his head. Could it be worth that much? "Isn't that a little steep?" he asked.

Maxwell laughed. "Jesus, you never change, do you?"

"You think it's worth trying another?"

"Sure." Maxwell stared at him a moment. "Look, I've still got a little of your stock, all in one box. I'm opening another shop down in the Queen Street area. Do you want me to keep it? I owe you around fifty dollars, by the way."

"Yeah, keep it. And hold the money till it gets over a hundred."

When he went to the shed the next day, he climbed under and studied the other koa slabs Benny had left there. He selected one and carried it up inside, and set it on the bench. Then he opened a beer and stood staring at the grain, waiting for it to speak to him. On the other end of the bench there was a little pile of dusty coconut shells, all cut for wind chimes. He had the odd sensation that they were now officially obsolete, that nobody wanted them any more, and the twenty-some year business of making them and all the other trinkets was finally over. Every shop that had such trinkets in Waikiki, he had noticed, had them packaged in cellophane, every trinket he saw had the look of sharp-edged mass production. There was something artificial and shiny about every object he saw, from the cheapest, the fists with middle fingers stuck out made of some black conglomerate that looked like hardened lava, to wind chimes that had been sloppily-varnished and had little red or green plastic collars around the hole in the dome where the fishing-line hanger was attached. There were even little black akua statues like the one he had carved from redwood long ago, some standing before what appeared to be a representation of a tide pool, until you saw the little indentations where the cigarettes were supposed to go. If cheapness and bad taste were what people wanted, then he was finished as a trinket maker.

Angela's business, on the other hand, had become one of the best-known on the Windward side. Her only problem was filling orders for leis, which, with the population increase in Kailua, became impossible. Kenika divided his weekday time between working out at the shed and helping her find flowers, tramping through the woods for nuts and seeds, running errands to Waimanalo to aunties' houses for plumeria, or buying them from farmers.

For two weeks prior to that day Angela thought would never come, she rearranged the kids' rooms, bought food, and ordered fish from Kenika: Lobsta—you know how dey love dat. Yes, the best cave is at Laie, how many you want? Menpachi? No problem. Odda kines, whatevahs, go get um. And as they had promised, they called from L.A. and told them when their plane would arrive. When Kenika left to go to the airport Angela was so excited that she thought she'd pee in her pants if she didn't calm down. The twins seemed not to have changed at all, but for the strange clothes they wore, bell-bottomed slacks and bright blouses, their husbands with long sideburns and goatees. So the house was suddenly full again, and the talking went on into the night, Angela listening intently to every tale about the exotic places they visited: the Tetons, Yellowstone, Black Hills, then Europe, Paris, Munich, Rome, Casablanca and so on, and they had thirty pounds of pictures to prove it.

One off-and-on tradition of the extended family was the Christmas season luau at the old house in Lanikai. This year they would do it New Year's Day. Recently it had seemed more and more like a gathering of old folks, because, like the twins, the children of the relatives from the leeward side and from Kaneohe and Waimanalo were usually "somewhere else," either on the mainland at college or working or having fun some other way. New Year's morning Kenika swept the sidewalk and street, bagging up the dunes of red paper, while Angela and the twins prepared various dishes in the kitchen before driving over to Lanikai. Although they had extracted from Keoki a promise to show face at the luau, he was not at home, and they assumed that he had gone surfing at the Mokuluas with his friends.

When he had not shown face by eleven in the morning, when two thirds of the people were already there, the kupuna sitting in the shade under the mango tree in the front yard, Angela caught up with Kenika who had been chatting with Frank Sakata and said, "Dat boy! He to' me he come."

"I'll go down to the beach and look for him," Kenika said.

He went across the lawn to the road that led to the beach and turned to look back. There they all were, sitting in the aroma of kalua pig and barbecued fish, the little group under the tree made up now of white-haired people: George and Irene, Momi, Aunty Clarice, the relatives from Waianae. And the house, once square and trim, looked to be almost melting downward, like the old house in Maunawili, which, the last time he had seen it, was so riddled with termite and wet-rot damage that he wondered if it was safe for Momi to be rattling around in it by herself.

He found Keoki's friends on the beach, lying in the sun, the expressions on their dark faces mixtures of fatigue and anguish, because they were all so badly hung-over that they seemed not to have the energy to stand up. "Where's Keoki?" he asked one of them, Tommy Ching he thought his name was.

"Oh, hi, Mr. McKay. He wen' cratah wit' Jimmy dem."

"What's that?"

"Da Sunshine Festival? We go laytahs."

"H'm, is that the hippie thing—flowers and rock and roll?"

The boy laughed. "Yeah, 'ass it."

Angela was not amused. "Everybody'll be here by two. Go get dat boy," she said.

"What festival?" Clarice asked.

He explained it, and she looked at her watch. Elizabeth looked up from one of Angela's old school yearbooks and said, "Count me out. I wanna stay here. Keoki should be here too."

"'Kay, but how do I find him?"

"Oh, he make me so mad," Angela said.

He wasn't sure how he would find him, but assumed that if he looked carefully, he wouldn't miss him. But the number of cars parked on the little streets off the mountain side of Diamond Head, near the tunnel that went into the crater, made him wonder. In the cool tunnel, his ears blasted by "Come Together" he could already see in the blazing opening on the other end the solid mass of people sitting before a raised platform on which a band performed.

It was hot and almost too bright inside, and he scanned the crowd. He went through a strange, almost dreamlike swoon because of all the colors, the clothes and tarpaulins and towels and tie-dyed hangings all over the place so rich in their blues and yellows and greens that he had to shake his head and orient himself to the visual intensity of it. All the way across the crater bowl, up on the platform, a band blasted out its music, the drum sounds so powerful that he could feel the echo ripple his flesh. He began walking the perimeter of the crowd, scanning faces. It struck him as strange that most of the people there were haoles, guys with long hair, a lot of them with beards and large chains around their necks with various things hanging from them, the peace circle, Indian-style beads, odd pieces of coral or shells. Because of the din of the music, to which many of the people were swaying, the air had an atmosphere of a kind of silence, the same silence you felt when a heavy rain made its continuous explosion of sound on a roof.

He made his way to the corner of the platform, where the sound was so loud that it hurt his ears. Just as he realized that it hurt his ears he saw one boy sitting leaning against a speaker the size of a refrigerator, his head tipped to the side, his face a strange mask of wan fascination, as if what was vibrating his brain was a soft whisper. Just away from the crowd, in some brush, a little group of people danced and, when they felt no one looked, passed around a little cigarette thinned out on either end. Marijuana. In fact he could now smell it in the air, a rich but flat tobacco-ish odor. One blonde girl who appeared to be very young, fourteen perhaps, and painted here and there with daisies and leaves, danced in a dizzy stupefaction, unconcerned about the fact that the bathing suit she wore left almost nothing to the imagination. In fact she seemed to want to point her undulating rear end and then her breasts at an appreciative man in his thirties who wore tight-fitting bell bottom jeans and stared at her through wire-rimmed glasses, a lecherous smile appearing through a beard so thick that only his eyes and forehead were visible.

Kenika went behind the platform to work his way around the other side of the crowd. Back there some people were sunbathing nude in the grass, and he looked away and walked on. When he got around the platform the music stopped, and then he heard voices from every direction, and they all sounded tinny and flat. The music and the sun had gotten to him, he thought, because he moved in a dreamlike numbness, feeling strangely hollow and light. It might have been the languidness of the crowd somehow contrasted with the variety of colors, so many that to his eye the effect seemed almost violent. When he did clearly hear voices what he got was a nonsensical intermeshing of multiple conversations—"At Berkeley, man, we—" "Waste more land is at it again, and do you think—" "No death, man, 'cause it's a fucking illusion," and then someone singing, "Everybody must get stoned."

He had made it almost all the way around the crowd when he saw Jimmy Chong, a friend of Keoki's, and went up to ask him where he was. "Eh, howzit? See da bushes o'dea? He wit' people we know."

"'Kay, thanks."

There was a blue tarp set up on poles near some bushes, and he went there and found a group of people, none of them Keoki. Haole and local bearded guys with loud clothes sat on beach mats and strange, oriental-looking rugs and drank wine from bottles in brown paper bags, blonde girls in bathing suits sitting next to them. When he stopped before them one of the men looked up at him with good-humored perplexity, as if unable to understand what this person was doing in their brightly-colored space. Another man snorted with contempt and turned around and put a little cigarette into a beercan.

As Kenika was about to speak he noticed that two of the girls and one of the men were now looking at him with irritated disgust. He looked down at himself, wondering if something might be wrong with his clothes: regular pants, a white tee shirt, what he considered good luau clothes.

"I'm looking for Keoki McKay," he said.

"Back there, man," the one with the wine said. He held his bottle up and smiled jovially.

"What are you, man," the irritated man said. "Some kind of narc?"

He didn't know what a narc was, and before he could speak the man said, "I mean we came out here to get away from guys like you, man."

"Where you from?" he asked.

"L.A.," he said. "L.A.'s dead, man. L.A. rotted away, man, and we escaped. We came out here and found our new country. I mean we like pledged our allegiance." Kenika stared at him, drew breath to speak, but he went on. "You come here to spoil this beautiful scene, man? I mean what is this, Altamont?"

"Look, I'll just go back there and—"

"He's occupied," the man with the wine said.

"He's following the tambourine man," the other said.

"What is he occupied with?"

"You mean who."

"All right, who is he occupied with? Never mind, I'll just—"

The jovial man put his wine down and jumped up, laughing and shaking his head. "Wait, wait," he said, stepping between Kenika and what looked like a little tent. "Give them a minute."

Kenika stared at him. "You're in my way."

"This is a peaceful gathering, man," he said. "What, you his parole officer? Is this Hawaii 5-0?"

"I'm his father."

The man stared at him.

"Tell him to get the fuck out of our space," one of the girls said. "Tell him to leave Keoki alone. Keoki's our man, let him be."

"Excuse me, man, but you don't look old enough to be."

Kenika snorted and tried to walk around him, but he grabbed his arm. When he did Kenika felt his scalp prickle, and reached out and took the man by the wrist, then squeezed.

"Hey man, you're—" He struggled to pull away, and Kenika let go.

The other man was up now, a look of belligerent wonder on his face. "Fuckin' toads, man," he said. "What, you some fuckin' L.A. cop? We ditched you fuckers, man. This is our turf, man."

The man who had tried to stop Kenika rubbed his wrist. "If you think you can push Keoki around, you're mistaken," he said.

Kenika walked toward the tent. Just as he was about to call out Keoki's name, his face appeared between the partly-open flaps. "Hey Dad!" he said.

Kenika had never been able to yell at the kids, and could not yell at Keoki now. "The luau," he said. "Time to come home."

Keoki was red-eyed and a little wild-looking, and he stared for a moment at the grass at the entry to the tent and then at Kenika and said, "'Kay." Then he looked back inside the tent, apparently listening to someone. "Hang on a sec."

Then the tent began to change shape, the sudden, flashing imprints of fists and heads appearing in the fabric. Keoki came out, followed by a pretty local girl.

She looked a little stunned, staring at Kenika, and then sidled up against Keoki, who said, "Dad, dis is Loke Soares." Kenika nodded to her, and she stared back with huge, confused eyes.

"Well, would you like to go to a luau?" Kenika asked her.

She looked to one side and then the other.

"Sure," Keoki said. "But she live dis side."

"We can bring her back, whatever," Kenika said.

"Eh, les' grab da stuffs," Keoki said.

On the way past the tarp Keoki stopped and looked down at the people sitting there. "Eh guys, dis my dad," he said, slapping Kenika on the shoulder. "He da man. Gotta go."

"Peace, brother," the jovial man said, and then he got up and approached Kenika. "Hey, sorry about all that."

"'Sokay," Kenika said.

"We didn't— I mean like, we didn't know. We're not as dumb as we act."

"'Sokay."

One of the girls snorted and whispered to another girl, and Keoki said, "Eh, 's go awreddy."

When they had finally made it to the car and got it going so that some wind could cool them down, Kenika turned a little and said, "Who're your friends?"

"Jus' not' shoah people from California."

"They sure say 'man' a lot."

Just as Loke stuck next to Keoki throughout all the introductions as if there were some invisible string that connected them, later Kenika noticed that the same invisible string connected Loke to Angela. Despite the distractions, with the twins going around to all the relatives to talk and the husbands doing the same, and Angela's function as the hostess, the fascination seemed mutual. Angela would look at her, then at Keoki, and then back, as if wondering just what it was that went on between them. The way Loke hung onto him seemed more than just a date thing, and the very un-Keoki-like way he looked at her was almost alarming. It was a totally alien expression for him. Kenika decided not to mention anything about the tent, not so much because he wanted to keep it from Angela, but more because she worried enough about Keoki without this.

If they really were involved in the same way Kenika and Angela had been, he reasoned that they were the same age as Kenika and Angela had been when they became involved, so there was nothing unnatural about it. And if there was any question about "approval," Kenika found himself looking again and again at the girl, thinking how pretty she was, and secretly he felt a warm exultation at the possibility that she might become Keoki's wife, because their children would consititute a gain in the blood balance. She was dark, had straight black eyebrows perched above large almond eyes, long black hair, and a face that was as Polynesian as Angela's. He knew that he was jumping the gun on this speculation, but he imagined that he would be able to watch with satisfaction the gradual disappearance of Caucasian blood in this part of the family, and his own blood running in the veins of his grandchildren would make up only a small part of it, a weak dilution of their own, whose lineage they could point to without any doubt: these two are my grandparents, and those two are my other grandparents, and three out of the four I know. Kenika, well, we don't know who he was, but—

As he made his way from one group of relatives to another, he had the feeling, or maybe the illogical hope, that this new development with Keoki was probably not a false alarm, because changes on the other end of the generational line were taking place. Momi was selling the Maunawili house because it was too much for her to take care of. It was true—she had become frail approaching seventy years old, and Angela had been worrying about her for some time, had even asked her if she would like to live in their house since the girls' room was empty. She declined because she said a man friend of hers was helping her acquire a condominium apartment on the Honolulu side. George and Irene were also very much slowed down by age, and George had been having trouble with diabetes and other afflictions, to the point that they, too, were considering moving. Darnay had met someone and would move back to Waikiki. Apparently Kenika and Angela and whatever children would choose to live in Kailua would be the only ones left.

"Momi," he heard Angela say with artificial distress, "now I gotta hire somebody. You cannot stay?"

"Angela, for heaven's sake, I can barely see what I'm doing any more. In fact, making leis is torture."

"Ho, a resignation," Angela said, waving chopsticks around in the air, and then turned to Darnay. "An' you, you kolohe o' man! Now what I do?" Darnay laughed with wan resignation. Now his pony tail no longer looked out of place. In fact Keoki thought it was "cool."

The luau lasted until late in the night, and at eleven, Kenika went and asked Keoki if he thought they should take Loke home. "Mommy call," he said. "She stay ovah."

Kenika thought it must be Angela's magnetism that caused it, but Loke seemed to be at the house almost every night, sitting at the table talking with Angela and the twins, and sometimes helping her down at the shop. Kenika finally asked her what she thought.

"Oh, she so sweet," she said. "An' she straighten dat bad boy out."

"Do you think they—" He didn't know how to put it.

"Yes," she said. "We awready talk about dat."

"Jesus," he said. "Did she ask the usual questions?"

"What usual questions?"

"You know, dakine, and so on."

She stared at him a moment, and then laughed. "When dey get married, den I get questions about tongues, an' sand, an' all dakine. Besides, dey nice people, not twisted pig like you."

"I like that—twisted pig. But anyway, do you think they'll really get married?"

"We awready talk about dat."

So, the world was advancing without his knowing it. But at eighteen, wasn't Keoki too young? "How old is she?"

"Eighteen summahtime."

"Makes me feel old."

"When kids get back from da beach?"

"Way later, but it makes no difference. I'm finished. I have no desire for, you know, dakine any more."

"I know. Me either. Jus' one dried-up o' gramma."

"Would you like a piece of candy?"

A week and a half after the luau the twins and their husbands packed up their things and left, amidst promises to stay in touch by phone and to come back, if not sometime in the summer then certainly next Christmas if things should work out that way, and again Kenika would wander to their bedroom door, open it and see the room as it had always appeared, with all the little mementoes of their earlier life, stuffed animals and records, posters and books all neatly arranged as they had been for years.

≈   ≈   ≈

After graduation, which Keoki just qualified for, he and Loke were married in the backyard of the house of Loke's parents, in Kaimuki. It was an immense gathering of people, mostly Loke's relatives and friends, and Kenika could easily see that they were from a higher-income level than his family was. Everyone seemed too well-dressed, and he looked down at his own clothes, feeling a little uneasy. Loke's parents took care of all the arrangements, and for this reason there was no kahuna present. The absence of a kahuna bothered him, as if without the blessing, some disaster awaited the couple. Angela had told him that Loke's family was "Catlick," and she had asked Keoki if he wanted a blessing from Kalani Chun, and he said, nah nah, 'sokay. Although Kenika felt that it was not okay, he said nothing, assuming that like other traditions that seemed okay in the forties or fifties, this one was of an old world, and the people of this new world would do without them.

The parents also provided for a honeymoon, and for two weeks the kids were in Las Vegas, a place in the middle of nothing on the map. Angela now added to her map-search for the twins a skeptical squint at the little circle that marked the desert city, and Kenika could tell that she looked at the map with a grudging wonder about that other world out there. The twins could not make it back for the wedding because they were in Greece, the explanation having something to do with Seth and Keith and their graduate studies, which were gradually becoming less and less understandable. Something to do with culture and business, far more complicated than the marketing of X-rated conversation hearts. But the twins had been able to keep Keoki's ear against the receiver for a half an hour, ragging him about getting married so young, and making speeches about what horrors awaited the poor young thing who was dumb enough to fall for him. And they thought that Vegas, rather than the Moana, was a bad precedent.

Kenika found himself churning through the water out toward the reef at Lanikai wondering whether or not there was any sense in getting more fish with only two of them left to eat them. Going back in, he surfaced and scanned the beach. Lanikai now had houses end to end, and motorboats sent up fans of spray behind them. He could just see the large blue tarp on Jerry Cambra's lawn, under which snoozed The Red Wind. In the foothills of the small mountain range separating Lanikai from Keolu Hills and his neighborhood, larger and larger houses were being built, two and three-story modern things that looked like boxes on stilts. He put his face back down in the water and pulled the bag to himself and looked in. Three aweoweo, one menpachi, shot through the body so that it would not really be that edible. Not much, but whatever glumness he might have felt at such a bad fishing day seemed pointless. These too would end up frozen and forgotten in the back of the freezer anyway.

But a kind of normalcy reemerged when Keoki and Loke came back from Vegas. They stayed in Keoki's room, and every evening there were four people at the table. Loke's father had arranged for Keoki to get a job with his construction company. It was good money, and Keoki wanted nothing to do with his own family business, such as it was. He was never a fan of woodwork, and these were new times, and wind chimes and seed leis didn't bring home the bacon, nor did one or two canoes every century. Well, a little more frequent than that, Kenika said, and Keoki slapped him on the shoulder. Eh, jus' raggin' you, Dad.

The renters of their other house, the Changs, had been for a couple of years trying to buy a house in Kailua, and when it came time to install Keoki and Loke in that house, Angela learned that the Changs were only three thousand dollars short of being able to make the down payment on one. Angela's solution was to loan them three thousand dollars, because it got them out of the house on good terms. Besides, she was not going to evict people who had taken such good care of the place, and anyway, where would they go? Gwen Chang was twenty-six and had three children and worked at the drug store just down the hill in the little shopping center built a few years ago. Angela could not stand the idea of kicking them out. When Kenika and Angela went around the block to the house to see them, Kenika could see on the couple's faces the look of doom at their approach. While Kenika talked with Ted Chang out by the mailbox, he could hear Angela explaining everything to Gwen, and then Gwen threw her arms around Angela's neck and cried. "What happened?" Ted Chang asked Kenika, who said, "Let Gwen explain it."

Which she did while Angela waited with Kenika by the mailbox. Ted Chang then turned and came back, and whispered, "Really?"

"You folks decide," Angela said. "No rush, 'kay?"

By the time the dead weather had come around again in September, the kids were in their new house, and Loke was pregnant. In an almost startling reversal, Kenika thought, there appeared to be family nearby after all.

$$\approx \quad \approx \quad \approx$$

With the dead weather came the suspicion on Kenika's part that he would be making no more canoes. He wasn't sure what it was, but there was a peculiar silence he felt around him, that despite the expansion of canoe racing as a sport, for some reason the canoe itself had stalled. No one used them for fishing any more, and if people wanted a boat, they bought one made of fiberglass that had a sixty-horsepower motor sticking out the bottom of the stern. As for racing canoes, there were apparently enough of them. There was talk of a new racing group that would use only fiberglass canoes, and in the possibility of that he saw the extinction of the koa canoe, because surely fiberglass canoes could be manufactured with that dead, alien material and ear-shattering power tools at such a promiscuous rate that he imagined drums of liquid being rolled into a warehouse front door and white, plastic canoes marching out the rear door day in and day out, price tags flapping on their artificial manus. In fact he learned from talking with a friend of Jerry Cambra's that fiberglass canoes were being made from what was called a "Malia mold." And he found himself thinking, here, pour yourself a canoe.

By the time the dead weather had passed, Loke was showing somewhat, and while Keoki was at work she was either down at the shop with Angela or sitting at the dining room table with her. Keoki had developed a strange tendency to occasionally head off for work at seven in the morning and for some reason careen off onto the wrong highway and find himself at the north shore, and from time to time he came home either smelling of beer or acting strangely. Kenika would feel a flash of heat and think, marijuana, acid, cocaine, heroin, peyote, and so on, running through his mind the list of drugs he had heard about watching television, and wonder just what it was that Keoki was fooling with. Those groovy friends of his out at the north shore, no doubt, had plenty of it. But the boy was on his own now, and most of the time seemed responsible.

In late October he got a call from a professor at the University of Hawaii named Ron Abel, who was part of an experimental program called Alternative Studies, in which students fashioned their own major programs. "It's like a roll-your-own thing, if you know what I mean," he said.

"'Kay." He looked over at Angela and Loke, who looked back at him, eyebrows raised.

"The project for this class is to build a canoe."

"'Kay."

"We want to offer you a position as a lecturer for the spring semester."

Kenika stared at the little grid of holes in the receiver. "I never did stuff like that before."

"Well, a dean at Stimson College told us that you were involved in a project with some students, and that—"

"Two students," he said.

There was a short silence, and then Professor Abel went on. "I tried to get the administration to offer you an instructorship, even assistant professor, but all they would allow was a lectureship. It comes with a salary of around two thousand dollars, and the class meets once a week."

"You can't make a canoe once a week. I mean—"

Professor Abel laughed. "Excuse me," he said. "We would make it according to your instructions, from scratch."

"Why?" There was another silence, and Angela and Loke continued their conversation at a whisper. "I mean," Kenika went on, "why do they want to build a canoe?"

"For the experience and for the cultural absorption. Some of the students are into Hawaiian history, about a third of them are local." He went on to explain that all Kenika would need to do would be to describe to the students all he knew about canoes, and to show them how to make one, or assist them in making one. He would have no papers to read, no tests to grade, no committees to sit on, no other university duties but that one project.

"What would happen to the canoe? Would they use it?"

Professor Abel remained silent for a moment. "I don't know," he finally said.

"Would the students use it?"

"I— Yes, I'm sure they would."

"Then what would happen to the canoe?"

"I'll look into that," he said.

Kenika then cleared his throat and went into his speech: "I require that the canoe have a name before we build it. I also require that the canoe be blessed in traditional fashion by a kahuna, and that those who will use the canoe be present at the blessing."

Professor Abel said that all those details could be worked out. Did this mean that Mr. McKay was agreeing to participate in the project? Yes, it did. "So could you come over next week and sign a contract?"

"We don't use contracts for canoes. We build them and then if the buyer likes the canoe, then the buyer pays for it."

"No, the contract is for the job. When you say 'we' are you talking about a partner?"

"I— No, it's only me. I was talking about my teacher, but he's gone now."

After another silence, Professor Abel said, "We'll provide everything, tools, the log, and so on."

"Where'd you get a koa log?"

"It's not koa, it's spruce or something. Found on the beach."

Kenika stared at the phone. Spruce. He remembered Benny telling him that Hawaiians prized those odd logs that sometimes came floating in to shore from far away, because some of them, pine, spruce, and so on, made decent canoes. "How long is the log?"

"Twenty-five or thirty feet I think he said. The student who has it, I mean."

"Then he takes the canoe when it's done?"

"I think so."

"What will he do with it?"

"I don't know," Abel said. "Is there a reason to be concerned about it?"

A reason to be concerned. If it was an alien spruce log, would its fate be to be further alienated by being sold, or stored in a garage? He couldn't really explain it to Professor Abel. The log was alive, at present lacking brains and lying somewhere snoozing in a fitful nightmare, its heart aching for life, its flesh waiting to feel water sweep under it in something other than the random, foam-tossed violence of a cross-ocean voyage. As soon as its fate was designated, to become a canoe, then all of those emotions, fears and doubts were immediately awakened in its hard flesh, suspended somewhere in that grainy tubular mass. It was lost, far from its home, and now its fate was in the hands of humans, and Kenika felt a surge of sympathy for it. He decided that for the log's sake it was a good idea that he agreed to do this, because the thought of any impropriety in its shaping made him feel a strange dread, not so much for the canoe inside the log but for the broad idea of the canoe itself, a sort of ideal image whose preservation and care he could not allow himself to ignore.

"This is ridiculous," he told Angela and Loke after he hung up. "But I'm teaching at the University next semester."

"Not," Angela said.

"Do you have to wear a suit?" Loke asked.

"I don't know," he said. Then he put his hands on his head. "What the hell am I thinking? I can't do that. I mean, what do I say?"

"Do what you did wit' Set and Keet," Angela said. Then she leaned over and patted Loke's stomach. "Eh, you li'l buggah, grandaddy one professah."

"I can still refuse to sign the contract," he said.

But he signed it. One factor was Professor Abel's clothes, bell-bottomed pants and a loud shirt with no collar. In fact, at the University he saw no one wearing a suit, and the students were dressed more or less as if they were going to a crater festival than to a college. The room where the canoe would be built was a moist, almost dank ground floor hall with a few desks and chairs piled in one corner and dust and pieces of paper strewn on the dull asphalt tiles, and the windowsills were perforated by termite damage. "Big enough, you think?" Abel asked Kenika.

"Sure."

"You'll get a paycheck every two weeks until the middle of July."

"'Kay."

With Set and Keet he had worried about the invasion of the shed, and recalled his insecurity about having to be their mentor, having to talk to them about how to make a canoe. As he drove home, considering what he had gotten himself into, he realized that this was far worse than two haoles coming to work on a canoe in the shed. Abel told him that there were twenty-five students in the class. He pictured himself standing there before them, trying to figure out what to say, and found himself mortified at the prospect.

Angela thought it was a good idea. "Since when do you get to talk to all those people at once? Think of it, you get to pass on your expertise."

No pidgin. She was serious about it.

"I'm a little scared."

She looked at him, then stood up from her chair and put her arms around him. "No be worried," she said. "Nobody knows this like you do."

He drew in a deep breath, with it the fragrance of her hair. "Hey, maybe you could come some time and watch."

≈   ≈   ≈

The No Mamao Wa'a. Or "From Afar Canoe," if that was the right combination. This canoe of spruce should simply announce its alien status and have done with it, so that fish, other canoes, fishermen, spirits, would all know its questionable lineage and then forget about it, so that the canoe could proceed with its life without that question hovering around it like a shroud. Whether or not its eventual owner would use it for its intended purpose of fishing wasn't his concern because he had no control over that. Probably those owners would not because after all, who fished from a canoe any more? But it had to be fashioned with its purpose in mind: 'opelu, fishing canoe, with a thick, sturdy hull, a broader beam, and high, regal manus. If he was the teacher and they were the students, then he would have them build it as if this were seventeen seventy-one rather than nineteen seventy-one, or rather seventy-two, since it would be spring. If there were people sitting around with nothing to do then he might even have them make sennit. He laughed at that. No, he wouldn't.

The night of the first class Angela fed him fried rice, chicken and Swiss chard which she grew (haole taro, she called it), and made him drink two beers, because as she said, it would loosen him up a little. At the door she stood there and looked him up and down.

"This is dumb," he said. "I didn't even graduate from high school."

She giggled. "Did you put on deodorant?"

"Yeah."

She sniffed his shirt. "'Kay, you all set."

The station wagon was so burdened down with tools that first evening that he imagined it looked like a junkyard on wheels, and he was glad that Professor Abel had set aside a parking space for him right at the door of the building. When he carried the first of the tools in, he found the log lying on the floor of the classroom, the bark stripped in places and the wood splintered and covered with hauling abrasions. But it looked like a good log. It was not spruce. It looked like pine, and he remembered Benny telling him that pine was also a good wood for canoes. Near the wall he saw three huge tool chests, and on top of one of them was a red chainsaw.

Because he was early he sat outside and tried to envision himself talking to a class. A few students wandered into the area of the building and sat down on wooden benches and large concrete planter borders inside of which were different kinds of trees. As he waited, he saw one student light and then pass a joint down the line, each student taking a puff and then holding the smoke in his lungs. When Professor Abel came walking through patches of waning sunlight toward the building, they did not put the joint away. Apparently not noticing Kenika, he walked into the hall. More students came down the walk, mostly girls, and went inside the hall. He could hear chairs scraping on the floor, and swallowed into a dry throat. Dumb, he thought. Dumb dumb dumb. Then he got up and went inside.

He stood there in a state of peculiar numbness, aware that Professor Abel was introducing him to the class. Then Abel went and sat down on one of the chairs. Kenika didn't at first have any idea of what to say, and went to the log and placed his hand on it. Then he said, "Uh, in the old days, a well-made canoe meant life and a badly-made canoe meant death. For this reason the building of a canoe took on an importance far in excess of what it might today. We're going to build this canoe as they did in ancient times, so in the process of building it there won't be any modern sounds. No chainsaw, no electric sanders, nothing like that."

With his hand on the wood he rattled on, and then worked backward into that region of antiquity Benny had described to him so many times. The log's soul leaked into his hand and up his arm and he felt no more discomfort. There were the dreams, the offerings, the chants, the 'elepaio, all of it leading up to the lolo 'ana ka wa'a i ka halau, "And without that last consecration, the canoe would be without brains and too dangerous to paddle."

As he went on he became more aware of the looks on their faces, some of them listening intently, some whispering to each other, some manifesting concealed skepticism if not ridicule. But he didn't really worry about those people, he worried only about being complete in his description. One male student off to the side appeared to sleep, his face buried down in the collar of an army jacket.

After what seemed like a long time, his voice growing hoarse, he paused and said, "Any questions about that part?" He noticed then that it was dark outside.

Professor Abel said, "It's a fascinating belief system, and a perfect example of how a belief system is created as a pragmatic response to a series of conditions." He turned to the class. Then he turned back to Kenika. "Sorry, go on. I was just interested in how they imbued inanimate objects with human characteristics."

"'Kay. I should say that I don't know anything about what made anybody do anything except where canoes are concerned. And I know only that I won't make one unless I know it will be given its brains."

There was a little rustle in the class, again he supposed a collective flinch of skepticism.

"Anthropomorphism is a disease the race has had from the beginning," one student said. The boy looked hapa, part Oriental and part haole. He was one of the cleancut ones. Kenika was confused for a moment, because he had forgotten the meaning of the word.

"'Kay, what does that mean?"

"It means assigning human characteristics to animals or objects or whatever." He heaved himself forward and put his elbows on his knees. "It's only that we've left that behind, or should have. But hey, whatever turns you on."

Kenika stared at him for a moment, his hand on the log. "'Kay, picture this—you're on a beach, and there are two identical canoes. Off in the distance is, say, Molokai, but there are angry-looking clouds over the water. You have to paddle a canoe to Molokai. A man comes along the beach—" At that a couple of the students laughed, and Abel held his hand up.

"I know," Kenika said. "It sounds strange. But anyway, the man tells you that this canoe was blessed in traditional fashion and this other was not. Which canoe do you take?"

The clean-cut student thought a moment, and said, "The one closer to the water. I'm a realist."

"How do you judge reality?"

"Science, verifiable perception, all that."

Kenika thought, his hand still on the log. Then he drew out his wallet and took out a dollar bill, and held it up, facing the student. "Read the number, the serial number I mean."

"I can't. It's too far away."

Kenika looked at the bill. "These numbers are, what, three-sixteenths of an inch high. Why can't you read them?" He held the bill up again.

"It's too far away."

"That doesn't tell me why you can't read it."

Abel now laughed.

"Why can't you read it?"

The student screwed his face up. "I told you."

"Actually you didn't," Kenika said. He looked around at the others. "Why can't he read it?"

After a few seconds a girl said, "Because of the physiological structure of his eye."

"There you go. Strange, but why don't we see things their actual size no matter what the distance?" he asked. "Because there's a limitation in the structure of the eye. We only trust what we can measure, and we can measure only what we can agree upon that we all perceive. But then remember that we're limited by the five senses peculiar to our species. We can't tell if we're right or wrong, because all we have to verify the objectivity of our senses is our senses. I'd bet that if you were alone, with nobody watching, you'd take the canoe that was blessed."

"Gotcha," Abel said, pointing at the student, who chuckled amiably and sat back in his chair.

Kenika walked along the log, running his hand over the remaining patches of bark and the splintered abrasions. "I guess 'belief system' is a funny way of putting it. I never question what I was taught and I never will. I know that all this stuff I described has been mostly abandoned, but I'm not keeping up with it because it's interesting old stuff like something you'd keep in a museum. I'm keeping up with it because that was the way I was taught. Whose log is this?" One of the boys in the middle raised his hand. "Where'd you get it?"

"It washed up at Waimanalo."

"This is Oregon pine, I think. It was highly-prized by the old Hawaiians for canoes. It made its way all the way across to Waimanalo, all by itself." Then he cleared his throat, thinking, you have to finish it right.

"'Kay, look at this log." They all did, even the one who had been sleeping. "As soon as any of us looked at this log and saw a canoe inside, it developed a rudimentary awareness, like a light being turned on, or like someone waking up from a long sleep. The image of the canoe was superimposed on the log and it happened. I can't say what happens when someone looks at a log and sees a telephone pole, whether or not another kind of awareness turns on like a light. Maybe it does. Maybe the log sighs and wonders how it will be to hold up wires for the rest of its life. But we look at this log and we see a canoe. Now it is aware of its flesh. Now it wants to emerge from the log as a canoe, and above all it wants water. Its greatest desire is water, like a baby wanting to be fed or like someone thirsty." He ran his hand over the wood again. "It feels my hand. Now it's up to us to bring her out, and we have to do everything right, all the way to the lolo ceremony. She will be called the No Mamao Wa'a, or the From Afar Canoe. I may not even have the words right, because I am not an expert in the language. It is called this because it is not anywhere near where it grew up. It is as if it is lost, so alienated from its native soil that I think it must be frightened. We have to reassure it, whisper to it, think to it while we make it. It is not an inanimate object. It is alive."

Professor Abel opened his mouth to say something, but did not. The students took their eyes off the log and looked at Kenika. "Are there any questions?"

"Like, when do we start?" one of the boys asked.

"Right away, I guess."

There wasn't enough time to do anything that first night, so he explained to them that all the words that had to do with building the canoe, tools and parts and so on, were Hawaiian words, so they all needed to buy Hawaiian dictionaries. He went to his tool pile and picked up an adze. "Ko'i 'ahuluhulu," he said. "Or planing adze." Then he picked up another. "Ko'i kalai, or carving adze." He picked up the long crowbar. "'O'o, which means digging stick, which means for us, crowbar."

Professor Abel stood up and looked at his watch. "Oops, ten minutes over," he said.

With that the class was over. When he was loading the tools back into the station wagon Professor Abel stepped up and said, "Man, that was great. That was something." Kenika knew that his enthusiasm was not for the truth of what he had said, but the novelty. It didn't matter.

"Thanks. You know, I was wondering how we were going to do this once a week for seventeen weeks and get it done. It's not possible unless they work other days too."

"Sure," Abel said. "That's the idea. Man, that was great."

Just as he was getting in the car, he saw a group of the students standing under a light next to a wooden bench. One of them sat down and then jumped back up, looking at the bench, and then said, "Oh! Would you mind?" and then sat down, and they all laughed. He started the car, thinking, oh well, you can't expect them all to take it seriously.

≈   ≈   ≈

Angela became increasingly worried about Momi being alone in the old house. She then became suspicious when Momi told her more about her man friend, a Mr. Richard Kemp, who came over from time to time and sat on the porch in the evening drinking wine with her. This was nothing new—Momi had many men friends, The Captain one of them, as Kenika knew. But Kemp was an investment couselor, and Momi had told Angela that he was managing some of Momi's money for her, investing in stocks, mutual funds, and short-term certificates. "Why now?" she asked Kenika. "She nevah worry about stuff li'dat until now."

Momi was seventy-one, Kemp in his fifties. That Momi might still have a little of that old spark where men were concerned was, Angela supposed, a possibility, but still she smelled a rat. "Jus' one nodda haole guy from mainlan'," she said. "Like dis skinny grease baw come out from whatchucall, Pattahson, come out fo' trick me into sleeping wit' him."

"What? Jesus, what did he do?"

"He try trick me into tink he col', den I try wahm him up and den what, feel dis snake creep up my side. Ho, what a slime ball."

"What happened then?"

"I go fine him asleep, an' he weave dis spell, make me take my clothes off an', oh, I cannot tell da res'. Shame 'ass why."

"You can tell me."

"What, you da terapis' now?"

"Yup."

But Angela's expression changed. "Really, I don't like it. Her sight isn't good, her hearing isn't good an' she has high blood presha. I wonder what this guy is up to. I talk to her and she just tells me not to be so ni'ele about her business."

Momi did continue to talk about selling the house during those times she came to sit and talk story with Angela and Loke at the shop or the house, but Kenika wondered just how much of a house would be left to sell. He frequently went over there to tend to repairs, and one Saturday went over to check on a plumbing problem. Standing in the doorway looking into the living room in which Momi sat, he put his hand on the doorframe and collapsed the wood inward with a light squeeze of his hand, which at that moment began to tickle, because the termites who had come out of the large cracks were running over his skin.

It was not a localized infestation. After repairing a leak in a kitchen sink drain, he checked the house foundation. In his old room, now a storeroom full of junk, he found little mud tubes snaking over the oozing lava rock and connecting to the walls, which were hollow, the boards like paper imitations of boards. Each time he poked a hole he smelled a dank, wet-newspaper odor, which was the remains of the wood along with the moist soil the ground termites had deposited in the hollow spaces where the wood had been.

Momi was not alarmed. "It'll be torn down anyway," she said. "It's the land that has the value."

"Do you have it on the market yet?"

"Dickie will tend to that," she said, and then added, "and you don't have to give me any grief about that."

Kenika looked at her. She still had echoes of that same regal bearing that had impressed him so long ago, but the look of frailty was overcoming it. "Is he a real estate dealer too?"

"No, but he invests in real estate, and please, don't worry."

Kenika nodded, then looked around. "I'm gonna get some of that can spray with the tube and needle," he said. "It'll hold them off for now."

"Thanks," she said. "Tell Angela I'll come over tomorrow."

During that period in early spring when he went week by week to pump the termite holes, Momi would tell him she'd be over Sunday, or on one weekday or another, and then not show up. Angela would scowl at the clock, and then go to the phone. When Momi did not answer, she would shake her head. "Dat o' lady! Go see if she awright."

He would find her in the living room. "Oh, Angela called," he'd say.

"I didn't hear the phone."

"Oh, it was just because you mentioned coming over."

"Did I?"

At other times, Mr. Kemp would be there. The first time, when Momi introduced them, Kemp shook his hand, his whole body hunched up as he squeezed with all his might, a broad, eager smile on his face. "How ya doin'?" he said. "Come on in and have a glass of wine." Kemp wore his shoes in the house.

Kenika kicked his slippers off and went inside.

So he sat and drank a glass of wine, and listened in on their conversation. More than once Kemp went on about how it was for a businessman like him, that at this moment the best place in the world was right here, and he patted the couch. "Hawaii, because there's a real estate boom coming. Do you know the effect of cheap air travel? It puts Hawaii in reach, and believe you me, I love this place." Momi smiled benignly at his speeches, and Kenika studied the man, wondering what it was that Momi saw in him, and then he began to see resemblances to The Captain, but also thought it might only be his imagination.

Angela was firm on the subject: after she met him the first time she wanted Kenika to talk man-to-man to him, to find out just what it was he was after. So he tried. He found an appropriate moment during another visit when Angela and Momi were in the house while they were in the backyard, and put it straight. "Listen, we wonder just why it is that you spend so much time with her."

Kemp looked at him, his eyebrows dropping. "Mr. McKay, puh-leeze. I am an investment counselor, and I take my work very seriously. I don't know what it is you imply, but I assure you, you are wrong." Then he shrugged, almost helplessly it seemed, and chuckled ruefully. "Oh I know," he said, "I make the wrong impressions on people. But believe me, I consider her a friend. A good friend, and that is all."

Kenika reported this conversation to Angela, who said, "I still don't like him."

≈   ≈   ≈

Each two weeks he received a check from the state in the amount of $153.80, gross pay, minus state and federal taxes and another deduction, retirement. Professor Abel explained that retirement was mandatory and that after the end of the semester Kenika could request that money, assuming that he was not planning to teach canoe-making until the year two thousand. Kenika had come to like Abel because of the way he assisted in the work on the canoe. Dressed in dirty shorts and a tee shirt, he draped himself over the pale hull and swept the plane along the inside wall until he dripped with sweat. He would also bring a cooler of beer to the class, and those who worked on the canoe and liked beer would leave the cans in different places as they took another crack at planing, or using the adze, and would find the beer gone when they went back for it. Or, as Kenika observed one night, one student took a final puff of a cigarette, dropped the butt into a can sitting on the floor, and then picked up a tool, while the beer's owner, gasping for breath and limbering sore muscles, left the canoe and grabbed his beer off the floor and took a lusty gulp, stared at the middle distance a moment, and then ran out the door to spit the foul mixture into the night.

Eric, his perpetually-stoned student, watched, his mouth hanging open, from time to time saying in a strained, almost agonized voice, "Man, that's heavy, that's so heavy. That blows all my wires, man. Oh, that's heavy." About his being stoned Abel seemed not to mind, or if he did mind, didn't show it.

Early on, just as they had begun to see a canoe emerging from the pile of pale chips that rose up as if to engulf the log, he told the class that the hardest part of making a canoe was the component parts, which they were learning the Hawaiian words for: wae, mo'o boards, pale kai, ama and so on. He told them that he needed help in finding the materials, which would involve long hikes into the woods, and asked for volunteers. Everyone raised a hand, even Eric, who, staring at all the hands held over heads, his face showing a slow, almost tortured laboring toward a kind of dumbstruck recognition, allowed his to float upward as if attached to the string on a helium balloon.

Sometimes on calm nights Kenika would be awakened at midnight or one, aware of barking dogs, or roosters with no sense of time, or the usual arguments which would float over the darkness as incomprehensible yelling, punctuated by the louder "Fock!" or "Bitch!" These sounds would come from different directions, the Kams' for instance, because after all these years it appeared that this was the way they related to each other, but then on other nights he began to hear what sounded like Keoki's and Loke's voices in the same harsh yelling.

When this happened he would walk out onto the back lanai, trying to better locate the source of the sound and tune in on the voices to see if it really was either of them.

And one afternoon he got home from the shed after muddling along on another relief, to find Loke and Angela sitting at the table,

Loke's eyes wet, her hands clasped over her swelling belly. Whatever it was they were talking about was not for his ears, he suspected, so he went into the backyard to hack at the hedge with the machete so they could continue without his overhearing.

Angela told him later what had been bothering Loke. Keoki had been walking off to see friends in the neighborhood and had come home stumbling, "wit' paint on his mout'."

"Paint?"

"Dey sniff paint, go' color paint."

"Isn't that bad? I mean on your brain?"

"Yes. I don't know what to do. Maybe call somebody? Why does he do that?" Her expression combined disgust and fear. "Dose friends of his, 'ass what it is. Why he wanna do dat?"

"I don't know. Pakalolo is— I don't know. Paint? I don't get it."

Loke had told Angela that when she asked him about it he said he didn't want to talk about it. It was just getting high, so what? It was cheap, so what? No big deal. Then he went to bed because he had to work in the morning.

The thought that Keoki would prefer a can of paint over all that was happening—a child on the way, a nice place to live and a good job—baffled Kenika, who imagined that there was now something about the environment that he should fear. And that was a sad idea. If there could ever have been an environment no one had any reason to fear, this was it, the little corner of six-hundred square miles in which happened everything good that had ever happened to him. But now something was wrong. He thought that whatever was wrong had been "imported." When he considered all the causes of the odd sensation that they had something to fear he always came back to that word: whatever was wrong had been imported.

The blessing of the No Mamao Wa'a took place in late May, delivered by Kalani Chun, now a wizened man with skin so dark and teeth so bright that the students seemed amazed by the contrast. Kalani Chun explained the Lolo Ka Wa'a Ceremony, and proceeded to circle the canoe, which was loosely lashed, its hau 'iakos looping over to a gleaming wiliwili ama almost as light as balsa wood. With the dropping of the match the No Mamao Wa'a was given its brains, and Kenika stood there satisfied that in every respect the project was a good one. "Listen," he said. "This is now Billy Soares's canoe, but before he takes it I think we have to use it. It has to feel the water. Then, even if it ends up in Billy's back yard, it will have the memory of the water."

Yes, they all agreed, even Eric, who nodded slowly, his eyes closed, saying in that same strained voice, "Yeah, man, water, it has to like feel it, man."

They would take it on Billy's trailer to Kapiolani Park and launch it right next to the Natatorium. Billy knew exactly where. "Just to the left of it, there's a nice calm place there."

"A picnic," another student said. The idea gained momentum, until it was agreed that the class would meet there Sunday afternoon, pot luck—hah hah, and one student imitated holding a joint—and would Kenika bring his family? Sure.

Only Angela went with him. Keoki and Loke, she said, were staying close to home because the baby was due, and anyway, he would watch his Knickernocker and Bullets game. Knickerbockers, he said. Yeah, whatevahs, and Momi was out somewhere wit' dat man Dickie.

They parked at Queen's Surf Beach, after driving through a Waikiki they barely recognized. When they were out of the car, Angela in her bathing suit and a sarong tied at the hip, carrying a tray of store-bought tako poke and some sashimi, she saw the refreshment stand and asked him to go get a big iced tea for her before the three-hundred yard walk to the Natatorium. Kenika found himself standing in line with a bunch of younger men, and idly studying the bare back of the one in front of him, he realized that the man's back had been shaved. He peered around at the next man. He was wearing a tiny bathing suit stretched over narrow buttocks. Kenika looked back, then around. All men. All of them were homosexuals, and he wondered if he should stay in the line. He reasoned that his old baggy bathing suit and fairly ratty tee shirt indentified him as a kind of alien.

Then he felt a warm hand on his shoulder, and turned quickly, then looked up.

"Brah, 'da fahk you dooen heah?" he said. It was Darnay. The men close to Kenika backed away, warily eyeing the monster. Then Darnay laughed.

He explained that his friend Evan was just over there, and Kenika explained the canoe-launching picnic and invited them over. "Angela's there too," he said.

"We come laytahs," Darnay said. "No tell her, 'kay?"

After Kenika introduced Angela to Abel and the students, they set up the food on the picnic table. Within a couple minutes he found himself watching the proceedings from a short distance—Angela stood there in the blazing sun, looking around at the food and explaining the poke and raw fish to a couple of the guys. The long, copper-black hair, curly now because of the humidity, went all the way down her brown back, a yellow plumeria tucked behind one ear, a bright bead of sweat making its way down her cheek. The students were looking at her and whispering to one another, and then two of the haole girls approached her with a peculiar caution, and then talked about the No

Mamao Wa'a sitting there in the sun just above the gentle shorebreak. Even as they chatted on he could see a look of wonder on their faces, as if Angela were some fascinating object. Professor Abel had that same look, of a kind of speculative appreciation, but concealed it better than the students did.

Kenika looked around toward Queen's Surf, and saw a very large figure walking with a very small one coming their way, Darnay and his friend, and then he looked in the other direction toward the Kaimana Beach Hotel peeking through the ironwood trees. He understood what it was. In this setting Angela was a beautiful, if not magnificent anachronism, a person from another age, tall, almost stocky, with so classic a Polynesian face that Kenika was momentarily struck as the students were. It was as if Waikiki were no longer Hawaii but something else, Los Angeles or Miami, because virtually every person he saw was Caucasian or Japanese, and then there stood a visitor from the past, a woman who seemed to radiate some pure aura that had struck the students almost dumb.

And when Darnay passed Kenika, his finger to his lips, everyone's eyes shifted to him, and some of the students backed away in wary confusion. The massive creature who moved with the powerful grace of some animal, tiptoed lightly up behind her and tapped her on the shoulder, and she turned, looked, and then threw her arms around him.

Kenika didn't know what it was, but that vision of her, and then of her and Darnay, was more troubling than impressive. He thought it must have been the setting itself, the gleaming hotel buildings, the powerboats in the water, the lines of cars parked just over there glinting in the sun, and in this setting Angela and all her kind now seemed so totally out of place that it caused in him a horrible swoon of either sadness or fear, as if the vision of her standing over the table suggested far more than he wanted to think about.

Five of the girls argued the boys out of the privilege and got Angela to go out in the canoe with them, and with that the No Mamao Wa'a felt water sliding along its hull for the first time.

Professor Abel watched the girls as Angela instructed them on how to paddle, and then turned to Kenika. "How long've you been married?"

"Twenty-three years," Kenika said, again staring back toward Waikiki, unable to shake that strange feeling.

"What, you got married when you were ten?"

Kenika laughed, and then went on to explain that it was just after Angela graduated from high school.

"I wondered," Abel said, "just what percentage Hawaiian you are."

Kenika squinted at him. "Well, none," he said.

"Really?"

He explained briefly where he came from, leaving out all the information about his "mother" and the prostitute who raised him.

"I was under the impression you were. You—" Abel stopped. Of course, it was his face, eyes, the curly hair, something about the nose and lips.

"That's okay," Kenika said. "My pedigree is mixed."

"The community advisory board had the impression that you were," Abel said. Then he shrugged. "Doesn't matter, of course."

"I know. Is Clarence Lum on the advisory board?"

"Yes, he is," Abel said, looking surprised. "Do you know him?"

Too hot fo' one blanket but den wit' no blanket he can get you.

Pua snores. Under the open louvred window she sleeps without any worry about him with his dirty clothes and his red manakuke eyes walking through Kailua with his long guava stick.

So. Put da blanket on an' sweat. Pua futs. Ten yeah ol' an' no mo' notting bodda her. Fricken animal. Eat like one pig an' fut an' no mo' notting bodda her. You said, you memba him? He mento.

Not, she said.

He one mento druggie an' he come fo' get us.

Not.

So you sweat. It more den dat. He get manakuke eyes an' he hiding insai da lie of one mento druggie, but insai is da dead man walkin' wit' one guava stick, walkin' troo Kailua lookin' fo' his keeds, fo' come wine dem up in his hair like da yellow an' black spidah do flies, roll um ovah fifty times an' wine dat dirty coppah hair aroun', den suck da life out wit' one kiss, one awful kiss.

Grandaddy Kenika got one to come out of the brush at Sandy's when you went to watch them ride the killer waves. It was behind the plate lunch truck, and he threw little gobs of rice in the weeds and the manakuke came out, brown like one furry spear snaking through the grass, its little black nose sniffing in on the rice, and then it chomped rice into its pink mouth and looked up, and its eyes were red, red like the ghost menpachi—like you could see into its head, into a nothing of red, into like a red sky. Kenika said they brought the manakuke to kill rats, but the manakuke comes out during the day and the rat at night, hey, how you doin', I'm goin' to work, 'kay, I'm goin' to bed.

Olomana out da window. Say da ashy light from Waikiki come fanning ovah da mountains an' make it so you see Olomana an' den da mountains behine, dat wheah he hide sitting wit' his guava stick, den he come all mentoed out, lookin' fo' keeds fo' wine dem in his hair an' suck life outta dem wit' one awful kiss.

Daddy.

Mento druggie.

He wine all kine people up in his hair an' suck da life out wit' one awful kiss.

Him wit' his red manakuke eyes, he suck da life outta people, he comin' across Kailua slow, tap tap tap goes da stick, to suck life. Kenika say, well, it's one of those things, but some day— An' tap tap tap, way inna night, he walk, an' suck life—Tutu Angela.

It is because he mento. He not know us any mores. 'Ass why he one zombie walkin', red eyes searchin' fo' us to wine in his hair. Because how could he oddawise? If he knew us?

Tutu Angela.

Jus' one real bad dream.

Wish.

≈　　≈　　≈

That strange feeling he had at the picnic didn't go away. He found himself awake in the middle of the night listening for the sounds of arguing from down the hill, and hearing none, went and got a beer out of the refrigerator and sat on the back lanai. Maybe it was all wrong from the start, that a person with a questionable pedigree who belonged nowhere had no place trying to belong here. It was not a question of whether or not he had a right to be here, it was more a question of whether he, like all those people from the other world, should be here. He supposed the situation here was something like the situation with Indians in the U.S., that The Captain would also have called them magnificent creatures out of the past. Homogenization was a by-product of technology, and he didn't like it, and at the same time knew nothing could be done about it. But the thought of any other life for him, in any other place, had long ago vanished as even a remote possibility.

The strange fears were now more or less overshadowed by the baby getting ready to make its way into the world. He simply stored that picture of Angela at the picnic in the back of his mind and went on with his work.

Loke's pregnancy was paralleled by the pregnancies of the twins. They sent photographs from a place called Malaga, in Spain, of the two of them in profile, their faces held in identical grins and their stomachs huge and perfectly round under some strange Spanish smocks fringed with colorful stitchery and beadwork. They could not come home, unfortunately, but would send more pictures. Angela stared at the pictures, and Kenika speculated on whether or not it might be a good idea for them to get on a plane and go over there. Angela said, "I want to be no higher than I can jump. I'm not getting on any plane."

On the Saturday morning that Loke started strong contractions, Angela reassured her and sent her off with Keoki to Kapiolani Hospital and got on the phone, to rally the relatives for a gettogether when the baby came home, two days maybe, eh, no rush. As usual, Momi didn't answer the phone, and Angela threw her hands up and told Kenika to go let her know about the baby, they would get the house ready for people coming over, shop for food and all lahdat. And she had to call the twins, and where the hell were they now? Timbucktoo?

Kenika found Momi's front door open and Momi sitting asleep in her easy chair before a cowboy movie on TV. She had a black line on her chin. "Momi?" he said.

Nothing.

On TV a cowboy said, "It ain't my business, Josh."

He went into the dark living room, and knew the moment he saw the ants on the doughnut on the coffee table and on the doughnut on her lap. "Momi?"

But it was no use.

"—fella works all his life and for what I ask you," another cowboy said.

Kenika turned and pushed the off button. The little black ants, each an eighth of an inch long, were industriously crawling into her mouth and back out, and the black line went down her neck and under her blouse and then out over her hip to the seat and down the chair leg onto the floor, where it then went under an electrical socket plate in the baseboard. He stepped to her, his breath held, and touched her hand. It was cold, and her arm was rigid.

Benjamin Lanakila McKay came home Monday to be received by the tutus and aunties, all of whom wavered from mourning the death of one of their own to celebrating the arrival of another. Loke's parents also came over along with two aunties and an uncle, so the total population of the house during the day reached twenty. As Kenika had observed before, whether baby shower or gathering of mourners, the atmosphere was the same. The men sat in the garage in a loose circle in the center of which sat a washtub with cans and bottles of beer bobbing around, and the women sat in the living room or on the back lanai, and each morning Kenika would go around and collect oily, teriyaki-stained paper plates, fish skeletons and chicken bones from various locations and put them in the garbage, and throw the shoyu-browned balls of rice into the backyard for the birds.

Loke, who was a strong girl, was up and about right away, and complained only of being out of balance when she walked, as if gravity were trying to tip her over backward when she least expected it. During the days she remained glued to Angela, who instructed her as to the mysteries of tending to the dark, chubby boy. Keoki, walking around with a stunned look on his face, finally stumbled into his old room and slept, getting up only to sit in the carport with the men and drink beer and talk surf and fishing. At those times Kenika would go out and check on them, and Keoki would pat an empty chair—"Eh, Dad, sit an' talk story."

According to the loose, practical traditions of the family, Momi's ashes were taken out in The Red Wind and released into the water off Lanikai. George and Irene did not accompany the paddlers because they claimed to be too wide for that canoe. Angela did the honors of spreading the ashes, and turned to Kenika holding the koa box, her face held in an expression of almost angry regret, because she blamed herself, in part, for not keeping watch over da o' lady. Momi had died of a massive stroke, which, Angela was convinced, needn't have happened if someone were there with her when she first had it.

They also learned from George that Mr. Kemp had appropriated most of Momi's assets and had left her in debt, something having to do with market speculation and margin-buying of stocks and other risky investments. As for Mr. Kemp, he was shocked at Momi's death, and claimed to George that it was Kemp himself who had been cheated by unscrupulous investment counselors, and that he was looking into this vigorously, don't you worry.

Kenika did not understand everything George told him, or at least didn't see how what he understood was possible. Mr. Kemp was being investigated by state and federal authorities, and there was even a small article about him in the newspaper, because he had left a number of clients broke, and in the article he manifested a confused indignation about the corrupt practices of certain people, without naming them. How these people, he said, could take the money of honest people and squander it, or worse, appropriate it for their own use, was beyond him, and he promised to get to the bottom of the problem by filing a series of lawsuits against those responsible. He declined to elaborate further. Within a week of the printing of that article he had left Hawaii, and his whereabouts were unknown.

It was left to George, Irene, Kenika and Angela to go clean out the house and rescue whatever objects were of value, either sentimentally or otherwise. Because they were selling the Lanikai house, they had little room for most of the stuff. But George was particularly interested in one closet which held old family documents, photographs and other objects, including wooden canoe and boat models his grandfather had made. "I show you some junks you like," he told Kenika. "Shoulda got dis stuff out yeahs ago but."

When he opened the door, and turned on the light, the familiar wet newspaper odor wafted out at them.

"Uh-oh," George said. Behind them they heard Irene and Angela sorting dishes in the kitchen.

George pulled one cardboard box along the floor and opened it. Inside was a strange, honeycombed mud labyrinth, busy with termites, the cream-colored soldiers perched on the edges, their brown mandibles open and waiting, the workers racing in lines further into the box. Whatever had been inside had been appropriated as building materials. Kenika could see the stacks of photographs eaten inward from the edges, and the remaining papers near the bottom were unrecognizable. The deeper they worked their way into the closet, the worse the damage was.

The furniture was not salvageable either. Many chair legs were hollow. The heavy piano might as well have been levitating considering what was left of its legs. Old tools lay in odd places without wooden handles, and one very nice model of a canoe, similar to Benny's demonstration model at the shed, stood on a box against a closet wall, and when Kenika went to lift it, one long half came off in his hand while the other remained glued by mud and termite secretions to the wall.

They saved what they could, which wasn't much. Luckily, according to George, the old deed to the plot of land where the shed was built was in the safe deposit box at the bank. "Not dat it mattah much," he said. "Still Pacific Combat Training Centah."

His mother, and then he and Benny had years ago written a series of letters to the army about the fence, but the result was always the same: they would look into it, and until such time as they did, the property was unfit for normal use because of unexploded ordnance, and off-limits to civilians.

"Yeah," Kenika said. "I trip over grenades every day."

About a month later they received a large box from Spain, and inside was a roll of eight-millimeter film, and a Kodak projector. The twins put in a letter that had the announcement, fringed with bright doodles of smiling faces, and it read, "Meet Angela Malia Williamson and Kenika Benjamin Davis." They had been born two weeks apart. Projected against one of the sheetrock walls Kenika had installed, the film was shaky and somewhat grainy, but they could clearly see the babies, Seth and Clarice's almost identical to Keith and Elizabeth's, with fine black hair and dark eyebrows, the twins above them mouthing words to the viewers: Hi grandma, hi grandpa.

≈   ≈   ≈

Benjamin became a fixture in the house because Loke went to work at the Kailua Liberty House store. Kenika wondered about Angela's being burdened this way, but she put her fists on her hips and said, "This is my grandson. I want to take care of him." Loke passed on working at the flower shop, and Angela reasoned that she liked clothes and make-up more than she liked flowers and seeds. She supposed it wasn't any mystery that Loke would prefer a more elegant job.

So the boy ended up spending his days at the shop, first sitting in a plastic carrier padded with a little blue Hawaiian-print quilt Angela made, then crawling around in a playpen, throwing cast-off orchids out onto the floor, and banging around generation-old toys that Angela had dug out of the closet. Loke would walk the two blocks from Liberty House to eat lunch at the shop, and talk with Angela about the multitude of problems involving intrigues among the workers, the employee pecking-order, the bitchiness of one manager or another, the whispers, slights, gossip and backstabbing. Angela told Kenika she could barely get a word in edgewise.

Keoki's habit of failing to appear at work surfaced again, but because Loke worked, she would not be aware of it until he brought home his check. On payday nights Kenika would be awakened by the sound of a shrill accusatory voice, followed by one male voice that sounded both apologetic and at the same time threatening. The argument culminated with the final "Fahk you!" along with more of Loke's yelling, and once, Kenika waited, listening, and finally walked around the corner and along the block to the house, fearing violence. When he got there the house was dark, and he cocked his ears, trying to hear beyond the sound of a barking dog, and heard them—they were making love. Confused, he tiptoed away.

He got a call from Mr. Maxwell informing him that the koa relief had sold for two thousand dollars. While that was good reason for celebration, it was offset by a lawyer's acquisition of the block of storefronts including the flower shop, and the first indication of the consequences of that was a letter informing Angela that the rent on the store would be tripled upon the renewal of her lease. After sitting and looking at figures, staring into space, and calculating on a sheet of paper, Angela told Kenika that the best she was going to do was break even. She could raise prices, but nobody would buy. For the present, she decided, she would hang on. A little shoestore next door to the shop closed within a month of the letter, and within another month opened again as Pacific Investment Corporation, with tinted windows and an interior that looked like a large dentist's waiting room.

Curious about what the store's title meant, Kenika wandered in and asked a very well-dressed secretary, "What do you guys do?" She explained that they had a series of interesting investment strategies including real estate, mutual funds, retirement accounts, tax-deferred or exempt certificates. Would he like their brochures? Noting the somewhat sour expression on the secretary's face, he glanced down at his clothes and said, "No, that's okay."

By the time Benjamin was running around the shop and talking—"Tutu Aga! I like dakine! I like seed!"—Keoki was away from work more than he was there, and the more and more alarming preference for drugs and his friends over a normal life began to dominate the lives of the rest of the family. One Saturday when Keoki, Loke and Ben came over to watch a University of Hawaii football game, which interested Kenika because one of the running backs had been in his class, Angela cornered Keoki in his room and started talking to, or at him. She didn't yell. Her voice had the same husky warmth it always had, and as Kenika and Loke watched the game, frequently looking at each other with their breaths held, it was as if they waited expecting the problem to vanish at that moment. And the miracle they hoped for seemed just on the edge of coming true when they came out of the room. Angela went to the kitchen to work on dinner, and Keoki settled down on the living room floor with his beer, a thoughtful and somewhat penitent expression on his face.

That same evening he disappeared. Loke came up looking for him, and then broke down crying, soothed by Ben who patted her on the back and said, "Da owee no mo'. Da owee no mo', Mommy."

She suspected he had gone to the north shore. "An' he no come back," she said.

Kenika looked at the clock. After ten. "Where would he go?"

It was on Ke Iki Road, just this side of Pupukea. He wrote the address on a grocery receipt and left. As he drove, he wondered if this was right, that he should be chasing after someone who was married and had a child. But Keoki was clearly not in control of himself, and Kenika reasoned that he would be justified in doing this even if Keoki were thirty. The boy had always been easy-going and good-natured, and now in a good-natured and easy-going manner he was bringing disaster on his family. It didn't make sense. He clearly remembered his mother going to AA meetings in a doomed attempt to quit drinking, but it never worked. It finally killed her.

When he found his way into the narrow beach road that paralleled the highway, he parked and heard the thunder of surf pounding the shore. He knew the area because it was a puka-shell beach, where Angela and the twins had collected the little white doughnuts for leis and necklaces. The house he was looking for was on a little street between the narrow road and the beach, perched on the back of a high dune among other houses that lined the beach. The noise of the surf drowned everything else out, although he was aware that at some of the houses inset from the dune that he passed, loud music was playing, and he could see the shapes of people moving on the high, tree-lined dune. It all had the atmosphere of a neighborhood party.

He went up the wooden steps and knocked. He identified himself to a young haole man, behind whom was a gathering of people drinking wine and beer. It did not look like the opium den he had expected. No, Keoki wasn't there. He was somewhere out on the beach. "I'll go find him," Kenika said.

The man had an odd look on his face. Then he shook his head with a sort of anguished perplexity. "Listen," he said. "He's a little wild, and I don't really care for who he hangs around with." He paused. "Are you the guy who makes canoes?"

"Yeah."

One of the girls jumped up and came to the door. "My sister was in your class. Sarah Whitman."

"Yeah, I remember her. She worked hard."

"Keoki," she said. "Look, he's—" She stopped.

"Put it this way," the haole man said. "He's burning his brains up. I'm a little—"

"What?"

"I— I just don't like who he hangs around with."

"Where's he get this stuff? I mean, what is it?"

The man looked at him, thinking. "You mean what kind of stuff is he into?"

"Where does it come from? Is it pakalolo?"

The man now appeared somewhat defensive. "Hey, look, I'm not—"

"It's just a question. I mean what do people— Get into?"

"Coke. Ludes, grass, pills. All kinds I guess."

"People just sort of bring it in? What's 'ludes'?"

The man stared at him again.

Finally Kenika shrugged and waved his hands around. "Never mind. I'll go look for him," he said. "Thanks."

"Hey," the man said. "Say hello to Loke for us."

Kenika nodded and headed for the beach. There was a concrete seawall with a flight of stairs down, and in the moonlight he could see the huge waves blasting the shore, and felt the powerful thumps of the water in the ground. He looked to the left toward Pupukea. There were rocks, sharp volcanic outcroppings there, and to the right the beach disappeared out of sight, and in that direction he saw figures moving near some ironwood trees.

He trudged through the heavy sand, and approached a man who appeared as no more than a ghostly silhouette. "Keoki?"

Nothing. The man turned to him. "I'm looking for Keoki," he said.

"Really," the man said. "Keoki. The man."

"Where is he?"

"Why?"

"I'm his father. I wanna talk to him."

"Really," the man said. There was a slight tinge of pidgin in his voice. "I didn't know he had a father. I thought he dropped out of the sky."

Kenika walked around the man and a little farther down the beach, the sand digging around the loops of his zoris. He felt his skin prickling because the man was now behind him. Another man materialized to his right, out from under an ironwood tree. "I'm looking for Keoki," he said to the man.

"What you want him for?" the man asked.

"I want to talk to him."

"I think you oughtta shove off, man."

"No, I want to find Keoki."

"No," the man corrected, "I think you ought to shove the fuck off."

"Look, he's my son and I want to talk to him."

"'Zat right?" the man said. "Maybe he doesn't want to talk to you."

Kenika snorted and walked on down the beach. He could see nothing in the near distance, and held his hand over his eyes, blocking the lights from the houses. Nothing. So he turned around and went back toward the seawall and the stairs, thinking that he might have gone in the opposite direction. When he passed near the ironwoods again, he saw the shapes of people sitting up on the dune, and trudged toward them. They were laughing, and he could see the faint glint of bottles.

"Hey, get the fuck outta here, man," a voice said.

Kenika stopped. The man approached, and he tensed up. "I'll go where I want," he said.

"No shit," the man said. "You will, huh?"

"Yeah. Where's Keoki?"

The man laughed as if the question were absurd.

"'Kay, I'll ask these people up here."

He took one step toward the group and was knocked down from the side, a glancing blow off his forehead. When he got up someone punched him in the center of his face, mashing his nose which immediately shot blood down over his upper lip and into his mouth. Then he was being shoved toward the stairs. "Shove off, man."

"Fuck you," he said, or tried to say, but it came out garbled and thick.

"'D'jou say?" the man said, pushing again.

Kenika spun and swung at the same time, and caught him in the face, and he went down cursing unintelligibly. When the man rose up Kenika slapped him on the side of the head so hard that he numbed his hand, and the man started yelling in the direction of the others, "Hey!" and then in an outraged growl, "God-damn! God-damn, you wrecked my goddamn ear! God-damn!" Kenika stumbled up the stairs.

He drove home holding a dirty rag over his face.

≈　　≈　　≈

He spent the next week with a thick bandage over his nose, to keep the broken bones in place, and dark circles under his eyes. His nose ran but he couldn't blow it because of the pain. He felt embarrassed about it, but he couldn't stop going out and seeing people simply because he resembled a raccoon.

Keoki did not come home. Whatever it was that made him do what he did was a cruel mystery to Angela, who would lean down to Kenika and study the shrinking-yellowish bruises under his eyes, and then sit down at the table to speculate further on how it could be that such a beautiful boy, who had always been good-natured and well-mannered and responsible, well, maybe not that, he could be a hothead too—how he could allow this to happen. And she was worried about the possibility that he would hurt himself. Worse, Loke was pregnant again, two and a half months already, due in June, and if this were to continue she would be burdened with two children and no husband. Of course Angela would take care of them too.

"I'll go out there again," Kenika said.

Angela shook her head with thoughtful skepticism. "He's grown up. I'd like to go out there with a guava stick and bop him onna head, but he's a man now."

The idea that he was on his own and could make these choices without any fear of his parents was not one Kenika was willing to accept. But it was true—he was allowed to do what he wanted to, even if it meant throwing a good life in the trash can.

Loke endured being alone, leaving Benjamin at the house or at the flower shop and going to work. Then, later in her pregnancy, she took time off and ended up every day helping Angela at the shop. Kenika would from time to time drive out to Ke Iki Road to ask about

Keoki's whereabouts, but no one knew anything. He tried getting help from people he knew who had kids Keoki's age, the Sakatas in Waimanalo, Larry Kam's kids who lived in Kaneohe, and so on, but no one knew anything except one friend who said he had seen him at Ala Moana Park. His absence went from being mysterious and saddening to infuriating, especially considering that he was most likely all right, because he was ignoring the coming of his second child and it made no sense. Kenika could not concentrate out at the shed, spent whatever free time he had walking the north shore beaches and wandering around Waikiki and the Sandy Beach and Makapuu bodysurfing spots. At night sometimes he would go back out to Ke Iki Road, but with a heavy, foot-and-a-half long iron pin he found stuck in a rotted log at the beach. He would see figures moving, approach people and ask for Keoki, and many times one person or another would stop, see the pin and say, "Hey man, we don't want any trouble." He would apologize and walk on, frustrated at the idea that the island was only about six-hundred square miles and Keoki was on it somewhere.

One evening after Loke dropped Ben off to drive over to visit her mother, Kenika was outside with the boy when he heard Angela calling him: "Kenika! Kenika, come quick!" He grabbed Ben and ran awkwardly into the house, bouncing the heavy boy in his arms, and found Angela staring at the television set, her hands on her face.

"You all right?" he asked.

She turned to him, looking stunned, then recovered and said, "Ben, time fo' play, come," and carried him off to Keoki's room where the playpen was set up for him.

Kenika stood there scratching his head, staring at a newsman describing some problem with the International Brotherhood of Electrical Workers and a contract.

Angela came back and whispered, "Keoki wen' rob two banks."

He laughed. "No, come on."

"Wait wait," she said. She switched to another channel.

Kenika's scalp began to prickle, because now he thought that it did make sense. Why, he didn't know. Angela stood there with her arms folded while different news stories were read. From Keoki's room they heard Benjamin banging a toy on the rail of his playpen. Then the news anchor read the story, with a look of jocular perplexity on his face: the bank robber did not demand money, rather he asked politely, claiming that he had a gun in his pocket. He was described as a local male, six feet tall and approximately one hundred-seventy pounds.

"The teller, a woman, reports that the robber was very cordial and in fact apparently a little embarrassed about what he was doing. He fled with an undisclosed amount of money." The newsman continued with a story identical to the first: at another bank the man asked very politely for some money, then corrected himself and asked for all the money, claiming that he was carrying a gun. After that there was a grainy bank photo of the man at the window. It was Keoki.

Angela called the police. Kenika sat on the couch staring into the middle distance listening to her tell them that she knew who it was and that she wanted them to understand that it was not like him, it was drugs, and she did not want any harm to come to him. He was not a violent person and he wouldn't ever hurt anyone.

Within ten minutes a police car was parked in front of the house. They were local cops, and they asked their various questions, and Angela answered. "You no hurt him," she said. "He a good boy an' you no hurt him."

The policemen nodded, one writing in his notebook. "No no, we no hurt da boy."

≈   ≈   ≈

Keoki Lanakila McKay became known officially as a fugitive, and two weeks after his crimes, Rhona Pualani McKay was born at Kapiolani Hospital. The house was visited by relatives from both sides of the family, the women socializing inside while the men, many of them slowed by age, sat in the carport drinking beer and talking. Mostly they speculated on Keoki, on where he might be and what he might be doing. Kenika asked George Santiago straight out, in the presence of the others, if he thought it was something Kenika had failed to do that had caused this, and the old man looked at him and then patted him on the knee. "Not you, not Angela either," he said. "No blame yourself, Kenika, I tink it have to do wit' da drugs an' all dakine. Keoki one good boy, jus' los' right now."

And Kenika thought, just lost right now. That sounded right, or at least it sounded optimistic.

Rhona Pualani McKay was a beautiful baby, with black hair and huge eyes, with which she would stare with a kind of gurgling fascination at Angela, who while holding her on the couch and cooing to her seemed in a world separate from everything else. Kenika watched from a distance, and it seemed as if deep down Angela wished they were all hers, and no child he had ever seen showed anything but an apparent desire to belong to her. That alone could convince him that Keoki was his fault, because it seemed to him that no child turned over exclusively to Angela's care could ever go wrong.

Angela learned that Loke's parents were advising, or trying to force her into filing for divorce, but Loke held on, returning to work, and then sitting at the table in the evenings with Angela and talking story about the latest assault by her mother. She wanted nothing to do with them now that they had even suggested this, and she was sure that bumbye Keoki would give himself up and do his time and then come out a new man. During this time, as the baby fattened up and showed more and more of a personality, stories about Keoki floated around in the news and by word of mouth. He had become a kind of hero to the younger people who were enthusiastic about rebellion, and to some people who regarded him as a kind of Robin Hood stealing from the Japanese and haole-dominated power structure of Hawaii. More than anything else he became a hero because no one could catch him, although there were claims of sightings on the north shore, that, yes, there he was cutting down the curved face of a fifteen footer while on the beach, oblivious to him flaunting himself on that huge wave, the police had no idea how close they were.

Kenika didn't believe it. He believed that no one caught him because he was holed up somewhere stoned out of his mind, protected by friends who could sit there and tolerate watching him kill himself. It infuriated him that it was even possible, and he slept badly, every night exhausting himself with an overactive imagination, dreaming up a multitude of horrible visions of what was becoming of him. An overdose, and his friends would then bury him somewhere and no one would ever discover where; or another robbery, where he would have a gun this time and kill someone. He made working at the shed a spare-time thing while he made looking for Keoki a job, driving day by day out past the surf spots to Kaena Point on the windward side where the road broke up and vanished into brush, or to Kaena Point on the leeward side where the road broke up and vanished into brush only a couple of miles from where it ended on the windward side, or Sandy Beach, or Pupukea, or downtown Honolulu or Waikiki. He told Angela he was working on the new koa relief, but he knew that she saw right through it. He would come home and she would be sitting at the table, and she would look at him with her eyebrows raised, and he would hold his shoulders up in a sustained shrug.

One night when Kenika was on his way home from an afternoon at the shed during which he sat and stared at the relief picture, another of a canoe emerging from the wood, he passed the street below his own and saw a number of police cars parked in front of houses, and there was a piece of yellow tape stretched across the street. His heart immediately began to slam in his chest because he either suspected or knew that it had something to do with Keoki, and he pulled in front of his own house and ran in. Loke and Angela were sitting there, Angela consoling Loke, who appeared to have been crying.

Angela glanced at the kitchen clock. "They've been down there two hours," she said. "He's in the house. He was asking for money."

"How is he?"

"Oh, he crazy," Loke moaned. "He all strung out an' crazy."

"Where are the kids?"

"Right here," Angela said, nodding toward the hall.

"I'm going down."

"Kenika, you can't," Angela said. "They tol' us to come up here."

"So what's he gonna do, shoot me?" he asked.

He walked down and around the corner. He was stopped by a cop who said, "Cannot come beyon' dis point."

"He's my son. I wanna talk to him."

The cop thought a moment, then nodded. "Come," he said, and Kenika followed him to within one house of Keoki's where other police stood behind a car. They were not crouched down. A sergeant explained to him that Keoki was in the house and claimed to have a gun, although they did not see one. They called up to him asking that he show it to them in the window, but he only waved. Kenika shook his head. "He doesn't have any gun. Lemme go in and talk to him."

"We can't do that," the sergeant said.

"Then let me go and call to him."

The police looked at each other, then moved away and whispered. Then they looked at Kenika, thinking, and came back. "Okay, you can call to him from the corner of the yard there by that car. But stay behind it."

Kenika positioned himself behind the car and looked up at the house. None of the lights were on. He called out Keoki's name, and waited. Then Keoki called back, "Hey, Dad! Howzit?"

"Can I come up?"

"Yah, come have a beah!"

Kenika walked around the car and up the front walk, while behind he heard one of the cops ordering him back, then another saying let him go, let him go. Other policemen were crouched around low next to the house, their guns drawn. It seemed absurd, but he simply walked up to the front door and went inside. "Keoki?" he whispered.

He heard the pop and hiss of a can of beer being opened. "Heah," Keoki said.

Kenika's eyes adjusted to the darkness, and then he saw him, sitting on the floor holding the beer out to him. "Thanks," he said.

"Is Mommy out deah?"

"No, she's up home."

"I no like her see me, 'kay?"

"'Kay. Hey, you look a little skinny."

"It's da drugs, 'ass all. No eat, 'ass why."

"You gotta come out."

"I know. Drink beah firs'."

Kenika went to a window and called out, "It's okay, give us a minute, 'kay?"

One of the cops ordered something to the cops at the house, but he couldn't hear all of it. The tone of his voice sounded affirmative. "Couple minutes!" Kenika yelled.

"How da boat business?"

"Not bad." He looked at Keoki, who sat there smiling back at him, not the slightest hint of fear on his face. "Why the bank?" Kenika asked.

"A dare. I— I wanted the money."

"Did you have a gun?"

"Nah, jus' tol' um I did."

"Well, that's good." He didn't know what else to say, so he said, "Why? I mean with everything, why would—"

He shrugged. "It was easy. I—" He shook his head. "Who was I takin' da money from? Not from people like us." He craned his neck to look out the window. "Mommy really not out deah?"

"She's up the hill."

"So anyway," Keoki said. Then the calm look on his face vanished, and he appeared pained. "Hahd fo' say," he said. "But drugs. I cannot get offa dem. I hate it, but I cannot get offa dem." He shook his head, then changed his expression again. "Dad, drink up, I got one nodda beah." He popped the top and handed it to him. "We finish dese an' go out, 'kay?"

"'Kay."

After a silence Keoki said, "I fucked up den ah?"

"We all do one time or another."

"Tell Mommy I sorry, 'kay?"

"'Kay."

"Ho, Rhona cute, yah?"

"Yeah, she's a good baby. Sleeps really well, just like Ben. Like you too."

Keoki came out with a loud belch and then chuckled. "'Kay, les' go. I tired."

"Wait, lemme tell them."

Kenika went to the front door and opened it, then waved to the blue lights. "It's okay," he called. "Hang on. We'll be right out."

So they went out. Kenika walked in front of him, feeling light and almost breathless. The thought of Keoki's being arrested, which he had known he would be, was horrible. He was Kenika's boy and now he belonged to a jail, and he hated the feeling of that.

The whole process was strangely amiable. They patted Keoki's pockets. "'Ass on'y one comb," he said. "Dat my loose change."

Then they stepped up to him with handcuffs and he held his fists out before him, close together. "In back, brah," the cop said.

"Eh, you Tony Chang's braddah?"

"Yeah."

"Tell him hi fo' me, 'kay?"

"'Kay."

≈ ≈ ≈

There was no bail because he was considered a flight risk. He wanted to refuse the services of a court-appointed defense attorney and wanted to plead guilty to all charges. Because of his willingness to plead guilty there would be a non-jury trial. Two days after his arrest, before his arraignment, he was allowed a family visit, which took place in a room with simple vinyl furniture and a beefy guard posted at the single door. Angela put her arms around him and asked him what they were feeding him, running her hands over his back and saying, "You so skinny. I talk to dem."

"Nah nah, I eat good now, Mom, really."

Then they sat around and talked, Keoki sitting with Ben on one leg and Rhona in the crook of his arm. No, he didn't want a lawyer, but da state give him one fo' trial. No, he had used no gun. But he knew what he had done and had no problem with the idea of prison. Hell, some of his friends were there. Kenika sat throughout the visit studying him, trying to understand how it was that Keoki had come to this. But then he was only twenty-one, and even after he got out there would be plenty of time to put stuff back together again.

By the time the trial was approaching Angela knew far more about the possibilities than Kenika did. She had met the mother of an inmate of the Halawa Prison, whose son had stolen cars and had gone from the bad boys' home in Kailua and later to the prison, and knew what the dangers were there. No, there was none of that prison rape they mentioned on news shows, because too many of the men there were related. Yes, they were all well-fed, and had visiting days, could have food from home, had job programs and so on. If you had to go to prison, Hawaii was probably the best state to be in for that. It was not, however, a place for a hothead like Keoki, and that worried her, because the place was full of hotheads. Local boys, Hawaiians and Samoans, were the ones with the hottest heads. She kept a list of things to talk to Keoki about—no, you don't get into trouble with other inmates, not one, because if you punch one, his cousin or brother might be out looking for you. If you see one drug of any kind, run away, because there were stories about drugs in the prison. Behave and you'll get out sooner. Don't worry about the sentence itself—worry only about when you would be eligible for parole, because those who behaved usually got out when they were eligible. They had families. Keoki had a family, and if that wasn't enough to keep him straight, then she didn't know what was.

If they ask, tell them you have a job waiting for you, even if Loke's father wants nothing to do with you. When you come out you will be an artisan and canoe-maker, and the family had mountains of proof that it was a real job—after all, your father was even a part-time instructor at the University. Yes, you have a place to go, your own house. You have children and a wife, your parents live around the block.

By the time Angela was finished describing all this to Kenika and Loke, who sat each with a child on a lap, all Kenika could think of to say was, "H'm, maybe it's not that bad after all." But Angela sat there studying Loke, who bounced little Rhona on her knees. Kenika knew what Angela's expression was saying: and you, you will wait for him. No hanky-panky wit' odda guys or I do sometin' rash.

He was sentenced to fourteen years and would be eligible for parole in five, possibly four contingent on review board deliberations. When the sentence was read by the judge, Angela whispered, "Not," and Keoki looked down, then turned to the family and nodded. With the firm numbers in their heads, they sat in the court and waved to Keoki as he was led out. As Kenika drove home Loke sat with her children in the backseat of the station wagon and cried as did the children, and Angela went the entire way from downtown Honolulu all the way over the Pali with her left arm draped over her seat, patting Loke on the knee and talking: "No worry, we take care of you an' da keikis. You can work an' come every day an' talk story. No worry, Loke. Five is not dat bad, really. He one good boy inside, he'll be good, an' we go see him alla visiting days, 'kay?"

"'Kay."

"Lemme hol' Rhona," she said, and Loke passed her over the seat. Then she draped her arm over the back of it again while the baby slept on her shoulder, and she patted Loke's knee all the way home.

With Keoki's incarceration, Kenika found himself able to work again. Leaning up from the relief picture, his back aching, he knew the irony of it, that his boy was in prison and now there was a strange energy coursing through him. He knew what it was: the boy was safe, he and Angela now knew where he was and how long he would be there. It created a peculiar kind of stability. If they had anything to worry about, it was now only what kind of trouble he got himself into in prison, and as far as they could tell, he got into no trouble. During their visits, Angela bearing various foods she had spent the previous day making, he got the impression that Keoki was even popular among other prisoners and especially the guards, who always joked with him as they led him to the visiting room. Angela then fell into the habit of bringing various foods, poke, haupia cake, local delicacies, to give the guards so that they could carry them home to their wives. Visiting day had the atmosphere of a complicated family gathering, and in this case the family was a huge-misdirected collection of men visited by their wives and their children, all of whom so resembled Ben and Rhona that Kenika thought of visiting day as the instant creation of a village gathering. Ninety percent of the inmates were local as were ninety percent of their wives, and Loke and the children, walking through the gate with other young mothers and their children, seemed to fit in far more than she did in any other public place, shopping center, beach or park. And it would sometimes stop him, so that Angela would turn and say, "What?" when he fell into a distracted musing on what he saw. Was that why Angela seemed so out of place that day on the beach when they launched the No Mamao Wa'a? That those who would normally be there fishing or playing with their kids in the park were here?

During the third visit he was again hit by the picture—the highest percentage of the men here were Hawaiian or part-Hawaiian it seemed. And again he thought, why? The answer came to him in a breeze that swirled grit and dust up off the boiling parking lot, and he thought of Benny, and then it seemed to him so obvious that he found himself amazed by it: over the years he had heard all the arguments about local people and social problems, and in his mind he countered all of them with one question. Would Benny have objected to the forced donation of his blood if the judge pronouncing the sentence had been Kelemeneke Makaila?

Within six months the strange cloud of the abnormality of things had vanished. Rolls of film came in the mail and they watched their other grandchildren running around on a lawn, their mothers in the background pregnant again. The Hawaii children were as strong as their father and aunties had been, and Kenika thought that except for Keoki's incarceration, everything could be thought of as running smoothly. When Loke gathered them up and left to walk around the corner to the house, Kenika and Angela would be left alone, and the old habit returned:

"Ho, seven o'clock an' notting on TV. Junk."

"H'm, what's that I smell?"

"Not me. Pig."

"No, I do smell something, a strange chemical smell," and he got up and walked around the living room sniffing, working his way in a circle toward her. "It's ethylbromopolyester. I read in U.S. World Report and News that ethylbromopolyester is highly toxic. What fabric is that made of?"

"Eh, get back, you pervert. It cotton."

"No, it's ethylbromopolyester. You've got to take them off. You'll get sick. I need to take a close look at you to make sure your skin isn't flushed."

"What, I cannot get one doctah do dat?"

"It may be too late. I've got to look now."

"You tryin' fo' con me into showing you dat! Nevah!"

"I'll pay you then."

"Fo' what?"

"I told you, if you aren't examined right now, you might be in serious medical trouble."

"How much you peh?"

"A million dollars."

"'Ass not enough. Besides, I don't even know what you wanna do."

"Give me a check. If that's the only way for me to save you, then I'm willing to spend it."

She sighed and pulled out the book, and tore one out.

Very carefully he wrote out a check for a billion dollars, making sure to put in the correct number of zeroes. "There, that should get rid of your stupid, self-destructive hesitation. Is your modesty worth your life?"

"Ho, a billion dollars. Cannot turn dat down. Hey, what dis? Mrs. Angela Jungle Bunny McKay?"

"Your name."

"Okay, so what do you want me to do?"

≈   ≈   ≈

Rhona Pualani McKay became Pua, because the one syllable from of her middle name was pronounceable by her and her brother: "Eh, Pua, like poi?" "Yah, Pua yike poi!" Angela had them both in the shop every day and then sometimes at home in the evenings when Loke, thirsty for a social life, went out with her Liberty House friends.

Those evenings Kenika and Angela would sit on the lanai or watch TV with the kids running around the house, Pua following her brother first on all fours and then on powerful little legs, running so fast that Kenika would watch with his teeth gritted. Once, at the Safeway store in the little shopping center three blocks down the hill, Pua motored full tilt around a corner and ran smack into a shopping cart and ended up sitting on the floor, the aghast shopper standing there with her hand over her mouth. Surely the child had knocked herself out or broken her nose. Kenika went to check the damage, but Pua jumped up, laughed, and ran on down the aisle, her black hair bouncing on her head. Like Ben, like the twins and Keoki, she was strong, healthy and almost ferociously energetic, her skin a rich brown and her face a miniature of Angela's, with black eyebrows perched above large brown eyes.

Angela's shop was the last holdout among the line of little shops in downtown Kailua. There was the investment counselor next door, beyond that an old building bulldozed away to provide space for another gas station the town didn't need, and on the other side, a real estate dealer's office that once had been a dry cleaning place. She discovered that with the rent tripled, she was in the red each month, and finally gave in. Nineteen seventy-five was the new world, she guessed, and the only small businesses that could survive were ones that didn't really sell anything anybody could use. She thought the lawyer who had acquired that block and kicked out all the old shops was no more than a pilau mainland bandit, and Kenika had to agree. Little modern-design lines of shops popped up here and there, and although he imagined some logical identity based on the principle of the old village—bookstore, coffee shop, flower shop, shoe repair, deli—what surfaced as a line of storefronts would be a real estate office, branch bank, investment counselor, floor tile shop, and a take-out pizza shop. It was not exactly a place you would go to for the purpose of browsing or talking story.

One odd contrast to this was that although the very identity of the little town was vanishing in the advance of the bulldozers and the arrival of those strange businesses no one he knew had any use for, elsewhere on the island there was an increasing upswell of the return to old times. The Polynesian Voyaging Society was building a huge double-hulled sailing canoe called the Hokule'a, which they planned to sail by old navigational methods to the south seas. Pictures they showed on TV, drawings and plans, showed it to be designed as if built five hundred years ago, and he wondered about what kind of logs they must have found for the manufacture of that canoe with its tall manus and a draft that looked to be the height of a man. Along with that, Hawaiians had begun illegally beaching their canoes and surfboards on Kaho'olawe, the military's bombing practice island, in an effort to reclaim it, and in the various protests Kenika saw on TV, the word "sovereign" began to be used, and with that, he realized that Benny had been born a generation and a half too early. Kenika often speculated on meeting those who worked on the huge canoe, but the nature of the enterprise along with all the other events suggesting Hawaiian reclamation of a magnificent past were really matters for those who could claim indigenous status, which he could not. As for Angela, she thought it was about time that someone decided to remember the past, and as for Kaho'olawe, the sooner they got it back from those jerks and their bombs, the better.

One of Angela's double-door, stainless-steel coolers ended up in the carport sandwiched between boxes of junk and topped by the roof-sheeting over an outrigger canoe called the Wa'a Aka, or "Laughing Canoe" which, when Ben saw it, suddenly became an object of such obsessed desire that the boy went on strike, refusing to play or eat until Kenika promised to let him use it.   ·

Just twenty years ago he had hoisted Keoki out of the water and into the seat of that canoe to teach him how to paddle. Pua, tiny as she was, demanded to be included, and one Saturday Kenika placed the two of them in the canoe and gave them their little paddles while on the beach Angela and Loke watched, Loke approaching and coming in the water up to her knees aiming a camera. Pua took a lusty swipe at the water with her paddle and missed, and in the series of pictures there was one which showed Ben taking the flat of her paddle in the face, with little bright beads of water spraying away from the point of impact.

Although Angela continued to sell leis and seed necklaces by order, there was a kind of emptiness at not having her friends from downtown present to talk story. The carport was cleaned up to make room for all the stuff she had at the shop: foam-blocks, wire, boxes. The rest she sold or gave away. Her shop was now a travel agency. Ben and Pua were deposited each day at the house, and Loke didn't come home for lunch. With that temporary custody of the kids, the atmosphere of twenty years back surfaced—Kenika would get up, consider the prospect of staring all day at the koa relief, and then tell Angela he would take the day off. If there were no pressing orders for flowers they would pack a lunch, get the kids into their little bathing suits and go to Lanikai Beach, now with a small inflatable boat that had a four-horse Seagull engine. They would go out to the Mokuluas and set up on the beach there, within just a hundred yards of that little hidden area and "their beach."

Hovering over all of this was the date of Keoki's probable release. "You'll do this when your daddy comes home," Kenika would say to Ben, showing him a menpachi hanging on his spear. "He'll teach you how to fish and all that. Someday your cousins will come and you'll meet your aunties."

"I like fish now."

"No, you're too young yet."

"Not."

Then they began to wonder about Loke. Weekend nights she went off with her friends to Waikiki, to a hangout called "The Point After" and Angela began wondering who these friends were, especially when she came home late, sometimes so late that Angela told her to leave the kids sleeping where they were. And then it was weeknights. Kenika asked Angela again if she thought they were being taken advantage of having to watch the kids all the time, but Angela said, "No. My grankids, 'asswhy. Besides, Keoki come out an' den dey go home."

Loke was always around for visiting day, and as they sat around and played with the kids and talked, she mentioned nothing about her social life, nor did Angela or Kenika. Yes, everything was fine, Keoki told them. He was okay, and ready to come out when they would let him. And yes, he would work with Kenika. He liked the woodshop in the prison, and had already made some small things—benches, lamps and so on. By the time he was out he would be able to show Kenika a few things. Electricity, for one. And then he laughed, slapped Kenika on the knee. "You too o' fashioned, Dad. 'Lectricity no bite, you know."

When Ben went to school it was then only Pua to watch, and Kenika became aware of a strange moodiness in Angela, as if something were bothering her that she didn't want to tell him about. Then one day he found her sitting at the table wiping her eyes, just after putting Pua down for a nap. He walked over to her and said, "What?"

She looked up at him and shrugged. "Keoki come out, dey go home."

"Well, it's better that way. They need a father, and it'll be great when they're back to normal again. Kids can come up whenever."

"Yeah I know, but—"

She didn't continue. He said, "You wait, it'll be all right."

≈   ≈   ≈

Although four years seemed like a century at the start, four years seemed almost nothing at all as the end approached. Kenika had discovered that he had to go down around the corner every two weeks or so to keep up the yard, which Loke ignored so that it became overgrown, the hedges ten feet high and the grass knee high with tassels of seed on the tops. He found himself staying longer to scrape and paint, repair rotted steps out the back door. Inside the house there was a hopeless mess, with piles of little cosmetic bottles and burger wrappers on the living room floor, clothes piled all over, and drywood termite damage on all the windowsills. If the place were going to be really shaped up when Keoki came out, then he'd have to say something to her. He realized that all his extra work outside was for that, for the day Keoki returned, so that he wouldn't have too much maintenance to mess around with while he was getting back on his feet.

As the release date approached, and it did appear that Keoki would get out on his first try, Angela became more moody and distant. She was convinced that the kids would no longer be hers to care for, and she apparently hated the idea, normal though it was. Besides that, she was more and more suspicious of Loke, whose nighttime galavanting had begun to appear like near total-abandonment of her children, and she worried about the implications of that once Keoki did come out. And was she fooling around? There was no way of knowing.

On those nights when Loke came home late, Kenika and Angela got into the habit of watching the ten o'clock news because of a number of alarming reports about shakedowns at the prison and about drugs making their way in. Angela would watch with her breath held any time the prison was mentioned. Along with these reports there were more and more reports about various kinds of protest by people against development in different parts of the island, Kalama Valley, Waiahole Valley, He'eia just past Kaneohe. One night they were watching the news and Kenika began to fall asleep, and was then nudged by Angela. He looked at her, and it was as if she had seen a ghost. "What?" he said.

"Wait, listen."

"—the Lualualei Naval Reserve," the reporter said. "The group cut a fence and hiked up toward Kolekole Pass to what they claim is a sacred site." Then the film showed the marchers standing there facing police and MP's. Kenika sat up. The woman glaring at the policeman was one of the twins, or— "No," he said. "My God, she looks like—" It seemed like some bizarre flash-dream. "They're not here," he said.

The woman was speaking: "—on the mainland, and it was no good. It was all false, and now only this is real."

"What'd she say?" Kenika asked. "What's going on here?"

"My God," Angela said. "My eyes popped out of my head."

The woman was tall, wore a head lei and pareo, and was so regal and formidable a presence that the police seemed tongue-tied. The newsman went on to explain that the marchers were simply going to worship at a site within the reserve, and claimed that they owed no allegiance to those who were trying to stop them. "You are on stolen land," the woman said. "I owe allegiance only to my queen."

"Who is she?" Angela asked.

"Hey, I know who it is." The newsman then confirmed it for him. It was Lehua Makaila, one of the sisters who had helped old Kelemeneke make it through the consecration of The Red Wind, and her resemblance to the adult twins was so complete that she could have been their mother, or older sister. She was escorted back toward where they had cut the fence, explaining first to the policeman that he did not need to hold her wrist. She would follow him out.

Angela got up and turned off the TV and sat back down, her face still crossed with that shocked look. "I thought it was one of them," she whispered. "I thought—" Then she stopped. She looked at Kenika. "I miss them," she whispered. "Kenika, I talked wit' some ladies, read some stuff too."

"'Kay."

"Don't tell me I'm crazy, 'kay?"

"I won't."

"Now I know afta—" She looked at the blank TV screen. "I know now."

"What?"

"I want another baby."

Kenika stared at the blank screen. After a few seconds he said, "But you're forty-seven years old."

"No mattahs any more," she said. "Dey get every kine—" She stopped and cleared her throat. "From what I have read, I understand that modern medicine has made it possible. There's actually little or no danger."

"'Kay."

"'Kay what? Kenika, aren't you going to say no? I mean argue about it?"

"No."

"Why?"

"I like babies."

"I don't believe you. You're just saying it because I want one."

"Maybe. I want what you want."

"Not. You're forty-seven too. What would you want with another baby?"

He remained silent. The idea appealed to him but he didn't know why. "I know," she said. "You want someone to learn what you know."

"That's probably it."

She looked at him, and he felt her breath on his face. "When do we start?" he asked. "I have some good ideas."

"Loke not here yet. Afta she take kids home?"

"No whatchucall. Condoms."

"Nope. I get good ideas too."

He looked down at her lap. "I can't do this without condoms. It's a chemical imbalance of some kind. You'd have to come up with some extraordinary means of counteracting what is in effect a toxic level of latex in my skin, which now—"

It was not only because Lehua Makaila resembled the twins, or the twins her, he knew. The incredible vision of the woman, dressed as she was in that setting, seemed to have shown them both what should have been but was not. Angela had been thinking about a baby even before they saw the news show, and the clip simply brought it out of her. After Loke left with the kids, they turned off all the lights and got into bed, and with the first hot immersion, it seemed to him that both of them were hurled back twenty years, her flesh hot against his, and sweat erupting from their bodies. With that he was sure that he wanted the same thing she did.

≈　　≈　　≈

Angela had a cork bulletin board in the back hallway leading to the carport on which she tacked pictures of the twins and the four grandchildren. Kenika would sometimes find her standing there staring at the pictures, and the expression on her face was strange, not the look of hope that one day they would all appear at the door but a contemplative objectivity, as if now her children had receded into the region of some lost dream. They talked about it often, Kenika explaining that kids their age did this, went out into the world to see what was there, and in the twins' case the fact that they were married to two adventurous guys made it such that they went to explore places no one of Angela's generation thought about: North Africa, Madagascar, India and so on. Now they were in Morocco, exporting fine Berber artifacts and importing things for the businesses in major cities—calculators, digital watches and business machines. Because Seth and Keith remained in business together, the cousins could grow up together.

Keoki's impending release took away the protracted sadness of that, as did the other, her conviction that any time now she would miss a period and they would be at the point of starting over. After all, on those days they had the chance, they were putting a lot of work into it. It was normal at night, and ridiculously creative by day, where going to the bedroom would be preceded by absurd conversations: I to' you I hate men, even if we inna same hotel room. You touch me an' I'll rip your face off (Kenika was convinced that he had a shoulder separation before conquering the surly woman).

So it went on: I have a shyness complex, especially in the presence of a woman like you. If you come anywhere near me, I'll pass out, and besides, I can't bend my knees, never could. Friddleak aptobu, skorik! (pointing to her stomach) I see, you do not speak English. Bobbaloo comsat Liberty House! Ah, you lost something. What did you lose? Skork! What is a skork? Very well, come with me and I'll see if I can find your skork.

The expectation sent a surge of energy through Kenika, so that he finished the relief in what seemed like no time at all and then went down to the foundation of the shed to study a splintered log that he once thought was useless, but now realized that with patching, joining of other pieces of koa, he could make a good thirty-five foot canoe. The what? 'Opua Hae, he whispered. The Wild Cloud. Its core was rotted a third of the way into one end and it was split, but it would not become coffee tables. He had no buyer, but decided to go on with the project anyway. He needed to do it because he had that energy and no direction for it.

At times he would have flashes of dread that something could go wrong with a pregnancy, but Angela's confidence seemed boundless. He would find himself looking at her, wondering. She was only a little heavier than when they were married, and had a couple of long gray hairs snaking through the thick copper black, and if anything, was physically far stronger than she had been. And any time people found out her age, they were amazed—she looked thirty.

Keoki came out of prison in March, and without any luaus or get togethers, because he didn't want any. He wanted to get back to work and put stuffs back togeddah. Kenika explained to him that they had a canoe they could build, and he thought it over and told him no, he'd go into construction. He knew people in the prison who knew people in the business, and it was good money.

So they tried to settle into what Kenika hoped was a stable life. But after a week he began hearing voices from down the hill, and at first assumed that it had to be someone else. It wasn't. Keoki vanished the eighth day after returning, and Loke and the kids ended up at the house at midnight, Loke crying and the kids so groggy that they didn't know what was going on. Kenika put them in their beds in Keoki's room. When he went back out, he heard Angela say, "Why you tell him?"

"He kep' asking an' I— I jus' tol' um."

"I to' you not to say anything," Angela whispered. "I don't know what you wen' do, but no tell him. Now he has an excuse."

"He no need excuse," Loke moaned. "I could see it in his face. Firs' chance, he go."

"I'll go look for him," Kenika said.

"Cannot," Loke said. "He's not a kid."

It was true. If it was strange for him to go looking for him back there when he did, it was absurd for him to go looking for him now.

Loke was afraid to go back home and went to bed in the twins' room. It wasn't that Keoki would hurt her, but she was still afraid. Then, in a whisper, Angela explained what had happened: Loke had become involved with a guy on the other side, a well-off haole who lived in Hawaii Kai. She had explained part of it to Angela just before Keoki's release, leaving out the details. And now, in an argument, she had blurted it out, and it reminded Kenika of his mother and Lon Carlson, and he was, in the back of his mind, frightened at the idea that some disaster might attend Loke's confession as one had his mother's.

The routines went back to the days before Keoki's release. Loke dropped Pua at the house each morning and took Ben to school, then went to work, Angela continued her business, and Kenika went to the shed. The prospect of making another canoe was no longer particularly attractive, but he had committed himself by staring at the log and seeing a canoe inside, and could not back out now. With no help, he worked on it outside in a cloud of black mosquitoes, planning to rough shape it and then winch it into the shed later. When Angela told him that she had missed a period, the prospect of making a canoe suddenly suffused him with energy, and he would leave for the shed early. She still had to confirm it by going to a doctor, but she claimed that she could feel it. No question.

On the day she had her appointment he left the shed early, and when he got home he found a note on the table, so shakily written that he could barely read it: "Accident, mom Queens, went there. Loke." His knees instantly felt weak, and he whispered, "No," and ran out to the car. By the time he got to the hospital he was so tense that he could barely pull his hands off the steering wheel. He ran in and asked the receptionist where she was. Intensive Care.

He found Loke there. She jumped up and ran to him. "She's unconscious," she whispered. "They no let me see her. I— I'm scared."

"'Kay, where are the kids?"

"Neighbor's. I gotta go back. Dey had to go someplace by now almos'. I—"

"Why don't you go ahead. I'll stay. I'll call her folks after I find out what the problem is."

She looked at the door of the room Angela was in.

"It's okay," he said.

She started to cry. Kenika put his arm around her. "It's okay, I'll stay."

She left. There was another smaller receptionist's counter in the intensive care section. He went and asked about her condition, and was informed by the nurse that the doctor would be out shortly.

He waited, pacing in the hallway. A man came out, introduced himself as Dr. Tanabe. "Let me explain what we know," he said. "She has both a whiplash injury and trauma to the brain. We have her on a respirator and we're now trying to stabilize her. Her condition is critical." Dr. Tanabe then nodded—follow me—and he and Kenika went into the room. What he saw so frightened him that he had to put one hand on the cool wall for support. She was attached to a machine that ran a thick, accordion-pleated tube into the base of her neck in front, and her eyes were covered with patches of cotton taped down from her forehead. There was an intravenous tube attached to a needle taped on her arm. The machine clicked and wheezed, at which her body moved, inflated slightly, and then settled in an artificial sigh.

"This is a respirator," Dr. Tanabe said.

"'Kay."

"We did an emergency tracheotomy, and today we'll set up an intracranial pressure monitor, which we'll watch every hour or so, for swelling and so on."

"'Kay."

"These wires go to this," he said, indicating a machine with a red line that blipped slightly and then snaked off the screen. "It's an electroencephalogram we use twice a day, which measures brain activity. This one here is an electrocardiogram for monitoring the heart—see?" and he pointed to another machine. The heart one showed the even, upward double-spikes of a slow beat. "The IV tube is for Levophed, which maintains her blood pressure."

"'Kay."

Tanabe looked at him. "The impact was severe," he said softly.

In his confusion Kenika had not thought of the specifics, only visualized the collision of metal on metal. "How— What happened?"

"A rear end collision. The other vehicle was going quite fast. There's apparent spinal damage, but we don't know the degree of severity yet. She has to be stabilized."

"'Kay."

"Would you like to stay a minute?"

"Yes."

"I don't have to mention this I'm sure, but please don't touch any of the equipment or try to move her in any way."

"'Kay."

Tanabe left. Kenika stood with his hand on the wall, and listened to the click-wheeze of the respirator. The way it shocked her body with that harsh inflating movement seemed as if it would hurt her. He stared at her chest, covered by a sheet, the accordion tube snaking over it. The surges showed the absolute limpness of her body.

He took his hand from the wall and went the two steps to the bed, and supported himself by placing his hand on the hard mattress, next to hers. There was the little circle of shiny skin on the index finger of her left hand, from the string she used in making the leis, and on the third finger, her ring. Her face, what he could see of it, was smooth and brown, her hair swept back from her forehead and then vanishing under her neck, the occasional strands of grey peeking out.

"Hey," he whispered.

Nothing. He looked at the two screens. The heart one continued, but the other—it was either nearly flat or showed a lazy wave sweeping across the line almost like some weak, arbitrary static. The respirator kept wheezing and clicking, and he found himself staring again at that series of harsh surges of her chest followed by the limp settling.

He touched her finger, then the back of her hand. "Okay," he whispered. "We wait. You wake up, 'kay? Oh God, you please wake up."

He tiptoed out of the room, and his knees were still weak enough that he did not trust his balance. The receptionist stood up from her chair and said, "Mr. McKay?"

He went to her. "Do you feel up to filling out these forms?"

"'Kay."

"Which medical insurance do you carry?"

"Medical insurance? None, I guess."

She stared at the form. "Oh."

"I can pay," he said.

When he sat down to fill out the form, he found that he could barely grip the pen, and had to wait about five minutes before he felt steady enough to try to write.

Then, his hands shaking, he called George and explained everything he knew about her condition, and told him he would stop by their apartment when he could.

He had assumed that he would sit there and wait for her to wake up, but long after it got dark outside, Dr. Tanabe came back out to tell him that it would be best if he went on home and returned the next day.

"It's okay," Kenika said. "I'll wait."

Tanabe looked at the middle distance off to his right and then said, "This takes patience. If you leave her care to us and get some rest, it would be better for both of you. We'll call if there's any change."

Kenika went home. Driving up the Pali he whispered, "She will wake up," over and over, and again found that his hands were sore from gripping the steering wheel. The house was dark. Loke and the kids were home, probably.

Inside, he turned the lights on and looked around. "She will wake up," he whispered. He got a beer out of the refrigerator. Ten o'clock. News.

It was a habit they had, to sit on the couch and watch the news, so he did. The first story was the accident, and he considered turning it off. But he left it on, felt his heart begin to slam in his chest. He barely heard what the newsman said, something about the man in the car being a parolee and the van he drove unlicensed, unregistered, uninsured. There was a white van with its front end mashed in, and then Angela's station wagon with the rear end crumpled forward, one tire parallel to the ground, rusted chassis beams twisted and sticking out. He felt his stomach heave, and just made it into the bathroom, where he vomited into the toilet.

He did not sleep. He sat on the couch and rocked slowly, his body so tense that his trunk and back began to hurt, and at dawn went outside to water Angela's plants, and the 'ilima bushes, the papaya trees. Then he went back over the Pali to the grandparents' apartment.

He took a deep breath approaching their door. It struck him that all of this was somehow his fault, going all the way back, that had he been left in that garbage can to die then none of this would ever have happened, that all of them would have experienced some far more preferable future than this.

They were up, and when Irene saw him she said, "Kenika, you look awful. Come eat something."

"'Kay."

He tried, but managed to swallow only a small part of the toast and eggs. He explained again what he knew of Angela's condition, and both of them listened in silence, Irene dabbing at her eyes with a kleenex, George sitting forward and leaning on his cane. When it came time for him to go, George said, "Eh, in da bat'room is my razor. Go shave, 'kay? We go later an' visit."

He did so, his hand shaking, and left.

Her condition remained the same. The respirator forced air into her lungs and wheezed it out, her hand stayed palm down on the sheet where it was that first day. When he got a chance to talk to Dr. Tanabe later in the day, he told him that yes, there were similar cases in which people did regain consciousness without serious damage to either function or acuity. But he had to be honest—the likelihood was not great that this would happen. Kenika remembered to ask him about a possible pregnancy, and Tanabe said that a simple test would show it. By the end of the day the results came back—she was, but he should understand that for the present it would not be a good idea to cultivate any expectations.

He did not. He worried about the possibility that when she did wake up they would discover other problems that would make a pregnancy a hindrance. He could not stand being alone in the house in the evenings, and welcomed the prospect of watching the kids when Loke went out. During the day Ben went to school and Loke dropped Pua off, and each day he spent the time they were not at the hospital watching her, and it took up the time in a way that felt almost comfortable. Because Pua heard more than once the phrase "when she wakes up," at home she began doing different things, making stick drawings and picking flowers in the yard, "Fo' when Tutu wake up, yah?"

≈   ≈   ≈

After nearly two weeks he tried calling the twins, using the number of Seth and Keith's Tangier office, and got a wrong number, then static, then an answer. No, a secretary with a British accent said, the families were in Marrakech, but he could leave a message. He described why he was calling as succinctly as possible, and the tone of the woman's voice indicated that she knew full well the seriousness of it, and promised to get in touch with them as soon as possible.

Two and a half weeks. Her condition did not change, the machine forced air into her and wheezed. By this time they had moved her to another room. The electroencephalogram showed the weak waves sweeping off the edge of the screen, the other showed the double spikes of the slow heartbeat. He would stand there holding Pua's hand and stare at the limp movement caused by the machine, and then, weary and trembling with fatigue, he would settle Pua in the front seat of the car and drive home. On Loke's days off he stayed away from the house, driving over to Waimanalo and then to the North Shore to look for Keoki. None of his old friends knew where he was. He told them all, if you run into him tell him his mother is in critical condition at Queens. Tell him to call, tell him to come home.

At three and a half weeks he was overcome by a stultifying fatigue and a fear that had dulled back from the horrible flashes of fright into what felt like an advanced state of some kind of a debilitating disease. At times the hot sweep of the fright would race through him, and he would suddenly be slick with sweat, but the worst of it was that protracted dread that weighed on him. Each time he visited George and Irene she would look sadly at him and try to make him eat, and he ate what he could, but it was never much. George told him that he had to get himself ready, that these things did happen, and although Angela was their daughter, she was Kenika's wife and he suspected how hard it must be, but it might be time for him to accept her dying, if that was what God had in store for her. He had to get ready to let her go. He nodded, thinking, no. No.

One day he woke up after a fitful sleep and realized that Loke would have the children all day. He had the sensation that he had forgotten something, and, standing in the backyard watering the 'ilima bushes, staring at Olomana and beyond it the dark-green curtain of mountains hanging out of the clouds, he remembered the shed, the path, and that parched square of rocks up on the mountainside. He turned off the water and went into the house and found a mango and a banana and got in the car.

When he got to the Marumotos' house he remembered that he had not told them about Angela, and went to their door. They already knew—Irene had called. Mrs. Marumoto invited Kenika in but he told her he had something he had to do at the shed, and promised to stop by when he could.

He experienced a strange sensation taking that little jump across the brook, as if the shed and the environment around it were a place he had not seen in years. Something else wasn't right—there were footprints in the muddy path, and inside the shed on the floor were little cubes of mud, from someone's hiking boots. He looked around— nothing seemed to have been taken, either from the tool rack or from inside the little sleeping alcove. Below the shed the partly-shaped hull of the 'Opua Hae sat undisturbed, and he could see going toward the path up the mountain the swipes of mud and water-filled footprints of different sizes indicating that people had hiked up there.

He went up the mountain. He realized now how long it had been since he had done this, and wondered if he would have trouble finding the place where he was to turn right and find the heiau. At the same cluster of ti plants he had stopped the last time, he picked leaves and wrapped the banana and mango, and then went on. As he walked, he stepped on the cleated-boot tracks, and they too went all the way up the ravine. At the point where he recognized the gentle slope beyond which was the arrangement of black rocks, he noticed that the tracks went both toward it and on up the ravine. At his feet there was a yellow film box and a cigarette butt.

He approached the little rise, and then stopped, feeling a sensation of wariness. He went back to the path and stood there, thinking. Then he decided to put off his visit for a while and follow the trail further up the ravine to see where the tracks led. He left the wrapped mango and banana on a rock. As he went further up the trail, the dark face of the mountain loomed closer above him, the tops vanishing into the clouds. The tracks continued to a point where it was apparent that the hikers had stopped, and then either eaten a lunch or something, because the grasses were trampled down and there was more trash—a kleenex, another cigarette butt, a soda can. Off to his right there was a large red mesh onion bag of the type people used to gather fruit, but there was no fruit around here. There were kukui and 'ohi'a trees and other brush he didn't known the names of.

He was about to turn back when he realized that this was the area Benny had taken him to long ago, that the little cave was right here somewhere, up to the right at the base of a rock face. He made his way through the weeds and brush, and then saw the long opening that was shaped something like a mouth. By the opening there was another mesh onion-bag. He felt an odd sensation sweep over him, one that he remembered from the first time, of being watched. But he shook it off and went to the little cave opening and got down on his knees. Inside the dirt had been dug up and pushed to the edges, and the skulls were gone. The rock walls of the cave bore pale abrasions from a tool of some sort. The wooden images were still there, but little was left of them. Parts seemed to have been removed. Beyond the dryrotted remains of one he saw a single bone, bright gray against the black recesses of the cave. He backed away, his heart beating rapidly.

He turned and went back down to the trail. Someone had put the skulls and hacked-off parts of the images into onion-bags and carted them off, and he stood there trying to figure out why. What use would anyone have for a skull? He had been here thirty years, and he imagined that no local person he had ever met would do something like this. It would be like visitors from, say, China, coming over to the U.S. to some town like Paterson and digging up the graveyard because of all the interesting bones they might find there. That sensation of being watched came back again, and he started back down the trail. He had the feeling that somehow he was being held responsible, and he whispered, "Not me, not me," but it did no good. He felt something in the air, a peculiar electrical charge, and made his way down to the heiau with his body held in a kind of protective rigidity, as if he expected to be struck from behind.

At the entrance to the heiau he stopped, holding the mango and banana before him. His reason for being here returned, and he tried to think of what to say, or to think, out on that parched square. Please. One word. He took one tentative step, then another, and then went out from under the shade of a large bush into the sun, the bits of rock making little grating sounds under his slippers. He put the fruit down on a flat rock and whispered, "That's for you," and as he rose up straight he suddenly felt as if he had been painlessly gutted, and his heart was high and too light in his chest. The sensation of dizzy airiness made him yaw a little, and he caught himself before losing his balance and stood there trembling and numb. She was dead. The strange sphere of stone and grass and air told him that and he could feel it as surely as he felt the heat of the sun. The sensation of airy emptiness settled itself into his flesh, and he felt its permanence, as if from the inside the simple truth of it had seared every square inch of tissue in a white-hot branding, had in an instant scorched every nerve. He wanted to mouth the word "why?" but there was no why. The air answered that before he asked it. Carefully he backed out of the stone square. Walking back down to the shed, he felt the same horrible, yawning emptiness in his chest, and he felt locked inside some strange dream, dry-mouthed and numb.

Her heart stopped two days later. Dr. Tanabe explained that they used an injection of adrenalin, but she did not respond. Kenika was allowed to go into the room, which had been emptied of all its machines, but standing there at the edge of the bed feeling that airy lack of balance, he found that he could not really focus his eyes on the brown, placid face, nor could he stand the stillness of her body. His breath held, he picked up her left hand and held it a moment, and touched the ring, but the cold stillness made him shudder. She was not there.

He would go out to the receptionist and ask for help with the arrangements. The mortuary on Nuuanu Street would do the cremation. The services would be held on the beach at Lanikai, so there would be nothing else the hospital would need to do. There were all the people he would have to call, Kalani Chun for the service, every friend he knew her to have, every relative, no matter how distant. They would have food at the house, and the people would stay as long as they wished. But first they would have the service on the beach, borrow canoes from anyone who would loan them so that as many people as wanted to would be able to go along as they took her out into the water on The Red Wind.

≈   ≈   ≈

He knew he was doing everything he was supposed to do but felt the same distant numbness that had hit him at the heiau. George and Irene came to stay at the house, which he appreciated, because Irene knew the relatives better than he did, and seemed able to intervene and help him out with the various arrangements. She shuffled slowly around the house using her aluminum walker, while George passed the time in the yard, or talked with old friends in the carport, his hands resting on the handle of his cane.

Kenika tried to socialize, but then found himself sitting in a stupor staring at the middle distance between himself and the wall. Then he would sneak into his room and fall exhausted on the bed. He would wake up hours later and step out of the room, and find the old folks sitting in the living room, and Loke, or Ben or Pua or Irene would try to draw him there to sit and eat. He would put food on a plate and sit down next to Ben, say, "So, how you doin'?" and then take a plastic forkful of rice to his mouth, but it would sit in his mouth like sand, and he would barely be able to swallow it. The only thing he could get down was beer.

After long negotiations with her walker Irene would sit down next to him and put her hand on his knee. "Kenika, you have to eat," she would say, and he would say, "Oh, I'm okay, just not hungry is all. I'll be okay."

"And you know," she said once, "you two gave us all these beautiful grandchildren."

"Yeah."

"So I want you to eat."

"'Kay."

"So tomorrow we take her out, and you'll feel better."

He nodded. Darnay would pick up the small koa box of ashes that day, and the next day was the ceremony at the beach. George and Irene had arranged for a Methodist minister to be present to say a prayer. Darnay had been contacted on Maui by Irene and was on his way. And the twins. He didn't know when they'd come, but the idea forced a lump into his throat. They had called from Europe when he was not there, and Irene had told them everything. He thought that of all things the loss of your mother, if she was real, had to be one of the worst things to bear. Then, one look at the sad, wistful expression on Irene's face would convince him that the loss of a child had to be worse. Kenika vowed to die if he could before any of his children.

When it was dark he would leave the soft voices of the old folks and go out to the corner of the yard behind one of Angela's 'ilima bushes and stand and look at the profile of Olomana backlit by the ashy light of Honolulu glowing above the mountains, and he would stand and breathe, and wonder why it was that he didn't burst into tears, surely some aberration of natural behavior. The strange, blank numbness that had settled into the hollow portions of his bones where marrow had been seared out seemed the only sensation he could identify of what was left of him. The name Angela became a recurrent whispered echo in his head and it gave him a peculiar comfort, if there was any possibility for that. And as for food, he had the feeling that he was done with food and would no longer need any because he had been hollowed out, and he knew that he would never get it back, that his life was now over. He was an animated corpse. What he had had, from the day he first saw her, was a dream that became so far in excess of anything he could ever have imagined, and now it was over.

The morning of the ceremony he opened his eyes, wiped the sleep from them, and rolled a little in the direction of Angela's pillow. He had not taken it off the bed. On it he saw a long black hair, and he lay there staring at it, and heard the voices from the living room. It was the twins. Outside, Pua, Ben and the twins' children were picking and eating tangerines. The two older ones, a girl and boy, would be Angela and Kenika. The little boys Pua's age would be Robert Williamson and Grant Davis, both named after their paternal grandfathers. He suddenly felt a swoon of embarrassment—did he even know the twins after all this time?

He needed to shave, clean himself up. Just as he was about to get out of bed there was a soft knock, then the door opened a crack, and one of the twins, he couldn't tell which, peeked in, then came in and sat on the bed, and he knew by the stricken expression on her face that he did not look good. It was Elizabeth, and then Clarice came in, and they both were on the bed with their arms around him, and whispered at him, Dad, you've got to eat, please come out and eat something with us. They did not seem to have changed at all.

He found himself able to eat, and they sat around and talked around Angela's death because Irene had filled them in on all the details. Seth and Keith, no longer with sideburns and long hair, took turns watching the kids in the backyard. Kenika went out to talk to them, and Seth took him aside and said, "Look, both girls had a really bad time with this, and I think they're still in a kind of shock. That's why they seem to act, well, sort of normal."

Kenika told him that he understood. He himself didn't know what to do or say. Before long they were on their way to the beach, and Kenika fell back into the airy numbness, the hollow feeling that he knew would never go away. There was a large crowd on the beach, and an astonishing profusion of flower leis, as if in response to some unspoken unanimity, and The Red Wind had nearly vanished under a display that looked more like the offerings at a convention of lei makers. The minister gave a short talk about Angela's spirit having gone home, and they left the grandparents and Darnay on the beach, paddled out through a cool morning breeze and spread the leis and her ashes on the water.

Three

Time seemed to pass like an evenly-turning wheel, day by day, as the children played and the adults sat either in the living room or in the carport, and Kenika got up every morning to collect paper plates and fish skeletons. All the kids were staying at Loke's house, George and Irene in Keoki's room, and the twins and their husbands camping in their old room. He would end up sitting listening to the twins and the grandparents talking, and more than once found himself studying the faces of his daughters, thinking that it was true as Irene had said, he and Angela did really produce these beautiful women, and through them those beautiful children in the backyard. It could be that even though they would leave soon because they had their own lives to live, the fact that they existed, no matter where in the world they were, was what Kenika's and Angela's lives had been about. Keoki too might someday pull himself free from the grip of whatever held him, and would be as whole as they were.

The day came when George and Irene had to go back to their apartment. Then the day came when the two families had to return to their lives, and Kenika followed them to the airport, waited while they turned in their rented van, and said goodbye to them at the gate, Loke, Ben and Pua sending them off with plumeria leis around their necks. It was the second time he saw the twins shed tears, the first being at the beach. They promised to write, to keep in contact, but had to admit that their location, so far away from even the U.S. mainland, made it difficult at least for now for them to visit. And with that, they had to turn and make their way down that tubular entryway to the plane, the children turning to wave, and the twins keeping them all together.

Finally, as if no one had visited and nothing bad had happened, he once again watched Pua and Ben when Ben was not in school, or Pua when he was, while Loke went to work. She promised to get a sitter for them, reminded him that Pua would be going to school soon, and he told her not to worry, he liked watching the kids and they were no burden to him, providing that they were allowed to go up to the shed with him from time to time. He could teach them some things. Sure, that was all right with Loke as long as they didn't wander off into the woods. So his life seemed to have settled back into something resembling months ago, but for the absence of Angela, and the presence of the blank, flat hollowness in the core of his being.

The arrangement would have seemed normal to him but for one problem: he owed the hospital, the neurologist, the cardiologist, around seventy thousand dollars. He knew that it was not their fault, that that kind of care, lasting for around a month, was expensive. He did not have the money, and told Loke one night that he had to sell the house down the hill.

"Which house?" she asked, pausing on her way to the door.

He pointed in its direction. "The medical bills," he said.

"That's our house."

"No, it was Angela's and mine," he said. "Look, if I sell this one, then we all have to move down there. This one is bigger and in better condition."

"Can you sell my house?" she asked. "I mean, is this really my problem?"

He looked at her. How was it her house? She had never even paid any rent, and hadn't kept it up. "Loke, it isn't really your house. It's in our name, we bought it so you and Keoki would have a place to stay. Now I have to sell it."

He studied the look on her face. She was obviously furious and trying not to show it. She snorted, and went outside to where Pua and

Ben were playing, and walked them down the hill to what she had assumed belonged to her.

She said no more about it. He tried to figure out the bills, and contacted a real estate agent, who informed him that the market was hot, and he would have no trouble selling the place. What was left of the family settled back into the normal routines, Kenika watching the kids during the day, and sometimes at night when Loke went on her Waikiki jaunts with her friends. Within two months she had to move into the house, and took over Keoki's room while her children slept in the twins'. She did the kids' and her laundry and cooked for them, but her part of the house was a mess similar to the mess she lived with in the other house. The fact that she now lived in the house seemed to make her even more a visitor than a resident, at least in spirit—she worked overtime, she went out more frequently, she appointed him the "parent" for visits to the PTA meetings and teacher conferences. He took Ben to soccer and baseball practice, then took Pua to soccer practice when she became old enough to play. He took them to the beach on weekend days, took them sometimes to the shed, and there showed them the intricacies of building a canoe. They liked the shed most of all because they always stopped to see the Marumotos, who sent them off with crackers, seed and candy. Of all the things Kenika did to occupy their time he liked most of all taking them to the shed, where they would sit and watch while he planed away at the hull of the 'Opua Hae, all the time telling them the things that Benny had told him, and all he had learned since. Those days he would start a fire in the rust-perforated drum, and take food he could heat, laulau and rice and fish, and feed them at the bench and talk on while they chewed and looked up at him with their huge, dark eyes.

Gradually the empty feeling faded, because he always seemed to have the children with him, and their contact gave him a reason to get up in the morning. At ten Ben began paddling, for the boys' twelve team of the Olomana club, and their canoe was The Red Wind. In the months preceding the season he would take Pua to the beach and they would watch Ben, smaller than the other boys, digging away as the canoe knifed along in the near shore water. The sale of the house seemed to make Loke more and more distant, to the point that she went on about her business as if Kenika did not exist, and he had to sympathize with her, because after all her husband was his son, and he had run off, may not even have been on the island, and the house she had assumed was hers had been sold, for eighty-five thousand dollars, which, minus all the fees, was enough to pay off all the bills for Angela's care.

He found that in the evenings he drank more and more beer, but it comforted him, and gradually Angela began to visit him in his sleep.

He did not know how it worked psychologically, but in his sleep her form would materialize somewhere and he would feel the warm, airy presence of her flesh sliding around his, and would wake up in the morning to discover that he had had what they used to call a wet dream. He knew that men who had lost their wives sometimes became involved with other women, and at the beach with the kids he would sometimes see them walk past, and study their bodies, the fluidity of their movement, their expressions as they said hello to him or marvelled at the beautiful, dark children he watched. But at the same time he felt a deadness where the possibility of desire was concerned. The uncomfortable sensation of a stirring in his body, he knew, was nature trying to tell him to continue that sexual release that he had been lucky enough to have with Angela for more than thirty years, but when he looked at those women in their scanty bathing suits, something shunted the desire off, and he knew why—he could not imagine himself touching any other woman than Angela. Then, after he had downed ten or twelve beers in the evening he would stumble off to bed and sometime later in the night, or in the morning around dawn, she would waft into the room like a warm vapor and settle down over him, her breath hot against his neck, and he was convinced, at least in the dream, that the flesh was real and that it was her dark hair that tickled his face.

≈　　≈　　≈

He continued working on the ʻOpua Hae during the week, and helped coach the kids when he could, those weekday afternoons when Jerry Cambra had the three koa canoes in the water for practice. The Red Wind remained the children's canoe, and Ben had settled in to the practice schedule with his friends Junior Sakata, who was Frank's grandson, Skipper Moniz and the rest. They were good boys but because of the unevenness of their weights and experience, not a team likely to win much of anything. When it came time for the first race, the Kamehameha Regatta at Kailua Beach, Loke was away visiting her mother, so he stood there on the beach holding Pua's hand and looking around at the other adults. When the time seemed right, he went to the boys and repeated the same little speech he had used when the twins had won their first race. The boys, their hands on the smooth, red hull, listened, their faces thoughtful masks of almost trancelike concentration.

"'Ass it, I feel um,"

"Ho, da wood alive,"

"But my skin not red, it brown."

And he said, "That doesn't matter. It's just the meaning of the word. As long as you can feel the life in it, you're okay. You do the best you can, and she won't be disappointed. But you have to feel the life inside the wood leaking up into your backs and arms, and that'll make them stronger."

He was amazed at the number of people at the beach. There must have been eight or ten thousand, quadruple what there had been back in the twins' days, as if the sport were experiencing some resurrection. He watched with Pua near the finish line, looking again and again at the tents of different colors and the kids all along the arc of beach fronting the race course, and listened to the Hawaiian music blaring from the speakers, and wondered what the new popularity of this sport meant. The boys did well, fighting the chop and sending sprays behind them as The Red Wind cut the water. They came in third.

The boys flipped The Red Wind at the regatta in Waimanalo, and came in surly and ashamed. Ben walked over to Kenika, his head hanging and water dripping off his brown skin, and said, "I sorry we huli da canoe," and Kenika explained that these things happen, don't worry about it, there's always another race.

Although there was no buyer for the 'Opua Hae, he did learn from Jerry Cambra that there were people interested in buying canoes, even if the 'Opua Hae were to turn out shorter than most racing canoes. So he continued working on the canoe with the help of Ben and Pua, who turned out to be good workers despite their ages. Like the students at the university, they soaked up everything he said, and worked with total focus, pausing only to complain about the incompetence of the other.

"Eh Ben, dat junk! I can feel lumps heah!"

"Not."

"Can!"

"I not finish deah 'ass why."

"Den why you o'dea, hah?"

"Shaddap!"

"'Kay guys, we gotta go up the mountain and look for 'ohi'a root now."

"Fo' real?"

"After lunch."

He wondered if in the new world all this information would be of any use to them. As he understood it, the information kids needed had more to do with how to make money in the commerce of the new world than in dying traditions like this. But he reasoned that it couldn't hurt. Whenever he told Loke about what either or both of them had accomplished at the shed, she just nodded her head with her eyebrows raised, always seeming distracted by something else. He was aware of her maturity now as she neared thirty, and was aware of her lessening tolerance for the circumstances of her life. Although he had no idea who her friends were, he imagined that she was still involved with someone on the other side of the island, because of the time she spent there, even staying over weekends sometimes while he watched the kids. He couldn't blame her for her feelings about her circumstances either. After all, at her age she should be enjoying some kind of security and normalcy. She had a place to stay as long as she wanted, but he knew she didn't really care for what he was so willing to offer.

When they did talk, over dinner while the kids sat and ate, she complained about the cost of living, particularly about the cost of real estate. This house we're sitting in, she would say, is worth two hundred thousand dollars. How could she expect to buy one any better? Or even as good. He wasn't sure she was right about her estimation of value, but at the same time he knew that a lot of people complained about the cost of real estate or bragged about how much they had made in real estate. If she was right, the house which cost him eight thousand dollars in the late forties would be far too expensive for him and Angela, even with her skill in handling money, to ever afford.

But the circumstances Loke seemed to find barely tolerable remained the status quo as she went off to work and the kids went off to school. He woke up every day to help them with breakfast and then took them in the car to the school, then, if he did not go to the shed, which was about half of the time, he went back home to sit and stare at the overgrown backyard, the dying 'ilima bushes, the little mounds of termite droppings on the windowsills, and would find that he did not have the energy to do anything about those problems. He found himself looking at the clock, waiting for the time when he could go and pick up the kids. Once in a while she took them for the day either to visit her family or do something else on the other side of the island.

His hair was graying, and in the mirror his face took on a strange, dark gauntness which he assumed to be no more than advancing age. During those nights when he drank a lot of beer he would be visited by the vapor-like figure of Angela, who, in his dreams, also turned gray. He even laughingly pointed this out to her at some dream beach where they were sunning themselves, and she got that familiar look of good-humored indignation and said, "So?" It made no difference to her.

With the approach of summer the practice for the regatta season started again, and Ben was bigger and stronger than he had been the previous year. Pua, too, had become interested in the sport, and pestered him to get her on the girls' twelve team, but she was too small. "But I like paddow!" she snapped, her fists on her hips, and Jerry Cambra settled it by suggesting that she work out with the girls' twelves by being an alternate this first year, and maybe a starter next. That was fine with her. Again, Loke's response to this was to raise her eyebrows and nod, as if the idea intruded on something far more important.

The season opened with the Kamehameha Regatta, and Kenika again found himself standing in the sand at the finish line, squinting over the water at the fourteen tiny canoes in the distance, all ready, and the flags went up, the horn sounded. He had given the boys the same pep talk, and this time Junior said, "Eh, I Japanee, I no mo' Hawaiian," but the other boys took care of his doubt.

It was a perfect repeat of the first race he had ever watched. He could see the canoes inch out from the start line, and then crawl slowly in that strange, narrow angle so that he could detect no movement. The Red Wind was the fifth canoe, and he counted out to it again and again, trying to determine where they were. A third of the way into the race the canoes seemed to stop, sitting in the water as the eighty-four boys fought, arms and fists pumping and spray shooting out behind them. He could hear the screaming from down the beach, but could still detect no movement, and the brightness of the water and the sky drove his eyes down into blazing slits of vision. Then the canoes were moving, but the line was jagged, and three, four, five, The Red Wind was out ahead, just a little, and as they drew closer he began to see the fury of their effort, their bodies heaving forward and pulling back, the canoe sweeping through the water with its manu rising and sinking, rising and sinking. Four-fifths of the way the canoes were all shooting along in that jagged line, and this time The Red Wind was clearly one of the front canoes, and the boys dug at the water, the sound of screaming approaching. The closest canoes raced at the line, the ones farthest out inched at the line, and number five swept at it, the last forty yards a single, furiously-synchornized blast of energy on the boys' parts, and it nosed across a third of a canoe out front, Keoni with his paddle over his head, Ben wilted over, his head on his knees.

They won four gold medals, two silvers and a bronze during that season, and came in second in the state races at Keehi Lagoon. Ben and Pua both had become children of the water, as Kenika and Angela's had. He kept the inflatable boat pumped up and leaning against the house, because they wanted to go out to the Mokes and help him fish often in the summer. Loke had no problem with this because she worked, even hinted at times that she thought Kenika ought to work too. There were small problems that bothered her where his watching the kids was concerned.

"Why did Pua come home with a smelly rag wrapped around her arm?"

"Portuguese man-o'-war sting—the old remedy. We were out on the Mokes and she showed me, you know, the little line of purple dots? I told her that the old remedy was urine, because of the ammonia, and she asked for a rag and went into the bushes."

"God, that's gross."

"Well, it works."

He tried to work on the relief picture, which was now years in the making. When the canoe was nearly finished, he got names and phone numbers from Jerry Cambra to see if any of those people would be interested in buying it.

"What about The Red Wind?" Loke asked one night while they ate. "How much would that bring?"

"I don't really wanna sell that now," he told her. "The kids are using it."

"And this other, this Opu whatevahs, how much would that bring?"

"Jerry thinks fifteen thousand."

Loke raised her eyebrows thoughtfully. Her expression said, in effect, hey, not bad.

"I've got just a couple little things to do, then we get the blessing."

Loke came out with a snort. "My God," she said. "You still do that? You're still into the mumbo jumbo?"

"It's not mumbo jumbo."

"Hey, whatevah turns you on, but don't fill my kids' heads with that."

"'Kay."

As for trinkets, canoe models, all those other bits of tourist shit as Benny called it, he was through with that. One trip to Waikiki could convince him of the impracticality of trying to work his way back into that market. Besides, he didn't have the heart for it. The relief, on the other hand, was the only non-canoe type of work he could get himself interested in, although he had not had any contact with Mr. Maxwell in years.

Unlike his father, Ben seemed attracted more to what was under the surface of the water than the waves on top. He did surf with his friends Keoni and Junior Sakata, but if he had the choice, he apparently preferred spear fishing and paddling. By the time he was twelve he had caught enough fish that he and Kenika had lost count of what kinds and how many. Pua learned to spearfish too, and by the time she was ten was strong enough to paddle in the girls' twelves, and with her crew on The Red Wind, began pulling in the medals as Ben did. Kenika understood by this time that if he were to line up his priorities, he had to place canoes and reliefs second to the kids. He knew that he would at times seduce himself into thinking of them as his, and would then experience a flash of fear that something would happen to upset the status quo they lived by. Loke, tiring of her forays over the mountain to Waikiki, seemed to look around the house and out at the overgrown yard with an expression of sarcastic distaste, and he wondered just when it would be that she would decide to leave.

But the status quo remained. Some days late in the summer he would put the rubber boat over the roof of the car and they would go out to the reef between the Mokes and Lanikai and slide off the tubular side into the water and work their way along the reef, Kenika always behind the kids so he could watch them. One day Pua speared a hinalea, a ten-inch fish with a greenish-red body speckled in a pattern of tiny pale gray dots, and she asked if they could go on to the little beach on the left Moke and cook it. Sure, he had matches, they could make a little fire, eat that and a couple of other fish along with their sandwiches.

About two hours after they ate the fish on the little beach, Pua eating the hinalea, she told him that her lips tingled and felt numb. It was a reaction to the fish, he knew, and they packed up their gear and put it in the boat. By that time she was vomiting into the sand, and he became more alarmed—he went to pick her up to put her in the boat, and she was sweating and her skin felt cold. "C'mon, we'll get you home," he said, but when she looked up at him, she did not seem able to focus.

He gunned the old seagull full-throttle, but they seemed to crawl over the waves, then wash back. "Grandaddy!" Ben said, "she wen' sleep!" She had passed out in Ben's lap, her eyes rolled up. The panic Kenika felt made the time go more slowly, and he kept looking at her to make sure she was breathing. When they finally got to the beach he dragged the boat up over the high tide line and took Pua from Ben, and they ran out to the car and took her to Castle Hospital and then waited, standing near the emergency room door covered with salt and sand.

The doctor called the poison ciguatera. Kenika had heard of it, but never in connection with Kailua. Pua would be all right. The doctor gave her an injection of a muscle relaxant to calm her stomach. She had vomited out most of the toxins, he believed, and he prescribed a simple regimen: no fish for now, drink plenty of liquids, don't let her drink any alcohol, at which he smiled.

"But why here?" Kenika asked him.

"When something changes the balance of things, this kind of thing can happen," he said. "Midway Island, for example, has so much of it that the fish are inedible, and that can be blamed on the war. Here I would guess it's runoff from the developments, runoff of fertilizer, stuff like that. It's far worse in Kaneohe and around some Leeward areas."

He drove home, Pua resting on Ben's lap, now fairly comfortable but tired.

He explained everything that happened to Loke, who listened, and then turned and went into the kids' room to check on Pua. After that, Kenika was aware that Loke was angry about it, but would not broach the subject until the kids were not in the house. So Kenika waited, as she seemed to wait, until Pua was better and the kids were invited to play and watch movies on TV over at Mr. Kam's house. His grandchildren were visiting and they had a swimming pool.

Loke came back from dropping them off around the corner and sat down at the dining room table. Kenika sat on the couch, waiting. Finally she said, "We're leaving."

"Where you goin'?"

"Hawaii Kai. There's—" She paused, shrugged, and then began to do something inside her purse. "I'm involved with a man, a lawyer who lives in a big house there."

"Well, I guess that's natural. After all, Keoki— I guess that's to be expected. You guys can come over whenever you want, you can leave the kids, whatever."

"No, that isn't likely," she said. "To tell you the truth I'm glad to get out of this situation, out of this family for good, what is left of it, anyway. Those children are going to a good school like Punahou, they're going to have everything kids their age should have."

"Well—"

"What on earth did you think you were doing anyway? Cooking some goddamned fish you caught out on the island."

"Pua caught it, and it was a hinalea. Good eating fish."

"Oh sure," she said. "Look what it did to her."

"So what will you do when you want to eat fish? Go and buy it from Safeway, imported from Taiwan or something?"

"Yes, that's where I'll buy my fish, at Safeway. And then we'll eat fish at restaurants, that's what we'll do. My friend, he is up to his knees in money, you know that?"

"I'm sure he is," Kenika said, and then took a deep breath. So, the time had come, and there was nothing he could do about it. They were her kids.

"So about their coming over here, whatever, no, I don't think so. I'm tired of hearing them tell me all about how wood has a heartbeat, how spirits hide behind trees, about how you have to whisper and behave around a fucking piece of carved log." He flinched a little, watching her expression, which had gone into an angry condescension. "I don't want that superstitious bullshit in their heads," she went on. "I don't want them fishing with spears or doing any of that. I just don't want them to think it's just so great to go back to living in a grass shack. It's embarrassing."

"I didn't know you felt that way."

"What's next, huh? Is it restoring the monarchy or whatever the hell you see on TV every night, people saying that they owe allegiance only to their queen? Is it some stupid jerk with a fruit in his hand chanting away? Give me a break."

"That would only be a kahuna. They mean no harm."

"Well, for my kids that stuff is harm! I'm telling you that I'm leaving and soon."

"Are you divorcing Keoki?"

She laughed. "Of course! My God, are you so—"

"Backward?"

She stared at him. "Man," she said, "you are something, you are some piece of work. You can't believe how glad I am or how excited I am about getting out of this dump, getting clean of this whole family."

"You didn't think that way when Angela was here."

That statement did not seem to impress her at all. She shook her head and snorted, looking at her nails. "You people belong to some other age. I never met anyone so impractical in my life, and just to let you know, grandpa," and she stressed that word with condescending sarcasm, "what excites me the most is getting them away from you. Hinalea, Jesus." She shook her head and then waved her hands around. "Poisoned fish. At least if it was from Safeway, I could sue. But you? For what?" She paused, thought more. "Hey, I have nothing against you. Go build your canoes and talk to them, fawn over them, whisper, hey, do whatever kind of silly little ritual you like, but you can forget trying to freak the kids out with that from now on."

"I never tried to freak them out. It's just a tradition. It more or less guarantees that we make good canoes."

"Who the hell is 'we?'" she asked. "You and who else? Oh!" and she snapped her fingers. "Of course! Those double-hulled guys. I forgot. Yes, the upswell of ancient tradition, ooga booga Lono and Kane protect me. How cute." She snorted again. "I don't want Ben ending up to be some dumb blala with a can of beer in one hand and a cane knife in the other, like most of his friends'll end up. You never look at those boys and realize what they are. They're a bunch of losers, and believe me, Ben's checking out of that."

He didn't know what to say. He was even a little amazed at the degree of her hatred, so much so that he sat and stared at her, almost numb to the whole thing. Even the idea of trying to defend himself was pointless, he knew. "Do you need any help with the moving?"

She burst out laughing. "My God," she whispered. "That's all you can think of to say?"

"I was offering help."

"No, thanks. What would it be, some crummy clothes, a few pieces of ratty furniture? The hell with that. We're starting over."

"'Kay."

"We're out of here before school starts. Don't trouble yourself about anything. I'll do it." She thought a few more seconds, then said, "I don't mean to be mean about it. I'm just being honest. This man I am involved with has it all, and he's apparently willing to share it with me. He loves the kids and wants the best for them, wants them to have it all, too. Just a stroke of good luck, I guess. It's what I've dreamed of for a long time, and I'm not passing up on this chance."

Then she got up and went to her room, her heels thumping the floor, leaving him sitting there staring at the chair she had sat in. He thought he should feel some indignation, but he did not. If anything he felt the familiar airiness, a kind of nonsubstantiality in his flesh. The notion of trying to fight back against that hatred was so remote that he wondered if his reaction was normal. Beyond what he had just heard, he saw before him a blank span, a strange isolation that now left him with absolutely no one he could identify as his, and he was amazed that this had happened in such a short time, that a house that had once been full of people most of the time would now be empty. But his amazement was more scientific than anything else.

≈   ≈   ≈

One Saturday Loke packed, and a man drove up in a new van. The man did not come into the house. Loke took bags and boxes to the carport, and he loaded them into the back of the van, and then got back in to wait. Loke still had some sense of propriety, because she had each child give Kenika a hug, and promised to let them call from time to time. Then they all climbed into the van and slid the door shut, the children just barely visible as they waved through tinted windows. When they were gone Kenika went into the house, got a beer, and sat down on the couch. He sat there for the remainder of the afternoon, staring at the wall across the room and drinking beer, laboring at some idea of what to do without getting close to anything. His mind did not seem to want to function.

In the days following he did come up with a few things: he still had the relief to work on, he could still stop and talk story with the Marumotos, now so old that they shuffled from here to there with a kind of tortured concentration. One of their children was coming to live with them, and that was good, Kenika thought, because he worried about them alone in the old house. Along with the relief was the business of trying to sell the Wild Cloud, and from time to time he made phone calls in an attempt to get a buyer.

By the time he did get a buyer it was October, and the lawn was three feet high, the hedge twice its normal height, and brush sprouted all along the foundation posts of the house, and became tall enough that at night when it was windy he would be kept awake by the sound of them scraping the outside wall of the house. He arranged for Kalani Chun to do the blessing, and he would be brought to Mr. Marumoto's by his grandson, a high school student. As for the buyer, a man who lived in a house on the beach in Kahala, his interest in the canoe was more just to have one, as he had a catamaran and a speedboat. The price was fifteen thousand dollars, and the man agreed to buy it sight unseen. He had heard of Kenika McKay's work, he said over the phone. As for the blessing, he would do his best to get out there, but if he did not show up, could Kenika leave the canoe in Mr. Marumoto's yard so that he could pick it up at his convenience? Sure, Kenika said, aware that if the man did not show up, it would be an incomplete blessing. But he did not argue. The canoe had languished long enough without water, and even if it would not be used for fishing or for racing, it would at least feel water after the man took it away.

Kenika got it out of the shed and up to Mr. Marumoto's lawn by himself, using a device he had made up out of old bicycle wheels and wood. The canoe weighed three hundred pounds, and he was surprised at how pretty it looked when he came to a stop at the blessing spot and, bathed in sweat and gasping for breath, he tipped the bow of the canoe down so he could work it off the dolly. The refinement of its components, and the finish of it, he thought, were partly Ben's and Pua's work, and he would tell them if he got the chance.

Kalani Chun now bore a strong resemblance to old Kelemeneke Makaila. He walked with a cane, was thin and stooped over, his hair white. His grandson helped him out of the car and led him to the canoe and then opened a folding chair for him to sit on. Then he went back to the car, got out a skateboard, and disappeared zigzagging down the potholed blacktop road, the high-pitched grating of the wheels audible long after he vanished. Kenika stood there before Kalani Chun, and said, "The buyer said he'd try to show up, but I don't know. Maybe he won't."

"'Ass okay," Chun said. Kenika gave him two fifty-dollar bills, which he folded carefully and slid into his pocket. Then Kenika looked around. Nobody. The Marumotos were visiting family in Kaimuki.

"How da family?" Kalani Chun asked.

"Fine, Loke's moved to Hawaii Kai, the twins are back on the mainland. The kupuna back in their apartment."

"Ho, you all alone den?"

"Yeah."

"Any wahines in your life now?"

"No," he said. "I— No."

Kalani Chun stared at him, then nodded. "'S hahd yah? Angela, she—" He thought a moment, then nodded. "'S hahd."

Kenika looked at the canoe. It occurred to him that there might be no more blessings of this sort, in his life anyway, and looked at the old man. "This ceremony," he said. "Do you have it written down?"

"Nah, but relatives, dey know."

"Benny mentioned it wasn't standard. I was wondering how different it is from—"

"Is different," Chun said. "Yah. Dis da way we do um. Odda people do it odda ways."

"It occurs to me that I've been here all this time and I don't know anything," Kenika said. "I don't know the language, I— I mean I feel like I don't know anything."

"Eh, take doctah, 'kay? You tink he one great cook too?"

Kenika laughed. "Okay, I know canoes."

"'Ass one beeg job, 'kay? Cannot be cook and doctah too, ah?"

"'Kay, I got you."

"So les' do dis now, 'kay?"

Kenika stepped back, out to what he imagined to be part of the circle formed by people, if there had been any there, and Kalani Chun took out his salt, and began his chant. Kenika stood and watched while the old man did his work, closed the circle, and gave brains to the Wild Cloud.

≈   ≈   ≈

The only contact he had with Pua and Ben was a Christmas card. He got long letters from the twins, whose husbands were still in the import business. Their children were growing up, were quickly becoming multilingual, played soccer and tennis, loved school. They all wanted to come back to Hawaii, but the whole business of raising the kids and keeping up with Seth and Keith's business galavanting ate up all their time. In fact, this time in their lives was, they admitted, more or less pulling them into family things, to the point that they were lucky if they got to do any traveling. They would figure out how to do it though, promise. In every letter they asked him how he was doing, if he was all right, and when he wrote back, he told them he was fine, even invented upbeat things so they wouldn't worry. I'm growing cherry tomatoes, lilikoi, sweet potatoes. He wasn't, but planned to.

His life settled into a routine in which one day became indistinguishable from the last. He looked around at what was left of all the logs—splintered stumps, long sections that could, if worked properly, be made into a canoe, but he had no heart for it. There were still large slabs of different kinds of wood under the shed, relief-picture material, and so he started two more, one a fanciful woodland scene with plants and wild pigs and birds and then a foreshortened sweep up the swirling grain to mountains in the background, and the other a broadside of two canoes racing, but only the fronts, coming out of a huge wave that would be made from the swirling grain on the left side of the slab. He still had not finished the one he had worked on for what? two years now, but he didn't care. The act of making something was more important than the finished product. All the things he had ever made except The Red Wind had more or less vanished from his mind once they were out of sight, because he always automatically looked to whatever he would make next.

He knew he could do his work at home, but did it at the shed because that was where he had always done his work, and he felt a familiar comfort there.

At home he would sometimes cook fish and rice for himself, would keep himself stocked up on poi and bags of frozen laulau from Safeway, but as time went on, he did this less and less. Three or four times a week he would take home a plate lunch from either the Korean barbecue down in the little shopping center, or from Andy's Drive-In downtown. He would sit and watch movies or sports on TV and drink beer, usually twelve or more cans a night. Sometimes days would go by without his speaking to anyone, and the only predictable contact he had with people came in the form of his visits to George and Irene, and months away, the canoe season, during which he would help with the coaching if asked.

He made halfhearted attempts to control the almost otherworldly growth in the yard, hacking away with his machete and bagging up grass and cuttings, but it was as if he would place the stuff out on the street for the refuse guys, walk back into the house, and find that it had all grown up again while his back was briefly turned.

Working on reliefs and helping Jerry Cambra coach left him with time, and on those days he did not go to the shed, he began walking the beaches, vaguely thinking that by luck he would run into Keoki, talk to him, and bring him home. He fantasized about that—the boy would be through with drugs, he would come home and they would work at the shed, some arrangement where Keoki would be able to see Ben and Pua would be made, and then some semblance of a family might spark and then take fire. He knew this was not likely, but would park the car in Kahaluu, or Kaaawa, or way out near Kaena Point, drag out his fishing gear and begin walking, looking at the people, sometimes stopping to ask them if they knew of a Keoki McKay. No one did. It was as if he had vanished off the face of the earth. Besides, now he would be thirty-four years old, and Kenika wondered if he would even recognize him. And that thought made him realize that Ben and Pua were growing up without his even seeing them.

He imagined that he watched Ben and Pua growing up, but only through watching the kids from the canoe club: Keoni, Junior, Skipper Moniz, who at fourteen or fifteen looked to him as strong as fullgrown men, and Pua at twelve must have resembled those dark little girls with their long, graceful limbs, dark hair and pretty faces.

He thought of existence as a tolerable fog. He did his work, but slowly. He managed to make contact with Mr. Maxwell, who now dealt only in Pacific artifacts, wooden masks and spears from New Guinea, carved animals and so forth. Maxwell looked frail and sick, but he was impressed by the two relief pictures that Kenika struggled out of the old car, and promised to try to sell them for him. Price, he said, he would negotiate up, but couldn't promise anything. Kenika told him he would stay in touch, and shook his hand, which felt warm, bony and soft. Then he left, and more or less forgot about the reliefs because he had started two new ones.

The apologetic letters continued to come from the twins, and he wrote back that he understood, their families came first. He told them what he was doing, and again lapsed into a positive over-exaggeration of how things were going with him. How they were going he could tell by looking in the mirror: he was dark, gaunt, and that he drank too much beer was written all over his face. He was fifty-six and had grown tired, and sometimes had strange sensations in the night, of a ticklish, magnetic sweeping away into oblivion. Only the visits by Angela's ghost rescued him from preferring that oblivion.

≈   ≈   ≈

Mr. Maxwell sold one of the reliefs for five thousand dollars, which amazed Kenika, and he drove over to get the check, minus Maxwell's thirty-percent take. So, he would be thirty-five hundred dollars richer. When Mr. Maxwell gave him the check he said, "Listen, I'm handing the business over to a friend. He'll treat you fairly."

"'Kay."

"You've heard of AIDS, I presume?"

"Yeah."

Maxwell laughed. "Okay, of course you're not that isolated. Well, I've got it, just like Rock Hudson."

"I'm sorry," Kenika said. He shook his head, wondering what he could add to that.

"It's all right," he said. "Nobody really knows what to say about those of us who have brought this nasty biblical plague upon ourselves. Certainly it's just punishment for our twisted lifestyle, eh?"

"I'm sorry, really."

Maxwell looked at him. "You know, you were my favorite, from the start. I actually bought one of your model canoes. Still got it at the house."

Kenika nodded. "Well—"

"No, don't say anything. After all you never did, did you?"

He drove home thinking of Maxwell and his disease, and wondered also if Darnay was all right. It seemed as if all the people from the old days were on their way out, and he was left here fumbling with his tools.

While he was watching the news and drinking a beer the phone rang, something that happened rarely. It was Junior Sakata, who said, "We was out wit' da Red Win' practicing fo' rough wattah, an' we crash um onna rocks asai da Moke. We no mean fo' do dat, we—"

"Listen, Junior, was anybody hurt?"

"No. We los' um an' da waves push um at da rocks, den she wen' huli us out, den one beeg wave tchrew um up an' it broke onna rocks. Broke all to pieces. I sorry."

"Which Moke, the left one?"

"Yeah."

"As long as nobody was hurt. Listen, Junior, these things happen. She flipped you out and nobody got hurt. That's all I worry about."

"But da Red Win'," he moaned. Now it sounded as if he had begun to cry. "We no mean fo' do dat."

"It's all right," he said. "These things happen to the best paddlers, really."

"Not mad?"

"No no no, not mad. Look, we'll make another one. Don't worry about it, 'kay?"

"'Kay."

"I want you to tell the other guys not to worry, 'kay?"

"'Kay." There was a silence, and then Junior said, "I caw Ben an' he tell me to caw you an' tell you, an' he say you no be mad."

"I'm not mad. How'd you get his number?"

"He caw. We make it kinda secret so his mom no fine out. I caw 'im up two tchree times a week when she not home."

"Well, look, don't worry about the canoe. Jerry's got the other two, so you can practice. Just tell him what happened so—"

"He wen' Big Islan'."

"Oh. 'Kay, just tell the other guys not to worry. When Jerry gets back, you can work it out."

"'Kay."

He hung up and sat back down on the couch. His mind was full of images of The Red Wind, and he shook his head sadly at the idea that it was gone. But it did flip the boys out because it was a smart canoe. It turned itself over before being heaved by a wave up on those rocks, and he knew them. That part of the island on the outside was a black, barren series of jagged rock formations rising up, and it resembled some forbidding landscape of another planet. It was just around the corner from a beautiful little cove formed by a single square rock separated off the oceanside corner of the island. He and Keoki had fished there a couple times, and he had had to order him not to try swimming out the back side of the cove into the breakers. The waves out there would slam the canoe into nothing, into boards small enough for little coffee tables. Then people would collect what was left of her off the beach at Lanikai and say, what pretty wood, can we use this for something? Can we make picture frames?

As the night wore on he drank beer after beer, unable to erase from his mind the picture of the canoe rising up in a wave and then crashing against those rocks, ama and 'iakos flying up with the spray, the hull twisted and broken to smithereens. But these things happen, he reminded himself. He knew he should eat, but had the appetite for no more than a banana, and then after another beer, he went to bed, flopping down on the oily sheet thinking, I should wash this.

In his sleep he was aware of a consistent pounding, and then whispers, as if Angela might be asking him something, or as if other voices from different directions were trying to keep him awake. The horrible sound of splintering wood shocked him in his flesh, and then the strange hammering sound became a call, a far-off voice he could not recognize or interpret, and then other voices whispered about him, whispered amongst themselves about Kenika, and he could not overhear what it was they said. Powerful desire on the part of something other than himself moved like expanding worms through the hollow portions of his bones. The consistent thumping increased in volume until his flesh hammered, seemed to be shocked with each beat as if surging with an electrical charge. The expansion in his bones pushed outward until he thought they would all shatter, explode through his flesh, but with everything, the hammering and the pressure, there was still that voice from far away.

He sat upright in the bed, his heart slamming and his body bathed in sweat. He wiped his face and looked at the clock. Four-thirty a.m. Outside it was still, heavy, the air sodden. In the distance a dog barked, and then he heard the faint sound of a rooster crowing. He was outside in thirty seconds, running on the spot from the flashlight and pulling the rubber boat out from under the house. But the pontoons were soft, and he flipped it over to find out why. He had placed it on old four-by-fours, and termites had eaten little holes through the heavy rubber. He ran to the tool shed in the backyard and found the patch kit, and on his way out grabbed the seagull motor and set it down on the grass. Then he stopped. "Tides," he whispered. He ran into the house and found the chart. He looked at the previous day—a low high last night just past midnight, which meant a low at six-thirty a.m. That was lucky, because the greatest damage would have been done at the high, but the high was a low high. He had only two hours.

He squirted water into a garbage can, standing there impatiently holding the hose. When it was half full he locked the engine on the side of the can and wound the rope around and tried to start it. Nothing. After fifteen times he opened the tank and sniffed. The gas had turned. Now off in the east he could see the faint, ashy light of dawn. It wouldn't work. Once the tide turned— He kept pulling on the rope, but the motor didn't start, and when he paused, he thought he heard it again, the whispering. Too much beer, he thought.

It was hopeless. If the motor started he would still have to put the patches on and wait for them to dry. Coffee tables, picture frames. He stood looking at the sky in the east, and the vision of people finding those pieces came back—could we make something out of this? It's so pretty, look at the grain—what kind of wood is that? Well, we could make a small coffee table.

He had a coil of strong quarter-inch rope in the shed. He had his innertube float. No, he would not need the float. It would slow him down. Just the rope, his mask and fins, his belt and knife. Gloves too.

There was a cool breeze coming off the ocean, and out toward the Mokes the surface of the water was glassy and flat, a light haze hovering over it. It was still half dark, but he scanned the water looking for wood. Nothing. He put the fins on, and walked backwards into the water, up to his knees. When he turned, he looked once more at the islands and whispered, "I can't do this."

But with that thought came the image of pieces of wood lying in the high-tide line with sodden coconuts and chunks of plastic and disposable diapers, and then people staring down at it—is that koa? Could we sand that and make a plaque for our mailbox to put the number on? Oh, I know, nice door stops.

He churned his way out, aiming for the left-hand side of the left island. The drag against the coil of rope over his shoulder chafed his skin. All the way he scanned the water for wood, but saw none. The breakwater was an extension of the side of the island, and after he made his way through the breakers the bottom dropped away to twenty, then fifty feet, and in the advancing light he could now see it. The waves turned into swells, and the water crashed against the rocks around the little cove on the oceanside corner of the island. He worked his way through the waves coming out of the cove, and inside, floating in the calmer water, he found a ten-foot section of mo'o board with a ridge of split-off koa attached. He left it there, figuring it would stay, and went out to the opening at the back side of the cove and into the deeper water. As soon as he made his way out from the island he heard it, a deep, resonant sound of wood hammering on rock. It was fifty yards or more to his right, in the center back of the island, and he followed the sound, rising and falling in the swells and studying the waves crashing up on the black, jagged rocks.

When he saw it he spit out the snorkel mouthpiece and fought a wave that pushed him at the rocks. The Red Wind rose out of a crevice with the surge of water and then fell, slamming against the rocks, and he was both shocked at its condition and astonished that it still appeared to be in one piece. "Oh God," he said. "Oh my God."

It had no hull walls, but as it rose up again, the stump of its manu-less fore end heaving fifteen feet above the crevice and then pausing like a giant wand, he realized that the hull base was still in one piece. Then, after the wand paused, the canoe fell behind the rocks to that sound of wood on stone, and the shock of the sound hurt his flesh as if someone had struck him. He couldn't stand it. That The Red Wind was apparently in one piece seemed somehow more horrible now, and the grinding shocks of the sound of the wood hitting the stone shot like pain through him, and he could not stop himself from doing it: the next wave pushed him at the rocks, and he watched the swell ahead of him rise up and then blast against the rocks and then sink away in white foam in the crevices, and he moved toward the rocks, feeling the next swell roil at his feet, and then he felt himself rising and being hurled forward, and he put his hands and feet out, staying level in the swell, and a black rock pillar came at him. The contact blasted the wind out of him and he clutched the black rock and gasped for breath, pulled the rope away from the snorkel, and then only ten feet from him the hull of The Red Wind rose up again, and he recognized, through the deep gouges and scrapes, the grain of it, and as the swell washed away he was left hugging the rock, pain searing his chest and legs, waiting for the next one, and he looked down quickly, through the half-fogged lens of the mask, and saw that the skin on his chest had been shredded by the impact. He heard the next swell and pressed himself against the rock, and the water slammed his back and drove his face into the rock, the mask mashing his nose, and then receded, and he pulled himself around the pillar and found himself at the edge of the crevice in which sat the canoe. It was floating free in the foam, but a jutting section of the rock prevented the aft end from rising when the fore did. Because he had worked his way past the face of the rock pillar, the next swell tried to push him into the crevice, and he had to turn and grip the sharp surface to hold himself through the swell, and then The Red Wind rose up again, right before him, and he could almost touch it.

Another wave blasted against his back and tore his grip from the rock, but instead of falling into the crevice he felt the white foam racing powerfully around his legs and hips, and the sharp-edged side of the hull base scraped up the outside of his thigh and then hit him on the hip, but it was enough for him to scramble over to the far side of the crevice. His body flat against the rock, he struggled to get the rope that had uncoiled from his shoulder. It trailed to his right, down a kind of flat incline toward the roiling whitewash at the edge of the rocks. From here he could see more, long pieces of board, part of the pale kai, split sections of hull, the ama higher on the rocks. He saw no seats, and the U-shaped wae spreaders were broken off where the hull walls had been broken off. The Red Wind rose up again, just three feet from him, and he watched it hover and then drop back, then slam against the rocks.

When he finally got his breath he realized how much his body hurt, the skin of his chest searing with the sting of salt, his hands scraped despite the gloves, his forehead cut. The blood on his chest ran down into the fabric of his bathing suit and the outside of his leg was scraped pink, little rivulets of blood running down to his ankle. He was exhausted and trembling, and did not want to move from the rock. The sun was coming up.

The ferocity of the waves had lessened, and now when The Red Wind rose it did not go up as high as it had, but when it receded the slamming of wood on rock was harsher, because there was less water now to hold her up. He tried to make his hands work, to form some kind of a loop to try to put over the shattered end of the canoe. He would try to pull it out at the highest intensity of a set of waves. Once it floated, he should be able to pull it in the water until it was free of that jutting rock and it could slide away over the flatter section, but once it was on its way, there would be no way to stop it. He had to take the chance.

The other pieces were higher up in the rocks. He wrapped the rope around the rock he held onto and then, fumbling with the knife, cut off a ten-foot section. Then he pulled himself up the rocks toward the ama, again trembling with fatigue and gasping for breath, banging his knees, his feet sliding inside the fins. He got the ama, two long sections of hull wall, a large section of the pale kai and another section of mo'o board, and then scanned the rocks for more. He pulled the pieces together and wrapped the rope around them, his hands shaking. When he was finished he realized that this awkward bundle was too heavy to carry, so he tried sliding it toward the flat section of rocks. The pain from the cuts and scrapes was such that he became anxious to get back in the water.

He tried pulling the bundle, scraping it over the rocks. When it got to the flat incline it began to slide on its own, and he held it back, studying the water at the bottom of the incline. There he saw more pieces of wood bouncing in the foam. That meant that anything he got to that water would stay there. In fact that was how the mo'o board got into the cove—it was at the edge of that roiling white water. He took a deep breath, and then pushed the bundle and it slid down, then ran into an incoming wave, heaved up to vertical, at which the rope binding it snapped and all the boards fell into the foam.

He felt almost too weak to move. The Red Wind rose up again and slammed down. He worked his way back to the crevice, falling once on his hip, but on a smooth rock. When he got back to the rock jutting up to the crevice he untied the rope and tried making a lasso. He began to giggle at how badly his hands worked, fumbling at the knot, but when it was finished he shook off the fatigue and waited for the hull to come up again. Once more The Red Wind rose up, and he flipped the loop over the stump of its fore end and jerked it tight.

With the rope secured on the nose, he stepped away from the rock toward the incline, but it was so slippery that he fell on his hands and knees. He managed to hold onto the rope, and waited. Again the slamming of wood against stone echoed out of the crevice, and he gritted his teeth, then rose to his knees. He saw the swell, and waited for it to wash into the crevice, and with it The Red Wind came up. He pulled on the rope, and the nose moved a foot toward him, and he felt the scraping in the rope. The swell was not finished. The nose rose another foot, and he pulled at the rope, and then fell back. The shattered fore end rose straight over him, hovered a second, and then the hull came down. He rolled out of the way as it slammed down and swept past him, hissing and grating on the incline. When it was past he let go of the rope, and the canoe knifed into the foam and then surfaced upside down, rolled on its side, and bobbed in the water with the other pieces.

He felt a surge of exhilaration, and began working his way down the incline. He continued to shake with fatigue, but felt a powerful desire to get in the water, and allowed himself to slide down the incline. He hit nothing when he went in, and the coldness instantly shut off the pain. He bobbed in the foam, then swam to the fore end of The Red Wind and got the rope. On his way to the other pieces he was hit gently on the head by something, and grabbed it—the fore manu with a foot of its neck, as smooth as the day he had varnished it.

It took a long time to lash all the pieces to the hull. By that time he was so tired that he would pause and hang in the water, gaping down at the bubbles and, during sudden calms, the coralheads and rocks angling down into the gritty rubble on the bottom. He went to the foreend and grabbed the rope, and began churning toward the cove. The bottom did not move under him. He worked his legs, pulling the rope, and then saw the bottom begin to inch slowly, and knew that as long as he maintained the pressure, the momentum would increase.

He was afraid that The Red Wind would be too long to turn in the cove, so he left it at the mouth and went in for the mo'o board. He also found another long section of hull, and took them out to lash to the canoe.

Towing it in, he thought he slept. He had no energy left, and the pressure he was able to maintain on the rope was so small that he wondered if he moved at all. Bright fish darted under him, and gentle swells urged him forward. He closed his eyes and worked his legs, now numbed to the pain and dreaming. He was dimly aware that his heart might stop, but could do nothing about it. The ocean lifted him and allowed him to settle, the pressure on the rope pulled back and then relaxed as the waves pushed The Red Wind forward. A third of the way toward the shore he swept over coralheads and saw more fish, then a sea turtle that placidly moved out of his way as he passed. Then, in what felt like a currentless dead spot, he went into that region of marginal consciousness where voices came to him through the water, soft whispers in soothing tones, almost like singing. He was being accompanied by others who urged him forward although he had no more strength to pull, and he felt the rope slacken, then go tight, saw the bottom inch under him. He could not fix his direction because he could not lift his head from the water, but thought vaguely that the current would carry him just a little bit west, as it had so long ago when he caught the ulua. But it didn't matter. The comfortable delirium felt so good that he thought it might be a disappointment to reach the shore, and he hummed low in his throat with each breath.

After a long period of that strange half-sleep, he saw the sand slowly coming up to meet him, the water becoming hazy, and forced his head out into the air. He did not recognize where he was—there were two huge new stucco houses with tiled roofs looming behind the beach, which was thirty yards away. A few people sat on towels, others walked or jogged along on the sand. Jerry Cambra's house was hundreds of yards to the left. Now that he was close to shore all the abrasions and cuts began to sting, and he tried to pull himself out of his dizziness. His legs barely worked. His gloved hand, clutching the rope, had seemingly cemented itself into a fist.

But the waves pushed The Red Wind forward, and soon his knees scraped the sand. He turned back, and draped his arm over the canoe, his fist still locked on the rope. He pushed the canoe forward, and its fore end nosed into the sand. When he rose from the water onto his knees and pulled the snorkel from his mouth he saw the blood begin to ooze off his chest and legs, and felt it run down into the corner of his mouth. He could not stand up, and stayed on his knees in the shorewash. Voices came from different directions, and the water nudged him, and he rose and turned, and sat there still holding the rope. With his left hand he peeled his fingers one by one off the rope. People were around him.

"—a log? He pulled a log in."

"It's not a log," he said. "It's a canoe."

The voices seemed flat and harsh, and he sat trying to make his eyes focus, trying to make himself get up. One man was leaning down to him. Doctor? Did he want to be taken to the clinic?

"No."

Before him were thick, hairy legs. He looked up. "Could you help me get this up on that lawn there?"

They were boys, two haoles with curly hair. They looked strong. Hey, it was no problem for them.

Then it was four of them. When they lifted The Red Wind out of the water, Kenika struggled to his feet, wanting to help, but found himself half-draped over the hull stumbling with them, steadying the parts lashed to it. When they set it down on the lawn a woman came out of the back door of the stucco house, then two children, a boy and girl. He looked down and saw that he had dripped blood on the wood, and the woman, trying to figure out what was going on, stepped closer, saw it and grabbed her kids. "Don't touch that!" she snapped. "Stay away."

Kenika took his gloves off and put them on the hull. "I have to leave this here for a while. Would that be okay?"

"I'll have to ask my husband," she said. She sounded suspicious and frightened. One of the curly-haired boys went over and spoke to her. Kenika imagined that he was negotiating in his favor, and she appeared to grudgingly accept.

Another boy held a towel to him. "Here, take this, wrap it around yourself."

"No, that's all right."

"It's okay," he said. "It's only a towel."

"Thanks."

"Is this your canoe?"

"Yes."

The boy who had talked to the woman came over. "She says it's okay, just to move it into the weeds there," and he pointed to a hedge next to which odd pieces of lumber and stones were piled in high grass. "Mainlanders," the boy said. "That's why they built that ugly piece of shit. Hey, your head's got a bad cut."

"I'll go over to the clinic."

"Need any help? We can take you."

"No, that's okay. Hey, thanks for the towel."

"You go ahead. We'll swing the canoe over."

He walked along the wall out the right-of-way with his hand on it for balance.

When he got to the clinic downtown, he found that he was too stiff and sore to get out of the car right away, and the receptionist and doctor came out. The doctor peered in, looked at his forehead and then at the bloody towel around his trunk. "Woah," he said. "What have we here?"

He slept for two days through dreams whose background sound was a steady thumping, an even, familiar beat, and was visited by rich images of canoes, of people of the present and those long gone like Benny and Momi and Kelemeneke Makaila, and then Angela settling over him in a warm blast of her breath, and often he felt a sweeping in which salt air blew over his face, a strange ticklish soaring which he knew to be the sensation a canoe had when parting the water under twelve strong arms. He got up only to check on the bandages and take the antibiotics prescribed as a hedge against infection, and to eat what he could find in the refrigerator, half-consumed plate lunches and fruit. He had a trailer, and prepared a space for The Red Wind in the narrow strip of grass between the hedge and the house. Each time he woke up he found that he was so stiff that it took five minutes of slow movement to limber himself up enough to get to the bathroom.

On the third day, still sore and weak, he drove through rain to Lanikai towing the trailer, and after an hour of struggling, during which he tugged at the long hull until blood began to bloom like flowers on his gauze bandages, he brought The Red Wind home.

≈   ≈   ≈

He routed tongues and grooves in pieces that could not be matched to the hull, collected leftover pieces he found under the shed, cast-off chunks of wood he recognized as being from the original log, the surfaces now silvered by the quarter-century of their storage. Each time he took a chisel to that wood and peeled off the surface so that it rose up and curled away ahead of the blade, he was amazed that the same fiery hue remained underneath, as if there had been no passage of time. But as he recovered, his desire to repair the canoe faded.

He did not put any more than an hour or two a week into the restoration. As if some other directive drove him, he put his fishing gear into the car and drove to one beach after another, and spent day after day wandering, looking dully at the junk in the high-tide line and then staring off into the salt-misted distance for Keoki or anyone else he might know. The calm solitude reminded him of that time when he was recovering from the eel bite and wandered without any purpose along the beaches, both wishing to run into someone and at the same time hoping not to.

He still had his responsibility to the old folks, and visited them once every two weeks or so. They were now both in their eighties and very frail, and had attached themselves to a church whose minister was an enthusiastic Baptist in his fifties. The man had pink skin and hair dyed so black that it appeared to have been dipped in ink, and Kenika had difficulty believing that anyone could look at him without a kind of astonishment. In addition to that, some of the possessions that had some antique value vanished from the grandparents' little apartment, and he learned that they had "donated" them to the church. Apparently a lot of old folks in the building had done the same, and he suspected the minister's motives. But Angela's parents appeared blinded to the man's apparent greed. They now spoke in soft wheezes, and only of things in the present, and he wondered how much exactly they remembered of the old days, if the image of Angela were as fresh in their minds as it was in his.

At least they were comfortable, he reasoned, and after all, things were only things and it didn't really matter that objects of sentimental value were being taken away, especially if they had trouble even remembering why something had that value.

Two days a week he went to the shed to work on the relief picture. The other days he walked the beaches. He put his hour or two a week into the restoration of The Red Wind, which now sat on wooden cradles next to the house, covered with blue tarp, only feet from where he slept. With each improvement, each piece carefully fitted into the hull, he was aware of a sensation of a peculiar security or comfort as he slept, as if the canoe slept safe next to him like a gradually healing child.

Up the Pali Highway, Jim Berger's head swiveling sideways every three seconds to say something to Mommy, and Pua looks back back back. Can still see the marsh, the buildings in Kailua and the ocean beyond that, and ahead the tunnel sits black under the green face of the mountain, and Pua looks, her eyes huge, at the ocean behind us, and then Jim Berger's head swivels, he nods, and Mommy sits sideways with her elbow over the seatback, and smiles. The baseball glove sits on top of a Huggies box full of clothes, and rocks with the motion of the van. Pua looks at you, her mouth open like she is about to say something, but she doesn't. She looks back back back.

"Can we go fishin' at dakine Hawaii Kai?" she asks.

Mommy's eyebrows up, and Pua says, "Can we?"

Mommy laughs.

Pua looks back and now the van turns and part of Kailua goes out behind the mountain.

"We no mo' hafta see um."

"Who?" Pua asks.

"You know."

The tunnel expands, and whoosh in the van goes so you look at the squiggly lines of spray-can letters racing by. Pua looks back at the tunnel opening. Right in the middle of the opening is Flat Island, off the Kailua boat ramp. Her eyes are so big.

"I like get on one baseball team," you say.

Pua doesn't hear because she is crying, looking back at the bright, shrinking opening of the tunnel behind.

≈   ≈   ≈

He got a phone call from Ben. Everything was fine. Ben was going to college, to UCLA. Kenika congratulated him for that, and asked about Pua. "If she isn't a millionaire by the time she gets out of high school," Ben said, "she'll be disappointed."

"Why?"

"Hey, she's a model," Ben said. "You don't see her much here, more on the mainland and Japan. She's got an agent and everything."

"She's only sixteen."

"Michael Jackson was a billionaire by that time. So really, how is everything?"

Kenika launched into the same upbeat explanation of his life that he used in the now less-frequent letters to the twins. Sure, he was working along at the shed, was planning another canoe, which he was not. Almost hectic, he told him.

"Two things," Ben said. "The good one is this—one of your relief things is in the judiciary building downtown, hanging on a wall."

"Really."

"I asked the guy where they got it, and he said the state routinely buys art, and this probably came from some private collector."

"I'll have to go down and look."

"You should. Your name is on it, too."

"I wonder what they paid for it."

"You know, Keoni told me about The Red Wind."

Kenika paused. He was about to say, I went out and got it, but decided not to. If anything he felt a little foolish about having done that and paid the physical price he did, so he said, "Yeah, that was too bad. Nobody's fault though."

"We always want to come out and see you, but Mom, well, she's got this thing about—"

"I know. Don't worry about it. She's had her troubles, and right now I wouldn't do anything to upset her."

"There's something else," Ben said. Then there was a pause, and Kenika knew it was something about Keoki, and a flash of horrible terror went through him. He was dead.

"I— What?"

"I saw Dad."

"Is he okay? That's all I was—"

"Sort of. Grandaddy, he didn't recognize me. Or at least I don't think he did."

"Where did you see him?"

"Downtown Honolulu, just Ewa of Fort Street, you know, the top of the old honky-tonk?"

"I'll go look for him."

There was another long pause. Kenika felt his heart beating rapidly, and he had the sudden impulse to run out the door to the car and drive over there. "Well, to tell you the truth he looks pretty bad," Ben said. "I mean dirty, disoriented, all that. He just walks around."

"Did you talk to him?"

"Yeah. I mean I tried to but he— He didn't seem to know me. I mean he talked a little, but he just didn't seem to be looking at me."

"I'll look for him."

He could hear Ben breathing, but he didn't say anything else. "Is something else wrong?"

"You know, I saw him a couple times when we were in Kailua, down by Aikahi walking along North Kalaheo, another time walking toward Waimanalo. I was with some friends? I knew who he was but went right by."

"But that was years ago."

There was another long silence. Finally Ben said, "I know. Shame, that's why. I shoulda told you."

"That's all right. You had a reason not to, I guess."

"I mean during those years I was afraid he'd come home."

"I know what you mean. It's understandable."

"I wish—"

"I know. I do too."

"Anyway," he said. "I swear we're coming over to visit you sometime, but—"

"Good you're goin' to college though."

"I guess."

"What's your major?"

Ben went on to explain that his mother's program for him was pre-law. The opportunities in Hawaii in that profession were endless, and down the line, Ben looked like the perfect candidate for something like the state senate. Ben laughed at the idea. "I don't have any interest in that stuff," he said. "I remember something you told us once, up at the shed. You said that you thought it was better to make something. I told Mom about that, and she said, 'Yeah, money.'"

"I told you that?"

"Yeah, a lot of other stuff too."

"I guess I kind of remember."

"And Mom, the more money she's got, the more she wants."

"Well," Kenika said. He went on to more or less defend Loke, and reminded Ben to remember what she had had to go through years ago, and how it takes a long time for stuff like that to fade away. "She just wants the best for you, that's all," he finally said.

Within another minute they hung up. Kenika checked the clock, five p.m. The rush hour would be over soon. He patted his pocket for his keys and went to the car.

A few years earlier Fort Street had been changed into a walking mall, and he had to drive around to find a place to park, inching along until he saw someone in a business suit jump into a BMW and pull out. Then he went and checked out the mall, and went partway down Hotel Street. The first derelict he saw was too short to be Keoki, but the vision of him scared Kenika. The man looked very busy, running from a shopping cart full of junk to a corner and back, animatedly talking to no one. He had stuffed either toilet paper or kleenex into both ears, and he was barefoot, his feet black with grime.

The two or three other homeless people he saw were more languid, sitting next to their carts full of dirty clothes and watching the people go home from work. One, off in the distance, stood staring to the west, leaning on a long cane, and he wore a heavy coat despite the heat. His copper-black hair was matted in back and hung all the way down to his waist, and even though he wore the heavy clothes, he was barefoot. The man then turned, and Kenika squinted, then began walking in his direction. He passed a line of dark men squatting in the narrow strip of shade in front of a Chinese herb shop. He nodded to the men, and picked up his pace. The heavily-dressed man seemed tall enough, but looked older than Keoki would be.

When he got within twenty feet he recognized him. His face was very dark and he was bearded, and his eyes appeared bloodshot. Keoki then looked at him and opened his mouth to speak. Some of his teeth were missing.

"Brah," he said. "Can you gi' me one dollah?"

"Keoki," Kenika said. "Listen—"

"Jus' one dollah."

Kenika fumbled in his wallet and pulled out a dollar, which Keoki took. He drew a little purse out of his pocket and with the cane held in the crook of his arm fumbled with it, then stuffed the dollar in. "Keoki," Kenika said. "I've been looking all over for you. I want you to come home."

"I no go back dat room."

"What room?"

"I no go back."

"Keoki, do you know me?"

"I no go back dat room."

He turned to walk away, and Kenika stepped around in front of him. "Here," he said, drawing out his wallet. "Lemme give you another—"

He took two tens out, all he had. Keoki's eyes widened a little and then he took them, and again drew out the little purse, which he fumbled with slowly, staring down at the money he pushed in with his dirty finger. Kenika could now smell him, a rich, oily odor of sweat and grime and foul breath. Kenika put his hand out to touch him and he backed away, still fussing with the purse. "I'm Kenika, don't you remember? I'm Dad."

"I no go back dat room," he said.

He walked up Hotel Street toward the Fort Street Mall. Kenika followed him. Ahead he saw two policemen, and wondered if he could reason with them about Keoki's condition. But he had heard the story before. Keoki was a grown man and no one could tell him what to do.

"Keoki," he said, walking beside him. "I'll make a deal with you. Come with me and I promise you'll never go to that room."

Keoki stopped. He still fumbled with the purse, trying to work the latch, and when Kenika moved to face him he turned slowly, like a child protecting a toy. Kenika put his hand on the grimy sleeve, and Keoki looked up with muddled alarm, and there Kenika saw something that stopped him, so that he stood there gaping open-mouthed at his son: still evident through the beard and the dirt was the beautiful boy, and the alarm had transformed Keoki's eyes—they were Angela's, huge and brown and now questioning, as if surprised that he should be accosted this way by a total stranger.

Keoki moved on and Kenika walked beside him, trying to think of what to say. Keoki now seemed irritated with his presence, and the two of them walking had drawn the attention of the two policemen.

"No chase me!" Keoki said, walking faster. "No t'row rocks at me!"

"Can I come see you again?"

"No, I no go back dat room!"

One of the policemen stepped toward them, and Kenika stopped while Keoki went on.

"Sorry," Kenika said. "Do you know that man?"

"Yah," the cop said. "Eh, he hahmless. But you cannot try prevent him from going wheah he likes, 'kay?"

As he drove home he went over various plots to see Keoki again, figuring that if he did not recognize his father, he would after a while, even if it was in the form of a new acquaintance.

When he got home, feeling a fatigue creep over him, he wandered out in the twilight to The Red Wind, pulled part of the tarp off, and then put his hands on the still-shattered fore end. He closed his eyes and whispered, "Oh God, the poor boy, the poor boy." It was not merely drugs or rebellion or an alternative lifestyle. The most horrible of all things had happened: he had lost his memory and his identity.

He could not give up on at least maintaining him. The next day he grabbed some money from the drawer, figuring that twenty would be enough this time. Maybe twice each week he would go give him a little more, enough that he would not have to eat out of garbage cans. Keoki might grow to trust him, and then some little wires and resistors in his brain would connect up and he would remember. He went over to Fort Street to find him, the money in his front pocket so that he would not have to mess with his wallet when he gave it to him. But Keoki was not there. He asked a couple of the other derelicts if they had seen him, and one man, a haole in fatigues, said that Keoki had simply moved on and there was no telling when he'd be back. As to where, the man said that he should try Waikiki at night, or Ala Moana Park at night.

So he waited, got something to eat at a little plate-lunch place downtown, and then drove over to Waikiki. He had assumed that he would be able to park on Kuhio Avenue as he had years ago whenever they went to Waikiki, but when he drove in there he was amazed at the effect of the continuing development since he had last been there for the kids' regattas. Fifteen and twenty and thirty-story hotel buildings crowded the sidewalks, and he could see no grass as he drove through. He parked on Ala Wai Boulevard instead, and walked down Seaside Avenue, then over to Royal Hawaiian Avenue toward the Kalakaua strip. He supposed the cottage would no longer be there, and it was not. Instead there was another tall building.

He walked the length of the Waikiki strip three times, looking for Keoki. He did see derelicts here and there, but then almost forgot his reason for coming in the first place. Prostitutes ambled along the sidewalk, very pale and wearing short skirts and boots, mesh stockings and low-cut tops. And there were a lot of police, tourists, tall buildings, and the features of the Waikiki of the old days, lei stands and tiki torches and open grassy areas fronting various businesses, were gone, replaced by expensive shops with brass-decorated doorways, pocketbooks and three-piece suits and jewelry in the windows, and then every block an ABC convenience store, so that as he walked, he began getting a strange, almost comical, deja vu sensation, as if each block were a replica of the last. The prostitutes did not approach him, probably because of the more or less businesslike way he walked and because of the way he dressed, with faded corduroy shorts and a tank top. He stopped only a few times, once before the still magnificent facade of the Moana Hotel, now fronted by stretch limousines with gold fittings, Japanese tourists in black suits making their way inside. He did go across to the beach entry at the Diamond Head end, and trudged through the sand most of the length of Waikiki. There were more derelicts and tourists and police. The hotel buildings were so tall that the sensation he got was of the beach sitting at the base of a three-hundred foot cliff, crowded by the looming mass so that sound was peculiarly muffled, or made into a strange, dreamlike echo off the planes of concrete and glass. Driving home, he felt a strange semi-dizziness, the sensation resulting from overstimulation of his senses, the feeling he used to have after seeing a loud double feature when he was really too tired to do that.

≈   ≈   ≈

He made periodic visits to Fort Street and Waikiki, and to the other places he suspected Keoki might show up, but to no avail. If there was anything positive about the whole thing, it was that the phone call from Ben opened up a sporadic communication between Kenika and both Ben and Pua. Ben was in college in California, Pua was at an expensive private school, and also doing modeling in California. One day Kenika got a large manila envelope in the mail, and drew out a magazine called You, and Pua's picture was on the cover. She was very thin, dressed in a slinky satin dress which draped over small breasts, but her face had that same regal beauty that came from Angela, especially the eyes. The letter enclosed described the hectic pace of her life and resembled the letters he got from Clarice and Elizabeth, at least in the implied message that she did not have time to visit. He stared at the picture a long time, looking for Keoki and Loke in the features, but ended up seeing Angela, probably because the face he looked at was a more or less emaciated version of the prototype of the Polynesian beauty. He noted with a dim stab of satisfaction that the name next to the photograph read "Pua McKay."

He went and looked at the maps. There, on the world map, in a place he would never go, were the twins. On the Oahu map, Keoki stumbling around in downtown Honolulu. Now, Ben in California, Pua there in the summers. It impressed him that the circumstances of her work had in effect exported Pua to the mainland. It was obviously her beauty that they wanted. He could imagine people in California looking at photographs of Pua and thinking, this is unique, exotic beauty, this goes on the cover, and then those same people considered what other things they might want from the same tiny string of islands, and he supposed that they could not look at the place without thinking that they had to have a part of it for themselves. In their minds they easily laid claim to whatever their romantic notions concocted: the style of life, maybe land, a hideaway, Oriental or Polynesian beauties to pay to have fun with, and of course the opportunity to exploit the beautiful place. There must be fortunes to be made there in real estate or in somehow tapping into the tourist industry. After all, rich Japanese businessmen had already bought up a good part of it. Why don't I get some of that action?

He stared at the world map and squinted. In his imagination all land was now water, and all water land. Connection with the outside world had established a kind of canal from Hawaii to the USA. There was a great quantity of water the USA was made of, so it crashed through the canal to Hawaii and filled it up as the smaller quantity that was Hawaii emptied into the USA and dispersed into the cities and deserts, its beauty and identity vanishing into the vastness of that continent. The twins, now Ben and Pua. Whatever there was that remained of Hawaii before the canal you found in odd pockets, in prisons or on beaches or in old neighborhoods like his own. Or wandering around dirty and confused, like Keoki.

≈   ≈   ≈

The strange insularity of his life would occur to him especially when he watched the news on TV and there would be stories about homeless people in tents at Makapuu Beach Park or Makua, and then people talking of sovereignty for Hawaiians, reparations for the theft of their nation. There were stories about occupations of land under development for highways. He saw Lehua Makaila often because she was elected to the state House of Representatives and was well-known as a kind of mainstream activist, and popular with local people because of her unyielding political stance and her classic, mature Polynesian beauty. Benny would have loved it. Many of the things he had done in the fifties, things he had seemingly made a fool of himself for, were now done routinely. Kenika thought of himself as having no politics, but sided anyway with the beach squatters and with anyone else protesting development on state lands that should have belonged to Hawaiians. It was not for him to do anything about it, but he was aware of the real reasons those people camped on the beaches. They had no place else to go. The house he and Angela had bought for that whopping sum years ago, and which he had sold for far more, had a For Sale sign on the front lawn, and he went down one Sunday afternoon during open house time to find out what they wanted for the house. The fact sheet said that it was a bargain at four-hundred thousand dollars. The only difference with the house was that the previous owners had tacked on two bedrooms, a bath, and surrounded it with a rock wall.

He asked the real estate dealer why the price was that high, and got an enthusiastic speech about the greatest sustained real estate boom ever. It was just a great time to be in the business. By the way, did Mr. McKay own a home in the area? Really? You should refinance. Kenika told him that he owned the house outright, and got another speech about the lucky position he was in because of that.

Just as he had found it odd that at the prison when they had gone to visit Keoki he saw only local people, Hawaiians and various dark mixes, he now saw that when he walked the beaches and passed those elaborate tents built of bamboo and blue tarps, that the people inside were Hawaiians, or various mixes.

With no success at finding Keoki in Honolulu, he began looking for him again at the beaches. His silent walks along the different beaches took him one day to Waimanalo, and as he walked that bay, studying the water and deciding whether or not he wanted to make the quarter-mile swim to the breakwater, he ended up near Sea Life Park, and in the distance could see the cluster of tents and blue tarps, centered by an upside down Hawaiian flag on a long bamboo pole; the signal for distress, the TV had said. He kept on walking, around the jetty and research shed near Sea Life Park, then along a short bay to the beginning of the tent area. When he got to within a hundred yards of the tents he stopped, and decided to look in the water in the little bay. He had fished there before, and it was a good spot for palani and other cattlefish. There was no point in invading the territory of those people—they moved around their tents, cooked, and the kids played in the tide pools at the other end of the little bay.

Then he remembered Keoki. What if he had taken up with someone in that group? If he somehow had made his way back into the ocean and awakened something? He decided to walk the beach between the tents and water just to check. So he walked on, carrying his gear. Between the tents and the water were black rocks jutting out of dry dunes, and he walked over the dunes, looking at the people. The women wore either cut-off jeans and tank tops or pareos, and dark children ran all over. Inside the tents he could see the shapes of men and hear radios playing Hawaiian music.

Halfway he saw a dark, burly man with gray hair watching him, then walking parallel with him, but closer to the tents. He moved on, thinking, look, this is a public beach. But the man stayed with him, narrowing the angle until he was only fifteen feet away. "Brah!" he said.

"Yeah?"

The man approached, and Kenika studied him, thought that he had seen him somewhere before, but had no idea where that might have been.

The man stepped on something that hurt his foot, then picked something out of it and stood up straight. "Shit," he said, "I step on one tack. Eh, I know you."

It was Junior Kaaiai.

"McKay da canoe man," he said.

"Junior, howzit?"

"Come, come," he said. Junior stepped to Kenika and put out his hand. "Long time ago I heah 'bout Angela. So sad." He looked straight at Kenika's face. "Funny, you get gray hair too. No opu like mine but," he said, patting his stomach. "Come da tent." Kenika followed him. Under the blue tarp it was cool, and Junior pointed to a lawn chair set in the sand. The woman who was apparently Junior's wife looked warily at Kenika, and Junior whispered, "He braddah, braddah, family, no worry."

Talking story. He sat there for three hours, ate tako poke and ahi poke and potato chips, and drank five beers. Junior had spent the past forty years or so on Maui, working as a maintenance man for a small beach hotel which had become a big beach hotel. Japanese investors bought it and he was fired, after those forty years. No pension, no mo' notting. He and his family came back to Oahu to see what there was for them here. What there was for them here was an apartment they could not afford to rent and finally, this beach, and when periodically the police came around to order them off, they would go out to Waianae or Makua and camp there. As for jobs, sure, he could get five dollars an hour in a fast-food joint, or cut people's lawns, but that would be not enough for a little shack that cost a quarter of a million dollars, would it?

"If I had to buy my house I wouldn't be able to afford it," Kenika said.

"Even wit' da canoes?"

"Not even close. When we bought our house it was about three and a half canoes. The same house today would be about twenty-five canoes, and it would take thirty-five years to make twenty-five canoes."

Junior laughed, then as quickly, frowned uncertainly. "We had a good life dere," he said. "But it got spoiled."

"It got spoiled here too once people saw a chance to make money. Statehood was just the beginning." He went on to explain Angela's lei shop business and the changes in Kailua since the fifties. After that they both filled each other in on family things. Junior had four children, three now living on the mainland, one in jail at Halawa, who left four kids, and he swept his hand around at the bright opening of the tent, where two of them were playing. He had twelve grandchildren. Kenika nodded. Yeah, Halawa, that was what happened to Keoki, and he went on about him and about the twins and their grandchildren, then about Ben and Pua.

"So you alone den?" Junior asked.

"Right now, yeah. Some day though, I think the twins might come back, I mean after they get tired of the world."

Junior got the same look of frowning uncertainty, and said, "I don't know 'bout dat. My keeds, I— I don't know 'bout dat."

The company of Junior was such a stimulant that he worked at the shed with more enthusiasm, worked on The Red Wind with a focus he had not felt in years, to the point that he was three-quarters done with the reconstruction. He took days off to go over to Makapuu and fish with Junior and his grandchildren, and felt the presence of family again, even though it was somewhat remote.

One coincidence occurred while Kenika and Junior were talking in the presence of Junior's granddaughter Kim, who was a pretty, somewhat stocky, fifteen-year old with long, curly copper hair. Kenika mentioned Ben and Pua and she giggled and said, "Pua McKay."

"Yeah, that's her name," Kenika said.

"Same as Pua McKay," she said.

"No, I mean she models. Are we talking about the same—"

"Not," she gasped. "Fo' real?"

"Really."

Every girl in Hawaii knew who Pua McKay was. Kim went on about how a friend of hers went to school with her and was in the same hula class with her, how they even had gone to movies together.

"I think she's too skinny," Kenika finally said.

"Not," Kim said. "She da mos' beautiful of all. Ho, she so cool."

"Well, I still think she's too skinny."

The little tent village was in constant danger of being closed down by the state, and as it grew in size so did the speculation about it on TV. He wondered where the people would go if they were evicted. He got an idea, and began picturing Junior and his family staying in the house if they needed a place to stay. Junior was family. He knew also that making any offer like that had the potential for being a kind of insult, but went ahead and cleaned the house anyway, thinking that at least they could come over and eat some of the fish that now crowded the freezer, or maybe teriyaki done on the hibachi outside.

He began to feel that the isolation and distance he had felt was being narrowed, if not by Junior and the comfort he felt sitting in that tent with his family, then by the connection he now had with Pua and Ben. He wrote to them although he did not really know what to write to a model or to a boy who would become a lawyer. When he wrote to the twins he described what was going on with Pua and Ben, and in the few letters he got back he had the sensation of connection reinforced. He could look at the Hawaii map, or the world map, and see lines between that little spot designating the house, moving outward toward locations only miles away, then thousands of miles away, but they were like lines in a spider web, all leading to his house. Keoki had no line, would probably never have one, and he had to accept that for now, although he hated it.

≈   ≈   ≈

In late winter he got word that a wave of Asian flu had run its course through the retirement facility where George and Irene lived, and both had come down with it and both died, quietly, of congestive heart failure. George went first, and Mr. Nolan, the minister of their church, did not know for sure if Irene even understood that he had. In any case she was very sick, and passed away one day later. We were all shocked, Nolan said. They were so sweet. Nolan went on to praise them for their generosity to the church, that Mrs. Nolan was in tears for a full day after learning of their deaths. As per the old couple's wishes, the church would handle all the arrangements for their funeral and burial. Would Mr. McKay alert all family members about those arrangements? Sure, Kenika said.

What little they had, after the costs of medical maintenance at the facility, they had donated to the church, and although there would be a reading of the will, Nolan was sure that there was little if anything that would need Mr. McKay's attention. Interesting small mementoes, he said, were being kept in a church collection—old things like a couple of poi pounders and some odd stone tools, some bone hooks, pieces of jewelry that had been in the family since the nineteenth century, these would all be kept by the church and from time to time displayed for educational purposes. And as Mr. McKay knew, of course, the apartment itself became the property of the facility upon the passing of its occupants.

Kenika did his best to alert the family, but he was aware that after all the folks were over ninety and the twins, far away as they were, would not be able to get to Hawaii for the funeral. Ben and Pua might, but then he wondered if Loke would scoff at the idea of their having anything to do with it. Since the funeral would happen immediately he decided to write letters rather than call people, and explain that he would represent them.

He went to the church by himself, feeling a sickness in his stomach that had come and gone over a number of weeks. The mourners were mostly old haoles, from the retirement home, and Mr. Nolan gave a brief sermon about their passing on and about how we should not grieve for them because they were going home to God. Sitting there Kenika felt out of place, as if not properly dressed. He did not recognize a single person in the church, and recalled that George and Irene's old friends were all dead, and that in the interim they had somehow lost contact with the next generation, except for Kenika. When the ceremony was over Nolan strode down the aisle and out the front door of the church, his face crossed with a look of almost overly tragic moroseness, and then out into the sun, which reflected off the ludicrous, jet-black hair.

Outside, standing among the old people near the two Cadillac hearses, Kenika again felt out of place, in fact so alien to the proceedings that, imagining that his sense of propriety had been defeated by a stomach ache, he skipped the drive to the cemetery and went home.

The deaths of the old folks sent him into one of those strange periods of contemplative silence during which he worked lazily on the relief, tried to do more for The Red Wind, whose hull was now built up and nearly finished but for refining the component parts. He continued his periodic visits to Makapuu until one day he found the place vacant. He went looking for Junior at Makua and Yokohama way out toward Kaena Point on the leeward side, but did not find him. He went along those beaches where local families camped, and the ones Junior had mentioned, and asked if they knew where Junior was. They speculated that he may have gone back to Maui.

It bothered him that he had no means of contacting Junior, as it bothered him that he never got the chance to ask him if he would like to stay at the house. He wished he had not been so hesitant. As with Keoki, where his hesitation may have cost him his one chance to get him back, he now went over and over in his mind all those opportunities he had let go simply because he did not have the nerve to ask.

He knew that during the school year Ben and Pua and the twins' kids were all tied up in school things, and he heard less from them. He found himself back in that pattern of working with slow, careful diligence on the relief picture, and when he finished it and took it over to Mr. Maxwell's place to sell, now through an associate of his, he learned that there was a buyer waiting, and within a week was five thousand dollars richer. This pushed him into another, this time a mountain nature scene loosely based on his memory of the long path at the point where he and Benny had sat the first time he went up there, the ginger and the little open spot where Benny had sat down, behind which stood the trunks of kukui trees. The prospect of spending a year on a project like this felt right, and he carried water to a galvanized tub so that during the day he could reach over and pull out a can of beer from the dozen or so that bobbed there, softly clicking against each other. The Marumotos were now so old that, like Angela's parents had, they spoke in soft wheezes, moved around their house in walkers or sometimes in wheelchairs. Richard, their grandson, took care of them, and from time to time wandered into the woods to have a beer with Kenika and talk sports and local politics. When he did not see Richard, he would spend an entire day working on a line of vine leaves, and then go home to sleep, and be visited deep in the night by a gray-haired Angela.

Just into the Christmas season he got a call from Ben, who asked if he and Pua could come over and say hello, day after tomorrow. Sure, Kenika said, and when he hung up he turned and looked around the cluttered house. At least the boy had given him some warning. But he could not figure out what brought on the sudden desire to visit. Ben was twenty-one, Pua nineteen. Their lawyer stepfather had bought a house in Los Angeles, and that was why they spent so little time in the islands. Loke loved Los Angeles, Ben told him. As for Pua, well— And Kenika asked him what that meant, and he said that Pua was going through a phase of bitchiness that had something to do with all the demands of her work.

While he cleaned the house, dragging Angela's old vacuum cleaner around, which looked like a bomb on wheels, he felt a series of cramps high in his stomach, and snorted at the idea that he might end up with one of those stomach flu things that would require him to go running off to the bathroom every ten minutes while they were at the house. As for the yard, he could do no more than mow the open areas. Along the side the hedge had grown up and over The Red Wind so that the branches scraped the house when it was windy, and the haole koa that had grown there along the narrow strip of dirt had shaded all the grass out. The blue tarp covering the canoe was covered with rotted leaves and bird and gecko droppings.

He was startled by both of them. Ben was over six feet tall and Pua had to be at least five-ten. It also amazed him that Pua was as familiar with him as she had been at ten, throwing her arms around his neck and kissing him on the cheek. Ben had not changed that much either, at least in his facial expressions. He still had his boy's face but now atop the body of an athlete. He looked a lot like Keoki.

They sat in the living room and talked while Kenika hid the cramps in his stomach. Pua had photo-shoots all the time, although she ended up mostly in magazine ads. There didn't seem to be any TV in her immediate future. Ben wasn't going to graduate yet because he had changed his major too many times.

After a while Kenika said, "You guys want anything to eat?"

"You got any fish?" Ben asked.

"Sure, I can do the whole thing. How about a beer first?"

"'Kay," Pua said. "An' I like aweoweo if you've got it."

"They've been in there a while, months in fact. I mean I still fish but there isn't anybody around to eat all of it."

"Let's do the aweoweo," Pua said. "You can't buy that anywhere."

Kenika got them out of the freezer. They talked for a half an hour, and then he cooked the fish and made rice and mixed vegetables from Safeway. They ate and went on talking, but he had little appetite. In what seemed like too short a time they were all back out in the driveway saying goodbye and climbing into the rented car. Could they come back and maybe stay a while at the beginning of the summer? Of course, he told them.

After they left he went into the house, and then, feeling what little he had eaten roiling in his stomach, just made it to the bathroom before he got sick.

Whenever any sickness hit him he simply rode it out until it ran its course. In the case of the upper abdominal pain, which felt like a vague ballooning of pressure, it didn't go away, and he had bouts of diarrhea and indigestion. His instinct was to ignore it and go on with his work, but he would find himself trying to concentrate on part of the relief, and realize that even though it was cool his forehead would be beaded with sweat and his body would remain rigid around the pain, as if trying to hold it in with a muscular contraction. Beer aggravated it, unless he drank a lot of beer, and then it seemed to numb the pain down, so he used beer as a kind of pain-killer.

After about three months of holding himself tense around the area that hurt, and experiencing flashes of powerful, almost debilitating pain, which would make sweat burst from his skin, he went to a doctor. The doctor listened to his complaint, felt around his stomach in a way that gave him the impression that he was driving his fingers through the skin to his insides, and referred him to a specialist. The specialist, a Dr. Morse, went over some notes on a clipboard and recommended what he called a barium test, where he would drink a liquid, and then later be X- rayed to determine what it might be that was wrong.

The result of the barium test was an ash-white curve on an X-ray showing what Dr. Morse called an enlargement of the duodenal loop, which indicated a growth on the pancreas. Kenika studied the bright shape, like a curved sweet potato tucked under the faint glow of his lungs. In order to determine the status of the growth itself, Kenika would undergo an aspiration of stomach juices which would be studied under a microscope.

"It is called duodenal drainage," Dr. Morse said, "and is accomplished by inserting a tube through the mouth into the duodenum. Then we aspirate juice and analyze it." Dr. Morse then paused, nodding slowly. "These are the possibilities," he said. "It may merely be a growth that has not spread, or it may have spread, in which case it would be pancreatic cancer."

"What would you do about that?"

"Well, unfortunately there is nothing we can do about it if it has achieved an advanced state," and he turned to the X-ray. "The degree of enlargement right here," and he tapped a pen on the picture, "is severe. We can almost rule out other pancreatic afflictions because of the symptoms, and the results of the test will show us what we have."

≈   ≈   ≈

He didn't return to the shed until a week later, and when he jumped over the little stream and stared up at it, he dropped his shoulders and felt a wave of nausea course through his trunk, and then sweat began to slick his skin. He breathed deeply, trying to control the sensation of fright that made his knees weak. Then he went on.

Inside sat the relief picture, curled shavings on the floor under the bench, beer still bobbing in the tub. In the hush that followed he felt calm again, almost exuberant, and he didn't know why he felt that way, considering his prospects. On the desk in the study at home was a pile of brochures and informational folders Dr. Morse's nurse had given him, some on how to care for yourself, a couple on hospice care, which, according to one brochure, would provide a loving and nurturing environment during your final passage. He shuddered whenever those words echoed in his head.

He had to credit Dr. Morse, who had approached every aspect of dealing with a terminal illness with a kind of sympathetic objectivity: there may be new or experimental treatments, but I suspect they're expensive. Kenika told him that he was not going through anything that would cost him his house. It was all he had, and was meant for— And there he paused. For whom? he wondered. But Dr. Morse had gone on to discuss what was available to him in terms of care, pain management, and so on. His condition, considering its advanced state, meant that he could expect to experience a somewhat rapid decline in health, six months maybe, before he would need to arrange for his care.

He had driven away from the hospital with a kind of shaky impatience, and had gone home to the only medicine that appealed to him at the moment: beer. And at home, he sat on the couch staring into the middle distance between himself and the far wall thinking of Angela, about how she was taken away from the world far too young, and now he, Kenika, would follow, not really young he supposed, but before he really wanted to die. Death itself did not frighten him that much, but the process did. Most of all he was frightened by that loving and nurturing environment mentioned in the brochure, and kept saying to himself, don't think about that now. When he had finally exhausted himself thinking of everything from hospice care to the kids to wills to spontaneous remission, over and over, he went to bed, only to wake up the next morning with that gnawing pain across the top of his stomach. He opened another beer and sat and stared into the middle distance.

Finally he had bored himself enough that he felt a desire to be at the shed, to be doing something. If he was going to roll over and croak, at least he would prefer to do that with a chisel in his hand.

He worked on the relief for a week, with a concentration that was almost furious, his entire upper body tensed around the tools. But he realized that you could not rush a job like this, as you could not rush a canoe. In his work he forced himself to calm down, and day by day worked his way along vines, up over trees in the distance, the optical effect achieved by the illusion of foreshortening that was aided by the grain of the wood. He stayed sometimes until it grew dark. But gradually impatience won him over again, and he would curse under his breath, and then throw tools on the floor. It was no good.

One evening he quit working on the relief, and sat and drank a beer. The problem was that he did not want to work on the relief picture. He downed the beer thinking that he would go home and not come back. When he walked down the steps he had to catch himself because a wave of dizziness flashed through him, making his eyes perceive bright spots which swept like tiny comets before him, and he had to sit down. As he sat there he felt something, a peculiar density in the air that pushed at him, and then he thought he heard whispering, but could not discern what was being whispered. He waited. When it came to him what was wrong he got up from the mossy stair and made his way through the weeds to the foundation of the shed, where the remaining chunks of koa log sat half-buried in mud, the splintered ends rotted partway in. There was one chunk fifteen or more feet long, another about twenty feet long, but split so that it formed a long cone.

He stared at them, the black shapes now nearly invisible in the increasing darkness. From the black shapes came something like a breeze with a shape, and the breeze had a smell, the ocean maybe. He felt the radiation on his face and arms but not the back of his neck, and it occurred to him that the sleeping wood had been trying to make its sentience known most likely for many years, but the inattentiveness of the human dweller in the area had left it unheeded.

"Night," he whispered. "Po."

So night would be in its name since it was not heard until a particular night. But what kind of night? That he had perceived bright lines while sitting on the stair came to him, and he whispered, "Rainbow." What was the word? Anuenue. Night Rainbow.

This sleeping wood would be named Po Anuenue, and would be somewhere between thirty-three and thirty-six feet, depending on the condition of the wood. There was not enough for a complete hull, at least as he might imagine a hull suspended inside a log, but there was more than enough for him to complete a hull as long as he could find a way of firmly joining the logs for the hull base. Like The Red Wind, or what was left of it, if he could make the bottom, the top would take care of itself. First he would need to go up the mountain looking for 'ohi'a root because of the time required to cure the spreaders. Hau for the 'iako and wiliwili for the ama required less in the way of curing, so he could wait on those. He would abandon the relief and begin the Night Rainbow the next day.

Although the pain was manageable, it was mentally irritating to the point that he would drop a tool, stand up straight and growl with frustration because he could not escape it. He tried the prescription pills Dr. Morse had ordered for him and discovered that they made him painlessly groggy, and he hated that more than the sensation just below his ribs. He worked on hollowing out the two halves of the Po Anuenue outside the shed, fueled by beer and a sustained impatience to get it to the point of joining the two halves, whose grain would go in one direction so that there would be no resistance from the wood.

Unless he wanted to send himself off into that bleary land of mindless nothingness that the pills caused, he had to hold himself around the pain and simply endure it. Over the weeks he realized that he was losing weight, and tried eating more.

He went fishing, and in the water found that he could escape the pain. There was something about the pressure of the water, something also about the coldness that leaked into his flesh, a familiar sensation that was now a kind of medicine. He would stay in long enough that the coldness caused a numbing of his senses, to the point that he floated along with the reduced awareness that he imagined a fish might feel, that there was no past or future, there was only a now that he existed in, and it was a comfortable now. He needed only to get past the shivering and the sort of helpless feeling of having no apparent warmth left, as if his organs would be refrigerator-cold to the touch. Once he managed to dominate that discomfort and bypass the one necessity for warm-blooded animals, that their blood remain warm, he found himself moving along in a stupefied, blissful hypothermia, and the colors of water and reef and fish were dream-bright and pinpoint-sharp in his vision. When he had to emerge from the water, feeling pain-wracked and heavy in the unwelcome gravity, he would find the arc of irritation over the top of his abdomen even more horrible than when he had gone into the water.

He got a call from Ben in April. "We'll be in town for the summer," he said, "and Mom's staying in L.A. Pua's gonna love that."

"Why?"

"They're at each other's throats all the time, Mom yelling at her for not controlling her weight, Pua pissed because she hates modeling, hates L.A., the whole thing."

"I always thought she was too thin."

"Know what she said to me?" Ben said. "She said, 'Take a look. I'm a five-ten, one hundred twenty-pound Polynesian, which is a contradiction.'" Ben laughed. "She's got guts, man. I think she's gonna chuck the whole thing, go back to Hawaii and buy herself the greasiest plate lunch there." Kenika waited through a silence. "Anyway," Ben said, "her career's on the skids. The shutter jockeys don't like the idea that she's growing up, and now she ends up in dress pattern catalogues."

"Are you guys staying at your house in Hawaii Kai?"

"Yeah, house sit, but we'll come over. Do some fishing, like the old days."

"That would be good," Kenika said, and then he began to sweat, because he knew he might not be in any condition to fish, or do anything else for that matter.

Ben said something else which he didn't hear. "—interviewed these people there. There was an upside down flag and everything."

"Where'd you say that was?"

"Makapuu. And they showed it on L.A. television."

When they hung up, with promises to get in touch as soon as they arrived, Kenika got a beer and sat on the couch. The loss of weight, the strange, bland fatigue he had been feeling, and the relentless pain all aimed at one thing: his death. What would happen if he went downhill when they were here? Of course they would want to do all they could for him, and would hear no questions about how much it would cost, because after all, wasn't his life more important than any house?

It wasn't, not at least in the shape his life was in. He had a sudden, horrible picture of himself in a hospital all wired up and full of tubes, lingering on and on when there was no point. The kids would visit, sustain him emotionally, be with him until the last moment. They were good kids and he could not imagine them ignoring him while he was dying.

He threw the thought off. Who said he would start to go when they were here anyway? When a surge of the pain began to balloon across the top of his abdomen, he got up and went for another beer. He had not been watching the news, and looked at the clock, thinking he'd see if there was anything about the Makapuu thing. Junior might be there. When the news did come on, there was no reference to anything about Makapuu, and he sat there trying to remember what Ben had said, if it was new news, or old, that he had been talking about.

≈   ≈   ≈

The Po Anuenue would be thirty-three feet long, perfect as a racing canoe for kids. Because he had roughed out the hull sections, he was able to slide the halves up the slimy logs into the shed without much trouble. He experienced a feeling of ticklish exultation, because now he could refine the hull and make it as smooth as ice. Rain or shine, he would chisel and sand until it was perfect.

He had assumed that when the kids came back they'd be around the house all the time, but it turned out not to be the case. They did have their friends and their own lives to live. They came over shortly after their arrival in mid-May, sat around in the evening and talked story and then left. They came back two weekends in a row and immediately dragged Kenika off to the beach at Lanikai so that they could fish.

Ben's claim that Pua was surly seemed not to show itself. Rather she seemed simply sad about everything, as if all she had ever done had had better alternatives that she had not opted for. Once, sitting in the sand and warming up after spending an hour in the water, she turned to Kenika and said, "It's funny how there's one place you always see as the center of everything," and then she nodded toward the two islands offshore. "Right here," she said. Then Ben went into an exaggerated imitation of someone weeping in bitter misery, and Pua hurled sand at him.

Then there was a long stretch when they stayed on the other side, except for one brief visit by Ben and a pretty local girl named Anika. They came by on their way to the North Shore, and Ben introduced her, they had a quick beer, and left. Pua had to be in L.A. for two weeks, Ben was taking a course at the University and on weekends hung out with his friends, including Keoni and Junior Sakata. Kenika continued on the canoe, trying to control his impatience. His illness had seemingly gone into some sort of a holding pattern, although he became more and more suspicious of the sensation of weakness in his hands and arms, and suffered from bouts of violent diarrhea. He tried to ignore his symptoms, worked on the canoe, and in the ocean got relief from the pain.

His need to be in the ocean brought about a trip to Makapuu, and he got out of the car and scanned the cluster of blue tarp and bamboo structures in the center of which was a flagpole with an inverted Hawaiian flag flapping on top. When it had been reestablished he had no idea, because he had not seen it on the television. The cluster was three times the size of the one he had seen at first. He got out of the car and grabbed his gear, and walked along the beach toward the tents. When he was within fifty yards he realized that something was wrong. In the parking section sat a number of police cars, and he could see women in pareos arguing with police who stood here and there at the perimeter of the cluster of tents. He looked around for Junior, and believed he saw him in a small group of men standing in the parking lot, their arms folded. As Kenika approached, he could see the police apparently preparing to arrest people.

There were two men and a woman standing on the beach near the activity, holding fishing poles and a cooler. One of the men, a beefy local guy, was laughing and pointing at the tent village. The other two, both haole, looked on as the man gestured and spoke. Kenika made his way through the heavy sand to them. "What's going on?" he asked the local man. All three turned and looked at him, and then their expressions changed into a questioning standoffishness. Why, he didn't know—something about his appearance, he guessed.

The local man guffawed. "That's the Nation of Ku," he said. "I mean for chrissakes, get a job why don't you."

"The Nation of Ku?"

"Hey, don't you read the papers? They declared this beach their nation."

Kenika stared at the man, then at the tents. "I don't think they have any other place to go," he said, and then felt the pain begin to radiate under his ribs, and then sweat formed on his forehead.

"The Nation of Ku," the man said. "I mean, like this is a public beach."

"Well, they mean no harm. They just have no place to go."

"Shit, you see them trash the place? Fish it out?" The man sneered in their direction. "Go look for a Help Wanted sign, man."

"Well, you might not know everything about it," Kenika said.

The man studied him for a moment. "Really? What is it I don't know?" His two companions began to appear somewhat uneasy, and Kenika smiled amiably at them.

"All I'm saying," he said, "is that you might not know everything about it."

The man's expression now changed. "All right," he said. "So now I know whose side you're on."

"Bill," the woman said. "Let's go."

"I know enough," the man said. "They don't have drivers' licenses, they don't pay taxes, they don't register their cars."

"Well," Kenika said, squinting at the camp. "See that pile of stones up there? Near the parking lot? That's what's called a koʻa kuʻula, or fishing shrine. Now if you were here alone you might pull the stones off the top and start a fire and fry hamburgers, right?"

"Hey," the man said, "you don't have to try to educate me on this culture stuff. You know what comes after this? Sovereignty, and then poof, casinos with them keeping all the money."

"Well, I don't know about that. They're just trying to do some things the old way."

"But welfare is the new way. I'll bet they don't pass up on that, eh?"

"I don't know."

"This is a state," the man said. "I was born here. Facts are facts."

"Well, that there is a fact, too," Kenika said, gesturing at the camp. "That's what's called civil disobedience. They may look foolish to you, but you know, every revolution has its what, uncompromising elements? They just decided not to play the game. You're looking at the point of the spear, so to speak, that's all. The U.S. prides itself on being fair, and now it's time for them to prove it."

Kenika shrugged again and nodded at the man. Then he walked on.

"Let 'em pay taxes first!" the man called after him. He waved his hand without turning around. "Man the barricades!" the man yelled, and laughed. Kenika walked on.

At the general perimeter of the tent area a policeman, baking in his dark-blue shirt and pants, stepped in front of Kenika and said, "Sir, you can't cross this point right now."

"Why?"

"We have a disturbance."

Kenika looked at the parked cars and the groups of people. He could not see Junior. Another slow surge of pain began working its way under his ribs, and then he felt dizzy in the brightness and heat. Sound seemed muffled, and what he saw came across as flat and two-dimensional. It was as if all that talking had exhausted him. Police were putting handcuffs on some of the men while women and kids yelled at them, and newspeople hovered nearby aiming video cameras at the action.

Finally he saw Junior in the parking lot lifting coolers into the trunk of an old K car. "Would it be okay if I talked to that man?" He pointed. "He's my cousin." The cop looked at him, thought for a moment, and said, "Yah, go ahead."

He went to Junior.

"Eh, Kenika!"

As he approached, he could tell that Junior looked at him with an increasingly skeptical doubt. "Eh, sammatah? You no look so good."

"Yeah, had flu or something." He asked Junior about the police.

It was a kind of standoff. The authorities had cut the water lines. Most of the people awready lef', he told him. A few were stayin' aroun' fo' get arrested. "An' ho, I miss cause I loadin' da cah!" he said. "So no mo' place fo' go again."

"What about the kids? I mean, where do you folks go then?"

Junior shook his head, watched the police marching one man after another toward vans and cars. "Maile, she no wan' me arrested, 'ass why we leave. I got traffic stuffs from Maui."

"So where are Maile and the kids?"

"Makua. Get frien's out deah."

Kenika looked over at the arrest process, then turned back to Junior. "Listen," he said, "I have plenty of room at the house. You guys could come stay until— I mean, as long as you need."

Junior studied him for five seconds, thinking. "No," he said. "'Ass nice, but we gotta stay wit' dis stuff heah."

"Where does everybody go?"

"I donno. Dey say dey negotiate fo' lan' Waimanalo. I donno."

"Look," Kenika said, and the long knife of pain slid through his trunk, and he paused, waiting it out.

"You okay?"

"Yeah, just a stomach thing. Look," he said, wiping sweat from his forehead, "can I help you out, like with money or something?"

Junior patted him on the shoulder. "Nah nah nah. 'Sokay."

"Here," Kenika said, and he drew his wallet out of his fish bag. "Think of this as a gift, 'kay?" He had eighty dollars. "Here, take this. It'll help you get set up a little, maybe."

"No, I no take dat," Junior said, laughing.

"It's okay, I got plenty. I mean, extra."

Junior considered this, staring down at the four twenties. "'Kay, I take half."

Kenika gave him the two twenties.

"Listen," Junior said, "you go home an' take care, 'kay?"

"You'll be at Makua?"

"Yeah."

"'Kay, I'll try to come out. We'll fish."

"Lay some net," Junior said. "Ho, aftah dahk, good fish."

At home Kenika lasted ten minutes before he became sick to his stomach and had to rush to the bathroom, and this time, the powerful cramps that ripped through his trunk made him so weak that he could barely stand up to brush his teeth.

≈   ≈   ≈

With no word from Ben and Pua, he focused all his attention on the Po Anuenue. He found that if he drank enough beer and ate bland foods like poi, rice and fruit, he could manage the nausea. He worked on four heavy ribs, each about eight feet long to inset where the hull halves joined, planning to leave the hull base three and a half inches thick. The beam of the canoe would be narrow, sixteen inches, and the hull would calabash more than usual in order to compensate for the narrow beam.

In early August he got a call from Ben. They would come over and do some fishing. Again Kenika worked a little in the yard which had flourished while his back was turned. The side of the house where The Red Wind was stored he left alone, because it had now become a dark tunnel so overgrown that he could not walk the length of the canoe without hacking his way with the machete. Now that The Red Wind was nearly repaired except for one moʻo board, he wanted to show it to them, but the fatigue he felt was so debilitating that he was afraid he wouldn't be able to fish, much less fight his way in there and drag the tarp off The Red Wind.

As it turned out they came over too late in the day to fish, which was a relief to him. Pua wanted to look at photographs, especially of the old folks and Angela. Ben was interested too, although he appeared to be not particularly happy.

"Gotta go back," he finally said. "I don't want to."

"Well, pretty soon you'll have a degree," Kenika said. "Then you'll come back."

"Grandaddy, who's this?" Pua asked, setting the album in his lap.

"That's Darnay Santiago, who'd be your what? Granduncle I think."

"He's huge. Is he still alive?"

"Yeah, but I haven't seen him in years. When your great-grandparents died I tried to call him, but his phone was disconnected. I have an address, but it's no good probably."

Then Pua giggled. "Ho, look da aunties." She was looking at beach pictures of the twins. "They shoulda been models," she said.

The evening was nicer than he had imagined it could be, because he had to get up only to get beer and check on the pupus, ahi poke, chips and salsa that they brought, and fruit.

He wondered if it was some odd paranoia on his part, but as the night went on he thought the kids looked at him more and more strangely, as if they knew about his condition and would bring up the subject of his care. He would undergo flashes of fear that some process was already underway regarding hospitalizing him, and he mentally prepared a kind of defense: I will take care of myself, and that will cost nothing. My death is my business. But they would not accept that, he was sure.

After they left, with promises to keep in touch, he sat in the study in a cone of dusty light. He took out a sheet of paper, and wrote, having some trouble controlling his hand:

Lapa Uila (with Benny)
Malolo   "
Leilani   "
Moana   "
Puaho Akua   "
Aukai   "
Makani ʻUla
Peniʻamina

Hokulele O Kamali'i
Moanapahi
Hihimanu
No Mama'o Wa'a
'Opua Hae
Po Anuenue

So that was it. He didn't know if he should be proud of what he had done or not. Certainly the list was too short. If he had been able to live to be a hundred the list would still be too short. But his life was now nearly finished, and he had to do something about the house, get that out of the way so he could finish the Po Anuenue. Sitting there he realized that even the act of writing the canoe list had fatigued him, and his hands shook and felt oddly numb, as if they had been asleep. There was just no tension left in the muscles, and more than anything else, more than pain or vomiting or those awful phases of sweating profusely for no reason, he hated most of all the loss of his strength.

He forced himself to go through the process of finding a legal book at the library and then typing out, pecking letter after letter, a simple will, which left everything he and Angela owned to the twins, Keoki, Ben and Pua in equal shares. Then he went to the bank and signed the will in the presence of Mrs. Loo, the manager, who witnessed the signing.

≈   ≈   ≈

One day he picked up a chisel and it slid from his hand onto the bench. His knees were weak, the pain had now mushroomed throughout his trunk, up to his neck and all the way down to his groin. As he had worked he had felt its increase in intensity but tried to ignore it. The deliberate denial of his own death was at war with a pain so aggravating that he almost looked forward to dying. The beer didn't help. He moaned involuntarily with each breath, and no matter how deeply he breathed he felt that he did not have enough air.

He looked at the dust-covered relief picture, then at the long, graceful hull of the Po Anuenue. He would not finish it. He had to go home. But he was afraid of going home, as if anyone who saw his condition would demand that he get help, a loving and nurturing environment for his final passage. He giggled with helpless fatigue. He could not let anyone see him.

Then all the hair stood up on his head and arms, and his heart began thumping in his chest, because he knew he had reached the point where no options were left. Outside the path snaked through the ginger up the ravine, and he stared blearily at it. He didn't have the strength to make one last visit up there but at the same time felt that it would be the only compensation for not finishing the Po Anuenue. He either had to finish it or go up. The idea of doing neither attracted him, but he wanted to finish everything correctly. He would not finish the canoe, and that caused a warm flash of sadness and shame to radiate through his flesh. He had to go up. There was no other alternative.

The recent rains had made all the vegetation flourish, and as he went up the path moaning, going from sapling to sapling to keep his balance, he felt whatever was left of his strength evaporating off him with his sweat. But apparently his legs were stronger than his arms and hands, and he was half-surprised to feel his diminished weight rise with each surge of a leg.

He was not sure if he would be able to find the place considering how overgrown the path was, and he staggered, sometimes giggling in a bright, stupefied delirium. It seemed to have something to do with the physical effort, but at one point he stopped, and all awareness seemed to drain from him, so that he stood staring at the bright-green foliage and the sky, with no idea of why he was where he was, or even who he was. He placed his hands on his chest, felt himself, and then remembered that he existed. That lapse of awareness, once he remembered it, was frightening and at the same time fascinating. The effort of walking had screwed up his perception to the point that he felt almost no pain, and the blank, floating numbness felt like a kind of death.

He stopped to rest at the place where he and Benny had sat that day long ago. It had not changed at all, and he thought of the relief in which those trees and that ginger were represented. For a gift he snapped off a fountain of flowers from one of the ginger plants. The pain had returned, and with it an impatience to keep going. Above him, the mountains loomed almost black, with clouds curling at the tops. He went on.

The rough square was the same except for some shrubs that had crept up over the cliff side. The air above the parched stone boiled in the heat, and he stepped into the square and placed the flowers on the stone. His dizziness robbed him of balance, the horizon tipped, and he felt a sweeping faintness. He landed on his elbow and hip. The sharp point of pain in his elbow woke him up, and he looked down at it. Little drops of blood fell off into the dirt and stood there each with a bright pinpoint of reflected sunlight. He stared at the little drops and then sat up, feeling the heat leak through his shorts.

He tried to stand up but couldn't, and settled back down, gasping for breath. Finally he whispered, "I can't finish the Po Anuenue." He looked around, suddenly calm, and then lucid. He squinted at the horizon, the sharp division between the dark blue of the ocean and the light blue of the sky. "I'm sorry. I tried." His elbow had stopped bleeding. "I did what I could," he whispered. "Now I have to—" He stopped, and again his heart began to bang in his chest, and the dizziness returned, followed by that strange, mesmerized delirium.

Do you love the ocean?

He held himself still, the echo of sound hovering around him. "Yes."

Is the ocean your home?

"Yes, the ocean is my home." He felt them. They were not visible but he could feel their presence as surely as he felt pain, and their presence eased the pain.

Are you the ocean?

"Yes."

Are you the ocean?

"Yes," he whispered, and then he understood, and he shuddered and felt a rush of strange excitement.

"I will," he whispered. "I am the ocean."

Then you have done well. You are now one with us in blood.

And he thought, no, and then giggled, feeling the ground tip under him. So the theft of their bones and the trashing of their sacred place left them confused, and in their sympathy they were willing to lie to make him feel better. "I visited," he whispered. "I visited your place."

You are one with us in blood. You are the ocean.

"I am the ocean."

Then a breeze carried them away, and he sat there staring at the division of ocean and sky.

He did not think he would be able to get back down the hill, and was again surprised at how his legs held up. At the edge of the woods he waited until it was clear that nobody from the Marumotos' would see him, and drove home, his foot trembling on the gas pedal and his knees weak. He drove hunched around the horrible pain in his stomach. Whenever he envisioned the ocean, or looked at it through the side window, his heart would beat rapidly and he would experience a powerful charge of excitement, a strange, frightful ecstacy.

The exhaustion caused him to fall on the floor as soon as he entered the house. He pulled himself up and went to the refrigerator for a beer. His hands shook so badly that he could barely open it. He drank some of the beer and felt it coming up, and when the gulp he had downed forced its way into his mouth he leaned over and spat it into the sink, and saw that it was a strange brick-red. He tasted the salty, metallic taste of blood, stared at it disappearing in an oily slide down the drain. He took another gulp and swished it around and spat it out. After that he was able to drink it.

The kids would be coming over one more time before they left, and he had to do it before they came. Again his hair stood up on his head and arms, and his heart pounded. The sensation of that ecstatic anticipation was frightening and at the same time suffused him with awe. When? he wondered. That was the only question left. He wondered how severe the internal bleeding was, if he would be prevented from doing anything simply because he would have become too weak to act.

Did he want another day? "Not like this," he whispered. "Not this way."

He took two beers with him and went slowly to the study. Inside, he sat at the desk before pictures of Angela and the kids. He would write something to the kids, first the twins and then Ben and Pua. They would walk into the house without knocking as they always did. The wisest thing to do would be to leave the letters and the will on the desk where they would find them.

He drew a sheet of paper out of the drawer, and picked up the pen. He aimed the point at the spot where the first word would go, and his eyes refused to focus, his hand began to shake, and the shaking became so wild that he dropped the pen. He tried a second and a third time but could not do it. The effort of trying to concentrate sent a powerful stab of pain through his trunk, and he ended up slumped down and moaning, sweat bursting from his skin. After that he felt so weak that he wondered if he would be able to get up from the chair.

He closed his eyes, and in a strange, serene phase of half-consciousness he felt a strong pulse he knew to be his heartbeat, but felt also the sensation of movement, of sliding effortlessly through water, and he felt wind against his skin, and the patient rhythmic surging with each strong pull. He had already discovered that his only escape from his pain was the ocean, and now began to anticipate and even feel some impatience for that serene, narcotic numbness that he would find there. And he thought about Angela, and felt some comfort at the idea that out there he might join her on some other level of existence.

≈   ≈   ≈

He vomited on his legs in the car, and then giggled at his own pointless embarrassment. It was beer and blood. In the night-long contest between pain and alcohol, the pain had finally won out. He had drifted in and out of consciousness sitting there at the desk, and Angela spoke to him in a warm, breathy whisper, sentences he did not understand but with a tone of sympathetic encouragement. Finally the raw, searing power of the pain had frightened him into action, and at four a.m. he put the little twelve-pound anchor and the mesh-floored innertube float into the car, and then went back for his mask, fins and knife. Then he went to the walk to stare blearily at the house. He had left it open and had left the study light on.

Although he existed on the border of full consciousness, his heart still rose into fits of powerful thumping, which were followed by that sensation of bizarre exhilaration. He parked the car at the right-of-way they had used all through the kids' childhood, piled the gear on the float and dragged it to the beach, feeling the cool wind drying the blood on his upper thighs. Now that he was doing it he felt a strength he had not felt in weeks.

Someone had left floodlights on at the back of a house, and the shorewash he faced was illuminated into a milky, pale green, beyond which was blackness. With the breeze that came off the ocean he felt so powerful a dread that he turned to go back to the car. But then that strange excitement returned, and he took a deep, shaky breath.

When he backed into the water and eased himself in, the raw coldness against his flesh robbed him of what strength he had, and he floundered, trying to pull himself free of the shorebreak. The coldness shocked him and he yelled into the snorkel, and then vomited again. He cleared the snorkel and tried to pull himself into the water. Then, with a burst of angry thrashing, he was afloat.

He scissored his legs for ten seconds, then rested. The pain had consumed him to the point that he closed his eyes and felt the waves pushing him back in. Then the pain drove so hard at his flesh that he yelled in anger at it, and scissored his legs powerfully, as if to leave it behind. When he opened his eyes he saw that he was moving parallel to the shore, and changed his direction away from the floodlights.

He achieved a rhythm, breathing and scissoring his legs, moaning with each breath and trying to ignore the pain, but the numbness and pleasant delirium he was so impatient to achieve did not come. Even the smallest wave stopped him and tugged on the innertube so that the pain was too debilitating for him to do anything but float, and when he did that he felt himself moving back toward the shore, and it was only his frustration and anger that made him move once again.

A few hundred yards out he experienced a lapse in which he did not know what he was doing. He was aware that he was in water, but did not know why, and wondered what he was doing without his spear, if Angela and the kids— He gaped into the black nothingness under him, and could not remember telling them. And why fish at this time of the night? He floated, trying to understand what was happening, and then began to remember. Then the pain in his stomach flashed into a series of surging thumps which caused bright points of light to sweep across his vision. He pulled the rope tied to his waist and felt inside the mesh. Anchor, knife. He turned and continued scissoring his legs.

He labored like this for what felt like hours. The Mokuluas, always tauntingly out ahead of him, gradually moved to beyond his right shoulder, and that gave him new will. In time the division of ocean and sky was clearer and that caused him to push harder.

He could see, fairly close now, the straight line of breakwater from the Mokuluas all the way across the bay. He churned on, aware that as he cleared the snorkel he was clearing stuff that came up into his mouth. Then, in a strange, slow flash, he felt no pain, or became aware that he had been feeling no pain but in his dreaming delirium was unaware of it. The crashing of the breakers was muffled, and he felt a strange warmth. He had made it into the state of narcotic hypothermia, and when he met the breakers and felt the racing bubbles tickling his skin all the way to his feet, then the powerful tug of the rope attached to the inner tube, he laughed, the sound of his own voice hollow and flat.

Then he was in open ocean, where the water was fifty or more feet deep. The gentle swells picked him up and then allowed him to settle. He had little feeling in his hands, but could now just see the rope tied to the anchor, which bobbed there in the mesh inside the circle of the tube. He slipped the rope around his neck and under his right arm and pulled it tight, then clumsily knotted it, and felt around in the mesh bottom for the knife.

Then he had no idea of what he was doing or who he was. Hanging on the innertube he lapsed into a strange blankness, a dream in which he was no more than a pair of eyes, and he labored over what or who he was, over the question of why he was where he was, but could not make himself know the answers. The blankness was fascinating and horrible at the same time, and he gaped at the black rubber, at the ghostly movement of his appendages. And then off to his right behind him he saw the black, sharp outlines of two islands, and beyond them the horizon was pink, with a bright yellow glow beginning to divide it in the middle. He did not know what that was, and stared, trying to make sense of what he saw. It was rich and bright and beautiful. Then he saw something clutched in his hand, a knife, and believed he knew who and where he was. The bright blade glinted, and he looked again at the pink and yellow light on the horizon. Then he remembered what it was.

Dawn.

Epilogue · 1994

Far away in the blue-black distance there is a beat, some strange sound. You float toward that tangible sensation in the air, a thumping or maybe a heartbeat. It becomes louder, and you feel it as a series of soft shocks in the air. Then you hear it as wood on wood, the rhythmic thumping of paddleshafts drumming against a hull, and you feel yourself float toward it through the blackness in a long, sweeping sigh. The thumps are as steady as a heartbeat, or it is your own heart beating, or your own heart beating is the sound of paddleshafts thumping on wood.

≈   ≈   ≈

The light through his eyelids was red overcoming black, and he heard the squeak of sneakers on floors, then the distant rattling of pans, and closer, the soft electrical hum of machines. He moved his arms, thinking of rolling over, and a stab of pain in his chest and shoulder took his breath away.

Someone in white walked past a doorway. Now wait, he thought. Now just wait a minute here. His eyes went first down, seeing white across the bridge of his nose, and then to the foreshortened view of his own body under a sheet, and he ran the hand that did not hurt down over his stomach. Underneath the sheet he was naked. Now wait a minute.

He smelled plumeria. Not California. He had not gone back. But he had gone to the airport and said goodbye to Anika and left. Then he remembered that he had not gone to the airport. He had been so ready to go that he had assumed that he had gone to the airport, because he had wanted to go and get away.

Then he remembered the practice green, the building, remembered being hit, kicked, and the man who told him to relax, people were on the way. Anika was on the Mokes, that was it. But he had left her there to go plant the taro, no big deal, an hour or so, and Keoni was going to meet her out there, and Ben had gone up to the place and planted the taro and had been hit and kicked. Anika was— He began to feel sweat on his forehead. Oh boy, did he ever fuck up.

On a chair near the door there was a yellow plumeria lei. Next to the bed there was a little console on a pipe neck and it had buttons, one of which read "nurse." His hand hovered over it, and then he paused. There was something else, dreams. In a number of those his father hulked off in the distance, leaning on his stick, sometimes calling his name—Ben, eh Ben. And in the dreams Ben always faded away, trying not to be seen, trying to get away. His father was on the practice green. No, why would he be on the practice green? The last place Ben was. But then Anika, Keoni—

A nurse poked her head in the door, then squeaked over to his bed. "Good afternoon," she said. "Now you lie still, you're okay."

"What hospital is this?"

"Castle. Your visitors went off to get lunch," and she clicked her tongue. "Two very pretty young ladies."

"Two?"

"One is your sister. Now you just hold on. Dr. Chang is making his rounds, and you're, oh, third in line from—" She peeked out the door. "Second," she said.

She left, and he waited. Now his face began to ache, and he lifted his hand to it, felt the bandage that went over the bridge of his nose. Then he pulled his hand away. Oh boy, don't touch that, don't sniffle, don't sneeze. Oh boy. Then, hovering in the air, was the smell of fish, and he raised his hand again. It was on his fingers. The kala.

The man he assumed to be Dr. Chang came in beeping. He pulled the little beeper off his hip, studied it, thinking, and then pushed the button. "Mr. —" and he held the rrr for two seconds. Then he pulled a chart off the end of the bed.

"McKay."

"Yes, sorry. I'm no good on names," and he approached the bed, aiming his attention at the left shoulder. "Let's just have a look."

"What is it?"

Dr. Chang stared at him a moment. "A gunshot wound."

"Jesus."

"You're all right, though," he said. "Let me go clinical for you." He slowly lifted one corner of the bandage and peeked. "Yes," he said. "Looks fine. It was a Mag three-five-seven. The bullet went through and broke the top of the scapula and was deflected upward. On its way there it caused damage to the supraspinatus muscle. On its way out it chipped the acromion, or point of the shoulder. You were apparently leaning slightly back with your arm raised because the entry was lower, under the collarbone. The problem there was that the damage nicked a somewhat important artery, hence the blood loss."

"Oh." He sniffed his fingers again. Then he remembered that he had buried the kala in the sand.

"So, we repaired that and piped in a couple of units, and now you're in good shape."

"Units?"

"Of blood," he said, and nodded reassuringly.

Ben stared at him. Dr. Chang continued to speak but he didn't hear because he could only think, blood. And then he began to shake, and a strange swoon raced through his flesh and made more sweat form on his skin.

"Whose blood?"

"Oh I assure you, we have a clean blood supply. You needn't be concerned about any contamination." Dr. Chang stepped toward the door. "You relax now," he said.

"But—"

Chang was gone. Ben lifted his bad arm and looked at the bluish lump of a vein snaking down, from a skin-colored bandage on his wrist and into the back of his hand, and touched it with the shaky index finger of his other hand. "But whose blood?" he whispered.

Then it seemed as if every cubic inch of his flesh itched from inside, rebelled to the point of contracting with a nauseated irritation, down to the squirming of every capillary. Flesh was not supposed to be sentient by the cubic inch but now his was, raging with a ticklish, intolerable discomfort. This caused a sensation of nausea in his stomach, and he was afraid that he would become sick, but the soreness in his shoulder and nose made him tighten up and try to hold himself steady against it. "No," he whispered. "Hold on now, hold on." Now he felt himself sweating, and held himself steady against the nausea, his eyes beginning to water, and whispered, "Whose blood?" He gritted his teeth, staring at the veins on the backs of his hands.

Then Anika and Pua were at the door. Pua came out with a little gasp. "He's awake," she whispered. They came in.

"We were so worried," Anika said.

"You guys know each other?"

"Now we do," Pua said. There were padded metal chairs against the wall, and they each grabbed one and sat at the edge of his bed, near his good shoulder.

After a few seconds, he said, "It was stupid."

"I called Mom," Pua said.

"Oh boy."

He looked at them, at their dark hair and eyes. "Hey, you look alike," he said.

Pua and Anika looked at each other. Pua giggled and said, "One of my goals is to look even more like Anika. I like gain twenty pounds."

"Don't do that," he said. "Mom'll give dirty lickens."

"Fuck her," Pua said. Anika's face went into a mask of good-humored, indignant surprise. "So?" Pua said. "She's my mom. Can talk stink if I want."

"What day is it?"

"Day after yesterday," Pua said. "It's Sunday," and she looked at her watch, "August seventh."

"All this happened only last night?"

"'Ass right," Pua said. "The police have the guy who did it, named Kimo Malama. I suspect they want to have a chat with you too, rebel without any clothes."

Anika laughed, looked again at Pua, and it struck Ben that they liked each other. Then he remembered that name, Malama. "What's the name Malama mean to you?"

"It means 'to take care of' or 'preserve,' shithead. Are you really awake?"

"I didn't mean that. I just remembered the name from somewhere."

"Beats me," Pua said, and then frowned at her lap. Something else was on her mind. "Look," she said. "All day today I've been on like a Nancy Drew jag, and I got some bad feelings, about Grandaddy Kenika."

She went on to explain that Anika and Keoni left the island at about midnight after it was clear Ben was not coming back, and Anika called the house in Hawaii Kai and left a message. Pua got it early in the morning because she had been out all night, and came right over. Anika stayed in Waimanalo at Keoni's place, after calling her mother. When they heard the story on the radio while they were driving to

Kailua they suspected that it was Ben who had been shot, so Pua went over to Kenika's house at about seven.

"He's not there, right?" she said. "I mean I just went in and called out for him, then went to the study where the light was on. What do I find? A will, a list of canoes he made, and two empty beercans."

So then they came to Castle and found that Ben was going to be okay and so on. So what's next? Did Kenika go fishing? They drove over to Lanikai and looked on the beach and found Ben's wallet, and found slippahs next to the usual right-of-way, and nothing else. So on their way out they walk right past his car, and they're driving away before Pua recognizes it. She gets out of the car and runs over. The keys are in Kenika's car.

"And look," she said. "On the front seat there are these stains, like blood. Blood an', you know, maybe something else. Smelled a little off."

"When can I get outta here?"

Pua shook her head. "We asked Dr. Chang. A few days was all he said."

"Fish blood?"

"What, he drives around with a dead fish in his lap? No. Something's wrong."

"He loaned the car out? He could be at the shed."

"I don't know."

"Maybe he went fishing on the Mokes? Like he always did? Maybe he's still out there."

Pua considered this. "Kayden, we go check."

"Walk the beach," Ben said. "You know, maybe he decided to come back in more toward Flat Island and the boat ramp?"

"I don' know," Pua said. "Maybe go back to the house and look again."

"I want outta here," he said. "I mean, what if—"

What if what? He stared again at the backs of his hands, at those veins, and felt a swoon of sudden wooziness. "What's wrong with me?"

"You're still a little sedated, I'll bet," Anika said. "Maybe we should go and let you sleep."

"'Kay, but come back, 'kay?"

They would. They paused at the door for one look, nodded, and were gone. He was left staring at the doorway, and then the wooziness swept ticklishly through his flesh, and he dozed.

In that area between sleep and awareness he saw the shifting phantasms of people, his father, then Kenika, a familiar but at the same time unfamiliar form, then his mother, her face crossed with an expression of irritated accusation. Behind it all was the shape of someone he would never know, and that person was the one whose blood now ran in his veins and squirted through the valves of his heart, and that made him aware of his heart pulsing, and then the awful, screaming, intolerable discomfort of his flesh cubic inch by cubic inch, desperate to purge itself of that blood but now unable to. And his mind conceived secret perversions of his identity brought on by the squirming alien infections hidden in that blood, perversions unknown to science or ignored by the happy, optimistic doctors who assumed that it was merely platelets and plasma while Ben suspected that it was far more than that in its insidious capacities.

He woke up sweating and needing to go to the bathroom. He pushed the nurse button, and in a minute a tiny Japanese lady came in. "Uh, I have to go to the bathroom."

"You no mo' hooked up," she said. "Doctah Chang say okay, jus' move slow. I stay."

It was not as hard as he had thought it would be, although he didn't care for the little smock he wore. He felt slightly rocky but had no trouble keeping his balance.

One of the other buttons was for the TV, which aimed down at him from the ceiling corner next to the door, mounted on an erector set frame. He turned it on and got a soap. He watched for five minutes, learning that Heather and Brad were hot to get in bed together, but had to endure such distractions as her husband's calling, and his fear of a huge stock deal going south behind his back. Ben could find no remote, so he was stuck.

He turned the set off, planning to doze some more, but turned to a figure blocking the door. Police. He took a deep breath and let it out, wondering what he would be charged with. But it turned out that the cop, an officer Lau, had no interest in his vandalism, only the details that he remembered of the shooting itself. "Look, I think it was a mistake. I had the little axe, and I'll bet the guy thought I was gonna hit his friend."

"And the man who kicked you was not the man with the gun?"

"I'm sure of it, yeah. I mean if it wasn't for the gun it would be manini, the whole thing."

"Tomorrow he'll most likely be let out on his own recognizance, and he said he wants to come by. Up to you, of course, but—"

"Sure."

After the cop left he stared at the doorway. As he stared he felt his eyelids drooping again, and lapsed off into that strange half-sleep that was full of faces, voices, and the steady thumping of his heart.

Near dark he sat up eating fried rice, beef broccoli and canned peaches, and his mother appeared at the door. "Oh Ben, we were so scared," she said, and then gave him an awkward hug, avoiding the injured shoulder.

"Hi Mom, come sit."

"Pua told me all about it, and about Grandaddy Kenika too. The poor man. I wonder if—"

"He might be out at the shed. That's what I was thinking."

"Well, as long as you're all right."

He looked at her. Jeans, a jogging jacket, little strands of gray hair. "You got a good flight?"

"Well, I should've been here hours ago. There was a delay."

Ben looked at her and sighed. "You mad, huh?"

"I'm not that cold," she said, laughing. "A prank, they said. Actually when they explained it I thought it was, what? Clever. Kagemori or Tagemori or whoever built that place is going bankrupt."

"My sabotage worked."

"Well, if they're not bankrupt now, they will be when we're through with them."

"What does that mean?"

"We'll file suit. No worry, it's routine."

It did not strike him as routine. "What about the guy who shot me?"

She snorted. "Trigger-happy jerk," she said.

"Does the name Malama mean anything to you?"

"No. Or, well, let's see. There was a Malama part of the McKay family like a hundred years ago. But hey, what difference does that make?"

"None, I guess."

"Right now I think you should finish your food there and get some sleep. You look like a raccoon."

He touched the bandage on his nose, smelled the faint fish odor again, and said, "Look, I'm sorry about all this."

She stared at him and then smiled. "As long as you're all right honey, that's all I care about." She leaned over and kissed him on the forehead. "Take care, 'kay?"

"'Kay. You come back tomorrow?"

"Uh-huh. I got some stuff to do on the other side. Like clean the house first of all."

"Oh, we didn't get around to that yet."

"How many pizzas did you guys eat?"

After she left he stared again at the door space. He had no more appetite, and pushed the tray table down toward the end of the bed. Something was still wrong and he didn't know what it was. He looked again at the veins on the backs of his hands. That things did not feel right was nothing new to him, but what didn't feel right now was obscure and mentally cryptic, and wormed its way through his flesh in a sort of powerful but mysterious persistence. Then he thought, Kenika. That something may have happened to the old man saddened him, and then it frightened him more than it saddened him, and he didn't know why.

Pua and Anika came back during the evening visiting hours. Pua had continued her Nancy Drew trip, and told him that all the news was bad. "'Kay, so we're at the beach, an' I remember long ago how the current always goes toward Kaneohe? Memba dat? So we look way down by da point, an' inna high-tide line is a deflated innertube."

"Did it have like a mesh thing inside?"

"Yeah. And it had a cut in it, like it was slashed."

"Sharks?"

"No. Jus' one cut, straight line."

So they went back to the house. Pua poked around a little more in the study, even read the will. "He gave the house to all of us, Dad and da aunties, you an' me." She went on—the will was one thing, but the medical book was the one she got most scared about. The page that was marked by a business card was about pancreatic cancer, and the card was from an oncologist named Morse. There were pamphlets about hospice care, stuff like that. "I goin' call him tomorrow," she said. She looked at the window, shook her head. "An' his car? His keys were in it. We put a towel onna seat an' took it home."

"Jesus," Ben said. "He might have— No, he wouldn't do that."

"Ben, I think he did," she said. "He was sick an' took his own life. I no like dis girl-sleut' stuffs any more."

"Why would he?"

"I don't know."

"I don't believe it."

Pua shrugged. "Anyway," she said, "a little while ago on the news you got your fifteen seconds of fame. Actually thirty seconds. Check it out at ten. They had a picture of some blood and taro plants."

It was a bad night. If he slept, it was a fitful trip through the universe of odd dreams. He kept repeating in his mind, Kenika, Kenika, and when he lapsed into half-consciousness the faces returned, Kenika's with them, whispering to him. In his dreams he knew Kenika was dead.

In the morning he watched television. The nurse gave him the remote, which had been right there on the lower shelf of the little table, and he watched ESPN, auto racing, speculations about the pro football season. He felt better, could move his left arm. Dr. Chang came in to look at the stitches, and declared him on his way to recovery. Another day and he'd be out.

After Dr. Chang left he stared at the doorway. Nurses squeaked by, pans rattled, the hospital hummed. He hovered between boredom and anxiety, and wished he could get out right away.

The next form to flash across the doorway seemed to pause just beyond it, then go past again in the other direction. He wore a baseball cap and a dark-blue service station uniform. Then the head without the cap appeared, a dark local guy. "Eh," he said.

"Howzit?"

He came in. "I Kimo Malama," he said. "My dad tell me I should come o'hea see you."

Ben looked at him, then said, "Eh, come on in, have a seat."

He did so. After a few seconds he said, "How you doin'?"

"Pretty good."

Then Kimo Malama looked embarrassed, and screwed his face up. "Jesus, look, I sorry."

"Eh, no problem," Ben said. "An accident."

"'Kay, I jus' come fo' tell you dat, 'kay?"

"Yeah."

"I bettah go."

When he stood up Ben said, "No no, hang around, 'kay?"

Kimo Malama looked at him, shook his head. "It was dumb, da ho ting."

"Hey, I was the one who planted the taro."

Kimo Malama laughed. "Da' was cool."

"Look, I got a question."

"Yeah?" Kimo said, with a look of vague suspicion on his face.

"Where you from?"

"Waianae."

"The name Malama. We had Malamas in our family a long time ago. I was just wondering something. Like, do you know your grandparents' or maybe great grandparents' names and all 'at stuff?"

"Granfaddah Tom Malama. But he dead now."

"My great-grandmother's name was Irene Malama. Does that ring a bell?"

"No."

"You ever heard the name Santiago in your family?"

"No."

He now appeared uncomfortable with the cross-examination. He shook his head slowly, looked at the door.

"Wait wait wait," Ben said. "Sorry. Look, I got a problem with something here. I mean—"

"I got one problem too," Kimo said. "My problem is Halawa. I no like go back."

"You were in Halawa?"

"Yeah."

"My father was too."

"Fo' real?"

"Look, could you do me a favor? Is there somebody real old at your house? I mean somebody that would know any of this stuff? Look, it sounds stupid, but could you call and ask a couple questions for me?"

Kimo squinted at him. "Why?"

"It's—" But he couldn't explain. It was far too complicated.

"Hey," Kimo said. "Shit, I shot you. What you like know?"

"Just ask what those old people's names were."

Kimo shrugged and left the room.

While he was gone, Ben stared at the doorway, waiting. Kenika was dead, probably. Kenika went and drowned himself, tough old fart that he was, and now there was nobody left. No, there were people left, but something was wrong anyway. It was the old people who were gone. That Kenika was the last one had never occurred to him, and now if he was really gone then there was nobody, as if Kenika somehow had stood for far more than the individual he was.

Kimo Malama came back into the room and sat down. "My great-grandfaddah name Kimo, like me. Great-grandmaddah name Clarice. An' get Santiagos too."

Ben stared at him, studying the features. Features of the race, he supposed. "My auntie is named Clarice. You're my cousin."

"Not. Fo' real?"

"Yup."

Kimo stared at him, and he could see him thinking, wondering what all this meant.

"Lemme tell you something," Ben said. "There's nothin' like bein' shot for straightening out your brain."

Again Kimo screwed his face up.

"I got an idea. You know Lanikai?" Kimo nodded. "Let's say, next Sunday, we're gonna have a get together of some kind. I think my grandfather just died, but we don't know." He went on to explain to Kimo who Kenika was, how he was connected to the Santiagos, what had apparently happened in the last few days. "Today's what? Monday. I'm gonna make some calls, try to scare up whoever I can, and have a little thing over there, over where we used to fish, where we spread my grandmother's ashes when I was little. I don't know, maybe some kind of a little ceremony." He shook his head, stared at his hands. "I know.

Canoes. I wanna get some canoes and—" What? He didn't know what he wanted to do with canoes.

"I ustedto race Hui Waʻa. My uncle Joe, he get one nice one."

"Could you bring it?"

"Eh, if I not inna slammah."

"Not if I can do anything about it. Hey, I'm not pressing charges, I'll try talking to them. I no want you go jail."

"Fo' real?"

"Yeah, an' my grandfather, he had an old canoe by the house, but it's probably junk. If we really had to we could get that one. Maybe borrow another from Lanikai Club?"

"Eh, you want canoes? I bring canoes."

"You gotta bring yourself, brah. Really."

"'Kay."

"I'm not kidding."

"'Kay."

He stared at Kimo, who looked down, then at the door. "I gotta go work li'dat," he said. "Second job, pumpeen gas."

"'Kay. Eh, promise?"

Kimo nodded. "Garans," he said. Ben put out his hand and Kimo grabbed it local style, hands up. "Hang loose den," he said.

"You too. Look, bring anybody in your family who can come, 'kay? And I gotta give you my number. You give me yours—we'll get times, an' I'll let you know which right-of-way an' all that." Kimo pulled a little pad and pen out of his shirt pocket, and Ben gave him Kenika's address and phone number. It hadn't occurred to him until that moment that he would stay there.

He was waiting for Pua and Anika to show up when the doorway was filled by a large man in an aloha shirt. Ben thought it might be another policeman, but the man put out his hand and said, "Hi, I'm Andy Sturdevant." He sat down and explained that with Ben's mother's permission, he would discuss with Ben the coming litigation as per the incident at the Kagemori project. They would file suit for wrongful injury against both the owners of the complex and the individual or individuals responsible for the assault. "And it looks like they did a job on you," he said, studying Ben's face and then wincing with vicarious pain.

"Are you my mother's lawyer?"

"I have done legal work for her on occasion, yes," he said. "In this case though we're talking about a rather substantial and I would say important action, and your testimony will be central to that action."

"It was my fault."

"We can easily separate a prank, something done in harmless jest, from attempted murder, I assure you."

Ben reached up and felt the bandage across his nose, and then looked at the man's shirt. Reverse print—hala leaves.

"I don't want to do that," he said.

Andy Sturdevant laughed. "Come on, now," he said. "We're talking about a settlement that will be of considerable benefit to you."

"I heard that the place went bankrupt."

"That means little. The owners are very rich. This is just a defensive maneuver."

"What about the guy who shot me?"

"He is central to this, and was employed by the project."

"He's my cousin."

"Really?" Sturdevant said. "How do you know?"

Ben explained his conversation with Kimo Malama, and noticed that Sturdevant was surprised to learn that it had taken place. "But what it comes down to is that we have the same great-grandparents, or great-great, I'm not sure."

Sturdevant shook his head, passing the explanation off. "He's what, a third cousin, probably removed? He's hardly related to you."

"No, you don't understand what I'm saying here," Ben said, sitting up in the bed. "This is Hawaii. Nobody is removed."

Sturdevant thought this over. "This is a mistake," he said. "I think this is bad judgment."

Ben bristled a little at what he said. "No," he said. "It's no mistake, and I think it's good judgment."

"I don't think your mother will be particularly pleased about this."

"I'm over twenty-one. Do I have the right to decide whether or not this goes on?"

"Of course."

"Then I don't want it to go on."

"I suppose it remains to be seen if she can sue on your behalf, but—"

"Tell her not to, 'kay? I won't sue my cousin."

≈   ≈   ≈

He was released the next day. Pua was on the other side, in Hawaii Kai. She had taken it upon herself to file a missing persons report, and told the police everything she had told Ben. The police pointed out that because there appeared to be no evidence of foul play, they could do no more than put his name on the list. Anika also reported that Ben's mother was not happy, with capital letters, about his conversation with Andy Sturdevant. But the momentum of the idea Ben had hatched while he talked with Kimo Malama was now strong enough that he simply shrugged off the idea that his mother was pissed.

"I can't help that," he told Anika in her car. She drove, glancing with a kind of motherly concern at his bandaged nose and his arm in the sling. "I wanna call up some people. There's only four days left."

"Aren't you supposed to go back Friday?"

"I'm not going. You wanna talk pissed? Wait till she hears that one."

"Do you think anybody'll come?"

"I'll be there. Pua. You. Keoni and Junior dem, Kimo Malama I hope." He looked out the window at the profile of Olomana. "But before that I think I gotta go up to the shed, just to make sure."

"Can I come too?"

"Sure."

By the time they got to Kenika's house he was beginning to feel doubts about the whole let's-get-together thing. After all it would be no more than a penance for his own stupidity, that he had always thought, hey, I'll see the old fart some other time. He didn't know how Pua felt about it either, but suspected that she was somehow freer of those guilt jags than he was. So it might be no more than a sort of foolish hysteria on his part to do something, anything, to try to make some of it right.

He showed Anika through the rooms of the house she had not seen before: this one here is the twins' room, and sure enough there was an old record player and a bunch of thirty-three and forty-five records, even seventy-eights, old clothes, little teenagers' nicknacks on shelves, as if the room were a museum. Some of Pua and Ben's old toys were there too.

"This is where Pua and I slept, and it's exactly the same as when we left. I took the good baseball glove, and look, there's the one I didn't want. This is my Dad's room—my Mom put all his stuff in the closet. Then here's Kenika's room."

He didn't want to go poking around in there right now. He could see from the partly-open door that the sheet was dirty, and was a little embarrassed. He would wash that stuff.

"The study of course you've seen, but look at what kinds of books they had—flower books, nature books, encyclopedias and on and on. There's one of his little canoe models—see the scale? The damn thing is perfect in every detail."

Staring at it, he began to shake a little, and Anika must have seen something in his face, because she put her arm around his waist and said, "It's okay, it's okay."

"I gotta make phone calls. No, make phone calls later when people'll be home. Go to the shed first. Pua'll want to go too." He picked up the phone, getting ready to dial the house in Hawaii Kai, and said, "Well, if my mother answers, the shit's gonna hit the fan."

It didn't. Pua answered, and said she'd be right over. Besides, she and her mother had had a little tiff over a gig she was supposed to do in L.A., and Pua had held firm. She wasn't going to any dumb photoshoot when her grandfather was missing and probably dead, and her mother had yelled at her about the misery that half of the family had caused since the beginning, and now here it was happening again. Pua had yelled back that she was of age and could do what she wanted. Her mother threw up her hands.

So it was with an attitude of ebullient liberation that she came over, ready to go out to the shed. Ben sat as Anika drove her car, with Pua in the backseat leaning up with her chin on Ben's seat back so she could talk story with Anika. Ben lapsed into staring at the buildings, the trees, lines of papaya trees at the bases of Waiahole and Waikane valleys, the hau clogging the shoreline. He kept thinking that the whole thing was pointless, what the hell was he doing? and realized his whole body had been stiff with a kind of sustained tension. He found himself again staring at his arms, at the veins snaking under the skin, and each time he looked at them, his body went into a strange shudder, as if by looking he was reminding his flesh, cubic inch by cubic inch, of the presence of the alien blood.

They found the old road and drove up, but when they reached the area in which he was sure the Japanese family lived, they found other houses, and could not identify the one they wanted. "What was the family's name?"

"I don't remember," he said.

They asked a haole couple at one house. Nothing. They tried another. Nothing. Finally he figured the best thing to do was to look for the oldest house on the hill, which they found, but there was no name on the mailbox.

Ben got out of the car and walked partway across a large lawn, and then recognized it. He nodded to Pua and Anika, and walked to the front door. He knocked, but apparently nobody was home. He was about to turn and leave when he heard something inside, a shuffling and a series of thumps moving toward the door. Then it opened, and inside was a tiny, wizened man leaning on a walker. He must have been in his nineties.

"My name is Ben McKay. I wonder if—"

"Kenika," he rasped.

"You know him? 'Kay, lemme just tell you—" and he told the man the story, including the fact that he, Ben, came up here when he was a boy.

"I memba you keeds," the old man said. "Ho, Kenika no mo'? I sorry."

"That's what we think. But I wanted to check to make sure he wasn't in the shed."

"Whatchu say, you tink he wen' go ocean? He sick, den he do dakine, I shuah. Kenika tough boy."

"That's what we think."

"Go look den. Come tell, 'kay?"

"'Kay."

The path ran through the fence, then down, and just as they entered the darkness of the woods he recognized it, could see in the distance the hulking shape of the building and the little stream half way. "Dis so pretty," Anika said. "Look da ginger."

"Down in dat tick grass get Job's tears," Pua said. "Come, I show you." She and Anika picked their way through the brush toward the grass, and Ben walked down to the stream. Pua had done that, he thought, because she was afraid of what they might find in the shed.

He stepped carefully across the stream because he did not want to jounce his shoulder, and when he was across, he had a strange feeling, a kind of buzzing in the air, and the sound of Pua's and Anika's voices seemed flat and distant although they were only fifty feet away. It was as if the effort of going across had made him a little dizzy, one of those zoning things where he had to wait for his head and vision to right themselves. Then he looked down at the back of his hand, at the veins under his skin, and followed one up his forearm toward that branch where the tiny blue-edged scab was. It struck him that it was all right, that he needn't fear what he had feared at the hospital. Cubic inch by cubic inch his flesh rested, felt whole.

He had trouble, still, righting his brain. He walked to the steps, went up and opened the screen door. A canoe hull, over there a large slab of koa, partly-carved. He stepped inside and went toward the canoe, and the sound, like the call of a weird bird, came from the other side. He remembered it: the singing floor. He stepped on it again and heard the sound, something like "why?" He went to the back and peeked in the little screened bedroom. There was the cot, empty. He looked around. The tools were not rusty—Kenika had been here recently. In fact the canoe looked as raw as if someone had been working on it when he came inside. He ran his hand on the smooth hull, and then realized that the last option had been used up, and Kenika was dead. He also realized that what he was doing was proper, and that there was no reason to feel strange about it. It was as if everything that was hazy and out of focus had now sharpened into something lucid and obvious. He went back to the doorway and looked out, and Pua and Anika were standing side by side a few feet from the stairs, looking up at him. He shook his head.

≈   ≈   ≈

When the clock read four it would be ten in Savannah, Georgia, and he checked in Kenika's little book and dialed his Aunt Clarice's number, at least the one Kenika had added after crossing out fifteen or twenty others. A woman answered. He introduced himself, feeling a little nervous, and the woman said, "I'm Anne Douglass, a friend. They're in Key West, why at this time of the year I can't imagine. I'm babysitting cats, plants, fish."

"Do you have their number?"

"No, but she's going to call here tomorrow."

"Okay, could you do me a favor? This is like a long-involved message." He started from the beginning, and his story was punctuated by interjected responses: "Oh my," "Oh, the poor man," "Dear God, are you all right?" "Let me write that down." Finally he told her he did not want to keep her up, and said goodbye.

Next, Auntie Lisbet. A recording. He said after the beep, "This is Benjamin McKay, and it's important, please call—" and left the number.

Next, Darnay Santiago. He got the irritating three-tone beep meaning his phone had been disconnected. The book said that he lived at an address on Date Street. He knew the area—a low-rise, low-rent district along the Ala Wai golf course.

This time he went alone. The address was a two-story brick apartment building with an oily-looking dumpster blocking one parking space, and trash and beercans flattened on the sidewalk. Approaching the door, he began to feel uneasy because the place was badly lit and heavily-graffittied. It was just getting dark, and he was then reassured a little by the smell of teriyaki wafting down the line of doors. He knocked.

The door opened and a little man with a thin, ridiculous mustache looked at him, feigning shock. "Heavens, did your parachute fail?"

He introduced himself and said that he would like to see Darnay Santiago.

"Oh really?"

"It's important, a family matter."

"Oh really?"

"Really."

"What mischief do you want to perpetrate here?"

"I have a message for him, that's all."

"Oh really?"

"Look, I—"

A hall light went on, transforming the man into a black silhouette, and then the hall was filled by a huge creature of a man, wearing shorts and a tank top with a round logo made into an unreadable horizontal oval. His legs were as big around as the average man's trunk, and he shuffled up to the screen door as the smaller man slid around him and vanished through a doorway.

"Can I help you with something?" he asked, but in a voice as soft and feminine as any grandmother's. Ben was so startled, staring up at him, that he was unable to speak.

≈   ≈   ≈

Lanikai Beach. On the average Sunday it would seem crowded from the point of view of locals, even though you would have your own thirty feet of sand. Ben stood there next to the three large coolers, his arms folded, right hand twined into the sling, and looked out at the two islands. He had seen beaches in other places, California and once New Jersey when he had visited a friend during summer vacation, and he thought, there is no place like this. Anywhere. He had always known that, but still the fact of it impressed him. He had learned to swim here, his father had learned to swim here, his grandfather fished here, even his grandmother so he understood; his great-grandfather fished here, in fact, lived right near here somewhere. It impressed him that if he stood with his back to the houses, the view was identical to what it must have been a thousand years ago.

Pua and Anika were picking up more ice, and he had arrived early in case anyone showed up early. He did not want anyone who was invited to come down, look around, shrug and leave. Keoni and Junior would bring one canoe, and Kimo Malama, he hoped, another. Keoni also promised to borrow one from a Hui Wa'a friend of his in Waimanalo, which would make three, enough to accomodate whomever wanted to go out. What they would do with the canoes was a question until Pua had the idea that they should drop one of his spears and one of his chisels into the water, along with leis. After all, the Buddhist offerings to the souls of the dead, she said, included sending imitation money and clothes into the other world, and so they would send a spear and chisel into Kenika's other world. It wasn't ashes, but those objects were Kenika, and Ben understood the simple logic of that.

He heard the deep drumming sounds of something being moved in the right-of-way, and turned to look. The fore end of a white fiberglass canoe bobbed out, followed by Keoni, then Junior Sakata in the middle, then Tom Sakata, Junior's uncle, and finally the other end of the canoe. It was a shorter one, twenty-five feet or so. They struggled under it while the canoe itself turned in a slow, stately quarter-circle, and then floated on their shoulders in Ben's direction, the manu going up and down with the rhythm of their walking.

They eased the canoe down. "I go get da riggin'," Junior said, and ran up the right-of-way. Tom Sakata walked over to Ben, and squinted at him, pausing on his eyes and the fading yellowish bruises. "Ho, dey kick you good, ah?"

Tom was very dark, from being out in the sun all the time. "Wouldn't show with you. Jesus, you're black."

"Eh, my dad come bumbye. He know Kenika from long time."

Keoni came over. "Eh, I t'ought regatta season ovah. Not odda dakine all gone, some invitation ting li'dat. Only get dis little one."

"Let's see," Ben said. "Kimo's makes two."

"I get da Hobie."

"Better if it was a canoe. What about Jerry Cambra?"

"No mo' heah. Big Island."

"Okay," Ben said. "There's one beat-up one by the side of my house, I mean Kenika's house. We'll go get that, or at least see if it's got its rigging."

"Get one trailer?" Tom asked.

"Yeah, by the side of the house. Might hafta pump tires though."

"Juniah, me go den," Tom said. Junior came out of the right-of-way carrying the 'iakos and ama and rope, and Tom went to talk to him, and they left.

Keoni was about to say something and then stopped. "Ho, who dat?" Coming out of the right-of-way was Darnay Santiago carrying a cooler, then the little man Ben had talked to, leis draped over his arm. Darnay shuffled through the sand, his huge body rippling with fat, the skin of his legs patchy, purplish at the ankles. His gray hair was pulled back into a somewhat greasy-looking pony tail. His friend went off to a spot high on the beach, just in the sparse vegetation between the sand and a yard, and opened a multicolored umbrella and began screwing its pole into the sand. Darnay approached Ben, and said, "Howzit?"

"Hey," Ben said. "This is Keoni, Keoni, Darnay," and Keoni, his face crossed with a look of caution, reached out and grabbed the huge hand.

A few minutes later Pua and Anika and a couple friends Ben didn't recognize came down the right-of-way carrying more coolers. Pua came over. "Who is that man?"

"Darnay Santiago."

She looked in his direction and her face had a slight tinge of disgust on it.

"No worry. He's a nice guy. Just hope we have enough food."

"Plenny," she said. "'Kay, inna coolers, eh you listen too, Keoni, da pepsi and li'dat on top, da beah an' wine onna bottom. When you guys finish one beah, put um inna trashbag, 'kay?"

"Yeah," Keoni said vaguely. She walked away, and Keoni watched. "Ho," he whispered. "Wop jaw, da girl."

She and Anika went and introduced themselves to Darnay and his friend, and then Pua brought her friends over to Ben; Carrie Wong, Tricia Jackson, Darla Lum, all friends from school.

Within another fifteen minutes there were around twenty people there, mostly young. Frank Sakata, Junior's grandfather, showed up, and immediately went to sit with Darnay and his friend. It didn't appear to be particularly chummy to Ben, and he thought the younger people might drift over to talk to them, but they remained where they were.

Then another fore end of a fiberglass canoe bobbed at the right-of-way. This time it was Kimo Malama, under the manu, then three older men Ben did not recognize. They were big, dark and obviously part of Kimo's family. They put the canoe down, and Kimo introduced them to Ben and Keoni, all the time looking a little awkward. They were Kimo's father and uncles. Pua and Anika watched, whispering to their friends, and Ben knew what she was whispering: "Dat da guy wen' shoot Ben, an' he related to us." "Not. Fo' real?"

Charlie Malama, Kimo's father, took Ben aside and said, "Look, tanks fo' dis. An' I got stuffs I sen' you. One family tchree ting. My dad Tom knew you' granfaddah, way way back." He looked at Kimo, who was talking with the other Malama guys. "Dat babooze no tell me til las' night about what you ask 'im, so I get no time fo' do it right. But we get Santiagos two mo' generations back. I sen' you dat, 'kay? Kimo say he get dakine. Address."

"Yeah, I'd like that. Hey, I'll introduce you guys around, 'kay?"

After that Kimo's older relatives appeared lost, and gravitated toward Frank Sakata and Darnay. Ben observed as they chatted, and then when they began to smile and their voices rose a little, he realized that they knew each other, but from so far back that it had taken minutes for them to find that out. Then, when Keoni's mother and Junior's mother and two aunties came, carrying an aluminum folding table, he had the feeling that the older generations were well enough represented.

Ben stepped to Kimo and said, "Eh, c'mere."

"Yah?"

"How things wit' da cops?"

"Get one pretrial hearing tchree weeks, den I don' know."

"Look, I'll be there. Can I speak up for you?"

Kimo looked at him, then nodded. "Eh, if you like do dat."

"'Kay. I will."

Then Junior and Tom came down the right of way and looked around. They spotted Frank and the other beefy Malama guys, and went to talk to them, and Malama uncles and Frank left with them. In a few minutes another fore end bobbed at the opening, then a grunge-covered koa canoe made its dignified turn under the shoulders. They set it down in the sand, and the Malama guys, with Tom Sakata's help, pulled out the 'iakos, ama and rigging, and went to work. Junior stepped over to Ben. He was covered with dirt. "Jesus, it's like black fungus—goddam ting filty." He went and dove into the water.

Ben wandered over to the canoe. The men discussed the positioning of the 'iakos, moving them around and unravelling the rope, their hands black. "'S everything there?" Ben asked.

"Yah," Tom Sakata said. "One gunnel boa'd missing but oddawise—"

It was an older canoe. The manus were higher and more rounded. Ben turned and went back to the cooler and dug down in the ice for a beer.

Because it was a Sunday there were more and more people walking the beach and spreading out towels, and it seemed to dilute their gathering somewhat. Pua took care of that by announcing that they could eat anytime—here are the plates, there's, let's see, tako poke, ahi poke, sesame chicken wings, potato and mac salad, fruit, there's spam musubi, there's Chinese chicken salad, an' put da beahcans inna trash, 'kay?

After that the people gathered in at the table, bumping into each other as they dished out their food. The older folks stayed up in Darnay's area while they ate, the younger ones stayed by the coolers or sat on the clean canoes and talked. Kimo Malama seemed confused as to where to locate himself, until he began talking with Junior and Keoni, about the only thing common to them, Ben imagined—wheah you surf? Fish too? Ho, da fish out deah bump into you, so many.

Ben shook his head, watching, wondering why it was that these people seemed shy. He had the feeling that the whole thing was going badly. Pua had brought an old chisel and a spear that had no barb that she found in the carport, so old that it had nearly worn through in the middle. The idea of making something out of dropping that stuff in the water now embarrassed Ben, but at the same time he thought he should go through with it. Besides, they had what looked like fifty leis. Why else were these people here but to give Kenika a proper sendoff?

He had planned to take the canoes out at about four, and had just a half hour to go, when a tall, very well-dressed woman came down the right-of-way. He recognized her immediately as one of the twins, and then was almost shocked at her resemblance to his grandmother, something he saw after seeing her clothes and hairdo.

Her hair was done up in a perfect French twist, and she wore what appeared to be a leather dress. She stood at the opening for some time, staring at the islands, high heels dangling from the fingers of one hand.

Ben went over to her. "Hi," he said. "I'm Ben."

"You look just like Keoki," she said, and then squinted at his face. "I'm Clarice Davis. My God, are you all right?"

He paused a second, staring at her earrings and a gold eagle pendant at her throat. "Yeah."

She looked at her shoes, thinking, and then said, "What happened? I mean my friend told me, but—"

Ben went into the same explanation he had now used for dozens of people, he now realized. As he spoke she shook her head slowly, sighed, and finally wiped her eyes a little. "I wish he'd told us," she said. "I mean if it was a question of money," and she shook her head again. "We could have gotten him any treatment that—"

"I guess he didn't want anybody to know."

"Keoki's not here," she said. "Kenika did write about his leaving, but—"

"We don't see him any more."

Ben tried to think of what else to say. She appeared so totally out of place that he scratched his head, then looked around at the others. "Do you know—"

She had already seen him. "Is that Darnay?" she asked, appearing amazed.

"That's him."

"Oh, I'd better go say hello."

And she made her way toward the gathering of the older folks. Ben watched her, thinking that the class and elegance were so alien to the setting that it was almost absurd. And others noticed it too, probably because she was beautiful. Pua and Anika watched and whispered, and then stopped whispering when she leaned down and kissed Darnay, whose face opened up in a mask of surprise. In fact he appeared so happy to see her that Ben relaxed, thinking that at least the strange woman would have someone to talk to.

She then went around and introduced herself to some of the others, at least those who were close by, and Ben could tell again that nobody knew exactly how to respond to her. In fact when he watched her talking with Pua and Anika, he could tell that Pua remained somewhat wide-eyed and even a little awed by her, and Anika, whose expression seemed almost jovially hostile, appeared not to like her at all. He wandered over to them after Clarice Davis moved on to talk to someone else. "You met Auntie Clarice, I see," he said.

"I think she's a little formal," Pua said.

"Ho, tell me story," Anika said, watching her. "I wonder how much that ridiculous dress cost."

"And the hair," Pua said. "I thought people stopped doing it that way twenty years ago."

Anika giggled. "Snob," she whispered.

Poor Auntie Clarice then found a place to sit, very carefully because of the dress, near Darnay, the only person she could apparently talk to. Ben thought then that it was time to get everyone together to go out. He sat with Pua and Anika, sipping his beer and watching Clarice because he was embarrassed about the whole thing, especially for her. She leaned back and faced the sun, her eyes closed, and Anika squinted at her and laughed. "Look," she whispered. "J' like one haole getting a tan."

"No talk stink," Ben said.

Clarice was so pretty, he thought, and so sort of classic-looking, that he wondered about what mainland life had done to her. The contrast was bizarre. As Polynesian as you could get, and you'd think it was Sophia Loren after having fallen asleep at a tanning salon.

He was about to get up when he saw her staring at the old canoe. She had a beer in one hand and shaded her eyes with the other. Then she leaned forward, something having caught her attention.

Pua and Anika had been looking, too. "What's the matter now?" Anika asked. "A bug crawl up her thousand-dollar dress?"

Clarice Davis got up, then stepped closer to the canoe, and then did a strange thing: she poured a little beer into one hand and hesitantly wiped it off on the canoe. Then she poured more, and began sweeping her hand over the hull, and her hand was black. She looked around, holding her hand out. She poured more beer on it. "Ben! Try come!" she yelled.

"Oooo," Anika said. "Pidgin. She tryin' o' what?"

"Uh-oh," Ben said. "Something's got her going."

He went to her. "Look," she said.

"What?"

"It's The Red Wind."

"Not, that crashed years ago."

"Look," she said, and poured beer on the manu and followed it with her hand.

The wood was a darker red than most koa. He leaned over and looked at the hull. There were repair seams running along under the mo'o board, inset with little, perfectly-shaped koa bow-ties. He went along the hull and then rubbed in another spot, next to his seat. Under his hand the eye-knot appeared. "Jesus," he whispered.

Clarice came to him and leaned close to his ear. "We are The Red Wind," she said, and giggled.

"You know that?"

"He told us that before we raced." She shook her head, smiling at the canoe. "We won so many races with her."

"Really? I thought he built this when we—"

"No, late fifties, I think. Fifty-nine? We were at the blessing up at Mr. Marumoto's."

"He's still alive you know."

"Not. What, a hundred-fifty?"

"Nineties maybe. But how did Kenika—" He looked at the two islands. "He went out and got it? I don't believe that."

"He loved this canoe," she said. "He—" She stopped. "I'm sorry," she said, turning away a little. "Oh, I hate this," she said. "I don't know why the time went so fast, why we didn't—" Then she looked at the islands and sighed. "I'm sorry. I can't talk about them without—"

"Yeah."

"We loved them. You get into doing your own thing and all of a sudden it's twenty years. I feel so bad about that."

"Well," he said. She stared at the islands. "Okay, I guess it's time to go out," he said. "We won't be gone long, just to drop a chisel and a spear and some leis is all."

She looked down at her dress. "Shit," she whispered. "No bathing suit either."

"Well, we'll be back," he said. He turned to go back to the others, but she followed.

"I'm going out too," she said.

"'Kay, you should."

She walked over to Anika and Pua, and looked at them both. Pua and Anika looked at her.

"Do you have an extra bathing suit?" she asked Anika. He knew why. Anika was more the full proportions of Clarice, and Pua was just too thin.

"No," Anika said. Ben didn't appreciate the standoffish tone of her voice. Clarice seemed to give in there, and shrugged and went back toward Darnay and the older folks.

Ben backed down toward the water and yelled out, "'Kay, we're gonna go out and drop this stuff. Pick a seat anybody who wants to go." Darnay and his friend would not go, nor would the Malamas he figured, except for Kimo. Eighteen seats, no, sixteen because of the small canoe, just about right.

Anika and Pua were again looking at Clarice. Then everyone looked at Clarice. She was unbuttoning the leather dress and speaking to

Darnay, who nodded to her. She stepped out of the dress, carefully folded it and handed it to Darnay, then took off her jewelry.

"Ho," Anika whispered.

There Clarice stood in black underwear, and one of those bras that was cut so low that her breasts surged out the top. She then undid the French twist and her hair fell all the way down her back, and she shook it out, animating her body with the kind of movement that turned men's heads. Three haole men walking on the beach, one carrying a video camera, stopped and stared at her, in fact everyone did, but she remained unconcerned about all those who were part of the gathering. When she saw the three men gawking at her, and the man with the camera began to raise it in her direction as if it were some involuntary bodily reaction, she put her hands on her hips and glowered back, and Ben sensed before she spoke what was coming.

There was a little pause of anticipation, and then, in a haughty resurrection of the pidgin of her youth she bellowed out, "What! I owe you money?"

Anika was impressed. She turned to Pua and said, "You heard dat?"

Clarice wanted her seat, just in front of Anika in the powerhouse. Ben could not paddle, so he did his best to steer, holding the paddle in his right hand and helping with his left when the situation would allow it. The water sweeping over The Red Wind's hull cleaned it, and if he had had any doubts before about whether it really was The Red Wind, they vanished when he saw the color the length of the hull.

Because it was between tides, it was easy to knife through the breakwater, and when they had reached the deeper water Ben lifted the old spear and the chisel out of the water sloshing in the hull and waited a few seconds while everyone watched, then dropped them in. After that the paddlers sailed the leis out onto the water one by one so that the brightly-colored circles bobbed around the canoes. Then they turned the canoes and got ready to return to the beach. Once the objects had been dropped, everyone got back to their good-humored socializing.

Clarice turned in her seat and peeked around Anika. "Ben, who is that man steering that canoe?"

"Tom Sakata? Didn't you meet him?"

"I wasn't listening I guess," she said. "Could we pull closer? I don't think he remembers me."

Ben churned the paddle and edged the aft end of the canoe closer to the other one. Clarice leaned out a little, and called, "Eh, you pilau little shit, you like race?"

Tom Sakata turned with his mouth open, and Anika looked back at Ben, her eyes wide with shock.

Tom Sakata stared at Clarice, thinking, and then burst out laughing. "Eh, you bitch, I slap you!" he said, and then they were both laughing. Then Tom looked at Ben and said, "My bitch of a babysitter. Ho, we wen' at it." He dug his paddle into the water and said to Clarice, "Eh, eat futs, you."

The two fiberglass canoes pulled out ahead, racing, and The Red Wind remained behind although Clarice pulled in a muttering fury that impressed Ben. When they reached the shore the others were already carrying the two canoes up on the sand. Clarice got out of The Red Wind and dove under the water, and then came up, and Ben watched her, thinking that whatever pretentiousness she may have had before, the ocean had washed away like dirt.

And he imagined that Anika noticed it too. From then on they and Pua hung out together, and Clarice, with her hair down, sitting with them in the sand, a towel around her shoulders, looked like a combination of sister and mother to them both.

People began to leave when the sun slid behind the mountains. The air felt suddenly cool, and Ben walked one and then another contingent of visitors out to their cars; the younger friends of Pua and Anika, the Malamas, the Sakatas, who helped Keoni and Kimo load the canoes. He spent a few minutes at the Malamas' car, getting information on Kimo's court appearances. We keep in touch, his father said. Then they offered to help Ben with The Red Wind, and he told them that he, Clarice and the girls would take care of it.

When they were gone he wondered if he'd made a mistake. But then he saw Darnay, still sitting there talking story with Clarice and Pua, and figured they had enough help.

He wandered off by himself, thinking that after all it had worked out well. After they brought the canoes back in the whole thing took on the appearance of a family gathering.

In a few minutes Clarice joined him, still wrapped in a towel. "Ben, that was beautiful," she said. "I feel a lot better now."

"Thanks."

"I like your friend too. Anika. And Pua? She reminds me of my mother."

"Listen, where are you staying?"

"Moana, for old time's sake."

"You could come stay with us. You know, your room is exactly as it was."

She laughed. "Amazing." Then she stared at the islands. "I might take you up on that. Hey, I can see the leis." He looked. The little spots of color rose up and went down in the waves. She laughed again. "Besides, I'm now sort of on my own. Mr. Davis has traded me in for a younger squeeze. We were in Key West to try to patch it up, but it didn't work."

"I'm sorry."

"Well, the kids are grown up. He's just fallen into it. Nothing to be done I guess. You know, your cousin is named Kenika, and he didn't like the name. He knew it meant Dennis in English, so now he calls himself Dennis." She stared at the islands again, the upper elevations lit by a rich copper sunlight. "Maybe I'll take you up on that, if I won't be an imposition." She sighed, still looking at the islands. "I had the taxi take me over there before coming here." She laughed. "Up on top of my mother's cooler I saw the little corrugated-roofing canoe we made. I lost it a little there, or else I'd have been here sooner." She pulled the towel around her shoulders. "Okay, I'll stay until the kids come out to get me, and then I'll finally get to show them this, and have them meet you and Pua."

"You know, the house is one-fifth yours."

"Really?" she said. "Kenika."

"Yeah."

"My sister— I called her, and she's coming too, but not until next week. Years ago when—" She didn't continue. Her expression turned into one of a strange devastation that made her look suddenly older. "When our mother died— Well, I talked to her about that after. Neither of us remembers it that much. We were both zonked out on tranquilizers, or else we wouldn't have been able to take it. I think we were both so stunned that—"

She shook her head. "We never got over it."

"I remember being confused," Ben said.

She looked at Ben, drew her breath to speak, and then shrugged, pulling the towel tighter around herself.

"What?"

She shook her head, staring at the islands, and then turned to him. "Was there ever a cleaner or more beautiful time or place?" she asked. "Do you think? Was there, I mean ever?"

"No."

"I guess I knew that. I've known it from the day we left. It's a big world, but it's overrated. I don't know why it took all this time for me to figure that out."

She continued staring at the islands, then wandered down to the water. Anika came up and put her arms around him, and the heat of her skin made him realize how cold he'd become. "Hey, you got your bandages wet," she said. "Here, lemme look."

She peeled the bandage away from his shoulder, and he looked at the top of her head. Then she said, "Look, you got sand on it, right on the stitches. An' da scabs are all green."

"It's okay," he said.

"What about infections?"

"It's just sand. I'll change it later. Listen, are you like— I mean are you like around?"

"Yeah," she said.

"I mean I wonder if you're staying around? I mean sort of— All the time, I mean?"

"Are you?"

"Yeah. I mean I'm not going back right now. Not— Well, not this year anyway."

She looked at him, and he didn't understand the expression. As if she might be thinking about it. Then she nodded, and changed her expression.

"Hey, I'm gonna go talk to auntie," she said. "Ho, what a babe."

"She's staying at the house a while."

"Fo' real?" She looked at her as she walked through the shallow water. "Maybe I come an' stay too den," she said, and went and joined Clarice.

He looked at the islands, and then down the beach. Most of the people were gone. There were still a few sailboards out in the water, and kids splashing in the shorebreak. Far down the beach toward Kailua he saw people walking, one of them a black shape, which appeared to undulate with movement, but was warped by what was left of the heat rising from the sand. It was a person walking in his direction. He squinted, trying to define what he was seeing, and chuckled, because it was a habit that went back more than ten years. He was just beginning to wonder if he was seeing the person he thought he might be seeing, when the black shape shifted, and in a strange, amoebic movement, became two people walking.

He let out a breath and whispered, "Well," and shook his head.

After all what would he have seen? Judging by the man's condition four years ago, he would now be even more decrepit. Somewhere out there he was walking, in Kaneohe or downtown or maybe even in Kailua. It struck Ben that his father was a special kind of casualty, an extreme, because he was lost even to himself, cut off, and it was so hard to understand why he ended up that way. He could still remember him, and had seen photographs of him when he was eighteen or twenty. As Ben had grown old enough not to fear him any more, in his more hopeful speculations he envisioned someone the circumstances of life had not wasted. Even now if you looked at the scarred face, you would see the broad nose, the high forehead, the thick lips, and if you squinted and forced yourself to look beyond the rotted teeth and red eyes and grime, you would see a face befitting an ancient chief or warrior. But right at the moment Ben stood there, he saw him as he imagined hundreds of people had already seen him on that same day, lifting a ball of cold rice stained with shoyu from a trash can, or biting bits of chicken away from castoff bones, brushing away the little black ants and finishing unfinished sodas, all the time seeming to think, as if trying to remember something important, perhaps even who he was, and then walking on, lost.

GLOSSARY

'aha: Sennit cord braided of coconut husk or human hair

'aka: To laugh, laughter

akamai: Smart, clever

akua: God, goddess, spirit, image, idol; divine, supernatural, godly

'alas, 'ala'alas: Volcanic stone, hula stones; (slang) testicles

ama, ama kaka: Outrigger float, arched, curved from end to end

anuenue: Rainbow

'a'ole, 'a'ole loa: No, not; certainly not

apopo: Tomorrow

aweoweo: Various Hawaiian species of priacanthus, red fishes

boroboro(s): (slang) Worn-out clothes

chichis: (slang) Breasts

'e'epa: Extraordinary, incomprehensible, as persons with marvelous powers; such persons

'elepaio: A species of flycatcher with subspecies on Hawaiian Islands

haku: Lord, master, overseer; to compose, invent, put in order; to braid, as a lei

halalu: young of the akule

halau, halau wa'a: Long house, as for canoes or hula instruction

hana hou: To do again, repeat

hanabutta: (slang) Mucous

hanakokolele: (slang) Shame on you

hapai: Pregnant

hapa: Portion, fragment; of mixed blood; person of mixed blood

hapu'u: Endemic tree fern

he'e: Squid, octopus

heiau: Pre-Christian place of worship

hihimanu: Various stingrays; lavish, magnificent, elegant

hoku, hoku'ae'a, hokulele, hokuwelowelo: Star, wandering star, shooting star, comet

ho'o, ho'oipoipo, ho'opilikia, ho'oponopono, ho'owa'a: Causation (to make), love, trouble, to correct, canoe

honu: Turtle

huhu: Angry, offended

hui: Club, association

huli: To turn; to curl over

'iako: Outrigger boom

'ie'ie: An endemic woody, branching climber

'ilima: Small to large native shrubs, species of sida

'ina: Young of the sea urchin

kaekae: Smooth, polished; perfect; to rub smooth

ka'ele: Empty and hollow, as of a bowl, poi board, hull

kahuna, kahuna kalai wa'a, kahuna la'au lapa'au: Priest; carving expert (canoe); medical/herb doctor

kala: Several species of surgeonfish; money

kamali'i: Children

kamani'ula: False kamani or tropical almond tree

kapakahi: One-sided, crooked, lopsided

kapu: Taboo, prohibition

kaukau: Chant of lamentation; (slang) food

keiki: Child, offspring

koa, koa la'au maia, koa awapuhi, koa'i'ohi'a: Largest of the native forest trees (Acacia koa); koa of different densities, light, medium, high

ko'i, ko'i ahuluhulu, ko'i 'auwaha, ko'i kalai, ko'i kupa 'ai ke'e: Axe, adze; planing; grooving; carving; swivel

kokua: Help, aid, assistance

kolohe: Mischievous, naughty

kopa: Soap

ku: Ancient Hawaiian god of war

ku 'ohi'a laka: God of canoe builders

kuamo'o: Backbone, spine; canoe keel

kupe 'ulu: Canoe manu made of one piece

kupuna: Grandparent, ancestor

la'au hope: After-endpiece of a canoe

lapa, lapa uila: Lightning flash

lauhala: Pandanus leaf, esp. as used in plaiting

laulau: Wrapping, wrapped package; packages of ti leaves containing pork, beef, fish, or taro tops, baked

lave: To take, transport, carry, bring

Lea ka wahine: Goddess of canoe builders

lilikoi: Passion fruit

lolo: Brains, bone marrow

lolo (with macrons): Paralyzed, numb, feebleminded, crazy

lolo ka wa'a, lolo ana ka wa'a i ka halau: Canoe consecration ceremony

lomi: To rub, press, squeeze, massage

lupe: Flattened end of the forward end of an outrigger float

mahu: Homosexual, of either sex

mai: Toward the speaker, this way

maika'i: Good, handsome

mai poina: Don't forget

makani: Wind, breeze, gas in the stomach

maku'u: Neck cut on the stern end of a canoe hull hewn in the mountains, hauling knob

mana'o: Thought, idea, belief, opinion

mane'o: Itch, itchy; sexually titillated

manini: Surgeonfish; stingy

mano: Shark

manu: Bird; ornamental, elliptical expansions at the upper ends of the bow and stern endpieces

mo'o: Lizard; succession, series; story; path; gunwale board

ni'ao: Edge, as of a canoe

niele: Inquisitive, curious, nosy

no, no mamao wa'a: From; from-afar canoe

no'o: Thought, reflection, thinking

oeoe: Whistle

'ohi'a: Native tree (Metrosideros macropus)

o'ia mau no: Same as ever

okole: Buttocks

'ono: Delicious; to relish, crave

'o'o: To pierce; digging stick

'opelu: Mackerel scad; strong

'opua, 'opua hae: Puffy clouds; hae; wild, fierce

'opule: Spotted wrasse

pa'ani: Play, sport, game

pakalolo: Marijuana

palani: Surgeonfish

pale kai: Taffrail of a vessel; sea guard

pau: Finished, ended

pehea oe, pehea lakou: How are you?; how are they?

pepeiao: Ear; blocks inside a canoe hull to which booms are fastened

pilau: Rot, stench, rottenness; to stink

pilikia: Trouble, nuisance

po: Night, darkness, obscurity

poi: Staple food made from cooked taro corms, pounded and thinned with water

popolo: Black nightshade: (slang) Negro

pua: Flower; arrow, dart

puka: Hole

pupule: Crazy, insane, reckless

tako: (slang) Octopus

'uhu: Parrot fish

uku, ukubillion: Louse, flea; (slang) quick, numerous

'ula: Red, scarlet; brown, as skin of Hawaiians; to appear red, to blush, flush; to redden, make red; sacred, sacredness, regal, royal; blood, blood of great value, as royal blood; a ringing in the ears, as due to rising in altitude, believed by some to be a sign that one is being talked of; ghost, spirit; footprint of spirits

ulua: Certain species of Crevelle, jackfish

vana: Sea urchin

wa'a: Canoe

wae: U-shaped canoe spreader

wiliwili: A Hawaiian leguminous tree

AUTHOR'S NOTE

Although I have lived in Hawaii since 1966, the idea of writing a book set in Hawaii did not seriously enter my mind until the early 90s, and then only as a possibility. I had written books set in places I have never visited, about events I could have no firsthand knowledge of, had even written a science fiction novel set in the future. The other things I wrote, short stories mostly, were set in upstate New York, a place I had lived in only about seven years. But then at the back of my mind I reasoned that more than a quarter of a century of familiarity with Hawaii stood for something. I had vague ideas about who my protagonist would be, and vague ideas about what would happen to him. But the first attempt was abandoned because I couldn't find a focus.

In the process of thinking up the book, I recalled things that had been right there in front of me for years, particularly my longtime love of spearfishing and my younger daughter's paddling for the Lanikai

Canoe Club. I recalled that the first time I took her to practice I saw a koa canoe up close, and was fascinated by its sleekness and beauty, particularly the beauty of the wood. Later I became interested in the complexity of the canoes' construction. But like my spearfishing, her paddling was just another of our family activities.

The first race my daughter was in took place at Kailua Beach, and I wondered before it started how they would do. Clearly she was too small, her paddler friends too skinny. She was in the girls' twelve age group; other paddlers from other teams were bigger, and I did not expect much in the way of results. But they won the race. Of all the sporting events I have witnessed firsthand in my life, I still regard that first race, more than ten years now, as the single most electrifying sporting event I have ever witnessed. Obviously I am biased because she was one of the participants, but I still hold this opinion—there were thousands of people at the beach, all of whom took this sport as seriously as others take football, basketball or baseball. It was clear that the results of the races were important, as were the traditions associated with canoes and canoe racing, for example the traditional blessing of the canoe. As I tell my writing students, stretch your imagination and take it as far as you can, but start with something you know. For me, the old-fashioned fishing spear and that forty foot object of carved koa became the focus of this novel.

The books most informative on this subject are: Tommy Holmes' *The Hawaiian Canoe*, and Te Rangi Hiroa's (Peter Buck) *Arts and Crafts of Hawaii (VI Canoes)*. Hiroa's book is shorter but packed with interested information, and Holmes' book is a splendid, beautifully written and researched work.